Handle with care . . .

I hadn't done a raku firing in some time, and I realized I'd like to. The process was simple and offered spectacular results. I'd take pieces we'd already bisque fired, then after glazing them, bring them to my backyard, where I had my equipment set up. After a quick firing in my outdoor gas-fed brick kiln, I'd pull out the red-hot pots and bury them in wood shavings or wadded-up newspaper. Thermal shock caused the glazes to shrink and crackle. It was a process I loved, partly because there was no way to exactly predict what the end result would look like.

Leaves had collected in the pit area where I moved the pieces after their firings; I'd need to clean up the area if I was going to fire again.

As I walked closer to the pit, I noticed the leaf pile had a peculiar shape to it. It was as if—no, it couldn't be. I brushed a few leaves from the pile, and my worst fears were confirmed . . .

The
Cracked Pot

Melissa Glazer

BERKLEY PRIME CRIME, NEW YORK

THE BERKLEY PUBLISHING GROUP
Published by the Penguin Group
Penguin Group (USA) Inc.
375 Hudson Street, New York, New York 10014, USA
Penguin Group (Canada), 90 Eglinton Avenue East, Suite 700, Toronto, Ontario M4P 2Y3, Canada
(a division of Pearson Penguin Canada Inc.)
Penguin Books Ltd., 80 Strand, London WC2R 0RL, England
Penguin Group Ireland, 25 St. Stephen's Green, Dublin 2, Ireland (a division of Penguin Books Ltd.)
Penguin Group (Australia), 250 Camberwell Road, Camberwell, Victoria 3124, Australia
(a division of Pearson Australia Group Pty. Ltd.)
Penguin Books India Pvt. Ltd., 11 Community Centre, Panchsheel Park, New Delhi—110 017, India
Penguin Group (NZ), 67 Apollo Drive, Rosedale, North Shore 0632, New Zealand
(a division of Pearson New Zealand Ltd.)
Penguin Books (South Africa) (Pty.) Ltd., 24 Sturdee Avenue, Rosebank, Johannesburg 2196, South Africa

Penguin Books Ltd., Registered Offices: 80 Strand, London WC2R 0RL, England

This is a work of fiction. Names, characters, places, and incidents either are the product of the author's imagination or are used fictitiously, and any resemblance to actual persons, living or dead, business establishments, events, or locales is entirely coincidental. The publisher does not have any control over and does not assume any responsiblity for author or third-party websites or their content.

Kilns, cutting knives, and other craft tools can be hazardous, if used carelessly. All participants in such craft activities must assume responsibility for their own actions and safety. The information contained in this book cannot replace sound judgment and good decision making, which can help reduce risk exposure, nor does the scope of this book allow for disclosure of all the potential hazards and risks involved in such activities.

THE CRACKED POT

A Berkley Prime Crime Book / published by arrangement with the author

ISBN: 978-0-7394-9588-9

BERKLEY® PRIME CRIME
Berkley Prime Crime Books are published by The Berkley Publishing Group,
a division of Penguin Group (USA) Inc.,
375 Hudson Street, New York, New York 10014.
The name BERKLEY PRIME CRIME and the BERKLEY PRIME CRIME design are trademarks belonging to Penguin Group (USA) Inc.

PRINTED IN THE UNITED STATES OF AMERICA

For my agent, John Talbot.
"Thanks for everything."

Chapter 1

I've lost a great many things in my life, including my temper, my car keys, my mind, and—a long, long time ago—my virginity, but I'd never lost an entire person before Charles Potter came into my life. Or didn't. I know it sounds confusing, but the truth sometimes is.

Let me assure you, there are some things that are certain in my life. My name is Carolyn Emerson, and I run a paint-your-own pottery shop called Fire at Will in the quaint little town of Maple Ridge, Vermont. I've been married to the same man for nearly thirty years, I've got a great assistant, a nearly perfect best friend, and a group of potters known as the Firing Squad who are always there when I need them. And before it became clear exactly how and why the man who called himself Charles Potter disappeared, I would have to lean on every last one of them.

* * *

"Is he here yet?" my assistant David asked breathlessly as he rushed into Fire at Will. Barely into his twenties, David was a nice-looking young man who just happened to have a long blond ponytail that was still hard for me to get used to seeing on a guy. Tall and a little on the skinny side, David had fingers that any potter would covet, long and slim with a strength to tame the wildest clay. "I didn't miss him, did I?"

"Honestly, David, he's not a rock star. He's a potter, just like you are."

"Come on," David said, "he's Charles Potter. That man can do things with clay I can only dream about."

"I know, I know, he's your hero, but to be honest with you, he didn't sound like a hero when I talked to him yesterday. He was kind of scatterbrained." At David's urging, I'd called Mr. Potter and asked him to come by the shop before his presentation at Travers College, the small liberal arts school on the edge of town. To my surprise, he'd agreed. He was giving a lecture and demonstration at Travers later that night, but he said he'd be delighted to come by Fire at Will on the way. I glanced at the clock and saw that he was now a half hour late. David had gone to the bank for me earlier, albeit reluctantly, and now, waiting on the potter's appearance, he was panting like a dog after a steak.

"I'm not entirely certain he's even going to show up," I said. "Maybe he forgot about us."

My accusation didn't faze David for a second. "He plays by his own set of rules. The man's a genius."

"I've never met a genius before, but if this is the way one acts, I haven't been missing anything. What time is he scheduled to talk at the college?"

David looked at his watch. "He should be starting in less than an hour. I hope nothing's happened to him."

"Don't be so dramatic. What you should really hope is

that he remembered at least one of the appearances he agreed to make today." I'd had enough hero worship to last me a month.

"If he misses it, I know he'll have a good reason," David said, already making excuses.

"Is Annie going to the demonstration with you?" Annie Gregg was David's first serious girlfriend. The relationship had begun because of Annie's remarkable resemblance to Julia Roberts, the lovely and talented actress—and David's other infatuation. Annie was cleaning houses to save up for Stanford, and David often complained that she spent more time amassing her tuition than she did with him.

"She's busy cleaning a house, but as soon as she finishes, she's going to meet me there."

"Maybe you should go on to the school," I suggested. "You wouldn't want to get a bad seat for the demonstration." Or stay here and keep driving me crazy, I added to myself.

"Don't worry about that. I've got two seats reserved in the front row."

"You don't have Hannah holding them, do you? Your mother has better things to do than sit in an auditorium all day saving you seats." Hannah was David's mother and also my best friend, an arrangement that sometimes led to complications but was generally a good thing for all concerned. She was also an English professor at the college and the push behind David getting a formal education there.

"Are you kidding me? She thinks I'm crazier than you do. I paid Kelly Winston to do it. In exchange for reserving two seats for me, I'm giving her a free lesson in throwing a bowl on the wheel. You don't mind, do you?"

"Why should I mind? It's just my business and the way I earn my living. If you want to give my money away, what right do I have to object?" When I looked at his face, I saw that I'd gone a little too far with my teasing, something I had a habit of doing with young David. "Relax, I'm kidding. Of course I don't mind."

"Thanks, Carolyn." He glanced at his watch again. "Maybe I should call the hospital, or even the sheriff. He'd know if Mr. Potter had been in an accident, wouldn't he?"

"I doubt Sheriff Hodges would know if he had hit the man with his own patrol car." John Hodges was our sheriff, an older man who was hanging on until he could retire with full benefits. Many townspeople thought he was a little less than diligent performing his duties, and I was ready to admit that I was one of the first to come to that conclusion.

David waited at Fire at Will as long as he could. After glancing at the Dali-like melted wall clock for the sixtieth time in twelve minutes, he said reluctantly, "He's not coming, is he?"

"It doesn't look like it." The man had some nerve, agreeing to come by one day and completely blowing me off the next, without so much as a telephone call or an explanation.

David sighed, and as he left the shop, he said, "Promise me you'll get his autograph for me if he comes by here first." He thrust Charles Potter's book, *A Study in Clay,* at me. "Have him personalize it, too."

"Shouldn't you take this with you? It will mean a lot more to you if you see him sign it yourself."

David grinned. "Don't worry about that. I've got another copy out in my car."

"Why am I not surprised." I turned the cover over to get a look at the author, but the back held only a blurb from another author. "What, no photograph?"

"He won't allow pictures of any sort to be taken of him,"

David explained. "In fact, this is his first public appearance, and I mean ever."

"Then how did he get so well known?"

David shrugged. "He's sold his work through galleries, and he has a presence online. This is his first book, though. There are all kinds of articles about his techniques on the Internet. You really should get a computer, Carolyn."

"What on earth would I possibly use it for? I'm fine with my portable typewriter."

He shook his head. "There's a whole world out there waiting for you."

"Then it'll just have to continue waiting." I wasn't in any mood to be lectured by my assistant on the modern age and the joys of technology. "Hadn't you better go?"

"You're right. Bye, Carolyn."

"Good-bye, David. Have fun, and don't forget to curtsey when you meet him."

"Don't be ridiculous," he said.

"Oh, that's right, boys don't curtsey; they bow."

He rolled his eyes at me much as my own two sons had done once upon a time, and I felt a stab of nostalgia for when they were younger.

After David had gone, I had the shop to myself for the last half hour of my regular business hours, though I wasn't finished with my workday by any means. Tonight, the Firing Squad was meeting, and it was my turn to provide the snacks. Jenna Blake, a retired judge, had instituted a practice where we took turns bringing refreshments to our meetings, since I couldn't afford to feed them without charging more. I contributed whenever it was my turn, and I didn't hesitate to sample what they brought in. It made me feel like a member of the squad instead of its sponsor. Tonight I was

hurrying home to make my famous not so Swedish meatballs, and if I knew my husband, Bill, he would be hovering
just underfoot, complaining about being hungry as he ate
more than his share of the treats.

"How much is this costing you?" Bill said later that evening
at home as I was preparing the night's fare. "Are you going
to actually make any money tonight?"

"I'm doing fine; you don't have to worry about my bottom line. This is a goodwill gesture for my group."

"That's all well and good, but don't forget about your
husband," he said as he polished off another meatball and
picked up one more. "I need some goodwill, too."

"I'm sorry, what did you just say? I couldn't understand
you with all that food in your mouth."

He pouted when I said that, something my dear husband
was inclined to do, so I quickly added, "Eat all you want. I
made a double batch, so there's plenty."

Out of sheer cussedness, he put the toothpick-skewered
ball he was holding back on the platter I was filling. "I
wouldn't want to deprive your guests."

"Fine, if there are any left, I'll try to remember to bring
them back home."

He looked at the meatballs another few seconds, then
said, "Knowing you, you'll probably forget. I'd better get
my share right now."

"Suit yourself," I said as I turned my back on him. A
minute or so later I looked toward him again and saw several more empty toothpicks on his plate. At least I knew Bill
wouldn't go hungry tonight. I covered the platter, then
leaned over and kissed his cheek. "Don't wait up. We're try-

ing a new technique of weaving clay tonight, and it might take us a while to get it right."

Bill pointed a toothpick at me. "Have you ever done anything like it yourself?"

"No," I admitted reluctantly, "but it looks easy enough."

He shook his head, so I asked, "What?"

"I'm not saying a word."

"You don't have to. I'm perfectly capable of learning how to do something from a book."

I was expecting some kind of retort, not the grin he gave me. "Why are you smiling?"

"Was I? Sorry, didn't mean to."

"Sometimes I'd like to trade you in for a hat."

"You hate hats," he said, still grinning.

"Then I'd give it away, too, and be done with you."

"Come here, woman." He wrapped me in his arms, and I tingled at his touch; even after all our years together he still made me feel that way. As I gazed up at him, a gooey and romantic expression on my face, he leaned down and whispered in my ear, "Don't forget to bring home the leftovers."

I broke away, smiling despite his less than seductive comment. "Don't worry, I've never forgotten yet, have I?"

When I got to the shop, Sandy Crenshaw—a reference librarian and a charter member of the Firing Squad—was standing out front. Sandy was a cute and curvy young brunette with sparkling brown eyes and a sunny smile.

"Have you been waiting long?" I asked as I tried to get my keys out of my purse while balancing the platter of meatballs in the other hand.

"Here, let me help you with those," she said as she took them from me. "Sorry I'm so early."

"Nonsense," I said as I opened the door to the shop and

held it for her. "I could use a hand setting up." I flipped on the lights as I walked inside. The front part of Fire at Will was devoted to folks who wanted to paint their own pottery pieces. There were tables and chairs set up, and along the perimeter were shelves stacked with bisque-fired pottery ready for paint and glaze. The front display window had pieces for sale, along with a table by the cash register for more items. I was amazed at how many of the pieces I sold were already finished. Not that I minded, but I much preferred folks to come in and actually paint or work with the raw clay themselves. Behind the paint studio, in the back, were the potter's wheels and the worktables for shaping raw clay. I had as many customers who liked hand-building as I did those who liked throwing on one of our wheels. Behind that was my office, a bathroom, and a storage area. Fire at Will didn't have a big footprint, but I'd managed to cram a lot of activity into it.

"What would you like me to do?" Sandy asked as she put the meatballs down on our snack table.

"You could get out the hot plate so we can keep those warm," I said.

As she did that, I started laying out some of the tools we'd need tonight. There were five of us in the Firing Squad. I never counted David, since he usually had night classes at Travers. He had brokered a deal with his mother early on. If he could work at Fire at Will during the day creating the pottery he loved, he would attend night classes at Travers for her benefit. Hannah had reluctantly agreed, so whenever the two of them had a conflict, I always managed to get stuck squarely in the middle of it.

After arranging the tools for the evening's activities, I cut off five chunks of clay from one of the bags I stored in a broken refrigerator and started kneading them. It would

save some time if I had the clay ready when the others arrived.

"Can I help you with that?" Sandy asked.

"Sure, that would be great."

As she took a slab of clay and started working it on the
board, she said, "I'm really excited about this."

"Then you need to get out more," I said as I worked out a
particularly stubborn air bubble. "How's your love life? Are
you still seeing Jake?"

"No, that kind of fizzled out," she admitted.

"Not your one true love?"

Sandy laughed. "Not even in my top ten. To be honest
with you, he found someone else."

"Oh, Sandy, I'm so sorry."

"Don't be," she said. "I kind of set it up myself."

I stopped kneading for a second and stared at her.
"You're not going to get away with just telling me that
much. I want details."

"I had a friend I thought would be better suited for him
than I was, so I planned a double date with Jennifer, and I
promised to introduce her to a great guy."

"Okay, I'm with you so far."

She grinned, then said, "I got an emergency phone call
when we were standing in line at the theater. I had to leave,
they went to the movie without me, and now everyone's
happier."

"What happened to her blind date?"

"Now why on earth would I go to the trouble of fixing
her up with somebody else when I had a perfectly good plan
in place to get them together. Jake really is a great guy. He's
just not the one for me."

"I don't know how you keep up with it all," I said, laughing. I started thinking about eligible young men I knew who

might be right for Sandy. I'd have to do any matchmaking surreptitiously, though. I'd promised Bill years ago that I'd stop meddling in other people's lives, and I always tried to keep my oaths. Most of the time. Okay, I wasn't great at it, but why couldn't he admit that sometimes people needed a little nudge in the right direction, and if I could provide it, didn't I owe that much to my friends? Why shouldn't they be happy, too?

I heard a knock at the front door, so I left the clay at the table and went to the front of the shop. Jenna Blake, the retired judge, along with Butch Hardcastle, the reformed crook, were standing outside. Butch looked like a thug at first glance, big and burly with an intimidating countenance, but he was a teddy bear inside. At least he was with us. Jenna managed to look dignified no matter what the circumstances. She had allowed the gray creeping gently into her hair to remain, and she absolutely exuded power and confidence.

I opened the door for them and stepped aside. "Come on in. Have either one of you spoken with Martha today?" Martha Knotts was the final member of the Firing Squad, a young mother of five who somehow managed to stay reed thin, a quality I had to work not to hate her for.

"She can't make it," Jenna said as I locked the door behind her. "Angie has the flu, and it looks like the others may be coming down with it as well. She sounded rather harried when I spoke with her earlier."

I couldn't imagine that crew of hers all getting sick at the same time. "Is there anything we can do to help?"

"No, she said her mother-in-law was coming to pitch in. The poor girl."

"Don't feel sorry for her," I said. "Martha told me the woman is an absolute dream."

Butch said, "You two can stand here and talk all night, but I want to get started."

"You're impatient tonight," Jenna said.

"Sorry. I've just got an appointment a little later on, and I want to be sure I don't miss it." I wondered at times just how reformed Butch really was, but I was afraid to press him too much about it.

On the other hand, Jenna was not. "Butch Hardcastle, I can't imagine any appointment that late being legitimate."

He grinned at her. "Then you don't have enough imagination, Judge."

"It's Jenna, and you know it. Now stop changing the subject. What possible reason could you have for a business appointment so late in the evening?"

"Who said it was business?" Butch asked, grinning.

Jenna looked embarrassed. "I'm sorry, of course it's none of my business. Your affairs are your own."

Could the oaf not see that the judge was just as interested in him as he was in her? These two were going to need a nudge if they didn't figure it out soon. Foolishness in love wasn't strictly a problem just for young people.

It finally occurred to Butch what Jenna was saying. He frowned as he explained, "It's not a date, if that's what you're thinking."

Jenna said stiffly, "It's none of my concern, even if it is."

"But I just said it wasn't."

They weren't getting anywhere on their own. I was about to say something to help when Sandy came through. "Aren't you coming back? The clay's ready."

"So am I," Butch said as he brushed past us.

Jenna looked at me and said, "Men," putting enough into it to supply a thousand gradients of meaning.

"They're not perfect, but they usually do their best."

"How sad for them," Jenna said. She was in a bit of a sour mood, so I decided not to press her further.

When we were all gathered in back, I suggested, "Why don't we get started, and when we get hungry, we can all take a break."

No one dissented, and we all took up our places at the table. "We're going to weave some clay tonight. First we have to get our balls into flat sheets. Sandy and I have already kneaded these, so they're ready to go. Take your dowels and roll the clay out until it's about a quarter of an inch thick."

They did as I directed, and we soon had our balls converted into sheets of equal thicknesses. "Now we square off the edges, and then we cut the sheet into uniform strips about an inch wide. If you want to be precise, use one of the plastic rulers to mark your clay before you cut it, but you can usually just eyeball it and get a pretty nice set of strips." At least that's what the book had said. Maybe Bill was right. I probably should have made one of these myself ahead of time, but really, how hard could it be? I hoped this experiment didn't bite me, as some had in the past.

There was no turning back now. As confidently as I could, I said, "Lay half your strips out in one direction, keeping the edges pretty close together. Next, pick up another strip and start weaving it in and out of the strips you've laid out." I demonstrated briefly, and then I stopped working on mine so I could help them when they needed it.

"Now what?" Butch asked as he looked down at the woven mat. "It doesn't look like much, does it?"

"Now we bend it up on all four sides. Use a rib to help the turn." A rib was a piece of wood or rubber—many times shaped like a large kidney bean—that helped the potter work clay. They came in various shapes and sizes, but I'd put out simple ones for our evening's work.

"I can't get it right," Sandy said as she stared at her lumpy basket.

"Let me see what I can do," I said. I worked the rib harder into the weave and managed to get a decent turn. "How's that?"

"Better, but the top's kind of ugly, isn't it?"

That's when I remembered I was supposed to have told them to save four strips to go along the perimeter to create a nice, finished edge. I started dismantling my bowl to supply them with the extra clay. "Use these to dress up the edges," I said as I handed out all but two of my own strips.

"But you don't get a basket this way," Jenna protested.

"I can make one whenever I want. So, what do you all think?"

They all agreed their baskets were nice, but they also wanted to try again.

"That's fine," I said, "but before we do, why don't we clean up so we can take your snack break?"

Butch nodded. "That's a great idea."

As we sat around the break table enjoying the meatballs and coffee from my new pot, Jenna asked, "Where's young David tonight? Does he have a class?"

"Yes, but I doubt he made it. He's still probably starry eyed about meeting Charles Potter."

"From what I've seen, he's good," Sandy said. "We ordered his book for the library, and I read it before we put it into circulation."

"Shame on you," Jenna scolded her lightly, obviously teasing her friend. "You should let your patrons have priority on the new books you get in."

"How can I honestly recommend a book if I haven't read it myself first?" Sandy asked, laughing. "Or movies, either, for that matter."

"I suppose you have a point," Jenna conceded. She turned to me and asked, "Have you read it, Carolyn?"

"I glanced through it earlier," I admitted as I pointed toward David's copy. "If you want my opinion, it's long on photographs and pretty short on technique. Just don't tell David I said that."

"There's no way that's his real name," Butch said as he glanced at the book.

"Why do you say that?" Jenna asked.

"Come on, a potter named Potter? Isn't that a stretch?"

"Not necessarily. I know a banker named Cash," Sandy said.

"And I know a farmer named Fields," I admitted.

"This sounds like a delightful game. What else can we come up with? A plumber named Flush?" Sandy asked.

"How about a carpenter named Woods?" Jenna asked, getting into the spirit of it. "It's your turn, Butch."

He frowned. "I just meant it sounded like an alias. I didn't mean to start something."

"Come on, don't be a spoilsport," Jenna said.

"Okay, give me a second," Butch said. "How about a construction crew chief named Foreman?"

"That's wonderful," Jenna praised him, and Butch decidedly glowed.

"How about a short-order cook named Frye?" I suggested.

"Or a golf pro named Link?" Sandy asked.

We were still coming up with names that matched their occupations when we heard the front door of the shop burst open. Goodness, had I forgotten to lock it after I'd let Jenna and Butch in?

It took only a second to realize that it was someone who had a key. David rushed back to us, but before any of us could say a word, he said, "It's Charles Potter."

"What about him?" I asked as David fought to catch his breath.

"He's missing. He never showed up at the lecture, but they found his car. The door on the driver's side was standing wide open, and the keys were still in it."

"Where did they find it?" Butch asked.

David looked at me for a long few seconds, then said, "It was parked right in front of your house, Carolyn."

Chapter 2

"What on earth was he doing there? How did he even know where I live?" Honestly, I never went looking for trouble, but somehow it always managed to find me.

"You talked to him last night on the phone," David said. "Maybe it had something to do with that."

"I didn't give the man my home address. I don't even think I gave him my telephone number."

"Then why would he go there before he disappeared?" David asked, still looking at me askance.

"Are you under the impression that I had something to do with this?" I asked with more than a little edge in my voice.

"Take it easy, Carolyn, David's not accusing you of anything," Jenna said.

"Well, it surely sounded like it to me."

Sandy added, "He's just concerned. Carolyn, should you call Bill? Just to make sure he's all right?"

That hadn't even occurred to me. I dialed our home number, my fingers shaking as I punched the buttons. After seven rings, the machine kicked on. "Bill, it's me. Pick up. Bill. Bill? Call me as soon as you get this."

I hung up. "He's not answering. I'm going home."

"I'll go with you," Butch said.

"We'll all go," Jenna added.

The last thing I needed was a parade, especially if my dear husband was in the tub instead of lying dead or wounded on the kitchen floor. "I can manage."

Butch said, "Not without me."

"I'm coming, too," David said.

Sandy touched Jenna's arm. "Why don't we stay here and clean up? Would you like us to do that, Carolyn?"

"That would be great," I said as I grabbed my coat and my purse. If I were being honest with myself, I would have to admit I wasn't all that eager to go home alone.

Butch said, "Come on, we'll take my car."

I got into his Cadillac without a word of protest, and David climbed into the back seat. It wasn't much of a trip from Fire at Will to my house, but it seemed to take us a lifetime to get there. Parked in front of the house was Sheriff Hodges's patrol car, its lights flashing. The second we got there, I could see why Bill hadn't answered the telephone. He was standing right outside beside the sheriff, deep in conversation, and obviously surprised to see me tear up the road in someone else's car.

As I got out, Bill rushed over to me. "Are you all right? Is something wrong?"

"I was just going to ask you the same thing. When you didn't answer the phone, I got worried."

"So you brought the cavalry? Hey, Butch. How are you doing, David?"

David nodded an abrupt greeting as he approached Hodges. "Is there any sign of him? What happened?"

The sheriff ignored the question and stared at me. "What do you know about this, Carolyn?"

"I just heard about it," I said. "Is there any sign of him yet?"

Hodges shook his head. "One of your neighbors was out walking his dog when he found this car sitting here with the door open and the keys still in it. I was kind of hoping you might be able to shed a little light on it."

"I was at Fire at Will all evening," I said stuffily. "That car was certainly not there when I left." It was a beat-up Ford Escort, and I wondered how little the potter must have made publishing his opus.

"We can vouch for that," Butch said. "Not the car being there, but her presence at the shop. She never left the place all night, and I'm willing to swear to that in court."

"Why am I not surprised you'd vouch for her?" he said.

Bill piped up. "Wait a second here. We've already had this conversation, Hodges."

"It's *Sheriff* Hodges," the man said curtly.

"I've known you forty-five years, and I'll call you whatever I want. Carolyn didn't have anything to do with this."

The sheriff shook his head slightly. "I can't exactly just take your word for that, either, now can I?"

Bill looked like he was about to blow, and I didn't want the sheriff to have any more reason to dislike me or my family. "Why don't we go inside and let the police deal with it, Bill? I assume you're finished with us, Sheriff." The Firing Squad was just going to have to get along without me for the rest of the night.

"I'm done with you for now," he said. "I'll probably have more questions for you later. Right now, I've got my deputies coming. We're going to search the area for Mr. Potter."

"I'll help," David chimed in.

"Thanks, but we've got it covered," the sheriff said just as another squad car pulled up. He walked over to greet them.

I touched Butch's arm. "Thanks for bringing me home. Would you mind taking David back to the shop? I'd better hang around here for now."

"How are you going to get your car?" Butch asked.

"I'll take her later," Bill said. "Thanks for coming, both of you."

Butch nodded. "Call me if you need me. Don't worry about the time."

I smiled. "What about your appointment? I'd hate to interrupt anything."

"Friends come first," he said. Then Butch turned to David. "Let's go."

"I want to help look for him," my assistant said.

Butch replied, "I know you do, but the sheriff's already turned you down. Come on, there are bound to still be a few meatballs left back at Fire at Will."

Bill blanched a little at that, probably rightly believing he wouldn't be getting any leftovers tonight.

Once they were gone, my husband and I walked up to the house. "It's getting chilly, isn't it?" I asked. I glanced back at the abandoned car and added, "I hope he's all right."

"I just wonder what he was doing here in the first place," Bill said.

"I'm sure the sheriff is wondering the same thing," I said.

Once we were inside, Bill looked hard at me. "Are you sure you don't know why he'd come here?"

"I don't have a clue," I said. "And I'm not all that crazy

about everybody asking me that. Why won't anybody believe me?"

"I do," he said gruffly. "I was just asking. It's too bad about the meatballs. I'm feeling a little peckish."

"You didn't look in the refrigerator, did you?" I walked into the kitchen and grabbed a covered dish. "I left you some, you big goof. All you had to do was look."

"Well don't just stand there, let's eat."

As Bill waited for the microwave to do its job on reheating our late snack, I asked, "Aren't you the least bit concerned about what happened to Charles Potter?"

"Why should I be? He's a grown man, isn't he? I'm sure he's fine."

"Then why would he just abandon his car like that, and what was he doing at our house in the first place?"

"I don't have a clue," Bill admitted as he took the dish out of the microwave. He stabbed a meatball, ate it with relish, then asked, "Do you want one?"

"How can you eat at a time like this?"

"I can eat anytime," he said, "And if you want any of these, you'd better grab them now."

"I've lost my appetite," I said as I stared out the back window. I could see bobbing lights in the yard, and from the look of things, the sheriff had every deputy in the county searching for the lost potter. I just hoped when he did turn up, he'd be able to tell us what had happened, and why.

An hour later there was a tap on the door, and I jumped up to answer it. Sheriff Hodges looked upset, and I wondered what he'd found.

"Is he dead?" I blurted out. Probably not the best thing to

ask the sheriff, but it had been weighing heavily on my mind.

"I have no idea. We couldn't find him."

Bill was right behind me. "If you want to search the house, you're going to have to get a warrant."

Hodges asked, "You'd actually make me do this the hard way? What are you hiding, Bill?"

I wanted to intercede, but I knew from the set of my husband's jaw that the best thing I could do was get out of the way.

He wasn't even trying to keep his voice reasonable now. "I'm not hiding; I'm standing on my constitutional rights, and I'm telling you to your face. I'm not about to let you or anybody else bully me into doing something I don't want to do."

"Fair enough. Then we'll have to do this my way. I'll be back in half an hour with a search warrant, and in the meantime, there will be a deputy sitting in your living room."

"He can wait outside," Bill said.

This had gone far enough. "You both need to grow up. Come in and get it over with," I said.

"No," Bill snapped. "He's not going to parade in here acting like he owns the world."

"Hang on a second, Sheriff," I said. "We'll be right back." I closed the door and looked at my husband. "What has gotten into you? It's a reasonable request."

"I didn't like bullies in school, and I don't like them any better now. Carolyn, I'm surprised at you. I thought you despised that man."

"I'm the first to admit that I'm not his biggest fan, but he's got a job to do, and for once, it looks like he's actually trying to do it. If we get stubborn about this, we're costing the police time to make a more thorough search of the area. What if Potter is hurt, and he dies because nobody found him sooner just because we were posturing? How are you going to be able to sleep at night then?"

Bill returned my stare, then lowered his gaze. "Let him in, then."

"Not unless you agree to it, too. It's just as much your house as it is mine." I rubbed his shoulder gently. "I promise, you can chuck him out as soon as he looks through the place."

He grinned slightly. "I guess that's something."

He opened the door. "Come on in." As a deputy started to follow, Bill added, "Just you, Hodges."

The sheriff must have decided not to chide Bill about his means of address, or his demand. He turned to his deputy. "Wait here. I'll be right back."

"I should go in with you, sir."

The sheriff snapped, "What you should do is obey orders. In case you didn't hear me the first time, I said to wait outside until I'm finished."

Properly cowed, the deputy took a few steps back and Hodges came inside. After a quick but pretty thorough search of the place, he nodded once we got back to the front door. "Thanks for letting me cross this place off my list."

"Just let us know when you find out what happened to him," Bill said, the snap gone from his voice.

"Will do," Sheriff Hodges said as he left.

Once the door was closed again, I turned to my husband. "What happened? I thought you were going to rub his nose in the fact that Mr. Potter wasn't here."

"You were right. It would have been petty, and I'm a bigger man than that. What? I am."

"I never said a word," I said, trying to suppress my grin.

"Woman, are you looking to pick a fight with me?"

"Me? Not on your life. What are you going to do now?"

"What else is there to do?" Bill asked. "I'm going to bed."

"How are you going to sleep until they find out what happened to Charles Potter?"

He smiled at me. "Like a newborn with no conscience, a clean diaper, and full belly," he smiled.

I waited up, hoping for a knock on the front door during the night, but none came. When I woke up the next morning on the couch, my neck was stiff, but sometime in the middle of the night my dear husband had covered me with a blanket. Why hadn't the old fool woken me up so I could sleep in my bed instead of out in the living room? I decided to give him credit for thinking of me at all. When I peeked out through the drapes in the front window, I saw that the police were gone, along with Charles Potter's car. What had happened to the man? I wanted to call Sheriff Hodges to see if he'd learned anything after he left us, but for once, my curiosity was defeated by my desire to keep the lowest profile I could. I'd been under the sheriff's suspicious gaze before, and I hadn't enjoyed it, not for one second.

"I don't think David slept more than an hour or two last night," Hannah said as we ordered coffees at In the Grounds before I opened Fire at Will. It was our ritual to meet at the coffee shop to start the day.

"I slept on the couch myself," I said as I rubbed my neck. "You're looking chipper, though."

Hannah was a slim brunette whose fortieth birthday was fast approaching, and I'd have to decide soon whether I was going to have a surprise party for her. When I'd turned forty,

I'd invited the world to celebrate with me, whereas my husband had crawled into a hole the day before and had refused to come out for a week. I was still feeling Hannah out to see which reaction she was going to have, but so far, she'd neatly avoided all my queries.

"Am I?" she asked lightly.

"Hannah, what's up?" There was a gleam in her eye I hadn't noticed before.

"I'm sure I don't know what you're talking about," she said, but as she started to sip her coffee, I saw an unmistakable grin.

"Okay, give."

She shrugged. "If you must know, I have a date tonight."

I'd been badgering her for months to go out again. "How did that happen?"

"He asked, I agreed," she said smugly. "It's as simple as that."

"Do you really think I'm going to let you get away without more details than that?"

"Don't push me on it, Carolyn. I don't want to jinx it," she said.

"Fine, but I expect a full report when you get home, even if it's just long enough to change your clothes for work tomorrow."

"You've got a dirty mind," she said with a smile.

"One of us has to," I countered.

Hannah glanced at her watch. "I've got to run. I'll talk to you later."

"I'll be waiting by the phone."

As I walked to Fire at Will along the River Walk from the coffee bar, I marveled yet again at the foresight of our

founding fathers. They had taken an average little stream called Pig Snout Creek, changed its name to Whispering Brook, then made the land beside it their retail shopping area, and all of this was done a great many years before San Antonio came up with their much showier River Walk.

"Hi, Rose. Is that new?" I called out to the proprietress of Rose Colored Glasses, a stained glass shop along the walk. Rose Nygren was a tall, skinny redhead with a complexion that would burn under a 40-watt lamp. She was standing in front of her shop, hanging a mobile made up of varied hues of colored glass.

"I'm wondering if it might attract more customers," she said, then turned to me and added, "Carolyn, the whole town's buzzing about what happened last night."

"Did I miss something?" I asked, knowing full well what Rose was referring to.

She raised one eyebrow. "From what I've heard, you're right in the middle of it. Again."

"I can't help it if trouble seems to come looking for me." I studied her mobile, then added, "If you ever want to add any glazed pottery pieces to these, let me know. We could work something out, I'm sure."

She studied her creation a second, then said, "Let me think about it."

If Rose was aware of Charles Potter's disappearance the night before, then the rest of the town must know about it as well. That meant that Kendra Williams—the owner of Hattie's Attic and the biggest gossip in all of Maple Ridge, Vermont—was no doubt dying to grill me about what had happened. We'd been through an ordeal together earlier, and she'd been under the mistaken impression that we'd bonded. I didn't have the heart to tell her otherwise. Maybe if I hurried past her shop and kept my gaze on the creek, I could pretend not to see her, something hard to do, given her proclivity for wearing faded muumuus over her abundant frame, regardless of the weather or the temperature.

"Carolyn," she called out. "Carolyn!"

I'd have to have been deaf to not hear her. "Hi, Kendra. Sorry I can't stay and chat, but I've got to get to the shop."

"This will just take a second. Tell me all you know."

This woman was relentless. "That will take less time than what you've given me. I don't know anything about anything."

Would she buy it? I doubted it, even though it was the truth.

"Come on," she prodded in a stage whisper, "whatever you tell me will be just between the two of us."

For as long as it takes me to get inside my shop, I wanted to say, but didn't. Kendra had an information network that beat satellites and relay towers by a mile. I knew she would take the slightest gesture of mine and turn it into a full revelation without bothering with anything as mundane as the truth.

"Sorry, but it's the truth. I really don't know anything."

She was frowning at me as I brushed past her, but I was too deft to let her stop me. As I neared Fire at Will, I took in the tumbled brick exterior, the forest green awning with the shop's name written on it, the jet black front door, and the display window in front showing some of our best work to the world. In the window, I'd put out a lovely Japanese tea set my pottery instructor Robert Owens had made, a delicately painted porcelain Buddha Butch had decorated, an interesting vase Jenna Blake had created, and as always, a handful of my glazed and fired tree ornaments. It wasn't vanity that made me include my work with the others. I'd found early on that if I offered something inexpensive to average window-shoppers, I might be able to coax them to come in and browse our other offerings. If I was really lucky, they'd try their hand at painting some pottery of their own, the entire purpose of my business. I believed that painting pottery was not only fun but also therapeutic. The world was full of its own set of woes, and my shop offered a distraction from all of that.

"Have you heard anything?" David asked me before I even had the chance to walk into Fire at Will. "There's nothing on the news, and the paper just mentions finding his car."

"Did you go to the café and eavesdrop?" I asked as I stepped past my assistant into the shop. Shelly's Café was where many of the locals hung out, and I was certain if there was anything to learn outside of the sheriff's office, the café would be the place to hear it.

"I didn't think of that!" he admitted. "Do you mind if I go right now?"

"We open in fifteen minutes," I said, glancing at the wall clock. It was a Salvador Dali–inspired piece that nearly dripped off its hook, something quirky that I was fond of, nevertheless.

The look of disappointment on David's face was too much to bear. "Be back in half an hour," I said.

"Thanks, Carolyn. You're the best."

"That's what I've been saying all along, but nobody seems to believe me," I said with a smile as he raced out the door.

I just hoped I'd have a quiet time of it until he returned. Of course, my hopes were dashed twelve minutes after he left.

*   *   *

The front door chimed, and I looked up to see a man in his early forties walking in the door. His face was vaguely familiar, and I tried to study him without being too obvious. He had a scruffy beard and long hair, and if it weren't for his nice clothes, I would swear he lived on the street.

"Aren't you even going to say hello?" he said.

The voice was even more familiar than the face. I looked past all the hair and realized who it was. "Richard Atkins. I thought you were dead."

Hannah's ex-husband and David's long-lost father was standing before me, and it was all I could do not to go for his throat. He'd deserted my best friend the second he'd found out she was pregnant, an act of cowardice that rated flogging in the town square, at least in my opinion. Then again, he was David's father, and if he'd come to see his son, to try to make some kind of amends for his desertion, I didn't want to be the reason he turned away.

Richard grinned. "A lot of folks probably have that at the top of their wish list, but so far, I've managed to disappoint them. How have you been?"

"Richard, do you honestly care?"

He shrugged. "Fair enough. Is David here?" He actually sounded nervous at the prospect of seeing his son.

"No, he's out at the moment. A potter disappeared last night, and he's trying to find him."

Richard ran his hands through his hair. "Sorry about that. I guess I kind of freaked out at the last second."

It took me a full ten heartbeats before I realized what he meant.

"Are you trying to tell me that you're Charles Potter?"

"One and the same," he admitted.

That was just a little too much, even for me. "Prove it."

He looked startled by the suggestion. "What do you want me to do, throw a pot? It's a pseudonym. My God, I thought everyone would see through it. I wasn't exactly trying to advertise my presence to the world, for a great many reasons."

Butch had seen through the obviousness of the name, at any rate. "Then why did you ever agree to come back here in the first place?"

"I was hoping to reconnect with my son," he said.

He had to be kidding. "In order to do that, you'd have to have some kind of connection with him to begin with, wouldn't you agree?"

"Hey, I was there at the very beginning."

"And then you left." Honestly, the man was insufferable. "Why on earth did you abandon your car in front of my house last night? The police thought I killed you and buried your body in my cellar."

"I thought you might be able to help me break the news to David and Hannah. But I couldn't ring the bell. I panicked, and I ran away. Sorry for the trouble."

I was about to snap at him when the door chimed.

It was David.

I hissed, "Don't say a word about who you are, do you understand me?"

Richard looked puzzled. "Why not? That's why I came back in the first place."

"You wanted my help. Let me at least prepare him for this."

"Okay, if you think it's best."

David nodded to me, started to speak, then saw his father standing there. "Good morning," he said, then looked at me. "Nothing but idle rumor and speculation at the café."

"It was a long shot at best," I said, trying to find the words to introduce David to his father.

Richard saved me the trouble. "Hello, son."

David's face went white, and then without a word, he ran out of the shop.

Chapter 3

"I thought you were going to let me tell him," I said as I ran to the front door. Richard was right on my heels.

"I couldn't help myself. Where did he go?"

At first I couldn't see David, but then I caught a glimpse of his jacket as he ran down the River Walk. "We'll never catch him on foot."

"We can't just let him go."

"I don't know that we have much choice," I said. "Oh, no."

"What's wrong?"

I stared at him a second, then said, "I have to call Hannah. She needs to know what just happened."

"I'll call her if you want me to," he said.

"I think you've done enough damage for the moment," I said as I hurried back inside Fire at Will.

I tried Hannah's office, and I thought I'd missed her, but she picked up after the seventh ring.

"It's me," I said.

"Make it dance, Carolyn, I've got a class in seven minutes."

"Your ex-husband is back in town."

She must have dropped the phone, from the way it sounded. I asked, "Hannah? Are you all right?"

After a second, she came back on the line and said, "I'm fine. Where did you see him?"

"He's standing right in front of me. He came into my shop a few minutes ago, and before I could stop him, he introduced himself to David."

I heard nothing but silence on the other end of the phone, not even breathing. "Hannah, are you there?"

"What did David do?" she asked softly.

"He ran away. I'm sorry, I couldn't stop him. I thought you should know."

"Thanks. Let me talk to Richard."

I looked at him as I said, "Are you sure that's a good idea?"

"Put him on."

"Take it," I said to Richard, offering him the phone.

Richard looked as though he'd rather take a beating than my telephone, but after a few seconds, he accepted it.

I don't know what Hannah said to him, but it must have been flame broiled. The man turned three shades of white, and then suddenly his face erupted in red before he handed the telephone back to me and started for the door.

"Where are you going?" I asked him as he rushed out.

"I'm going to find my son."

"Hannah, are you still there?" I asked into the receiver. Nothing. No doubt she'd hung up after delivering her scathing message.

I wanted to follow Richard and help find my assistant,

but I had no idea where David might have gone, or what to say to him even if I did find him. There was nothing I could do but be there in case he came back to the shop.

I called Bill to tell him what had happened, but he didn't answer the phone. I left him a message to call me as soon as he got it, and hung up.

The door chimed just then, and I half-expected to see David or Richard walk in. To my surprise, it was Sheriff Hodges, and he had a scowl on his face that was darker than usual.

"I've got some news about that car," he said.

"It belongs to Richard Atkins," I said before he could continue.

"If you knew that, why didn't you tell me last night?" He looked angry enough to lock me up, which wasn't all that odd for him. "You could have saved me a great deal of time and energy."

"I just found out myself. He was here to talk to David."

"How did the boy react?"

"How do you think? He tore off like his shoes were on fire. He's never met the man."

The sheriff shrugged. "That's tough, but at least he's still alive."

"I'm not sure for how long. When I told Hannah her ex-husband was back in town, she was ready to kill him."

Hodges put his hand back on the front door. "Tell her to watch her temper. We don't need any more violence around here."

I rolled my eyes as he left, and wondered yet again how the man managed to get reelected time after time.

The phone rang, and it was Bill. "What's going on? I just got your message. Are you all right?"

"I'm fine. I thought you should know that I found out who really owned the car that was parked in front of our house last night."

"Did the sheriff come by and tell you?" he asked.

"I knew it before he did," I said, trying not to sound too smug.

"Carolyn, have you been snooping again? That's a bad habit that's going to get you in big trouble someday if you're not careful."

"Thanks for the lecture. Now, do you want to hear what I found out or not?"

"I already know it belongs to Richard Atkins," he said.

"How on earth did you know that?" Honestly, the man drove me absolutely mad sometimes.

"The sheriff came by first and told me."

"Here's something I'm willing to bet you don't know," I said. "He's also Charles Potter."

"Who are you talking about? You don't mean Sheriff Hodges, do you? Have you been smelling fumes from the kilns again?"

"No, you nit, I'm talking about Richard Atkins. He made up the name to hide his identity."

Bill said, "Hannah's going to have little baby kittens when she finds out. Carolyn, I know how much you love to meddle, but stay out of this."

"It's too late for that. I already called her."

Bill sighed heavily. "How did she react?"

"She wants to kill him."

"You know what? I don't blame her a bit. Does David know?"

A customer walked in, and I held up a hand. "I'll be right with you," I said to her. "Bill, I've got to go."

"Did you tell David?" Bill asked again.

"No, Richard did that himself, right here in the shop. Good-bye, Bill."

"Call me right back," he said as I hung up.

"May I help you?" I asked my new customer.

The woman, a petite young thing who would probably be swallowed by a size 0, pointed to the display window. "I was wondering if you gift-wrapped."

"We can, for a nominal fee," I said. "Which piece are you interested in?"

She pointed to the Japanese tea set Robert Owens had created. "I'll take that."

"Wouldn't you like to know the price first?" Owens was charging an outlandish premium for the set, and I didn't want to shock the girl when I rang up the sale.

"It doesn't matter. It's for my mother. It's her birthday."

I told her the price just the same, but she didn't even flinch. "That's fine. When can I pick it up?"

Maybe I should have jacked the price up a little. I would make a nice commission on the sale, but every little bit helped. "I'll have it ready in ten minutes, if you can wait that long."

"I'd be delighted. I'll browse around while you wrap it."

I ran her card through the register, and after she signed the receipt, I boxed up the set and wrapped it. While I worked, she kept returning to the window for more items, and by the time I was finished ringing her up, she had just about wiped out the display. The only omission was my work. Out of everything she'd purchased, there wasn't a single ornament. In a fit of largesse, I retrieved one of my prettiest pieces and added it to her stack.

"I don't want that," she said.

"It's on the house," I said. "You get one free with every purchase over five hundred dollars."

She plucked it from the pile, a look of distaste on her face as she handed it back to me. "That's all right. If it's all the same to you, I'd rather not."

I wanted to kick her out onto the curb in that instant, but the commissions I'd make on the sales would more than make up for my hurt feelings. Plastering a smile on my face I didn't feel, I boxed everything up, and when she wasn't looking, I slipped the ornament back into one of her bags. What could she do, return it?

Hannah stormed into the shop two minutes after the young woman left. "Where's my son?"

"I wish I knew. Hannah, I'm so sorry. Richard just showed up and blurted out that he was David's father."

"I'll deal with him later," she said, with murder in her voice. "I just have to make sure David's all right first."

"He didn't come back here," I said. "You might want to call Annie."

I knew David's new girlfriend was a bone of contention between the two of them, but I never realized how deep the conflict was until Hannah said, "That's all right; I'll find him on my own."

"Swallow your pride and call her," I snapped. "She might be able to help, and you can't afford to be stubborn about this."

Hannah glared at me for several seconds, then calmly asked, "Do you have her number?"

"I can ask her if she's heard from David myself, if you'd like," I said as I dialed Annie's cell phone.

"No, that's all right. I'll talk to her," she said.

After a few moments of whispered conversation, Hannah handed the telephone back to me. "He's not with her, but she's going to call if he turns up."

As Hannah started to leave, I asked, "Where are you going?"

"I know his favorite places in Maple Ridge. If anyone can find him, I can."

I touched her arm lightly. "If you find Richard first, don't do anything rash."

"I'm not making any promises," she said, and then she was gone.

I hadn't even had the chance to tell her that Richard was going by the name Charles Potter, if it was indeed the truth. All of that would come out soon enough. Hannah was right. The only thing that mattered at the moment was that she find her son.

An older man with a luxuriant gray mustache and an elegant three-piece suit walked into the shop. "Are you open for business?"

"Certainly," I said. "How may I help you?"

"Are you sure you're open?"

Was he deaf? "Yes. Why am I having trouble convincing you of it?"

"Your front window's empty," he said, gesturing to the uncluttered space up front. I hadn't had a chance to restock the display.

"I'm trying to decide what to feature next," I said.

"I'd put something there, if I were you. I nearly passed on by the place."

"But you didn't, did you? Are you looking for a gift?"

He looked around. "Is this a gift shop? I thought it was a pottery painting place."

"It is," I said, though I couldn't imagine this man painting a bowl or a mug.

"I don't want to do that," he said stuffily.

"You don't want to buy anything or paint anything. I'm curious. Why exactly did you come in?"

"Perhaps I've made a mistake."

I had another thought. "If you're looking for a rifle or an antique pistol, you have."

He looked quizzically at me. "Now why on earth would you assume that?"

"It's the name," I said, gesturing to the sign out front. "Some folks think Fire at Will means we're a gun shop."

"Then they're idiots," he said soundly.

I still had no idea why he was in my shop, and I wondered if I'd ever know. I decided to wait him out, and thirty seconds later, he said, "I'd like to make something out of clay. You do that here as well, don't you?"

"Absolutely. We have pottery wheels in back."

"I have no desire to learn to throw pots," he said in his stuffy tone.

"Of course you don't."

He nodded. "I'm glad we understand each other."

I couldn't help myself. I laughed. "I haven't a clue what you're talking about."

"I want to build something from clay; a house, to be precise. Is that something I can do here?"

"I don't follow you."

He looked at me as if I were insane, grabbed a paper bag with "Fire at Will" emblazoned on it, then removed a pen from his suit pocket and proceeded to sketch out a house. "Here, this is what I want to do."

"What scale would you like to build this?"

"Life-size, of course," he said.

"It's a little more than I can handle in my kilns."

The man shook his head in obvious disgust. "Why does

no one get my humor? I want to make something about the size of a tissue box."

"That we can do." I handed him an apron. "You need to put that on. I'd hate to get any clay on your suit."

He shunned the apron. "I'm most careful, I assure you. I won't need that."

"Suit yourself," I said. "I can help you with the basic shape, and then you can embellish it however you'd like. Fair enough?"

"I believe so."

I handed him a thick round dowel and a lump of clay. "You have to work the air out of that and get it ready."

He studied the clay in obvious distaste without touching it. "Would you mind?"

"Not at all." I kneaded the clay until it was a smooth consistency and handed it to him. The only problem was, he refused to take it. "What's next?"

"You have to roll it out," I said.

"Show me, please."

If he hadn't added the "please," I would have refused, but what else did I have to do at the moment? I rolled the clay out into a wide sheet until it was about a quarter of an inch thick, my favorite thickness for hand-building. "Now cut your walls and I'll show you how to put it together."

"I'm afraid I wouldn't be very good at that," he said.

Why wasn't I surprised? I cut the walls, floor, and roof out of three-quarters of the clay and quickly assembled the house. "I don't have any idea how you want to embellish this, but there are plenty of tools to cut out the shapes you'd like."

Instead of taking my not so subtle hint, he said, "Let me sketch out what I'd like."

He quickly embellished the house he'd drawn earlier, adding window boxes, a grand front door, and a chimney along one side. "You can do this, can't you? Or is it too difficult?"

"I can do it all right. But I thought you came in here to do it yourself."

He said nothing, just kept staring at his drawing. I decided it would be easier to do it for him than argue with him about it, and after a few seconds, I nearly forgot he was there. I added the chimney and door, then started to cut out the windows.

"What are you doing?" he asked.

"I'm trying to match your windows."

"I want it to be solid," he said. "Can't you apply windows to the walls?"

"Sure," I said. He was awfully picky. "How's that?"

"Perfect," he said as he looked at the house. "Shouldn't there be shingles or something on the roof?"

"How about a thatched roof instead?" I was really getting into the model building.

"No, I'd prefer shingles."

I took my knife and scored in lines of shingles on the rooftop. "Is there anything else you'd like?"

He studied it a moment, then said, "No, it's perfect. Do we paint it now?"

"It has to be fired first. If you come back in a few days, we can add the coloring then."

He frowned. "Does it really take that long?"

"I have to wait until I have a full kiln," I explained. "It's too expensive to fire a single item."

"I see," he said as he dipped his hand into his jacket. And why shouldn't he? The man hadn't bothered to dirty his hands the entire time he'd been in my shop. He retrieved an eel-skinned wallet and plucked a brand new hundred from it. "Will this cover your firing fee?"

"I think so," I said as I accepted the bill.

"Good. Then I'll see you this time tomorrow."

He was gone before I could even get his name, but if he wanted to be anonymous, he was paying for the privilege. I had a few other pieces to fire, so I decided to do a bisque-firing immediately. It was against my normal policy, but then again, I wasn't in the habit of hand-building projects for my customers, either. If it paid that well all the time, I'd have to start, though. I was just about to close the kiln and turn it on when I realized that I really wanted to see what the cottage would look like with a thatched roof. No one was in my shop, so I had time to make a cottage of my own. I set to work, creating a cottage completely different from that my customer had designed, and the results pleased me. Maybe I'd have to add a building segment to one of my classes.

My stomach growled as I turned the kiln on, and I realized that I'd nearly missed lunch. With no prospect of David's return, I had two choices: I could either raid the paltry contents of my shop pantry, or I could shut the place down and go get a decent lunch. If I hadn't just earned that hundred-dollar firing fee, I might have made do with the remnants in my shop, but that bill was pure profit as far as I was concerned, and I was determined to spend it. Normally every dime I made went into my shop books, but this once, I was going to make an exception. There was a hat I'd been admiring on my strolls past Hattie's Attic, and though I wasn't all that eager to do business with that busybody Kendra Williams, I did think it would look smart on me. I got out the sign that said, "Gone to Lunch," put it in the store window, and locked up.

As I glanced back inside to see if I'd left any lights on, I noticed just how stark the front window really was. My gentleman customer had been right. It wasn't very inviting; it made the shop look more like a place for lease than a going concern. My stomach growled again, but I ignored it and headed back inside.

Grabbing what I could from the sales area, I filled up the window without too much concern for themes or even basic principles of display. The window was full again, that was what really mattered, and I could go eat with a somewhat clear conscience.

I'd planned on trying the hat on after I ate, but if I was going to avoid Kendra until then, I was going to have to stear clear of Hattie's Attic. It was amazing how often I ate lunch at Shelly's Café simply because it was located in the opposite direction from Kendra's shop.

"Carolyn Emerson, have you been avoiding me?" Though she was busy grilling for her big lunch crowd, Shelly Ensign took the time to wave a spatula at me as I walked into the café. She was a petite woman, but anyone who had ever been on the other side of one of her tongue lashings knew her small size belied her feisty personality. I'd gone to school with Shelly, and not only had we sat beside each other in alphabetically ordered classrooms, but we also had consecutive birthdays: Shelly's birthday was May 11, mine, May 12.

"Shelly, why on earth would you ask me that?"

"You haven't been here in a week. Did I say something to offend you?"

"Nothing out of the ordinary," I replied as I took a seat at the counter that stood between the grill and the other tables. The café had last been decorated sometime in the 1950s, sporting black and white scuffed tiles, red vinyl tabletops, and mismatched chairs, the motif worked for Shelly.

Ken Marcus, the town's only doctor and the man who had delivered both of us, said, "Wait a second, you two are nearly exactly the same age. Yes, I remember that May well. Shelly, you were born at 11:57 P.M., and then I had to rush over to the next room to deliver you, Carolyn. It was 12:06 A.M., if I remember correctly."

"Nothing wrong with his mind," Shelly said.

"He's as sharp as ever," I added.

"Are you two youngsters making fun of me?" Dr. Marcus asked.

"Us? Why, we'd never do that," Shelly protested.

"No, sir, not for one second."

The good doctor stared hard at each of us in turn, threw a ten-dollar bill down beside his plate, and then headed for the door. "One of you bit me right after you came out, but I won't say which one did it."

Shelly and I pointed at each other automatically and said in near-perfect unison, "It had to be her."

The doctor shook his head and walked out without another word.

I looked at Shelly, fighting to hold my laughter in, but the second her smile broke free, I couldn't restrain myself. I didn't care that some of the other customers in the café were looking at us a bit oddly. It felt good to laugh.

"What can I get you today?" she asked as she went back to her grill.

"I'll have my usual." I thought about facing a salad on what I'd dealt with so far that day, and changed my mind. "On second thought, give me a hamburger and some French fries."

"Do you want a chocolate shake to go with that?"

"No, I'd better not. Make it a Coke. Diet."

Shelly smiled. "Sure, because you wouldn't want any unnecessary calories, now would you?"

"What can I say? I'm watching my figure."

She let that slide, so I asked her, "Are you feeling okay?"

"Why, what have you heard?"

"You let an opening like that sneak past you, I'm ready to call the paramedics."

"We're right here if you need us," a handsome young man said from a table in the back. I hadn't spotted him coming in, but sure enough, he and his partner were wearing EMT uniforms.

"False alarm," I said.

He nodded, and they went back to their meals. I turned back to Shelly. "I mean it, what's gotten into you?"

"Wayne thinks I'm too much of a smart aleck."

Wayne Campbell was her latest boyfriend, a man eleven years her junior. I would never dream about teasing her about that, though. Shelly had lost her first husband to cancer and the second to a car accident. I figured my friend was entitled to whatever happiness she could find. "Tell Wayne I like our relationship just fine the way it is," I said with a smile.

She nodded. "I do, too. Let me get that food for you."

I looked around the café as I waited for my order. It was jammed full with folks from town. There were restaurants where the tourists liked to go, but Shelly's was for locals. Not to say we'd throw somebody out if they weren't from Maple Ridge, but it took a brave soul to look past the run-down exterior of the café and actually step inside. I saw the mayor having lunch with his secretary from the car dealership he owned, and I wondered who they thought they were fooling with their innocent act. They were involved in something—romantics would call it a love affair; more pragmatic types would label it a sleazy relationship on the side. Either way, I doubted they'd be able to get away with it much longer. As some folks around our parts liked to say, "There's a storm a brewing."

Shelly slid my burger and fries in front of me, well before I was due to get my food. I lowered my voice. "You didn't have to bump my place in line."

"You've got a business to run, and no one to help you at the moment. I don't hear any complaints, do you?" She gazed around her restaurant, and not another glance met her stare.

"You heard about David already?"

Shelly nodded. "The whole town knows about it by now. Imagine the nerve of Richard Atkins just showing up like that. He ought to be shot, and I've heard a few folks think he will be."

"David and Hannah would never do anything like that, no matter what the provocation."

Shelly shrugged. "Who's to say what folks would do, given the right circumstances? Don't forget, though, Richard Atkins has more enemies in Maple Ridge than his ex-wife and his son."

"Like who, for instance?" I asked. I was not normally a gossip. Well, I wasn't. Okay, I admit that I might have shared a tidbit or two in the past, but this was different. Well, it was.

Shelly nearly whispered as she spoke next, and I had to strain to hear her. "There are a few folks sitting right here, our dear mayor being one of them."

I looked at Harvey Jenkins, who kept his rapt gaze on his curvy secretary, Nancy Jane Billings. "What could Harvey have against Richard?"

"You didn't know? They were in some kind of business together, and when Richard disappeared, evidently he took some of Harvey's money with him."

That was interesting, and something I'd never heard about. "Who else?"

Shelly looked toward the front door. I turned to see Kendra Williams making her way to the café. "Speak of the devil and she appears. Kendra has a reason of her own to make him regret showing up here."

"Kendra? Don't tell me she and Richard had anything in common."

Before Kendra could get inside, Shelly said softly, "Some folks say Richard did the antiquing on some of her pieces and started blackmailing her when she balked at paying him for his silence."

"That was a long time ago," I said.

"You know what they say. Elephants don't forget."

That was a cheap shot at Kendra's weight, but I wasn't about to defend her, not after Shelly had scalded me so many times with her whiplash tongue.

"Who else?" It was fascinating to me that I'd missed so much dirt.

"Can't talk about it now," Shelly said.

There was an empty stool beside mine, and I knew Kendra would head straight for it. Could I stop her somehow? Tell her it was saved for Bill, or someone else? Knowing Kendra, I was sure she'd stand there and wait, and when no one showed up, she'd start in on me. My best option would be to wolf down my food so I'd be exposed to her for a minimal amount of time.

"Is this taken?" she said loudly in my ear.

"Feel free," I said as I jammed a large bite into my mouth. "I'm just about through here."

"Don't hurry on my account," she said.

Shelly asked, "What can I get you?"

"The usual," she said. I wondered what that might be, but not enough to hang around to see for myself.

Kendra somehow managed to settle her bulk onto the counter stool and said, "It's a terrible shame about poor David, isn't it?"

"What about him?" I said through the fistful of fries I had crammed into my mouth. These weren't the skinny little fast-food fare, either. They were honest potato wedges, and I could barely mumble with them in my mouth.

"Imagine, that father of his just showing up like that after twenty years. He took off about the time the jewelry store was robbed, didn't he?"

I somehow managed to swallow, and said, "I guess so. I understand you knew Richard pretty well back then."

Kendra's eyes narrowed. "Who told you that?"

"I can't remember," I lied, trying not to look at Shelly.

"It's a bold-faced lie," Kendra snapped. "And I don't want to talk about it."

That was a switch. I didn't think there was anything on the planet Kendra wouldn't discuss. I thought about pressing her further, but if I did, it would have to wait. I ate the last bite of my burger, slipped my payment under my plate, then turned to Shelly and said, "Thanks for lunch."

She pointed to my money. "There'd better be enough for a tip in there, too."

"You know me, I always tip a solid 9 percent," I said with a grin.

Shelly collected the money as she cleared the plate. "It's nice to have something in this world I can count on."

I walked outside, grateful for the respite from the noise in the café. It hadn't sounded that loud when I was inside among them adding my own voice to the fray, but it became extremely noticeable once I was away from it. I didn't know how Shelly took it all day.

I thought about the hat I'd wanted to look at in Kendra's shop, but as she was at the café, I knew Hattie's Attic was closed. Now that my belly was full, I was starting to feel guilty about shutting my shop, especially with David missing. Had he come back while I'd been gone? I found myself hurrying back to Fire at Will. The sign was still in the door, and the place was dark inside. If he'd come back, he hadn't bothered opening up.

"David?" I called out as I walked inside after unlocking the door. I had the weirdest feeling, as if expecting to find a dead body in my shop. To be frank, it had happened before, though I hadn't had a premonition about it as I was now. A part of me wanted to call Bill, or even the sheriff, but I had no idea what I would say to either one of them. One thing I knew for sure. I wasn't about to admit that I had a gut feeling that something was wrong. I could hear them now, cackling about woman's intuition, something I believed in wholeheartedly, and I wasn't in the mood to be teased or scorned for it.

"David, are you back there?"

Still no reply. I wasn't convinced the place was corpse-free until I'd searched every bit of space big enough to hold a body.

Carolyn, I chided myself after shutting a closet door, you are letting your imagination take control of you.

I turned on the lights, flipped the sign to "Open," and tried to get rid of that sick, dull feeling that was still lingering in the pit of my stomach. I called David's cell phone, and then Hannah's, but I got their voice mails. Had my friend managed to find her son, or were they both ignoring any summons from the world outside their own? I hoped Hannah had found him, or would soon. She'd be able to settle David down. At least I hoped she could.

Blast Richard Atkins anyway. What nerve he had showing up like that after all those years. I was still cursing him under my breath when the telephone rang.

It turned out to be a call I wasn't particularly pleased to receive.

Chapter 4

"Sheriff, I don't know anything I haven't already told you," I said for the third time in the conversation. "David's still gone, and so is Richard. I haven't heard from Hannah, either. Why the sudden interest in their lives?"

"It's not all that sudden," he said. "I don't want this to develop into more than it has to. If you hear from any of them, call me."

"You'll be the first one on my list," I said, not even trying to sound sincere.

"That's good," he said, apparently missing my sarcasm. "I'd hate to see somebody get hurt."

"For once we have something we can agree on."

Without another word, he hung up. I had half a mind to call him back, but then the telephone rang.

"Where have you been?" My husband started in on me before I could get out an answer. "You were supposed to call me right back."

"I got distracted," I said. "It's been crazy here."

"Okay, I understand. Let me take you out to lunch, then. I'm starving."

"I really can't leave the shop right now," I said, failing to admit that I'd already eaten.

"Then I'll bring you something. How about a hamburger from Shelly's Café?"

There was no way I was going to put my friend in the position of lying to my husband for me. "I had one a few minutes ago," I admitted.

"I thought you were too busy to eat." His voice had that distinct sullen tone I knew all too well.

"I'm sorry, I should have called you back. I was wrong. Forgive me?"

Sometimes, the only thing to do is throw oneself on the mercy of the court.

To my delight, my husband accepted my apology. "If you had a burger, I'm getting one, too. And fries. And a shake."

"Hey, I had a Diet Coke with mine."

"Tough for you," he said with just a little too much glee in his voice.

"Enjoy your meal," I said. After all, being gracious in return was the least I could do.

"And pie," he added before he hung up. I thought about calling Shelly and vetoing the dessert, but Bill had probably earned it.

I was trying to figure out a new way to arrange the front window when I looked up to see Hannah tearing down the street. I raced out onto the sidewalk, but she blew past me, nearly knocking me over.

"Hannah? What's wrong?" I yelled at her back.

"I can't talk right now, Carolyn," she said, barely turning around.

"What is it? Did you find David?"

She didn't answer. In all the years I'd known her, I'd never seen my best friend act like that. Did it mean that she'd finally caught up with David, or had she found Richard instead?

This insanity had gone on much too long for my taste. It was time to call out the reinforcements. That meant the Firing Squad, my team of amateur potters, as well as one of the best informal investigation crews in our part of Vermont. If they couldn't find David, I wasn't sure what I would do, but at least we had to try. Butch answered on the first ring.

"Are you waiting for a call?" I asked him after I identified myself.

"I had a feeling you'd be giving me a ring," he said. "I haven't seen him."

"How on earth did you know I was looking for David?"

"Give me some credit, Carolyn," he said with a chuckle. "I know more about what goes on here than I let on. I've asked a few friends to keep an eye out for him, too, but so far, no luck."

"I appreciate your help," I said. "I need to call Jenna and Sandy, too."

"It's taken care of," Butch said. "I'm coordinating things from here, and I'll let you know as soon as any of us hear anything."

"I feel useless," I admitted. Butch had taken it upon himself to organize a search party, probably while I'd been stuffing my face at Shelly's.

"Don't say that," he said. "We need you."

"That's sweet of you to say, even if it's not true."

"Don't sell yourself short, Carolyn." He hesitated a second, then said, "We probably shouldn't tie up the line."

"I thought you'd have call-waiting," I said.

"I do, but the last time I checked, you didn't. What happens if David tries to call you and gets a busy signal?"

"I hadn't thought about that. I'd better get off." I hung up. I'd have to thank Butch for his efforts by making a batch of my peanut butter and Hershey's Kiss cookies. He'd loved them since the first time I'd brought a batch to one of our meetings, and every now and then I liked to surprise him with the treats. He'd earned a double batch today.

I waited on a few customers, but the day still dragged. I kept expecting David to walk in. I had a funny fluttering in my stomach, and it wasn't because of anything I'd eaten at Shelly's. I feared something had happened to my young assistant. The phone rang a dozen times during the rest of the afternoon. The Firing Squad kept checking in, all with null reports, unfortunately.

It was seven minutes past my regular closing time, but I couldn't bring myself to lock the door and go home. What if David needed me, and I wasn't there?

The door chimed, and I called out without looking up, "We're closed."

"You're not, but you should be," my husband, Bill, answered.

"What are you doing here? I thought you'd be ankle deep in sawdust." He was busy working on new furniture pieces for Shaker Styles, a local furniture business, and I'd grown accustomed to his late hours.

"I was. Now I'm not. Let's go home."

"Are you telling me you stopped work to take me home? I'm not some kind of feeble old invalid who needs watching after."

He frowned. "That's not what I meant. I've been working too hard lately. I miss you."

What a sweet old bear. I hugged him, then said, "That's one of the nicest things I've ever heard you say. What exactly do you miss most about me?"

"Well, the first thing that comes to mind is that I haven't had a home-cooked meal in weeks," he said.

I jerked away from him. "And you're not getting one tonight." He had a decidedly crooked smile when I looked at him. "Why are you grinning like an old fool?"

"I was just kidding."

"Well, it wasn't very funny."

He shrugged. "You were fishing for compliments. You know how I hate that. Come on, let's go home."

I could have fought him on it, but he was right. We hadn't been spending much time together lately, and I'd missed him, too. "I don't know if I should leave."

"I said I was sorry."

He looked hurt. "Actually, you didn't. But that's not why I want to stay. What if David needs me and I'm not here?"

"He knows where we live, Carolyn," Bill said. "If he finds this place empty, we're less than ten minutes away. Come on, I'll make you dinner tonight."

I wasn't in the mood for one of his evening breakfast meals. "Thanks for the offer, but I've had stew simmering away all day."

"That beats my eggs, I won't deny it. Let's go."

I looked around the shop, still not sure if I should leave. But Bill had a point. I had no idea if David would show up, and it didn't make sense for me to wait for him. "Let me just do a few things to close, and then I'll meet you at home."

"I can wait," he said.

"Are you going to just stand there and hover while I work?"

"No," he said. "I think I'll sit down instead."

My husband dead-bolted the front door, flipped the "Open" sign to "Closed," then walked to the back of the shop and flopped down on the new couch. It had been an extravagant splurge, but one I'd happily made, eager to replace its predecessor.

I took the day's receipts from the till, totaled the report, then slid everything into my store safe—a ceramic piggy bank. It wasn't all that secure if someone knew where to look, but honestly, who would look in a piggy bank in a pottery store for money?

"Let's go," I said as I finished my nightly tasks.

"Do you have a firing tonight?"

"No, I've got one going already, and I'm waiting until tomorrow for the other one."

"Good enough. Let's go get some stew."

Out on the sidewalk, I bolted the door and turned to my husband. "Whose car should we take?"

Bill smiled at me. "You'd better drive. I went home and parked my truck, then I walked back here."

"What's gotten into you?" I asked. My husband wasn't exactly an exercise fanatic. "It must have taken you an hour to get here on foot."

"More like half that," he said smugly. "It was a pretty evening, and I've been stuffed inside that woodworking shop too much lately. I needed some fresh air."

"You're perfectly welcome to walk back home, then."

He raised an eyebrow. "There's no need to be obsessive about it. Let's go."

The first thing I did when we walked in the door at home was check our answering machine. It was dismally blank. I'd hoped that David would have at least checked in, espeically given his hasty exit from the shop, but I knew he wasn't obligated to call. Even our sons didn't call us regularly. Bill and I had raised our boys to be independent, to live their lives on their own. Some of my friends demanded daily or weekly calls and visits from their children, but I thought they were a bit daft. I, for one, refused to wait by the phone. I had a life of my own to live, and while I loved my two boys more than anything in the world, besides my husband, I was proud of them for making their own way it the world. Birthdays, holidays, and a few times in between were usually the only occasions when we heard from them.

"Nobody writes, nobody calls," Bill said as he caught me staring at the phone.

"No news is good news," I said. The aroma coming from the kitchen was divine. "Let's eat, shall we?"

"I'm one step ahead of you. I already set the table."

After we ate, Bill asked, "How about a movie?"

"You're actually staying here? What about those deadlines?"

"They can wait. I want to spend a little time with you, and to be honest, I'm flat worn out. So, what would you like to watch?"

"We haven't seen *Casablanca* in a while," I suggested.

"Bogart it is," he said.

The movie hadn't even flashed back to Paris before Bill was sound asleep. Truthfully, it wasn't holding my attention, either, and I thought it was the greatest movie of all time. I nearly turned it off, but then remembered Bill's reaction to silence. As long as the movie played on, he wouldn't stir, but if I turned it off, or even lowered the volume, he'd shoot out of his chair as though it were on fire. I grabbed a light sweater, tucked the portable phone in my hand, then went outside. The Vermont summer was fast approaching, by far my busiest season of the year. Not only did tourists descend on Maple Ridge, but also the town's children were out of school, so I would have summer camps and classes going almost continuously. We needed the cash influx to stay open the year round, but I didn't look forward to the rapid pace life would soon hold.

I hadn't done a raku firing in some time, and I realized I'd like to. The electric kilns did a fine job back at the shop, but the raku process was simple and offered spectacular results. I'd take pieces we'd already bisque fired, then after glazing them, bring them to my backyard, where I had my equipment set up. After a quick firing in my outdoor gas-fed brick kiln, I'd pull out the red-hot pots and bury them in wood shavings or wadded-up newspaper. Thermal shock caused the glazes to shrink and crackle. It was a process I loved, partly because there was no way to exactly predict what the outcome would be. Oh, I'd have an idea of what the end result would look like, but it almost never completely matched the finished product.

Leaves had collected in the pit area where I moved the pieces after their firings; I'd need to clean up the area if I was going to fire again.

As I walked closer to the pit, I noticed the leaf pile had a peculiar shape to it. It was as if—no, it couldn't be. I brushed a few leaves from the pile, and my worst fears were confirmed.

It was a body, and the instant I saw the man's long hair, I knew it was David.

*   *   *

"Bill, wake up. Call the sheriff."

"What?" he asked groggily as he sat up. "What happened?"

"Where's the phone?" Why wasn't he listening to me?

"Take it easy, Carolyn. It's right there in your sweater pocket."

I'd forgotten I had it. My fingers were shaking too much to dial the numbers, and I shoved it into his hand. "Call Hodges. I found David. By the kiln. He's dead." The sobs were coming now, stealing my breath, and to my husband's eternal credit, he ignored the phone and wrapped me up in his arms. After a few minutes, I managed to catch my breath and I pulled away from him. "Sorry. I lost it for a second there."

"You're entitled. Are you going to be all right?"

"I think so," I muttered.

"Good. Stay right here. I'll be back in a second."

The last thing in the world I wanted was to be left alone. "Where are you going?"

"I have to check myself."

"You don't believe me?" My voice had a hysterical pitch, but I couldn't seem to suppress it.

"Of course I do. It won't take a second."

"I'm going with you," I said.

"You don't need to."

"You're wrong. I do."

He studied me a second, then said, "Come on."

Why on earth had I volunteered to see David again? I couldn't decide which was worse, the prospect of seeing Bill turn him over and staring into David's lifeless eyes, or being in that house alone, waiting for my husband to return.

"Let me grab my flashlight," he said. A minute later, we were outside by my kiln. I wondered if I'd ever be able to bring myself to fire there again. I doubted it, with the image of David constantly hovering in my mind.

I stayed back a few paces, but Bill walked up to the body and knelt beside it. "What are you doing?" Why was I screaming?

"I've got to make sure he's really dead."

Oh no. I hadn't even considered that possibility. What if my reaction had robbed David of his last chance to be saved? Hannah would hate me for eternity, and I wouldn't blame her.

My husband reached down and tried to find a pulse. I stood there watching, afraid to utter a word.

He shook his head, then stood. "He's dead all right, but it's not David."

"Are you sure? The hair looks just like his."

Bill said, "That's because you looked at it in the twilight. It's too gray to be David's, but unless I'm missing my guess, it's his father."

I felt a momentary flood of relief wash through me, but it was soon gone.

"What's wrong?" Bill asked me. "I thought you'd be happier about the news."

"I'm glad it's not David, but you know who the sheriff is going to suspect. Hannah had every reason in the world to kill him, didn't she?"

"From what I've heard around town, she'd have to get in line." He started dialing the phone, but I put a hand on his. "Do we have to call him right now?"

"You know we do," Bill said. "It's the proper thing to do."

"I guess," I said, "but I'd like to see if I can get Hannah first and warn her about what's about to break loose."

"It'll have to wait until I call Hodges," my husband said firmly.

Thirty seconds later, after listening to Hodges's warning not to touch anything, Bill handed me the phone. "I'd call her as fast as you can. You're right; she deserves a heads up about what's about to happen."

At least my hand wasn't shaking anymore. I dialed Hannah's number, and instead of saying hello, she answered with a question. "David, is that you?"

"It's Carolyn," I said. "I'm afraid I've got some bad news for you."

"It's David, isn't it? He's dead." There was an utter lack of emotion in her voice as she said it, as if she already believed it in her heart.

"I found a body, but it wasn't your son's. It's Richard. Somebody killed him and his body is in my backyard."

"Oh, no," she said, and then hung up the telephone before I could warn her that the sheriff would likely be coming after her and her son.

Bill asked, "What did she say?"

"As soon as I told her about Richard, she hung up on me."

He shook his head. "I hope she doesn't run away from this. Panicking is the worst thing she could do right now."

"She didn't kill her ex-husband," I snapped at Bill.

"Take it easy. I didn't say she did. But you know how she can be."

I was saved from answering by the sound of sirens nearing. A minute later, Sheriff Hodges came into the backyard, followed by half a dozen other officers.

"You can go inside," he said to us after he heard how I'd stumbled across the body. "I'll be in later to get an official statement from you."

"I just told you all I know," I said.

"Bill, will you take her inside? We've got work to do."

He nodded and put an arm around me. "Come on, Carolyn. Neither one of us can do anything out here."

"You're taking orders from the sheriff now?"

He whispered, "I'm doing this for you. Do you really want to see them examining the body? I thought I'd save both of us from that nightmare."

"Okay, I understand that."

I walked inside with my husband, who said, "You might want to put a pot of coffee on. It's getting chilly out there."

"They can go to the convenience store and get their own coffee," I said.

"They can, or we can do the right thing and offer them something ourselves. Carolyn, I know you don't like the man, but it wouldn't hurt to be civil. He's just doing his job."

"I'm not sure I agree with that."

"Blast it all, I'll make it myself then." As Bill started toward the coffeepot, I waved him off. "I'll do it. After all, I don't want them to arrest you."

"Why would they do that?"

"Some folks might think having to drink your coffee was a crime."

At least it gave me something to do. After the coffee had brewed, Bill grabbed a tray and filled it with mugs, and I got the pot.

To my relief, the body was gone by the time we got out there. The sheriff said, "I thought I told you to stay inside."

"We brought you and your staff some fresh coffee," I said as I took in the scene: crime tape surrounded my kiln, portable lamps lit up the yard, and an officer was filming the whole thing.

"That would be nice," he admitted as he took a mug from me.

"So, do you know what killed him yet?" I asked as casually as I could manage while Bill handed out mugs to the rest of the force.

"Is that why you're suddenly being so nice?" he asked. "Are you out here trying to mine me for information?"

"Forget I said anything," I said.

After a few sips of coffee, Sheriff Hodges said, "Sorry. Murder always puts me on edge. I'd tell you if I could, but it's not time to release that information yet." He gestured with the cup. "Thanks for the brew."

"You're welcome," I said.

After he was finished, he handed me the mug. "That was mighty hospitable of you, Carolyn."

"It was Bill's idea," I admitted.

"Tell him I said thanks, then." He paused and said, "He was beaten up pretty bad." Then asked, "Did David ever turn up?"

"You honestly can't suspect him of killing his own father, can you?"

He paused a second before answering. "There's no telling what a shock like that might do to his system. Now, don't get in an uproar. I need to talk to him, that's all. Surely you can see that yourself. How about Hannah? Why isn't she here?"

"What do you mean?"

"Carolyn Emerson, I'll give you ten to one that you called her right after your husband called me. Don't make me pull the phone records to prove it."

"What makes you think I didn't call her before I called you?"

"I doubt Bill would let you. So let me ask you this. Why isn't she here? She's got a stake in it—even you have to admit that."

"I don't know what you're talking about," I said as I turned and walked away.

As Bill and I collected the rest of the mugs, I did my best to avert my gaze from the raku pit. It was as dead to me now as Richard Atkins.

My thoughts returned to David. His disappearance would look bad for him, but why would David kill Richard? The man was his father, albeit an absentee one. Then I realized that Richard, in the guise of Charles Potter, had also been his hero. There was no telling what he might do given that combination. Could Hannah have killed him? She had reason enough. At least she had twenty years ago. But that was a long time to hold a grudge. Or was it? There had to be other suspects, including the ones Shelly had mentioned earlier that day. I wondered if the mayor, Harvey Jenkins, or that gossip Kendra Williams had alibis for this evening, or if Sheriff Hodges would even get around to asking them. No, most likely he'd focus on David and Hannah, two of my favorite people in the world. I was not going to let him pin this murder on either one of them. Whether Bill liked it or not, that meant that I was going to have to do a little digging on my own.

Chapter 5

"I'll see you this evening," I told my husband the next morning after I kissed his cheek.

"Where are you going at this hour?" he asked as he sat up in bed. "It's the middle of the night."

"It's 6 A.M.," I corrected him. "I have some errands to run before I open Fire at Will."

"Hang on a second. Let me get dressed and I'll go with you." He started to get up, and I put a hand on his shoulder.

"Go back to sleep. I'm perfectly capable of being on my own."

He rubbed his eyes. "Have you talked to Hannah already?"

"No, but I'm hoping she meets me for coffee this morning. She usually calls to cancel if she can't make it, and I never heard from her last night." I was painfully aware of the extenuating circumstances that might have kept her from calling, but that didn't mean I was going to give up on my friend. I was hoping the regularity of our morning coffee breaks together would bring her to In the Grounds out of habit, if nothing else.

"Who are you going to talk to this early?"

"No time to chat. I'll call you later." I knew if I told my husband I was going to Shelly's Café, he'd refuse to stay home in bed. He loved her pancakes more than he loved mine, a point of contention between my dear husband and me since he'd first disclosed it.

Shelly looked surprised to see me as she worked at feeding what was currently a light breakfast crowd. "I didn't know your alarm clock worked," she said as she slid three eggs, bacon, and a short stack of pancakes on a platter.

"I'll have one of those," I said.

"I don't care what you get, but you can't have that one," a burly man said from the other end of the counter. "That one's mine."

"Or is it?" Shelly asked. "How do you know Carolyn didn't phone ahead?"

"You don't take telephone orders," he said smugly.

"I do for my friends," she replied.

He looked as though he might cry.

"Let him have it," I said. "I'll wait my turn."

For a moment, I thought the man was actually going to kiss me. "Thanks."

"My pleasure," I said.

Shelly leaned forward. "Is that really what you want?"

"Make it two eggs, one piece of bacon, and some dry toast," I said, vowing to stick to my diet.

"Not even one pancake?" she asked.

"Well, just one," I said, promising myself I'd try walking home sometime myself.

She had my breakfast ready in no time, and since no other customers had come in, Shelly pulled up a stool and sat across from me at the counter. "Mind some company?"

"Actually, I was hoping to talk to you."

She nodded. "The sheriff came by. I figured the murder last night brought you in this morning. It must have been awful finding the body like that."

"It wasn't the most pleasant thing I've ever experienced," I admitted, "but at least it wasn't David." I explained the similarities between David's and his father's hair colors and styles, and my confusion when I'd stumbled into the pit the night before.

"I never even thought of that," she said. "Have you seen him? How's he taking it? It's got to be tough losing a father you didn't even know."

"I haven't talked to him, or his mother. It wouldn't surprise me if the sheriff has them both locked up by now."

Shelly frowned. "I know you're not a big fan of the man, but he's not as bad as you think."

"I don't know how he could be," I said. "The real reason I'm here is that I'm looking for more information."

"About Richard Atkins? Carolyn, I don't know anything I could swear to. All I hear are rumors and idle speculation around this place. You'd be amazed by what folks say here. It's almost like they forget I'm working back at the grill."

"I need to know what you've heard," I said. "I'm not about to accuse anybody of murder without facts, but I do need to know where to look. You mentioned the mayor and Kendra Williams. Do you have any other suspects in mind?"

She bit her lip, so I added, "Besides the obvious ones like Hannah and David? I'm not even going to consider either one of them at the moment."

She didn't look all that happy when she said, "It's possible, though. You have to admit that."

What was Shelly getting at? "Do you know something I don't?"

"Knowing and proving are two different things, aren't they? Each one of them had motive enough, didn't they?"

I stabbed a bite of pancake and ate it before I trusted myself to speak. "I'm not going to even think about that possibility. Let the sheriff worry about them. I want to talk to people Hodges won't. Come on, Shelly, if you know something, tell me."

She hesitated, then said, "As soon as I heard about the murder, I started thinking about who might have killed Richard Atkins. Besides the four people we've talked about, I know of two other folks who might have hated him enough to kill him."

I waited ten seconds, then asked, "Who are they?"

She lowered her voice. "Remember, you never heard this from me, okay?"

"I promise I won't tell anyone where I got my information." What more did she want, a blood oath?

"Richard was seeing someone on the side while he was married to Hannah," she said softly. "When he took off, he left her high and dry, too."

"Who was it?"

"She has a shop near yours."

"Kendra was sleeping with him, too?" I couldn't imagine that particular union, and I would have paid good money to get the thought excised from my mind.

"No, I'm talking about Rose Nygren."

I was nearly as surprised by that name as I would have been by Kendra's. "Timid little Rose, of Rose Colored Glasses? Are you sure?"

"She hasn't always been that soft-spoken," Shelly said. "I never caught them doing anything, but a few folks around town saw some things that made me wonder. I remember after Richard left, Rose was nearly inconsolable."

That would definitely bear looking into. "Who else? There wasn't another woman, was there? How did the man find the energy, let alone the time?"

"No, it was just Hannah and Rose; at least those were the only two I was aware of."

"So, who else would want him dead?"

Shelly frowned, then said, "If you repeat this, I'll deny it and call you a liar, okay? It's not something I want to talk to you about anyway."

"I already gave you my word," I said. "What more can I give you to convince you?"

She appeared to think about it a few seconds, then nodded. "You should talk to the man Rose was seeing at the time. He never forgave her for the affair, and I doubt he'd have given up his grudge against Richard, even after all these years. Rose was the love of his life, and he never forgot her, even if he couldn't get past what she'd done."

"All you need to do now is give me a name," I said.

"I will, but you're not going to like it. I hate to have to be the one to tell you this, but it's your uncle Don."

"What? I'm not one of his biggest fans, but I can't imagine Don killing anyone, can you?" Don Rutledge was my mother's youngest brother, a slim, hard-eyed man with a fiery temper and such a generally bad demeanor that he was an outcast at every family reunion. He'd gotten drunk at my wedding, dove headfirst into the cake, and somehow managed to knock off my mother's wig in the process. I'd stopped calling him "uncle" years ago, and I avoided him whenever I could, though we lived less than twenty miles apart. Still, I'd have to talk to Don, even if it meant dragging up a past I'd just as soon forget. I loved David and Hannah more than a disenfranchised uncle. Some folks cared only about blood relations. What mattered to me was what was in someone's heart. Hannah and her son were more a part of my real family than Don would ever be.

"Is there anybody else I should talk to?" I asked.

"How about a psychiatrist? Are you really going to try to solve this murder on your own?"

"I don't have much choice, do I?"

Shelly stared hard at me. "You could always butt out and let the sheriff do his job."

"I suppose I could, but I'm not going to. Whose side are you on, anyway?"

She touched my hand lightly. "Yours, always yours. You shouldn't even have to ask."

I slid a ten under my plate and started to get up.

"Hey, that's too much," Shelly said.

"Think of it as a nice tip."

"I don't think so," she said as she made change. I took the money and jammed it into my purse.

Shelly frowned. "Do you mean I don't get any tip at all now?"

"Make up your mind," I said as I slid a single under my plate. "If you think of anything else, call me, okay?"

She cracked the single in her hands. "With tips like this, I'll be burning up the phone lines hoping for more."

I left her place and glanced at my watch. I'd tarried much too long over my meal, and if I was going to make my standing date with Hannah, I'd have to rush to get to In the Grounds.

*   *   *

I needn't have bothered. Hannah never showed up, though I lingered over my coffee much longer than I should have. After all, I had people I needed to see before it was time to open Fire at Will. I hated the thought of closing up shop during the workday again, but with David absent, and without any idea of when the boy was coming back, I knew I might not have much choice. Out of my list of suspects, Don was the one I least wanted to speak to, so I put him at the head of my roll. I'd discovered long ago that the more I dreaded doing something, the quicker I needed to do it. Otherwise it would linger over me like a black rain cloud until I took care of it.

I got into my Intrigue and headed toward Autumn Landing. It was time to see if Don might have had something to do with Richard Atkins's murder.

I was half hoping my uncle wouldn't be home as I drove to his house. I would have rather had a sleepover with Kendra Williams than talk to Don.

He kept a nice yard and house, I had to say that for the man. The grass was manicured, the shrubs were precisely trimmed, and the paint on the house wasn't more than six months old. It was as clean and sterile as a magazine layout, and I knew the inside would be just as stark. I was idling in his driveway, trying to work up the nerve to approach the house, when his front door opened.

It was a pretty unusual welcome, since he had a shotgun in his hands.

"Hi, Don," I said through my open window.

"Carolyn, what are you doing here?"

"Trying not to get shot at the moment. Do you mind lowering that thing? I'm looking for some information." I wasn't all that comfortable staring down those double barrels.

"What? Sorry," he said as the gun muzzle dipped. "I thought you were somebody else."

"Care to give me a hint who you're waiting for?" I asked as I got out of my car, wondering who my uncle had ticked off recently.

"The government says I owe more on my taxes than I do. We've been having a little disagreement about it."

"So you greet federal agents with a shotgun?"

He grinned. "It's not like it's loaded." He pulled the trigger, and I heard a thunderous boom as the turf at his feet exploded with the impact of the pellets.

"I thought I took those shells out," he said calmly as he breached the gun and pulled out two shells, one spent and one fresh. "Sorry about that."

"No problem," I said, my knees feeling a little weak. I expected the neighbors to come pouring out of their homes to see what had happened, but not a door opened, though I saw a few curtains fluttering without the aid of a breeze.

"Blast it all," he said, staring at the ground where the buckshot had gone into the dirt. "I hate that that happened."

"No one was hurt, but you should be more careful," I said.

"You're telling me. Do you have any idea how long it took me to get this turf just right? I'm going to have to start all over on this patch. It's ruined."

So much for my uncle's familial concern.

"I'll leave you to it, then," I said as I started to get back into my car.

"You never said why you came by," he said.

"Forget it." The last thing I wanted to do was get on this lunatic's bad side. If anything, he'd gotten worse over the years.

"That's the problem," he said. "I can't just let it go."

I didn't want him stalking me. "I came to talk to you about Richard Atkins."

He frowned, then said, "There's a name I'd just about forgotten." He twisted the ring on his right pinky, a bright green stone of adventurine mounted on gold. The twisting appeared to be a nervous habit, and I wondered what he had to be concerned about. "What happened, did he finally get himself killed?"

"Now why do you ask that?"

"It was bound to happen sooner or later, the way the man acted. Don't tell me it happened in Maple Ridge?"

"In back of my house, actually. I understand you weren't his biggest fan."

My uncle grinned, but there was not an ounce of warmth in it. "He took something of mine, something I didn't want to let go."

"So it's true? You actually went out with Rose Nygren once upon a time?"

Don looked shocked by the suggestion. "Now where on God's green earth did you hear that?"

"A friend told me," I admitted.

"Well, your friend lied to you. My relationship with Rose was a little different than that. She was a good friend of mine, and Richard ruined her."

"It's obvious you didn't care for the man, but did you hate him enough to kill him?" I asked softly.

He raised the shotgun in the air again, and although I knew it was unloaded, I still felt uneasy having it pointed straight at me. "You didn't chuck that pottery store of yours and join the police force, did you?"

"No, I still run my shop." I certainly wasn't going to say "Fire at Will" while he was holding a gun on me.

"Then why are you snooping around?"

I wondered what our front-yard conversation must look like to Don's neighbors, but I doubted any of them would try to rescue me. "Hannah Atkins is my best friend, and her son, David, works for me. I'm not going to let the sheriff's suspicions settle on either one of them."

"So you'd rather pin it on family than have it pinned on your friends, is that it?" I swear, I could see his finger tighten on the trigger. The gun *was* unloaded, wasn't it? I was growing less sure with every passing second.

"I just want to find out the truth," I said, attempting to keep my voice from quivering.

"The truth's a slippery thing, Carolyn," he said.

I was still trying to figure out how to reply to that when he said, "Leave Rose out of this. Do you understand me?"

"Are you actually threatening me, Don?"

"It's Uncle Don, if you don't mind. And no, I'm not threatening my sister's kid." He stared long and hard at me, then added, "But I am warning her. There are a dozen other folks around town who wanted to see that man dead. Go try looking at them."

"Anybody in particular you have in mind?"

"Start at the mayor's office and work your way down."

It was clear I wasn't going to get anything else out of him. I started to get back into my car for the second time, and managed to shut the door before he spoke. "Where are you going?"

"I've got a business to run," I said. "Remember?"

"Just as long as it's not mine." He held the shotgun firm in his grip. "Heed my words, Carolyn."

I managed to muster a weak grin in reply before backing out of the driveway.

As I drove away, I felt an itching in the back of my neck where the pellets would hit if my uncled fired, and it didn't go away entirely until I was out of sight of his house. Would Don Rutledge have actually shot me? On purpose, I mean. I hadn't been worried until Rose Nygren's name had come up. At that moment, I honestly believed that my uncle was capable of just about anything.

But I wasn't going to let that deter me. In fact, I was going to visit Rose before it was time to open Fire at Will. Maybe I could get the truth out of her. At the very least, I doubted she'd take a shot at me.

Rose was playing with her front window display when I walked up to Rose Colored Glasses. I'd always enjoyed a clever name, and Rose's was perfect, even without knowing the proprietress's name. I could see through the glass that Rose's red hair was pulled back into a ponytail. I tapped on the display window and she jerked up, so startled that she dropped a lovely red stained glass hot-air balloon. It shattered on the brick floor, and I felt sick at the sight of the broken pieces.

I walked inside and said, "Rose, I'm so sorry. I didn't mean to startle you."

"It's fine, Carolyn. It happens more than you'd imagine." As always, her lilting voice was almost a whisper.

"Have you ever thought about carpeting the place?" I said. The bricks had to be torture on stained glass.

"Carpet is so sterile," she said. "I love the textures of the bricks, and if it means I lose a piece now and then, so be it."

"I'll be happy to pay for it," I said, reaching for my purse.

"Nonsense. It was an accident. You weren't even the one who dropped it."

"No, but I caused it as surely as if I'd knocked it out of your hands. How much is it? I insist."

"They're thirty-nine dollars," Rose said almost apologetically. Thirty-nine bucks for that? I was in the wrong business. I counted out four tens from my wallet and handed them to her.

She wouldn't take the money. Instead, she said, "At least let me sell it to you at cost."

"No," I said, despite being tempted. "I robbed you of a sale, so I won't hear of it."

She accepted the money, folding it up and putting it into her apron, rather than the register, and I wondered if my money would ever see her till. I thought about the single I had coming back to me in change, but decided not to make an issue of it.

"Since I'm here, I'd like to talk to you," I said. At least my forty dollars might grant me an interview.

She glanced at her watch. "I've got few minutes. What's it about?"

She started to rearrange the window display now that one of her hot-air balloons was gone, but I couldn't afford to pay any more breakage fees. "May we sit for a moment?"

She reluctantly agreed, and we moved over to her sales counter where she had two chairs poised nearby. "What would you like to talk about?"

"It's about what happened last night," I said.

"Why? What happened?"

"You mean you haven't heard?" I asked. I'd been sure some branch of the Maple Ridge grapevine would have reached her by now, but evidently I was mistaken.

"I went to bed early last night, and I haven't spoken to anyone this morning. What is it, Carolyn?"

"Somebody killed Richard Atkins in my backyard last night."

I was watching her face, but she showed no reaction at all. It was as if she already knew, but that didn't match what she'd just told me.

"So, it finally happened," she said after a moment.

"You don't seem all that surprised, if you don't mind me saying so," I said.

"I'm long past letting anything catch me off guard," she said. "If you'll excuse me, there's someone I need to call before I open."

I hoped it wasn't Don. "Do me a favor, don't tell anyone I told you, okay?"

"Why not? Is it some kind of secret? You did call the police, didn't you?"

"Of course I did," I said as I stood. "I just don't want anyone to think I'm being cold, talking about it like this."

"Certainly. Now I really must make that call."

I walked outside, and Rose locked the door behind me. I gave her twenty seconds, then I took out my cell phone and dialed my uncle's telephone number. It was busy. Perhaps it was just a coincidence, but I doubted it. Until I knew different, I was going to assume that Rose had phoned my uncle. Why would she call him, though? To tell him the news, or perhaps to thank him? I wasn't sure how I could find out, but I didn't want to attract unwanted attention by standing in front of Rose's locked shop hitting redial every seven seconds. I headed toward Fire at Will.

As I walked past Hattie's Attic, I didn't even think about Kendra Williams, I was so focused on wondering what my uncle and Rose were up to. Kendra wasn't about to let me just pass her by, though.

"How dreadful for you." I didn't need to see the faded muumuu to realize Kendra was talking to me.

"I could say the same thing to you," I said.

She looked taken aback by my comment. "Whatever are you talking about? Are you in some kind of shock after finding that dreadful man's body?"

I leaned in toward her, something that made her uncomfortable, if the sour expression on her face was any indication. "I'm fine, but I wonder if you are."

"You're talking nonsense," she said, taking two steps back toward the safety of her shop.

"Am I?" I followed her, matching my steps with hers.

"I've got to go." She was in full retreat now.

"I'm right behind you." It was nice unnerving her for a change, but it wasn't going to get me any information. Before she could escape inside Hattie's Attic, I said, "You must be relieved the man's dead."

"Carolyn, I'm willing to make allowances, given what happened last night, but I won't stand here and be insulted like this."

"Would you rather go inside and sit down?" I asked. "We can do this in your shop, if you'd like."

"I don't know what you think you're doing, but you're not going to browbeat me in front of my own place of business. I'll thank you not to come back until you can act normally."

"No promises there, Kendra," I said.

She nearly ran inside, and I waited to hear the dead bolt slam shut, but apparently even my behavior wasn't enough to keep her from losing a sale. Kendra was jumpy, but I didn't know if it was because of what had happened the night before, or the way I was acting. No matter how much joy it gave me to see her off balance, I couldn't afford to alienate her by applying too much pressure.

I walked over to Fire at Will and unlocked the front door. A part of me was hoping David would greet me as I walked in, but there was no sign of him—until I walked in back. There I saw my comforter spread out on the couch and some wrappers from a convenience store on the floor beside it. It had to have been David. While I would have normally fussed at him for not cleaning up his messes or warning me he'd be camping out in my back room, I didn't care. At least it meant he was still all right.

I picked up the phone next to the couch and had started to dial Hannah's number when I heard tapping on the front door. I still had two minutes until I officially opened. Whoever was out there would just have to wait. Hannah's phone kicked me straight to voice mail. I said quickly, "It's Carolyn. Call me as soon as you get this."

I hung up and looked out the front window. It was my dapper elderly gentleman from the day before. He was back to finish up his house. I vowed not to lift a finger, to make him do the glazing himself.

After turning on the lights, I unlocked the door, and he bolted in past me. "Sorry to be so impatient," he said, "but I just couldn't wait."

"That's fine," I said. "Let's see how it turned out." I led him back to the kiln and opened the top. It was cool enough to reach in and pull out his clay house. "There it is," I said.

"It's all pink," he said, obviously a little disappointed in the hue of the building.

"Remember, we're going to paint it next, so it won't stay that way."

He looked over my shoulder and saw the nearly full kiln. I said, "I had a few other things to add at the last second. Things fire more uniformly if it's a full load."

"Rightly so," he said. "You don't want to waste the electricity either. It is electric, isn't it? I don't see any gas lines."

"I have a gas kiln at home," I said, "but we use electric ones here." I wasn't going to finish unloading the kiln with him standing there, but he must have spotted the house I'd made after I retrieved his. "Did you do another one?"

"It was fun, so I decided to make one, too," I admitted.

He looked delighted. "Well, bring it out. Let's see what you've come up with."

He took my decidedly more eccentric house and studied it as carefully as if it were an architectural rendition instead of a flight of my whimsy.

Finally, he declared, "It's perfect. You must glaze yours along beside me."

He was paying for the privilege, and besides, it sounded like fun. "Let's pick out some colors then. Do you have anything special in mind?"

"Of course. The exterior should be a gray pristine enough to represent a weathered shade of white, while the windows should be painted forest green. The roof needs to be a brown, the tint of autumn loam, and the chimney should be faded red."

Okay, that was a little more specific than I'd been looking for, but he certainly gave me a good set of guidelines. I started pulling out paints and mixing to get the shades he was after. He looked at the palette with obvious disappointment. "My, those are rather muted, aren't they?"

"Wait until they go through the kiln. I think you'll be happy with the colors I've come up with."

He frowned at the paints as if he didn't believe me.

"Look, it's as easy as this," I said as I grabbed a brush and started laying on the main body tint.

When I finished, I handed him the brush. At least I tried to. He refused, saying, "I just don't have the touch you seem to. Would you mind?"

It was beginning to look as though this project was all mine, but I didn't have any other customers, and he had paid for the privilege with his firing fee the day before. Besides, I enjoyed painting pieces. "How's that look?" I asked when I'd finished.

"Rather bland, I'm afraid."

"I'll tell you what, if you're still disappointed after it's been fired, I'll refund your fee. How's that sound?" What was I saying? I'd already spent some of the hundred he'd given me, and here I was offering a full refund. I suddenly had more at stake than I had intended.

"I couldn't do that," he said. "Will you be firing again tonight?"

I didn't want to, since there weren't enough pieces to make it worth the expense, but I was feeling bad about taking so much before. "For you, I'll run it through tonight."

"Excellent," he said. "Do you mind if I watch you decorate yours? I'm in a bit of a rush, but I'd love to see your preliminary step."

"Why not?" I chose a rusty red and dusty blue to decorate my cottage, then added some ivy outside as an afterthought.

"What was that last bit?"

"I thought some ivy would look good crawling up the outside of my place," I said. "Would you like some on yours?"

"No, there's no ivy on mine," he said resolutely. I had to

give him credit. He had the most specific imagination I'd ever run into. "Same time tomorrow?"

"I'll have it ready for you," I said.

I don't know if I would have taken another hundred if he'd offered it, but it didn't matter, because he didn't. Where was Hannah, and why wasn't she calling me back? I thought about trying her again, but I knew she was extraordinarily conscientious about returning her calls. I'd give her more time. In the meantime, I decided I might as well fill up that kiln, so I decorated another batch of my ornaments that I'd bisque fired the week before. I enjoyed doing them, letting my imagination run wild with the colors and designs. After I'd stacked the kiln, I decided to go ahead with the firing.

It was a good morning's worth of work, but I was increasingly uneasy about how much time had passed without any word from David or Hannah.

I was just about to pick up the phone and try her again when I saw Hannah outside rushing toward my front door. From the expression on her face, I could tell something had gone horribly wrong.

Chapter 6

"I don't know what I'm going to do," my best friend said as she nearly collapsed in my arms. "David never came home last night."

If Hannah had gotten even an hour's worth of sleep the night before, she certainly didn't look it. Normally stylish and sharply dressed, she appeared to have slept in the suit she was wearing; uncharacteristic bags shadowed her eyes. Her hair, usually so well tamed, was frazzled and frayed, no doubt much like the woman's spirit.

"From the way I found my back room this morning, I'm guessing he stayed here," I said as I held her.

She jerked away from me as if I were on fire. "He was here? Why didn't you tell me?"

"I tried to call you this morning when I got in, but you weren't answering your phone. I left you a message."

"Oh, no," she said as she pulled her cell phone out of her

purse. "I forgot to charge it. The battery's dead. What if David's been trying to reach me?"

"Let me see it." One glance was all it took. "I have the exact same phone you do. Take my battery. I charged it last night."

"That will leave you without a phone, though."

I fumbled with the back of my cell phone, took out the battery, and pushed it at her. "If anybody needs me, they can call me here. Your need is a little more urgent than mine."

We swapped batteries, and I plugged my phone into its charger. I kept one charger at home and another at the shop, since I was always forgetting to plug in my cell phone, or turn it off, for that matter.

She checked her voice-mail messages and had four waiting, but only one of them mattered to her. It was from David, and after she listened to it once, she handed it to me.

"Mom, I'm okay. I can't come home. I'm in . . . ," and then the message died. What had he been trying to add? Was he in love? In trouble? In England? In jail? The dead tone of his voice didn't betray much additional information.

"What does it mean?" Hannah asked.

"It means he was okay last night, and probably this morning, too. That's got to count for something."

"Carolyn, I need to know."

"I know you do, but there's nothing you can do about it right now, is there? If you can think of anything constructive to do, I'll help. You know I will."

She frowned at me, then started to cry. As I held my distraught friend, I tried to imagine how I would feel if one of my sons were in trouble. I didn't have to think about it for very long. Without a doubt, I would be ready to rip the world apart to find him.

"I don't know what to do," she stammered out.

"I know. It's okay, Hannah. He's going to be all right."

She blew her nose into a tissue. "I wish I could be as sure about it as you are."

"It's easier for me," I said as I handed her the whole box. "It's not my son we're talking about."

"He thinks of you as his other mother. You know that, don't you?" She wiped at her tears, but the tissues were no match.

"I love him, too. Listen to me. David is smart, he's resourceful, and he's got a good head on his shoulders. He's going to be all right."

"Doesn't he know he's just making things worse hiding like this? The sheriff's certain he killed Richard. That's why he keeps hounding me."

I picked up a mug from the sale table that someone had painted, paid for, then abandoned. It was an ugly little thing, but at least it gave me something to do with my hands. "Does the sheriff suspect anyone else?"

"Besides me, you mean?" She rolled her eyes. "He's already determined that if David didn't kill his father, I did it myself. I'm not afraid to admit that I had more reason than most to do it, but I didn't, and David didn't, either. He wouldn't. He couldn't. I wouldn't believe it if he himself told me he'd done it."

"Of course he didn't do it," I said, trying to soothe her. I hadn't lied. I did love David, but that didn't mean I was blind to his faults. He had a temper sometimes, and it was quick and sharp and strong when it reared its head. If he were in one of his moods, and Richard's sudden reappearance had triggered it, I wasn't sure what he might do.

"I can't stay here," Hannah said, "but I just had to come see you."

"If I hear from David, I'll call you, or make him do it himself. Don't worry. What am I saying, of course you're going to worry. If it helps, I'll be worrying, too."

"It does," she said as she squeezed my hand. "You're a true friend."

"So are you," I said.

"I've got to go," she said, fighting back another jag of tears. "You'll call me. You promise?"

"I swear. Where are you going?"

She thought about it a minute, then said, "I need to be home. It's the first place David will look for me."

And the first place the sheriff would expect, too, I thought. But I didn't say it aloud. Hannah didn't need to hear that from me, or anyone else.

After she left, I was trying to decide what I should do when the front door chimed. In walked Butch, followed by Jenna and Sandy. The Firing Squad had come to help me in my hour of need, and I knew if Martha hadn't had a house full of sick children, she'd be right there with them.

I just wished I knew some way they could help.

"We need a course of action," Jenna said as we gathered in back. I stood in the doorway where I could keep an eye on the front, just in case a customer happened to wander in. Hey, stranger things had happened.

"Where could David be?" Sandy asked.

"That's the question, isn't it?" I asked. "Folks, I appreciate you coming by, but I don't know what any of us can do."

Butch put a big paw on my shoulder. "That's not like you, Carolyn. Finding that body must have been tough on you."

"I do seem to stumble across more than my share," I admitted. "But that's not why I'm so pessimistic. David was shattered when Richard told him he was his father. You should have seen his face." I didn't want to say it, but I had to tell these people what they might be dealing with. "He wasn't himself. I don't know what he might have done."

Butch squeezed my shoulder, and I tried not to wince. "Carolyn, in his worst hour, David's not a killer. But the kid has to be pretty shook up by what happened. Finding, then losing your old man in a span of a few hours would be hard on anyone." He released his grip, and I tried to hold in my relief.

Jenna said, "Let's find him. I'm sure we can do it if we just use our heads."

"If it helps, I'm pretty sure he spent last night on my couch," I said.

"He was at your house?" Sandy asked. "Why didn't you tell us that from the start?"

"Not my couch at home," I said as I pointed to the one in back of the shop. "He slept there, and from the look of the way he left things, he was in a rush when he took off."

Butch walked around the couch as if it were a fascinating artifact instead of the discount sofa it really was. "It looks clean to me."

"That's because I just couldn't leave it like it was."

"Where's the trash bag?" he asked.

"I tossed it in the Dumpster in back. You're not going to dig through my trash, are you?"

"I've done a lot worse in my life," he said with a grin. "I'll be back shortly."

I appreciated their help, truly I did, but there was no way I was going to let him sort through my rubbish in my shop. "Don't bring that bag back in here. Please."

Butch nodded. "You got it."

At least he was abandoning that plan. Or so I thought.

"I'll do it out back. No offense, but I need room to work anyway."

Was he serious? "Go on, then."

"Don't worry, Carolyn, I'll clean up after myself. Where are your spare trash bags?"

I pointed to the bathroom. "I keep some back there."

He grabbed a few bags, then headed out back. As he reached the rear entrance, he stopped and asked, "Anyone care to join me? No? Okay, suit yourselves."

When the door shut, I asked Jenna and Sandy, "Has he lost his mind?"

"No, the police do it all the time," Jenna said, "a fact that's not lost on our friend, I'm sure. Let's see if we can come up with something ourselves while we're waiting for Butch."

Sandy walked over and picked up the telephone. "Have you used this phone since you came in this morning?"

I remembered my frantic telephone call to Hannah when I'd first found the mess. "Sorry, I called Hannah this morning."

"That's all right, how could you know? Redial would have been nice, but there's got to be something here." She started digging under the cushions of the sofa.

"If you're looking for spare change, I've got some in my purse," I said.

"I'm looking for clues," she said.

Jenna smiled. "I thought the Internet was your specialty."

"Hey, a gal's got to branch out sometimes, doesn't she? What's this?" Sandy held out a wadded-up sheet of paper and started to open it as Jenna and I approached so we could see it as well.

We looked at the paper and saw the numbers 06-07-91 written on it in what was unmistakably David's handwriting. Sandy frowned at it and said, "What is it, some kind of combination? I wonder if it's to a safe."

"Yes, David is so rich he needs a safe to keep his money in," I said dryly.

"It could be a birthday," Jenna suggested. I glanced at a calendar I got from my glaze supplier. "It doesn't mean anything to me."

"It's got to mean something to him, though," Sandy said, too proud of her discovery to allow any dispute.

"Sandy, we have no idea how long that's been there. David could have left it months ago."

"You haven't had the couch that long," Jenna said.

That was true. I'd been forced to replace the old one when I'd discovered something about it that I preferred to forget. I'd had the new one for only a few weeks. "That still doesn't mean he left it last night."

Butch came back in holding a soiled piece of paper.

"What did you find?" I asked him.

"This was torn from a pad. There's an impression of something, but I can't see what it is. Hand me a pencil."

I gave him one from the counter near where I was standing, and he rubbed the edge of the graphite along the sheet. After he'd done that to his satisfaction, Butch held the paper up to the light and read, "I think it's a six up front. Let's see, that looks like it might be a one right there."

"Could it be a seven, by any chance?" Jenna asked, trying to suppress her grin.

"Hang on, let me see. Yes, I think you're right. It does look like a seven. Now how in the world did you know that?"

Jenna grabbed Sandy's paper and handed it to him. "We found the original. Or Sandy did, I should say."

The librarian was grinning broadly.

"You're quite proud of that, aren't you?" I asked.

"That's not why I'm smiling. The paper Butch has proves that David wrote this last night. It's got to mean something."

"I suppose you're right," I admitted.

"It has to be."

Jenna said, "But we still don't know what it opens. Or if it even opens anything."

I looked at Butch, and he was frowning.

I couldn't have that. "You gave us valuable confirmation. Don't look so glum."

"That's not it," he said. "This could be something else."

"We're listening, if you have any ideas," I said.

"What if it belongs to a security system for someone's business, or even their house?"

Jenna said, "Surely you're not accusing David of being a burglar, are you?"

"No," Butch said patiently. "He doesn't have the skills for it. But if we knew where it matched, it might tell us where he is right now."

Sandy asked, "What kind of skills do you need to steal?" Her tone of voice wasn't accusatory. She was obviously fascinated by the subject, but we didn't have time for one of Butch's discourses on the art of thievery.

"Never mind that right now," I said. "There can't be that many homes in Maple Ridge that require a security code, can there?"

"You'd be surprised," Butch said. "There are more around here than you'd think."

"I'd really love to know how a reformed thief would know that," Jenna said sternly.

"I can't help what I notice," Butch said. "Once you've trained your eyes to look for certain things, you can't just ignore those observations, even if the information isn't pertinent anymore."

"Would you two please hush?" I asked. "I'm thinking."

I dared Butch to say something about my scolding, but he kept silent. Why on earth would David have a security combination for someone's house? Where would he get one? Then I remembered what his girlfriend did for a living.

As I reached for the telephone, I said, "I've got to make a call."

"Who are you calling?" Sandy asked.

"Annie Gregg. Hush, it's ringing."

After seven rings, she picked up. "AG A1," she answered.

I knew that was the name of her cleaning business. It was clever, catchy, and had the distinct advantage of being listed first in the Yellow Pages.

"Annie, it's Carolyn."

She sighed deeply and then said, "Carolyn, I haven't seen David since yesterday morning."

"But have you spoken with him?" I asked. "Perhaps long enough to give him the security code for someone's home who happens to be out of town, maybe a client who is trusting you to care for their property while they're away?"

Okay, perhaps I was being a little heavy-handed, but I needed to find David before he got into any more trouble. I added, "You're not helping him, Annie, despite what you might think."

In a voice that was nearly a whisper, she said, "He made me promise not to tell. I talked to him this morning."

"I won't say anything," I said as reassuringly as I could. "Where is he, Annie? I need to know. It's for his own good."

"I can't tell you anything," she said after a long pause.

"Could you at least give me a hint? I found the security code here at the shop. That is what 06-07-91 means, isn't it?"

"Yes," she admitted. Again in a near whisper, she added, "Look up and you might see him."

"What?"

"I won't say anything more, Carolyn. Good-bye." She hung up before I could say another word.

Had the dear child spent too much time breathing in cleaning fluid fumes? Look up. Was she kidding me? And then I realized what she had to have meant. There was one place, a stately mansion indeed, that looked down on all of Maple Ridge, and I'd been there a few times myself.

Tamra Gentry was in New York the last I'd heard. Her estate on the mountainside would be the perfect place for David to hide out.

"Let's go," I said as I started for the front door.

Butch said, "Let me lock up the back entrance. You can't trust people these days. Carolyn, you really should update your security system around here."

"What are they going to take, a few bags of clay and some glaze? I'll risk it."

"Those kilns might be expensive to replace."

"Enough of this. Where exactly are we going?" Jenna asked.

"Tamra Gentry's place. I've got a pretty good idea that's where David is hiding out."

"Let's go," Sandy said.

"Don't you have to work? I don't want to get you in trouble with Corki."

"I took a sick day as soon as I heard about David. Do you honestly think I could work and not help him? He's my friend, too, Carolyn."

I hugged her quickly. "I knew there was a reason I was so fond of you."

"Hey, I'm coming, too," Butch protested.

I hugged him as well, then turned to Jenna. "How about you?"

"I'm coming, but we can skip the embrace," she said. "Are you all quite ready?"

"Absolutely." I grabbed the "Closed" sign and hung it in the door without another thought. If it meant I lost some business, so be it. David took precedence over everything else at the moment.

Butch said, "I'll drive," and none of us argued with him. His Cadillac had plenty of room, and if there was an option he didn't have on it, it was purely by accident.

As we drove up the steep, winding road to Tamra's place, I thought about what I would say to David. Should I scold him for running away like he had? For that matter, should I even bring up his father's death? I'd have to figure it out on the fly.

The leaves of a hundred maple trees obscured the drive, but I could still see Tamra's place through gaps in the canopy. It truly was a stately place, a three-story colonial with massive white columns in front that loomed over all of Maple Ridge.

It was impossible to tell if Tamra, or anyone else, for that matter, was in residence. Had I guessed right? David didn't have to come out if he didn't want to. Although I had the security code, I suddenly realized that I didn't have a key, something I had neglected to ask Annie about.

Butch parked in front of the house.

I reached for my phone, but couldn't find it anywhere in my purse. Then I remembered that it was still in the charger at the shop, the good battery now on Hannah's phone. "Can I borrow one of your cell phones? I need to make one more call."

"We're already here," Sandy said. "Let's just go in."

"I have the code, but we still need a key," I said.

"Sorry, I forgot all about that."

I shouldn't have snapped at the poor girl, since I'd forgotten that myself. I smiled. "To be honest with you, so did I, until thirty seconds ago."

"We don't necessarily need a key," Butch said in a soft voice. Before Jenna could protest, he added, "I'm just saying."

"Make your call, Carolyn," Jenna said as she handed me her cell phone.

This time, Annie picked up on the first ring. I said, "Annie, it's me again. I know there must be a key hidden out here somewhere. That's the way Tamra is." It was a guess, but I thought it was a good one.

"Where are you?" I detected a little bit of fright in her voice, as if she'd said too much earlier.

"I know David's at Tamra's, but I'm afraid if I ring the bell, he'll try to run again."

That wasn't really true; I had no idea how David would react, but I needed this girl's help. "I want the best for him, too. Surely you know that."

Was she crying? I wasn't sure, and the sound stopped nearly as soon as it had started. Finally, she said, "Look under one of the columns. There's a bit of detail work hiding the key. You have to push on a slight paint smear and it opens up."

"You've got to be kidding me," I said as I got out of the

car in search of this secret hiding place. It was obvious the others wanted to know what I was up to, but to their credit, they followed me in relative silence. I studied each column's base and couldn't see a thing that looked out of the ordinary. "It's not here."

"The key's gone? David must still have it," she said.

"No, I'm talking about the paint smudge. It's simply not on any of the bases."

"Are you sure you're looking carefully enough?" Annie asked.

"I can see a smudge without my glasses," I said abruptly. "Which column is it in? Do you remember?"

She paused, then said, "I think it's on the right side. It's not the key I use, but Tamra told me about it in case I lost mine."

"I started from the left," I said, "but I'll keep looking."

"I'm sorry, I'm just not myself."

"It's all right, dear," I said. "I can't imagine how hard this is for you."

"Thanks for being so understanding, Carolyn."

"That's what I do," I said. "I'm looking, but I still don't see it." The others must have thought I'd lost my mind, but they didn't say a word as I stared intently at the column bases. I explained what I was looking for, then Butch got down on his hands and knees and started studying one himself. He frowned a second, then poked a spot I'd missed. To my surprise, a small door opened, and there, inside the base, lay a key.

"We found it," I said.

"We? You didn't bring the police with you, did you?"

"Of course not, Annie. Now I've got to go."

"You won't tell him I told you, will you?"

"I promise," I said, and then I hung up. I stared at Butch

as he handed me the key. "How on earth did you know to do that?"

"It was pretty obvious, wasn't it?" he said, trying not to sound too smug.

"Maybe to you," I said.

I took the key and approached the door.

Jenna put a hand on my arm before I could try it. "Are you sure we shouldn't ring the bell first? We might frighten him off if we just barge in."

"I'll call out his name as soon as we get inside," I said.

I slipped the key into the lock and gently turned the knob. As I slowly pushed the door inward, I saw a handgun leveled at my chest, and David's finger nearly white on the trigger.

Chapter 7

"Would you mind pointing that somewhere else?" I asked David as calmly as I could manage. This was the second weapon pointed at me today, definitely a trend I wanted to discourage.

"Sorry, I didn't know it was you," David said as he lowered the gun to his side.

Butch walked past me and took it from David's grasp. "You should never point one of these things at somebody unless you're willing to use it," he said. "And before you can do that, you've got to take the safety off, like this." He moved a small lever and handed the gun back to David. "Now it's ready to shoot."

"Give me that," Jenna snapped, and David handed it to her. She put it gingerly in Butch's hands. "Put the safety back on, unload it, and then, David, put it back where you found it."

"Fine," he said. "What are you all doing here? Annie told you where I was hiding, didn't she?"

I wasn't about to tell on her. "It wasn't that difficult to figure out," I said before the others could stop me. "You left the security code wadded up on the couch. The alarm's not set right now, is it? We wouldn't want the sheriff showing up." I added with a frown, "Nice housekeeping in the shop, by the way."

"Sorry," he said sheepishly. "I was in a bit of a rush to get out of there. That still doesn't explain how you knew to come here. Annie must have told you where I was, and where to find the key."

Butch grinned at him. "I used to be a crook, remember?" The man was taking a page from my book, lying convincingly by telling the truth. There was an art to it, one Butch had obviously mastered long ago.

"I can't even hide right," David said miserably.

Sandy approached him. "Do you know about your father?"

David's head shot up. "That man is not my father. He walked out on my mother before I was born. What was he thinking, coming back here after all this time?"

Jenna asked softly, "You know he's dead, don't you?"

David looked wildly at us. "I didn't kill him!"

"We believe you, but if you didn't have anything to do with his death, why are you hiding?" I had to know.

David looked at me as if I'd lost my mind. "You're the one who keeps saying what a fool Sheriff Hodges is. If I show my face, he'll arrest me for sure."

"You don't know that," I said. "And I never said Hodges was a fool. He's a lot of things, including lazy, but he's not stupid, David. You're just making things worse for yourself hiding like this."

"I can't just walk into town now, can I?"

Butch stroked his chin. "Why not? You haven't done anything." He paused for a few seconds, then smiled. "In fact, that's exactly what you should do. David, you need to head back into town with us, go to work with Carolyn at the shop, and call your mother. She's worried sick about you."

David looked ill at the suggestion. "I tried to call her this morning, but she wasn't picking up her cell phone."

"That's because she left her phone on all night so you could call her," I said. "I agree with Butch's plan, with one change. You'll borrow Jenna's cell phone and call your mother on the way down the hill."

"So you honestly think I should just act like nothing's happened? What about you, Jenna? What do you think?"

"I have to agree with them, David. If you haven't done anything wrong, there's no reason to hide. Don't forget, I was a lawyer long before I was a judge. I'll stay at the shop for the rest of the day, in case you have any trouble with the sheriff."

"You'd do that for me?"

"Of course I would," she said. "We will all do whatever we can to help you. We're here, aren't we? Now let's forget this foolishness and go to Fire at Will."

He looked relieved that we'd stepped in. At least until Jenna handed him her phone. "Call your mother," Jenna and I said in unison.

He nodded reluctantly. "Fine. Can I call her before we go, though? I'd like a little privacy."

"Need I remind you all that we're here unlawfully?" Jenna asked. "It wouldn't do to tarry."

"I won't be long. I promise," David said as he walked back to the bedroom area.

The four of us waited in the living room, and I saw Sandy frowning. "Is that what I think it is? No, it couldn't be."

She was admiring the Monet I'd spotted on my first visit to the house, but before I could confirm it, Butch glanced at the painting and said, "It's the real thing, all right."

Jenna said, "Now how could you possibly know that? You barely glanced at it."

"Would you really like to know?" Butch said, barely able to hide his grin.

"Forget I asked," she said as David rejoined us.

"That was quick," I said.

"She's going to meet us at the shop," David said. After expressing her relief, Hannah undoubtedly had blistered him for taking off the way he had. I wasn't looking forward to being privy to part two of their little chat, but Fire at Will wasn't anywhere near the size of Tamra's house, and if they raised their voices above whispers, we'd all be able to hear what they were saying.

After David put Tamra's gun away properly and set the house alarm, Butch locked up and returned the key to its resting place. We then rode down the hill in relative silence. I half expected to see Sheriff Hodges waiting for us when we got back into town, but there was no sign of anyone in front of Fire at Will as Butch pulled into a parking space near my doorway. I normally liked to keep those spots open for new customers, but I wasn't about to ask Butch to move, not after all his help this morning.

He must have caught my glimpse, because as we were getting out, he stayed put. "I'm going to move this to the upper lot. I'll be right back."

"You don't have to," I said.

"But you wouldn't mind, would you?"

I was still looking for a polite way to answer when he grinned. "It's fine, Carolyn. I know the way you like to do business."

I unlocked the front door, and everyone went inside.

David looked around the shop, then asked, "So what do we do now?"

"There's not much we can do but wait," I said.

Sandy said, "I don't know about you guys, but I'm going to have a little fun while I'm here."

"That sounds delightful," Jenna said. "What shall we do?"

"Help yourselves," I said. "I've got some things I need to take care of. David can teach you anything you'd like to learn. Don't worry about fees; this lesson is on the house." I walked up front to work on my display a little more while they continued discussing which new project to try.

The front door chimed a few minutes later, and I looked up, expecting to see Butch returning from parking his car, or even Hannah making an appearance.

What I had not expected to see was our illustrious sheriff.

At least not so soon.

"Where is he?" the sheriff demanded as he walked in.

"Who exactly are you looking for?" I asked. Not that I really had to guess, but he was using a tone of voice in my shop that I didn't approve of, at least not when it was directed at me.

"Don't get cute, Carolyn. I'm not in the mood for it."

"I wouldn't dream of it."

David poked his head around the corner. "Are you looking for me?"

"Where have you been?" the sheriff said as he moved toward him quickly. "Let's go. You're coming with me."

"Hold on, Sheriff," Jenna said as she joined us. "David has a right to an attorney, and I'm going to represent him, if he agrees to it."

"Sure, that would be great," David said.

Sheriff Hodges didn't look happy about the prospect, but there wasn't much he could do about it. "Are you really going to hide behind her?"

David started to reply, but Jenna touched his arm. "David, from now on, you're not to speak without express permission from me. Do you understand?"

Instead of answering, he just looked at her and nodded.

"Let's go," Sheriff Hodges snapped.

When I started to follow them out of the shop, he said, "Not you. You have no standing in this."

I looked at Jenna, who shook her head slightly.

Taking her cue, I said, "Fine, I'll stay here."

Jenna said, "Don't worry, I won't leave his side, and I'll call you the second I learn anything."

Butch came back in after they were gone. He found Sandy and me discussing what had just happened. "I leave you alone for five minutes, and now half the group's gone. Where's Jenna?"

"She's with David. The sheriff came by to talk to him, and Jenna agreed to represent him."

Butch smiled, and I added, "This is not the slightest bit funny."

"I'm just thinking about how Jenna's gonna shred him. Come on, don't you find that a little amusing?"

Sandy smiled. "I don't envy our sheriff. If we're not going to work on anything else, I'm going to go."

"Back to work?" I asked.

"Are you kidding? I'm taking a sick day, remember? No, I'm going to snoop around and see what I can find out about Richard Atkins."

Butch asked, "Would you like some company?"

"Sure, why not?" She looked at me and added, "Carolyn, you're more than welcome to come, too."

I was tempted, but I finally said, "No, I'd better stay here. I might get a customer. Stranger things have happened. Besides, Jenna expects me to be here, so I'm going to stay."

A little arm-twisting and I would have gone with them, but they both left, and I was at Fire at Will alone.

Not for long, though.

"Where is he?" Hannah asked as she stormed into the shop. "Where's David?"

"He's not here, Hannah." Before she could explode, I added, "The sheriff took him in for questioning, but don't worry, Jenna Blake's with him."

"And you just stood there and let it happen?"

"Well, I thought about stopping them, but the sheriff had a gun, and all I had was some pottery."

"Don't be ridiculous," she said.

"Then give me a little credit, will you? David's in good hands."

"I can do better than a retired judge," she snapped.

"In Maple Ridge? I doubt it. Let Jenna handle it, Hannah. She knows what she's doing. I'd let her defend my own sons, if it came to that."

"Good for you. I'm going to find someone else."

Before I could talk her out of it, Hannah was gone. Wow, a great many people were walking out on me today. The phone rang, and as I picked it up, I asked, "Jenna?"

"No, it's Bill. Your husband, remember?"

"Oh."

He paused a second, then said, "I've had warmer welcomes in my life. What's wrong?"

"What makes you sure something is? You don't know everything about me."

He chuckled, a sound I normally enjoyed. Just not at the moment. "What's so amusing?"

"I know enough. Now quit stalling and tell me what happened."

"If you must know, the sheriff came into the shop and took David in with him."

"When did he finally turn up?"

"The sheriff? About ten minutes ago. Why?"

"Not the sheriff, David. Stay focused, woman."

"David came to the shop this morning."

Bill hesitated, then asked, "Are you trying to tell me he just waltzed right in there of his own free will? Why don't I believe that you didn't have a hand in it?"

"You're just not very trusting, I guess," I said.

"With reason, from the sound of it. Does Hannah know where the boy is?"

"She left here thirty seconds ago. From the way she was talking, I expect to see Clarence Darrow's heir-apparent show up at any minute. She was pretty fired up when she left."

"Wouldn't you be? I don't suppose there's a chance in the world you're going to stay out of this, is there?"

"What do you think?"

"I know, I know, that's why I said that. Just be careful, okay? There's a killer loose in town."

"Why on earth would he come after me?" I asked, honestly startled by the premise.

"We don't know why he got Richard, do we? You could be next on his list."

"Or you," I retorted.

"Me? Why would anybody want to do me in? You're the closest thing to a threat on my life."

"Bill Emerson, why would you say something like that?" Sometimes my husband could utter the most inane things.

He laughed. "Cause you're the beneficiary on my life insurance policy."

"What is it, fifteen grand? You're worth more than that to me alive. Barely, but still."

"Hey, as long as it's in the plus column, I should be okay. If you need me, call. I'll be in my shop at the house, though, so leave a message and I'll get back to you as soon as I can."

"I'll be fine," I said, then I hung up the telephone. I'd grown accustomed to my husband's disappearances into his workshop. He was almost impossible to reach there, with all the constant sawing and hammering going on. I'd be in dire shape if I were depending on Bill coming to my rescue, especially if I had to get him on the telephone. My cell phone was charged enough, so I put it in my purse in case I'd need it later.

It was nearly lunch when Hannah came back to Fire at Will. She had two bags from Shelly's Café with her. "Feel like a quick bite with me?" she asked.

"That depends. Are you going to take my head off again?"

She looked contrite. "Carolyn, I'm sorry. When it comes to David, I tend to be a little overprotective sometimes."

"Really? I hadn't noticed. I'm surprised you're not with him right now. Is he still with the sheriff?"

"With the way Jenna was watching out for him? Hardly. She's quite vigorous defending him."

"So you're not getting a hired gun from New York or Los Angeles?"

"What gave you that idea?"

"When you left here, you said you were going for a legal-eagle gunslinger."

Hannah smiled. "I got one, too, didn't I?"

"David hired Jenna, remember?"

She snorted. "Does it really matter who chose her? They're back at Jenna's house now, deciding how to handle this. I was asked to leave, since the attorney-client privilege doesn't extend to mothers. Now are you going to accept my apology and eat with me, or do I have to have both burgers myself?"

"I forgive you," I said as I reached for one of the bags.

"You're too easy," she said, smiling.

"Hey, what can I say, you've found the best grease there is."

"Don't you like Shelly's burgers?"

I nodded. "Of course I do. I'm not talking about that kind of grease. I mean to make an apology go smoothly. Relationship lubrication is what I'm referring to."

"What can I say? I do my best," she said.

As we ate, we tried not to talk about what had happened to Richard, or why the police were focusing on David. It made for a strained conversation, but by the time we were finished eating, we were both at ease with each other again. I hated when Hannah and I fought, and I always felt better when we'd patched things up.

After we cleaned up, Hannah said, "I hate to eat and run, but I've got a class to teach."

"I thought you had TAs for that," I said.

"Believe it or not, some of us in the profession actually

like to teach. Besides, my dear assistant is in love again, and that means her focus won't be on the modern novel."

"So, you feel pretty comfortable about Jenna helping David?"

"For the moment," she said. "I don't have much choice, do I? David insists that Jenna is the only lawyer he trusts, and if I'm hard-pressed, I'd probably have to agree. There's nothing I can do now, so I might as well teach my class."

I shrugged, and she must have read more into it than I'd meant to convey. "Do you think it's heartless, me teaching the day after my ex-husband died? I know women who would still be partying."

I looked her dead in the eyes. "But you're not that kind of woman, are you?"

"No, I'm not. I was devastated when Richard walked out on me, but that was a long time ago. Being with him wasn't all bad. We had our share of joy, and I got David in the bargain. Don't get me wrong, I wasn't about to nominate him for sainthood, but I didn't hate him. Now if I could just get the sheriff to believe me."

"Has he been pressuring you as well?"

"Let's just say he's keeping an eye on me. What are you doing about the situation?"

I picked up a glazed mug and pretended to study it. "What do you mean?"

"Carolyn Emerson, there's no way on earth you're standing idly by. I know you too well. You're looking into Richard's murder, aren't you?"

"I might have asked a few questions around town," I admitted reluctantly. The sheriff had already scolded me about my behavior, and my husband had as well. I wasn't in the mood to hear it from Hannah, too.

She shocked me by saying, "Well, keep it up. Don't let anyone talk you out of it."

"Excuse me for saying so, but you're usually not this supportive when I start snooping." That was an understatement.

"I've got a vested interest this time. Besides, if the sheriff is focusing on David and me, somebody else has to look for the real killer. Keep me posted, okay?"

"Sure," I promised.

After Hannah had gone, I wondered about her change of heart. Did she want to be notified of my progress for David's sake, or for her own? I might have to wonder about that, if I were a suspicious person, which normally I wasn't. Well, I wasn't. Okay, maybe sometimes, but only if it was merited. Anyway, it could be argued that Hannah wanted to know what I was up to so she could see if I was getting too close to the truth. Could she have had something to do with Richard's murder, despite her earlier declaration? Or did she believe in her heart that David had killed his own father in some kind of fit of rage? Nonsense, I couldn't believe it of my best friend in the world, or her son. Still, just to be cautious, I decided it couldn't hurt to keep quiet about what I found out, at least until I was able to come up with something definitive.

"Hi, is this where I can paint my own pottery?" a petite young woman with fine blonde hair asked as she came into the shop an hour before closing.

"This is the place," I said, trying to keep my sarcasm to myself. I looked around at the bisqueware, the bottles of paint and glaze, and the tables, and wondered what else she thought it might be. "Is there anything in particular you're interested in?"

"I think I'll look around first," she said.

"Be my guest. If there's anything you need, just let me know." I wasn't exactly worried about shoplifting, at least not from the unglazed section; some of the pieces I had on display were worth quite a bit of money, but I figured it'd be difficult for her to get a teapot under her dress, as snugly as it fit.

It was fascinating watching her study each item in turn, picking it up, looking at all sides of it, then placing it delicately back down. Forty-five minutes later, she was still just halfway through my stock. "I'm afraid if you don't make a selection soon, there won't be time to decorate it," I told her.

She looked pensively at me. "I just hate to rush my decision."

"I understand," which was a total and complete lie if there ever was one. "I just thought you should know."

"Perhaps I should come back tomorrow."

People took less time to choose a mate. "I'll be here."

She thought about that another minute. "That's what I'll do then. I'll come back tomorrow."

That's what she said. What she did was just stand there, staring at the pottery she'd yet to examine. Finally, reluctantly, she left. I couldn't wait for her return. If David managed to come into work the next day, she was all his. Maybe with my handsome young assistant she'd make a decision in less than a month.

I normally hated to close the place early, but that woman had gotten under my skin. So what if I lost a customer or two? I flipped the sign, dead-bolted the door, then started cashing out the register.

I'd just started my report when I heard a knock at the front door. "We're closed," I called out without looking up.

"Open up the door, you daft old woman," my husband, Bill, called out from the sidewalk.

I walked over to the door, but I didn't unlock it. "You'll need to talk a little sweeter than that if you expect me to comply."

He stared at me a few seconds, as if deciding what to do, then grinned slyly. "If you don't let me in, you won't know why I'm here. Let's see your curiosity stand that."

"I can take it if you can," I said, turning my back on him. Honestly, the man should have learned by now not to order me around. I gave it thirty seconds, then turned back to him.

He was gone.

But where? I leaned out through my display window trying to catch sight of him, but my field of vision was limited to a few squares of the sidewalk on each side of my shop. I unlocked the door, and the second I did, he popped out from next door.

"Got you," he said with delight.

"Get inside, you old goat."

"Now who needs to talk sweet?" he asked. "It's not nice, calling your husband an old goat."

"Which part do you object to, 'old' or 'goat'?"

He frowned. "Both of them. What do you think?"

"I think they fit, sometimes," I said. I noticed a few window-shoppers looking our way. "Now get inside. You're making a scene."

As he followed me into Fire at Will, he said, "You were the one yelling."

"I was not yelling," I said, trying to keep my voice soft. I had a tendency, when aggravated, to increase my volume, or so I've been told. I wasn't sure it was true, but enough people had pointed it out that I was beginning to doubt it could be a conspiracy. "Now what is your news?"

"Speak up. I can barely hear you," Bill said, cocking one hand behind an ear.

"You heard me just fine, and you know it. What's going on?"

"I got another commission," he said. "It's for five Shaker-style nightstands for a bed-and-breakfast over in Newberry."

"Olive Haslett is working you too hard." Olive owned the business Shaker Styles where my husband was employed. What had started out as a hobby after his retirement had developed into a full-time job.

"Olive's got nothing to do with this," he said. "I got this order on my own."

"Do you mean to tell me you're soliciting business on the side? Don't you have enough to do?"

He said, "I thought you'd be happier about it. I'll make twice as much as I do working for Olive."

"We don't need the money," I said. "Besides, you're supposed to be retired and enjoying yourself."

"If I had to sit on that rocking chair on the porch all day waiting for you to come home, I'd climb up on the roof just so I could throw myself off."

"Gee, thanks. I was wrong before. You know just what to say to get my heart fluttering."

He took me in his arms, something that still managed to take my breath away after all the years. "You know what I mean."

"I do," I said. "You need to stay busy to be happy."

He pulled away and smiled. "That's what I just said."

"In what language, Urdu? That might be what you meant, but it was certainly not what you said."

"Don't quibble," he said as he reached into his pocket and pulled out a card. "What do you think?"

I looked at it and saw an old-fashioned wooden hand-plane on it, along with my husband's name and telephone number. Above it all, in bold letters, it said, "Old-Fashioned." I handed it back to him. "Is that the best name you could come up with for your business?"

He took the card back, studied it a second, then frowned. "What's wrong with it?"

"Since I know for a fact that you're not a bartender or a spinster, I'm not sure what you're trying to say."

"It's furniture, and you know it."

I tapped the card. "I know it because I know you, but someone else might not. Why don't you add the word 'furniture' below it, if you're stuck on the first part."

"I could write it in with a pen," he said as he looked at the card yet again.

"You will do no such thing. You're handwriting's a mess."

"You could do it, then," he said.

"I could, but I'm not going to. Let me think about it a minute." I started playing with names, trying to come up with something more clever than "Old-Fashioned." It certainly shouldn't be that hard. "How about 'Brand New Antiques'?"

He thought about it, then said, "Yeah, that's kind of nice. I'll have new cards made up when I run out of these."

"How many did you have made up?"

"I got a deal on a thousand. That's not bad for twenty bucks, is it?"

I reached over into the till and pulled out a twenty. "I'll trade you this bill for the rest of your cards. That way you'll break even."

"You should make it forty for me to do that," he said.

"If that's the way you're going to be, give me back my twenty and you can pay for the new ones as well."

"Not so fast. I was just kidding," he said. "You free for dinner? I feel like celebrating."

"That sounds wonderful," I said, dreaming of a night out on the town. "What did you have in mind?"

He scratched his chin, then said, "You haven't made meatloaf in a while."

"Thanks, but I'll pass."

"How about fried chicken? You make the best in town."

I stood toe-to-toe with my husband. "Bill Emerson, my idea of celebrating isn't cooking for you at home. You should take me out to dinner."

He nodded. "Sorry, I guess you're right. There's just nothing in the world I'd rather have than your meatloaf."

How sweet. I knew when he was conning me and when he wasn't, and the expression on his face told me that my husband was sincere. "Tell you what. Why don't we go out some other time. All of sudden, meatloaf sounds great to me, too."

"I didn't think you wanted to make it."

"Are you going to argue with me, or are you going to take a list and pick up a few things at the store for me?" We had a routine when I was cooking a meal he'd requested: I'd do the work, but he had to shop. I knew how much he disliked the grocery store, and if my dear husband was willing to do that, then I knew he was serious.

"Just tell me what you need," he said.

I jotted down the ingredients, along with potatoes and some frozen peas. He took it from me and studied it. "There's no pie on here."

"You didn't ask for pie," I said. "I don't have time to make a crust."

"We could get a lemon meringue from the store," he said.

I knew it was his favorite dessert. "Go ahead, pick one up, too. You're going to get fat if you keep eating those things. You know that, don't you?"

"Are you kidding? For pie, I'm willing to take the risk. Any chance you want to come with me to the grocery?"

I could have managed it, but I still wanted to check in with the Firing Squad members before I left the shop. "I'll be along in half an hour. Now shoo."

He started for the door, then said, "Thanks."

"For what?"

"Understanding your crazy old husband," he said with a grin.

"I don't know that I'll ever understand you," I said, returning his smile, "but after nearly thirty years of being married to you, I've learned to just accept you the way you are."

"Then it's been time well spent," he said, a surprisingly gushy remark coming from my normally gruff husband.

"I think so," I admitted. I locked up behind him, and suddenly regretted not going with him to the store. After all, he was being such a dear. On a whim, I shoved the cash from the till into the pig, turned off the lights, and locked the shop up. The investigation could wait.

For now, I wanted to be with my husband.

"I'm sorry to call you at home, but this is kind of important," Butch said after I picked up the phone later that night.

Bill and I had enjoyed the meatloaf, and I'd even joined him in a piece of pie. I'd walk to the shop tomorrow to make up for it, I promised myself.

"It's okay," I said. "What's going on?"

"I've been talking with Sandy, and we'd like to get together tonight, if it's not too much trouble."

"I'm surprised you didn't wrangle Jenna in, too," I said.

"That's part of what we need to talk to you about," Butch replied. "Can you come down to Fire at Will?"

How could I say no, especially since I was the one who'd gotten them involved in the first place? "Give me ten minutes," I said.

"That's fine. We'll be there."

I grabbed my purse and my jacket, then nudged Bill, who had fallen asleep in front of the television, the Discovery Channel blaring out. "I'm going out for a while," I said.

"You want me to come with you?" he asked groggily.

"No, I'd hate to interrupt your program."

He glanced at the television. "What happened to *Myth-Busters*? Did you change the channel?"

"They went off twenty minutes ago," I said. "You fell asleep."

"I was just resting my eyes," he said.

"Then you should have given your snoring a rest, too," I said. "I won't be long."

He nodded. "Do I even need to ask what this is about?"

"You can ask, but I'm fairly certain you won't like my answer, so maybe we should just leave it at that."

"Maybe we should," he said. "Be careful."

I leaned over and kissed his forehead. "I promise."

"I'll be here when you get back."

"I'd expect nothing less," I said.

I could have walked to the shop and atoned for my slice

of pie, but it was dark out, and the wind had picked up enough to put a chill in the air.

The exercise would have to wait. Butch had sounded urgent, and I needed to get to the shop and learn what my crew had found out.

Chapter 8

"Thanks for coming," Butch said as I walked up to the pottery shop. "I hate to drag you out like this."

"Where are the others?" I asked as I fumbled with my keys. "Or did you already let them in?" Butch was a reformed burglar, so I knew my feeble security system was no match for his skills. Sometimes I wondered just how "former" he really was, but I was too afraid he'd tell me the truth if I asked him.

"I'd never do that," he said. "At least not without your permission. Sandy will be here any second. In fact, here she comes right now."

Sandy approached us with a tray of coffees and a bag from In the Grounds. "I've got treats," she said.

"You didn't have to do that," I protested. "We could have made coffee inside," I added as I opened the door.

"This way's quicker," she said.

After I locked the door behind us and flipped on a few lights, I asked, "So, why isn't Jenna coming tonight?"

"That's the thing," Butch said. "When I called her and asked her to come, she said she couldn't."

"That's perfectly understandable," I said as I sipped some of the warm coffee. "We all can't drop our lives at a moment's notice and come running."

"You don't understand. She didn't bail on us because she was busy. Now that she's representing David, Jenna didn't feel that it was right for her to help us with our snooping."

"It's all for the same cause, Butch," Sandy said. "I still think you're overreacting."

"Sometimes she gets a little carried away with those ethics of hers," Butch said.

"We have to respect her position," I said. "Until Martha gets back, the three of us will have to just muddle along. Was that it, then? We could have had this conversation over the phone."

Butch shook his head. "No, we're just getting started. Sandy and I have found out a lot of important information today."

"That doesn't surprise me at all," I said. "Let's hear it. We're all here, and I'm listening."

"You go first," Butch told Sandy.

"Okay. I went back to the library after hours and tapped into some records for the county."

I wasn't sure I liked the sound of that, even if it was for a good cause. "Is that legal? I don't want you getting into trouble on David's account. One member of the Firing Squad in the sheriff's sights is enough."

"Don't worry, it's all a matter of public record. The thing is, you have to know where to look. They do their best to obfuscate the information, but I'm on to their tricks. It turns out our fair mayor isn't quite the success he wants everyone to believe. Harvey Jenkins is not really the sole proprietor of his business at all. He barely has a quarter share of ownership."

"Sandy, forgive me, but what does this have to do with Richard Atkins?"

"I'm getting to that. It turns out that the majority owner is a company called ClayDate."

"I'm sorry, perhaps I'm slow because it's getting so late. What's the significance to our investigation?"

"ClayDate is a dummy corporation, and I saw a reference to an R. A. Potter in the incorporation papers. It has to be Richard Atkins. Don't you see? Richard Atkins, Potter."

"It doesn't have to be," I said, a little impatiently. "It could be Regina Ann, Reginald Allen, or Rebecca Alison."

Sandy frowned. "I have a hard time believing that. I would have dug a little deeper, but I wanted to get back here to tell you. I actually thought I'd found something."

"You may have," I said. "We just need to investigate a little more. It's true that Richard and Harvey were in business together a long time ago, but from everything I've heard, it ended when Richard left Hannah twenty years ago."

I turned to Butch. "How about you? What did you find out? I don't suppose you were digging around on the Internet as well, were you?"

"Hardly. I like a more direct approach when I snoop around. I was talking to an old friend of mine, and he had an interesting light to shed on this mess. I know he's your uncle, but Don Rutledge is not a good guy."

"Do you think that's news to me?"

"No, but this might be. From what I heard tonight, he was out at the college asking questions about Charles Potter. He doesn't strike me as the crafting type, but I could be wrong."

"You're not," I said. "My uncle is many things, but that's not one of them. So, you think he knew that Charles Potter and Richard Atkins were one and the same before the rest of us?"

"He had to."

"I'm not as certain as you are, but I have to admit, it doesn't look like he's completely innocent in all of this, does it?"

Butch shrugged. "I don't care so much about guilt and innocence. I'm more concerned with results. We find out who aced the potter and David walks. It's as simple as that."

"It doesn't sound all that straightforward to me," I said. "Anything else?"

Butch scratched his chin. "There's Rose to dig into, and Kendra Williams, too."

"What a joy. If you're right about either one of them, I'm working on murderer's row."

"As long as you're not next in line," Butch said.

"I'll second that," said Sandy. She glanced at my Dali-inspired clock. "Is that the time? I've got to go."

"Late for a big date?" I asked.

"I wish. No, I've got a meeting first thing in the morning. Corki's got a big announcement to make, and she asked me to come in early."

"What's she up to?"

"With her, she's probably going to take a sabbatical and climb Denali."

"The bottled water?" Butch asked.

"No, the mountain in Alaska, and stop pretending you didn't know that. Good night."

"Let me walk you to your car," Butch said.

"I'm perfectly capable of making it on my own," Sandy said.

"I know. I was kind of hoping you could protect me in case there are any bad guys out and about tonight," he said with a grin.

"Come on, you big lug," she said. "Carolyn, are you coming with us?"

I thought about catching up on my account books since I was already there, but it was late, I was tired, and I had no desire to walk to my car alone later.

"I'm right behind you."

"It's a lot more fun if we're side by side," Sandy said.

"Just go," I replied.

When I walked back into the house, Bill was still awake and the television was off. I took my jacket off and asked, "What happened? I thought your next program was on."

"I couldn't enjoy it knowing you were out there by yourself."

"Don't give me that nonsense," I said as I hung my coat up. "You know I can take care of myself."

"I can still worry about you, can't I?"

"I suppose," I said as I leaned forward and kissed his forehead. As I did so, I brushed the remote control with my knee, and the television jumped to life. It was tuned to his usual channel, but the program wasn't the one he normally watched. "Preempted, was it?"

He shrugged. "I still would have watched it. You know me."

"I do at that. Coming to bed?"

"I'll be up in a bit. This looks kind of interesting."

I left him to his show and decided to take a quick shower

before bed. As I scrubbed up, I thought about what Sandy and Butch had said. Was there any possibility that the R. A. Potter she'd found referenced to was actually Hannah's ex-husband? That would mean that he'd kept in a lot closer contact with Maple Ridge than anyone had realized. Then again, it was probably Ramona and not Richard, just one big coincidence.

Butch's news, on the other hand, might have more substance to it. Don had a reason to want to see Richard suffer, and knowing how long my uncle could hold a grudge, I wouldn't put anything past him. I knew he believed in his heart that the reason he was alone was because of Richard Atkins. I didn't buy his story that he and Rose were just friends. I wondered if Rose felt the same way about Dan. It would certainly give either one of them a motive for murder if they believed that Richard had robbed them of their one chance for happiness.

And what about Kendra Williams and Harvey Jenkins?

Could I imagine Kendra killing the man? Or Rose, for that matter? I'd never been all that fond of car salesmen, including the mayor. I could easily believe that Harvey Jenkins had killed Richard, but wishing didn't make it so.

David and Hannah were decidedly not on my list of suspects. And if I was being honest about it, I wouldn't have added their names to the list even if I'd seen either one of them do it myself.

I was just falling asleep when something occurred to me. If Richard had been keeping tabs on Maple Ridge from afar, what would have made him come back, thereby blowing his cover identity as Charles Potter? Had he returned to get to know David, as he'd told me before he died, or did he have a more sinister motivation? He'd managed to build a new life for himself, so why risk it all now?

I wasn't sure, but I was only getting more muddled trying to figure everything out when I was so tired. It was going to have to wait until tomorrow.

"You're up early," Bill said as he joined me at the breakfast table the next morning.

"I've got some errands to run before I open the shop," I said.

"Carolyn, you're not going to give up on this, are you? What's it going to take, someone whacking you in the middle of the night like they did Richard Atkins?"

"No, but thanks for that thought. What a perfect way to start the day." My husband had a way of pointing out my sometimes foolish behavior in ways that were a little more descriptive than I liked.

"You need to remember what could happen to you," he said. "You're not bulletproof."

"I'm careful, and you know it," I said. "Don't worry so much. I'll see you tonight."

"I surely hope so," he said as I left. What a glum mood my husband was in. I couldn't help but take some of his bleak outlook to heart as I drove to Fire at Will. Was I wasting my time, trying to investigate a crime the police were already looking into? Knowing Sheriff Hodges as I did, I was skeptical about just how hard he would investigate. If he had David and Hannah already pegged as his only two suspects, it would certainly take more evidence than what I'd uncovered so far to dissuade him of the idea. I needed proof. The only problem was, I wasn't exactly sure how to go about getting any.

Breaking my own rule, I decided to keep the Intrigue close, so I parked on the street four storefronts down from my shop. I wanted to be able to go when I needed to, not slog halfway through town before I could get to my car.

I glanced in the window of Fire at Will, but I kept walking. Everything looked normal enough inside, and I had plenty of work to do, but my errand had to take precedence. I knew Kendra was usually at her shop, Hattie's Attic, by seven every morning, doing what, I had no idea. It was nearly eight, but the shop was dark and the sign still said she was closed. Where could she be? Was she sleeping in, or was it something more ominous? Stop it, I chided myself. You've jumped to enough conclusions this week, thank you very much. If Kendra isn't here, she must have a good reason.

Rose was already at Rose Colored Glasses, though I knew that she never opened before ten.

I tested the door, and sure enough, it was unlocked. As I walked in, Rose said, "Sorry, we're not really open yet."

"It's me," I said.

She looked up, obviously startled by my sudden appearance. "Carolyn, what are you doing here?"

"I'm fine, Rose. How are you?" She was trying to be rude, in her own way, but I wasn't going to let her get away with it. The sarcasm in my voice had to be evident.

"I didn't mean to snap at you. Sorry," she said again, her face reddened. It was the curse of her complexion. Rose Nygren couldn't hide her discomfort from me, or anyone else.

"I'd like to talk more about Richard Atkins. We didn't get a chance to finish last time we spoke."

"I don't want to discuss him, Carolyn. That's all ancient history. I've moved on."

I looked around the shop. "Have you? Rose, have you even dated anyone since Richard left town?"

"I've had an active enough social life," she said. "Not that it's any of your business." The woman looked ready to bolt from her own store, but I stood my ground.

"When he was murdered in my backyard, it became my business," I said. "I've spoken with my uncle," I added softly.

"How is he?" she asked, all the anger suddenly gone from her voice. "I regret what happened between Don and me more than anything about the whole affair." She paused, then amended, "Okay, that was a bad choice of words. 'Incident' doesn't sound much better. Let's just leave it at that."

"My uncle's as mean as ever. I can't imagine you two were ever friends, let alone anything more." I was baiting her, I couldn't deny it, but I meant what I said. Even though we were blood kin, I could barely stand to be around Don Rutledge. Why should Rose feel any differently?

"He wasn't always like he is now," she said.

"He has been as long as I can remember, and that's at least forty-five years."

Rose blushed again, slightly this time, then said, "I should have said he wasn't like that with me."

"You had a crush on him, didn't you?" The words just popped out of my mouth, but that didn't mean I didn't believe them. There was no denying the look in her eyes when she spoke about my uncle.

"We were friends," she repeated.

"But you wanted it to be more, didn't you? You lost something dear to you when Don found out about you and Richard. Where were you the night before last, Rose?"

"Carolyn, are you asking me for an alibi?" She was ready to snap, and for once, I was happy to supply the extra nudge she needed. If I could get her to break down, maybe I could get the truth out of her.

"I'll do one better than that. I'm asking you if you killed Richard Atkins."

I had hoped I'd pushed her enough to get a response, but not the one she gave me. Rose Nygren's eyes rolled into the back of her head, and she fainted dead away.

I grabbed some water from her bathroom and splashed a little on her face. "Rose? Are you all right?" I thought about calling 911, but I wasn't sure if I should. I'd try to wake her on my own, and if that failed, then I'd call for the paramedics.

Her eyelids fluttered, and then opened. "Carolyn? What happened?"

"You fainted," I said. "Are you feeling any better?"

The memory of how I'd accused her must have swept across her because she said quickly, "You need to leave."

"I'm not going to go and leave you lying on the floor," I protested.

She struggled to stand, then leaned against a shelf and pulled herself up. "I'm fine. Now go."

"You should see somebody, a doctor," I said.

"I skipped breakfast, so I was a little light-headed. I mean it. You aren't welcome here."

"Fine, but I'm going to check in on you later." She couldn't keep me from doing that, could she?

"If you do, I'm calling Sheriff Hodges and telling him that you've been harassing me. That's what you're doing, you know."

"I'm just trying to find out what happened to Richard Atkins," I said.

"Leave me alone." Her voice was shrill, and I didn't want

her to faint again, so I did as she asked and left. How curious her behavior had been. I wasn't quite sure what to make of it. I didn't have much time to dally, though. If I was going to speak with Harvey Jenkins before it was time to open my shop, I'd have to hurry. I rushed back to the Intrigue and headed for his car lot.

Harvey was out front, changing the cardboard sign he had in the window of a Subaru. That wasn't his only manufacturer; since Maple Ridge was a small town, Harvey carried a variety of new vehicles.

"Have you finally come in to trade that Intrigue?" he asked the second he saw me. "I can make you a sweet deal on a new Subaru. We've got a new shipment of Honda CRVs, too."

"Thanks, but I'm just here to talk to you."

"Unless it's about a new car, I don't have the time. This is a busy season for me."

I looked around the deserted parking lot. "I can see you're just swamped with customers."

"You never know, a crowd could be five minutes away."

From the intent jut of his jaw, I realized he was serious. "Fine. I'll test drive that one."

"Sounds good. Let me get a plate and we'll be off."

I looked at the red vehicle, and found that I liked its sporty style. My Intrigue was great, and I loved it, but that didn't mean it was the last car I ever wanted to own. Besides, if we were riding together Harvey would be a captive audience.

Harvey attached the plate and handed me the keys. "You're going to love this. It's really got some pep."

I took the keys, got in, and started it up. We were twenty feet out of the parking lot when Harvey started to press. "Now let's talk about this ride. It's got four-wheel independent suspension, a 173-horsepower engine, and sixteen-inch alloy wheels."

"Stop," I said. "The more you talk, the less I like it."

He shut up as if I'd thrown a switch. We drove a few miles—and I had to admit, I liked the way it handled—then I decided to get to why I was really there.

"I'm sorry about your loss," I said.

"What are you talking about?" Harvey answered.

"Your partner died a few nights ago. That's got to be tough on you."

"I don't have a partner," he said.

"You might be able to fool the rest of the world, but I know Richard Atkins owned a percentage of your business through ClayDate."

I'd expected a denial, not the laughter I got instead. "That's a blast from the past. That particular business has been dead twenty years. You should do your homework, Carolyn. It's old news."

Could Sandy, in her haste, have found dated information? I had to press it, regardless. Now that Harvey knew what I was up to, I'd given away the advantage of surprise. "Are you trying to tell me you didn't lose a fortune when Richard skipped out of town?"

"I'd hardly call what I lost a fortune. I'd honestly forgotten all about the man until this week. I've had my share of good partners and bad ones, but I don't hold grudges, and I don't look back. Now, what do you think?"

"About what?"

"The car. She's a real beauty, isn't she?"

I'd honestly forgotten the ruse. "It's a machine, not a female. Why must men do that?"

"Not all men, not all the time," he said. "You've got to admit, this car handles better than yours."

"I don't have to admit anything," I said. "I love my Intrigue."

He grinned. "What happened to vehicles just being machines?"

"Are you trying to lose a sale?" I said. I turned the car around and headed back to his lot.

"Hey, I was just kidding."

"Sorry, I've changed my mind." I didn't want a new vehicle, couldn't afford the payments if I did, and wouldn't buy it from Harvey Jenkins even if the first two points didn't matter.

Back at the dealership, I pulled to a stop, turned off the engine, but kept the keys in my hand.

He reached for them, but I held back. "There's one more thing I want to ask you."

"Go ahead," he said warily.

"Where were you two nights ago?"

Harvey shook his head. "That's none of your business."

"What happened to treating the customer right?"

"You don't have any intention of buying a new car," he said. "Now give me the keys."

I thought about holding on to them, but changed my mind and dropped them in his extended palm. As I got out, I said, "Thanks for the test drive."

"Sure thing," he said, barely managing to suppress a snarl. It was gone as quickly as it had come, and as he turned to greet a new customer, I could see his usual smarmy smile plastered to his face. "Hi there, I see you're admiring the new model. She's a beauty, isn't she?"

I got back into the Intrigue and headed to Fire at Will. I wasn't sure I'd accomplished anything that morning other than alienating more people, but I couldn't worry about that. I had a murder to solve and a business to run, in that order.

Someone was waiting for me to open, and for a second, I didn't recognize him. As I neared the shop, though, I saw that it was my cottage-making customer. That was stretching things, as I'd done all the work, but it was nice to see someone interested in my shop, for whatever the reason.

"I know it's early," he said the second I pulled out my key. "I just couldn't wait."

"Impatient to see how it turned out?" I asked as I unlocked the door.

"No, that's not it, though I am rather curious. It's for my mother, and I'm afraid she won't make it until noon."

It stunned me the man's mother could even still be alive, given the years he must have logged himself. "I'm so sorry," I said as I led him in. I didn't care that I wasn't set to open for another ten minutes. He might not have that long.

"Don't be," he said. "She's had a good life, made a great many friends, and helped scores of people over the years. Her last wish was to see her cottage in Haymore one last time, and since the sweet old thing would never last the trip, I commissioned you to make one for me. All the old photographs were lost in a fire, and I'm hoping my memory is strong enough to match Mother's."

It was the sweetest thing I'd ever heard. "It should be ready. Let's go check."

I opened the kiln, holding my breath as I peered inside. We lose things sometimes when we fire them. It's the nature of the business, and not a pleasant part of it, at that. I just hoped and prayed that the cottage we'd created made it.

I reached in and pulled it out. The glazes and paints had turned out beautifully, and I could see why my costumer's mother would long for it in her last days. I wouldn't mind living there myself.

I handed it to him, which he took reverently. "It's perfect," he said, his voice muted.

"It did turn out rather well." I retrieved my effort, and was pleased with it, too.

"That's very nice, too," he said. "Pardon me for asking, but is it for sale?"

I smiled at him. "If it's not bolted down, it's for sale. And don't worry about offending me. I'd be delighted to sell it to you."

He nodded his approval. "Wrap them both then, would you, please?"

"I'll take care of it." We hadn't yet discussed a price, and honestly, what he'd paid to have the firings expedited would cover the bill for both of them. I wasn't sure he'd stand for that though; I decided I'd give him a great price on the pair of cottages.

I came back up front and handed him the two cottages, each wrapped carefully and boxed. "Here you go."

He took them from me and handed me an envelope. "And here you are."

"Thanks. But we didn't discuss a price."

"I think you'll find that suitable," he said, and then he was gone.

I opened up the envelope, not sure what I would find, and was startled to see only a letter inside. It was a flyer for an antique auction in Bloodsbury.

I couldn't believe he'd stiffed me. He'd seemed like such a nice man. It wasn't that I'd lose any money on the transaction given his earlier firing fee, but it was a rather petty way of getting out of paying the final bill.

I took out a pin and tacked the flyer to the board behind

the register where I kept the delinquent checks I got from time to time. It would serve as a reminder that I was running a business, not a charity shop. It served me right. I'd neglected to name a price, so he'd neglected to pay it.

I did hate losing that cottage for nothing, though. I decided to make another one and put it in the display window. Something good might come of this after all.

I was just putting the walls of my latest effort together when David walked in.

"I wasn't sure I'd be seeing you today," I said.

"Sorry I'm late. I had some problems I had to deal with." He looked absolutely hangdog.

"Is the sheriff giving you trouble?" Had Hodges amped up his pursuit of David as the killer?

"I almost wish it had been that. You know what? I don't think I'm one of his major suspects anymore."

"What makes you say that?"

David shrugged. "He wants an easy arrest, but I think he knows I'm not guilty."

"Then why are you so glum?"

He looked as if he wanted to cry as he said, "Annie broke up with me."

"How awful for you," I said. "Did she say why?"

"Oh yes, in complete and thorough detail. It appears that I've been less than the ideal boyfriend, and she kindly pointed out several ways I could improve myself in the future, were I ever lucky enough to make the acquaintance of a girl of her caliber again."

"Ouch, that had to sting," I said as I added the roof. It surprised me when I realized that I was making a cottage just like the one I'd done for my customer. I wasn't sure why, but something about the place seemed to beckon to me.

"You don't seem all that sympathetic," David said a little truculently.

"For sympathy, you should go to your mother. For the truth, I'll do just as well as anyone else will."

David's face dropped. "So, you think she's right?"

"David, my dear, sweet friend, how should I know? Only two people ever really know what goes wrong with a relationship, but it sounds as though Annie gave you some things to think about. Take her advice, and maybe you'll do better next time."

"I wanted to do better this time," he admitted.

"Sorry, I can't help you there, either. Annie's a fine young woman, but I'm sure she's not the only eligible one in Maple Ridge."

"I guess," David said. Then, for the first time since walking in, he seemed to notice what I was doing. "Model building?"

"No, this is real construction. We should do more of these for our paint crowd," I said.

"They'd have to cost a fortune," David said. "Making them looks pretty labor intensive."

"All it costs us is time and clay, and we've got plenty of each at the moment. Grab some clay and start building."

"Sure, why not? What should I build?"

"Visualize your dream house," I said, "and then make it happen."

"As easy as that?"

"It can be, if you want it to," I said.

By the time I'd finished my replica of the cottage, David was lost in a design of his own. He was right about his concerns of how much to charge for them. A great deal of time and effort went into each piece, but I didn't care. By building cottages and bisque-firing them for our customers, we were offering them more choices than the norm of cups, mugs, plates, and saucers.

David studied the house he was building, then said softly, "You know, the worst part of it is that she was right, all the way across the board."

I patted his shoulder. "Just remember, where there's life, there's hope. Nobody's born knowing how to date. That's why you do so much of it. Believe it or not, you get better with practice."

"Then I'd better get started. Do you have any candidates for me?"

"No thanks, I'm not about to set you up on any blind dates," I said, as the front door chimed.

I was ready to wait on a new customer when I saw it was my uncle Don.

"We need to talk. Right now," he said, the fire leaping from his glare.

Chapter 9

"Go ahead, I'm listening."

"Not here. Out there," Don said as he pointed to the sidewalk in front of Fire at Will.

David looked at me, and I shrugged. If my uncle didn't want to talk in front of my assistant, that was fine with me.

I followed him out, and I was barely onto the street when he snarled, "Don't you ever go after Rose Nygren again, do you hear me?"

"What are you talking about?"

"I understand you went by her store and was browbeating her," he snapped. "You have no right."

"How did you hear about it?" I asked.

"Rose called me," he admitted.

"I thought you two were estranged." This was getting interesting. I'd meant to stir things up in Maple Ridge with my inquiries, but I was beginning to realize that I might be stirring up more than I'd bargained for.

"We were, but she didn't know who else to call."

"I find that interesting, don't you?" I asked. I never would have believed it, but my uncle's voice actually softened whenever he talked about Rose. "After all, it's been a long time."

"Too long," he admitted, "but you're missing the point."

"Am I?"

"Don't be that way, Carolyn. It wasn't cute when you were a kid, and it's surely not attractive now. Leave her alone, or you'll wish you'd listened to me." He smacked one hand with the other, and the ring I'd noticed earlier caught the light. I'd hate to think what it would do if he hit me.

"Are you threatening me? What happened to blood being thicker than water?"

"Don't count too much on that," he said, then stormed off.

I looked around to see if anyone had witnessed the confrontation, and saw Kendra ducking back into her shop. She'd no doubt seen and heard everything.

I still needed to talk to her, and David was minding the store, so I pulled off my apron and hurried over to Hattie's Attic before Kendra could call half of Maple Ridge and tell them what she'd just seen.

She looked startled to see me enter her shop, and as I'd suspected, Kendra had her telephone firmly in her hand. "Carolyn, I wasn't expecting to see you."

"Put the phone down, Kendra. We need to talk."

She looked at me warily. "I'm busy right now."

"So am I," I said. "This won't take long."

There wasn't a soul in her shop besides the two of us, so at least I had that in my favor. "I want to talk to you about Richard Atkins."

"We've had this conversation, Carolyn. You're repeating yourself."

"Where were you two nights ago?"

Kendra just smiled. "Wouldn't you like to know."

"I'm not digging into your social life. I just want to be able to eliminate you as a suspect."

Kendra shook her head. "I'd love to help you, but I'm afraid I'm not at liberty to discuss that. There are other people's lives involved."

"Just give me a name, Kendra, and I'll get off your back. I promise."

"As I said, it's none of your business."

"Why does everyone keep saying that? It's a simple question."

The door chimed, and David hurried in. "Carolyn, I was hoping I'd find you here."

"What's going on?" The look on his face told me something was seriously wrong.

"You'd better get back to the shop. Something's happened."

Kendra butted in. "What is it? What's going on?"

"Sorry, I need to talk to Carolyn about it first."

I followed him out of Hattie's Attic, but I wasn't going to wait until we got back to the shop to find out what had brought him out searching for me so urgently.

I put a hand on his arm to stop him. "David, what is it?"

"It's Bill. There's been an accident."

I felt my heart stop. "What happened?"

"I don't know all the details. He was working in his shop and something happened."

I raced toward Fire at Will to get my car keys. "How bad is it?"

"Carolyn, all I know is that he's in the emergency room. Come on, you're in no shape to drive. I'll take you."

"I'm not riding on the back of your motorcycle," I said.

"We can take your car, but you don't need to add to your problems right now. I hope you don't mind, but I already locked the shop up and I grabbed your keys."

"Of course I don't mind. Let's go." As we got into the car, I asked, "What exactly did the hospital say?"

"They didn't call," he admitted. "Annie was there visiting her aunt and she saw him come in. That's all I know."

I nodded, too numb to speak. What had happened? Had Bill had an accident with one of his woodworking machines? Had he had a heart attack? A thousand scenarios raced through my mind. I'd have to call the boys, but not until after I knew what had happened. They'd want to come back home to be with their father. I'd need to change the linens in the guest room and pull a cot out of the garage. Then there was food to worry about. Oh Lord, what was my mind doing? I was probably thinking about the arrangements because it was something I could actually control. What had happened to my dear, sweet, ornery husband?

David pulled up at the ER doors. "You go on. I'll park and then join you."

I shot out of the car without even thanking him. There were several people in the waiting room, but no sign of Bill. It must have been urgent if they'd taken him straight back. I approached the nurse's station. "I'm here to see my husband."

The nurse, buried in paperwork behind her desk, held up one finger. "Hang on a second."

"His name's Bill Emerson," I said.

"You're going to have to wait."

There wasn't much chance of that. Since she wasn't being helpful, I decided to find someone who was. I started back to the treatment area when the security guard on duty blocked my path. "I'm afraid you can't go in there, ma'am."

"If you think you're going to stop me, you'd better pull out that gun, because I'm going in."

Then I heard a voice I knew behind me. "Carolyn, what are you doing here?"

I whirled around to see my husband standing there, a sheepish look on his face and a bloodied rag wrapped around his left hand. "What happened?" I asked as I hugged him.

"I'm fine," he said as he pulled away from me. "Watch the hand, okay?"

"You're bleeding. Why are they making you wait? What did you do to yourself?"

"I had the table-saw blade set a little too high. It's nothing," he said.

"Bleeding like that isn't nothing. Come on, we're going to get you looked at."

I was ready to unleash on the nurse when she looked up and said, "Bill Emerson."

My husband said, "Wow, you get results."

"Just your husband, ma'am," she said sternly to me.

"If I can't go with him, he's not going in."

"Hey, don't I have a say in this? I really would like somebody to look at this. Go back to your shop. I'll call you when I'm finished."

"You've lost your mind as well, haven't you? I'll be right here when they're finished with you."

He shrugged, then followed the nurse through the forbidden double doors. Before going through, he paused and asked, "How'd you know I was here?"

"A little bird told me. Now go on."

A minute later, David came in. "The parking lot's jammed, so I had to go to the overflow area. How is he?"

"Not nearly as dire as we thought," I said. "He cut his hand on his table saw." The rag he'd wrapped around his hand had been soaked through with blood, but I was hoping it wasn't as serious as it looked. I'd long given up on warning my husband about the dangers of the power equipment he worked with every day. Wood was tougher than flesh, but up until now, he hadn't had an accident. At least not that he'd told me about. "David, why don't you take the car and reopen the shop? There's no telling how long we'll be."

"Sure, I'll be glad to. Listen, I'm sorry if I got you worried over nothing."

I kissed his cheek. "You did exactly the right thing. Now go on. I'll see you soon."

After he was gone, I paced around the waiting room, then sat and picked up one of the year-old magazines lying on a table. I was catching up on old news when I felt a presence in front of me. I looked and was surprised to see Sheriff Hodges standing there.

"What are you doing here?" he asked me.

"I always come here on my lunch hour," I said. "They have the best magazine collection in town."

"Don't be smart with me, Carolyn."

"Bill had an accident," I said.

"Is he all right?" Was that actual concern in the sheriff's voice? Why not? He liked Bill, which was more than he could say about me.

"He seems to think so."

"What happened to him?"

"He cut his hand working on his table saw," I explained.

"They can be nasty things," he replied.

"What brings you here, Sheriff?"

I never thought he'd answer me, but to my surprise, he did. "I'm here checking out an alibi."

"Does it involve someone you suspect in Richard Atkins's murder?" This could be something I could use in my own investigation.

"I'm not at liberty to say," he said, almost by rote.

"Come on, what possible harm could it do?"

"It could give you the false impression that you actually have a right to keep snooping into this when it's none of your business," he said sternly. That was more like the sheriff I knew. His earlier amiable mood had indeed been a fluke.

"The man was killed in my backyard, and I'm the one who tripped over the body. Doesn't that mean anything?"

"I'm sorry you had to find him like that, but that doesn't give you the right to dig into his murder, Carolyn." He tipped his head to me, then left.

I approached the nurse's station and waited patiently until the nurse who had scolded me earlier looked up.

"Yes?"

"I just wanted to say I'm sorry about the way I acted before. I was worried about my husband. I didn't mean to snap at you." I saw one of the other nurses behind the desk smile, but not the woman I was addressing. I was beginning to wonder if her frown was permanently attached.

"Fine. Now take a seat, you're blocking my station."

I looked behind me, but no one was there. "I didn't mean to, but if you've got a second, would you mind telling me what the sheriff wanted? We were talking about checking alibis for one his suspects, but he was called away. I'm sure he wouldn't mind if you told me." That was a whopping big lie, but I was past caring. I needed to know who else was on the sheriff's list of suspects.

"If you want to know, ask him, not me." There was an overhead page, and the nurse I'd been speaking with abruptly turned to the one who had smiled at me and said, "Betty, that's for me. Take over."

After she was gone, I looked at her replacement. "I don't suppose you could help me."

"We're not allowed to give out any information that involves the police. I'm sorry."

"That's all right," I said. I hadn't expected to learn anything, but it hadn't hurt to ask.

I was ready to find a seat again when she said, "You're Carolyn Emerson, aren't you? Don't you run Fire at Will?"

I admitted as much. "Have you ever been in? I don't recognize you."

"No, but I've been meaning to come by. Isn't Rose Colored Glasses near your place?"

"It's just down the River Walk," I said. "Do you shop there?"

"No, I'm new in town. Would you do me a favor? The owner, Rose Nygren, was here a few nights ago, and she left her reading glasses in the waiting area," Betty said. "I've been meaning to return them, but I haven't had the chance. She seems like a nice lady."

"She can be," I said. "I'd be happy to return them for you." As I took the glasses, the magnitude of her words hit home. "Did you say two nights ago?"

"Yes, she brought a friend of hers in to be seen. She must have sat in that waiting room three hours waiting for Mrs. Sampson. Who knows? It could have been longer than that. She was here when my shift started at seven, I know that much."

"Are you saying she was here the entire time?" I asked.

The nurse frowned, then said, "I really couldn't swear to it. Things were kind of crazy that night, so I wasn't keeping tabs on her. But yeah, I think so."

"Thanks," I said as I returned to my seat. Did that mean that Rose had an alibi on the night of the murder? My house was less than five minutes away from the hospital. Did she have time to sneak out, club Richard in my backyard, then make it back here without anyone noticing she was gone? I looked around the room, trying to see if the nurse's station offered a view of the entire waiting area; a few large plants and a television definitely blocked the view. It certainly gave me something to consider. I'd learned earlier that someone had beaten Richard to death, a particularly hideous way to die. How much did you have to hate someone to bludgeon him to death?

I was still pondering the possibilities when I heard Bill's voice. "Are you going with me, or would you like to hang around here all afternoon?"

"What did the doctor say?" I asked as I looked at his hand. It was wrapped in a white bandage held on by a gauze strip two inches wide. A yellow liquid—no doubt, some kind of salve—had discolored part of the bandage.

"I'll be able to play the piano in no time."

"So there's a downside to this," I said. "Would you be serious for one moment and tell me what happened?"

"Carolyn, when you work with power tools all day, something's bound to happen now and then. It's nothing, not much more than a scratch."

"So he just put some salve on it and wrapped it up?"

"No, the doctor put in a few stitches. Anyway, what makes you think it was a man? My doctor happened to be a very attractive young woman."

"She sounds too good for you," I said curtly.

Bill looked surprised. "Are you honestly mad at me about this?"

"I was sitting out here worried about you, and now I find out you were in there flirting with your physician. Somebody should report her."

"She didn't do anything wrong," Bill said.

"Then they should report you."

"What for, talking to my doctor? Hey, I'm all right," he added softly. "I'm glad you came, but it's going to be fine."

"Let's go home, shall we?" He was right. I wasn't sure why I was snapping at my husband, but I clearly was. "Give me your keys. I'll drive."

"How'd you get here? You didn't walk, did you?"

"Don't be ridiculous. David brought me, then he took the Intrigue back to the shop."

My husband still hesitated.

"Hand them over," I said.

"Thanks, but I'll drive."

"Bill Emerson, I'm perfectly capable of driving that precious truck of yours." Honestly, sometimes I thought he cared more about that vehicle than he did about me.

"It's not that," Bill said. "I want to drop you off at Fire at Will."

"I have no intention of going back to work as if nothing happened," I said.

"That's just it. Nothing did happen, at least nothing deserving this much fuss. Carolyn, I'll call you if I need you, but right now, what I need is some rest. I've got a prescription for the pain, and I think I'll fill it on the way home. The doctor told me they might make me sleepy, which is fine by me. Just because I'm going to take the rest of the day off doesn't mean that you should."

I knew that tone of voice. He didn't want to be pampered, and I'd just end up getting frustrated if I went home with him. I let him drive me to the shop, then hesitated before I got out of the truck. "You'll get your medication, then you're going straight home, right?"

"I promise," he said. "I'm not exactly feeling up to going bowling."

"Call me if you need me," I said.

"You can count on it."

"Bill?"

He had put the truck in gear, but stopped. "Yes?"

"I'm glad it's not worse than it was," I said.

"Me, too," he said with a grin.

I walked inside and found David working on his clay cottage. "How is he?"

"He needed a few stitches, but he's going to be all right."

"You didn't have to come back," David said. "I can handle things here."

"I know you can, but Bill asked me to give him some peace and quiet, so I'm here. Did anything happen while I was gone?"

"Nothing too exciting," he admitted. "A man called here looking for you, but when I told him you were gone, he said he'd check back later."

"How odd. Did he say what he wanted?"

"No, not a word."

"I think I'll make another cottage myself. It's quite fun, isn't it?"

"It's got potential," David admitted.

We were still working side by side when the door chimed. It was my cottage customer from before, and he had a bittersweet look on his face.

"Did you come back to give me a brochure on skiing this time?" I asked him.

"No, I'm sorry about that. I grabbed the wrong envelope from my jacket pocket."

"I wasn't sure it was an accident," I said. He looked sufficiently contrite, so I decided not to give him a hard time about stiffing me. "What did your mother say?"

"She adored it," he said. "You should have seen her eyes."

"I'm glad she liked it."

He coughed once, then said, "I'd like another, if you don't mind."

"Did something happen to that one?"

"No, but my sister wants one as well."

"How about you?" I asked. "Wouldn't you like one?"

He shook his head sadly. "I'm taking Mother's. We lost her an hour ago."

"I'm so sorry," I said. I hugged him, and he let me.

"Thank you. You've been so kind about the entire thing, I just wanted to come back and tell you how much it meant to her."

"It was my pleasure," I said. How often did I get to give someone their dying wish? "I'm just glad she liked it so much."

"She did." He reached into his jacket and pulled out another envelope. "Sorry about the earlier confusion."

"You don't have to do that," I said, refusing the envelope. "I was happy to help."

"Nonsense. You provided me a wonderful service, and I won't hear of you not taking payment. There's one thing, though."

"What's that?"

"Would you mind terribly if I had that auction leaflet back?"

I'd forgotten all about tacking it to the board behind my register. "Of course not," I said as I retrieved it.

"I'll be back for the cottage in a day or two," he said.

When I looked inside the envelope, four crisp one-hundred-dollar bills looked back.

I started for the door, and David asked, "Is it another brochure?"

"No, but it's too much."

I caught him on the sidewalk, just getting into a Jaguar. "You overpaid me," I said.

"Nonsense. If anything, I didn't give you enough. Please, keep it with my sincere thanks. I'll be offended if you try to return any portion of it."

I grinned. "Well, I wouldn't want that. Thank you."

"I should be the one thanking you," he said.

I walked back inside, and David asked, "What did he say?"

"He told me to keep it."

"Well, the customer's always right," David said with a grin.

"I suppose I'll have to live with it, then." I put the money in the till, then rejoined David at the bench. "Now I need to make another one."

"I thought you already were," he said, pointing down at my clay.

"I've got one already bisque-fired," I admitted, "but I wanted one for the window, too. We should make these to sell."

"Carolyn, not everyone's going to be willing to pay what your last customer did for these things."

"I know that," I said. "But it might make a nice addition to our display."

"Just as long as we don't mass-produce them," David said. "You know how I feel about production work."

I knew all too well. There were two types of potters in the world. One kind, those who had been raised to throw for production, worked incredibly fast and could generate a great deal of stoneware in a short amount of time. The other type, the category that David fell into, felt that pottery was an art form that should be developed, with careful consideration given to the options each step along the way. I liked both types, for different reasons. Without the production potters, I wouldn't have all of my bisqueware for my paint-your-own customers to enjoy, and without the artistic potters, I wouldn't have some of the breathtakingly beautiful pieces I owned, including some of David's work.

The phone rang, and I answered, "Fire at Will."

"Carolyn, it's Sandy. I was wondering if you'd had a chance to talk to Harvey Jenkins yet."

"As a matter of fact, I did. He claims the ClayDate information dates from when Richard Atkins was in town twenty years ago."

"What? How can that be? I was sure it was more recent than that."

"It's an easy mistake to make," I said. "I shouldn't have rushed you like I did."

"I could have sworn I tapped into the current database," Sandy said. "I feel just awful. I must have made you look like a fool."

"It wasn't that bad," I assured her. "I appreciate your help."

"For all the good it did you. I'm not giving up. I'll keep digging. You can count on me."

"Sandy, it's fine; believe me."

She hung up, and I felt bad about telling her what the mayor had told me. I'd learned that it was easy to run into dead ends investigating without the benefit of the police department's resources. I never would have had the brashness to do it in the first place if I didn't believe that Sheriff Hodges was going to fail to follow all leads in his investigation. I wished the man would just go ahead and retire. Then perhaps we'd get a real sheriff, and I could go back to what I loved to do best, running Fire at Will.

David and I spent the rest of day making cottages out of clay; a lull in our foot traffic, as happened quite frequently, left us virtually undisturbed. As we loaded the last kiln and turned it on, I asked, "Shall we call it a day? I don't think anybody else is coming in."

"It's fine with me. I've got something I have to do."

"It's not about your father, is it?" I didn't want David going off on his own to investigate.

"I wish everyone would stop calling him that," David said, the irritation thick in his voice. "He walked out on us before I was born, and the first time I laid eyes on him was this week. As far as I'm concerned, he was a stranger, no more, and no less."

"That's kind of callous, isn't it?"

He slammed his hand down, smashing a cottage he'd been working on. "After what he did? You can't be serious."

I couldn't let him go out so angry. It wouldn't do to have the sheriff run into David and get a whiff of the young man's temper. "If you're not doing that, what's this urgent mission?"

He shrugged. "I'm going to talk to Annie. She's got to see that we belong together."

"David, it's her decision as much as it is yours."

He scowled, and whether I liked it or not, I could see some of his father in him. "Carolyn, don't you think I know that? I can't make her want to be with me, but I can at least try to get her back." He looked at me a second, then added, "I'm open to any suggestions you might have."

"I think pleading and groveling couldn't hurt. Also, if you can work it into the conversation up front, tell her what an absolute idiot you've been, and promise her you'll change. But only if you're really willing to."

"I am," he said. "Thanks. How about flowers? Should I take her some?"

"You've been dating her awhile. What do you think?"

"No, Annie's not one for frills. She'd probably be mad I wasted the money on them."

"Then there's your answer. Good luck, but remember: it's her decision, too, and you should respect whatever she wants."

"You know I will. Mom drilled that into me from the day I could talk."

After he was gone, I closed out the books on the day, turned off the lights, and locked up. It was time to go home and check on my husband. Looking into Richard Atkins' murder would have to wait. I decided to take some of my own advice and put my love life ahead of everything else. Just because Bill and I had been together since dinosaurs roamed the earth didn't meant that I still shouldn't show him how much I cared about him.

Chapter 10

Though it was barely seven by the time I got home from work, with a trip to the grocery store thrown in to get some of Bill's favorite foods, my husband was fast asleep; his snoring reverberated through the house. What kind of prescription had they given him? I envied him the sound sleep, but not the pain he must be feeling. Though he'd protested that it hadn't been that bad, I knew my husband. That cut had hurt, and not just his pride, which was considerable. He fancied himself an accomplished woodworker, and he was—that was easy to see in the beautiful pieces he made— but even pros had accidents. I saw it as a mark of his skill that it had taken this long for him to have an injury that drew enough blood to require stitches.

I'd planned to make him his favorite dinner, homemade chili hot enough to blow the top of his head off. Even though he was sleeping, I decided there wasn't any harm in making it now. I'd simmer it on the stove, and when he woke up from this drug-induced nap, a bowl of it would be waiting for him.

I made two batches, a big one for him full of spicy additions, and something a little more bland for me, though it was still hot enough to bring tears to my eyes. As both pots simmered on the stove, I looked in on him again. He hadn't even shifted his position on the bed. It didn't make sense for me to wait to eat with him, since it could be hours until he woke, and I was hungry now. I dished out some of the milder blend, cut off a chunk of sharp cheddar cheese, grabbed some crackers and a cold glass of milk, then set a place at the table and ate. The meal was fine, but I missed my husband, even though he was just in the other room. Was this how it was for my friends who had lost their spouses through death or divorce? I wondered how many meals Jenna, a widow, had eaten alone. How did she stand it? I'd have to be a better friend and invite her over more often than I did, which was hardly ever.

After I ate, I cleaned up, took Bill's pot of chili off the stove, and mulled over what to do next. Television didn't interest me, and I wasn't in the mood to read. I was still upset about somebody murdering Richard Atkins in my backyard, but I wasn't going to let them drive me from my land. I grabbed my coat, jotted a quick note to Bill, and propped it up beside his awaiting bowl. Then I walked outside, grabbing the flashlight by the back door as I left.

It was a crisp evening, and the moon was full and bright, obscured only occasionally by scudding clouds. I loved our property, especially the way the land went back into the woods behind us. It gave me the illusion that we abutted some great, wild wilderness, though I knew the next street over was just a hundred yards away. I thought Bill had been foolishly extravagant when he'd bought the abutting lots along with our property, but I had seen his wisdom a thousand times since. While our neighbors were surrounded by each other, we had the luxury of space around us, something that I cherished.

I found myself drawn to my raku pit for the first time since I'd stumbled across the body. The police tape was gone, and there was honestly no indication that something dire had ever happened there. As I stared at the pit where I buried the pots freshly removed from the gas kiln beside it, I began to wonder something that should have piqued my interest from the start. What on earth had Richard been doing in my backyard in the first place? Did it have anything to do with him abandoning his car practically in my driveway the night before he was murdered? It was an odd place for a rendezvous, that was for sure.

I'd asked Bill about putting a security light in back so we could see if someone was out there, but my husband had protested that a light would just make it easier for a burglar to see what he was doing. Why help him break into our house?

I heard a noise in the woods in front of me, but the flashlight beam was too weak to penetrate very far into the darkness. I knew raccoons frequently ran through the woods, and neighborhood cats came and went as well. I'd just about decided that whatever it was had left when I heard a branch crack. From the sound of it, this was no raccoon. For once, my survival instinct was solid, and I raced back to the house, dropping the flashlight as I ran. There was enough moonlight to show the way, and the light I'd left on in the kitchen was like a beacon drawing me home. My heart was racing when I got back inside, but I didn't slow down until the door was safely dead-bolted behind me.

"What happened? Did you see a ghost?"

My husband was sitting at the kitchen table, polishing off the bowl of the chili I'd left him.

"No, it was nothing. I just decided to go for a walk out back. How's your hand?"

He flexed it slightly. "It's better. That medication knocked me out. Sorry about that."

"Sleep has to be good for you," I said. "Did you enjoy your chili?"

"I still am." He smiled as he took another bite. I sat across from him, happy that he was awake. "Thanks for this."

"You're most welcome. I thought you might like some comfort food tonight."

He stared at his hand. "It's not that bad, really."

"I know. Accidents happen."

He searched my eyes and saw no sarcasm in them. I heard his sigh of relief as he realized I wasn't going to say anything about what had happened.

"Maybe I'm getting too old for this foolishness," Bill said.

"You don't have to keep making furniture," I said, "but I know how much you love it. You shouldn't let this stop you. In fact, I think you should get back to it as soon as you're able."

He shook his head. "The doctor told me to lay off until I've finished my prescription. It makes me kind of loopy."

"I didn't mean tonight," I said. "But don't let this stop you for good."

He nodded. "I have to admit, it was scary looking down and seeing that blood."

"Did it hurt when the blade hit your hand?"

He rubbed his chin with his good hand. "No, as a matter of fact, it didn't. It took me a few seconds to even realize that I'd been cut. Seeing the blood was what triggered the pain." He shook his head briefly. "The medication's taking care of it right now." He pushed his bowl away. "That was perfect. Carolyn, I hate to be this way, but I think I'm going back to bed."

"That's a splendid idea," I said. "When are you due to take more medication?"

"I've got another half an hour." He winced slightly. "Do you think it would hurt to speed it up a little bit?"

"As long as you don't make a habit of it," I said. "Let me get it for you."

"That's all right. I've got it on the nightstand. I'll see you in the morning."

I kissed him quickly, then said, "Sleep tight."

"With this stuff? That's not going to be a problem, believe me."

It wasn't even nine yet, too early for me to go to bed. As Bill's snoring reached a particularly loud level of buzz-sawing, I thought about making up the spare bedroom and bunking in there for the night. No, then I wouldn't be nearby if my husband needed me, and that was more important than a sound night's sleep. I sat in the living room for an hour or so, doing not much of anything and had just about decided to turn in myself when I heard a tapping at the front door. Who on earth would come visiting this late? I flicked on the porch light and looked out the peephole, prepared to ignore whoever had come by.

I changed my mind and opened the door the second I saw who it was.

"Come in," I told Hannah. "What's going on?"

"I didn't wake you, did I?"

"No, but Bill's already asleep."

saw that I was nearly out. "Okay, no Darjeeling. I've got a jasmine blend, and some sassafras tea as well. I know I have both of those."

"I haven't had sassafras since I was a little girl," Hannah said. "Isn't it bad for you?"

"This has been processed, so it's high time you revisit it. You still like licorice, don't you?"

"Occasionally," she admitted, "though I'm afraid I haven't had that in ages, either."

"Then you're in for a real treat." I pulled the sassafras chunks from the freezer where I kept them and dropped some in the kettle. "Now, let's see, I've got some cookies around here somewhere."

"Carolyn, I don't need a snack. Would you sit down here with me? There's something we need to talk about."

"That sounds serious," I said. "Perhaps it should wait until after our tea is ready."

"I suppose," she agreed. I was in no hurry for the kettle to whistle. Hannah was visibly upset, and I was almost certain it had something to do with Richard Atkins.

Impatiently, she said, "You know what? I can't wait for the kettle to boil. I'm here to talk about David."

"What about him?" I asked as the kettle began to whistle. "The sheriff didn't arrest him after all, did he?"

"No, at least he hadn't half an hour ago when I left him. This is about Annie."

I reached for the kettle and strained two mugs of tea. The sassafras had a strong licorice smell to it, and to be honest, I kept it just as much for the mildly sweet aroma it gave off as I did to drink the brew.

"I've made it a point to stay out of David's love life," I said as I handed Hannah a mug.

"Well, you're not his mother," she replied.

She looked uncomfortable. "This can wait."

"Hannah, he's on medication for his hand. I doub
hear us if we started a drum and bugle corps."

She didn't come in. "I hadn't heard. What happen
him?"

"There was a little accident in his shop," I said lig
trying to disguise how I really felt about it. "He need
few stitches, and he's on something for the pain. You
saved me from endless boredom. Now are you coming
or should I join you outside?"

"I'll come in, but I'm just going to stay a minute."

"How's tea sound?" I said as I closed the door behind h
and bolted it. "I'm in the mood for some Darjeeling."

"I'll take anything but iced," she said. "It's really gettin
chilly out there."

"Why don't you come back into the kitchen with me an
we can chat while I put the kettle on."

She joined me in the kitchen, and as I filled up my bu
nished copper teakettle, Hannah said, "I didn't think an
one made tea on a stove top anymore."

"There are a few of us relics still out there," I said.

"Carolyn, I didn't mean anything by it."

I laughed as I said, "I know you didn't. I was jokin
self. I know I can just as easily microwave the wat
there's something safe and reassuring about a te
don't you think?"

"I never thought about it before," she said, "but
you're right."

"If nothing else, it's a great deal more fun
crowave." I rummaged through my cabinets ur
the tin with Darjeeling in it. It was awfully ligh
container with tea leaves. My fears were real

"No, but I care about him, and I hate to see him get hurt as much as anybody does, with the possible exception of you."

"I know, excuse me for being so snippy. He's just devastated this girl has broken his heart."

I looked at her closely. "Have you talked to him today?"

"No, that's the problem. He was mooning all over the house last night, and now he hasn't even come home. I'm worried sick about him."

"He's a grown man, Hannah. The last time I saw him, he was going to try to win her back. Have you considered the possibility that he was successful, and that they're together right now?"

"Which is worse?" she asked softly, most likely thinking I hadn't heard.

"If you have to ask that, you're not the mother you think you are. Hannah, you can't keep him your baby boy forever. He has the right to a life of his own. Look, don't borrow trouble. Wait to hear what he has to say before you condemn him for something he may not have even done."

I don't think she could have looked any more shocked if I'd slapped her. With an expression devoid of all emotion, she put the mug down and left, without a peep, a whimper, or a single word. Perhaps I'd gone too far at last. This might be the breach that couldn't be fixed with club sandwiches or tea. But the words needed to be said, and Hannah needed to hear them. Suddenly I was very tired, of everything. What I needed now was rest, and time to lock the world away.

With the collection of nightmares I had, I might as well have stayed awake. Bill's snoring beside me didn't help matters, though I couldn't say it hurt all that much, either.

After my restless night, I wasn't ready to face a new day when my alarm went off, but I didn't have much choice.

Bill was annoyingly refreshed as he popped up beside me. "That was some night. How'd you sleep?" he asked as he practically leapt out of bed.

"Barely," I said.

"Really? I had a great rest. My hand's not even that sore. I think I'll go back to the shop today."

"Don't you think you should take a little more time off? You don't want to rush it, and if you even get near those pills, I won't allow any woodworking. Do you understand?"

Normally my scolding would set him off, but not today. "I don't need them, I tell you. Maybe tonight, though." The grin on his lips made me uneasy.

"Pain pills are the easiest thing in the world to get addicted to," I said. "Easier than heroin, alcohol, or cocaine." I wasn't entirely sure that was true, but I didn't want my husband hooked on the medication. That wasn't the whole story, though. For some reason, my dear spouse was aggravating the fool out of me, and I felt the need to come down hard on him.

"Hey, I'm the one who said I was done with them, remember? If I don't hurt, I don't need them, and I won't take any more."

"That's a slippery slope, and you know it. Tell you what. Why don't I hang on to them for you."

"I'm not a child, Carolyn. I'm perfectly capable of dispensing my own medication. I'm going to go take a shower," he said grumpily.

I felt a twinge of guilt about crushing his good mood. But I was still upset with his jaunty attitude. Out of aggravation more than anything else, I stole into the bedroom and put his bottle of pills by the cleaning supplies in the kitchen. He'd never look there; I had full confidence in that. If he asked, I'd turn them back over to him, but he was going to have to make the request.

After he got out of the shower, he didn't mention the pills again, and I certainly wasn't going to bring it up. I made us eggs for breakfast, and he headed back to his workshop.

Or so I thought.

"Carolyn, you might want to come out here," he said as he called to me from the back porch.

"What happened, did another dog make a deposit on our deck?" Some of the neighborhood dogs loved leaving us little presents, and Bill had threatened to electrify the entire place on more than one occasion.

"No, it's nothing like that. Come out here. Now."

"All right, I'm coming. There's no need to be so gruff about it," I said as I joined him outside.

The second I got outside, I saw what had disturbed him so. Someone had scrawled the words "BUTT OUT" on my car windshield in big block letters with a black Sharpie pen.

"That's rather clear, isn't it?" I said.

"Who did this?" Bill asked. "Do you have any idea?"

"It could have been a dozen different people," I said, more honestly than I wanted to admit.

"I'm going to call the sheriff," Bill said as he started back inside.

I grabbed his sleeve, being careful not to touch his hand. "Don't, Bill. It's not going to do any good."

"He needs to be told someone's threatening you," Bill said, shaking off my grip.

"Let me deal with it in my own way," I said. I couldn't

imagine Hannah writing such a terse message, but she'd been angrier than I'd ever seen her in my life. I couldn't rule it out, not completely.

"Are you at least going to take the advice?" he asked.

"What do you think?"

"I think I wasted my breath even asking you the question," he said as he started to walk away.

"Where are you going?" I asked.

"If you're not going to let me call the sheriff, I'm going to my workshop."

He stormed off to his shop and went inside. It was a hundred feet from my raku pit, on the other edge of our property line, and I wondered if my woodlands visitor might have done something to my husband's shop. He didn't come back out, so I had to assume it was undisturbed.

I went back into the house, grabbed the phone, then stared at it a full minute before I had the nerve to dial the number I had to call.

"Yes?" Hannah said, her voice full of frost.

"It's me," I said. "I want to talk to you about what happened last night."

"There's nothing to talk about," she said.

"You didn't leave me any messages, did you?" There, I'd said it.

"I haven't called you. Why would you think I had?"

"I'm not talking about on the telephone. I mean on my windshield."

"Carolyn, what on earth are you talking about?"

"I didn't think you'd do it," I said.

"What was the message?"

I had to tell her. "It said 'butt out.' "

"I can understand the sentiment, but I didn't leave the message," she said, and then she hung up.

That answered that. I knew Hannah well enough to know that if she'd done it, she would have at least admitted it to me. So, who else wanted me to mind my own business? It could have been a message from Rose Nygren, Kendra Williams, Mayor Harvey Jenkins, or my uncle Don Rutledge. Then again, it could have been half a dozen other people I didn't even realize I'd offended with my impromptu investigation. Whoever it was, they were going to have to do better than that to get me to stop.

If anything, I was more determined than ever to find out what had happened to Richard Atkins in my raku pit, and just as important, why.

Butch Hardcastle was waiting for me in front of the shop when I got there thirty minutes later. He handed me a cup of coffee. "I thought you could use this."

"How did you know I didn't meet Hannah this morning?" Was the man watching me?

"I didn't. Here, give it back and I'll drink it."

"Not on your life," I said. "I need this."

"Two cups already? I don't want to be the one responsible for you getting the jitters."

I opened the door and let him in. "As a matter of fact, Hannah and I skipped our morning ritual," I said as I deadbolted the door behind us.

"Are you two squabbling again?" he asked.

"I'm afraid I might have pushed things a little too far this time." I told him what I'd said to Hannah about David and waited for his reaction. All he did was listen. "No comment?"

"Are you kidding? I've got enough problems without getting involved in a fight between two strong-willed women. No, I'll stay on the sidelines for this one."

I snorted. "A fat lot of help you are, then. So, what brings you here so early? I wouldn't think you'd be up at this hour."

He grinned. "I've found it's a whole lot easier if you don't go to bed first."

"You've been up all night? My mother always told me nothing good happens after midnight."

Butch pulled up a chair and sat down. "Then we wouldn't have had much in common. Sometimes I think just the opposite is true."

I grabbed a seat across from him. "Butch, you haven't been backsliding, have you?"

He patted my hand. "Carolyn, I appreciate your concern, honestly, I do, but I'm a big boy. I can take care of myself."

"I know you can. I just worry about you sometimes. I can't help it, so don't ask me to stop."

"I won't," he said. "I'm here this early for a reason."

"Not just my company? I figured as much. What's up?"

He reached into his pocket and pulled out a folded envelope. "I may have found something about Richard Atkins's first disappearance." He slid the envelope across the table to me. "See what you think."

Inside was a faded and yellowed newspaper article, and it broke in two as I unfolded it. "Sorry about that."

"That's all right. Read it."

Holding the pieces together, I scanned the article, then looked up. "It's about a jewelry store robbery. I remember reading about it back then." In fact, Kendra had brought up the subject when she'd first heard that Richard had returned to Maple Ridge.

"Look at the date," he said as he tapped the paper.

"Okay. It doesn't have much significance to me. I'm sorry, I must be a little slow this morning."

Butch sighed. "Think about it. You know David's birthday, don't you?"

"Of course I do. It's March eleventh."

"You know the year as well, I'll wager. Take that date, count back seven months, and what have you got? I imagine it's about the time Hannah knew she was pregnant with him."

I frowned at him. "Are you saying that the two events are related? Do you honestly believe Richard Atkins found out his wife was pregnant, then decided to go out and rob a jewelry store to celebrate? The owner was shot and wounded. It hardly seems the proper way to celebrate."

"I don't believe in coincidences, Carolyn. This has to be related."

"But how?"

"Give me some time. I'll dig into it and get back to you. But first I've got to go out of town today."

As we stood, I said, "I'm not even going to bother asking you where you're going."

He smiled. "Good. Then I won't have to lie to you. If you're in a hurry for the information, it won't hurt my feelings if you look into this yourself."

"I've got a better idea. Why don't I ask Sandy?"

"That works for me. I'll stop by when I get back into town."

I couldn't let him go yet. I held his hands in mine, then said, "Be careful. Promise me that much."

"Yes, ma'am."

Once he was gone, I dialed Sandy's number at the library. Before I could tell her what I wanted her to investigate, she said, "Carolyn, I haven't had a chance to look into that ClayDate thing since we spoke yesterday. Things have been kind of crazy around here."

"That's fine." It looked as though I was going to have to research the robbery myself.

Before I could hang up, she asked, "That was why you were calling, wasn't it?"

"No, but it can wait."

"You can't tease me like that," she said. "I'll fret about it all day."

I quickly relayed Butch's hunch to her, expecting her to dismiss it out of hand. Instead she said, "I can get back to you in half an hour."

"I thought you were busy," I said.

"I've got time for this. It's an entirely different kind of search. This is all open information. Will you be at the shop this morning?"

"Who knows? I think so, but that's no real indication, given the way my days have been going lately."

"I'll track you down, then," she said, and then hung up.

David wasn't due in for an hour yet, and though I had a hundred things I could do, I didn't want to do any of them. Was I losing my drive for running Fire at Will? No, I still loved working with clay, glaze, and paint. It was just that I had so many distractions to deal with, I couldn't enjoy my real purpose in life.

I decided to open my kilns to see how the cottages had turned out. As I unloaded them, I marveled at the simple little structures, and how much fun they were to make. Though they were all the reddish pink of bisque-fired clay, I could imagine the many variations we could make with paint and glaze. Taking one of the cottages I'd created, I sat down at one of the painting benches and lost myself in decorating the structure. When I looked up from my work, I saw that I should have opened my door twenty minutes earlier. I'd been so wrapped up in what I'd been doing that the time had flown past me. As I unlocked the door, I was a little disgruntled that no eager customers had brought my tardiness to my attention.

I'd just flipped the sign on the front door when David came trotting up. "Sorry I'm late. I slept in."

"Is that good news, or bad? Did you have any luck with Annie?"

"She's thawing, but it's still kind of chilly," he admitted as he took off his jacket and hung it on a peg. "Speaking of arctic blasts, I talked to my mom this morning."

"Did you? What did she have to say for herself?"

He whistled. "I thought I was the only one in the world who could push her buttons like that, but you must have found a few I didn't even know existed. You probably should know that you're not one of her favorite people in the world right now."

"I didn't think I was," I said as I returned to my cottage. I'd suddenly lost interest in working on it, but it was nearly finished. It had been for ten minutes, but I'd been enjoying adding little details, like a black cat perched on the front stoop. The next house I did would have a three-dimensional feline on it. I had a core group of customers who would buy anything I made as long as it had a cat on it. The only catch was, it had to be unique, so I was constantly searching for more ways to add cats to my pieces. I loved them myself, but it was strictly a marketing decision. Okay, that wasn't true. They were fun to do, and I considered it a challenge making the felines fit in.

"Do you want to talk about it?" David asked as he put on his apron.

"That's the last thing I want to do," I said. "Let's finish these cottages, shall we? I want to get them fired and in the window as fast as I can."

"We're not doing production work, are we?"

"No, but if these little buildings help pay the rent, we should embrace them."

"Okay, I get it," he said. As he looked at the pieces spread out on a table by the kilns, David said, "We've got a lot of work to do."

"I think we should just glaze half of them," I said. "We can put the others out on the open shelves for our customers."

"Have you thought about what you're going to charge for them?"

"Not yet," I said. "For now, just put them in the most expensive pricing section and we'll figure out an exact amount later."

I had my shelves of bisqueware organized, from the least expensive saucers to the fanciest jugs and teakettles. The system wasn't perfect, but it was the best I'd been able to come up with in the years I'd owned Fire at Will. Pricing the pieces I bought wholesale wasn't that difficult. But David liked to add his own work to the shelves, and Robert Owens, the potter from Travers who sometimes taught classes at the shop, often put the pieces he didn't think were quite good enough on the shelves, too. I hadn't seen him lately, because he was on some kind of research trip in Europe—nice work if you could get it. I seemed to be stuck in Maple Ridge. Not that I didn't love our little corner of Vermont, but sometimes I got the itch to grab my husband, get the next flight out, and see what the world had to offer. The funny thing was, I knew if we ever actually did it, in three or four days I'd be yearning for my kilns and pottery again. It was something that drove my husband crazy, but I couldn't help myself.

I saw David holding one of the cottages he'd made. "Are you going to do that one for the window?"

"No, I thought I'd keep this one myself. You don't mind, do you?"

"Of course not. Is it going to be a gift?"

He grinned. "It might be. It depends on how well things go later, I guess."

"You could always give it to your mother."

"Or you could make one for her yourself as a peace gesture."

I looked sharply at him. "David, I thought we weren't going to talk about that."

"Hey, don't blame me. You're the one who brought her up."

I wasn't about to argue, especially since he was right. "Are we going to decorate these or not?"

"I'm right behind you."

We quickly lapsed into our old habits of conversation as we worked on our pieces side by side. Business at the shop was slow, but at least David and I were doing something productive with our time. Summer would be upon us soon enough, and we wouldn't have much opportunity to work on our own projects. Still, I was a little concerned about the lull in revenue.

When Sandy came in, I forgot all about those concerns. The look of sheer exuberance on her face could mean only one thing. She'd uncovered something she thought was significant in the case.

Chapter 11

"Can we talk?" Sandy asked me, her eyes darting quickly to David.

"I won't tell, I promise," David said. "You can say whatever you want to in front of me."

"Don't be that way," I told David. "This might not concern you. Why don't you take an early lunch? Don't worry about the mess. I'll clean it up."

"In that case, be my guest. Sandy, you can come by the shop any time." He washed up, traded his apron for his jacket, and then David was gone.

"Sorry about that," Sandy said as soon as the door closed. "I just didn't think it was right talking about his father in front of him."

"So you found something else?" I asked.

"I'm not sure if there's any fire, but I'm close enough to something to smell smoke."

"Well, don't hold out on me. What is it?"

"I didn't get this on the Internet. My boss Corki gave me the scoop about what happened. She was married to one of Hodges's deputies around the time that Richard left town."

I knew Corki had gone through a pair of dud husbands before she'd found a keeper, but we hadn't been friends back then. "What did she say?"

"It's about the jewelry store robbery. The police believed two men were in on the theft, though that never made it into the papers. They never had any idea who one of them was, but they were looking hard at one of our prominent citizens as the accomplice. Harvey Jenkins opened up his first car dealership around then, and it wasn't entirely clear where he got his backing."

"Did your boss actually say the mayor of Maple Ridge is a thief?"

Sandy shook her head. "No, apparently Harvey had an alibi, but that doesn't mean he wasn't in on it. And there's something else."

"Go on," I said. For a reference librarian—someone who made her living telling people things they wanted to know—Sandy sure seemed to enjoy ratcheting up the suspense.

"Corki's ex also interviewed Richard Atkins. They couldn't find any hard evidence against him, but not long after the robbery, he left town, so it made the police wonder."

"That's what Butch thought, but I'm still not convinced."

"Here's the part where it gets worse," Sandy said. "The jewelry store owner who was shot and wounded died a few years after the robbery. They say he was never the same after what happened."

"How does that fit into the rest of this?"

"He was Annie Gregg's dad," Sandy said.

"That would give her a motive for killing Richard, if he had been involved and she knew it," I said.

"And if that's true, then the mayor better watch his back as well."

I tried to picture the sweet young woman I knew doing something so cold-blooded. "No," I said after a moment, "I can't believe Annie would have anything to do with what happened to Richard. She's not that kind of girl."

"What, the kind who kills to revenge her father? Face it, Carolyn, it's hard to say who would or wouldn't be capable of that, isn't it? I'm sorry I don't have more, but there was really nothing official ever filed. As far as I know, the case is still open."

"You've given me plenty to think about," I said.

"Well, I'd better get back to the library, but I wanted to tell you what I'd heard as soon as I could."

"Thanks," I said as Sandy hurried out.

Was it possible that Annie had been dating the son of the man who'd killed her father? Could that, rather than David's behavior, have spurred the break up? I found it difficult to imagine Annie killing anybody, but Sandy was right. Who knew what a person was capable of, given the right circumstances.

I was still mulling over what Sandy had told me when David poked his head in through the front door. "Is it safe to come back in?"

"The coast is clear," I said, trying to lighten my dire mood. "How was lunch?"

"Is was good," he said. "I called Annie and she actually agreed to have a bite with me. I think there's a glimmer of hope there somewhere."

"Hope is a wonderful thing, isn't it?" I couldn't exactly warn David that his girlfriend might be a killer, but could I just let it go? Evidently not. "You're sure you're doing the right thing with Annie, right?"

"What do you mean, Carolyn?"

I really was out of line, especially if Sandy was wrong about Annie's actions. Whatever happened to being innocent until proven guilty? "Don't listen to me. I'm just an old poop sometimes."

He shrugged, dismissing it. "Are you ready to do some more decorating?"

"What I'm ready for is my lunch, young man. Watch the shop. I'll see you soon." I grabbed my coat and got out of there. Until I was sure about Annie, I had to watch what I said around David. I didn't want to poison his chance at love if my suspicions were unfounded.

"Annie, it's Carolyn Emerson. Do you have a minute?" I figured the best place to get information about the girl was to go directly to the source. At least I'd remembered to charge my cell phone, so I could make this call in the relative privacy of a bench overlooking the brook.

"Hi, Carolyn. I just took my lunch break with David, and it put me behind. Sorry."

"This won't take long," I promised. "All I need is five minutes. I can come to you, if you'd like."

She paused, then said, "No, I can meet you. Are you at the shop?"

"Actually, I'm getting ready to go to Shelly's. I know you've eaten, but how about some pie?"

"Please, I'm getting plump as it is. David loves to eat out, and I've been gaining weight from the moment we met."

"Okay, no pie. What about coffee? We could meet at In the Grounds."

"I suppose so. Carolyn, there's no chance we can do this right now over the telephone, is there?"

"I think it would be better face-to-face," I said.

"If you say so. I'll see you soon."

I hurried over to the coffee shop, securing a table by the window where I could watch for her. Nate Walker, the owner of the place, approached.

"Hi, Carolyn. I was beginning to think you'd forgotten we were here. Are you and Hannah fighting?"

"What makes you ask that?"

"Come on, I can set my watch by you two, but lately, neither one of you has been coming by. I'm beginning to wonder if it was something I said."

"It's not you, it's us. I'd like two coffees, please."

He looked out the window. "Does that mean Hannah's going to join you?"

"No, this one's for someone else."

He nodded gravely, then left to get my order. Twenty seconds after the coffee was delivered, Annie arrived. I was struck again by how much Annie resembled the actress Julia Roberts. It was easy to see why David had found her attractive, but I knew Annie's charms went far beyond her appearance.

"Thanks for the coffee," she said as she took a sip.

"Don't you even want to know what I ordered for you?" I asked, smiling.

"If it's got caffeine, we're good," she said. "I was up pretty late last night."

"So I heard," I said without realizing how it must have sounded. "Sorry about that. I didn't mean to butt in."

"It's fine. I fully expected David to talk to you about our situation. I know you two are very close."

"We are. I'd hate to see him get hurt," I said, refraining from adding any more to that statement.

"I don't want to hurt him, believe me. I care for David." I could see in her eyes that it was true.

"His father's sudden reappearance was pretty shocking, wasn't it?" I said.

"I guess. It's been hard on him all these years not having a dad."

"The same can be said for you, can't it? You two have a great deal in common in that regard," I said. Then I sipped my coffee.

"It's true. I never knew my father, either," she admitted. "Somebody stole that from me."

"What an unusual way to put it."

For an instant, she looked furious. "How else would you say it? That robber killed him, just as surely as if he'd put that gun to my dad's head and pulled the trigger again."

"It sounds like the wound is still raw for you." Annie's emotions were breaking through her normally happy demeanor.

"Carolyn, what was so urgent that we had to meet? I don't have much time."

"It's about David," I said.

I was still struggling for words when Annie said, "No offense, but I'm not sure it's any of your business. I know you two are close, but you're not his mother, and I wouldn't even be discussing this with her, if she cared enough to ask."

"Hannah loves him a great deal," I said softly.

"There's got to be room in his life for someone else." She threw two ones on the table. "I've got to go."

I picked up the bills and tried to hand them back to her. "This was my treat."

"Thanks, but I pay my own way."

After she was gone, I stared at my coffee. Suddenly, I wasn't nearly as sure as I had been that Annie wasn't involved in the murder. If she suspected that Richard had committed that robbery twenty years ago, I doubted she would hesitate to exact her revenge. Whether or not I liked it, I was going to have to add her to my list of suspects.

"May I join you? All the other tables are full." I looked up to see Mayor Jenkins standing in front of me.

I moved Annie's cup to my side and motioned to a seat. "Help yourself."

He nodded, then settled in across from me. Harvey Jenkins was fighting his spreading waistline, and was obviously losing. His clothes, while nicely cut, were too young for a man his age, as was his fancy haircut. He looked like a man trying to hold on to something that was long gone.

"Listen, I'm sorry about our earlier conversation during your test drive. You caught me at a bad time."

"We all have them," I said. "Don't worry about it." Clearly, he was trying to put our earlier encounter behind him. I wasn't sure I was going to let him, but I'd see what he had to say.

"You're looking a little ragged around the edges, Carolyn," he said. "Are you getting enough sleep?"

"My, you know just what to say to turn a woman's head," I answered. "No wonder you keep getting reelected."

He smiled. "Granted, that was probably a little harsh." He stifled a yawn. "I had a rather late night myself. A mayor's work is never done. I keep pushing for it to be a full-time job, but so far, nobody wants that but me."

"You'd miss your dealership, wouldn't you? I'm sure you make a killing off it."

He raised one eyebrow. "You'd be surprised. How's the pottery business?"

"We're getting by," I said. "Actually, I had an interesting conversation about you this morning."

Harvey rubbed his ears. "I thought I felt my ears burning. Only good, I hope."

"That depends. We were talking about the robbery twenty years ago at Quality Jewelry."

Did I see a flinch when I mentioned the name of the store? "How on earth was my name tied to that?" Harvey asked, seemingly perplexed.

"We were discussing things that happened around the time Richard Atkins took off. The jewelry store robbery and the opening of your first car dealership all happened at about the same time, didn't they?"

"It was a long time ago," he said. "I'm sure they weren't all that close together. The years have a tendency to blend together, don't they?" He sipped his coffee, but the mayor's gaze never left my face. If nothing else, I'd certainly managed to pique his curiosity. "Who exactly were you discussing all this with, your husband?"

"No, Bill was already at work by then. It's a small world, isn't it?"

"And getting smaller by the minute," he said as he looked over my shoulder. "Thanks for the seat, but a booth just opened up."

"Don't rush off on my account," I said.

"Of course not. I've just got a few calls to make while I drink my coffee, and it would be rude to do that in front of you. Good bye."

"I'll see you later," I said.

I'd delayed my lunch hour long enough, but I didn't want

to eat at the coffee shop. Neither did I feel like going under Shelly's microscope, so instead, on a whim I got into the Intrigue and drove home.

Bill's truck was parked in the driveway, and I was happy he was home. My husband wasn't the most romantic man in the world; in fact, much of the time he could be downright gruff. But something about his presence soothed me, made me feel safe, like I belonged. I'd never tried to convey that in words to him, and even if I did I doubted he'd understand. But that didn't matter. I knew, and that was enough.

"Bill? Are you in here?" No answer. He must still be in his shop, though with his injured hand, I wondered how much work he'd be able to accomplish.

I walked out through the back door and started for his woodworking shop. As I walked, I noticed something odd about the backyard. The lawn was filled with small holes and looked as though it'd been invaded by a horde of gophers. Bill wasn't all that keen on landscaping, and neither was I, but I was sure we couldn't allow this rampage to go unchecked.

I finally found him in his shop leafing through plan books. "What's going on?" I asked.

"Carolyn? What in the world are you doing here? Why aren't you at work?"

"I thought I'd come home to see my husband. That's allowed, isn't it?" He didn't look all that pleased to see me.

"You know it is. I just thought you'd be too busy. You don't usually pop home for lunch."

"Listen, if I've interrupted some grand plans of yours, I can make a quick sandwich and take it back to the pottery shop with me." I'd had warmer welcomes at my dentist's office.

"I'm sorry," he said abruptly. "This blasted hand hurts too much when I try to do anything, and if I take a pill for the pain, I'm too loopy to work. I can't win."

"So why are you sitting out here feeling sorry for yourself?"

"I don't have the slightest idea," he said, trying to scare up a smile but managing only a sickly grin.

"Come on in and I'll make something for both of us." I offered him my hand, and he took it.

"That's the best idea I've had all day."

"I believe it was mine."

"Don't quibble. What's for lunch?"

I thought about what I had in my refrigerator and freezer, and realized a real shopping trip to the grocery store was long past due. "Let's go see, shall we?"

As we walked back to the house, I said, "The gophers are getting pretty aggressive with our backyard. There are lumps everywhere."

"Fine," he said absentmindedly.

"I was thinking about getting some dynamite and taking care of it myself."

"That's good," he said, still lost in thoughts of his own. "Wait a second. Did you say dynamite?"

"I did indeed."

"There's no need for anything that drastic," he said.

"Don't scold me. I was just trying to see if you were paying any attention to me, which you weren't."

"I've got deadlines to meet, Carolyn. This is serious."

I stopped at the door and turned to Bill. "You are retired. Stop acting like you have to earn a living, because you don't. We're fine. If you have to, give back the money you took as a down payment."

He pulled away from me. "It's not the money, and you

know it. I gave my word, and now I'm not going to be able to keep it. You know how I feel about that."

"You can't heal yourself," I said, suddenly angry. "The harder you push, the longer it's going to take you to get better."

"I keep telling you, it's not that bad."

"It's serious enough to keep you from working. Do you really want to have this argument again?"

"No, not particularly," he said gruffly.

"Then let's find something to eat."

I poked around the kitchen, but the supplies were low in nearly every department. "How about an omelet?" I asked.

"For lunch?"

"No, I'm thinking about breakfast three weeks from Thursday. Do you think you'll be in the mood for one then? I can pencil it in, then you can change your mind if you'd like."

He looked surprised. "There's no need to snap."

"Then don't ask silly questions. I'm not in the mood for it. Is it going to be eggs, or would you prefer peanut butter sandwiches?"

He smiled, then said, "Eggs sound fine."

"Just fine?" I was in a snit, and I couldn't do anything about it. It would wear off eventually, but for the moment, I couldn't seem to stop myself from snapping at my husband.

"Grand, wondrous, joyful, delightful. That's what I meant to say."

I stared at him for ten seconds, then returned his smile. "Eggs it is."

"I'll do the toast," he volunteered, "and I'll grate the cheese, too. Let's make omelets."

"You're a model of helpfulness," I said.

"Are you kidding? I'm afraid if I don't, you won't feed me at all."

I put the pan down, but before I cracked the eggs, I said, "Bill, I am sorry. I know I'm being a little abrasive, but this murder is digging up things that might be better off left buried."

"You don't have to investigate it yourself, you know."

"I can't just let it go," I said as I rinsed the eggs and cracked them open. As I put them in a bowl and stirred in some milk, I added, "It's not in my nature."

"I know. It was just a suggestion. What are we going to do with ourselves? I'm a woodworker who can't use his shop, and you're a shop owner who doesn't have time for her business. We're quite the pair, aren't we?"

"I like us, despite our varied flaws," I said.

"So do I." He hugged me briefly, then said, "I'll have that cheese for you in a minute."

I made the omelet big enough for both of us, and it was delicious, especially with the sharp cheddar cheese we both preferred.

After we ate, Bill pushed his plate away. "What's for dessert?"

"Do you have to have something sweet after every meal?"

He shrugged. "I don't have to, but it sure tastes good."

"There's one slice left of the lemon meringue pie, but I thought you were saving it for tonight."

"Forget that. Grab two forks and I'll split it with you."

"I'd better not," I said. "I've got to get back to Fire at Will. I've left David there long enough."

"Suit yourself," he said, happily sliding out the pie tin from the refrigerator.

* * *

"I wasn't sure you were coming back," David said impatiently as I walked back into the shop.

As I hung my coat up, I said, "I didn't realize there was any rush."

"There you were wrong."

I looked around the shop, and there wasn't a single customer in sight. "I can see you're just overwhelmed with work."

"It's not that," David said. "Annie called a few minutes ago and said she wanted to talk. I hate to do this to you, but can I take the rest of the afternoon off?"

This could be trouble. "Did she say what she wanted to talk about?" I asked.

"No, why do you ask?"

"David, there's something you should know before you meet her."

He narrowed his gaze. "Carolyn, what have you been up to?"

"What makes you ask me that?"

"Come on, I've known you my entire life. Spill."

There was no use denying it. "I had a talk with her an hour ago."

"You had no right," he said fiercely. "I swear, you're worse than my mother."

"High praise indeed," I said. "Don't you want to know what we talked about?"

"Do I even need to ask?" He had his hand on the door, but I had to stop him. David deserved to hear my suspicions, whether he wanted to or not.

"Move your hand, Carolyn." The calm resonance in his voice was a sure sign that he was angry.

"Not until you listen to what I have to say. I can be just as stubborn as you can be, you know that, don't you?"

He took a step back. "Talk."

"Do you know what happened to Annie's father?" I had to tread lightly here.

"Sure. He died pretty soon after she was born. Neither one of us had a dad growing up. It's something that's brought us close. What does that have to do with anything?"

"You know about the jewelry store robbery, don't you? The one where he was injured?"

He scratched his chin. "She mentioned it."

"It happened about the time your father left town," I said, not able to look into his eyes.

"So what? Wait a second. You can't be serious." I could hear his breathing become raspy. "You think my dad had something to do with it, don't you? Is that why you think he left town, because he was afraid of getting caught? You didn't even know him."

"Surely you don't think you did, David. He left before you were born, and you didn't see him again until the day he was murdered."

"He wasn't a crook. I don't believe it."

"I'm not saying he was, but think about it. If Annie held your father responsible for what happened to her dad, she could come after you, too."

"Carolyn, you've breathed in too many fumes from the kilns. I can't believe you're even suggesting this."

"I'm not saying it's true, but it's a possibility, and isn't that reason enough to be careful?"

"I'm leaving," he said. By the tone of his voice, I knew better than to try to stop him again.

I probably shouldn't have said anything, not without more evidence than a gut feeling, but at least David would go to the rendezvous with his eyes open. At least I hoped he would. I felt guilty about accusing Annie, but if she had been involved with Richard Atkins's murder, David needed to be careful around her.

I knew I'd fret about David until I heard from him again, but after the way we'd left things, I didn't expect that would be anytime soon. In the meantime, I had more avenues to explore. Unlike our esteemed sheriff, I couldn't afford to focus on one suspect. Too many people had had reason to want Richard Atkins dead, and unfortunately, several of them were either friends or family of mine.

Chapter 12

I couldn't shut down Fire at Will again; I'd done that too many times in the past few months. The bottom line was starting to suffer, and I was never that far away from being in the red as it was. I didn't know many small stores that could afford to stay in business with the kind of hours I'd been keeping.

To my surprise, I had a few customers come in over the course of the rest of the afternoon, though none of them wanted to paint anything, or work with the raw clay in back, either. Still, by the time I closed out my register, I'd made enough to prove that staying open had been worthwhile, even if it did mean that I was no closer to solving Richard Atkins's murder.

I had locked up the shop and started for my car when I saw Kendra Williams and Rose Nygren huddled together in conversation in front of Hattie's Attic. I couldn't pass up a chance to listen in on two of my suspects colluding about something.

I tried to get close enough to hear what they were talking about, but their voices were too low for me to understand what they were saying.

"Hello, ladies," I said the second I realized that Kendra had spotted me approaching.

"Carolyn," Kendra said stiffly. Rose merely glared.

"What's going on?" I tried to keep a sunny and harmless expression on my face, though I doubted either one would buy it.

"None of your business," Rose said in an uncharacteristically harsh tone.

"Is that any way to talk to me? I've never done anything to you."

"Other than accuse me of murder?" Rose asked.

"I never accused you of anything. I've just been trying to find out what happened to Richard Atkins. Is that such a terrible thing to do?"

"That's why we have a police force," Kendra said.

"We both know that not much goes on in Maple Ridge that you don't know about," I said. "I'm sure the police could learn a thing or two about our fair town, if you chose to tell them."

Kendra shrugged, and I could tell she was weakening, but Rose said, "Don't let her flatter you. She just wants to know what we've been talking about."

Kendra nodded. "You're right. It's none of your concern, Carolyn."

"Fine, be that way," I said. "When Sheriff Hodges asks me about you two, I know just what I'll say."

Kendra snorted. "As if the sheriff would ever consult with you about anything."

"You see how often he comes by my shop," I said. "What do you think he's doing over there, asking for pottery tips?" Okay, that was a flat-out lie, but I didn't care. After all, the sheriff did spend an inordinate amount of time at Fire at Will, albeit only to scold me for my amateur sleuthing efforts.

Before Rose could dissuade her, Kendra said, "If you must know, we were discussing our alibis."

"Do you mean making them up?" I asked.

Rose snapped, "No, we were talking about whether we should step forward and tell the sheriff where we were the night of the murder, so he won't suspect us."

"You two were together?" I couldn't believe they hadn't told me sooner. Could it be true, or were they each covering for the other? Wait a second, what about Rose's glasses being left at the hospital? "But Rose, you were in the hospital waiting room three nights ago. I've already looked into that, and I've got your glasses to prove it."

"So you have been checking up on me," she said, the accusation thick in her voice.

"Are you telling me it's not true?"

"I took Edith Sampson there, but I couldn't wait the entire time for her. I had other things to do, so Kendra picked me up at the hospital, then dropped me off later so I could give Edith a ride home."

"Okay, that explains that, but then where exactly were you both the night of the murder?"

"In Burlington," Kendra said in triumph. "We were meeting with the new owners of our buildings."

"Wait a second, whoever bought your places owns mine, too. Why wasn't I told about this meeting?"

"I'm sure you got the same notice in the mail that we did, but since you were so busy with your investigation, you probably forgot all about it. Don't worry, we told the new management team all about you."

"I'll just bet you did," I said. If Kendra Williams was my character witness, I was already sunk. "What did they say?"

"Rents won't go up, at least not until the current agreements expire," Rose said. "We made sure of that. If you don't believe us, you can call them yourself."

"Do you have their number?" I asked.

"Are you seriously going to check our alibis?" Rose asked.

"I might, but I want to talk to these people myself. After all, they're going to be my landlords, too."

Kendra turned to Rose and said, "We might as well give her the number. She's going to find out sooner or later."

"Oh, go on, then."

Kendra nodded, then said, "I've got one of their cards. I'll be right back."

While she was inside, I turned to Rose and said, "You know, you could have saved me a lot of grief if you'd told me about this before."

"Why on earth were you under the impression it was my job to make your life easier?"

"You sound just like my uncle," I said. Taking a stab in the dark, I asked, "Are you two back together?"

"I told you before, we were never a couple in the first place." She hurried back to her shop, and when Kendra emerged a minute later, she looked around, then asked, "What did you do to Rose?"

"Nothing. She got tired of waiting and left," I said. "Is that for me?"

She nodded and handed me a business card. "Here, you can call them if you'd like."

"Kendra, I'm going to ask you the same thing I asked Rose. Why did you hint that you were on some mysterious tryst when I asked you about an alibi before? You made it sound as though you were with a man, not Rose."

"I don't approve of your snooping, and you know it. Besides, I thought if I spread a little rumor that I was seeing someone mysterious, it might make folks talk. I knew you'd never be able to keep it to yourself."

"As a matter of fact, I haven't told a soul," I said, then I walked toward my car.

Once inside my Intrigue, I pulled out my cell phone and called the management group. The secretary confirmed Rose and Kendra's alibi easily enough, and echoed the news that rents would stay the same as long as the current leases were in effect. That was something, anyway. I could strike two names off my list, and I felt positively giddy doing so. That just left Mayor Jenkins, my uncle, and Annie Gregg. At least the field was finally narrowing.

I'd just walked in the door at home when I heard the telephone ring. "Hello?"

"You sound positively out of breath," Sandy said. "Did I catch you at a bad time?"

"No, I just got in. What's up?"

"I've been doing more digging into the ClayDate Corporation, and I found something I thought you'd like to know."

As I looked through the mail, which Bill had deposited on the counter, I said, "That's old news, Sandy."

"That's exactly what it's not," she said smugly.

"What do you mean?"

"ClayDate has been paying its business license fees

every year, including this one. Does that sound like a defunct company to you?"

"No, it doesn't," I admitted. "Why would the mayor lie to me about it?"

"He's a politician, isn't he? It must be second nature for him. Doesn't that mean he and Richard were doing business more recently than he admitted?"

"It has to. Thanks, Sandy. I'm going to ask him about this the first chance I get."

"You're welcome," she said. "I'll keep rooting around."

"Do that," I said as I hung up. The mail was mostly bills and the rest was junk. Didn't anybody write real letters anymore? I used to love getting mail. Of course, I hadn't written any letters myself for ages. I'd have to do that sometime soon if I expected to get any in return.

I walked back to Bill's workshop and noticed that the gopher had dug even more holes. I promised myself I'd look up gopher eradicators in the phone book after we ate dinner.

Bill wasn't in his shop. Where could he be? His truck was parked out front, and I hadn't seen any sign of him in the house. I hurried back inside, worried that something might have happened to him.

"Bill? Are you here?" No answer. I could feel the knot in my gut growing as I searched the house. Our bedroom was empty, and that just left the boys' old bedroom we'd converted into a guest room years before. If he wasn't in there, I'd call the sheriff.

At first I didn't see him, but as I flipped on the light, I breathed a sigh of relief. "Bill, what are you doing in here?"

"Didn't want to get in your way," he mumbled. "My hand was hurting, so I took a pill and went to bed. Turn off that light, will you?"

I did as he asked, then sat down on the edge of the bed. "Can I get you anything?"

"Just sleep," he said as he jammed a pillow over his head. I took the hint and left him alone.

There wasn't a thing in the world I could do for him, and I hated the feeling of helplessness. Since our two sons had moved away, Bill and I relied on each other for so much. Having him out of action left me feeling odd and uneasy.

Since it appeared that I would be dining alone tonight, I looked through the cabinets for something to eat. I couldn't face eggs again, and I hadn't yet shopped, so peanut butter and jelly would have to do. Except a layer of something was growing on top of the jelly, so that was out, too. Peanut butter sandwiches might be wonderful fare for a ten-year-old, but they didn't do much for me. I promised myself I'd go to the grocery store tomorrow. After eating my unfulfilling sandwich, I decided to pop some popcorn as a supplement. I wasn't in the mood for regular television, so I put *Casablanca* in the DVD player and settled in for a night with Bogart, Bergman, and friends.

Darkness dropped like a coin outside, and I shut off the lights in the den so I could enjoy the movie. But something started flickering on the television, and for a minute, I thought the set was going out. Then movement outside caught my eye, and I paused the movie so I could get a better look. Someone was in our backyard with a flashlight! I peered out through the glass, but I couldn't see anything but a bobbing beam of light. Creeping into the guest room, I whispered, "Bill? Are you awake?"

No response but a snore.

"Bill?" This time my voice was louder, but it had no effect on his drug-induced slumber.

I could call the police. I should call the police. But first I wanted to see if I could catch a glimpse of who was out there.

Standing by the back door, I flipped on the back porch light, ready to catch whoever was out there, but the light didn't go on. The bulb must have burned out. It was going to be up to Sheriff Hodges to catch the interloper.

I got through to him on the telephone without too much trouble. "This is Carolyn Emerson. Somebody's creeping around outside my house with a flashlight."

"Have they tried to get in?"

"No. Right now, it looks like they're just standing there holding a flashlight."

"Can you see who it is?"

I peered into the darkness again, but I couldn't make out who the trespasser was. "I can't tell. Should I go outside for a better look?"

"No! Lock the doors and I'll be there in two minutes."

At least I'd managed to shake some of the rust off the sheriff. I didn't have any weapons in the house, but I did have a mop handle I could swing like a bat. I grabbed it and watched outside, waiting for something to happen. I had just about given up any hope of the sheriff coming when I saw another light and heard him shout, "Freeze."

The flashlight dropped and I heard running. My first thought was to go outside, but I decided it would be better to wait for the sheriff to come get me.

After the longest ten minutes of my life, I heard a tap on the back door, and I was so startled, I dropped the mop handle.

I could make out a man's shape, but I couldn't see his face. "Carolyn, let me in."

There was no mistaking the sheriff's voice. After I unlocked the door, he asked, "Where's Bill?"

"He's sleeping."

Hodges stared at me a few seconds, then asked, "You didn't think this was important enough to wake him?"

"He's on medication for his hand," I said. "Who was it?"

"I don't know," he admitted. "I lost him in the woods. I found this, though. Any chance it's yours?"

He reached back and collected a brand new shovel with dirt on its blade. "Are you kidding? I haven't bought a new yard tool in ten years. Where did you find it?"

"It was in the yard. It looks like your friend was digging holes. Any idea why?"

"I thought we had gophers," I said.

"Maybe the two-legged variety," he replied. "Why didn't you turn the back porch light on when I came up to the house? I could have been anybody."

"It must be burned out," I said. "Besides, I waited until I heard your voice before I let you in. What should I do now?"

"I'd get a new bulb if I were you."

"I'm not talking about the light. I mean the intruder."

"I doubt he's coming back tonight, but just in case, I'll have someone come by every hour or so to check on the place. If you don't mind, I'll keep this shovel."

"Be my guest," I said. Despite the problems I had with the sheriff, he had been prompt about coming out when I'd needed him. "Thanks for getting here so fast."

"It's part of my job," he said. "Don't forget to replace that bulb in the morning."

"I promise," I said.

Not even *Casablanca* could hold my attention after that. I popped the movie out of the DVD player, brushed my teeth, and decided to go to bed. The guest room was a single mattress, and there was no way Bill and I both would fit on it, at least not now that we were nearing our thirty-year anniversary. Not that I didn't love my husband—I probably loved him more after all our years together than I did the day I married him—but I wasn't willing to fight him all night for the covers on a bed two sizes too small.

Our bed seemed vast and empty without him, and I thought I'd never fall asleep, but the exhaustion from the day finally kicked in. I found myself drifting off as I wondered why on earth anyone would dig holes in our yard, at night to boot.

"I can't believe you slept through all of the excitement last night," I told my husband as he came into the kitchen for breakfast the next morning. I'd been up for hours and was dallying so I could see him before I had to leave to open the shop. Since Hannah and I were at odds, it meant we weren't meeting for coffee in the morning, and that left me with more free time than I liked.

"Why, what happened?" He was not nearly as fresh as he had been the day before. "Those pills really knocked me out."

"We had an intruder."

He sat up in his chair. "What?"

"Well, not in the house. Somebody was digging holes in the backyard last night with a flashlight."

"You can't dig much of a hole with one of those things," he said.

"He was using the flashlight to see, you nit," I said. "He had a shovel for digging. The sheriff took it with him."

"Hodges came out here? Why didn't you wake me?"

"I tried," I said, "but you were too far gone."

He walked over to the sink, took the bottle of pain pills, and tossed them in the trash.

"Why did you do that?"

"You needed me last night, and I was too doped up to help you. I don't need that kind of comfort."

I'd threatened to do the exact same thing myself, but now I had a change of heart. "Bill, don't be so rash. Everything was fine."

"But it might not have been," he said. "Why didn't you turn the porch light on and scare whoever it was away?"

"That's another thing. You need to put a new bulb in the back porch light. That one's blow out."

"I changed it last week," he said.

"You don't have to do it right now," I said. "Eat your breakfast first."

"Just a second." He opened the back door and stepped outside. Twenty seconds later, he was back. "Flip the light on."

I did as he asked. "It's working perfect now," he said.

"Well, it wasn't last night."

He frowned. "The bulb was loose. I could have sworn I tightened it up all the way when I put it in."

I thought about that as I took a sip of coffee. "Maybe somebody unscrewed it."

"Now you're just being paranoid."

I pointed outside. "You said we had gophers, too."

He shrugged. "You made your point. I'll poke around a little after I eat."

"I'll go with you," I said.

"Don't you have a shop to run?"

I glanced at the clock. "I've got plenty of time. What would you like for breakfast?"

"I'm just going to have some orange juice."

As he poured a glass, I said, "You need to eat more than that."

"I'm not hungry. Those blasted pills kill my appetite. That's enough reason to throw them away."

As he got dressed, I wondered again why anyone would invade our backyard. With the broad daylight to reassure me, I decided to go out and look around myself. Sure enough, I could see a clump of grass the digger had failed to replant. The hole was nearly six inches deep and twelve inches across. What could he have been looking for?

"What are you doing out here by yourself?" Bill said gruffly behind me.

"It's perfectly safe at the moment," I said. "What do you make of this?"

He peered down and studied the hole. "I may be wrong, but it looks like a hole to me."

"We've already established that," I said. "But why?"

"Hey, I answered a question. Now it's your turn."

"I don't have a clue," I said.

"Maybe you should get that shooting gang of yours to take a swing at it."

"They're called the Firing Squad, and you know it. I might just do that; it's not a bad idea."

"I was kidding, Carolyn."

"Well, I'm not." I glanced at my watch. "I have to run. Try to stay out of trouble today, okay?"

"It's always my goal," he said, "but I'm not always that successful at it."

As I drove to Fire at Will, I continued to ask myself what the digging meant. Was there something back there worth excavating? I couldn't imagine what it might be. No pirates had ever made it to Maple Ridge, and as far as I knew, the closest gold strike had been hundreds of miles away. Something was out there, though. Or at least someone suspected there was.

I was surprised to find David in the shop when I arrived, a full half hour before he was due to punch in.

"You're here early," I said as I traded my jacket for an apron.

"I wanted to make up some of the time I've been missing lately," he admitted, a full-blown apology for David. "Our first batch of cottages is finished. Would you like to see them?"

"You bet," I said. He'd pulled them out of the kilns and lined them up on the table in back. They were unique, each beautiful in its own way. "It's like a tiny village."

"You read my mind. We should do snow-covered ones at Christmas. I bet we could make a fortune."

"That's a great idea," I said as I picked one up. "This is nice. You did a good job."

"Feel free to put it in the display window. You're welcome to get what you can for it."

I frowned at him. "I thought this was for Annie."

"It was, but I'm afraid she'd just throw it at me if I tried to give it to her."

"I thought you two had patched up your differences," I said.

"So had I. Evidently, I was wrong. I don't want to talk about it, if it's okay with you."

"That's fine," I said. David had a right to his privacy; I quickly turned the discussion back to the cottages. "We could do a winter display now. I've got some spun fiber from last year."

"Not with summer almost here, but we should do something with them. Let's see what we can come up with."

We tried a dozen different layouts in the front window before we came up with something we both agreed on. I walked out onto the street to get a better look at it from the customer's perspective. As I stood there assessing our efforts, I heard someone calling me from the street.

I turned around to see Mayor Jenkins sitting in a brand new car. "Carolyn, do you have a minute?"

"I suppose," I said. "What can I do for you?"

He eased the passenger-side door open. "Why don't you get in so we can talk?"

I saw something in his eyes that I didn't like.

I said firmly, "No thanks. I'm fine out here."

"Carolyn, I don't want to have to crane my neck to look at you. Come on. Get in." That was more of an order than a request, and I didn't obey commands very well.

"I don't think so. You can get out, if you want to."

He did just that, slamming the door. "You're a stubborn woman, you know that?"

"I like to think of myself as independent," I said. "What did you want to talk about?"

"This snooping you're doing. It needs to stop, and I mean now."

"Harvey, were you under the impression you were my boss? I don't take orders from anybody; not my husband, and certainly not you."

"Maybe you should reconsider that policy," he said.

"And perhaps you should tell the truth when someone asks you a question."

He scowled. "What are you talking about?"

"ClayDate. I found out it's not old news after all. You've been renewing it every year, and I know you, Harvey. You wouldn't spend a penny on it if that business weren't still active."

"You don't know what you're talking about," he said. "There's a lot more to me than you realize."

Why was he being so defensive? "Prove me wrong. I'm willing to listen to what you have to say."

"Carolyn, what I do or don't do is none of your business."

"Is it really worth having me on your case about this for the next month or two? You know I won't back off until I know the truth. Come clean with me, Harvey."

He shook his head, then spat out his next words. "Fine. If it will shut you up, I'll tell you. I made a promise a long time ago to a man who did me a favor when he didn't have to, and I'm enough of a blamed fool to keep it. As long as I'm drawing breath, ClayDate will stay in business. It's as simple as that. Now, are you satisfied?"

"Not really. There's got to be more to it than that."

He snorted. "That's your problem, not mine. You're never content, even when you get the truth." He stopped and stared at me a second before adding, "Remember what I said about nosing around things that aren't any of your business."

"It's etched in my mind forever," I replied with a smile. "Don't think for a minute that it will alter my behavior in any way, though."

He shook his head, got in the car, and drove off.

David had been watching openly from the window. "What was that all about?"

"I don't think the mayor wants my vote during the next election."

"It didn't look like it, did it? What did he say, Carolyn?"

I thought about shrugging him off, but David had a right to know. We worked together, and he was more than just an assistant to me, he was like another son. "He told me to quit snooping." I wasn't about to get into the mayor's rationale for keeping an old corporation in business long past its earning potential for him. Was it really as simple as that? Was ClayDate still viable because of a promise he made long ago? I couldn't be sure. Men baffled me sometimes. I've seen sterner and harder men than the mayor do things for sentimental reasons that would make a schoolgirl blush. Maybe he was telling the truth.

David wasn't about to let up. "He was more specific than that. You've been stirring up a dozen different pots, haven't you?"

"At least. I don't want to talk about that right now. We need to work on our display some more. Are you sure you don't want to keep the cottage you made for Annie? It might make a nice apology."

"Thanks, but I'll pass. I'm tired of saying I'm sorry. I don't even know what I'm apologizing for at this point."

I kept my mouth shut, something that would surprise Bill, if he knew about it.

We opened Fire at Will, and to my surprise and delight, by the time our lunch hours rolled around, we'd sold three cottages, with four more on order. "Can you believe how these are selling?" I said as I added our last one to the display.

"I've got a feeling I'm going to be making more of them."

I patted his shoulder. "Look at it this way. You get to work in clay, and that can't be all bad."

"I don't want to mass-produce anything."

"I don't want that either, David. Make them all unique. Give them your special touch. And add a cat to one every now and then, though, would you?"

"I don't do requests," he said, his smile softening his words.

"Come on, that's usually all we do around here. If you don't want to add any cats to yours, I'll make a few and add them to mine. I think making these cottages is fun."

"I guess," he said. "Do you want to take your lunch break first, or should I?"

"You go ahead," I said. "I want to finish up a few of these."

David had been gone ten minutes when the front door chimed. It was my uncle, and I could tell from the scowl on his face that he was not at all happy with his only niece. Yet again.

Chapter 13

"Why do I get the feeling you're not here on a social call," I said.

"Maybe you're smarter than you look after all, but I sincerely doubt it."

"You always were a charmer. What's wrong now?"

"You."

"That encompasses a lot of ground. Could you be more specific than that?"

Don Rutledge frowned as he looked around my shop. "Butting into other people's lives is bad for business, and it's going to be bad for you."

"Are you threatening me?" Here was my own flesh and blood, standing in my shop trying to intimidate me. Sadly, it was working.

"I'm trying to help you," he said. "Don't you get it?"

"Apparently not. How is your blustering supposed to do me any good?"

"Carolyn, life is not just one big game. This is serious business."

"I never said it wasn't, but that doesn't mean I've got to stop digging. Speaking of which, do you mind if I look at your hands?"

"My hands? What has that got to do with anything? Have you completely lost your mind?"

"Probably. Let me see them." I'd made it a point to look at the mayor's hands when we'd had our tête-à-tête earlier; they'd been clean and without calluses or blisters. So had the sheriff's the night before. Okay, I hadn't really suspected him of digging up my backyard, but I'd looked all the same.

My uncle, shaking his head in obvious disbelief, held out both hands. They were tough and calloused, and bits of dirt embedded around his nails made it clear that he was used to working in his own garden soil. "What's this about?"

"Just checking," I said.

"What, are you on cuticle patrol now? Stay out of this, Carolyn."

When was everyone going to stop trying to tell me what to do? "Fine," I said, just to get him off my back.

"I don't believe you," he said.

"I can't do anything about that, now can I?"

My uncle stared at me a few seconds, then left the shop. I was aggravating a great many people lately, and I didn't envy the sheriff his task if someone decided to get rid of me. The suspects would be too numerous to name.

Just then Butch walked into the shop. "Those are new, aren't they?"

"Are you talking about the cottages?"

"Yeah. I'd like to try my hand at one of those sometime. Are they hard?"

"Not for you. Why don't you grab an apron and we can make one together right now?"

He glanced at his watch. "Sorry, but I'm running behind as it is. I just thought you might like to know something I just found out."

"You bet. At the moment, I'm at a complete loss."

Butch looked around the shop. "You don't have to keep after this, you know."

"Why does everyone keep telling me that? I need help, not discouragement." I was becoming increasingly exasperated with people. They could either lend a hand, or get out of my way. There wasn't room for any other option.

"That's why I'm here. I've been asking around about what really happened twenty years ago, and I may have finally gotten the right guy to talk."

"You didn't do anything drastic, did you?" I was in constant fear that Butch would slide back into a life of crime, and I certainly didn't want to do anything to encourage that kind of behavior. Then again, it was a little hypocritical of me to take so freely the information he offered.

"No, this guy was thrilled to have somebody in the business to talk to. We don't exactly form social clubs when we retire, you know what I mean? Anyway, this fella used to be a fence in Marston, and he handled some of the jewels from the robbery that happened in Maple Ridge about the time Richard disappeared."

"Just some of the merchandise? How can he possibly remember that after all these years?"

"The man could tell you every piece he's ever touched. He's like a baseball nut who can recite the batting averages for every player in the 1958 World Series, you know?"

"I don't suppose he gave you the name of the thief, did he? Or is that a question of honor among thieves?"

Butch laughed. "You've been watching too much television. As far as I've seen, that bunk is just that, pure hogwash. No, my friend didn't cooperate that much, but he did say that some of the best pieces weren't offered to him for sale. He only handled a few items, so he started to wonder how many partners had held the place up. Evidently there were some onyx brooches, a handful of gold rings, and lots of diamonds that never turned up. When my friend asked the guy about the things that were missing, the guy said that the rest of his share was someplace safe, stashed away where nobody would ever find it but him, and then he added something odd. He said that it was in the pits and kind of chuckled something about poetic justice. Kind of a crazy comment to make, wouldn't you say? It's not typical behavior for a crook."

"I didn't think there was such a thing as typical behavior," I said.

Butch laughed. "You've got a point. Listen, I've got to run. Call me if you need me."

"I will. And Butch? I'm sorry I snapped at you earlier."

"Hey, you're entitled to unload now and then. I'm a big boy; I can take it." He shot me with his finger as he left, and for some reason, the gesture made me smile.

When David came back from lunch, he asked, "What's up, Carolyn? You've got the oddest expression on your face."

"Do you know what it's like when you've seen or heard something that you know is significant, but you don't know how?"

"It happens," he admitted.

"So, what do you do to figure it out?"

David thought about it a few seconds, then said, "I always try not to think about it. Do something else, put it out of your mind, and it will come to you."

"Like not thinking of blue elephants, right?" I asked.

"What? Did I miss something?"

"It's an old parlor game. For the next thirty seconds, you can think of anything in the world. Just not blue elephants. Ready? Go."

I stopped him three seconds later. "Quick, what were just thinking about?"

"Blue elephants," he reluctantly admitted. "Why don't you try having lunch, then? That might jar something loose."

"It might, but even if it doesn't, I still get to eat, so there's no real downside, is there?"

I left the shop, but instead of going to Shelly's or In the Grounds, I decided to swing by the grocery store and pick up some things for a proper lunch with my husband. I'd fed him an omelet the day before, but today I pulled out all the stops. I grabbed some roast beef and provolone cheese from the deli, along with some crisp French bread, and on a whim, I added a bottle of wine to my basket. Bill and I were going to dine in style.

I drove home, trying not to think about holes, or blue elephants, for that matter, but I didn't have much luck.

Bill wasn't in the house—I even checked in the guest bedroom—which meant he had to be in his shop. I put everything out on the counter and stared out the window as I started making our sandwiches.

Then it hit me. I knew what the fence had really told Butch, and why someone was digging in our backyard. It all came together, as if a jigsaw puzzle had just fallen from the sky and landed in perfect alignment.

Leaving everything where it was, I rushed to our garage, grabbed an old, rusted shovel, and headed into the yard. If I was right, I might just have the answer to all my questions. And if I was wrong, we'd have one more hole in the yard.

I didn't think I was wrong, though. The sandy indentation had been there twenty-five years, first as a horseshoe-throwing pit, and then as a cooling area for my pottery. The missing jewelry was literally in the pits. It had to be. I wedged the shovel into the ground around the perimeter of the sandy area, searching for any sign that I was right. The digging was hard, since we hadn't had much rain lately, and I was beginng to fear I wasn't going to be able to go deep enough when my blade hit something between the edge of the pit and the gas kiln.

It was a pot, but not one I'd ever made. I moved as much dirt as I could with my hands and finally uncovered a small, earthen pot buried deep in the soil. Something was inside it, and as I hefted it out of the hole, the pot cracked open, most likely as a result of that first blow from my shovel. Inside, I could see a dirt-covered box.

This had to be what my backyard digger had been looking for! My hands were shaking as I worked the box free from the remains of the clay container. Despite the dirt, I could tell it was from the jewelry store robbery so long ago.

That's when I heard a voice behind me say, "Good job, Carolyn. I knew you could do it, if I gave you enough time to look." My blood chilled in my veins as I realized my uncle had been behind it all from the very start. I couldn't believe someone close to me, a member of my own family, could be capable of the things he must have done, but the proof was pretty clear. If I was going to survive this confrontation, I had to come up with a way to stop him before he hurt anybody else, including me.

My right hand started drifting toward the shovel, but I felt a foot crash down on my fingers. I yelled out in pain.

"Not so fast. I don't want you getting any ideas. I've got your husband tied up in his shop, and if you do as you're told, you'll both walk away from this alive. Let's go; he's waiting for us."

I knew the threat was real. If I didn't do something quickly, I was sure Bill and I would soon be dead.

I turned slowly, and Don ordered, "Bring the box with you. You just couldn't let it go, could you? Curiosity might end up killing more than just the cat."

My flesh crawled at the sound of his words. Dutifully, I grabbed the box, wondering if I could use it as some kind of weapon. The edges had sharp corners, but I'd have to move quickly and decisively at just the right time, or I'd only anger the killer more.

He said, "Nice and easy. That's right. Let's go over to the workshop, shall we?"

I knew that once we were inside, Don would be able to deal with us easily. If I could keep him outside, there was a chance that one of my neighbors would see us and get suspicious. It was worth a shot, anyway.

"I knew it had to be you," I said as I turned to my uncle and looked him straight in the eye. He had a handgun pointed at me, partially concealed by a folded towel, but it was clear enough to me what it was.

"Don't try to tell me that," Don said. "I was careful not to leave any clues behind."

"They're everywhere, if you just know where to look."

"Go on, I'm listening."

"Let's take that ring for starters. It's from the robbery, isn't it? That was careless of you to keep wearing it, because it matches the general description of one that was taken," I said, recalling what Butch had told me.

He glanced at it, then said, "It suited me. Besides, everyone who knew that it was part of the haul was either dead or gone. To be honest with you, I nearly forgot where I'd gotten it. You've got to have more than that."

"You were too quick to unload on me the first time I talked to you," I said. "That was a red flag from the start. When I came out to see you after the murder, you didn't lower that gun barrel until you found out that I was looking for information and not there to accuse you of murder. What happened, Don, did your guilty conscience get the best of you?"

"Why would you think I would kill him after all these years? Rose got over it. So did I."

"It wasn't about Rose at all," I said. Where was everybody? Normally I couldn't take out the trash or go get the newspaper without someone butting into my business, but now a man was threatening me with a gun in broad daylight, and no one was around. "You were looking for this box from the start. Richard was blackmailing you with what's inside it, wasn't he? Don't bother denying it, it's the only thing that makes sense. Were you two partners in the robbery?"

My uncle laughed coarsely. "What's it going to hurt to tell you now? Do you think I'd be stupid enough to be partners with him? I committed the robbery myself. It was just dumb luck that he saw me coming out of the store that night and demanded a split of the take. I thought about killing him then, too, but he was too smart for me."

"So that's why you've been digging in my backyard the last few nights. Did you follow him here the first night he was back in town?"

Don nodded. "I saw him leaving your shop and followed him the rest of the day. I knew he had to have come back to Maple Ridge to check up on his stash. Richard wouldn't tell me where the box was when I confronted him that night, and I lost my temper. He was going to dig it up. I knew it had to be somewhere around here, but I wasn't having much luck on my own. It was nice of you to dig it up for me."

"So the rest of it was just a smokescreen," I said. "Seeing David, the lecture, all of it."

"It was enough to fool Hodges. That's all of the questions I'm going to answer. Let's go back to Bill's workshop where we can talk about this without your neighbors around. Go on, Carolyn, and don't get any funny ideas."

"There's nothing remotely humorous about all of this," I said.

Poor Bill. Was he already dead? It was clear that my uncle was capable of murder. If he'd killed my husband, I'd find a way to stay alive long enough to make him pay for it.

"Go on inside." He nudged me with the gun when I hesitated at the doorway.

I walked in expecting the worst, but relief flooded through me when I saw that Bill was still alive. Don had bound him to a chair and had taped his mouth, but I could still see Bill's eyes. He was trying to tell me something, I knew it, but I couldn't figure out what it was. As my uncle started to raise the gun, I said, "There's nothing in the box. You know that, don't you? It's too light."

"You're bluffing." A worried expression crossed his face, though I knew it would pass when he felt the weighty box.

"See for yourself." I started to offer it to him when there was a noise behind us. Bill had somehow managed to free himself, at least one arm. He ripped the tape off his mouth and screamed ferociously, like a wild animal attacking.

Don's aim shifted from me to my husband, and I hit his gun arm as hard as I could with a sharp corner of the box. A shiver went through me as I struck him, a physical memory of defending myself once before.

He dropped the gun and yelped in pain. That was all the opening I needed. As he knelt down to retrieve the weapon, I grabbed a length of oak Bill had turned on a lathe and shaped like a baseball bat, and I struck Don in the back with everything I had.

My uncle hit the floor hard, like a bag of dirt.

I started for Bill when he shouted, "Get his gun first."

"He's not coming around anytime soon," I said.

"Just do it, Carolyn," he commanded, and I obeyed. I took the gun, and stared down at my uncle. Had I killed him with the force of that blow? If I had, I promised myself I wouldn't let it destroy me. The man was a cold-blooded killer, and he deserved what he got, even if he was my kin.

As I started to untie Bill, he said, "Get that knife on the bench and cut me free."

"These ropes are expensive," I said. "Give me a second. I'll get it."

"Carolyn, don't push our luck."

I gave up on the knot and grabbed the knife. "Don't move," I said.

As soon as he was free, he leapt to his feet and threw his arms around me. "I didn't think you'd get my signal."

"What signal? I could see you were trying to tell me something, but I couldn't for the life of me figure out what it was."

"I was gesturing to my back," he said plaintively. "I managed to free one arm while he was out there with you, and I was working on the other one when you showed up." He cradled his cut hand against his chest. "I wish I hadn't thrown those pills away."

"Don't worry, we can get you more." My hand was

throbbing from the stomp Don had given it, and I might need a pill myself to get to sleep that night.

Bill shook his head, and I could see he was shaking. "That was too close. I can't believe how hard you hit him."

I couldn't believe it myself. The adrenaline that had been shooting through me was nearly gone, and I felt my knees weaken. "We're safe now; that's all that counts."

"Thanks for saving me," he said in a humbled voice. "I've never felt so helpless in my life."

I tapped him lightly under the chin. "You saved us both, you old fool. If you hadn't worked your arm free and taken that tape off, you never would have been able to distract him like that. Nice yell, by the way. You managed to rattle me, too."

"So I guess we saved each other," he said.

"I like that," I agreed. "There's a certain symmetry to it, isn't there? Would you like to call Sheriff Hodges, or should I?"

"I'll let you have the privilege." He looked down at Don and shook his head. "So, it was all for nothing. The box was empty."

"Hardly," I said as I started to open it. My hands were shaking as I worked the clasp free and lifted the lid. As I gazed inside, I asked, "I wonder if there's a finder's fee for this? There's a necklace in here that I absolutely adore."

"If there's not a reward, I'll buy it for you out of my woodworking money."

"That's all right," I said as I closed the lid. "It's probably too fancy for me anyway."

I heard Don groan, and despite what I'd vowed earlier, I was glad I hadn't killed him.

"You watch him while I go make that call," I said.

Bill picked up the turned piece of wood. "Go on, but hurry. I don't like playing guard duty."

"If he somehow manages to get up after the way I hit him, you should be able to glare at him hard enough to drop him again."

Chapter 14

The next day, I was working at Fire at Will when the sheriff came in.

"I just wanted to let you know that your uncle confessed to the murder."

"Don't call him that," I said. "He stopped being family a long time ago."

He shrugged. "I don't blame you a bit for feeling that way. Are we good?"

I looked at him, thought of about a thousand things I could say, but surprised myself by answering, "Never better."

"Sometimes worse though, right?" Was that a smile I saw on his lips? It happened so briefly I couldn't be sure.

After the sheriff left, the older gentleman returned for his sister's cottage, and I had it ready and waiting for him. As he paid the bill, he said, "I couldn't help noticing your front window."

I smiled. "In a way, it's all your fault. I enjoyed making those cottages so much, I kind of got carried away. What can I say? You inspired me."

"It's a nice scene. Most of us spend our lives trying to go home again, don't we?"

I smiled. "I don't know; I'm kind of happy the way things are right here and now."

He saluted me with two fingers as he made his way to the door. "Then you are a truly lucky woman."

"You don't have to tell me that," I said as he walked out with a smile on his face.

Twenty minutes later, three people I never expected to see together came into the shop, practically arm in arm. Hannah, David, and Annie looked as though they'd found a way to come to grips with their situation.

Hannah said, "We need to talk to you, but I get to go first." She smiled at the kids, and added, "I won the coin toss."

"I wanted to go two out of three," David chimed in.

"Let you mother talk," Annie corrected him, and to my amazement, David did just as she'd asked.

"Carolyn, anybody can say what their friends want to hear, but it takes someone special to point out something that might be tough to take. Thank you."

"You're welcome," I said. "But I'm disappointed in one thing."

"What's that?" She looked alarmed, so I decided I'd better stop toying with her.

"You don't have any presents with you."

"I'm taking care of that," Annie said. She came forward and hugged me. "Thank you for finding my father's jewelry."

"I imagine you have to give it back to the insurance company," I said. "That's a real shame."

"They never paid his claim," Annie said brightly. "Everything you found belongs to me. Do you know what that means? When I sell the jewelry, I'll be able to finally go to Stanford. It will be all mine as soon as the case is settled. I'm so happy."

"There wasn't that much in there, was there?" I knew the costs to go to such a fine school were astronomical.

"You'd be surprised. But don't forget, I've been saving for years. I was getting close, but the jewelry will put me over the top. I want you to have something."

She reached into her bag and brought out a brightly wrapped present.

"I can't accept that," I said.

"I insist," she said.

Well, it wouldn't hurt to unwrap it. Instead of the necklace, there was a nice ring with a diamond that, while not huge, was still substantial.

"Thanks," I said, "but I meant it. I can't accept it." She started to frown when I added, "Think of it as a small scholarship. There's just one condition, though."

"What's that?"

"You have to promise not to use the money from its sale on anything practical. Set up a fund for pizza runs and ice cream parties. There's more to school, and life, than working all the time."

She nodded, and I could see tears tracking down her cheeks.

"Are you crying?" David asked her.

"Of course not," she mumbled. "Restroom?"

I pointed to the back, and she ducked in to repair her makeup.

David said, "I never understood why women cry when they're happy. She was happy, wasn't she?"

"David, what am I going to do with you?" Hannah asked.

"He's too old to throw back, so I guess you're going to have to keep him," I said.

We laughed, and David scowled slightly. All was well with the world again.

Annie came out and gave me a hug. "Thank you."

"Just do as I ask, and I'll be happy."

"I promise," she said. "David, are you ready?"

"Let's go." He turned to me and said, "We're driving to Boston to talk to some jewelry appraisers and find one who'll give top dollar for what you found. You two don't want to come, do you?"

It was clear from his expression that our company was the last thing in the world he wanted.

"Sorry, I've got to keep the shop open."

"And I have a class to teach," Hannah added.

They were gone before we could blink.

Hannah said, "It's nice they asked. So, you don't get a present after all."

"You're back in my life. That's the only gift I need," I said. "I'm sorry I was so abrupt with you."

"You were brutal," she acknowledged. "But I needed it. I'm going to try to step back a little. I may need some help."

"Don't worry, if your apron strings start to constrict, I'll step in and say something."

"I know I can count on you. Do you really need to keep the shop open?"

"Why, don't you have a class to teach?"

"My TA can handle it. After all, that's what teacher's assistants are for."

"I'm game if you are," I said. "What did you have in mind?"

"Nothing as exciting as a trip to Boston, but I was think-ing a nice long coffee break might be in order."

"Lead the way," I said. As I locked the shop up, I glanced at the store window. Our cottages were lined up like a vil-lage street, making me think of our quaint little town. Maple Ridge was a wonderful place to live, but it wasn't perfect. Greed could have dire consequences. Richard Atkins's greed had gotten him killed, and my uncle's had nearly ended my life—and my husband's—all for a few cold, hard stones.

And unlike pliable clay that could be reworked and used again, Richard's and Don's lives were destroyed forever, like fired porcelain that was shattered beyond all hope of re-pair.

I chose to look at it positively, though. Annie had her education paid for, David had his life ahead of him, and I had my best friend Hannah and my husband, Bill, as well as two bright and healthy sons.

It was more than most folks had, and for me, it was everything I needed.

☙ Clay-Crafting Tips ☙

Weaving Clay

There's a real artistry in weaving clay. If you have access to a kiln, you can weave potter's clay, but don't despair if all you have is modeling clay. Many brands can be used to form a nice woven basket that you can temper in your oven. Be sure to read the package's instructions before starting your project.

As Carolyn demonstrated to the Firing Squad, knead your clay and then roll it into a flat sheet the thickness you want. If you're using modeling clay, you can dress up your creation by using different colors of clay. After you've rolled out the clay to a quarter-inch thickness, cut it into uniform strips. I like to make mine around an inch wide, but you don't have to be exact. Lay out half the strips side by side vertically, and then take one of the remaining strips and weave it horizontally in and out of the vertical strips, going over one and then under the next. Repeat until you've used all but four of the remaining strips.

After you've completed the pattern, you should have a woven square. Now comes the fun part. Using a bone or a rib, bend the four corners up until you have a bowl shape. You can squeeze and pinch the clay at this stage to get the shape you desire. To dress the edges after you're done, take the final four strips of the clay and bend them lengthwise over the rough edges of the basket. Then bake your bowl per the directions on the clay package.

And as always, the most important thing to remember is to have fun! If you're not happy with the results before you fire the clay, knead it all together again and start over. That's one of the beauties of working with clay.

THE
HOUSE
OF
MEMORY

THE
HOUSE
OF
MEMORY

A Novel of Shanghai

NICHOLAS R. CLIFFORD

For Paul Cooper —
Happy birthday — I hope you
enjoy this —
Nicholas R. Clifford

BALLANTINE BOOKS

New York

All rights reserved under International and Pan-American Copyright Conventions. Published in the United States by Ballantine Books, a division of Random House, Inc., New York, and simultaneously in Canada by Random House of Canada Limited, Toronto.

The lines from Lu Hsün appearing in Chapter Two are from "The Diary of a Madman" (Kuangren riji) and those in Chapter Five from his essay of 1926, "In Memory of Miss Liu Ho-chen" (Jinian Liu Hezhen jun), to be found in Volumes One and Three of the Complete Works of Lu Hsün (Lu Xun quan ji) *published in 1956 by the People's Publishing House in Beijing. The translations are by Nicholas Clifford.*

Text design by Ruth Kolbert

Library of Congress Cataloging-in-Publication Data
Clifford, Nicholas Rowland.
     The house of memory : a novel of Shanghai / Nicholas R. Clifford.
       p.   cm.
     ISBN 0-345-38149-1
     1. College teachers—China—Shanghai—Fiction. 2. Americans—China—
Shanghai—Fiction. 3. Shanghai (China)—Fiction.
   I. Title.
   PS3553.L4378H68   1994
   813'.54—dc20   93-41281
                                                                                  CIP

Manufactured in the United States of America

First Edition: June 1994

10 9 8 7 6 5 4 3 2 1

AUTHOR'S NOTE

The protagonists of this novel are, of course, inventions. The periods through which they lived are not. The events both of the Chinese revolution of the 1920s and the democracy movement of 1989 are, I believe, accurately depicted. For example, the role of Shanghai's underworld, both in the drug trade and in Chiang Kai-shek's purge of the Communists, has been known for some years, although the precise extent to which the city's foreigners were implicated is a bit less clear. And the response of Shanghai to the Beijing massacre of June 4, 1989, was generally as the novel states it to have been— including the episode of the train that was set on fire on the night of June 6. Moreover, those who know anything of Shanghai, in either of the incarnations depicted in this book, will, I hope, recognize the city as it was and is. Much of the novel's historical background is based on the research done for my *Spoilt Children of Empire: Westerners in Shanghai and the Chinese Revolution of the 1920s*, published in 1991 by the University Press of New England, Hanover, New Hampshire.

But *The House of Memory* is primarily about history: history as it is used, history as it is remembered, written, and read. Whether its writers and readers will recognize in this novel anything of the craft they practice is an open question, for here the ideas are my own.

THE HOUSE OF MEMORY

CHAPTER ONE

Morning. Outside, the sky gray-yellow, rain drifting in a thin scrim that softened the sullen shapes of the buildings against the smoky cloud. Pushing himself up on one elbow, Matthew squinted at the clock on the bedside table. Eight minutes past seven. The city already up, and here he was, just coming into a blurred consciousness that still felt itself only halfway across the Pacific. Just three days ago he'd left home: a six-hour flight from Boston to San Francisco, and then fourteen hours nonstop in a 747, roaring west at six hundred knots, high over the invisible lines steadily marking off the longitudes to Hong Kong, every seat taken, no room to stretch, impossible to sleep.

Yet the excitement of the trip, of arriving in China now, this spring, drove away the long hours of cramped weariness. For the past six weeks Matthew had found himself following with a passionate interest the reports of the Beijing spring, as the papers were calling it, the great wave of hope that was sweeping over much of China. Led by the students in Tiananmen Square, voices everywhere had been calling for a new birth of freedom, of national pride, for an end to the corrupt and autocratic government of the handful of old men who held power in the capital. Sitting at home, watching the demonstrations on the television screen, he had been struck by their resonances with the past, and had wondered whether the history he'd learned from books could provide any sort of guide to what might happen to them.

And after that long flight he had arrived. If not quite in China yet, at least in Hong Kong, that city on the edge, in China but not entirely of it, so long a gateway to the continent beyond. That evening, instead of the usual approach over the harbor, they had come down over the steep hills to the northwest of the airport, banking low above the concrete towers till suddenly the ground flattened, tires squalled and smoked on the tarmac as the aircraft touched down in the dusk, the circlet of lights of the Peak hanging across the water against a darkening sky. To the jaded traveler, all airports may be the same, but to Matthew, arriving at Kaitak was still different despite the English signs in the terminal, the advertisements for cigarettes and tape recorders, cognac and computers. The distinction lay in the sound of Cantonese, the intelligent liveliness of the crowds, and in the unforgettable smell of the city: a mixture of diesel exhaust, hot pavement, people, food—and the harbor, an evocation of the South China Sea hovering like fading incense on the warm and heavy evening air. And it lay in the sense of China's brooding immensity off beyond the darkness: Hankow, Chengdu, Harbin—the electric departure boards clicked their announcements of flights to places that geography and politics for so long had made inaccessible; now they were only hours away.

That was Friday. He had given himself three nights in Hong Kong to sleep off the trip, staying at the Y.M.C.A. on Salisbury Road, right next to the Peninsula, spending the time buying the necessities and little luxuries for his stay in China: extra notepaper for his research, film for his camera, Kaopectate for the inevitable, and at Swindon's on Lock Street a variety of paperbacks for bedtime reading: green-backed Penguin detective stories, but also Henry James and George Eliot, whom Laura had told him to read. Then yesterday, on Monday, he had flown up to Shanghai, the China Eastern Airbus filled, strangely, with tourists from Taiwan. Matthew had seen them arrive at Kaitak, lumbered down with plastic bags bearing their burdens of dried fish and duck, Dunhills and Winstons, Johnnie Walker and Courvoisier, luggage carriers piled high with cartons labeled Sony and Matsushita and Sanyo, presents for the mainland relatives they were at last allowed to visit after forty years. The aircraft, heavily freighted with its consumer cargo, had seemed to struggle slowly into the air, almost as if it had to overcome an affront to its communist principles.

The stewardess had come by, handing out customs forms to the passengers. Matthew had obediently filled his in, promising the authorities that he had no gold, no firearms, no seditious literature or videotapes. Then he had reached into his briefcase and pulled out the thick stack of photocopies he had brought with him. On top lay a neatly typewritten title page. "Typhoon Over Shanghai," it read. "Memoirs of a Changing China, 1922–." After the dash, the date 1927 had been written in by hand, obviously later. "By Simon Larsen." He had riffled through the pages until he found the passage he wanted, and then had begun, once again, to read it.

Saturday, May 30, 1925

Last night once again, for no apparent reason, I woke suddenly, almost as if startled out of sleep by the very depth of the silence that envelops me at two in the morning. As always, this waking to such a stillness brings with it a sense of alarm: lying there in the dark, I am suddenly appalled by the very vastness of this country, by the incomprehensibility in which it cloaks itself, a silent warning to unwanted guests such as I. I don't belong here; I have no place among those silent multitudes, those hundreds of millions of souls, in this land stretching endlessly west under the dark stars, and the thought of them arouses in me something of the terror of the infinite. Like Pascal's agnostic, I look on this universe and am afraid.

And in the wake of this fear comes an agonized yearning that I thought I had long since grown out of: a sense of home, of all I have left behind. It reaches me in vivid images, trivial enough in themselves perhaps, yet each one freighted with layer upon layer of memory and meaning; a vision of dogwoods and magnolias in the spring, the lovely faces of girls I have known at dances, the light of streetlamps catching the snow as it drifts down against the gray buildings of a winter evening, oarsmen in the spring sun on the stretch of river under the museum. A vision of security and order and rightness, of a world so different from this one, the world to which I belong. Slowly, sleep begins to come back, as in my mind I plot my return: calling on the steamship company in Peking Road to buy my ticket, packing, saying farewell to my friends, sailing east across the long reaches of the Pacific. Going home.

What do they mean, these midnight wakings, these thoughts, these visions and memories that have started to come upon me? Has the time come, then, to settle down to the life that my family expects? I know, of course, that my mother, my brothers, my sister, have almost given up on me. Willing at first to allow for a certain eccentricity in my behavior, they put no real obstacles in my way. Had I not, after all, both been wounded in battle and written a book—two accomplishments that set me off immediately from virtually all the rest of the fruit of that family tree so lovingly recorded by Aunt Caroline? Never mind that the first accomplishment was involuntary; they still gave me full credit for the supposed heroism that led my path to cross with the random trajectory of a German bullet. The second achievement they talked about less, as if it were somehow an embarrassment best guarded within the family. No doubt they found this discomfiting knack for literature to be like my wound, and like that wound under the surgeon's care, one that could be dressed until new tissues might grow over it, covering it, putting it out of sight, so that it could be decently forgotten. Then, once healed, I could give myself to life's proper concerns: business, or the profession of law.

Lately there have come suggestions, even importunings, that it is time to go back. "Dear Simon," writes Robert in a letter that arrived last week. "Mother is planning a great family reunion for Christmas." He's two years my senior, and after spending the war in Washington as an aide to General Mercer, has become well established as a partner in Morris, Waln, and Clothier on Chestnut Street. "I know she will not say so herself, for she does not wish to seem to interfere, but it would make her very happy if you were able to be with us." Behind it an unspoken reprimand: you've been away too long, Simon, and while we've made allowances for all you have been through, it is now seven years that the war has been over. You are neglecting your heritage and your duties to the rest of us.

Robert's right. Of course he's right. I know that the obligations of filial piety, that virtue extolled by Confucius and his followers, is by no means restricted to the Chinese. I belong to America, to my city, to my family, in a way that I will never belong to this alien land whose vastness wakes me in terror in the small hours of the night. It is now four years since I first arrived here in China: two years spent in Peking, and two here in Shanghai. And what have I to show for it, to justify to Robert and to the others, this continuing absence from them? I can imagine my own brother questioning me in a courtroom, where I must defend myself against a charge of breach of obligations—to my family, to my city, to my country. And to those memories of home.

I'm no lawyer, and my answers are weak and unconvincing. But some points I will try in my own defense. First, there are the students I have taught in my occasional forays into the classroom. Granted, most of them form a crowd of indistinguishable faces, and they want no more than the knowledge of English that will carry them to America for further study, or will help them find a job with one of the big foreign firms. But that memory is saved by the few that stand apart: young men and women in whom I detected, or thought I detected, that quickening of the intellect that marks an unfeigned curiosity, who bring with them into the modern world the love of learning that marked the best of the old China.

Second, I will tell the court that I am writing another book. Yes, it is true that only a few chapters exist. But it is no longer the book it was. Begun two years ago, when I set out bravely to explain the Problem of China to an expectant world, by now it is about Shanghai, a subject that only sounds more modest, for the more I learn of this extraordinary city, the more I realize how little I really know of the world that is contained here within the compass of a few square miles. Nor am I confident that I can do more than set the questions forth; the answers I must leave to heads better than mine. I plead with the court: I need more time, I cannot put it aside now.

Third, a passable command of the Chinese language. Is that an accomplishment the court will recognize? I pride myself on it, preen myself immoderately under the flattery of Chinese friends who compliment me on the purity of my Peking-learned Mandarin, or rejoice in my growing ability to salt my conversation with those tight idioms of four characters of which the Chinese are so inordinately fond. Since coming to Shanghai, I have made a start with the local dialect, but it comes slowly, and I am nostalgic for the accent, and the humanity, that fills the language of the northern capital.

That is all. Or all I care to state publicly, at any rate. Not much for four years, perhaps. Of course, I argue in my own defense, there are less tangible benefits from my sojourn here. I think of the friends I've made, both among my own kind and, I add with some pride, among the Chinese as well. I think of my travels, of sights that are unforgettable: the gardens of Soochow and Hangchow, the cliffs of Taishan, the precipices rising thousands of feet above the Yangtze beyond Yi-ch'ang, those peaks from whose summit the poet Tu Fu thought he could make out the snow mountains at the Great River's head. Above all, there has been the experience of a different climate, a different geography, a human world so utterly removed from my own in its imaginings, its suppositions, its conceits and prejudices, in the construction it places upon humanity.

Surely all that counts for something. Living here, a foreigner in a strange land, I have come to understand what makes me the man I am, a citizen of a particular country, of a particular time and place. Yet even as I speak, I am uneasily conscious of what I dare not tell the court: that I find a growing distance from the country that is my own, and from my countrymen who people it. And I fear the court will count that against me.

The prosecution responds: And if you finish this book you talk of, what purpose will it serve, beyond collecting dust as it sits unread on the back shelves of public libraries all over America? We put it to you that this book has become no more than an excuse to stay away from your duties.

When daylight comes, I am myself again, and the memories and fears of the night have vanished. No, I will not buy my ticket today; time enough to think about leaving next week, next month, next year. In any case, I have nothing to fear from China's vastness. I have seen that world that exists, only a few miles away, still untouched by the nineteenth century, to say nothing of our own. But here in Shanghai, we live in a city that is on the edge of China, yet not part of it, a city with all the reassuring comforts and conveniences of our own modern age. Including, above all, the convenience of living under our own laws rather than those of the Chinese.

So enough of these midnight thoughts. Today is Saturday,

the sun's shining, and I am giving myself a holiday. The horses will be running out at Kiangwan today, the oarsmen are holding their spring regatta at Hen-li, and there's to be a cricket match this afternoon at the Recreation Ground under the tall clock tower on Bubbling Well Road. Mr. Chu will not come again until Tuesday, and though the typewriter waits for me reproachfully on my desk, I have no intention of touching it today.

The book can wait. And so can I.

Outside, the steady roar of the aircraft's engines had suddenly changed. Matthew had put away the papers he'd been reading and looked out the window, reflecting on Simon Larsen's uncertainty. A few minutes later, as they let down through the broken clouds of the afternoon, Shanghai's gray immensity sprawled below them in the spring sun like a dream of the past, the Huangpu River curling north through the city to meet the Yangtze.

That had been yesterday. Today was Tuesday. May 30, 1989. Sixty-four years to the day after Simon's ruminations. A gray day, a late spring day. The sort of day the Shanghainese call *huang-mei tian*, yellow plum weather, the season of warm, soft rain when nothing is ever dry and everywhere there blossoms a delicate green mold: on clothes, shoes, books, even, it seems, on your body, in your hair. That morning, when Matthew left his hotel, the wet leaves of the plane trees on Huaihai Road shone a fresh spring green, undulled as yet by the summer's dusty air. Bicycles poured down the street in an unending river, thousands of bells trilling gently in the soft light, their riders wrapped in flapping plastic capes against the weather, looking like dark, dejected birds. Black cars, whose curtained windows shielded important passengers from common humanity, slicked over the shining pavement, horns skirling at the pedestrians who plodded undisturbed along the street, oblivious of the efforts of traffic guards, officious old men with red armbands, who were trying to herd them back onto the crowded sidewalk.

Matthew made his way slowly east toward the Bund, renewing his acquaintance with the city before his appointment with Zhao Shanling that afternoon. A research associate at the

Shanghai Historical Institute, he had been part of a delegation visiting both Harvard and Atherton when Matthew had met him two years before. Now, after ten months of negotiation by mail, he'd arranged to have the institute invite Matthew to come to Shanghai to do research for the book he was writing.

"Old Zhao is really one of the survivors," he had said to Laura one day at lunch in the faculty club that March. "I mean, imagine what a man of his age must have been through—the Japanese war, the civil war, God knows how many reeducation campaigns under the Communists, probably years out in the countryside during the Cultural Revolution in the sixties and seventies. And then last year he's suddenly touring America as an eminent intellectual, under Beijing's sponsorship."

"So you're going to go see him?"

"I hope so, if I can get all the paperwork done. Not that I really want to spend the summer in Shanghai, since it'll be ungodly hot. But he really sounds as if he might be able to help. And while I'm there I'm going to try to find out about your uncle."

"Great-uncle Simon? After all these years? I mean, even Sherlock Holmes would have had a hard time." Laura had finished her frugal lunch of salad and yogurt. A graduate student at Harvard in English literature, she was writing her dissertation, and making ends meet by her part-time teaching at Atherton. As she and Matthew talked, she cupped her hands around a mug of coffee, trying to warm them. It was a cold day, and as usual, the college was trying to economize on heat.

"Sherlock wasn't a historian, remember. We don't deal in bloodstains and footprints. We have other ways to make people talk."

"And what kind of third-degree methods do you propose to use to get my long-lost relative to come clean?"

"For starters, I'll finish reading the rest of those papers your mother found. I've been working my way through the draft of his book. That's mostly typed, and fairly neat. The journal's different. A lot of it's handwritten, and that can be pretty tough going."

"What do they tell you? Anything?" Laura watched him, her winter-pale face framed by her dark hair. She looked tired, he thought. He wondered what else might lie behind those gray eyes, but couldn't decide.

"Well, Simon obviously had a lot going on that wasn't ever going to find its way into his book. His private life. About Emily Ransom, for instance. What I told you before. But so far nothing to explain his disappearance. Still, he must have left something behind. A man like that can't simply walk off the face of the earth. Even in Shanghai. Even though it all happened years ago. But suppose I find something, maybe even some people who knew him. Zhao's almost old enough himself."

"And then what? All this so you can use my family as material for an article? Publish or perish: is that it?" Was she just teasing him, or did the sparring hide something deeper?

"Are you afraid I'll dig up some secrets the family wants to leave buried? Find out that Simon became a Communist, or a Japanese agent? Maybe he ran off with a beautiful White Russian princess and left a string of illegitimate children behind." He paused to swallow his own coffee. "It's just that I like detective stories, that's all. They're my trash reading, remember." Last summer she'd made fun of the Dashiell Hammetts and Elmore Leonards she'd found in his backpack. He looked at her, wondering again what she was thinking, then glanced at his watch. "I've got to be on my way," he said. "An appointment with the dean."

He signed the chit for both of them (his buying her lunch was a kind of challenge, he admitted to himself; would she object?) and got up to go, leaving Laura at the table, going over the notes for her afternoon class.

Now, almost four months later, he was back in Shanghai, three years after his first trip, ready to settle down to what he hoped would be the end of his research on the city's history. Publish or perish, Laura had scoffed, but like any new professor, Matthew needed a solid book to underwrite his career, whether it was to be spent at Atherton or elsewhere. Coming across Simon Larsen's papers had been completely unexpected, a stroke of pure good luck (though, of course, it was through Laura that he'd found them). Even though he knew he'd probably never find out why Simon disappeared so many years earlier, the writings themselves, with their record of life in Shanghai during the revolution sixty years ago, would help him to add some human flesh to the academic bones of what threatened to turn into a depressingly dry monograph. (Like most young scholars, Matthew was taking few chances; given the choice between soundness and liveliness, soundness usually won.) Let other people write the detective stories—but trying to solve one of his own would at least be an entertainment during the long hot weeks of a Shanghai summer.

By the time he'd walked several blocks, the rain was coming down harder, driving people into the shelter of open doorways. Though Matthew had planned to walk the two miles across the city to the Bund, the prospect of arriving at the institute thoroughly drenched obliged him to join the crowd waiting for one of the infrequent buses that would carry him downtown. Today luck seemed with him; within a few minutes a Number 26, his route, came along. Even by Chinese standards, it was full, and it splashed on by without even slowing. It took fifteen minutes for the next one to come. The doors banged open, crowds elbowed their way out, while others were already fighting their way in. A New York subway at rush hour seemed tame by comparison; this was more like a rugby match. Bracing himself to climb aboard, he felt literally swept up by the crush, carried into the dank interior, jammed hard against the side, something gouging a hole in his back, unable to see out the grimy window. Nothing to hold on to as the bus lurched awkwardly down the street, but that didn't matter; it was hard enough just to breathe, let alone fall down.

Half an hour later he sensed rather than knew that he had reached Szechwan Road, and at the next stop fought his way out, eager to escape into the air. He was about two blocks west of Zhongshan Road, as the street fronting the river was now designated. On maps, at least; the Shanghainese still called it the *waitan*, or the Bund, its name from the old days. By now the rain had stopped, and a wind brought some promise of clearing weather. Turning right, he walked east, picking his way through the crowds, the bicycles, the trucks, and the buses, across to the waterfront. Above him rose the familiar buildings of the harbor's skyline, their elaborate turrets and towers, their neoclassical columns echoing the architecture of empire and recalling in precise detail the old sepia photographs he'd seen, pictures taken sixty or seventy years before. In the appearance of this part of the city, at any rate, time had brought no revolution.

Simon Larsen would have recognized it instantly. But had it looked as drab then as it did today? All that Matthew had read or heard about Shanghai in those days spoke of a life of light, of color, an excitement and liveliness that seemed unimaginable among these gray buildings and the stolid crowds that moved through the streets. Glamorous, exotic Shanghai, it had been then the Paris of the East, the city of sin, Shanghai, the paradise of adventurers. But how many of those historical memories simply reflected a nostalgia for a vanished world that had never really existed? In any case, that kind of Shanghai had been only a tiny part of this city's past, remember; the good liberal conscience that had been ingrained in him reminded him sternly of the beggars dying in the streets, the exhausted rickshaw coolies, the children slaving in the cotton and silk mills. Wasn't it on their suffering that that liveliness and color had been built? The historian's house of memory must find room for them as well; they too had once been real, and no one would regret the passing of the particular old Shanghai they had known.

Yet what an extraordinary juxtaposition of images there was in the architecture of the Bund! In Simon's day, the great columned pile in front of Matthew had been the Hongkong and Shanghai Bank. Now it served as the headquarters of the municipal government and the local Communist Party, its high white dome incongruously crowned by a large red star, and its entrance guarded by soldiers standing at attention, bayonets on their rifles. To its south was the Dongfeng, the East Wind Hotel. Years ago it had been the Shanghai Club, haunt of the British taipans and their associates, no Chinese or women allowed, please. Now its famous Long Bar was gone, and the Italian marble entrance hall had been filled with glass counters under pale blue fluorescent lights, showing off dreary souvenirs for the tourists. On his right rose the brown tower of the Customs House, whose English bells still rang the hours with the Westminster chimes, as they had for decades. Except, of course, for the Maoist years, when they had played "The East Is Red," that anthem likening the Chairman to the rising sun, its portentous music coercing into joy the revolutionary masses of the new China. Behind him, ferries and tugboats with their lines of barges hooted in the brown waters of the Huangpu, now as always the life of Shanghai. An excursion boat advertised, in Chinese and English, three-hour tours of the harbor, and down on the old French Bund, a river steamer was loading passengers for Nanking and Hankow. Huge billboards, across the river in

Pootung, proclaimed the presence of Japanese and German electronics firms, testimonials to the new openness of Deng Xiaoping's China.

He lunched alone in the restaurant on the eighth floor of the Peace Hotel, sitting near a window, and looking out over the river. The waitress brought him *xiaolong bao*, delicious "little dragon dumplings" of lightly spiced pork flavored with ginger and black Chinese vinegar. As he ate, he read yesterday's edition of the *South China Morning Post*, the Hong Kong paper he'd bought at the hotel bookstore. The headlines spoke of a quarter of a million troops surrounding Beijing, where the tens of thousands of demonstrators, with their cries for democracy and an end to corruption, had been holding Tiananmen Square since April. Zhao Ziyang, the Party chairman, hadn't been seen for ten days, and there were persistent rumors that he'd been purged. Once again Premier Li Peng was warning darkly that firm measures would have to be taken to deal with the troublemakers who remained in the square. A few days ago he'd made the same threat, and nothing had happened. But now there were more troops. No one knew where the army stood, and that was the most worrying of all.

Saturday, May 30, 1925

Night has fallen on the city now, and the darkness that covers us hides the blood on the streets. But it cannot take away the memories of those who have seen it spilled, and so it is a night that brings with it no promise of a new dawn. Though in a few hours the sun will rise out of the China Sea, bringing the first gray streaks of morning in the eastern sky—even our vice and folly cannot interrupt the inexorable laws of the universe—for those who weep tonight, the grief has settled down like a black shroud, and not all the wide light of the approaching summer will lift it from them.

Death, when it comes in the spring, seems always to violate nature itself, and all the more so when it is the death of the young at the hands of the old. There is in this city a kind of habitual cruelty whose victims are the street beggars, the cripples, the children deformed by poverty. But it's an everyday cruelty, and its very familiarity gives it a commonplace air, so that you learn to look past it, and simply shrug, as if to say: After all, this is China. Today was different, today brought an open, naked violence, the violence of gunfire, of blood spilled in the streets, of sudden death. And the sight of it has brought surging back those memories that I have tried so hard to escape: of that spring seven years ago, when the drab countryside of Lorraine was suddenly bursting into life, and underneath the fresh green of the budding trees, we men were trying to kill one another.

Those terrible memories, recalled so sharply by what I have seen today. And with them, the pain, that heavy, dull pain, there in my left shoulder, that pain that I thought I had done with forever. At first, in the crush and panic this afternoon, I thought someone had hit me. When I reached home, I took off my shirt, which was soaked in sweat, and ran hot water over a towel, holding it up to the scar of my old wound, tenderly, almost afraid of it, remembering how the agony could undo me those first few years after I left the hospital. But today I could hardly feel it, and the scar itself seemed lifeless, insensitive to my touch. Yet beneath the skin the pain was there—and with it, the memory of terror and surprise on those faces I saw today, and that I will never forget.

In France, at least we had the excuse of war. Our countries praised us for what we did, and thus lifted from us some of the guilt of behaving in a way that contradicted everything we had been taught of civilization, every natural emotion. For what took place today, there is no such relief. Yes, I know what the papers will say, what those prudent and experienced men who govern our city will say: that there was danger, that the police had to act as they did to prevent even worse from happening. And they will believe it too, must believe it, for they are, in their own ways, kind men, humane men, sensible men who could never admit to any motives of fear, of contempt, of hatred, to explain their actions.

There is much I do not know, much probably that I will never know. But there is some value in writing down now, while the memories are still fresh, all that I saw, and all that I have been told. Ben Rogers was with me this evening, as we sat talking and drinking, trying to make some sense out of what we had seen happen just a few hours earlier. We were in the Broadway Bar, where the newspapermen gather at the end of the day, and where the sounds of the ships' sirens drifted in through the windows on the warm and heavy air, as if this were no more than an ordinary spring evening.

Rogers had known that today might bring trouble, growing out of the unrest in the Japanese and British mills this spring. Ten days ago he came back from a trip to Kuomintang headquarters in Canton, full of stories about how Borodin and his Russians have organized a communist takeover in the south, and are now looking to Shanghai. Like many reporters, he's a bit of an alarmist, but he has friends among the police, and they feed him information as long as he doesn't name them. He's also got friends among the Chinese, and they help him. Not that he really cares much about China one way or another—for him, the Shanghai beat is no different from Chicago or San Francisco. But he treats the Chinese well, and they trust him. "He's a rarity in this city," one of his friends said to me, "a white man totally without prejudice." That's one of the qualities that makes him a good reporter.

From his Chinese friends, Rogers had learned of the protests planned for today. From Canton, the Kuomintang has been sending in agitators to stir up the students. And now all the schools were ready, he said: Chinese universities like Nanyang and Fudan, even the missionary colleges like St. John's, and Aurora in Frenchtown. So, while most of his fellow reporters were out covering the races, or taking the day off, Rogers had followed the marchers from Chekiang Road up to Thibet Road.

"There were hundreds of them," he told me. "Boys and girls, carrying banners in English and Chinese, plastering posters up everywhere. On walls, on shop windows, on telephone poles, handing out leaflets, making speeches on street corners."

I'd seen some of them too. Early this afternoon I'd gone out, heading downtown to Foochow Road to spend some time in that street of restaurants, tea shops, and arcaded bookstores, with their bright red and gold banners hanging down, advertising the wares inside. All of Shanghai seemed to be outdoors, celebrating late spring, knowing that summer's terrible heat will soon be here. The Boulevard de Montigny was crowded with people out for a stroll, people shopping, people going to the Great World, that vast amusement palace of restaurants, theaters, and entertainments, all capped by its fantastic spire.

By the time I reached my destination, I could see the crowd filling Nanking Road three blocks north, and curiosity led me up there instead. A group of students—the oldest couldn't have been more than twenty—had built a platform out of old crates, and several were haranguing a crowd that was getting bigger by the minute. Others—mostly girls—were handing around pamphlets in Chinese and bad English. "Take back the foreign concessions!" *Shanghai shih Chung-kuo jen ti Shanghai!* "Shanghai belongs to the Chinese!"—foreigners are guests, and when they behave like bosses we must throw them out! A knot of Sikh policeman swung through, led by an English officer, towering above the Chinese, trying to break up the crowd, swinging their sticks to keep them moving. But the mass of people was now so thick that the traffic had come to a stop. Turning east on Nanking Road, I went about a block, and there found Rogers beside me.

By now it must have been about quarter past three, and Nanking Road was in turmoil. Nothing was moving because of the jam of people; the trams had stopped, cars were caught in the middle of the crowd, the rickshaw coolies were standing still, panting and sweating, barechested under the bright afternoon sun. In the middle of the road a red-faced British constable was trying to herd some students he'd arrested into the Louza police station in an alley across the road. More students surrounded them, cursing and shouting angry slogans. When the first group was led into the station, the others followed, and a few minutes later were thrown out, the Sikhs with their black beards and red turbans beating them down with their sticks while other policemen lined up to block the narrow lane that led to the station entrance. But the mood was getting uglier, the crowd growing all the time, shouting curses against the police, against the foreigners. Then the English officer in charge came out and started shouting orders to the crowd in English and Chinese to get back. I heard Rogers beside me: "My God, what's he going to do?" Suddenly the police raised their rifles, and the officer gave one last shout of warning. Then, not more than ten seconds later, he cried out "Fire!" A volley of shots— not many, but enough—and the front rank of the crowd crumpled, several of them killed outright, the others lying in agony on the pavement before falling still.

Then came silence. A sudden and horrified silence, following the crack of the rifles. An explosion of silence, an absolute quiet; that whole crowd, all those thousands of people filling the street in front of the police station, suddenly falling mute. A silence far more frightening in its way than had been the roar of a few seconds earlier. Though it must have lasted only an instant, it seemed as if whole slow minutes ticked by before the sounds began again. A terrified screaming this time, as the crowd ran—back down Nanking Road, up the side streets, the flood of people trying to vanish as fast as they could. Rogers and I pushed into an open doorway to get out of their way. And through the running figures, in the middle of it all, I caught a glimpse of the English officer who had given the order, white-faced under his khaki cap, while his Indian and Chinese constables stood there stolidly, their rifles at the ready in case they had to shoot again. Then, a few minutes later, we heard the sound of ambulances coming to pick up the dead and wounded.

An hour later, Rogers told me, the fire engines drove up, and with their hoses washed the blood off the street.

Tuesday, May 30, 1989

Matthew's interest in China and its history had evolved largely by accident. During his first year in college, unable to get into a class he wanted in English metaphysical poets (even at that age he was turning rather self-consciously intellectual), he had chosen instead to experiment with a course in classical Chinese literature in translation. Before long he'd found himself entranced by Arthur Waley's renderings of Han dynasty poems, and caught up by the appeal of the distant world that ripened in his imagination as he read the verses of Wang Wei, Tu Fu, Li Po, and the other great singers of the Tang dynasty. By the end of the year he was determined to begin to study Chinese (rather against the advice of his practical parents), and soon discovered a fascinated aptitude for making sense out of the ideographs he was learning. Ten years earlier, students like Matthew had been drawn to Chinese by the idealized picture of a Maoist utopia that was briefly popular among western intellectuals, but by 1977, when he entered college, the allure of the

Great Helmsman was rapidly fading. His fellow students, he discovered, were now less interested in the prospects of Chinese socialism than in the possibility of profiting from a China gradually opening to American enterprise and American trade (several years later, as that dream cooled, they would turn to Japanese instead, hoping for jobs after graduation with Nomura Securities).

By then Matthew had already decided (again, over parental misgivings), that the world of the intellect had no room for such materialistic considerations. So he plunged headfirst into his study of China's literature, her society, and her history. A junior year spent in Taiwan, followed by a month's travel on the mainland, overcame his fears that he, like Waley, might prefer the imaginary China of the past to the gritty China of the present. It also gave him a fluency in the language that his teachers found remarkable, and startled him with a passionate but inconclusive encounter, in the sulfurous air of a Taipei summer, with Althea Ma, a pleasingly ravishing if somewhat empty-headed Californian who had been sent abroad by her lawyer parents in the hope that she would discover her Chinese roots. Whether she did or not, Matthew never found out. For her ardor had unfortunately cooled before his own, and with more than a twinge of jealous regret he'd watched her disappear to Hong Kong in the company of a blond tennis star from Stanford named Hank, who was on his way to play a tournament in the British colony. Within a few days, however, he had been honest enough to acknowledge a sense of release, a deliverance from the possibility of an encumbrance that he had never quite intended to bear. But apart from its transient pleasures, his adventure with the enthusiastic Althea, and her mockery of his self-imposed eastern seriousness, had the salutary effect of breaking down a developing pretentiousness extraordinarily dangerous in one already virtually decided on an academic career.

After graduation he had spent another year in Taipei, working for an American accounting firm, before returning to the States to begin graduate work at Harvard. Two years ago, on the strength of a first-rate, if not quite stunning, doctoral dissertation on the early years of Shanghai's French Concession, and two articles that his adviser helped him to get published in small but respectable academic journals, he had landed a job teaching history at Atherton College, whose location in northern Massachusetts made the inevitable break with Harvard Square less painful for him than for those of his colleagues who found themselves heading west to Oklahoma, Idaho, or Illinois. Now he was at work on a book about Shanghai in the 1920s, those years when revolution and counterrevolution had fought their battles in the city's streets, and Chiang Kai-shek's victory over his leftist foes had seemed to save China from the specter of communism. Matthew found the period fascinating. But there was more than intellectual interest at work, for as Laura's irony had reminded him, in only four years Atherton would have to decide whether to grant him tenure, and a book in print and well reviewed would help his chairman and his dean reach the right decision. History has many uses, and for someone in Matthew's position, job security is by no means the least of them.

He found the Shanghai Historical Institute on Szechwan Road in the city's old business district, occupying a large granite-fronted office building put up some seventy years ago, and, like so much else in that dowdy city, very much showing its age. Just inside the entrance sat a plump, balding man in an undershirt, a cigarette in his mouth, checking people who went into the building. With some difficulty Matthew introduced himself and explained why he had come. "I'm looking for the institute," he said. "Deputy Director Zhao Shanling." "*Si lou*—fourth floor," grunted the gatekeeper. "There"—pointing to the elevator. A young woman in a white blouse put down the magazine she was reading long enough to take him up; she yawned and looked bored. Fatigued by its ascent, the elevator groaned up the shaft; inside it the air was rank with the smoke of old cigarettes. It came to a stop and the door clanged open. At the end of the dark corridor Matthew found an office with two men in it, reading newspapers. He knocked on the open door. "I'm looking for Mr. Zhao," he said. "The deputy director. I have an appointment with him."

"Come in," said the taller of the two men, rising to greet him. "I'll find Mr. Zhao." He went out into the hall. The other one poured hot water from a pale blue thermos over some tea leaves, and handed the cup to Matthew, who thanked him. "Please sit down," he said. "Mr. Zhao will be here in a minute." He turned on a fan, animating the hot air and setting a newspaper to twitch fitfully on a table in the corner. From the street below rose the blare of horns, and in the distance, a pile driver kept up its steady beat. Matthew sipped his tea. It tasted green and dusty, like the afternoon, and the leaves stuck to his tongue.

"Mr. Walker, how are you?" Zhao came into the room. He was a small man of about sixty-five, with a brown, bony face, his hair going white. His darting energy somehow seemed out of place in the damp heat of the room; he reminded Matthew suddenly of a sandpiper, moving along the beach in a fit of nervous stops and starts. "It was not as hot as this when we met last year, was it?" He spoke Chinese slowly and clearly, for which Matthew was grateful; his ear still had trouble with the heavy Shanghai accent. Zhao poured himself a cup of tea. The other two men left the room, shutting the door behind them. "Please sit here," he said, motioning to a large red stuffed armchair with a stained antimacassar on it; the sort of chair, Matthew thought, that Mao Tse-tung used to be photographed in as he greeted foreign dignitaries.

"You had a good trip, I hope? And your hotel is comfortable? Good, good. But you know the really hot weather hasn't come yet. Wait till July and August. That's the worst. And we don't have much air-conditioning, you know. There's a bad power shortage in Shanghai. Someday, perhaps, if they build the dam at the Three Gorges. But our environmentalists"—he used the English word—"don't like that."

Matthew knew that it would be impolite to try to get down to business right away. Half in Chinese, half in English, he and Zhao circled round each other, talking about America, talking about life in Shanghai. Zhao touched on the demonstrations that had taken place ten days earlier when Mikhail Gorbachev had visited the city, flying down to Shanghai after his meeting with Deng Xiaoping in Beijing. Right after the Soviet leader left, three American destroyers had steamed up the Huangpu on a courtesy call to the city, and outside the Party headquarters on the Bund, students had put up a replica of the Statue of Liberty to greet the visitors. Nothing of the sort had ever happened before. It was almost as if forty years of building a communist society had been forgotten, and China was suddenly faced with a bewildering variety of choices for the future. But when Matthew tried to ask him where he thought the extraordinary outbursts of April and May might lead, Zhao was noncommittal, and Matthew did not press the point. Wherever the "China spring," as the journalists were calling it, might be going, it would depend upon events in Beijing, and Zhao Shanling's vagueness masked the silence of prudence.

Perhaps to avoid the subject, he turned to business. "You're interested in old Shanghai," he said. "The national revolution—the *minzu geming*." He used the Chinese term for that brief period, more than sixty years ago, when the Nationalists and Communists had been allies in a great movement to drive out the old ways and to build a strong and independent country. For their own victory in 1949, the Communists used the term "Liberation"; by then they had no need of allies in imposing their rule over the country. "Several people here at the institute are also studying that period," he said, "and I hope we can help you."

"Of course I'd be most grateful for anything you can do," said Matthew. His carefully learned Chinese courtesies came out. "And I know that your institute has been making some very valuable contributions to the history of Shanghai."

Zhao was clearly pleased. "Fifteen or twenty years ago—under the Gang of Four—everything was different." He paused, a wry smile on his lips. "But of course I wasn't in Shanghai then. They sent me to a commune in the Chekiang mountains to do farm work. Did I tell you that? For seven years." Another pause. Matthew waited. "I learned a lot," he said diplomatically. "But today we are encouraged to work more freely." He talked of his own studies, and suggested people for Matthew to meet, materials to look at for his book. Finally, sensing it was time to leave, Matthew brought up Simon Larsen.

"There was that man I wrote you about, whom I'm interested in. The American—his Chinese name was Lai Shi'an. Do you think there might be anything about him in the records here?"

"I haven't forgotten the question," said Zhao. "I've been looking for materials that might interest you, asking people who might have heard of him. But you know, it's difficult to track down one person. This Larsen—well, there were so many foreigners in Shanghai in those days, and since then we've had so much trouble. The Japanese invasion, eight years of occupation. And then civil war. Even since Liberation there has been some turmoil in Shanghai, particularly under the Gang of Four." He paused, and then went on in English. "Have you been to see Xie Bona yet—Bernard Hilding?"

"Not yet. I've written to him, of course, and I'm going to get in touch with him." Hilding was one of a small group of expatriates who had stayed in China after 1949 when most foreigners had chosen to leave, or had been forced out of China. Born and raised in Lancashire, he had worked as a stoker on one of Alfred Holt's Blue Funnel liners, and had jumped ship in Shanghai in 1935 at the age of nineteen, making a living for himself by a variety of jobs in the city. Though he had little formal education, he possessed an extraordinary aptitude for language, becoming fluent in Shanghainese and Mandarin. Drafted into the British Army in 1939, he was assigned to an intelligence unit and sent to the wartime capital of Chungking to help the embassy keep track of the murky relations between Chiang Kai-shek's Nationalists and Mao's Communists in Yan'an.

What happened after that was not clear, though some said that Hilding's relations with the Communists in Chungking became closer than the embassy liked, and that in 1944 he was ordered back home. At that point he had disappeared; one version of the story had him going to Yan'an in the northwest to offer his services to Mao's Communists; another had him going back to Shanghai and Canton, working with the communist underground during the civil war that had torn China apart from 1946 to 1949. By the mid-fifties he was visible again, living in Beijing, writing laudatory works about the New China, translating for the Foreign Languages Press, meeting visiting foreign delegations. Occasionally he went to Europe, a star at international peace congresses in cities like Stockholm and Bucharest, and sometimes even to Britain, where he addressed little groups on the fringes of the Labour Party. Invariably he would assail the policies of his own government and of the Americans (the State Department would never give him a visa for the United States). By the 1960s, however, Mao had concluded that the Kremlin's new czars were more dangerous than Wall Street's old capitalists, and when Hilding began to denounce Soviet policies as well as American, he found himself less welcome in those modish London circles. Then, during the Cultural Revolution, he had disappeared from sight—jailed like so many others, Matthew had heard, for the crime of ultraleftism. Several years later, he reemerged, receiving a public pardon and a public apology from none other than Chou En-lai himself.

"As you know, Hilding's been living here in Shanghai for the last several years. He moved down from Beijing. He's quite old, but he still teaches at the Foreign Languages Institute. You may find that his memory is not as good as it used to be. I don't know. Life was difficult for him for several years. You should go see him anyway. He can tell you a good deal about old Shanghai. You know where he lives? at the Huaihai Hotel on Thibet Road?" Matthew nodded. He knew the building, a former Y.M.C.A. in the old French Concession. "Mostly overseas Chinese use it, but there are some foreign experts who live there too."

Zhao picked up the battered blue thermos to pour some more hot water over the green leaves in Matthew's cup. The door opened, and a young woman spoke to him. "*Yue Guanzhang laile.*"

"*Haode, haode, mashang jiu lai.*" He turned to Matthew. "I must go now; I have an appointment with the director, and can't keep him waiting. But as for our institute, we will of course do what we can to help you." Then, back to English: "But do go see Hilding. I know he'd like to talk to you, and I think that he might be helpful. In the meantime, come back the day after tomorrow, and we'll have the materials ready for you here at the institute."

Invariably in China the first meeting, the first day, is almost purely social. But such interviews were important. Living in China, trying to work in China, Matthew thought, had something of the quality of a dream, like being confronted by a maze, unsure whether the object is to find your way out or to plunge more deeply into it. There are many threads that may act as guides, threads that are all part of the web of personal connections that hold China together, that have always held China together, more important than government bureaucracies, police forces, armies, more important than political parties, more important even than Confucianism or communism. The world of China remained a world of human beings, and everyone was part of the web; no one, even Mao himself, had been able to control it, to determine how the web is spun. The important thing, Matthew knew, was to find out where the individual threads lead. Following one can steer you to a particular set of personal connections, which may be helpful. Or may not. Sometimes the threads cross one another, and you have to decide whether to go off in a new direction or stay with the one you've been following. The whole exercise, he reflected, was rather like trying to turn classical Chinese poetry into English. Written in a language that rejoices in ambiguity, in connections and allusions, in suggestiveness, it makes the translator choose which of the possible senses he must emphasize, knowing that in so doing he forces upon the words a concreteness of meaning that destroys the joyful indeterminacy of the original. Even the modern language could have the same quality, and the Chinese delight in ambivalence, in word play, in allusion, had never been effaced, even by forty years of dreary Marxist-Leninist pronouncements by the country's leaders.

And now Matthew, a foreigner, was back in China, trying to grope his way through the web, trying to translate the past, trying to make the connections.

CHAPTER TWO

Tuesday, May 30, 1989

The Jinjiang Hotel, where the institute had arranged for Matthew to stay, stands on Maoming Road, just opposite the site of the old French Club, the Cercle Sportif, where now a new skyscraper built by the Japanese was rising in the place of that once exuberant building. Several structures make up the hotel compound, the largest of which is a tall brick apartment house built in the late twenties by Sir Victor Sassoon, and known then as the Cathay Mansions. Matthew's room, however, was in a considerably more modest structure, an anonymous square building that harked back not to the free and easy days of the Sassoons, but rather to the time of China's infatuation with the Soviet Union in the early fifties, and though its years were fewer, it wore them with considerably less grace than did the older building. Large coffee-colored blotches of indeterminate origin stained the faded green carpet in his room, echoing the patches of damp that mottled the pale brown wallpaper. The furniture was covered with a cracked reddish wood veneer, and even on a hot day the bathroom felt clammy, pervaded by a smell in which disinfectant mingled with periodic exhalations from the plumbing.

By Shanghai's crowded standards, as Matthew well knew, he

was living in extraordinary luxury. Nonetheless, contemplating the room's dingy appearance when he got back, he found himself strangely depressed, a feeling that he told himself was only a temporary loneliness, and that would vanish as soon as he got down to work. Yet it followed him that evening into the nondescript shabbiness of the dining room, and there it combined with the indifferent quality of the food and the warm beer to bring a sudden wave of melancholy over him. He found himself, however, almost actually encouraging it rather than trying to drive it away, for Matthew had about him something of the disposition that can cherish sadness, and the very monotony of the scene and his own loneliness seemed to evoke, simply by contrast, a nostalgic but brilliant memory of last summer, and his three weeks in Europe with Laura. For an instant he wished himself not here, but back with her, nine thousand miles away, on a warm spring evening at home, with the chance to make everything right again.

They had met in the fall of 1987. It was his first year at Atherton, and Laura Donati had been commuting twice a week from Cambridge up to the college to teach her course. Matthew had been struck at first by what he saw as an intelligent rather than a conventionally beautiful face, with its alert gray eyes set under a high forehead, the glasses she occasionally wore giving her the look of a wise child sitting silently attentive to the world around her. From her Florentine ancestors had come her soft dark hair, its russet lights caught by the sun or the glow of a lamp, framing her face in its smooth loose fall, or tied back behind her, to reveal the fine bones of her head and her slim neck. As he had with Althea Ma, Matthew sensed in Laura, born and raised on the West Coast, something of a complement to his own eastern introspection, and they'd formed a casual acquaintance, finding themselves thrown together at the sorts of parties on rainy autumn nights where young faculty members down quantities of obscure Italian wine, deconstruct one another's remarks with an adroit cleverness, and complain endlessly about the obtuse deans and tyrannical department chairmen with whom they are burdened. He was attracted not only by her looks and her quick mind, but also by her admission that she, like he, tired of the interminable chatter of academic politics at such gatherings. The pleasant sense of superiority that this discovery gave them naturally drew them closer together, and by November Matthew found himself looking forward each week to the days she'd come to Atherton to teach, arranging his schedule so that he could spend some time alone with her. In her he found a combination of opposites that made her quite unlike any other girl he'd ever known, for her aspect of almost severe intellectuality contrasted with the slender limbs that moved with a kind of loose California grace, just on the verge of being gangly, as if she had only recently grown out of a rather leggy adolescence. She seemed to him one of those women who, for a while, at least, the years would continue to soften rather than harden, as age and experience brought a wider understanding to replace the rigid certitudes of youth.

From the very beginning, however, he was conscious of a certain reserve, a certain distance in her, so that he was never quite sure where they were going with each other. It had started when they'd first met, that evening when he'd spotted her across the room at a crowded party, recognizing her face as one he'd seen in the corridors of Van Ness Hall, where his office was. She was wearing a wine-red wool skirt and a white sweater, for the weather had suddenly grown chilly, and her dark hair was kept in place by a headband. He'd made his way across the room and introduced himself. They'd talked—the particular talk of couples who have just met, dancing around one another with the usual questions: Who are you, what do you do? I teach, I live here, I live in Cambridge, isn't the weather cold. But underneath, far more important than the words actually spoken, were the kinds of silently coded signals that were almost unconscious: Who are you really, what do you like, have we anything in common?

Do we speak the same language?

When he'd asked her about her work, she'd tried at first to deflect the question.

"Just another exercise in criticism." She laughed. "Someday perhaps it'll be a footnote in someone else's learned article." Upstairs a child had begun to howl, presumably woken by the noise.

"So are you keeping it a secret? I'm not going to steal your ideas, if that's what you're afraid of."

She looked at him, as if trying to make out whether he really was interested. Then apparently she decided he was.

"All right. I'm looking at novels about colonialism. Depictions of the colonial world, their institutions. Relations between men and women. The Westerner and his Other. That sort of thing."

"Joseph Conrad and such?"

"Conrad, yes. And Forster and Graham Greene. Maybe some others. Maybe Kipling. I haven't decided yet." They'd talked together for another half hour or so, Matthew feeling that he was sailing past unmapped headlands into uncharted bays, yet strangely reluctant to penetrate too deeply into that reserve he'd sensed in her. Finally she'd looked at her watch. "Look, I've got to go. It's been nice meeting you. But it's a long drive home."

She sounded as if she'd suddenly been afraid she was boring him. But he'd extracted a promise from her to meet again, and after that they began seeing each other with some frequency. Yet Matthew found that he always had to draw her out about her own work, and every time she'd tried to change the subject, as if convinced that he couldn't possibly be interested in it.

"Laura, come on," he'd said to her. They were sitting in a restaurant on Church Street in Cambridge on a Saturday, having lunch. "I want to know what you're doing. Unless you're trying to forget it." He did want to know. But more than that, he wanted to be with her. He didn't tell her—not yet, at any rate—that since meeting her, he'd taken to rereading Conrad and Forster, calling up dim undergraduate memories of *Heart of Darkness* or *Passage to India*. Hoping to sound more intelligent when they talked together.

"But I'm afraid I'll bore you." She laughed as she said it, but the serious look didn't leave her.

"Bore me? Would I keep asking if it bored me?"

She hesitated before answering, keeping her eyes fixed on the table, her finger drawing an imaginary doodle on its surface. For the first time, he noted that she was left-handed. He wondered vaguely whether it affected her outlook on life.

"It isn't that I don't like what I'm doing. I love it. That's the trouble. I've never done anything like this before. And it's almost become part of me. To the point where I almost feel I don't want to share it with anyone."

"But your adviser. He's going to have to read it. What'll you do then?"

"She. Not he. Joan Fennimore." She looked up to see if the name meant anything to him. It didn't. "I'll cross that bridge when I come to it. And hope I can trust her."

Matthew looked blank. "Trust her? Why not?"

Laura took a gulp of her wine, and then stared back down at the table, still tracing a design in the damp left by the glass.

"I guess there are parts of my life I'm jealous of. And I guard them. Carefully. I know it sounds odd to say my writing may be one of them. Not even writing, really. Just a dissertation. But there it is. Maybe it's because I have so much invested in it. My future, my career. More than that. Proving something to myself." She fell silent again, and Matthew looked out at the cold autumn rain that was pulling the dead leaves off the trees.

Then she looked up and smiled at him, as if trying to lighten the mood. "Beneath this sunny California exterior there beats the heart of a buttoned-up easterner. It's my chilly Philadelphia inheritance. Always at war with my Italian blood. Sometimes the Larsens win, sometimes they lose. Today they're winning, I guess. Larsens five, Donatis zero. Or perhaps Donatis one, but no more. Maybe coming east to grad school was a mistake; maybe it tilts the balance in favor of those Philadelphia roots."

"But if you hadn't, then I'd never have met you, would I?"

"I guess not," she said. "But I did, and you did. So here we are." She got up. "And you said you were going to help me with my groceries." She took his hand to draw him up. "Come on, Matt. Let's go to the Star Market. Then we can go see a movie."

When the term came to an end in December, however, Laura had been carried off by a fellowship to spend the winter and spring in London, working on her dissertation. From her room in Handel Street, off Russell Square, she had enlivened his winter by her wryly funny letters about life in latter-day Bloomsbury, about the quirks of the readers whom she saw gathering every day under the great blue dome of the British Library's reading room, and about her own indecision and the inconclusive nature of her work.

He found himself missing her more than he'd thought he would, looking forward to her return the following summer, vaguely hoping that her absence in London wouldn't lead her to drift away from him. Then, one bleak February day, he'd gone to see a distant older cousin who lived on Marlborough Street but who spent much of every summer at a villa near Ponte Cerrone, in the wine country just north of Siena. "Come and stay for a week or two," Henry Osborne had offered. "If you've nothing better to do. It's a wonderful place to relax. Bring your work. Bring a friend if you like. There's plenty of room."

Matthew had looked outside at the trees, winter bare against the gray skies and the dark red brick of the Back Bay. The idea came to him then, like a sudden, vivid, Technicolor dream of summer, growing in his mind all afternoon, so that he'd sat down to write Laura that evening. He'd almost called her—she'd given him a phone number—but then had decided that he didn't want to take her by surprise, and that his chances might be better if she had time to think over the idea in private. Even though he'd have to wait while his letter crossed the Atlantic. But he was also careful to remind her of his own number. So that she could call. If she wanted to.

She did. A week later—it was a Saturday morning, and he'd been home putting together his lecture notes for the following week—the phone had rung.

"Matt—it's me, Laura."

"Laura—where are you?" All the cheerful inanities of a phone conversation wanted to come out.

"I'm in a phone booth. On Charing Cross Road, if that's any help." An instant's silence. "I've got to make this quick, I'm running out of change." Another pause. "Matt, I got your letter."

"You did?" Stupid question, particularly over three thousand miles of ocean.

"Yes. And I think I'd love to go to Italy with you." Think? What did that mean? But a wave of relief and joy flooded over him.

"You would? That's wonderful."

"But, Matt, your cousin? Do you think he'd really want me along?" Again that note of doubt in her voice.

Of course he would, he'd assured her, and he'd gone on to start describing the plans he'd been making in his head ever since the idea had first come to him. But then her coins had run out, the line went dead, and after that it had taken more letters and more phone calls to set the dates.

So in June, when his classes were over and his examinations read and graded, he'd flown to Milan. He was in time to meet Laura as she stepped off the plane from Heathrow at Linate, and his first pleased reaction as she greeted him was that she looked younger and a good deal less like the graduate student he remembered. After lunch they had set off in a tiny rented car, heading south along the Autostrada del Sole, and by mid-afternoon were climbing out of the hot and dusty Lombardy plain, the road before them curving up into the Apennines above Bologna. Passing over the crest of the mountains, they drove down the western slopes toward Florence, watching the long light of the golden afternoon throw into relief a landscape where lines of tall cypresses, dark against the silver gray-green of sunlit olive orchards, marched over the Tuscan hills.

At Monteriggioni they had turned off the autostrada, and with the help of a map sent by Henry, had poked their way along little back roads leading up into the Chianti, finding, after a few false turns, the village for which they were looking. It was late afternoon, and the way led them out of Ponte Cerrone, half-way up a gentle ridge, then finally, in a sharp turn to the left, through the gate of the Villa dei Querci.

Henry Osborne met them at the door.

"You found it all right? So glad you could come," he said, shaking Matthew's hand. "And how are your mother and father? Good, good." He turned to Laura. "And you must be Laura Donati."

"Mr. Osborne," she said, taking his outstretched hand. "Thank you for having us. It's absolutely lovely here."

"It's I who should thank you for coming," he said. "And with a name like Donati, I'm going to guess that your forebears were Tuscan. Am I right?"

Laura nodded. "My grandfather was a Florentine," she said. A refugee from Mussolini's Italy, he had come to America in the thirties, living first in New York, before settling in San Francisco, where he had taught physics at Mills College. There his son had met Simon Larsen's niece, and the two were married in 1954, nine years before Laura was born, the youngest of three children.

He stood back and looked at her, without letting go of her hand. "Matthew tells me you're a student of literature, so you'll understand when I say that it's not often I have a guest here who calls to mind so clearly that other Laura—"

She looked at him, surprised. Then started laughing. "Hardly that," she said. "Anyway, she was French."

"But of course her poet was Italian, wasn't he? A Tuscan too. Francesco Petrarca, of Arezzo. I think that perhaps you too deserve a poet like that."

Laura flushed, and Matthew could see that she was both enjoying and embarrassed by the sudden shower of old-fashioned flattery, and he himself was rather relieved when Henry suggested they be shown their rooms, telling them they had time for a swim before dinner. In his room, Matthew changed quickly into a pair of bathing trunks, and took a towel from the chair near his bed. Then he stepped into the hall, just as Laura came out the door of her room. There in the dimness, a towel wrapped around her middle, she looked almost like a boy: slender-waisted and straight-legged, betrayed only by the fall of hair down her back, and now, as she turned toward him, and his eyes adjusted to the light, by the slim roundness of her hips and the slight swelling of the breasts under her bathing suit. It was almost as if he had never seen her before, had never seen how she really was, now that they were away from the familiar landscape in which they'd come to know each other earlier.

She looked at him. "I like your cousin Henry," she said. "He seems very kind."

He nodded. "Yes. He's a great guy." And he sure knows how to play the role of an aging gallant, he thought, turning on the charm for a woman not much more than a third his age. "He's obviously glad I brought you along."

When they reached the pool, Laura undid the towel, and he had a quick glimpse of her before she took a running dive into the water, slipping through the smooth green surface with barely a splash, swimming underwater in strong, graceful strokes, not coming up for air until she reached the other end. Her body seemed to him to fit in the water almost more naturally than it did on land, as if it belonged there, for now that she pulled herself out of the pool, the swimmer's womanly grace gave way to that angular gangliness, almost adolescent in its nature, that sometimes characterized her movements. Out of the water now, she stood up straight, then reached down with a gesture of unselfconscious modesty, trying without success to tug her bathing suit lower over her bare hips, and walked over to where he was sitting, watching her.

"Aren't you going in?"

"Is it nice?"

"Wonderful. Just the right temperature."

He got up and walked to the edge of the pool. Diving in, he knew that he had none of her swimmer's sleek grace, as he entered the water in an exploding splash. But he was restored by the cool smoothness of the water against his body, calming it, refreshing it, yet reminding him how tired he was after his night on the plane and the long drive down from Milan.

He swam slowly over to where she was now sitting on the edge of the pool, dangling her legs in the water.

"Laura," he said, resting his elbows on the concrete side.

"Mmm."

"Happy to be here?" He looked at her.

"It's wonderful. Just to think that a few hours ago I was in London. Gray, grungy, chilly London. Or at least that's the way it was this morning. Everything gray. Even all those dirty papers flying around in the wind, outside the Russell Square Underground when I left for Heathrow. Now look at this."

Behind them, a row of small cypresses stood, and beyond it lay a field of carefully tended grapevines, climbing up and over their wooden frames. The evening sunlight was low on the hills in the distance, and from the village below came the sound of a bell ringing, and voices calling to one another. From the house, half-hidden by trees, there drifted down the smell of cooking food. A smell of olive oil and garlic and something frying.

He sniffed it appreciatively. "Think that's dinner?"

"You're not hungry again already?" Laura asked.

"It's been a long time since lunch."

Just at that moment Henry came through the trees to the pool. "You found it, did you?" he said. "Good. I'm afraid the water's rather warmer than usual. It's been very hot for the last few days."

"It's perfect," said Laura, looking up at him. "Just perfect. Thank you so much."

Henry beamed at her. "That's what it's here for," he said. "I prefer to swim in the morning. Otherwise I'd join you. But now it's getting a bit late, and we're expected for dinner at seven-thirty. Half an hour; does that give you enough time? Camilla will have my scalp if we keep her waiting." Camilla, Matthew had discovered, was the formidable woman who ran the house, organized Henry's life while he stayed here, and made sure that his guests were properly treated.

"Can I go in once more?" asked Laura. "Do I have time? I promise to be quick."

Henry smiled at her, nodding. "No hurry," he said. She dove in again, once more cutting the surface of the water cleanly, then coming up to breathe, shaking the wet hair out of her eyes before she swam slowly to the pool's shallow end. There she climbed out, wrapped her towel around her waist again, and the three of them proceeded up to the house.

Dinner was a small plate of pasta with olive oil and herbs, followed by a chicken stewed with rosemary, surrounded by small fried slices of eggplant, all of it washed down with a dry Vernaccia di San Gimignano—"a local wine," said Henry, "and it goes best with the local food." He was holding forth, talking to them about living in Ponte Cerrone, about the people who farmed the countryside, about the land developers from Florence and Milan and Turin who were trying to get around the laws controlling building, to put up hotels, vacation apartments, condominiums. And he told them of its history, of the great battle that had been fought nearby, in 1260, between Florence and Siena, of the eccentric philosopher Andrea Massimiglio, who had lived in the villa in the eighteenth century, and of the Franciscan convent two kilometers away that had sheltered Allied airmen and refugees from the Nazis during the war. Matthew felt himself almost overcome by the pleasant magic of the night air, heavy with the scent of jasmine, punctuated by the fireflies that swam through the blackness beyond the table where they sat. Laura sat opposite him, silent, her gray eyes fixed on Henry, who was clearly entranced by having such an audience, and was launching into story after story. Matthew scarcely spoke, simply allowing himself to be swept up by the enchantment of the evening, by the faint sounds of the night coming from the village below, and by the sight of Laura, in the pale blue cotton dress that left her shoulders bare, glowing in the light of the candles.

"You must love this country," she was saying. "It must be wonderful to feel such an attachment to a part of the world that isn't yours but that you can come back to year after year."

"Every year since 1949," he said. "And you're right. It isn't mine, of course. Not in any proper sense. And yet I feel that in a way I've adopted it. And in a way, too, it has adopted me." He laughed. "*L'Americano stravagante*, the eccentric American. That's what they used to call me. But now I think I'm pretty well accepted when I show up every year."

He took another sip of his wine, holding it up and looking at it in the candlelight.

Laura turned her eyes up at him, smiling. "If you had to do it all over again," she asked, "would you be born Italian?"

He laughed. "Perhaps. At least if I could be the right kind of Italian. The kind that lives in a place like this. But then I might not appreciate it. I might always be wanting to go to someplace new. Like America, for instance. So perhaps if I were born again, I'd be an American, as I am now. And come to Italy every year. As I do now."

The talk went on, the bottle of Vernaccia was emptied with dessert, coffee arrived and was finished, and tiny glasses of *grappa* appeared—"it's very special," Henry assured them, "from the Veneto, the kind that Hemingway used to drink when he was feeling flush." He raised his glass and looked at them. "Here's to both of you. I can't tell you how delighted I am to have the two of you here, and may you have a good journey." Then, with a glance at his watch, he rose from his chair. "It's ten-thirty," he said. "I'm going to leave you, I'm afraid. But don't feel you've got to follow. Stay up as long as you like. Just blow out the candles when you leave. But I'm going to bed. Fascinating as the company is, I can't stay up as late as I'd like to sometimes."

"I think we'll go too," said Matthew. "It's been a long day."

"Of course it has. After that night on the plane. How thoughtless of me. I've probably kept you up far too late. Listening to an old man ramble on while you must have been thinking of nothing but catching up on your sleep."

Laura put her hand on his arm. "No," she said. "It's been fascinating. Listening to all your stories, I mean. And it's so kind of you to have us. Last night I'd never have dreamed that I'd ever be in a place like this."

"My pleasure, I assure you." Henry was clearly delighted. "Come down for breakfast whenever you want after eight. It's simple—rolls and coffee and orange juice. And fruit, if Camilla has it. But it's good. She does very well by me."

They bade each other good night, Henry going upstairs, and Matthew and Laura walking slowly to the guest wing where Camilla had earlier led them. They were next to one another, Laura's room the bigger and better of the two, with three large windows looking out over the valley, and a large bed with painted wooden headboard, while Matthew had to make do with a single window, and his bed was a plain iron frame of no particular distinction.

Outside her door, Laura stopped and looked up at him. "Good night, Matt," she said. "And thank you for bringing me here. I haven't been this happy for ages." She smiled at him. He looked down at her, at the dark hair tied back behind her head, at her slim neck, at the smoothness of her shoulders, the fine sculpture of her collarbones.

"Laura—" he began. Then he put his arms around her and pulled her to him, feeling her come to him, nuzzling up against him, her hair against his cheek, a faint clean smell of lavender in the night air.

For a minute they hardly moved, but just stood there, holding each other, as if this were the first tentative step in their discovery of each other, neither one quite sure enough to make the next move for fear that it might somehow break the spell. Through the thin cotton of her dress he could feel her body against his, and he sensed himself drifting off in a pleasant daze of wine and tiredness, felt his long trip, the night on the plane, the drive, everything in the past thirty-six hours falling away, as if it had all happened ages before, as if this were the only reality, right here, with Laura in his arms, the Italian night surrounding them, only the present counting for anything.

Then she reached her hands up and pulled his face down against hers, kissing him fully on the lips, her hands ruffling his hair. A loving kiss, but a firm kiss, which even—he reflected later—had something perhaps more sisterly than erotic about it.

Then she pushed him away. "Matt," she said. "Dear Matt, good night. You must be very tired. Get a good sleep, and I'll see you in the morning."

And before he could say anything, do anything, she was gone into her room, the door closed, leaving him standing in the hall almost before he was aware what had happened, not knowing quite what he should have expected, not knowing whether he should feel disappointed or not. Yet in some curious sense that he himself didn't quite understand, he found himself almost relieved that a decision had been made for him, as if he hadn't known what it was that he really wanted himself.

The next afternoon they were in a small café in Greve, late in the afternoon, after a day of walking and driving around the countryside. Above them a blue and white umbrella with CINZANO written on it sheltered them from the heat. Laura had fallen silent, and sat looking thoughtfully at the glass of vermouth the waiter had just brought her.

Then she spoke. "Matt," she said, her voice low and her eyes fixed on the table.

"Yes?"

"Matt." She sounded uncertain, not quite able to say what she wanted to. "I was thinking about yesterday. About last night, I mean."

He waited for her to go on, not knowing what was coming.

"It's just—well, it was just such a change being here." She looked up at him again, seeking his eyes, as if to read his face. "For me, anyway. I mean, from rainy London, down here to the sun and the warmth and the flowers. I think I've never seen anything as lovely as the landscape here. I was overwhelmed by it when we got here yesterday. Particularly seeing it with you. So, yesterday, you see, I just wanted to make sure that it wasn't all going to my head. To make sure that I knew what I was doing, not plunging into something I'd be sorry for later."

She saw his surprise. "Oh, Matt, I'm sorry. I don't mean that I'd regret having come, or being with you. Not at all, you mustn't think that." She put her hand on his arm. "I love it here, and I'm so glad you've brought me with you. But you do see what I mean, don't you?" She looked at him questioningly. "Don't you? Or am I not making any sense?"

"You're right, of course." He didn't know what else to say, wasn't quite sure what she was driving at.

"I didn't know what to expect, you see." Again she was looking down, running her finger over the bubbles of moisture on the edge of her cold glass. "I've been so much looking forward to it.

This trip. All spring. But now it all seems very sudden, somehow. Being here with you, I mean."

He hadn't known quite what to expect either.

"If we were two characters in a novel, it wouldn't matter," she went on. "Then I suppose the right thing to do would be to let myself be swept away by the strangeness of it all, by the beauty of it all. But I'm not like that. And I can't change. You'll have to take me as I am. If you want me around at all." She looked up at him, smiling.

"Even if this is one of those days when the Larsens win out over the Donatis?"

She looked uncomprehending at first; then laughed. "I wouldn't bet on it," she said. "But I needed today. Just some time to figure it out." She reached for his hand and gave it a little squeeze. Then withdrew her own, and glanced over to her right. "Look over there," she said. At one of the next tables, a little boy had just been taken up into his grandfather's lap, and sat there, crowing with delight, pulling the old man's beard while his parents and his grandmother fawned over him. Laura laughed. "You'd never see that in London. Or Boston. That's the difference between you and us."

He looked at her quizzically. "Meaning what? You and us who?"

"You Anglo-Saxons and us Italians," she said, smiling. "You cold, stiff, proper types, and we warmhearted, humane Latins." She laughed again. "Sorry, Matt. I don't mean to tease you. But maybe today it's the Donatis who are winning."

She went on, talking of different things, reminding herself of what they had seen that day, a sudden animation as if the earlier conversation had never taken place, as if no questions remained. But that evening, after they had returned to the Villa dei Querci, after their swim, after the dinner with Cousin Henry, sitting in the candlelight and watching the sun go down over the hills to the west, there was nothing sisterly, he thought, in the way Laura had kissed him outside her room. So after the household had retired, he quietly opened his door, stepped into the hall, and knocked gently at the door of her room. No answer. He knocked again, a bit harder this time, hoping that the sound would rouse no one else.

This time the door was opened, and Laura was there, rubbing her eyes, and looking at him.

"Did I wake you?" he whispered. "I'm sorry."

"It's all right, Matt." She looked at him expectantly, a light smile on her lips. "I was waiting for you."

She stood before him, illuminated by the pale light of a half moon riding over the Tuscan hills. Her white nightgown reached almost to her knees, and her hair, loosed for the night, fell over the scoop of the neckline above her breasts. She looked at him steadily, smiling. For what seemed like an age, neither of them spoke.

Then he said: "Well, here I am, Laura."

"Yes, Matt. Here you are indeed." She smiled, and then she came toward him, putting her arms around his neck and pulling his face down on hers. "Matt," she whispered. "Matt, I wanted you to come." She felt fresh and cool, and her hair smelled like almonds.

Then, gradually, everything he'd been waiting for had happened, and later, when it was over, Matthew had the sensation that he had suddenly found himself resting in the first evening of the world, a cool darkness descending after a sudden tempest had boiled up out of the day's furious heat, bringing a respite that no one, ever, anywhere, could have known before, a sense of release and of peace, a calming fatigue quite different from anything he'd ever experienced, or even dreamed possible. Yet even then, as they lay there together, he heard a train cry from the valley, and outside the window could see that dark moonlit landscape, so beautiful despite its long and terrible history, reminding him that they were not alone, that countless others before him, in that same house, in that same room, indeed on that same bed, must have known that sense of newness and peace, of refuge from the world that had now overtaken him.

"Laura." She lay on her back, the sheet drawn up to her waist, her arms above her head, hair spread out on the pillow.

"Matt. Dear Matt."

"Are you awake?"

"No." She laughed softly. "I've gone to sleep, of course." Then she rolled over on her side, facing him, reaching out her forefinger to trace the curve of his shoulder. "Did you want to say something?"

"Laura." He felt himself dumb, not possibly capable of finding the words he wanted. So he fell back on repeating her name as he looked at her. "Laura, Laura. Lovely Laura."

She propped herself up on her elbows, and looked serious. "Matt, I feel—I don't understand it—I feel somehow as if I'd come home."

He pulled her down against him and kissed her. "Come home. Signorina Donati comes home to the land of her ancestors. With a cold, stiff, proper Anglo-Saxon in tow."

She laughed again. "Whatever else you are, Matt— The land of my ancestors. Maybe that's it. Partly, anyway." She looked at him earnestly. "Explain it, Professor Walker. Something in the air, d'you think? the soil? Is that what does it?"

"The water."

"More likely the wine. Did I have a glass too many? Anyway, that's not what I mean by home, Matt. I mean because I'm here with you. It's as if there's been something I've always wanted, someplace I've always been trying to find." She raised herself up and looked at him. "And now I've reached it, and I'm here."

They were to spend the next ten days in a kind of idyllic indolence, a time that marked the beginning of a voyage of gradual discovery for both of them, an excursion into each other, an exploration of their separate temperaments: their expressions, their voices, their rhythms, their likes and dislikes, their passions, and their responses. England had somehow softened Laura, melting away the kind of intellectual brittleness that Matthew had seen at home, and in its place had grown a new gentleness, a responsiveness to emotions, to perceptions that arose from a kind of sensibility he had not seen in her before. She'd let her hair grow longer, and the effect was to temper the severity of her looks, which had earlier attracted him but which now would have seemed out of place in this setting of cypresses and olive groves, of wisteria climbing up the faded yellow walls of old houses, of wildflowers in the sunlit fields. Or so it had seemed then; had he, he wondered now, simply imagined all this, had he simply seen in her the kinds of qualities, the appearance, that the Italian countryside, by its own shapes and colors, its very air, seemed to call forth?

And together in those ten days, Matthew and Laura had explored the countryside around Ponte Cerrone, tramping along dusty roads that led deep into the Arcadian hills, wandering through small villages, dawdling over long lunches in little *trattorie* while the world slept, and escaping the afternoon heat in the cool darkness of village churches.

"There can't be any other landscape in the world like this," he had said to her one day as they sat on a hillside overlooking the valley of the Arno. It was a sultry afternoon, and above the green-blue hills in the distance a thunderhead was building splendidly into the sky, the sun catching the silvered complexity of its form like the cloud of a Tiepolo ceiling. His back was propped against the trunk of a tree, his arm around Laura, who lay beside him, her long legs stretched out straight on the grass, and her head nestled against his shoulder.

"Mmm," she had answered drowsily, moving against him. "Is it going to rain?"

"D'you remember that part in A *Passage to India* where Fielding comes through Italy on his way home to England? And what Forster says about the Mediterranean being the human norm? A landscape where nature and human beings work together rather than against one another? That's what it's like here. Everything fits."

Silence. Her soft hair blew across his cheek.

"Did I wake you up? Sorry."

"Just thinking. Yes, I remember. The world of the Mediterranean—such a contrast to poor chaotic India." She nuzzled him. "But I don't want an oral exam now." A distant rumble echoed across the hills. She looked up into his face. "Shall we get a gelato before it rains?"

"You're a philistine," he had answered. "This is the home of your ancestors, after all. 'Lovely Laura in her light green dress.' " She was, in fact, wearing light green shorts. But he kissed her and roused himself as the thunder sounded again, closer this time—"Come on, then, faithful Petrarch," she said, scrambling to her feet and pulling him up. "But his Laura was blond, remember?" Last night at dinner, Henry Osborne had quoted the sonnet describing Laura's hair, sometimes bound up with pearls and precious stones, sometimes falling loose about her shoulders, *sovra or terso bionde*, brighter than burnished gold, setting a snare about the poet's heart so tight that it could be undone only by death. Matthew, sitting and listening, watching his modern dark-haired Laura in the candlelight, had suddenly shared with that ancient lover a feeling that seemed to collapse the centuries separating them. He looked at her now against the afternoon hills, and then hand in hand they escaped down to the café before the first drops fell. Laura got her gelato, and by the time their Tuscan interlude was up, they had agreed that their journey had reached at least one of the destinations they had hoped for.

Poor India, thought Matthew now, looking back on that scene. Poor China. China, where nothing seemed to fit together: Shanghai, with its jumble of buildings and people, or the villages of the countryside, featureless gray buildings put up with no apparent sense of form, no sense of adaptation to the landscape. Was the Mediterranean really the norm, as Forster said? Or was it only that in Asia we insist on trying to impose a western sense of form on a human scenery so different from ours? As we try, all too often, to impose a western shape of the past on parts of the world with histories very different from our own? Perhaps it was no more than a matter of poverty; perhaps the kind of Italian sensibility that had so enthralled them a year before was not natural at all, but a privilege of the rich that China, poor China, could not afford. Any more than she could have afforded—even had she wanted it—a history shaped in the way of the West. The question spun in his head in a pleasant confusion of food and gentle Shanghai beer. It was the kind of question he and Laura would have discussed with great earnestness, and he found himself longing for her again, wishing that she could be there, with her intelligent face and quick mind. Perhaps then it would have been possible for them to have recaptured that closeness they'd known a year ago, before—for reasons that he still didn't quite understand—they had begun to drift apart. The thought brought back his lonely depression, and he rose from the table, paid his bill, and left.

Back in his room, he called Bernard Hilding. The telephone system was surprisingly cooperative that night, and he got through on the third attempt. Hilding sounded far away, uncertain why he was being called; as they talked, distant Chinese voices drifted over the wires, vague echoes blowing in from other conversations across the city. They agreed to meet the next morning in Hilding's hotel on Thibet Road. Matthew hung up. A warm damp wind blew in the window, spitting rain, rustling the papers on the desk, and bringing with it the smell of the city at night. On the television screen there was an earnest movie about the People's Liberation Army. He pushed the channel button, and a Hong Kong pop star appeared, wailing about unrequited love; another push, and in came a program from

America, carried by satellite from one of the networks. Matthew turned it off, and took from the desk his photocopy of *Typhoon Over Shanghai*. Slowly, he began again to read it.

Shanghai in the spring of 1925 had been a city of gathering tensions, of rising fears. Fighting between rival generals had broken out the previous September, had smoldered and sputtered for the next five months, occasionally bursting into flame with a violence that seemed to threaten the security and stability of the French Concession and the International Settlement, the two sections where almost all of Shanghai's forty thousand foreigners lived. No sooner had a doubtful peace been patched up in early February than strikes had broken out in the city's foreign-owned textile mills. There had been violence, brawls between workers and the police. Then in mid-May it was the death of a Chinese striker at the hands of a Japanese foreman that had touched off the great demonstrations of May 30, and thus provided the occasion for the shooting that Simon Larsen had witnessed in front of the Louza Police Station on Nanking Road that afternoon.

All this, of course, Matthew knew from his study of the city, from the research that had taken him to dry and learned monographs by other historians, to newspapers like the *North China Daily News*, the *Écho de Chine*, to the reports of consuls, of businessmen and their chambers of commerce, and to the writings of the many missionaries who had made Shanghai, for all its image as a city of vice, the center of Christian evangelism in China. Simon's papers, however, gave Matthew a privileged insight into this little foreign colony that had been built up in Shanghai ever since its opening some eighty years earlier. It was the view of an intelligent outsider, a man with no particular stake in the city, but with a natural curiosity, who was interested in understanding and recording different points of view, whatever might have been his own sympathies. In 1925 Simon had been twenty-nine, precisely Matthew's age now. But Simon had fought in the trenches of the western front, had been badly wounded and then decorated for his heroism, and thus on the eve of this thirtieth year had seen a great deal more of life and death than Matthew had ever known or perhaps ever would know. Matthew pictured him as a man who must sometimes have felt older than his years, detached from the world of his carefree contemporaries in jazz-age America—or jazz-age Shanghai, for that matter. His brush with mortality must have given him a conviction, if not of moral authority, at least of a kind of experiential authority, and there was sometimes evident in his memoirs a kind of condescension, even an impatience with those who had never yet been made to stare into the face of the infinite.

Like everyone else in Shanghai, he had been badly shaken by the violence in Nanking Road on May 30, 1925, and had watched helplessly the furious reaction that followed.

Wednesday, June 10, 1925

"Devils! Foreign murderers! You have made Shanghai a sea of BLOOD!" Smeared and tattered now, but still legible after the rain, the poster on the wall outside my house stares at me whenever I leave it. The last character, *hsüeh*, larger than the others, and scrawled in brilliant red, cries out the indictment. Like an accused felon, I try not to look at it as I pass; am I held to be somehow responsible, is it up to me to stop somehow what's happening here? But that's only my imagination. I can't be the target, for all over the city such placards have appeared, put up when the police aren't looking, on other walls, on shop windows, on telephone poles, even on tramcars. A few are in English, but most, like mine, are in Chinese: "Down with the foreign murderers!" "Never forget the bloodthirsty butchery of May Thirtieth!" There are cartoons too: fat British plutocrats extorting money from the emaciated bodies of Chinese workers, or sinister Japanese generals manipulating their tame warlords to suppress China's cry for freedom. And over and over again there is that same large character splashed in bright red ink: "BLOOD!"

Most of Shanghai is now on strike against the British and the Japanese, and with so many of the mills and factories idle, the dockers no longer working the ships, the crowds of unemployed fill the streets. A *san-pa*, the Chinese call it, a triple strike: workers leave their jobs, students boycott their classes, and shopkeepers put up their shutters. The International Settlement suffers the most, for the British are seen as the villains. Here in the French Concession we've had only a one-day shop closing, and life remains easier.

Most foreigners blame the trouble on a small handful of agitators, and are convinced it is they who keep the great majority of law-abiding Chinese from going back to work. No one forces the Chinese to live in the foreign settlements, after all; they do so of their own choice. Doesn't that show that they realize how much better conditions are here than in the Chinese city? Surely they must know that if we really packed up and went home—which is what the extremists are demanding—then they'd be left at the mercy of the warlords who've been ruining the country for the last ten years. Of course even in the settlements things aren't perfect, we admit; we're reasonable people, and we know that some changes have to come. But they must come peacefully, not because of threats and violence. Can't the Chinese see that?

So goes the tune that most of the foreigners sing. Ask them here about Chinese politics, and they'll tell you they know nothing and care nothing about them. As long as the wharf coolies work the ships, the women and children work the mills, as long as the boys bring us our drinks, Chinese politics are Chinese pidgin. What does it matter who runs the country? So long as they leave the settlements alone, today's General Wang is no worse than yesterday's General Yang. But the Kuomintang—ah, that's different now, with Borodin and his crowd of Bolsheviks down in Canton. Everyone knows they're behind this agitation. Have another drink, old man.

His Chinese teacher, Simon observed, had not gone on strike against him, and during those hot days of early summer had continued to show up every other day for a Chinese lesson. "An interesting man," Simon had noted when he'd first met Chu Hung-ying almost a year earlier, in August 1924, "with a handsome but mournful face, educated by the Jesuits at Aurora University, and now an accountant for Racine, the big French trading firm up on Peking Road. But he also writes occasionally for some of the more politically minded Chinese papers, and he moves in the kinds of circles that most foreigners here distrust: students, quondam students, young professors, intellectuals, many of them probably members of the Kuomintang, some of them perhaps even Communists."

Though Chu was the younger man, Simon knew enough of Chinese ways to respect the relationship between student and teacher, and they remained on formal terms with each other—"Mr. Chu" and "Lai *hsien-sheng*," or "Mr. Lai." Yet this had not prevented a friendship from springing up between them, and Simon had soon recognized Chu's value in giving him an opening through which he could get a glimpse of a particularly interesting aspect of the city's political subculture. That summer of 1925 they'd argued patiently about the bloodshed, the violence, the strikes—and about questions of responsibility.

Mr. Chu is honest enough to admit that not all their leaders are sorry for the blood that was spilled in Nanking Road.

But what good will bloodshed do? I ask. Don't the students see that they ought to be helping to rebuild their country rather than tearing it down?

"No one likes bloodshed," Mr. Chu responds, his face growing even more doleful, "but we Chinese have been passive too long. The West has its martyrs; perhaps China needs some too."

Think twice, I advise him. We've just been through a bloody and destructive war, and having almost been killed myself, I have no desire to be a martyr. Or to make martyrs of others. Anyway, China has never been governed by soldiers. Until recently, when she picked up bad habits from us.

Mr. Chu looks sadly at me, choosing his words carefully both because he is my teacher and because he wants to make sure I understand his point.

"Like all foreigners, Lai *hsien-sheng*," he tells me, "you read Confucius and you read Lao-tzu and you read the poets of the Tang dynasty. Then you think, of course, China has always been the way those books describe her, a country where harmony reigns between men and men, between men and nature." The picture evokes a Sung painting: gentle scholars seated in a secluded pavilion, taking a mournful delight in the cries of wild geese as autumn slowly makes its way down the mountains.

"But if you really look at our history," he continues, "you will see that it is not true. China's past is one of violence, of blood-shed, of the strong oppressing the weak. It is a record—we must admit it—it is a record of cannibalism."

The word startles me, and I say so. But it is not his, and he quotes a Chinese writer to me: "Every one of our histories re-peats the expression 'Humane feeling and virtue.' But if you read between the lines, you see that the whole volume has only two words—'Eat people.'"

The quotation, Matthew knew, came from Lu Hsün's "Diary of a Madman," a story that had been published in 1919, and in which it is the mad protagonist who, with the moral acuity of Lear's fool, has the clearest vision of the inner meaning of Chi-na's long past. Simon, patiently collecting information for his book, had recorded many such discussions with his Chinese teacher in those days, "sitting quietly," as he put it, "taking notes, interrupting only when I don't understand, a detached observer listening to what is being said. For much that he tells me cannot be found in the newspapers."

From Simon's reports of these conversations with the ac-countant who was also a Chinese teacher, there emerged a pic-ture of a man who must have stood at least on the fringes of the circle of radical students and young intellectuals, the men and women who had plotted the strategies of the great movement that spread from the Nanking Road shooting of 1925. At least he spoke with an authority that Simon took seriously, about the activities of the student and labor unions that summer, about the strains that developed among the leaders, partic-ularly between the activists (many of whom had been Com-munists, Matthew knew) and the Chinese businessmen of Shanghai, who wanted to turn the movement's outrage to their own purposes.

Mr. Chu says they don't like the strike [ran an entry of June 20th]. But since they can't stop it, they are going to try to use it for their own goals. They want a voice in governing the for-eign settlements, they want to sit with the taipans on the municipal councils of the French Concession and the Interna-tional Settlement. So they hope that the foreigners will be frightened enough by the demonstrations and the strikes to give way a little. Not to the revolutionary demands of the students and the demonstrators and the labor unions and the Kuomintang, of course, but only to them, the men of property and standing, who make reasonable requests.

Meanwhile the signs of violence are everywhere. In the days right after May 30 we saw more shooting, more deaths. Now the gray warships of the Powers—British, Japanese, American—lie off the Bund, their guns sheltering the banks and trading houses that stand above the harbor. Sailors and marines patrol the Settlement's streets, rifles at the ready, and the ugly armored cars of the Shanghai Volunteer Corps scuttle through the city, reminding everyone to whom this particular piece of Chinese territory really belongs.

It does not belong to me. This is not my country, not my city. I lay no claim to it, for here I am neither traveler nor tourist, but simply a visitor, with a visitor's detachment: one who looks through the window from the outside, trying patiently to record what he sees. But indoors the figures that are playing out this drama are real men and women, capable of real pain, real joy, and real hatred. Not simply those urbane scholars drinking wine in their pavilion set among the golden autumn mountains of an imaginary land seven centuries ago.

From Shanghai, the hot flame of fury ignited in Nanking Road had swept across the country, and day after day came in the stories of violence and rage from other cities. In Beijing, Simon wrote, a hundred thousand demonstrators had gathered outside the Tiananmen to shout their denunciations of imperialism, and there were similar rallies elsewhere, in Hankow, Nanking, Amoy, Chungking. But most terrifying of all was the outbreak in Canton, where foreign troops had killed more than fifty people marching in protest against the British. Meanwhile both the Chinese government and the foreign diplomats in Beijing sent their own teams of investigators to Shanghai to find out what had happened, and to try to patch up a peace so that the city could get back to business as usual. By late June, however, Simon noted that a good deal of the bite had gone out of the strike. "Every day the sun rises over Pootung to the east," he wrote, "drawing the damp out of the thousand stagnant creeks, ditches, and waterways of the Yangtze delta, and turning the heavy sky an oppressive yellow-white by noon. Summer's thick heat is here, a draining ordeal that does as much as the patrols of the police and the marines to bring a kind of sullen tranquillity to the city."

Yet neither side was willing to make concessions. Simon had recorded some conversations he'd had toward the end of June. This time they were with foreigners.

Eric Massingham, who's with Ilbert, the big British trading firm, told me the other day that things have been going from bad to worse ever since the Washington Conference three years ago, and that it was "you Americans," as he put it, who were to blame for making too many promises to the Chinese.

We sit in the dim coolness of the Shanghai Club's smoking room after lunch: green leather armchairs, tall oak bookshelves, three-month-old papers from Home—the *Spectator*, the *Illustrated London News*, the *Tatler*—lying scattered on the gleaming mahogany tables. Outside in the harbor, British and Japanese ships lie motionless under the burning afternoon sun, ensigns hanging limply from their flagstaffs in the still air. Their crews have walked off the job, and there is none of the usual commotion that comes from the tugs and lighters and sampans working their cargoes.

Massingham sits at ease, legs stretched out before him, digesting his meal. "A wonderful people, the Chinese," he says. His voice is rich, well fed, his collar unaffected by the damp heat, his striped tie impeccable. The smoke from his cigar spirals lazily upward toward the distant ceiling. "But they need a strong hand, mind you. Not this weak government in Peking that doesn't have the courage to stand up to the rabble-rousers. And we play along with it, your government and mine, leading the Chinese on with promises of new treaties, of handing back the concessions, putting foreigners under Chinese law. Someday, perhaps, but they're not ready for it yet."

He reminds me that he was here twenty-five years ago, in 1900, a young man just come to China in the middle of the Boxer Rebellion. "When you've been here as long as I have, old man . . ."

Massingham is a great friend of O. M. Green's, who edits the *North China Daily News*, and in his voice I hear the echo of that paper's contemptuous editorials. "Take all this talk of New China." He sits up and leans toward me, close enough that I can smell the lunchtime whiskey on his breath.

"Let me tell you this. There is no New China, old man. There's just old China, and the missionaries and the diplomats and the idealists aren't going to change what's been here for thousands of years. Too many of our people don't see that. Any more than they see that the Chinese are quite prepared to tear down everything we've built up here in Shanghai."

He leans back again, waiting for my response, ready to counter any argument I might make, disappointed, perhaps, when I don't rise to the bait. But I'm in no mood to argue with a man who has just given me lunch and who is as much an object of my study as the city of which he speaks. Anyway, he's right in a way. Shanghai's an extraordinary city, and newcomers never fail to be impressed when they come up the river for the first time and see the harbor full of ships, the massive buildings on the Bund, the motorcars and the trams. It almost looks like home; can this really be China? Then they find that they can dine every day on beefsteak washed down with claret rather than having to eat puppy dogs and bird's nest soup with chopsticks.

Seen from the streets of the foreign settlements, Shanghai is almost a new city. Since the war there has been building everywhere, from the immense banks and office blocks that are transforming the Bund and Szechwan Road into a replica of an English city, to the new apartment buildings on the avenue Joffre, to the hundreds of villas that spring up on Bubbling Well Road, the avenue Lafayette, or west of the Settlement out near Jessfield. All this gives a picture of a dynamism, a growth, that can be matched nowhere else in the world.

Yet to Mr. Chu and his friends, the sight of this new Shanghai stirs different emotions. "Think what it means for us who live here," he said to me the other day. "Think what it means to see these vast buildings, these banks, these shipping companies, these department stores. They are at once a sign of hope to us, and a sign of despair, because in our hearts we still think they exist only because of you foreigners."

Take another look, however—look carefully behind the façade of Shanghai as it is emerging today, look into some of the back alleys off the main streets. There you'll find elemental China: the poor, crowded together into filthy slums, the stench of sewage, wastes rotting in the sun. And the children with vacant eyes, the cripples, the beggars, with no hope, just as you would find them in a little provincial town in Hopei or Shansi, living the sort of life they have always known, a life still untouched by the twentieth century.

In Shanghai, a thousand observers tell us, China is meeting the modern age, learning from men like Massingham the ways of industry, of commerce, of science. All that is quite true. But Shanghai, with its modernity, with its trade, its factories, its universities, is built on a basis of special privilege enjoyed by the foreigners. Privilege granted by China in the treaties ("extorted," Mr. Chu would say, extorted when the Chinese were too weak to oppose it).

And indeed some of the privilege has no basis in the treaties. "Where in the treaties," François Verdier asked me the other day, "does it say we can maintain our volunteer militia?" He is a French vice-consul, one of the few men in Shanghai with which one can discuss matters other than business or sport. "Where does it say that we can land our sailors and marines? We do all these things and others because we have the gunboats and they have not." He looks around the room in which we sit. It is after dinner, and we are at the house of M. Freytag, a successful exporter of Chinese silks to Lyon. The doors are dark brown, paneled; the furniture heavy, Second Empire. On the wall, in an ornate golden frame, nymphs and shepherds disport themselves allegorically in a style popular forty years ago. I am reminded of the rooms of my childhood in Philadelphia; China might be on the other side of the world. Except for the street noises that come in through the windows, open to catch the air on this oppressive night.

I object: perhaps that's true of the French. Or the English and the Japanese. But America has never behaved that way.

Verdier raises an inquiring eye. "Why, Simon," he asks patiently, "do you live here in the French Concession and not in the Chinese city? Why are all those American warships moored off the Bund? Americans like to think they are not empire builders. But you Americans are in the game as much as anyone. A century ago you were selling opium to the Chinese, and today you sell other wares—and the ideas that encourage people to buy them." Look at your missionaries, he continues, with their schools, their universities, their Y.M.C.A.s, all of them devoted—to what? To religion? Perhaps. But also a kind of American political propaganda, a cultural propaganda. He smiles at me, a fellow conspirator, knowing that we agree. "A salesmanship not so different from that of the Ford Motor Company, *n'est-ce pas*, Simon?"

I concede the point, and I ask him why this summer the French Concession has been immune to the troubles that have overtaken the Settlement. Englishmen like Massingham are convinced it's because the French are pandering to the Chinese.

Verdier laughs. "We Frenchmen have our faults, Simon. But race prejudice is not one of them. At least as many Anglo-Saxons have it. Have you ever heard of a Frenchman kicking a rickshaw coolie? I don't think so. But I have seen an Englishman do it. Right on Nanking Road. And his companions, what did they do as they watched him? They laughed. And then, like the good fellows they were, they took him into the Palace Hotel to buy him a drink."

But we know this, he continues. If the Chinese are turning against the English today, your turn and our turn will come later. That is why we must try to save the Englishmen from the consequences of their own folly. Not because we love them. But simply to protect ourselves. So in public we stick together. "And that, Simon, is why you may not write what I have just told you in one of your articles. Not yet, at any rate."

CHAPTER THREE

Wednesday, May 31, 1989

Seventy years ago, when Simon Larsen had lived in the French Concession, Huaihai Road had been called the avenue Joffre. Both names evoke memories of war: that of the French commander who had first checked the German advance in 1914, and that of the great battle of early 1949 when the People's Liberation Army had broken the resistance of Chiang Kai-shek's troops and had opened the way to Shanghai. Other memories still float in the heavy summer air. Some are called up by the buildings that line the street: the Cathay Theater, whose 1930s modernism evokes the recollection of a thousand vanished movie houses in towns all across America; the pale blue or yellow stucco houses, shabby and neglected after half a century of war and revolution but that still leave hanging a faint echo of Provence or the Auvergne. Others have left no physical reminders of their presence: the thousands of White Russian refugees who had made this part of Shanghai their center after Lenin's revolution, lining the street with their shops, restaurants, cafés, and cabarets, talking endlessly, planning endlessly for the day they could return to their homeland.

It was a busy street then, and it is a busy street today, a street that has done well from Deng Xiaoping's reforms in recent years. The windows of the stores are filled with clothes and shoes, with cookpots and transistor radios, with electric fans and books. Walking is difficult, as it is everywhere in Shanghai, at least if you try to set your own stride; and Matthew, as he made his way to Bernard Hilding's hotel, found himself searching for the occasional openings that would suddenly appear, hurrying through them like a broken-field runner before they closed up again, trying to gain a few feet on the crowd drifting slowly along the sidewalks. The temptation is to seek freedom and to skirt the crowd by stepping down into the road itself, but the guardians of public order have anticipated you, and iron railings line the sidewalks to prevent such disruptions to authority. In any case, such a step might well be suicidal, thought Matthew; trucks and buses jumbled down the middle of the street, depending on their sheer size and the irritable shrieking of their horns to clear the way, leaving the sides of the road to the stream of bicycles and their trilling bells.

Hilding's hotel was a tall building of dark brown brick a block south of the Great World on Thibet Road. Designed by an architect trained in America, it was done in the style of the late twenties, capped by a Chinese green tiled roof, a genuflection toward the country's ancestral spirits. Inside the entrance, a clerk slumped behind the counter, chatting listlessly with a friend, while Taiwan pop moaned softly in the background. He perked up as Matthew approached: Xie Bona? Mr. Bernard Hilding? Yes, fourth floor. But you must walk up; *jintian dianti huaile,* the elevator's broken. Sorry. Actually it appeared less to have been broken than to have been commandeered by a group of workmen who were engaged, with no great success, in trying to fit a collection of pipes and plumbing fixtures into it for transport to the building's upper reaches. Matthew thought it a very Chinese scene—and then wondered what he meant by that.

Hilding turned out to look older than Matthew had expected, and thinner than he appeared in his photographs.

"Come in, Mr. Walker," he said. "Come in and sit down." The room was filled with books and papers, both English and Chinese. A small table served as a desk; on it sat an old Olivetti portable, with a sheet of paper, half covered with type, sticking up from it. "Sorry for the mess. I've been told I must write my memoirs, but I'm not very good at keeping things in order."

Matthew nodded. "I'm sure they'll be very interesting."

Hilding shrugged impatiently. "Not my idea, you understand. My family's. They want me to get everything down on paper. Probably afraid I'll forget it. But it's taking longer than I expected. Nothing wrong with my memory, whatever my family may think. It's just—" He paused. Matthew waited expectantly.

"It's just that it makes me wonder what sort of a past it is that finds its way into a book." He laughed. "Sorry. I shouldn't say that, should I? You study history, don't you?"

"I hope you don't stop," said Matthew. "After all, it's people like you who keep us historians going."

"But how do you make sense out of all these events so long ago? Everything seemed so clear then, but now, when I look back, so much has become murky, less definite. Sometimes I despair of explaining why I did what I did, or why I believed in what I did in those days. But at the time it all made sense, it was all so obviously right."

He cleared a pile of books off one of the chairs and motioned Matthew to sit down. "I don't know how much I can help you," he said. "I may be old, but I didn't come to China till the mid-thirties. Isn't that a bit later than you're interested in?" He looked at Matthew questioningly.

Matthew hurried to assure him he was very much interested. "Anything you can tell me about the city in those days would be very helpful."

They talked, Hilding rising from time to time to look for a book or some notes, or to pour more hot water from a thermos over the tea leaves in Matthew's cup. Listening to him, Matthew was impressed by the acuity of his memory, sharpened, no doubt, by the writing he'd been doing about his earlier life. Names, places, events, some new to Matthew, some familiar from his reading, came pouring out, drawing the picture of a young man whose surroundings had been his political schooling, driving him to the radicalism that was to color his life.

Finally it was Hilding who brought the conversation around to Simon Larsen. "Tell me more about him, then," he said. "I've been asking around a bit since you mentioned him in your letter, but I don't know that I'll be able to do you much good."

Matthew explained that Simon had first come to China almost seven decades earlier. A few years before that, a German bullet at Saint-Mihiel had brought his brief and involuntary mil-

"Yes," said Matthew. He felt he had to rise to Simon's defense. "But that's not why he came. He saw Shanghai as the political center of China. Labor unions, radical students. Communists, the Kuomintang. The new China being born. That sort of thing."

"Did he get involved?"

"No. At least I don't think so. But he started writing about what he saw. For magazines back in America." Matthew had run down a half-dozen or so pieces in obscure monthlies in New York and Chicago. But occasionally Simon had found a wider audience, and last winter Matthew had discovered a few articles in *Colliers* and the *Saturday Evening Post*. "Shanghai: City Forging China's Future" had been one of them.

"Where did he live?"

"Near here. In a flat on Ruijin Road—what was the route Père Robert in those days. He obviously had some money coming from home. Not much, probably. But enough to get by with his journalism. And he began to write another book. Not a novel this time. But a kind of a memoir. About what was going on here. Seen through the eyes of someone living in Shanghai. To explain it to the outside world. He never finished it. But he was going to call it *Typhoon Over Shanghai*." He smiled, as if apologizing for Simon's rather melodramatic title.

Hilding grunted, looking at him skeptically. "Good luck to him," he said. "To anyone who tries to explain China to the outside world."

"But he never went home for a visit, though his family wanted him to. And then he vanished. Utterly vanished."

"Lots of people vanished in 1927," Hilding broke in. "That was the year Shanghai went over to the revolution. Before Chiang Kai-shek and his gangster friends turned on the workers who had liberated the city. The unlucky ones were killed, and the lucky had to go into hiding."

"I know," said Matthew. "But it was Chinese, not foreigners, who were usually the victims."

"Still, it was easy to disappear in China in those days," said Hilding. "Much easier than it is now." His voice still had a trace of the Midlands in it. "There might be all kinds of explanations. Bandits, for instance. They might have taken him for ransom and then discovered that trying to get the money was too dangerous. Safer to kill him. Things like that did happen back then."

itary career to an end shortly before the armistice (
his time on the western front had come a brief no
Ridge, begun in the trenches and finished in a Su
Very much in the mode of Wilfred Owen and Sieg
it appeared in 1920, was flatteringly noticed by the
ics and totally ignored by an American public tir
already caught up in the joys of peace, prosperit
market. Restless, eager to continue writing, and
money to give him independence at least for a few
bid good-bye to his family in Philadelphia and sail
East.

For the first two years he had lived in Beijing, j
group of foreign expatriates, who in those days
ghosts haunting the old imperial capital, where ca
passed under the great gray city walls, somethin
grandeur that earlier had drawn Henry James's (
to Rome or Florence. There he had prowled arc
monuments, tasted its food, observed its seasons,
smells, and its colors. Drawn by his surroundings,
to learn Chinese, supporting himself by occasic
English at one of the city's missionary universiti

"He began writing another novel," said Matth
to. Something about Beijing at the turn of the
time of the old dowager."

"But he never finished?"

"No. Apparently the book just wouldn't come.
want to turn into just another expatriate living in
I think he also found Beijing too much cut off f
China. From what was really going on in other

"He wasn't the first person to make that com
made a wry face. "Nor the last."

"And he got interested in politics. From his i
probably."

"So that's when he went to Shanghai?"

"Yes. In early 1923."

"Shanghai was a good place to be in those yea

"For foreigners, anyway. Cheap living, lots (
chance to make a fortune. And above all, safet
wars." A censorious note had slipped into Hildin
still like that when I arrived a dozen years late
blew it all to hell in '37."

"Perhaps," said Matthew. "In any case, his family turned heaven and earth trying to find him. They were rich, well connected. His father had been a lawyer in one of the big Philadelphia firms. They went to the State Department, and the State Department told the consul in Shanghai to investigate. Which he did. But he never turned up anything. The family had the sense the French authorities were stonewalling. There were rumors. One was that he died of cholera and the officials hushed it up. Another was that he'd been caught in a shootout between Chiang's troops and the Communists. Or that he'd gone back north to Beijing or south to Canton. Two years later, after there was no word from him, his family held a memorial service in Philadelphia, and that marked an end of it."

"But now you think you have something more to go on?"

"Lots more. But nothing that helps to explain his disappearance. A few months ago his younger sister died—she was well over eighty—and when her family was cleaning out the house, they found his papers in a trunk in the attic. Letters to his family, to friends. The draft of most of his book. And a journal. Or part of it, anyway. I guess they'd been sent home after he disappeared. Apparently no one had paid much attention to them since they'd given him up for lost, and they'd been sitting for all these years in Aunt Kate's house."

"Aunt Kate? So Larsen was your relative?"

"No. He was the great-uncle of my—of a friend, a woman I know in the States. She knew I was working on Shanghai, and put me on to the papers."

"But they don't tell you anything? About where he might have gone, I mean?"

"No. The journal stops at the end of February 1927. About three weeks before the Nationalists took Shanghai. But we know that he was still alive as late as the second week in April that year."

"So it was just about the time Chiang Kai-shek purged the Communists that he disappeared?"

Matthew nodded.

"But the journal doesn't suggest any reason why he might have wanted to drop out of sight?"

"Not yet, anyway. Of course I just got the papers a few months ago, and I've only had time to give them a quick reading. So I've brought along photocopies of the journal—and the book, as far as he'd written it. They're very detailed in some places. The journal was obviously raw material for the book. Sometimes the book repeats it word for word."

Hilding looked thoughtful. From the hall came the noise of someone hammering on hollow metal. He got up, walked around the room looking for a match to light his pipe. "All that's very interesting." Having found a match, he paused to strike it, sending a little cloud of blue smoke into the stale air. "Why do you want to find all this out, may I ask? Are you writing his life?"

"No, not that. I'm writing about the city. Larsen's just a side-show. But he's telling me a lot about what it must have been like in those days. And somehow I think that if I could find out what happened to him, I might learn even more." He laughed. "Anyway, I promised this friend of mine—this woman who's related to him—that I'd try to find out what happened." But Hilding's question had made him vaguely uncomfortable. How much time could he afford to spend chasing down Simon's mystery when there was more important work to be done?

Hilding looked at him. "Very interesting. But as I said, I didn't come to China till about seven or eight years after all that happened."

"Larsen wasn't famous, of course," Matthew continued. "But he had a lot of friends. I know a good deal's happened in Shanghai since he was here, and that it's going to be hard to pick up the traces. But I'm hoping that somewhere in this city there may be some record of him. Old newspapers, perhaps. Old Chinese records, Kuomintang, communist. I know he was interested in investigating the drug trade. Maybe I could find out something about the Green Gang." The Green Gang had dominated the Shanghai underworld between the wars, largely monopolizing the city's illegal opium traffic.

"The Green Gang's still a touchy subject here in Shanghai." Hilding gave a wry smile. "Not all the old gangsters fled to Taiwan or Hong Kong like Tu Yüeh-sheng." Tu Yüeh-sheng had risen to become the Green Gang's boss in those years, controlling much of the city's criminal activity. "Some of them stayed right here in Shanghai. A few even joined the Communist Party, and won't be too happy at the thought of someone looking into their past." He paused. "D'you know, last year there was a series of television programs on the Green Gang? And halfway through, in the middle of the series, they were canceled. Taken off the air. Why d'you suppose that was?" He was quiet for a minute, and then rose. "I don't know that I can do much. But I may be able to help. Telephone me tomorrow afternoon. And now you must be hungry. The restaurant on the top floor's not bad. Why don't we have some lunch?"

Over the meal, Hilding had talked about his own life in China. He was, Matthew gathered, distrustful of the new course that the country had undertaken in recent years, still maintaining something of a loyalty to Mao Tse-tung as he'd first known him.

"I even spent some time in jail myself," he said. "During the Cultural Revolution. Did you know that, eh? But I blame it on the Gang of Four. Not Mao."

"I'd heard about it," Matthew said cautiously. He didn't want to interrupt the flow of words.

"I know that some terrible things took place during those years," Hilding went on. "Things that I was too blind to see. Or didn't want to see, or at least didn't want the outside world to know, since they'd be used against the revolution. But Mao at his best could be a man of extraordinary honesty. And he had a vision of the world in which everyone would be equal. It was a real inspiration to me. Today's leaders aren't the same. They're bureaucrats, and when a Communist becomes a bureaucrat, the revolution's dead. Going backward. Take Li Peng, the premier— there's too much of the smell of Stalin about him, and I remember the comrades I lost to Stalin. Or Yang Shangkun, the president. He's too busy making sure that his relatives are in positions where they can run the army. Mao would never have allowed people like that around him."

Mao also had liked his cronies around him, thought Matthew. But he kept his mouth shut. At the next table four men talked rapidly in Shanghainese, pausing only to drink loudly from bowls of soup. The remains of a meal littered the plastic tabletop. Through the open windows came the noise of the city, seven stories below. A waitress arrived, bringing them dishes of spiced pork and greens, and two small bowls of rice.

"What do you want to drink?" asked Hilding. "Beer, eh? It's the safest." Matthew nodded, and the Englishman gave the order. Then he went on.

"Every day, more stories about corruption—in Beijing, in the provinces, in cities like Shanghai, in the countryside. Not just rumor either. It's in the papers, on the television. And it's not always about money. It's about connections. You find me what I need to run my factory, and I'll find a way to help your son get into the university or the technical school that will set him up for life. It's the same with students going abroad: their families save up money, and then find they have to spend most of it getting permission from all the right offices to leave the country."

That spring his daughter had come to visit him from England. She was just twenty-one, born in 1968. Not a good year to be coming into the world in China, thought Matthew. The Red Guards had been on the rampage, taking over universities, government offices, newspapers, factories. And the hospitals.

"My wife was the daughter of a Kuomintang official who'd gone to Taiwan in forty-nine," said Hilding. "And I think they held that against her when she went to the hospital for her delivery. So that they didn't give her proper care."

She'd died. But the girl survived—Mary, she'd been named, Meili in Chinese. "I didn't know what to do with her. On the one hand, I wanted to keep her with me. But by 1969 I could see that things were starting to go wrong. I'd been very active in the Cultural Revolution myself, with a lot of my friends. Then they started being rounded up, sent down to the countryside— all of them accused of being ultraleftists. Even foreigners weren't safe."

"Was that before you were arrested?"

"Yes. All through those years I'd hung on to my British passport. And now it paid off. In 1970 I arranged to send Mary home to my sister in England. Just in time, because a few months later I was in a jail cell myself."

"So Mary grew up in England?"

"Yes—grew up, and now she's at the university. In Leeds. But she's been here this year. At Fudan. Come to study Chinese. She looks completely Chinese, of course." He laughed. "So she's always embarrassed when people speak to her, assume she can understand them. Then they discover she's foreign."

"So she's here now? In Shanghai?"

"She was until a couple of weeks ago. Then she went up to Beijing with some of her friends. To join the demonstrations in Tiananmen Square. I didn't want her to go, but she was all caught up in the enthusiasm of the movement, and told me not to worry. Now one of the friends she went with seems to have become one of the movement's leaders. Liu Meihua. Maybe you've seen her picture on television? Back in the States?"

Matthew, drowsy from the food and the beer, didn't recognize the name. "No," he said. "I don't think so." He watched a fly crawling slowly up the dingy green wall behind Hilding's head.

"A lot of what the students want is right, of course," Hilding went on. "And of course it's not only the students. Now it's lots of workers, even government employees and the police, reporters for the *People's Daily* and the television. But they're pushing their luck too far. The government was humiliated—absolutely humiliated—when Gorbachev arrived three weeks ago. Reconciliation with the Soviet Union—Deng Xiaoping wanted that to be his great achievement. They had enormous plans to greet him. Right there in Tiananmen Square. It didn't work. The students took over the square, and Deng's people had to cobble together a quick ceremony at the airport, drive Gorbachev into town almost in secret, and bring him into the Great Hall of the People through the back door. Deng's a proud man, and he's not going to tolerate that."

"At home the papers were saying that the army and police won't move against the protesters."

"I don't know what the army is doing. It's very strange. Thirteen years ago, in the spring of 1976, there were big demonstrations in Tiananmen Square. Supposedly to honor Chou En-lai, who had died that winter. But it turned into a demonstration against the Gang of Four."

And against Mao, Matthew thought, but said nothing.

"That time it was the *gong'an*, the public security forces, that moved in, not the army. There's an old slogan, goes back to the days of the war against Japan. 'Chinese don't fight Chinese.' It was supposed to shame Chiang Kai-shek's troops into not attacking the Communists. There's a lot of that spirit still alive in the army; they don't want to use their arms against civilians."

"Have you heard from your daughter?" asked Matthew.

"She called me several days ago, told me about life in the square. There's a lot of spirit there and a lot of courage. But the regime declared martial law on May 19, you know. Everyone thought that the army was going to come in last week, and the demonstrators decided to wait for them. They collected towels,

cloths, buckets of water, to protect themselves against the tear
gas attacks they expected. Mary found it an extraordinary experience. Half of them were terrified, and really wanted to leave.
Most of the others were undecided. But there was a group that
kept them there, telling them that the army would never turn on
the people, that the army commanders and the police were on
their side. And that they had to be ready to sacrifice themselves
for China's future. They sat there all night, waiting. And then
nothing happened. Absolutely nothing." He described his daughter's wonder at the coming of dawn, the early sunlight slanting
down Chang'an Boulevard into the square, where she and her
comrades looked around at one another, surprised still to be
there, alive and welcoming the new day that was beginning.
Then the surprise changed to joy as they realized that either the
troops had refused to move or the leaders had never given the orders. It didn't matter which, for it meant that the army would
never be used against the people. What mattered was that they
had won. All the posters proclaiming people's power, proclaiming
the advent of democracy, really meant something. They had won
the hearts and minds not only of the ordinary citizens of Beijing,
but of the government, the army, as well.

"Have they won?" asked Matthew.

"I don't like it. You don't win a victory like that simply with
slogans. It's meant another humiliation for the leadership. They
can't make a threat like that and then not carry it out without
taking the consequences."

"It must be very worrying," said Matthew. He wished he could
say something more helpful, or at least more intelligent.

"It is," said the Englishman. "I don't mind telling you. But,
you know, I'm also very proud of her, what she's doing with her
friends. If I were her age, I'd probably be doing the same thing.
But I'm not, so I wish she'd come home." He leaned back, lit a
cigarette, and stared thoughtfully at the ceiling.

After the meal was over, and Matthew had made his farewells,
he walked north up Thibet Road, past the Great World, still sur-
mounted by the extraordinary spire that Simon had noted, to
People's Square, a vast open waste of asphalt in the heart of the
city which had once been a racecourse. Twenty years ago and
more, he knew, when Shanghai had been more radical than
Beijing itself, hundreds of thousands of Red Guards had filled
this space, all wearing identical armbands, shouting identical slo-

gans of praise for the leadership of the Chairman, waving identical copies of the Chairman's quotations. In 1986, however, when he'd first come to Shanghai, Matthew had seen there a very different kind of demonstration. That autumn, thousands of students had taken to the streets demanding more freedoms, and an end to the rigid ideological indoctrination that still infused so much of their studies and governed so much of their lives. Matthew had watched the rallies, had talked to the students who had joined them, and had shared their sharp disappointment when Jiang Zemin, the city's mayor, had cracked down, peremptorily ordering the demonstrators back to their classes and their dormitories, warning that the masses of Shanghai would tolerate no disorder.

Though the brief movement had collapsed, its discontents had not been dealt with, and had flared up in a far larger form this spring. The demonstrations, begun in mid-April, had spread beyond Beijing, and in Shanghai they had reached a climax only about ten days ago, during Mikhail Gorbachev's flying visit to the city. Matthew, getting ready for his trip, had read of the tens of thousands of students and others who had poured into the streets here, to welcome the man they saw as living proof that a communist leader could guide his nation and his people toward openness and democracy. Even today the parades were continuing; right here in People's Square, Matthew saw a straggling line of young men and women, posters and banners held high above their heads, calling on their leaders to follow the Soviet example of *glasnost*. It all looked very friendly, he thought; if there were signs attacking official corruption, there were also many professing the students' love of their country and the Party that was guiding it to a brilliant future. Obviously the demonstrators were determined this time not to give the leaders any excuse to crack down on them again.

He watched them for a while, and then walked slowly home.

When he had first started reading Simon's papers, Matthew hadn't paid much attention to the personal revelations that he'd discovered in them. As he'd told Hilding, as he had to keep reminding himself, he wasn't writing the man's biography after all, but simply using him as a window through which to look into a particular place at a particular time. Simon, the impersonal observer and recorder of Shanghai and its ways, had been of more interest to him than Simon the individual, a man with his own particular combination of strengths and weaknesses, satisfactions, desires, and frustrations. Yet as time went on, Matthew found himself wanting to know more about this private Simon, this Simon the individual. It was partly—but only partly— because he occasionally wondered whether that private life might somehow be tied to Simon's disappearance. But now the desire came mostly from a natural human curiosity (and, of course, his own wish to solve the mystery, tie it up neatly, and present it to Laura as a trophy of the summer's hunt). Through his memoirs and his journal, through his observations and reactions to what was taking place around him, Simon was emerging as a human being in a world that Matthew had hitherto discovered only from impersonal sources: the yellowing newspapers, the economic and political reports, the diplomatic dispatches, and the other documents that make up the stuff of so much of the historian's world.

And, as he was now beginning to realize, an understanding of Simon the individual would help him better to read those other observations and analyses of the city and the society in which he had lived. *Typhoon Over Shanghai* was, for the most part, silent about the personal side of Simon's affairs. The journal, however, was different. Sometimes it was no more than a record of names, dates, notes of conversations. Sometimes it was far fuller, the pages carefully typed out, obviously rewritten from an earlier draft, where Simon had set down his ideas before putting them into his book. And very occasionally Simon would engage in a bout of what was almost confessional writing, setting forth details of his private life. Usually in longhand, these were sometimes hard to decipher, and Matthew had found some of them extraordinary, almost embarrassing in what they revealed.

Not so Laura, however, after she'd read some of the passages he'd shown her. "It's obvious," she said. "He was going to write another novel."

"Out of this? Some of it's pretty personal." He couldn't imagine exposing himself in such a way.

"He'd already written one novel about his experiences in the war. This one was going to be autobiographical about—oh, I don't know. Probing the human psyche, perhaps. His psyche, anyway. He'd have disguised himself, of course. Anyway, that's what I think he's doing."

One passage in particular had struck Matthew at the time. It came from late 1924.

> Impossible to describe—like passing over a threshold, perhaps, or entering a country that's new, uncharted, a country in which you follow a compass of your own devising. A fresh land, opening to you, first glimpsed in that smooth oval face, eyes wide under the soft black hair, whether long, in the old style of the courtesan, or bobbed in the modern fashion. Unmapped, its very topography, with its hills & valleys, invites exploration, calling you to make a journey deep into the interior. And once the voyage begins, while the landscape may at first recall others you have known, before long you realize you've crossed a frontier beyond which all the old rules of navigation fall away, and, with your compass now pointing to a different pole, you are led to the land's remote places, the secret palaces & hidden gardens that lie concealed in its innermost recesses.

When he'd first read it, he'd been thoroughly shocked. Not at the sexuality, of course, which he took for granted. But at the way in which it had seemed to reflect a side of Simon that he'd have preferred not to find. Clearly Simon was talking about an encounter with a Chinese woman, and was doing so in a way that seemed to modern eyes almost exploitative in its nature. Laura had shown him an unflattering passage in one of the books she'd been using in her work. "The eroticizing of the colonial landscape," the author had pointed out disdainfully (she was referring to Flaubert's Oriental travels), "is a typical feature of such discourse, valorizing the projection of a male sexual fantasy onto the Other, in which the colonized land is taken and penetrated, reduced from an aspect of humanity with its own signification to an It whose only purpose is the colonist's use."

Somehow that characterization didn't seem to fit with what Matthew knew of the man, and he wondered vaguely what Simon would have made of such a stricture. He'd been good-looking, apparently—Laura had dug up an old photograph of him, sent home from China and placed in a family scrapbook, showing him with a white scarf around his neck, a cigarette dangling from his lip, and doing something with his hands—Matthew couldn't make out what. "He looks like Robert Redford playing André Malraux playing an aviator in the Spanish civil war," he'd said. Laura had laughed, and warned him to be respectful of her family. But there must have been certain women in Shanghai's foreign circles who would have seen such a bachelor as a good catch. One of them appeared in a handwritten entry of May 15, 1925.

Rhonda telephoned again last night—why haven't I come to see her for so long? So long! Only a week, ten days at most, & besides, I know I'm not the only visitor at that little Mediterranean villa off the route des Soeurs. Not that she's ever said anything, but recently I've found unmistakable signs of the presence of others: a crumpled pack of Chesterfields (R. smokes Balkan Sobranie); a man's shirt, recently laundered & ironed, hanging in her closet (!)—and once, a safety razor in the bathroom. For a woman as excessively careful as R., the existence of these small memorabilia—trophies?—is hard to fathom. An appeal to some presumed sense of masculine jealousy? But my discovery of these little evidences of other conquests only convinces me the time has come to go our separate ways. I no longer fit into whatever vision she may have of her life. Nor she in mine.

Another entry, a week later, spoke of a growing impatience with the affair.

I was lonely, as was she; even here in Shanghai the life of a divorced woman's not easy, & ever since she left her sailor husband, Lt. John Sexton, R.N., many of her old friends snub her, take his side against her. R. says it's only because she used to have a little fling now and then—to get the sorts of satisfactions her husband couldn't provide her—or, she suggests, didn't have the tastes for. Some of my friends warned me in that jocular way that men use among themselves to conceal embarrassment: she had a certain reputation, old man, even when she was married to that stick of a husband of hers. Here in Shanghai you don't want to run the risk of being trapped by someone like that—if you have certain needs, I know where to find some nice Russian girls, very clean, very discreet—& you know, some of the Chinese aren't bad at all. And so on.

But I wanted more than that—companionship, intelligence, a certain spirit. R.'s had a wide experience, & I've learned a lot. But I can't be her pupil forever, & have reached a point where I can now learn more beyond the walls of the schoolhouse.

Neither Laura nor her family could shed any more light on Rhonda, and Matthew could conclude only that she'd been the sort of woman who in those days would have been called an adventuress: a divorcée, perhaps of uncertain years, moving from one affair to another before the fires of spring had entirely burned themselves out.

Yet there had been, according to a piece of folklore in Laura's family, another woman in Simon's life, someone who'd been close to him, had even seen him the day before he'd vanished. Laura herself knew little of the story, and her mother wasn't much more help. But Matthew, on reading the private journal, concluded that it must have had to do with Emily Ransom. Not only was she quite different from the women he'd known before, but the manner in which he'd first met her was unusual. Though the account came from his journal, it was typed, obviously after being written and rewritten with some care, and Matthew guessed that parts of it, suitably edited, might eventually have made their way into *Typhoon*.

Saturday, July 18, 1925

I sat in the Broadway Bar again late yesterday afternoon with Rogers of the *Shanghai Mercury*, the heavy air blue with cigar smoke, stirred up occasionally by a languid electric fan. As usual, he looked unaffected by the heat. He's a small man, with bright eyes, one of which somehow seems set higher than the other, giving his face a quizzical and unbalanced aspect, the look of a skeptical questioner. Not a bad point in a reporter, perhaps. Unlike the others of his craft, Rogers is always well turned out, and today he was wearing a light tan tropical suit with a sharp crease in his trousers, a bright red necktie, and a white handkerchief neatly folded in his breast pocket. A bookmaker, you'd think him, or a gambler—but the sort of gambler you'd be tempted to trust, to confide in.

I bought him a couple of drinks, and he opened up, telling me what's been going on that the papers don't say, making guesses about what's going to happen. About how the Bolsheviks are using the troubles here this summer to build up their strength. And about how some of their allies are beginning to worry because the Reds are getting just a little bit too strong.

"They can't go on together much longer," he told me. "Give them a year or two. Then the Reds and the Kuomintang will be at each other's throats. Just two more bloody-minded rivals fighting over the body of this wretched country."

We talked about what was happening, how all this would affect Shanghai. Rogers doesn't have much use for the Shanghai Municipal Council, or its American chairman, Stanfield Frothingham. "He's only there because the British know it looks good to have an American at the head, and because they know they can trust him to do their work for them. That's why he's been blocking every movement for change this summer. He's got the taipans behind him, he's got the British consul behind him. So he stands firm. Nothing's going to happen, because the British don't want it to happen."

Much of this is clear to anyone who reads between the lines in the local press, but I was grateful to him for filling in the gaps. It was getting late by then, so I rose to go, signing the usual chit to pay for the drinks. I said good night to him, and left him to make his way over to another table, where a game of poker had started. Outside, it was already getting dark—though Shanghai's not in the tropics, it's close enough so that you miss the long summer evenings of the north. Across the Garden Bridge, the offices along the Bund had closed for the night, and only the North China Building and the Palace Hotel next door were still brightly lit. Opposite the British consulate, the Public Gardens were beginning to fill up with people looking for a breeze off the river to break the day's heat.

Then, turning down into Foochow Road, I heard voices shouting in what sounded like an argument. Nothing unusual in that, for the Shanghainese can't seem to live without noise. The center of attraction was a rickshaw and its passengers—two foreign women, one young and one older. The rickshaw coolie was complaining that they hadn't paid enough, and the crowd beginning to collect around them was obviously very much on his side. Students, many of them were by the look of them, and several of them were egging him on, shouting the kinds of slogans that have become common in the last few weeks: "Down with British imperialism!" "Chinese will no longer be foreign slaves!"

I elbowed my way through the crowd to see if I could help, for no white man could leave two women of his own race alone to face a Chinese mob. The elder woman looked puzzled and rather frightened. They'd agreed on a fare before they started, she told me, or thought they had. But now the man seemed to want more, and they didn't know what to do.

I tried to talk to him but found it impossible. He spoke in the thick dialect of Su-pei, the region north of the Yangtze, where so many of Shanghai's poorest and most desperate workers come from. A hungry peasant in a city where he didn't belong, which he didn't understand, he looked as if he knew he must now fight to stay alive. A couple of the students were eager enough to translate into Mandarin and broken English for me, adding insults as they did so: "This man's very poor, he works very hard on a hot night to pull two ladies—too fat ladies, very heavy!—all the way from Bubbling Well Road. And now they won't pay him what they owe."

Neither of the women was fat, and, as it happened, what they had agreed to pay was already twice the normal fare for the trip. Now the coolie was demanding double that. I held out the fare, telling him to take it and be gone. He coughed, the long, racking cough of the poor that's so common here, bending over and spitting on the ground. Meanwhile, the crowd was growing angrier, though they kept their voices down, not wanting to attract the attention of the police. I turned to face the young man who was making the greatest nuisance, and advanced on him, fists clenched in what I hoped was a menacing attitude, though by this time I was rather worried myself, for you can never tell how a Chinese crowd is going to behave. It was all over, I said, time to go home. More insults: "*Yang-kuei-tzu!* foreign devils! capitalist turtles!" But the threat worked, and in the end I paid the coolie what his passengers had agreed on in the beginning. We left the crowd muttering angrily behind us as we walked away, heading toward the safety of the American Club in the next block. When I turned around to look back, the crowd had broken up. But there stood the coolie alone under a streetlamp, and the look of pain and hatred on his face is one that I shall never forget.

By the time I got home, I was furious with myself as well, for by then I'd cooled down a bit and realized that I'd behaved exactly like the kind of Shanghailander I can't abide. I poured myself a whiskey and went to bed, but as I tried to drop off to sleep, I kept seeing the thin face of the rickshaw coolie before me, glistening with sweat, his awkward words punctuated by that frightening cough. Poor fellow, he's probably tubercular, as so many of them are, and within a few years the strain of his work will get to him. Then one cold winter morning he'll be simply another nameless body picked up from the banks of the Soochow Creek or in a back alley of the Chapei slums. But I didn't think of that when I was arguing with him yesterday; I didn't think of the misery of his existence. All I thought of was his infernal cheek in trying to hold up a couple of white women, so that while I didn't kick him (as many would have done), I had lost my temper, had threatened him, and had threatened the ringleaders in the crowd who had taken his side. Not that I had anything to threaten them with, except my physical presence as a white man. But here in Shanghai, that's enough, of course. And yesterday evening it seemed right and natural, the chivalrous thing to do. This morning, it seems like mindless brutality.

In that somewhat melodramatic way, Simon Larsen had met Emily Ransom. Just graduated from college that spring, she had come to Shanghai with her mother to visit John Ransom, her uncle (Matthew recognized the name as one of the representatives of Standard Oil). "I know him slightly, but have never taken to him," wrote Simon two days after this episode.

> There's a kind of American you meet abroad, in places like Havana or Manila or Panama. Or Shanghai. And Ransom's one of them. At home he'd be a lawyer, or perhaps a banker, in upstate New York—a pillar of the community, a member of the Rotary, devoted to hard work and keeping up the standards of his town, holding a position that matches his abilities. But Shanghai's altogether different from upstate New York, and like so many others, Ransom has attained heights here he could

never have hoped for at home. So he has the manner of a man who has risen into a more elevated sphere than his abilities justify, and you have the feeling, when you talk to him, that he knows it, he knows that you know it, and that the two of you are never quite sure how long he can continue to get away with it. But the world—Shanghai's world, at any rate—thinks well enough of him, and he's spoken of as one of the coming leaders of the American community here, a man who one day will probably be nominated for one of the American seats on the Municipal Council.

Presumably out of gratitude for his intervention on Foochow Road, Ransom had shortly thereafter invited Simon to a gathering at his house, one of the large villas in the western reaches of Bubbling Well Road. A typical Shanghai affair of its kind, Simon found it, "the house all lit up, Japanese lanterns hanging from the trees in the garden, a Filipino dance band playing 'Dardanella' in the background, and the usual caucus of busy houseboys in white jackets scurrying around with trays of drinks and food. Whatever the troubles of the summer, social life must go on."

And there, of course, had been the charming Emily, being introduced by her uncle to Shanghai's eligible bachelors: a cluster of young white-uniformed naval officers from the warships in the harbor, junior members of foreign trading houses and banks and law firms, a few of the more presentable missionaries, and a vice-consul or two. She'd caught Simon's eye across the room, sending him a silent plea for rescue, and he'd come over in answer, moving to her side and managing to detach her from a partner who'd been boring her with stories about his service that summer in the Shanghai Volunteer Corps, the Settlement's foreign militia.

She thanked me for coming to her deliverance: are all men here in Shanghai like that? motioning toward the departing figure of Jim Henderson. Surely you're not. Of course I was flattered. Who wouldn't be? I've no wish to be considered an example of the genus Shanghailander, always nattering on about the natives and their shortcomings. Besides, she looked stunning, dressed in a simple white frock, her arms bare on a hot July night, and her face framed by bobbed fair hair, with a freshness that brought back memories of the girls I've known at home.

Though a newcomer, she mercifully does not start out by judging China, thank heavens, as so many others do, according to the standards of America. She told me, with a look of great seriousness, that she knew China to be an old and proud country, from which we no doubt had much to learn. It's an uncommon enough view here, and I teased her: fresh out of Bryn Mawr, and all her American ideals still intact. Yet as we talked, it soon became clear that there are some Chinese customs she's quite ready to question. Footbinding: do they still do that to girls? Not here in Shanghai, I assure her; we're far too modern. But yes, out in the villages, or in the upcountry towns. And even here in Shanghai most girls still have their marriages arranged for them by their parents, and never see their husbands until the wedding day.

I don't see why they stand for it, she told me. I reminded her that the Chinese have done things that way for thousands of years. For the Chinese, marriage is not simply a matter of two people falling in love. It's a contractual arrangement, and a successful marriage is one from which the two families stand to benefit.

Such things appall her. Yet she doesn't want to seem the bossy American telling the Chinese how to behave. Even in her short time in Shanghai, she's seen enough of that sort of behavior to dislike it.

I fetched her a drink from one of the scurrying houseboys. Though she comes from the land of Prohibition, she took it without demur, letting me know that such things are not new to her. We talked, we danced together, I told her about my life here, what I do, about the book I'm writing. Was I trying to impress her? Perhaps. At all events, I was pleased and flattered when she asked me to show her Shanghai. Real Shanghai, not the Shanghai of the tourists, she told me (how often have I heard that phrase!). And to meet real Chinese; since coming here, she's talked to none but her uncle's houseboy and the amah. So I've promised to introduce her to some of my friends, but warned her that she mustn't think them the real China. They're mostly university graduates—what the Chinese call *chih-shih fen-tzu*, intellectuals, a word that doesn't go over very well with Americans. She's not put off by it, however: I'm a

Bryn Mawr graduate, she reminds me with a beguiling smile, and thus a certified bluestocking.

Then her uncle came up and carried her off to meet some other people. Had Emily's smile been too beguiling, and did he think, perhaps, that we'd been together long enough? I stayed another half hour or so, for the sake of politeness, and then made my farewells and came home.

Thursday, June 1, 1989

Matthew woke the next morning to find the sun shining through a screen of high clouds that seemed to merge indistinguishably with the hazy smog that promised a hot day. At eight o'clock the television set brought in the evening news from New York, twelve time zones away, images of Tiananmen Square bouncing by satellite halfway round the world and back, swimming slowly into focus on the screen, a reporter describing the continuing standoff between the demonstrators and the government. But now there was something new to talk about, for two days ago—the same day he'd arrived in Shanghai—the students had brought into the square a thirty-foot-high white Styrofoam statue of a figure they had dubbed the Goddess of Liberty. There she stood in the sunlight, her hair streaming in the wind, arms outstretched before her, an extraordinary counterpoint to the Stalinist architecture of the square, to the great granite shaft of the Monument to the People's Heroes, to the huge portrait of Mao Tse-tung hanging on the Gate of Heavenly Peace at the entrance to the old Forbidden City. If Li Peng's armies wanted to tear her down, they were going to have to do it in front of the world's television cameras. Cameras like those that now closed in on two young men and a woman, leaders of the demonstration who looked tired but jubilant, and who left no doubt that they knew precisely what they had done in challenging the Party's authority and its prestige. Clearly the movement still had some life left in it, and Matthew wondered, a little uneasily, how the rulers would respond to this defiance.

That morning he had an appointment at the institute to meet Wang Baozhen. A professor at Fudan University, she was a specialist in the early history of the Communist Party, when Shanghai had been its headquarters, and when for a few years the city had been the hope of the Chinese revolution. A sensitive subject, as Matthew knew, for the Party is determined to control the vision of its own past, and he knew that it must have taken a certain adroitness on her part to make certain that the orthodoxy she embraced one year would not become the heresy of the next. "You'll like her," Zhao Shanling had told him. "She has done some interesting work."

"I know. I've read some of it." He didn't bother to add that he'd found it thorough, but highly conventional, in its approach to the Party's history.

"Yes," said Zhao. Then, after a pause, "Probably now she will have more to tell you." His voice had trailed off into near silence, suggesting that not everything that she carried around in her head could or would find its way onto paper.

"Come in, Mr. Walker," she said when they met that morning. They were back in the room with the overstuffed armchairs and the stained antimacassars, the battered blue thermos of hot water, and the china teacups with their lids. Through the open windows came the din of Szechwan Road, with its never-ending traffic jam, its blaring horns, its smell of smoke and dust in the hot morning air. "The director says we can talk in here. *Tamen dou kai hui*—this morning they're all holding a meeting, so they won't bother us."

Wang Baozhen was a woman of about sixty, with a plump, pale face and short black hair going silver. A woman who has made a place for herself in a man's world, thought Matthew: purposeful, no-nonsense, deliberate in her movements, and careful in her choice of words. She had about her the look of a survivor, the same toughness of mind and spirit that reminded him of old White Russians he'd met in New York, or old Jews who'd outlasted the German camps, seemingly through sheer will and force of character. No doubt, like so many of her generation, she'd endured the many campaigns that Chairman Mao had launched to stamp out the devils of heresy and counterrevolution whom he suspected of whispering in the ears of his billion subjects. There had been several of these, culminating in the Great Proletarian Cultural Revolution of the sixties, and in all of them, tens, hundreds of thousands of men and women like her, teachers, writers, scientists, journalists, had been jailed, tortured,

killed, or sent into concentration camps. Many had died, many
no doubt still remained in exile in the distant wastes of
Ch'inghai or Sinkiang. But some had held on with a dogged determination, inspired by a vision of China's future, of communism's future—or perhaps by nothing more than a stubborn
refusal to give their persecutors the pleasure of seeing them perish. Professor Wang, he imagined, was one of these; she must
have lived through all this, have kept her sanity, have kept her
faith—in what? Like Zhao Shanling himself, in the new openness that had developed since Mao's death thirteen years before,
she now found herself back doing the sort of work she had always done, this time with the Party's official blessing. As long as
she didn't step too far out of bounds.

"It's very good of you to see me, Professor Wang," Matthew
began. "I've admired your work, and have been looking forward
to meeting you." More Chinese courtesies, swimming through
the air like bright fish in an aquarium, conventional and confined. He hoped they didn't sound too forced.

"And I know your work," she said. "I read English better than
I speak it. This isn't your first time in Shanghai, is it? No? And
now Mr. Zhao tells me you're studying our history. The
twenties—those were exciting years. Years when our country
stood at the center of the world revolution." Was it an implica-
tion, Matthew wondered, that China no longer did so?

"Yes," he said. "But also a very complicated time, and I'm trying to understand it better." It was a cautious beginning.

"That was a heroic epoch for our Party," she said, almost as if
she hadn't heard him. "Men like Chou En-lai, Li Lisan, Ch'ü
Ch'iu-pai. They survived, of course, but many others didn't—
the ones who were killed by the imperialists, by the generals, or
by Chiang Kai-shek." Li and Ch'ü had both been among the
early communist leaders in China, young intellectuals attracted
to Marxism, inspired by the Soviet example, active in organizing
the Party in Shanghai. "Men of the sort knew who their friends
were and who their enemies were. And they knew what must be
done against the forces of imperialism, against the warlords, and
the feudal remnants."

Matthew's heart sank as he listened. Was she going to do no
more than simply mouth the platitudes of Party history? Wasn't
there some way he could draw her out?

"But were things really that simple?" he asked. "And in the

end, the revolution didn't work. Not then, at least. It was defeated in 1927, right here in Shanghai."

"Of course our views are not the same, Mr. Walker," she said, looking at him sharply with her black eyes, as if sizing him up. "And we look at history differently. But the revolution was not defeated. It was betrayed. Betrayed by Chiang Kai-shek when he turned against the workers in April that year. He and his allies among the imperialists, and among the criminals. Tu Yüeh-sheng and the Green Gang. You know that, of course? That when Chiang wanted to exterminate the Communists and the labor unions, he knew that the soldiers of the revolutionary armies would not take up arms against their own people. So he had to depend on the gangsters to do the killing for him."

"Yet the Party leaders might have been better prepared to meet Chiang," said Matthew. "After all—"

"History has its own rationality, Mr. Walker. And the people can be its masters, not its victims. The Chinese revolution proves that. But only if they understand that rationality. To explain that rationality is a function of the Party, and it is a lesson that Chiang Kai-shek never learned."

"But in 1927—" Matthew began.

She smiled at him, a friendly smile, as if she wanted no argument, and expected him, a foreigner, to take her word in such matters of her own nation's past. "Yes. But you know that in those days our Party lacked experience. And its leadership was in the hands of Trotskyists and opportunists." It was the conventional Party view, and while they talked together for about an hour, Matthew found it a disappointing conversation. While Wang Baozhen was clearly a woman who had a detailed knowledge of her subject, her learning appeared to be completely at the service of Party orthodoxy. A mind unclouded by doubts, he thought; she suggested no new ways of looking at those contentious years, and raised no questions about the simple black and white categories into which Party historians had always cast the players in the momentous drama of revolution.

So at the end, she surprised him with her suggestion. When they were through, he had brought up the question of Simon Larsen, to see whether the name evoked any sign of recognition. She thought for a while.

"Lai Shi'an," she said, looking at the three characters he had written out for her. "Yes, there were a few foreigners who played a role in the revolution. Was he one of them?"

"I don't know," Matthew answered. "Judging by his letters and his journal, his sympathies were pretty radical by 1927."

"Was he a Communist?"

"No. At least, I don't think so. There's no evidence that he was. Not a Party member, anyway."

"But perhaps in his heart?"

"It's possible," said Matthew. He doubted it, however. "Probably lots of his western friends in Shanghai thought he was a Communist. But they thought anyone was a Communist who wanted to change the way things were in China."

"I don't know the name," said Professor Wang. "But don't give up. Others may. And something may turn up." She thought for a while. "Are you busy this evening?"

"No," said Matthew. "No, I have nothing planned."

"Perhaps I'll come to your hotel," she said. "No, that's not a good idea. Do you know where Fuxing Park is? It's not far from where you're staying."

"Yes." Fuxing was a large open space with trees and gardens in it, south of Huaihai Road; Kouzaka, it had been called in the days of the French Concession.

"Meet me there, this evening. Is seven all right? There's a large statue of Marx and Engels, and near it are some benches. It's easy to find. I'll be there, and perhaps we can talk some more about these matters." She smiled, and for an instant Matthew had a glimpse not only of the intelligence that lay behind her orthodoxy, but even a glimmer of humor, a suggestion perhaps that she had reasons other than convenience for choosing the statues of the two great progenitors of communism.

Each of Shanghai's parks is an oasis of green in the midst of the heat, the noise, the dust, and the smells of the city. Originally laid out by the French, Fuxing has kept something of the comfortable formality of a place like the Luxembourg Gardens, which, Matthew thought, must have inspired its designers. It was already near dusk when he bought his entrance ticket, and the children whom he'd seen playing there on summer days had gone home, leaving the park to the young couples who could find under the dark trees a brief and private escape from the all-pervading public nature of life in China. He carried with him that day's edition of the *South China Morning Post*, with its dark rumors of a growing concentration of troops, tanks, armored cars, and artillery lining the roads leading into the capital. Meanwhile, angry voices thundered from Zhongnanhai, the compound off Chang'an Boulevard where the leaders of Party and nation lived, denouncing as an insult to the people of China the tall white statue that now dominated the square and looked toward the Tiananmen, the Gate of Heavenly Peace.

He found Professor Wang as she had promised, under Marx and Engels, who emerged from a block of reddish granite with a look of pleased optimism on their bearded faces. The sculpture was a new one, done in a style almost verging on the modern. Not quite Henry Moore or David Smith, Matthew thought, but at least a slight advance over the socialist realism that Maoist artistic canons had demanded for so many years.

"I came here early," she said. "I love the park in the evening. So peaceful." The day's heat had broken, and little groups of old men were sitting at the tables under the trees, playing cards. "And so private. It's a good place to talk." She looked around, breathing in the cooling evening air. Matthew waited, and said nothing.

"That period we were discussing this morning," she went on. "It was a time of heroes. I really do believe that." She paused. "But they were difficult years. Difficult and painful for those who lived through them. Reading the histories the Party has written, particularly the older ones, you sometimes feel that the triumph of the revolution was all inevitable, that men like Mao Tse-tung, and Chou En-lai and the others all knew that they were on the crest of a great historical wave that they would ride to victory."

Matthew nodded, not quite knowing how to reply; Professor Wang's own books had sounded rather that way.

She must have sensed what he was thinking. "Sometimes, perhaps," she went on, "it is better to write in the way that's expected of you. Even if you know that there was nothing inevitable about the victory of the revolution." She paused. "At the time of the May Thirtieth Movement in 1925, for instance, there were no more than perhaps two hundred Communists in all of Shanghai, in a city of over three million people."

Matthew was surprised; he thought there'd been many more. "But even so," he said, "by the end of the year there were thousands. Because of the movement."

"As I get older, I have more trouble reading," Professor Wang went on. "My eyesight was hurt when I was younger. An accident on a commune in Anhwei province. I lived there during the Cultural Revolution." She looked at him. "Did you know that? I was sent there to learn from the people, to realize what a soft life I had led as an intellectual. So I learned how to make bricks. That was easy. The hard part was carrying them, day after day, to where they were needed. We had to build a new headquarters for the local cadres. We rightists. And I learned how to plant vegetables, and to care for the plants. But one day an insecticide splashed in my eyes. The local doctor—a barefoot doctor—did what he could, even though the cadres told him he was spending too much time on someone with unreliable politics. He was a good man, but he didn't know much, and my vision has been fading since then. But in other ways I see more clearly than I did. And now I understand better what those early Party leaders must have faced."

"The warlords and their soldiers," Matthew prompted her. "And the hostility of the foreigners and their police."

"Of course." She dismissed his interjection as if it were of no interest. "That's what our books have taught us. But that's not really what I meant. Think also of what the books don't say; students and intellectuals trying to organize workers whom they didn't understand, who didn't understand them. I remember the world that separated us from those Anhwei peasants I knew twenty years ago. We didn't even speak the same language. I don't just mean their dialect. I mean that while we all used the same words, those words could mean very different things to us. Because of the way we had lived. Because of what we had seen—or hadn't seen. Or been through."

It was growing dark rapidly. But even in the gloom he could make out the animation in her face.

"And think of the apathy and ignorance of the people that those early Party organizers had to work with. The doubts, the fears, particularly when union leaders were arrested and tortured, often killed. What was it like wondering if you would be next? But worst of all must have been the uncertainty. Our Party histories say that we controlled the labor movement in those days. It's not true. In most places the unions were forbidden. And where they did exist, they were run by the Kuomintang as well as by the Communists. Or by neither. Lots of workers, you know, owed their jobs to the Green Gang. It was the gangs that recruited them, that made the deals with the factory bosses and the factory foremen to get their employment. And so they did what the gangs told them to do. They didn't understand the need for unions. They just wanted to get enough to stay alive, to feed their families."

The gangs, Matthew knew, had been powerful among Shanghai's workers in those days. By the early decades of the twentieth century they had come to control much of the city's underworld: prostitution, gambling, arms smuggling, and above all the distribution and control of the opium traffic after the drug had been outlawed in 1919. And labor recruitment and racketeering as well, though it did not fit the Party's view of an aroused and united industrial proletariat to say so.

"When we make history too simple," she continued, "we take away all humanity from the very people we are trying to honor. The Party tells us that the worldwide victory of socialism is inevitable. Perhaps I believe that; I don't know. But I do know that it did not seem inevitable to those men and women who were living in fear and uncertainty, struggling to keep the Party alive against their enemies. And that's why they were heroes. Not because they knew they were going to win—that would be too easy. But because they didn't know. That's what must have been really difficult. These are the things I should like to write about. Perhaps someday I will. About these men and women who kept fighting despite their doubts and fears, because they believed in the cause they were serving."

"The cause?" asked Matthew. "You mean an independent China with no more foreign control?" And realized once again that it was he, rather than she, who was speaking in clichés.

"That, of course. But more important was the dignity of their people. A dignity that has to be won by a battle against oneself, not against others. Have you read Lu Hsün?" Matthew nodded at her reference to that sardonic observer of the Chinese scene who had nonetheless become a hero in the communist pantheon. "Of course you have. So you know that he had little good to say about us, his fellow countrymen. And you know that what we Chinese are really most afraid of is that we'll discover that we're not as good as other people, not as good as the Japanese or the Americans or the French or the English. And so we put all the blame for our shortcomings on foreigners."

"But that was all sixty or seventy years ago," said Matthew. "Surely things have changed since then."

"Of course," she said. "Sixty and seventy years ago, Shanghai was run by the foreigners. Today it's run by the Chinese. Of course that's progress. You've walked around the city. You know that." A sardonic note came into her voice. "You've seen how much better things are here than in—in Hong Kong, which is still a colony."

Matthew said nothing. Here, in the solitude of the park, Wang Baozhen was giving voice to a bitter memory that she could never have spoken in the institute that morning.

"If the victory of socialism is inevitable, sometimes I wonder whether it has already come to China. Or if it will come. Sometimes I wonder if the China I see today, forty years after the victory of our Party, is the China I dreamed of when I was a girl, when I joined the Party back in those years before liberation. Dangerous years, years when just being a Communist was enough to get you arrested. Or even executed. Then, in 1949, we were told socialism had won, but twenty years later, in the Cultural Revolution, we were told that socialism still had to fight for its life against its enemies. And that those enemies were now to be found in the Communist Party itself! That some of us, who thought we were loyal members of the Party, were actually trying to destroy it!"

"That's when you were *xiafang*—sent down to the countryside?"

"Yes. From 1968 to 1976 I was in Anhwei. That's when I had my accident. Only after the arrest of the Gang of Four in October that year was I allowed back. And since then I have taught at Fudan."

"So things have gotten better in the last ten years? Under Deng Xiaoping?" Matthew asked.

"I suppose so. I've had no problems. But I've been careful, you know. And the Party likes what I've written."

He wondered if she still belonged to the Party, but was reluctant to ask her directly.

She must have guessed the question. "I am still a Communist," she went on. "Ten years ago I was told that there had been a mistake in my case, and that the verdict was to be reversed. That left me free to join again. And I did. Partly for safety, I suppose, but also partly because I believe—I believed—in all that the Party had done for China, despite its mistakes, and that now perhaps we really could work together for the reform of society."

Did she still believe, Matthew wanted to know, but held back, afraid that he might be probing too deeply. Instead, he asked her about the demonstrations that had been taking place that spring in Beijing, in Shanghai, in other cities throughout China.

"Are those students socialist?"

"Socialist? Yes—if socialism means that they want a better China," she replied bitterly. "But they've had it too easy, the young. Oh, I know they think that's what people like me always say. That's an old woman talking, they will say. And they're right. But we who are old have our memories, the memories of our experience. We remember our difficulties. The young don't know that, don't understand that, think that's all in the past, and it has no meaning for them."

"Those who forget the past are condemned to repeat it?"

"That's your Santayana, isn't it? I read him in university before liberation, and have never forgotten it. He was right, but try to tell that to the young."

"Our students are like that too," said Matthew, wondering if at the age of twenty-nine he was old enough to escape Professor Wang's strictures against the easy certainties of youth. "They study history—when they study it—as if they were reading about life on another planet. Sometimes I think nothing is real for them but the present."

"We've had a lot of excitement here recently," Wang Baozhen continued. "Not like Beijing, of course. But our students are very worked up by what's happening in Tiananmen Square. The city government and the Party tried to stop them, tried to keep them shut up on their campuses. Jiang Zemin—you know about him?" Matthew nodded. "The Party chairman here. He remembers 1986, the last time the students demonstrated in Shanghai, and the insults they shouted against the Party, against Mao, against him. He was determined not to let it happen again. But it didn't work. There were demonstrations, marches, when Gorbachev was here, and they put the Goddess of Liberty on the Bund. Even before the one that appeared in Beijing." She pointed to the photograph in the Hong Kong paper.

"It's a brave gesture. I was proud of them when they did it. They remind me of the way we were when we were young, here in Shanghai after the war, when the Kuomintang was still in control. But a Goddess of Liberty isn't going to change things. Today our young know nothing of the history of their own country—the Party has seen to that. Or if they do know anything, they know only the kind of history the Party gives them: the people are united, the Party is united, and victory inevitable. They believe it. And so because they believe that their own ideas are right, their own cause is right, they believe in the inevitability of their own victory. They have none of the experience of fear, of uncertainty, of disunity; they think that hope is enough to win."

She paused, and then looked at him. "What they don't know is what it means for counterrevolution to be stronger than revolution. That's what happened in the period that you're studying, when Chiang Kai-shek launched his white terror. In 1927."

"And today?" asked Matthew. "Will there be counterrevolution? And where will it come from?"

Wang Baozhen continued to look straight at him in the rapidly fading light. Almost, he thought, as if she were examining his face, his eyes, to see how much she could trust him. Then, in English: "Mr. Zhao told me that you met Xie Bona—Bernard Hilding, the Englishman."

"Yes," said Matthew, "I talked with him yesterday."

"I know his daughter," she said, still in English. "She's studying at Fudan, you know."

"So he told me," said Matthew. "He showed me a picture of her. She's in Beijing with the students from Shanghai. He seems very proud of her. As if he'd be there in the square himself today if he were still a young man."

"Will you see him again?"

"I hope so."

"See him soon," she said. "And tell him to bring his daughter back to Shanghai. As soon as possible. Now."

Then, back in Chinese. "Well, we didn't come here to discuss the present. We are both students of history, you and I. Tell me more about your Simon Larsen, and about what you hope to find here in Shanghai."

* * *

By the early autumn of 1925, Shanghai was beginning to relax again. All summer long the thunderheads had built up, towering into the pale Chinese sky, and distant rumbles rolled over the city, but in the end the storm had never broken, the electricity had dissipated, and the weather had begun to cool. As Chu Hung-ying, Simon's Chinese teacher, had predicted, the Chinese businessmen, the bankers and traders and shipowners who controlled the affairs of the powerful commercial associations, had become increasingly worried by the spread of radicalism, and were ready to see a return to normal life. Consequently they raised no objections when the police and the army of the local warlord began to crack down on the communist-led labor and student unions, and by September most of the strikes against the British and the Japanese had come to an end. Under Stanfield Frothingham, its American chairman, the Shanghai Municipal Council admitted no wrongdoing, but agreed to allow a panel of foreign judges to hold hearings in October to investigate the shootings of May 30, hoping that this would bring the movement to an end and that Shanghai could get back to the pursuit of profit that was its life.

Both Simon's journal and the draft of *Typhoon* discussed these subjects at some length, though they told Matthew little that he didn't already know. Meanwhile, more and more pages of the former were devoted to Emily Ransom. Mrs. Ransom had sailed home on the *President Jackson* in early September, leaving her daughter behind in John Ransom's care, and the enterprising Emily (no doubt with the help of a word or two from her uncle) had landed herself a job as a cub reporter, writing society notes for the *China Press*, the city's American-owned daily.

And Simon clearly had been captivated by her. Rereading the journal now, Matthew was astute enough to realize that he was not seeing Emily herself, but rather an Emily mediated through Simon's journal: the Emily that Simon wished him to see, and perhaps himself wished to see. He found her openness a contrast to the tightly bound and narrow circles of his own Shanghai, and he must have enjoyed playing the role of teacher to a girl ready for experiences beyond that of the world in which she'd been raised. So, too, she must have been an eager listener to this man whose knowledge of life and the world was so much broader than her own, and Emily—at least the Emily of the journal—had become his willing pupil.

So he had begun to make good on his promise to show her Shanghai. "We started out as any tourists would," he wrote in an entry dated Tuesday, September 15. "The Bund, Nanking Road, dinner and dancing in the Astor Hotel, the floor show at the Carlton Café." She dismissed it all; any one of her uncle's friends could have done the same, and she reminded him of his promise to show her the real Shanghai, Chinese Shanghai. So late one warm autumn afternoon they had gone in search of it, leaving the safe boundaries of the foreign concessions, to the original Shanghai,

> . . . the old walled city that lies just off the French Bund. It's a district many visitors avoid; they're put off by the dirt, the smells, the poverty, the narrow, airless lanes with their rough cobblestones, the danger of being drenched by a basin full of wastewater (or worse) thrown from one of the balconies above. But at least they're honest about their reasons for not going. Better than those who do go, and think that at last they've found the real China. Because what makes it real for them are the terrible examples of human suffering that they find here, toward which they toss a few copper cash and point their Kodaks, in a fraction of a second capturing the misery with which they can entertain their friends back home.
>
> E. (to my relief!) had left her own Kodak behind. We began with the Yu Yüan Garden, and its Willow Ware teahouse, the most famous of the old city's sights. A bit of a disappointment, she admitted—the building falling apart, & its pond is covered with the usual thick brown-green scum, lying under the bridge that jogs from the shore in a series of right angles—designed to keep away demons, because they can move only in straight lines. The explanation's one that is almost guaranteed to bring forth one of two reactions: "how charmingly quaint!" or "how appallingly superstitious!" E. gave neither; she keeps her eyes open, makes mental notes, passes no judgment.
>
> But beggars lie sprawled painfully in the corners, & what the missionaries call ladies of uncertain virtue ply their trade among the customers. Yet the crowd of small vendors around the building is always lively, their booths covered with scrolls, pottery, toys, musical instruments, and cheap knickknacks from America and Japan, like an open-air Woolworth's. At the Temple to the City God, the air is heavy with the blue smoke of

joss sticks burning before the altars, & the courtyard is filled with stalls and entertainers—the magicians and acrobats, the storytellers and jugglers, who make up the theater of the streets, the theater of the poor. Walking slowly through the narrow lanes north toward the Settlement, we peered into the stores: bird sellers, bamboo cages festooning their entrances and walls; pawnshops & silversmiths, herbalists with their strange remedies, money changers, jewelers, carvers of ivory and opium pipes; and the coffin shops, where woodworkers turn out the strangely shaped boxes that carry the Chinese dead to their final rest. Everywhere there were the beggars, of course, some of them diseased or mutilated; mothers exhibiting their deformed children, crying out that we were their last hope; & from open silent doorways there drifted the sweet sick smell of opium, strong enough occasionally to overcome the ever-present stench of the open sewers and human waste. It's a place that is at once fascinating and terrifying. But not the real China. No single place can be the real China.

E. was sobered by the experience, and I could tell that she was relieved when we crossed the avenue des Deux Républiques, emerging back into the broad streets and cleaner air of the French Concession. To read at home that China is a poor country is one thing; to see the poverty, and to smell it, is something else. Yet most of those who live in Shanghai do so by choice, for bad as they may be, conditions here are better than in many places in the countryside. There, even in good years, life is hard, & when the floods come, or the drought comes, or worst of all, when the warlords arrive, sacking villages, violating women, carrying off the able-bodied men, then there is no hope. Here, at least, particularly if you've got a family, there's some chance of survival.

Back on Foochow Road, E. was entranced by the shops: the silk stores with their bright bolts of red, blue, and green spilling off the shelves; the bookstores with their hundreds of sewn volumes of poetry, philosophy, the history of the dynasties; stores selling wen-chü, the "literary implements" of the Chinese scholar—writing brushes, some no more than tiny wisps of fine hair on slender bamboo holders, others so big that they look almost like shaving brushes; ink blocks decorated with golden dragons or phoenixes; and on the walls, scrolls of maxims drawn from the classics, their calligraphy forming moral and visual models for the aspiring artist.

They'd arranged to meet Chu Hung-ying for dinner at a Chinese restaurant nearby. "Not every 'restaurant' on Foochow Road is suitable for girls just out of Bryn Mawr," wrote Simon, "and many of them are no better than bordellos. But there's also probably no better place in the Settlement to introduce a novice to the joys of Shanghai cooking." Matthew wondered whether John Ransom would have approved of his niece visiting such a place after dark, but by now he had concluded that Emily was the sort of girl who told her uncle no more than she thought he needed to know. At all events, she'd apparently taken to Simon's Chinese teacher, and they'd spent the evening talking about the events of the summer, and about where they might lead. As Simon described it, there was something about the passionate reaction of the young Chinese accountant to the indignities suffered by his countrymen that she found attractive; it appealed to her American idealism, and made her determined to show that not all foreigners spoke the language whose vocabulary of contempt found daily expression in the editorial pages of such foreign papers as the *North China Daily News* or the *Écho de Chine*.

Several weeks later she asked Simon if Chu was a Communist.

We were standing by the wall that bounds the Public Garden, looking out over the river, where a British cruiser & three American destroyers lie moored, their riding lights coming on as twilight descends over the city.

Her question took me by surprise. I've never tried to ask Mr. Chu directly about his political opinions, though I've a pretty clear sense where they lie. But to ask him to spell these out—to say whether he's a supporter of the Kuomintang, or even of the Communists—would seem to invade a private domain of his own, and might not only break down the trust between us, but even be dangerous for him.

E., however, has repeated to her uncle some of the ideas that she'd heard from Mr. Chu during our dinner a fortnight ago, and he warned her that they sounded Bolshevik. She laughed as she told me this. But then she startled me. "I'd love to meet a real Communist. What would my parents say?" At Bryn Mawr there had been girls who called themselves Communists, who were always reading about Russia, trying to show how much better things are there than in America. But she didn't consider them real Communists.

I asked her what a real Communist is—a man with a black beard & a bomb?

She didn't want to be teased. A Communist is someone who believes in what he's doing. Someone who really wants to make the world a better place, who really believes that everyone's equal. Or should be. She looked around as she spoke. A chilly breeze blowing in from the river, reminding us that summer's nearly over. The great buildings on the Bund, the banks and shipping companies, dark and massive against the fading light of the western sky, & down on Nanking Road, the tall buildings hung with lights. The Great White Way, the tourists call it; it's one of the sights of Shanghai. E. looked at all this, & said, "I think perhaps if I were Chinese, I might be a Communist too."

I laughed, warned her not to let her uncle hear her talk that way. Whatever else he is, John Ransom is not a man of advanced political views, & sometimes he seems to take his ideas ready-made from the *North China*, spying the dangerous hand of radicalism in anything or anybody who suggests changes in the way Shanghai is run. But she was perfectly serious, wanted to know if I didn't agree with her, wanted to know whether, if I were Chinese, I wouldn't hate & resent these signs of foreign wealth and foreign rule, resent the way in which foreigners treated me.

I'm not Chinese, I reminded her, merely a writer, a sort of a journalist who has to stay calm, listening to what people tell me, not getting caught up in their political battles. I have to see both sides, weigh arguments, make judgments; I can't afford to let likes and dislikes get in the way.

But, she said, suppose I did take sides, join the battle? Wouldn't I understand better, see things more clearly? Even be a better writer?

I'm still startled by the passion in her voice. Of course E.'s right in a way, and I've thought a good deal of this conversation since then. Once, years ago, I felt the same way she does. But the memory of the past, of those months in the trenches, shooting and being shot at, and of those more months in the hospital—all that cured me forever of such idealism. If knowing that you're right leads to what I saw in France, the senseless carnage of those battlefields, rows of young corpses staring at the sky with vacant eyes, then perhaps it's time to retreat a bit, to try to look at both sides of an argument.

Still, perhaps Emily has a point. If I were Chinese, living in Shanghai this year of 1925, I might well feel differently. If I were Mr. Chu, or one of his passionate young friends, I might very well be following E.'s prescription. I'd never get my book finished, of course. But perhaps I might feel that there was more important work to be done.

CHAPTER FOUR

Friday, June 2, 1989

Matthew sat in the institute's reading room, sipping the tea that had been set before him, staring at the pile of documents for which he'd asked, and musing about the city through which he'd walked that morning, the city whose past he was trying to reconstruct, the city Simon Larsen had known almost seventy years earlier. Then it had been one of the world's great seaports, and the old shipping maps still showed the routes of the steamers, dotted red lines that led purposefully out from the Huangpu over thousands of miles of empty ocean to Bombay, Marseilles, Liverpool, Vancouver, New York. Under the house flags of the P.&O. and the Blue Funnel Line, the Messageries Maritimes and the Dollar Line, the ships arriving from abroad, and the cargoes filling their holds, had defined much of Shanghai's reason for existence. Perched as it was on the very edge of the vast continent of Asia, almost spilling into the ocean that gave it life, the city often seemed to have little connection with China itself, living like a tenant on an uncertain lease, strong enough for the moment to keep the landlord's agents at bay, yet never knowing when the rightful owner would claim possession.

Meanwhile the tenant improved his holding. The great buildings that still lined the Bund and the downtown streets were structures that spoke their makers' proud language of modernity, progress, and industry. Yet translated into Chinese, the words had somehow changed their meanings: the pride became arrogance, modernity became domination, progress became greed, and industry became exploitation (Matthew remembered the old photographs of those rows and rows of silent women and pale, exhausted children in the cotton mills). So that when the landlord did return, the monuments that the tenants had built were kept, but all the shadows of their past had to be exorcised. As China turned its back on the world, Shanghai had faced away from the sea to become inward-looking, a Chinese city whose destiny lay not with the world beyond but with the great movements sweeping across the country after the communist victory.

In Simon's day Shanghai had been a hybrid, neither fully a colony nor fully Chinese, but a frontier city spanning both worlds. And within the city, Simon himself must have seemed something of a hybrid as well. Conscious of a need to remain the impartial spectator, his observations were those of a man who listened with intelligent curiosity to what others told him: consuls and businessmen, missionaries and journalists, while his growing command of Chinese gave him an access to Shanghai's ordinary citizens that was denied to most foreigners. Though he had lived in that world for three and a half years, Simon always remained the skeptical outsider in Shanghai's foreign colony, unable or unwilling to enter fully into its ways, its customs, its beliefs, its prejudices, and its superstitions. "It's in moments like these that I wonder what keeps me here," he had written in early 1926, after describing an argument with a member of the Shanghai Volunteer Corps who had taken him to task for failing to play the role demanded of an American in Shanghai.

> I am continually tried by the shallowness, the pretensions, the everlasting boredom of life here. In this nondescript city lying jumbled together on a flat green-gray land, my only escape has come from my explorations of China and Chinese ways, with a guide such as Mr. Chu, who with infinite patience teaches me not only the language of his people, but also that other more difficult grammar of gesture, of tone, of look, of custom, without which even the most fluent mastery of the tongue is virtually meaningless.
>
> But when I move among my own kind here in Shanghai, the

sense of ennui almost overwhelms me. If there is a terror in the infinite vastness of China that lies beyond the city, so, too, there is another smaller terror in the quiet desperation with which so many men here lead their lives, lives circumscribed by the narrow confines of home, office, church, and club. Little men, escaping from little middle-class lives in provincial towns, enjoying here luxuries they could never have known at home, they have built themselves new prisons, whose walls are none the less real for their invisibility. Hardly daring to move beyond these little circles of self-importance, they form their own ranks and their own social orders, they arrogate to themselves their own privileges—and then cry out in protest when they discover that their own flattering view of themselves is not shared by the greater world beyond the foreign settlements.

Only occasionally do you find among them someone with a larger view, someone who talks of the ideas, of the events that are shaping the world of which we are a part—someone, in short, who sees Shanghai for what it really is, no more than a flyspeck on the vast map of Asia.

Or, a few weeks later, in one of the handwritten passages:

I wish I liked my fellow man better—at least my fellow man as I find him here in Shanghai. But what do I have in common with men like John Ransom or Eric Massingham & their friends? I'm not part of their world, & they, in turn, can fit me into none of their neat pigeonholes. Look at me: no steady job, a man who lives, or tries to live, by his writing. The newspaperman they can understand, or the globe-trotting correspondent who passes a few weeks in Peking & then blows through town, meeting the taipans, the consuls, the missionaries, perhaps a tame warlord or two, before sailing home to write a series of articles about the Problem of China. The adventurer, the crook, the con man; these are all familiar figures here, with the deadbeat and the remittance man who washes up on these shores.

But here I am—none of these descriptions will fit me. Let Ransom, Massingham, and their kind march on, setting the beat for the city they want to control. I follow a different tune.

Occasional passages like these helped Matthew gradually to build a picture of Simon in his mind, and he was astute enough to see in such outbursts a sense of superiority of social class as well as of intellect. Though he had wrenched himself loose from the narrow world in which he'd been raised, aristocratic Philadelphia had left its own mark on Simon Larsen, and he found little or nothing in common with what was decidedly a commercial middle-class society in Shanghai.

Still, was Matthew reading the journal the right way? "Never believe that the documents tell you everything you need to know about history," Hannah Bernstein had warned when he sat in her graduate seminar a few years earlier. "You must learn to look behind them. The simplest human actions come from reasons far more complex than any that can be written down on paper. That's one of the reasons most historians improve with age. Unlike physicists or mathematicians." A loud snort of laughter would follow this dictum. A formidable woman in her early sixties, she herself was the author of five books on modern German history, each more complex and nuanced in its view of the past than its predecessor. While her students sat gathered around a table in Robinson Hall on those darkening autumn afternoons, she paced the room, a cigarette in her mouth, dripping ash onto the ancient rust-colored carpet, oblivious of the university's moralistic exhortations for smoke-free classrooms. "Experience, observation, that's what counts, and that's something you don't learn in the classroom or in the Library of Congress or the British Museum. And never forget," she continued, "that everything, literally everything, is a historical document: not just diaries and letters and peace treaties and census reports, but propaganda, hymns, poems, novels, clothes, ships, buildings, turret lathes, farm machinery—everything! Every one of them will answer the historian's questions absolutely truthfully. But only if the historian"—and here her glance swept the room, challenging her students—"knows how to ask the right questions. And the right question is the question to which he can expect a truthful answer."

What were the right questions to ask Simon's journal? That spring, after Laura had given it to him, Matthew had taken *The Steel Ridge* from the library stacks, hoping to find in it some clues to Simon's character. The narrator of that novel (like Simon, a soldier, but not Simon himself) had moved through the topography of battle, recording the words and the silences, the gestures and the motions of other men as they came face-to-face with fatigue, fear, horror, and shock, all of them enemies more immediate than the unseen Germans who lay, several kilometers away, hidden in their own trenches. Yet this nameless, unidentified, almost disembodied recorder of war had then, step by step, begun to take on his own form, to become a person with his own human vulnerabilities, his own fallibilities and weaknesses, as if gradually aware of the essential inhumanity of maintaining such a detachment in the face of so much pain, so much terror, so massive a violation of human norms as the battlefield revealed.

But a novel is a work of art, Laura had reminded him, a text with its own integrity, its own truth, and not something to be mined by biographers and historians in the hope that they will find more than the artist chooses to give them. Nonetheless, Matthew, with his historian's training, could not help wondering what form Simon's writings would have taken had he lived to see them through into print. Them? Was there more than one book here in these writings Simon had left behind? *Typhoon Over Shanghai*—that was easy enough, a reminiscence of life in Shanghai, Simon in the first person educating his reader about the upheaval in China. Books like that had been common enough at the time, and no doubt had enjoyed good sales in the late twenties. But the private journal—that was something else. Perhaps Laura was right, and Simon's musings here might someday have been intended for eyes other than his own. But if that was the case, then how far did Simon the journal's narrator resemble Simon the man who had written it? Certainly, Matthew was coming to believe, there emerged from it a picture of Simon as he wanted his unknown, unsuspected reader to see him: a man dispassionate, patient, fair-minded yet unmoved, an outsider always distancing himself from the subjects of his investigation. Was that Simon Larsen as he really had been? Had he perhaps not insisted too much, even to the point of becoming tendentious, on this persona, this public face of his private musings? For occasionally Matthew would come upon a passage that seemed to subvert that carefully devised image—in his reflection on his own reaction to the rickshaw coolie's demands, in the few references to Rhonda Sexton, in his wish that Emily not see in him an example of the genus Shanghailander, for example. How far had those little betrayals, those contradictions, been knowingly introduced? If Simon's private journal was indeed the beginning of a novel, how far, as he planned it, had a conception of fictive truth begun to balance, even to outweigh, the kind of objective truth that the journalist (like the author of *Typhoon*), or the historian, likes to claim as his own?

How far, in short, could Matthew trust what he was reading? Educated in a time when the old certainties were crumbling, he knew that he could never return to the day, fifty years ago, a century ago, when most historians believed that they were called to practice not an art or a craft, but a branch of science. This comforting faith had taught them to think that with patience, hard work, and the right kind of imagination, it would be possible to reconstruct accurately worlds that no longer existed—the world of Cromwell and the Cavaliers, the world of Parisian aristocrats and sans-culottes, the world of twilight Luoyang awaiting the collapse of the Han dynasty. Some historians might still be believers today, but he knew that the worms of skepticism had been boring into the house of history as well as literature, and that the belief in scientific history, if not quite ready for the same fate as the belief in a flat earth, would need something more to shore it up than the replacement of a few rotting timbers.

Matthew remembered another one of his professors, a man very much of the old school, bemoaning the directions that the latter-day study of the past had begun to take. Like Jeremiah preaching to an unrepentant people, he warned his students that history, according to some of its new practitioners, was no longer the property of the men and women who lived and moved in a particular world of the past, and which it was the historian's task to reconstruct. Rather, it had become the property of the historian himself, who, like Prospero, now saw his business as the construction of a stage of his own design, on which these men and women would act out the roles in which he had cast them. And it had become the property of the readers, who were now invited to use their own imaginations to transform the historian's stage and the historian's actors into plays that had a present meaning for them.

For Matthew, this relativistic attitude toward the claims of the past had only been strengthened by those talks with Laura, who had imbibed, though perhaps with some skepticism, the views of the literary theorists. He remembered a long and at times heated argument with her last winter, in which she had challenged the whole notion of trying to reconstruct a particular story, a sense of a particular time and place. "Can't you see," she insisted, "that you're simply imposing a pattern—your own pattern—on all those supposed facts you've scribbled down on all those notecards, and tapped into all those computer files? And so what comes out is a fiction, your particular fiction, which has no more or less claim to truth than any number of others?"

In vain he'd come back with the historian's old defense: he was doing no such thing, but merely trying to let the facts speak for themselves. But he knew it sounded weak, and that he spoke without conviction. Anyway, he had been easily subverted by the new ways, temperamentally attracted by such views of the contingency of knowledge, for they left open an inexhaustible number of choices, an infinite indeterminacy, rather than forcing a commitment to a particular view, demanding a particular relationship with the past. Trained by her mentors in a fashionably post-modern vocabulary, Laura had gotten the better of him that evening, as she almost invariably did. It was only when phrases like "the hermeneutics of suspicion" and "crisis of epistemological contingency" began to fill the air that they had both suddenly stopped, gazed at each other in horror, and then burst into laughter at the appalling parodies of their professors that they themselves had briefly become.

And yet, trained as a skeptic himself, Matthew could not help wondering about the way such views seemed to entail the elevation of relativism to the status of absolute virtue. Last night, Wang Baozhen had complained about the way in which an optimistic inevitability of socialist victory suffused so much of the Party's version of history, almost as if the recognition of human complexity and confusion, the clouded and ambiguous nature of human indeterminacy, would somehow be an admission that history might not have moved so inexorably along the path that Marxist scholars claimed to have discovered for it. Yet how different, he wondered, was this view of the revolution's inevitable success from that which he himself had been given—more nuanced, more qualified, of course—in his own studies of the Chinese revolution? How far had his teachers, consciously or unconsciously, fallen into that ancient and seductive view that sees history as a process whose purpose is ultimately the ratification of the present?

The control of the public memory has always been important for rulers, especially in a country like China, where, ever since the days of the earliest dynasties, the government has assumed the task of setting forth the correct interpretation of the past. Whatever else communism may have changed, Matthew thought, it had not changed that. And indeed if history is no more than what historian and reader make it, why not accept the Party's version as valid—at least as valid as any other view? Of course, Professor Wang, like any historian, would have misgivings about being forced to accept a particular view of the past. But Matthew sensed in her words a greater objection than that, sensed that she was also rejecting the whole notion that histories are no more than arbitrary constructions, or that there is no firm basis on which to judge the adequacy of one and the inadequacy of another.

The door opened, and Zhao Shanling's head appeared.

"Good morning, Mr. Walker," he said. "I hope our staff is treating you well?"

Matthew looked up. "Thank you," he said. "Yes, I have everything I need."

"Good, good." Zhao smiled and disappeared. His daydream broken, Matthew turned to the stack of manila folders that had been given him, beginning slowly to read his way through the hundreds of pages they contained. The cheap paper was dry and crumbling at the edges, like that of old French novels, so that no matter how carefully he handled the individual pieces, brittle shards broke off, tiny brown leaves flaking the table like a woodland in October. Unless something were done to preserve them, these records would soon crumble, and with them would vanish another part of that ephemeral memory of the past.

The documents before him professed to record the deliberations and decisions of the committee that had planned the great communist insurrections in Shanghai in 1927. They told of the meetings of a little group of men, working in secret through that dark winter as they prepared to lead Shanghai into the springtime of revolution. Hunted by the police of the local warlord, by the police of the foreign settlements, they surely could have had no certainty that their cause would triumph, at least in their lifetime. Far from cultivating the detached objectivity of the scholar, or the journalist like Simon Larsen, the men who had kept these records had been passionately committed to the cause they were serving. What questions could he ask them if he expected a truthful answer?

"Minutes of the meeting of the Shanghai District Committee of the Communist Party," he read. "January 23, 1927." Then a list of the names of those who had come: Lo Yi-nung, the chairman, Wang Shou-hua, leader of the communist-dominated General Labor Union, Chou En-lai, in charge of military preparations, Peng Shu-chih, and others. Ghosts hovered silently in the room, called up by the very act of reading their names, their words. "Issues for discussion: the shortcomings of our propaganda, the need to build up our membership, the need to get arms for the insurrection, our relations with the Kuomintang." Questions and problems that betrayed their uncertainty: We are the Party of the workers, but the workers do not understand our purposes, they are uneducated and politically backward, they are afraid; how can we make our propaganda more effective? That was what the documents talked about, but from those lines of faded ink on the yellowing paper there emanated other unspoken apprehensions: How can we continue to believe, with our fears, our weaknesses, that we really are what we say we are, the vanguard of a historically irresistible force that will someday liberate these tired, hungry, and frightened people? Behind that, even more anxious questions shivered in the air: Which of us will have disappeared before we meet again? Which of us will have broken under torture, under the threat of death? Which of us, sitting here today with his fellows, may be a traitor, a double agent, ready to betray us to the Kuomintang, to the warlords?

How far can those who control historical memory allow such doubts, such questions, Matthew wondered. Surely they upset easy assumptions about progress, and progress is always defined by the victors. The victors' history must never endanger the present by introducing awkward ambiguities, suggesting other possibilities. No: it has to have the easy certainty of a propaganda poster, and Matthew remembered those heroic workers and peasants depicted by the Maoists, determination fixed on their handsome faces as they courageously marched leftward across the paper, driving back their enemies of feudalism and imperialism. Such history is a narrative constructed by those who win, in which fact follows logical fact, nothing is left unexplained, and all questions are answered by the time the curtain goes down on the happy ending. But what of the losers' narratives, those narratives that are so difficult to find, so easy to overlook even when they are right in front of us? Unless the historian turns propagandist, he must bring out the complexity of the past, understanding and making his reader understand what might have happened as well as what did happen. Only if he realizes that the future is one of possibility—fearful and dangerous as well as hopeful—can he respect the humanity of the men and women he studies, only then will they become morally free rather than simple actors playing roles in a script conceived by the victors. Matthew remembered a line from *Man's Fate*, André Malraux's novel of the Shanghai revolution of 1927: "In Marxism there is the sense of a fatality and also the exaltation of a will. Every time fatality comes before will, I'm suspicious."

A young woman, one of the institute's staff, came in. "It's time for lunch," she said, giving him an apologetic smile.

Matthew looked at his watch. It was eleven-thirty, the morning already flown.

"Thank you," he said. "I'll be back later," and he rose to go.

In October 1925, Shanghai—the Shanghai of the Chinese, at any rate—had undergone another change of rule. The uneasy peace reached in January had broken down, and now Sun Ch'uan-fang, the warlord of Chekiang province, had marched his troops up the railway from Hangchow, and had taken control of the city. The move had nothing to do with the summer's upheaval, and General Sun, like his predecessors, had no aim more exalted than a simple wish to control Shanghai and to put its wealth at the service of his military machine.

Certainly he proved himself to be just as active in harrying the disintegrating organizations of the radicals as his departed rival had been. On Thursday, December 17, Chu Hung-ying had told Simon about the fate of Liu Hua, a student who had emerged as one of the leaders in the mill disputes, and had later become head of the General Labor Union, helping to coordinate the summer's general strike.

According to Mr. Chu, the Municipal Police picked him up a few weeks ago in a teahouse on Foochow Road. Then they turned him over to the Chinese police, who took him down to the military headquarters at Lunghua, south of the city, and executed him. It's the usual way of getting rid of troublemakers so that the foreigners have no blood on their hands.

"He was a very gentle man," Mr. Chu tells me, "a man incapable of hurting anyone, who wanted only to help the workers, the women and the children who labor in the mills."

Though Sun Ch'uan-fang, our new ruler, is said to have more progressive ideas than his predecessor, Mr. Chu denies it. Some of his friends have been arrested, others have fled, or are in hiding while the police—both foreign and Chinese—look for them.

"Last summer we were so hopeful," he continues, "and yet now nothing seems to be left." I am struck by the way he puts it. *Our* hopes, *our* work—I've never before heard him identify himself so closely with the movement that burst forth after the bloodshed on Nanking Road last spring. I hear a new bitterness in his words, not only when he speaks of the foreigners, but also when he talks of the Chinese leaders of Shanghai. He takes no comfort from the common prediction that because of what we have been through, Chinese will at last gain a voice on the two councils that run the Settlement and the Concession. "We did not put ourselves through the pain and sacrifice of the summer just to be exploited by Chinese rather than foreigners," he says. "Look, Lai *hsien-sheng*, if Chinese join the councils, they will be the factory owners, the mill owners, the shipowners. Chinese *lao-pan*—bosses—in collusion with foreign taipans. We ordinary Chinese will have gained nothing, and will be as badly off as ever."

As he leaves, he urges me to go look at the textile mills. "You cannot tell the truth about the city, about what happened here last summer, unless you have seen what they are like."

Meanwhile, the judicial investigation into the Nanking Road affair had moved to its close, its findings (by a two-to-one vote) that the police had acted properly convincing no one not already convinced. Christmas came and went, and the bitter winter set in (Matthew recalled the words of a French journalist of the period, who had claimed, with some exaggeration, that Shanghai's climate managed to combine a Saigon-like summer with a Moscow-like winter). Simon had left a vivid picture of the city's changed aspect in the cold.

Monday, January 11, 1926

The holidays are now behind us, and our bleak city is gripped by the season's bone-chilling damp. At home, fireplaces and stoves help to keep the cold at bay, but outside there's no escape from the winds that blow through the bare trees of the French Park at Kouzaka, or sweep up the Huangpu toward the Bund, raising choppy waves in the harbor's brown waters. Shanghai's whole aspect changes during this darkest season of the year. For us, it's a time to stay indoors, a time to talk with friends over a drink in the early winter twilight. For others it's a time when the city flaunts its cruelty most openly: how many of those beggars that you see on the pavement today, outside your house, outside your office, will survive the next two months until spring comes? or the next two weeks? or the next two nights?

The city's smells, among the most evocative of its characteristics, change at this season too. In summer we live with the all-pervasive stench of decay, of rot, of human waste, in a city, a country, that seems often to have given up the battle against dirt. Now the cold dulls those odors, and instead the air seems to dance with the scents of food, from the little restaurants on the street corners of the Chinese city, the thousands of vendors with their barrows peddling noodles, bean curd, boiled dumplings, fried meats, and the sharp and ubiquitous reek of the pickled vegetables that are so much a part of the Shanghai winter diet. Above it all, under the rain-drenched sky, hangs the cloud of dusty gray-brown smoke from the hundreds of thousands of fires burning the coal that the city uses for cooking and heating. No wonder bronchitis in all its forms is a frequent visitor in the winter, and though the foreign councils try vainly to prohibit spitting on the street, it will be a long time before that particularly Chinese form of catarrhal enjoyment is brought to an end. In the meantime you have to be careful where you step.

Nor had Simon's own affairs done much at this point to cheer him up. A hastily written entry in his private journal spoke of another unhappy passage with Rhonda—or at least Matthew assumed it was her.

Tuesday, January 19, 1926

She telephoned today, said she had to see me. No ready excuses, so we met at the Odessa near the avenue Joffre. Usual seedy crowd there, homesick & unkempt—old cavalry officers now become bodyguards for rich Chinese, musicians reduced to playing in café orchestras, the unemployed whose pride keeps them from physical labor, all lamenting former lives in Mother Russia. The Odessa's one of many such places—though they depress the spirit, their anonymity makes them useful for meetings like ours today.

Same old song—why have I passed so completely out of her life? After all she's done for me here, in Shanghai, is this to be the way I treat her? She's thinking of leaving, going back to England, to her family in Hull—I can tell she's oppressed by the prospect: dreary town, rain, no friends, nothing to do. And yet what future lies here?

I'm on trial today, she's appointed herself prosecutor & judge. She's heard I'm seeing a lot of a little American girl—but I break in, tell her that I won't have E.'s name dragged into her quarrel with me. Naturally I resent my position, & I suppose it shows. What can I say in my own defense? Why do I need a defense at all? She knew what she was doing as well as I.

Of course I feel sorry for her. And anyone watching us might say that I should be more sympathetic, shouldn't let her provoke me. God knows, she's not had an easy life. So if her purpose is to make me feel a bit of a heel, it's worked. But she's got no call to make any more demands on me—never any agreement between us, anyway, save that we'd both keep our freedom—nothing said about the future, no promises either made or broken.

It's cold in the café as we sit there, & outside the rain is beginning to come down harder. Two men at the table next to us argue quietly over their chessboard—in the corner, a pair of dark-haired lovers gaze at each other; they've hardly moved in the past hour, their food gone cold in front of them.

And she sits there, finishing her drink, too much makeup on her face, her too-strong perfume emphasizing the room's unpleasant closeness, looking at me ruefully. Aren't they called crow's feet, those little lines that are beginning to form around her eyes?

From the journal Matthew could not tell how far Simon's affair with Rhonda had become generally known. But he seemed very much on the defensive about it, and presumably it lay behind another one of the scattered entries about his personal life.

Thursday, February 18, 1926

What does John R. suspect? What has he heard that makes him distrust me, that leads him to think that I'm not suitable company for his niece? Not that he has any cause for his suspicions—unless he thinks that a few visits to my flat are unsuitable for an unchaperoned young girl, even though we're living in 1926 and not 1890.

But if times have changed at home, in some way they've stood still here. Strange, isn't it? All the world knows that Shanghai is a city of sin, a city where the white man loses his morals. All the world, that is, except those of us who live here, for in some ways this self-styled Paris of the Orient would make even Peoria or Des Moines seem wicked.

Not literally, of course. There is sin here, if that's not too old-fashioned a word, a kind of abandonment that makes Shanghai quite unlike any other city in the world. Americans, coming from their dry land, discover here whole rivers of wine and whiskey, oceans of gin and rum flowing through our midst. But drink's only the beginning. Though prostitution's supposed to be illegal now in the Settlement, it's easy enough to buy a woman if you want one. Chinese, if the fancy takes you: in the native city, here in Frenchtown, even in the Settlement if you know where to look. If you're squeamish about the Chinese for one reason or another, there are the White Russian girls. Many of them even have titles—Princess this, Countess that—but most of those noble ranks seem to have been discovered only after their holders arrived from Vladivostok or Harbin.

Drink, women. Gambling too. Opium, for those who want to try it. And a whole range of other amusements, corruptions, vices, sins, and perversions of the sort that are only whispered about, catering to that whole variety of frailties, needs, desires, natural and unnatural, that are part of the common condition of man.

That's the world's picture of Shanghai. But the men and women who rule our society, the taipans of the Shanghai Club and their like, lead blameless lives of an almost startling rectitude. Outwardly at any rate. Everyone may know that the director of a certain British shipping firm keeps his Chinese mistress in a luxurious flat on Bubbling Well Road, or that the head of a certain American trading company pays frequent visits to a Russian soubrette on the rue Ratard. But never must you refer to such affairs. It's almost as if admitting that such men were prey to normal human temptations would be to expose the hollowness of our claim to moral superiority. And the moral superiority of our race, in the end, is all that justifies our position here, all that gives us the privilege of determining what happens in this city of some three million souls.

So you must not reveal the little indiscretions of others. Or let your own leak out. If you do, and they are cried about the town as a public scandal, you're cut off, ostracized, exiled from society. It's not the enormity of the sin itself—the tawdry affair with your partner's wife, the inability to pay the debts that you ran up in your infatuation with Mlle Krupensky or Mme Shchukin, before she began showering her favors on your successor. No, it's your carelessness in letting all the world learn of such matters. It brands you, marks you out as a visible danger to the others of your race and your class. And then they have no choice but to sacrifice you, to cast you out, in order to protect themselves.

Hypocrisy? Of course it is. But a hypocrisy justified by the need to maintain face among the Chinese. Emily understands this. She may not like it, but she doesn't need to be told it. Any intelligent girl like her imbibes, even if unconsciously, the moral sense of those among whom she lives.

So, whatever our feelings may be toward one another, our meetings are carefully circumscribed by this narrow morality. There's the paradox: back in Nebraska, young couples lie locked in each other's arms in the automobiles that they've driven out into the night under the huge prairie sky alive with its million stars. But here, in this most libertine metropolis in the world, we don't even have that freedom open to us.

In America, men tell me of girls they've taken to towns

where no one knows them, signing the register as husband and wife in hotels where being strangers confers on them the privacy they are denied at home, where the desk clerk asks no questions, and, a knowing look on his sly face, becomes a partner in your fraud. Of course I don't want that kind of tawdry deception. I don't want the regrets you wake up with next morning, staring at the cheap patterned wallpaper, brown stains near the ancient iron radiator with its flaking paint, the torn cover on the faded green chair, a smell of waste and decay in the chilly air, wondering how many similar scenes have been enacted in this same dusty room on this same tired bed.

Anyway, it's impossible here. Perched on the edge of Asia's smoky vastness, in this huge alien city, it's as if we were living in a small town where everyone knows everyone else and everyone watches everyone else.

But we must have a place where we can be alone together. Without that sense of constant vigilance.

In Shanghai we live on a small, barren island of respectability, surrounded by the dazzling blue ocean of sin. And all the signs read: No public swimming allowed.

By spring, however, there were indications that the problem had found a temporary solution, and that Simon's relationship with Emily had moved to a different level. Or so Matthew guessed from a couple of passages he'd found in the private journal. The first described a matinee concert he'd gone to in late March, given by the Shanghai Municipal Orchestra, "a somewhat ragtag collection of Russian refugee violinists, Filipino wind players, and the occasional German or Austrian left over from before the war." During the intermission he'd talked to an old friend, Agnes Simmons, a middle-aged missionary attached to the Y.M.C.A. She had reported that Emily Ransom looked tired, and told him to keep an eye on his young woman. He'd responded defensively.

E.R.'s not my young woman, I told her, & if she looks tired, it's probably because she finds a Shanghai winter difficult. Agnes gave me a quick & sardonic smile—of course, living in the same household with John Ransom & his wife would make me find the winter difficult too. Or any other time of year. Then laughed. Not quite the Christian spirit, is it, Simon? But again she commanded me to watch out for E., who's too bright to become just another Shanghai debutante going to an endless round of parties & winding up at the altar someday with one of those empty-headed young clerks from Jardine's or Standard Oil. Or even—again the same smile—with one of our missionaries.

The bell rang, summoning us back to our seats for the remains of the afternoon's entertainment: Glinka, Glazounov, and Glière. There's a great vogue for Russian music here.

I don't think Emily's likely to wind up with a junior clerk. But I also don't like her being thought of as my young woman. Because in these last few weeks we have found our place, a place away from the prying eyes of Shanghai society. If E. looks tired, it may not only be because of the winter, or her work on the newspaper. Or even because of the endless round of parties that Agnes thinks she is going to.

Then, a page later, came the following passage, in Simon's almost unreadable handwriting.

None of the awkwardness or uncertainty, none of the elusiveness I'd anticipated—her mind made up, a creature of grace, diving into the unknown pool full of beauty and deep danger—coming up for air, shaking her flaxen hair out in the sun, centering herself in this new world, wistfully joyful in what she has gained from her loss, knowing that she will never again be what she was before—& all my sense of gratitude and wonder, to have been there with her, since the day of her first plunge, watching her swimming become stronger, more certain of itself, fearless now in even deepest & darkest waters.

Friday, June 2, 1989

Back at the hotel late that afternoon Matthew found a message to call Hilding. "Can you come by this evening?" the Englishman asked him when, after three attempts, he got through. "I've got someone you should talk to. Wei Tiaoyuan—or Thomas Wei, as he calls himself. He's well into his eighties now, but when he was young he was in the French police. I've known him for a few years, and he's full of stories about life in old Shanghai. I thought you might be able to ask him about your Simon Larsen."

Whether or not Hilding's friend would be able to help him with Simon, Matthew welcomed the opportunity to meet him. By the middle of the 1920s, as he knew, certain members of the *Garde municipale,* the police force of the French Concession, had entered into a corrupt bargain with Tu Yüeh-sheng, the chief of the Green Gang that controlled so much of the underworld, and through it, the distribution of opium in the city. And Simon himself had apparently discovered—or at least had suspected—what was going on. As he noted, in the early years of the twentieth century the Chinese government had undertaken a drive to stamp out the production and use of opium, and by 1917 the drug had become illegal in both of Shanghai's foreign settlements as well as in the Chinese city. "But whiskey's illegal back in the States," Simon had written in *Typhoon.*

> That doesn't mean it doesn't exist. Opium poppies grow all over China. Most of Shanghai's supply comes down from Yunnan or Szechwan, not counting the foreign mud that's brought in from Persia and Mesopotamia. Warlords up in the western provinces force the peasants to plant poppies. Then they send the drug downriver because Shanghai's the distribution point. Every steamer coming down the Yangtze—Chinese, Japanese, British, even Norwegian and American, carries opium. The captains look the other way, and so do some of the customs men.
>
> Sometimes the opium is thrown overboard in watertight containers for junks to pick up later; sometimes it's landed on deserted beaches at night; sometimes, so go the stories, it's even put into narrow tubes and forced down the gullets of ducks, who carry it ashore. But most of it gets loaded onto Chinese Navy ships at Woosung. From there they carry it up the river under guard to the military headquarters at Lunghua south of the city, and then the local general makes arrangements with his friends in the opium ring to retail it.

Simon's information about the French role came from an unlikely source. Jean-Pierre Duchamp was one of the fathers at the Jesuit mission in Siccawei, a man who had been in Shanghai about ten years, and who had, Simon reported with some envy, an excellent command of the Shanghai dialect. They had talked about the events of the summer, and the reactions of the missionaries and others to them.

His sympathies are clearly very much with the Chinese, and he had little good to say about the way Frothingham and his friends handled the crisis in the Settlement. But he's also got little good to say about his own countrymen—and sometimes about his own churchmen, for that matter.

From him I've had an extraordinary story that seems to bear out some of the common gossip here about links between the French and some of the less savory elements of local Shanghai society. Every month, according to Duchamp, Tu Yüeh-sheng and his Green Gang pay off the French police, and they pay off two or three members of our *Conseil municipal*, which runs the Concession. In return, the French choose to look the other way while Tu and his henchmen go about their business. Particularly the side of their business that deals with opium.

It's an arrangement that makes both sides happy. The gangsters keep control of the opium trade and get foreign protection. The French don't have to pay for a large police force because Tu Yüeh-sheng and his friends are powerful enough to guarantee that when Shanghai suffers from one of its periodic crime waves, the Concession will remain an island of law and order, and foreigners won't be bothered. Meanwhile, a few members of the French administration get a tidy sum of money that doesn't come from taxes and doesn't need to be reported. Everyone profits—except of course those whose lives are being ruined by the drug.

Is the story true? I don't know. But Duchamp has pretty good ties with the Chinese, and he's not the sort of man to go spreading rumors. "Why don't you tell the authorities?" I ask him. "Or your mission?"

He laughs scornfully. "The authorities don't need me to tell them," he answers. "And my superiors wouldn't believe me, and would be much happier if I say nothing. They don't want to embarrass the police or the consul general. It would upset Paris too much—both the French government and the French church."

Duchamp is a big man, a Breton with the rough hands and the square face of his peasant father. He joined the church, he said, because he thought that through it he would be able to help the poor, though he never expected to come to China then. "Perhaps if I'd stayed in France I'd have been a Communist by now," he told me the other day. "Or at least a socialist—my father was a great admirer of Jaurès, and wept the day he was assassinated." There are other people like him who come to China full of idealism. But most who stay for a few years get caught up in the foreign way of life here: lots of servants, big houses, everything you want. It's true even of many missionaries, French as well as American and English. But living here ten years hasn't changed Duchamp, hasn't made him forget why he became a priest, or why he came to China.

Rogers isn't much help when I ask him about the opium traffic. Even though his information is usually so good. He tries to change the subject; perhaps because he's on to something himself and doesn't want me to scoop him. "Of course there's an opium traffic here," he says, "and of course there's bribery. French police, English police, customs men— they're all in on it. That's the way China works, and that's the way foreigners have to work, too, if they want to get anything done here."

I tell him I need the information for my book. Writing about Shanghai and leaving out its crime is like writing about Chicago and leaving out the Capone gang.

"You're wasting your time," he replies. "You'll never find out anything. Nothing you can put in print, at any rate. There's a story out there, all right, but nobody's going to talk. Either because they're in it themselves, or because they're scared. Just like Chicago under the Capone gang."

When he met him that evening, Matthew was struck first by Wei Tiaoyuan's eyes. Short, bent over with arthritis and walking with a cane, the old man fixed Matthew with a look of high intelligence, his black eyes set deep in a skull over which the skin was so tightly drawn that it left no room for wrinkles. But what was extraordinary about them was their clarity, as if they alone had kept their youth while the rest of the body that now moved with such obvious difficulty had aged. He must have been a formidable opponent, Matthew thought, and even now he wouldn't want to cross him.

Wei had brought with him a young man in his early twenties, and Hilding made the introductions. *"Enchanté, m'sieu, enchanté,"* he said, taking Matthew's hand in a surprisingly strong grip. "This is Daoming, my grandson. I do not move about as well as I once did, and he helps me in getting around the city. He is a student at Jiaotong University, but we hope that he will be able to go abroad to study—to America, perhaps." He smiled at Matthew, who suddenly wondered if he was supposed to pull a scholarship award from Atherton out of his pocket to present to Daoming. Then, rather to Matthew's relief, the old man added: "But first he must learn his English better." He eased himself slowly and painfully into the chair that Hilding had provided, and refused the offer of a drink.

In a mixture of French and Chinese, Matthew sought to draw on Wei's memories, and the old man was clearly pleased to have someone to talk to about his past. He had joined the French police force in 1923, he told Matthew, when he was only eighteen, and had remained in it until 1943, the year that the Vichy regime had handed the Concession over to the puppet government set up by the Japanese during the war.

"Mr. Wei became something of a hero at that point," said Hilding. "Tell Mr. Walker about that. I'm sure he'd be interested."

Wei smiled. "It was nothing," he said. "No more than any patriotic Chinese would have done."

"Please," said Matthew. He could see that the old man was flattered to be asked. "I'd like to hear about it."

"By the time I resigned, I was already a member of the *geming dixia*, the revolutionary underground."

"For the Communists?" asked Matthew.

"At first for the Kuomintang. Later the Communists."

Wei and others had used their contacts with the French to gather what intelligence they could about the Japanese, passing it on to the Kuomintang and communist undergrounds. It was difficult and dangerous work, and more than once he had thought of stealing out of the city to join the communist guerrillas operating in northern Kiangsu province. Later on, after the Japanese surrender, when the civil war broke out again between Communists and Kuomintang in 1947, he had stayed on in Shanghai, now working for the communist underground, using his connections and his knowledge of police methods to ferret out information that would be useful to the Red armies.

"And you were never caught?" asked Matthew.

"Yes, once. And I was afraid I was going to be shot."

"What happened?"

"Fortunately, the captain who ran the jail was a man I had once promoted when I was in a position to do so. He was grateful to me. So one night he looked the other way and I was able to escape."

"And after the liberation of Shanghai in 1949, Mr. Wei was decorated by the government," said Hilding.

"Yes," said Wei. "And that helped me to save the life of the man who had saved mine. As a Kuomintang officer, he had been convicted of counterrevolutionary activities by the People's Court. But the judge was a friend of mine, and he trusted me. I was considered an important figure in those days because of my service to the Party. So the captain's life was spared. At that point." He stopped.

"At that point?" Matthew prompted him.

"Yes," said Wei. "But two years later he was arrested again. In the *su-fan* campaign, the campaign to exterminate counterrevolutionaries. There was nothing I could do for him then."

A silence followed this bleak announcement. Matthew remembered his talk with Wang Baozhen the previous day. When the regime did not trust even members of its own party, there was little hope for those who'd once opposed it.

He changed the subject, to bring the conversation back to Shanghai in Simon's day.

"Did you know Étienne Fiori?" Fiori, a Corsican, had been the chief of the *Garde municipale*.

"Capitaine Fiori—yes, I remember him. But I didn't know him well. I was just an ordinary constable in those days, and he was always surrounded by important people."

"I've been told that Fiori was connected with the opium traffic—was that true?"

Mr. Wei was silent. "I can't remember," he said.

"It was a long time ago," Daoming interjected helpfully.

"Did he have any dealings with Tu Yüeh-sheng?" asked Matthew. "Do you know anything about that?"

"Tu Yüeh-sheng." Mr. Wei thought for a while. "Yes. He was a very important man. Lots of people knew him. The French thought very highly of him, you know. He did much for the

Concession—schools, hospitals, that sort of thing. A man fond of good works."

"What about opium?" Matthew persisted. "What about his relations with Fiori?"

"They were friends. So people said. But I can't tell you anything about that. It was so long ago."

Matthew went off on a new tack. "In 1927, when the Nationalist armies were closing in on Shanghai, how much did the police know about the communist underground? About men like Lo Yi-nung, or Wang Shou-hua, or Chou En-lai? The men who were behind the uprising that March? Lots of them lived and worked in the French Concession."

"We knew they were patriots," said Wei. "And we didn't care if they were Communists. Chou En-lai was a great man. We were all patriots in those days. Even though we worked for the French, wore French uniforms, we were all proud when the revolutionary armies came, and we could see the flag of the new China flying over the city."

"But what happened after the insurrection?" asked Matthew. "When Chiang Kai-shek turned against the Communists, what part did people like Tu Yüeh-sheng play? And what about the French authorities?"

"Tu Yüeh-sheng cooperated with the Communists," replied Mr. Wei. "At first, before the Nationalists came. They were both against the warlords. But they never trusted each other."

"And then—?"

"And then Tu began to work with Chiang Kai-shek. They had known each other several years earlier, you see. When Chiang Kai-shek had lived in Shanghai." Mr. Wei fell silent again, and Matthew had the sense that he was wondering how openly he should answer these questions.

"So Chiang and Tu began talking?" Matthew prompted him.

"Yes. Neither of them trusted the Communists. And Chiang knew that Tu could be very helpful to him."

"Against the Communists, you mean?"

"Yes. Chiang Kai-shek had to put down the Communists if he was going to control the city. And when the purge began, it was Tu Yüeh-sheng's people who did most of the killing. Many people died then. Hundreds of them, thousands, perhaps."

"And what did Tu get out of it?"

"He ran the opium traffic in the French Concession—in all Shanghai. The Nationalists promised not to interfere if he helped them."

"And what about the French police?"

"We just followed orders. Many of us did not like what was happening, but there was nothing we could do, you understand. And in those days many of us thought that Chiang Kai-shek was a great patriot who would restore Shanghai to China's control." He paused again. "I am sorry, *m'sieu*. There is much I do not remember about those years." He glanced at his watch. The interview was obviously drawing to a close.

Hilding broke in again. "Mr. Walker is also trying to find out something about one of his relatives."

"I know it was a long time ago," said Matthew. "But there was a man here in Shanghai in those days, named Simon Larsen. Lai Shi'an. An American. He lived in the French Concession."

Mr. Wei gave him a quick look. Then, after a pause he said, "So did many others."

"He disappeared," Matthew continued. "Sometime in the troubles of 1927. And I am trying to find out what happened to him."

"He was an ancestor of yours?" asked Mr. Wei.

"Not mine," said Matthew. "But of a friend. I promised her I'd try to find out about him."

"Lai Shi'an," said Mr. Wei. "I don't know." He looked abstracted. "It was so long ago. *Si longtemps—vous comprenez? Hen jiu yiqian.* There were so many people."

"I think he had some sympathy for the revolution," said Matthew. "Perhaps even with the Communists. I hoped you might know where I could find out something about him. Or even might remember something yourself?"

"It was so long ago," Mr. Wei repeated. A suspicious note had crept into his voice. "So much has happened since then, and my memory isn't as good as it once was." He sounded tired again, and his eyes had become dull. "I'm sorry," he said, looking at his watch. "I must go. Daoming will take me home." He looked around. Daoming rose and helped him to his feet.

"Monsieur Wei," said Matthew, "you've been of very great help indeed. What you've told me will help me understand better this affair into which I am inquiring." Matthew's schoolbook French came out in a strangely formal and stilted way, and he was suddenly conscious of the surrealist vision that the two of them must present: here he was, on a hot night in Shanghai in 1989, talking to an octogenarian Chinese in the kind of French that made him sound for all the world like a bad parody of Hercule Poirot. All I need is a reference to the little gray cells, he thought, and the picture will be complete. "Can we call you a taxi?"

"I'd like that," said Mr. Wei. "Thank you." It would be an unaccustomed luxury not to have to wait for the bus, and to be delivered to his own door. "And in return, I will think more about your Lai Shi'an. Perhaps after a night's sleep—but give me your address and telephone number." Matthew scribbled them on his card, and handed it to the old man.

"Of course, if you can do anything to help—"

"I will see," said Mr. Wei. "Thank you. Good night."

After he'd left, Hilding turned to Matthew. "What d'you think, eh? He knows more than he lets on. I think he wants to know if he can trust you."

"Trust me?" said Matthew. "How?"

"Not to get him in trouble," answered Hilding. "Anyone in the French police in those days is likely to have known a good deal about the underworld. Even to have had ties to the underworld. Maybe he was a member of the Green Gang himself. Lots of them were, you know."

"But that's all over and done with now, surely."

"That's what the government says. And it's what I used to believe. But since I came to live in Shanghai a couple of years ago, I'm not so sure. Oh, I don't mean the Green Gang still exists, or that the opium trade is still going on. It isn't—not in Shanghai, anyway. But not all the old gang members fled to Hong Kong or Taiwan or Singapore in 1949, like Tu Yüeh-sheng. They're old men now, the ones who aren't dead. Some are still alive, in positions of some influence. And so are their families. China's built on a network of relationships—*guanxi*. The Communists haven't changed that. And a lot of old *guanxi* survives from the days before Liberation. No reason why the gang relationships should all have disappeared."

"So Mr. Wei may have some loyalty to his old comrades, you mean?"

"Loyalty—call it loyalty if you like. Maybe fear. If he talks too much, particularly to a foreigner, life could become very nasty for him. It's a good sign he asked how to get in touch with you. If he does, treat him well. Buy him some American cigarettes in the Friendship Store, or a bottle of brandy. It might be a good investment." He paused. "And now," he said, "what about a nightcap yourself?" He extracted a bottle of Courvoisier from a drawer and poured two drinks into tumblers. "Sorry I don't have the proper glasses. But this is still a proletarian society, you know." He smiled.

"Thanks." Matthew took the drink out of politeness, though he didn't really want it on a night of such heavy heat. "Have you heard from your daughter in Beijing?"

"Nothing," said Hilding. "And I don't mind telling you I'm anxious."

"Did you see the paper?" Matthew asked. "With the picture of the Goddess of Liberty?"

"That's what worries me," replied Hilding. "They've put her right in front of Mao's picture on the Tiananmen. Mao's no longer the hero he once was up in Beijing, but there are limits as to how far you can criticize him."

"I had a talk last night with Wang Baozhen," said Matthew. "Do you know her? A professor at Fudan?"

"I've met her," said Hilding. "Mary knows her. What does she think?"

"She didn't make any guesses about what's going to happen. But she said it would be a good time for you to convince your daughter to come back to Shanghai."

Hilding glanced up at him. "I know," he said. "I've tried to do that. But you know what the young are—they don't think anything can happen to them. And it's not so easy to get hold of her. I can't just send a telegram to her in the square."

He sat there thoughtfully, sipping his brandy. "Professor Wang strikes me as the sort of person who knows what she's talking about. I wish I could do something." His voice drifted away, and it was clear that his mind was up north, as if worrying about his daughter could help her. "Maybe I should go to Beijing myself and see if I can find her. I've got friends there who might help. But traveling is difficult at the moment."

They talked on in a desultory way, finishing their drinks, wrapped in the hot dampness of the night that surrounded them, even in that room. Then Matthew got up to leave. "Thank you for asking me this evening," he said. "You've been very helpful to me, and I very much enjoyed meeting Mr. Wei. And if you think of any way I might help you, please let me know."

"It's kind of you to offer," Hilding replied. "But I'm sure everything will be all right. And in the meantime, good luck with your work, and good luck with the hunt for your uncle Simon. I'll keep my ears open, and if I hear anything more, I'll let you know. In the meantime, why don't you come have lunch with me on Sunday? Take some time off from your work. I'd like to talk to you about these memoirs I'm supposed to be writing, since you're a historian and you understand these things."

CHAPTER FIVE

When they had left Ponte Cerrone last year, Matthew and Laura had allowed themselves an extra week to spend alone together before returning to America. Back up north from Tuscany they had sped, beyond Milan, and along the placid shores of the Lago Maggiore (memories of Lieutenant Henry and his Katherine as they passed the Edwardian grandeur of the Grand Hôtel et des Isles Borromées; but they spent the night at a modest *pensione* in Domodossola). The next morning, the road led them through Iselle and up the narrowing gorge of the Val Divedro. At Gondo they crossed into Switzerland, pushing the complaining little Fiat up the steep curves to the summit of the Simplon, much to the annoyance of the more powerful cars stretched out in a column behind them. At the top of the pass Matthew pulled over to park, letting the others rush by, horns squawking loud Teutonic blasts of relief and aggravation. But here above the trees, the shining snows of the Weissmies climbed into the cloudless sky of early July, and the alpine meadows were alive with wildflowers: white marguerites and alpine fennel, yellow trollius and anemones, the deep blue of gentians, while farther up the slopes the red of the Alpenrosen burned darkly under the high gray cliffs.

That brief time in the Alps had been a magical one for both of them. Advised to avoid both the crowds and the expense of more favored spots such as Zermatt or Saas-Fee (every day the

119

Herald Tribune reported the dollar's downward plunge), they had gone instead to Arolla, a tiny town in the Valais, lying at the end of a perilously narrow road that rose high above Evolène and finished in a small larch-filled valley under the mountains. There they'd stayed in one of those small hotels that can still be found in the Alps, making few concessions to late-twentieth-century tourism: no business centers, no pale blond wood furniture, no saunas or whirlpool baths. Matthew, who some years earlier had found himself spending a rainy week in a summer house whose owner had collected old Baedekers, suddenly felt that he had stepped back into the kind of world described by those faded red guides. The crooked floorboards of their room supported two simple white-painted iron beds covered with an array of blankets and quilts that seemed to have come from a secondhand sale at a folk crafts store of perhaps thirty years ago. On the pale brown walls hung lithographs of famous scenes from Swiss history and myth—the oath on the Rütli, William Tell escaping from the boat carrying him to captivity across the storm-tossed waters of the Vierwaldstättersee—and, improbably, Gladstone addressing Parliament on Irish home rule. But the view from the window gave out on to the huge rock and ice-hung bulk of the Mont Collon, its summit touched by earliest rays of the morning sun, and ruddy in the evening's alpenglow.

Four days they had spent together there, exploring the countryside, walking up to the glaciers at the end of the valley, or climbing high above the trees into the summer meadows under the graceful snow slopes of the Pigne d'Arolla that curved white into the noonday sky. On their last morning they had left the hotel early, heading up to a pass that would give them a view of the adjoining valley to the west. It was a steep climb, and below the final slope they left the path to wander into a sun-warmed meadow, resting in the lee of a large boulder that protected them from the wind blowing down from the glaciers. Matthew, stretched out on the ground, elbows on the earth, his hands propping up his face, gazed at Laura, who lay flat on her back, looking up at the sky and at the occasional small clouds moving over the mountains above her. It was a moment of utter peacefulness, and he was captivated: by the day, by the surroundings, and by the sight of Laura lying there, her dark hair against the wildflowers, her long brown legs, and the light blue polo shirt that rose and fell steadily with her breathing.

"Laura?"

Silence at first. Then: "Yes. That's me, Laura."

"What are you thinking about, Laura?"

"What am I thinking? Oh, Matt, I don't think I had any thoughts." She smiled at him lazily. "Did I? Should I have?"

"I don't know. You weren't telling them."

"I wasn't telling them. No, I guess not." She put her hands behind her head, drew one brown knee up. "Maybe I was thinking—about the day, about the weather. About our time here. About you, Matt—about us. And what it all means."

"About what all what means?"

Silence again. "I don't know. I don't want to think about it now. About anything. It's so lovely here. I just want to enjoy it while we can. Look at the sky—I've never seen such blue." She glanced at him again. "Matt?"

He drew close to her, pulling himself along the ground until his face was above hers, looking at her eyes, now almost closed. But not quite. She lay there quietly, not moving. He picked a yellow daisy and put it in her hair, above her left temple. But he could see that her breathing had become quicker, the rise and fall of the blue shirt more pronounced.

"Matt—"

He moved closer to her, until his mouth was lightly brushing hers. She didn't move at first, but now her lips were slightly parted as he kissed her. Gently, gently, but then her hands took his head, and pulled him closer, tighter toward her. There was a passion in her kiss, a passion that almost made Matthew sad—a passion that seemed to say: I know that this is coming to an end, I don't want it to, but I don't know what to do about it, how to stop time.

After a while she gently pushed him away and got unsteadily to her feet. Smiling down at him lying there, she walked over to where he'd left his pack. "Lunchtime, Matt." Bending down to reach into it, she took out the food they'd packed and brought it back to where he was still lying. "We've got some climbing left to do." Above them, the path left the meadows and turned steeply up the rocks that led to the Pas de Chèvres, the Goat Pass, that was their objective for the day.

Sitting cross-legged, leaning against the rock, she carefully began putting slices of local cheese and some dried meat into the rolls they'd bought that morning at the bakery.

"Why do we have to leave this, Matt?" The sun brought out the russet colors of her hair, falling across her cheek, and Matthew, passing her a cup filled with pale gold *fendant*, the dry wine that comes from the steep vineyards of the Valais, suddenly thought: This is it, why must it ever change, why can't we keep it?

"D'you want to come live here? Run away, leave your friends and family, your home?" He wanted to forget that it was their last day, that in less than thirty-six hours they'd be in Boston.

"To come to a country where it's always early July, where the sun always shines on the mountains, where the sky is always blue, and where we can always eat bread and cheese and meat and drink cold white wine on a hot summer day? Leaving behind all my obligations, the things I have to do, and the things I should do? Of course. Why not?"

"And Conrad and the others? Are you going to leave them behind too?"

"Forget Conrad and the others. They can look after themselves, and there'll be plenty of other graduate students after me to take care of them. I can think of them now, slaving away in their library stalls, worrying whether the rest of the world will ever recognize their brilliance."

"And publish their articles and their books."

"I *can* think of them now, but I don't want to. Matt, perhaps at least someday we can come back."

"Years from now, when we're old and creaky, we'll hobble up these slopes together—"

"By then there'll probably be jet-propelled ski lifts or something—"

"—and look out over these same mountains, and remember the days of our youth—"

"And regret all the misspent years that came in between—"

"Years spent studying Conrad—"

"And Chinese history, and the book you have to write—"

"And teaching classes to people who don't care, and grading papers full of dangling participles and run-on sentences—"

"And then we'll say: we were wrong, we should have forgotten everything, settled down here in our Hôtel des Trois Suisses, and abandoned ourselves to the inspiration of the mountains, to thinking great thoughts like John Ruskin or Samuel Butler. So if that's what we're going to come to eventually, why don't we do it now?"

Public displays of affection upset the Swiss almost as much as the Chinese, Matthew had discovered. So he looked around carefully, and was disappointed to see a gray-haired Swiss-German couple coming slowly up the path. He caught Laura's eye and grimaced, but she smiled back at him: Wait till they get by. "*Grüezi miteinander,*" they called out pleasantly as they passed, and "*Grüezi,*" echoed Matthew, nodding at them.

"There we go," Laura murmured to him in a low voice. "A look into the future: forty years from now, trudging together up the mountain."

Forty years from now: Matthew couldn't imagine such an impossibly distant time in his life. Even ten years was too much. But as soon as they were hidden from sight behind a boulder, Matthew took her in his arms and kissed her again, tasting the wine on her cool lips, feeling her respond to him, clinging to him, her long body stretched against his. Yet she was trembling, and this time, when they drew apart, she was no longer smiling, her gray eyes were filled with tears and she looked away, unable to speak. They finished their lunch in near silence, and then, though the path upward looked steeper than ever, they finished their climb—"We came here to get to the top of the pass," said Laura, "and the Puritan conscience always wins out, even when you're supposed to be enjoying yourself." One hour and a thousand feet later they stood among the steep rocks at the summit, looking down the cliffs to the broad Glacier de Cheilon below, the thin, sharp wind from the snowfields cutting through their sweat-drenched shirts to the skin.

Two days later they sat crushed together in the aluminum anonymity of a DC-10, looking out the window as their plane headed northwest from Milan, over the Val d'Aosta, past the great south face of the Mont Blanc, an unbroken sweep of ten thousand feet of rock and ice rising above Courmayeur at its base. Then a sudden return to reality: plastic food appeared on plastic trays, followed by a movie about three women in a small town in Texas coping with divorce. A few hours later the choppy waters of Massachusetts Bay appeared below them, and beyond, the towers of downtown Boston rose darkly into a heavy summer overcast. Home: the life that lay waiting, of things to be done, of classes to be prepared, of scrawled notes and computer disks and printouts that marked the slow progress of Laura's unfinished Ph.D. thesis, and Matthew's unfinished book.

* * *

In the spring of 1926, the foreign voters of the International Settlement had at last grudgingly agreed to allow three carefully chosen Chinese to sit with the Shanghai Municipal Council as that body deliberated on the Settlement's affairs. Though the announcement was supposed to be an olive branch, it failed, for by that time even the relatively conservative businessmen of Chinese Shanghai were demanding nothing less than a council directly elected by all eligible voters—Chinese as well as foreigners—and thus, in effect, a council that they would dominate. "So they can run things as they want," Simon's journalist friend Ben Rogers had pointed out. "Run them without having to kowtow either to the bunch of thieves who run Peking, or the even worse bunch of thieves who run the Chinese city here. All the virtues of foreign legal protection and none of the drawbacks."

That spring, as Simon noted in *Typhoon*, there had been good reason, both for Chinese and for foreigners, to distrust the government in Beijing.

Friday, March 26, 1926

When men and women are killed, how much difference does it make what fingers are on the triggers, whose are the hands that fire into a defenseless and unresisting crowd? No difference to the victims, surely; the laws of physics that guide the flight of the bullets, the laws of physiology that determine how the bones will be pulverized, the blood vessels smashed, the brains and hearts cease their life-giving work, pay no attention to such matters. Perhaps we who are the witnesses to such events should try to emulate the detachment of the scientist when we consider what it is that we have seen. But we are subject ourselves to other laws, and when our first shocked horror has passed, we are driven, in our very makeup as human beings, to judge such acts, to praise or to blame, and to excuse in the one action what in the other we would have found intolerable.

Consider what has just happened in Peking, where once again scores of innocent people have died. This time, however, it was Chinese, not foreign, rifles that did the killing.

A week ago, several thousand men and women, some no more than boys and girls, gathered in the square outside the T'ien-an-men, the Gate of Heavenly Peace, that great red portal capped by a roof of yellow imperial tile that guards the entrance to the Forbidden City. They met to protest an intervention by the foreign powers in the endless civil war that this spring has once again flared up in north China. As others have before them, they cried out for an end to all control by foreigners, to the unequal treaties that continue to humiliate and shackle their country and force her to grovel to the outside world. They were harmless, utterly harmless, but the government, embarrassed and frightened by this outpouring of passion, fought back. The troops of Feng Yü-hsiang—the Christian general, as the missionaries like to call him—opened up on the unarmed crowd, and by the time their guns fell silent, forty-seven men and women lay dead. More than four times the number slain on Nanking Road last May. And yet—and yet—

And yet—how little anger there has been! Of course the Kuomintang has once again uttered its condemnations from Canton, and here in Shanghai once again the slogans and posters have blossomed briefly in the early spring sun, denouncing the unholy alliance between foreign imperialism and the warlords who are their running dogs, as the colorful Chinese epithet has it. But the affair has been quickly forgotten. To foreigners here, like Eric Massingham or John Ransom, it's just another proof of Chinese hypocrisy, proof that the Chinese, ever ready to condemn the foreign guardians of law, lack the stomach to deal with their own domestic tyrants.

So, as Eric Massingham predicts, there will be no boycott of Chinese goods to protest what the Chinese government has done. "In the foreign settlements," he complains, "we're forced to follow our own legal procedures, and the troublemakers know how to take advantage of them. Maybe the Chinese are wiser about such matters than us. They act first and ask questions later." He brings the side of his hand down firmly on the back of his neck to illustrate the point: "Chop-chop. You know what I mean." He looks around, seeking approval.

An American girl [this could only be Emily, Matthew realized], who is standing nearby, turns to him with her eyes full of innocent guile. "Do you mean," she asks, "that we should emulate the Chinese in such matters? And allow Chinese laws and Chinese ways to run in the settlements?" I admire her spirit, but Massingham is startled and falls back on the time-honored argument. "Wait till you've been here a bit longer," he counsels her, and I watch her jaw tense as that tired phrase tumbles out yet again. "Then you'll realize that Shanghai isn't London or New York, and that the traditions of English law mean little to the Chinese criminal mind."

Every instinct I have teaches me to object to Massingham's easy conclusions. They are so one-sided, so reflective of the common foreign view here that the Chinese are selfish and individualistic, lacking in any sense of common purpose or public spirit. And yet, seeing what has happened, it's hard to avoid conceding that Massingham and those like him have a point. Mr. Chu admits that he is shamed by the tragedy: ashamed because it was Chinese who killed Chinese, and ashamed that such an act does not make his people cry out as they would if the foreigners had done it. "Their fear explains the silence in part," he says to me as we sit in my rooms in the late afternoon. "But only in part, for even down in Canton, where there is no reason for fear, they have been quieter than they should.

"Yet some have dared to speak out," he continues, pulling a handful of magazines and papers from his briefcase to show me. From them he picks out an essay by a professor at a university in Peking. One of his students, a young girl, was among those killed in T'ien-an-men Square last week, and it is in her memory that he has written this piece.

He puts on his glasses, and reads me a passage, translating it into English as he goes.

" 'As I've said before, I'll never shrink from thinking the worst of the Chinese. But this affair really shows a side I'd never quite expected.... I never thought we'd act with such appalling barbarism.' " His voice breaks off, and he looks at me. "That is the way many of us feel."

He continues his reading:

" 'Time flows on forever: the streets of the city are quiet again, for in China, a few lives are of no account. At most, they give good-natured loafers something to gossip about, or evil-natured idlers the stuff of "rumors." But I doubt whether there's any deeper significance than this, since it was only an unarmed demonstration. History shows that mankind's fighting forward through bloodshed is like the way coal is formed: a great deal of wood produces only a tiny lump. But demonstrations aren't really like this, particularly when they're unarmed.

" 'This time, however, blood was shed, and no doubt that will attract some attention. . . . Those who are indifferent may catch a faint glimpse of hope in the pale color of the blood; those who are real fighters will now push on with a greater determination.' "

His voice is heavy with grief as he ends. He leaves me the copy as he goes. "Read the whole essay," he says, ever the teacher. "It will be good for your Chinese, for he writes our modern language well. And it will be good for you to know what a man of principle and intelligence is saying about the problems of his country. Good-bye, Lai *hsien-sheng.*"

The writer's name is Lu Hsün.

Then, in the late spring of 1926, Simon's relations with Emily reached a crisis. Somehow, somewhere—if it was a mystery to Simon, it was even more of one for Matthew reading it now— Emily found out about Rhonda. There was a painful scene: accusations, recriminations, arguments. The journal entry was for Tuesday, May 18, presumably the day on which Emily had taxed him with what she had discovered.

How did she find out? Isn't it enough that I broke off with R. almost a year ago? We're all through, have been through for months. E., unconvinced, insists it's not what I've done she minds, it's that I never told her.

I try to explain. Yes, I do know R., yes, at one time we used to see a good deal of each other. But that was ages ago, long before I met you. She never meant anything to me. But I was lonely, she was amusing to talk to—

Talk? Only talk?

I try to reason with her, but she won't listen, like so many women, lets her emotions get the better of her, says she knows men are like that, men have, well, certain desires that have to be satisfied.

Only men? I wonder, as I think back to all our meetings this past winter—but of course I don't say that.

She leaves in tears, saying that she can never trust me again.

Friday, June 2, 1989

Any swift change in the conditions of life brings with it a kind of immediacy. The insistence of an unfamiliar present makes everything else, even one's own past, seem suddenly distant, a series of disparate events that took place only in someone else's story. For Matthew, coming to China was to plunge into another world, a world so strange and foreign that even his own most intense and recent memories seemed to take on something of the character of history, a narrative of the past that had been mediated by others and was at the mercy of others. Not quite a year ago, he and Laura had made their unreflecting discovery of each other among the gray-green olive groves and sun-colored farmhouses of the Tuscan countryside. Yet here today in Shanghai, different Shanghai, dingy, crowded, and busy Shanghai, it seemed to Matthew almost as if all that had passed between them had happened to two other people, and that he was merely an observer.

What if I were to sit down and write about it, he thought. At home it would never even occur to him to undertake such a task, and even if by some chance the idea struck him, he knew he could never do it. Unlike Simon, he'd never kept a journal other than an occasional and impersonal record of events he wished to remember. Knowing that it would be incomplete because, even in privacy, he could never reveal himself, he therefore preferred not to do it all.

If I ever had to write an autobiography, a self-analysis, he thought, it would have to be in a place like this: foreign, distant, thoroughly removed from both the easy security and the constraints of the familiar. And he knew that what would come out would be like a historian's treatment of the subjects he discovers in his documents: detached, objective, a little dry perhaps, and analytical only because it was self-effacing, a record that seemed to be not really about oneself, but about others. Like the past that he was trying to evoke here in Shanghai, a past gotten not through experience but through his patient researches. A past, in other words, with which he had no more than an intellectual connection. (Do historians, Matthew wondered, write about other places and other times to avoid confronting themselves? Do they participate, perhaps, in the guilty pleasures of the voyeur, the unseen observer of the actions of others?) Suddenly he had a vision of himself and Laura here, sixty-five years ago, like Simon Larsen and his Emily: two characters out of someone else's history, someone else's novel, moving toward their undetermined and unplotted futures. Futures over which he had no more control than over those of Simon and Emily, and that long-ago world in which they had moved.

Matthew's break with Laura had come about quite differently from that between Simon and Emily. The split between them—and even that term had about it a precision that did not seem fully to fit the case—had begun to open much more slowly, much more gently, a division without tears or recriminations. Yet it was no more comprehensible for all that. Less so, in fact; even while he might have found her accusations unjust, at least Simon had known why Emily had turned against him.

They had returned from Europe, pleased with themselves and with each other, relieved that their travels, which like any journey had been undertaken with something of risk about it, had reached a safe, if perhaps temporary, haven. A few years earlier, Matthew had found himself almost on the point of a formal engagement with someone he'd known in college; then at the last minute, worried whether he was ready to take on such an obligation, he'd broken it off—or, more accurately, had brought about an understanding that they would both go their separate ways. The experience had left her hurt, and him scarred, not so much by the episode itself as by the fear of what his behavior might tell him about himself. With Laura, things would be different, for in her Matthew thought he had found someone whose intelligence gave her the kind of independence that would make few demands on him and yet would allow a continuance of the early closeness they'd achieved during their time together that summer.

Yet it hadn't worked like that. Back in America last year, the enchantment of July began somehow to fade. It happened gradually, and at first neither one of them realized what was taking place. That fall, as a visiting instructor at Atherton, Laura was teaching a course on nineteenth-century women's writing. As she told Matthew, she would have preferred a less restricted subject, but the English department, a den of satisfied males old and young, was faced with a growing demand for women's studies, and so she found herself unwillingly required to do not only Jane Austen and George Eliot (whom of course she would have taught in any case), but also such figures as Mrs. Gaskell, Elizabeth Barrett Browning, and the elusive Christabel LaMotte. So he saw much of her, both during her twice-weekly trips to the college and his own occasional visits to Cambridge, where her pile of note cards and computer files was steadily growing into her dissertation. Meanwhile they talked little about the future, about where their relationship was leading them, even though Matthew, at least, spent a good deal of time thinking about how Laura might fit into the sort of life he envisioned for himself. Yet while there was no one time, no particular event, that marked their separation, each was aware, as autumn declined into winter, that their relations were subtly but unmistakably changing. In ways that were never defined, a distance was opening between them, and they became like two countries sharing a frontier, still officially friendly but neither quite sure of the other's intentions. The border was far from closed, but on either side the frontier guards were wary, and a cautious traveler might decide that crossing the line was more trouble than it was worth.

Their natural reserve kept them not only from talking openly about what was happening, but even from facing it straightforwardly within themselves. Consciously or unconsciously, they each put their feelings down to the pressures of work. Laura was determined to finish her dissertation by the following summer, and was beginning the arduous and painful task of applying for teaching jobs in a market already thoroughly glutted by specialists in modern literature. Meanwhile Matthew struggled hard to stay ahead of his students in two courses that he'd never taught before, and, under the heavy weight of his approaching review for tenure, gave what little spare time he had to work on his book.

Then finally, one cold day in early December, the break—if that's what it was, Matthew thought, for even later he was never really sure—came out into the open. They'd been out one Friday afternoon walking in the countryside near Atherton, under the sort of flat, cold overcast that brings the threat of snow by nightfall. In the brief light of early winter, the earth was gray and brown, the bare maples on the hills stark against a dun-colored sky. Neither one had said much, and it was only when they got back to Matthew's apartment that, rather to his own surprise, he suggested that she leave Cambridge and come to live with him, commuting from Atherton to Harvard rather than the other way around.

He couldn't find his glasses, and was wandering distractedly about the room, searching for them, as he brought the words out. It was, he knew, a way of avoiding looking directly at her when he made the suggestion.

"I can't," she told him. "I've got to be near the library. And all my books and my notes are there. It would be too much of a disruption in my work, and I've got to finish up before next fall."

"But you could work just as well here, couldn't you?" He pulled open a drawer in his desk, hoping that the missing glasses might be in there. They weren't. "You could fix up the spare room as a study. Put your books and your computer in there, and everything you need for your work."

She tried another approach. "Anyway, I can't possibly break the lease on my apartment, and I'm not allowed to sublet it." She lived in the top two rooms of an old frame house behind the fire station on Garden Street.

Of course he thought she was just making excuses. He also knew that his suggestion had come because he was afraid of los-ing her, and he wanted to try to recapture the closeness that they'd felt last summer. Or at least that he had felt, and thought she had too. But now he wasn't so sure.

She looked at him, serious gray eyes searching into his, but said nothing. Outside it was already dark, and the two standing lamps that he had switched on threw off a light at once merci-less and dreary in its exposure of the room's shortcomings: the cracking paint on the window frames, the uneven molding that ran around the ceiling, the cheap patterned paper that he'd in-herited from an earlier tenant and hadn't ever gotten around to replacing. A place in which to survive rather than to live. In the silence, a quartz clock ticked off the seconds.

She turned away from him and stared at the night outside. "I've got my career to think of, and jobs in English departments are hard enough to get. And—"

"And what?"

"I don't quite know how to say this, and I don't want you to take it personally." Careful; a sign that trouble lies ahead. "Look, Matt, I like you very much. I loved being with you last summer, and I'll always remember our time together. I was ecstatic then. You know that."

"But?"

She looked at the floor, dark hair falling over her eyes. "But it's not just the dissertation and the lease on the apartment. It's just that—well, I'm not the sort of person who can just pick up and move in at a moment's notice." The toe of her shoe traced a design on the floor.

A moment's notice? He was hurt, and he must have showed it.

"Oh, I know that's not what you meant. It's just that I want to be sure of what we're doing. Sure for both of us. You must know that." Suddenly she got up and walked over to a pile of books and papers in the corner. When she came back, she had the missing glasses. "Oh, Matt, sometimes you really are the image of an absentminded professor. They were right there in front of you all the time, and you were looking right at them." She reached up and put them on his nose. "What are you going to be like when you get older?"

He heard in her voice a kind of weary, almost annoyed affection: the voice one might use toward a large, ungainly dog, a voice that seemed to suggest that she was asking herself not so much whether she really wanted to spend her life with him, as to spend it in the sort of world whose coloration he was already taking on.

He wasn't going to let her change the subject.

"But, Laura, I thought we'd decided—after last summer—"

"I don't know what we decided, Matt. Last summer was wonderful. I think of it all the time. Sometimes even when I'm in class, teaching." She picked a piece of thread off his sweater, and smiled. "But it was like being in another world, a world where what we did had no relation to this world, the real world that we live in now. Like the shipboard romances of our grandparents' generation. You know—five days of moonlit nights, orchestras playing on the *Île de France*, and then suddenly you're back in New York in the dawn and it's all over."

"Look, that's not the way I thought of it. Sure, I admit it, I do want you to come live with me here because I think we could be the way we were last summer. You could live here, do your work, I'd do mine. What's the matter with that?"

"What's the matter with that is that it's on your turf. And on your terms. I don't expect you to see that, because men never do. But there's something about men, good men, men with all the liberal values, like you. Oh, I know, you're all in favor of female equality, affirmative action, gender-neutral language, and all those other wonderful things. But you still think that once you have a relationship with a woman, you can possess her. And I'm not ready to be possessed. Yet or perhaps ever. Why is it that men with good liberal values continue to make life hell for women? Look at your friend Steve Richardson. It's all right for him to go renew himself at the fountain of youth, but what are Sally's chances at her age?" Richardson, a professor of English who spent his life fighting apartheid, saving whales, banning the bomb, and deconstructing the classics of nineteenth-century American literature, had recently left his wife of twenty years and the three children she had borne him, to move in with one of his former students. Sally, who worked in the college's personnel office, had been stunned, and suddenly looked far older than her years. The Ancient Mariner, one of Richardson's supporters had uncharitably called her. Laura, noticing the new spring in Steve's step, the new animation in his look, saw there nothing more than a grotesque caricature of youth, and it made her afraid. "I know you're not like that, Matt. But it does seem to be a common problem around here, doesn't it? The man, no longer in his first youth, but still handsome and vigorous, can always find an adoring student to bed down with when he gets tired of his wife. And she's left out in the cold."

"Laura." He looked at her, shocked. "I'm not like that, I love you." He did, and honestly meant it. "I want to be with you."

"Maybe, Matt. Maybe someday. But not till I'm sure. And till you're sure too. And we both know what it means."

What it means? He didn't see any mystery. "Think about it, anyway. You look tired, Laura. You're working too hard. Sleep on it—"

At that she flared up at him. "Tired—tired, tired! Why do all men say that when women don't do what they want? Aren't men ever unreasonable because they're tired?" She paused, and looked at him, and now her voice had a hard edge to it. "Matt, I trusted you. But, you know, sometimes I don't think you give a damn about what I'm doing. About my work, my career, I mean."

Matthew was totally at sea, shocked at the seeming unfairness of the remark. Remembering all those conversations when he'd tried to draw her out. What did trust have to do with it, anyway? "But don't you still?" was all he could say.

Laura relented. Partly, at least.

"Oh, I don't mean it like that. I don't mean you're trying to take advantage of me, trying to use me. At least not in the conventional sense. I know that what you're suggesting seems perfectly normal to you. I guess I mean I trusted you to see my position. Or at least understand it."

"Like—?" Of course he hadn't any notion of what she meant. But he was trying to draw her out to cover up his ignorance.

"To see why it wouldn't work. For me, anyway. And if it didn't work for me, it wouldn't work for you either."

She must have seen the hurt on his face. A hurt that came not so much from her rejection as from his sense that he might have said the wrong thing, done the wrong thing.

"Matt, look. We're not ready for this. I'm certainly not, and I don't think you are either. I've got my future to think of. And you—"

He waited.

"You've got—you've got—oh, I don't know. You've got to learn to see things—from other people's points of view."

He was stunned. "Laura, I'm sorry if I've hurt your feelings—"

That only seemed to make her angry again.

"Look, Matt, it's not my feelings I'm worried about. Well, maybe it is. Because I thought you were different. That you weren't the sort of man who'd insist on seeing things only through your own eyes. Who'd see that there'd be room for me as something more than—well, someone around whenever you want me."

By now he was wondering what could possibly have gotten into her. He'd never seen her like this before. Something must have happened to upset her, to make her react this way. Yet, unwilling as he was to admit it, he had a sense of unease, almost guilt, at what she was saying. Last summer's trip had been mostly of his own devising, and she'd fallen in so easily with his plans, content to let him make the decisions: where to go, what to see, where to stay. Had he, perhaps, assumed too easily her compliance? The trip had, as Laura had said, put them in an unreal world, a world of no troubles, no responsibilities. Was this the real Laura he was seeing now?

"Look, Matt," she said, her voice gentler now. "You're asking me to come live with you. I know you don't mean it this way, but I can't help feeling I'm to be companion and housekeeper while you go about your daily routines. Meanwhile, somehow I'm meant to get on with my own future." The edge had come back into her voice. "Unless maybe you don't think that's important." Her tone rose at the end: a question, a challenge?

"That's not what I meant." But what exactly had he meant? Was she really so wrong?

She ignored him. "And there are no promises, no commitments. As if—as if—I don't know. Maybe that's what made me a bit angry, feeling—well, let down." He was relieved that at least she hadn't said "betrayed."

"Angry, because like so many good, decent men, you just don't get it."

"Laura, let's drop it. I'm sorry I even brought the subject up." He was. He hated arguments—arguments like this, anyway, arguments on emotional subjects that touched him personally. Intellectual arguments he enjoyed.

Now her eyes softened again, and she became more like the Laura he knew.

"I'm sorry, Matt. I didn't mean to blow up at you like that. But I just don't think we're ready for this step yet. We've both still got some thinking to do." She came over and sat on the arm of his chair, her hands ruffling his hair, trying to soothe him. "Don't be angry, Matt. Please."

He felt miserable, felt almost betrayed himself. Why? Simply because she hadn't gone along with him? Or was it perhaps that he had betrayed himself by showing her how much he took for granted?

"Okay, Laura," he said. "Forget it. I'm not angry." But now he wanted her to leave so that he could be alone, take cover in his emotional foxhole, lick his wounds, and try to figure out what had hit him.

She sat in silence for a while, then seemed to sense what he was thinking, seemed to sense the time had come to go.

"Well, I guess I've got to be on my way. I've got lots of work to do."

She rose, and stood there, the glow of the lamp picking out the tawny lights in her hair, her gray eyes looking at him, kind now, as if she wanted to console him. For what she'd done—or what he'd done to himself.

"Good-bye, Laura." He kissed her distractedly on the cheek, feeling it a meaningless gesture. "I'll see you next week, I guess."

"Sure, Matt. See you then." She gave him a wan smile, and then moved distractedly to the door. "I'll still be here."

So she'd gone back to Cambridge then rather than spend part of the weekend with him. Though he'd never admit it, even to himself, he recognized, way down deep, a slight sense of relief that his own routines wouldn't be disturbed by Laura's presence. Much as he would have liked to have her there. So they'd gone on seeing each other, feeling each other out in conversation, as if trying to discover without ever talking openly about it what sort of a change had taken place, why it had taken place. Occasionally they lunched together on the days that Laura was teaching at Atherton, and several times Matthew went to Cambridge to see her. But it was a chaste and reserved friendship in which they talked about ideas, about their work and the books they were reading, even about the academic politics they had once disdained.

A friendliness, as of dwarfs shaking hands, was in the air—the odd phrase from E. M. Forster came back to him. Last summer he and Laura had laughed over it—but now he thought he understood what it meant.

After Emily's break with him in the spring of 1926, Simon's journal made far less mention of her, though Matthew sensed that she was still very much on his mind. Occasional brief passages, sometimes no more than a sentence or two, spoke of his attempts to talk to her again, all of which she rebuffed, of the letters which were returned unopened, and of the way in which the sight of her, in the company of others, in a restaurant or a club, left Simon feeling both hurt and jealous. And, now in his fifth year in China, he began once again to ask himself what point was served by his continual absence from home.

Wednesday, June 9, 1926

Not for a year, not since that harrowing day that changed us all, have I seriously thought again of leaving. What is it, I wonder, that keeps me here, in a country that is not my own, among people whose ways are not mine? I tell myself that it's China, of course, that I must stay to the end, to see played out the last act of the drama that opened twelve months ago with its scene of death and terror on Nanking Road. But deep within me I know I'm making excuses for myself; I know that it has been Emily's presence in Shanghai that has helped me to reach my easy conclusion that at this time, at this point in my life, my place has been here.

So from time to time I write home that I must postpone my departure for yet a few months, regretting that my work isn't yet finished. Of course I don't expect my family to believe me any more than I believe myself. But both they and I know how important it is to maintain a civilized pretense, a kind of a fiction that will give them a way of explaining my prolonged absence, to make it seem as if I have an honorable reason to continue ignoring what, in their eyes at least, are the duties that I owe them.

We have nothing to learn from the Chinese about saving face, my family and I, for both in our need to do it, and in the way we go about it, we play out a thoroughly American, thoroughly Philadelphian, charade. Perhaps all mandarin societies are alike in this; except for the accidents of time and geography, my father, my uncles, my brothers, might all have been Confucian scholars of a vanished time, serving their dynasty just as they serve the tight little world in which they find themselves, the world that revolves around Rittenhouse Square and its families.

Now, perhaps, the time has come for me, at any rate, to drop this polite game. The turmoil is over, played out to its conclusions in the changes that have come to Shanghai. My excuses, never very convincing, have lost what little potency they enjoyed. A summer's work, and I shall have all I need. Then there will no longer be anything here to keep me from going home at last.

Then, at the bottom of the last typewritten page, a longhand note had been added.

> Other reasons not to stay, to put China behind me, not just because my work is almost done. Without her, the color of my life has changed, & Shanghai's coming to seem almost a prison—small, provincial, insufferably narrowminded, a place where there's no longer any room for me.

Sometimes, in a mood of bitterness, he blamed Emily for what had happened—"she had no right, absolutely no right, to dredge up something that was in the past. It seems to have brought out in her a jealousy, an emotionalism, that I hadn't seen before, and whose absence I thought set her apart from other women." But in one passage, which Matthew read with a slight pang of uneasiness, not to say guilt, Simon reproached himself for never having suggested to Emily where she might fit into his vision of the future—a vision that must have included marriage.

> She's far too proud & independent even to want to seem as if she had a claim on me, determined to convince both of us we needed no such contract to bind us together. And in her behavior, I saw—or thought I did—a desire for a freedom like my own. But how blind I was not to realize that she gave me that freedom expecting that, undemanded by her, I might use it to embrace a future that would join us by the sort of bond that would enlarge us together rather than diminish us separately.
>
> Perhaps only after a loss such as this does one begin to understand what might have been, to realize how little justified we are when we take for granted the present circumstances of our lives, & how frail the base on which those circumstances are built. So that even a slight miscalculation in the balance may weigh too heavily to one side or another, & bring falling to earth the structures that we have erected almost unconsciously on what turns out to be no more than the tightrope of our own imaginations.

Clearly Simon wanted to believe that it was his tactless silence, not his adventures and misadventures with any other woman, that had led to the break, and Matthew guessed that he still didn't want his affair with Rhonda to be seen as anything culpable. So in the summer of 1926, he plunged once more into his work with an almost desperate intensity, to finish it, to complete the book, to prove to himself that he had not wasted his time in China. Despite the heat, he became tireless in his investigations, in his conversations with others, with businessmen like Eric Massingham, with municipal councillors like Stanfield Frothingham, with junior consuls like François Verdier, with police and military officers, with spokesmen for the Chinese authorities, and sometimes with the authorities themselves. As Matthew himself had done, he spent hours reading the back files of newspapers, buried himself in the records of trade and shipping kept by the Maritime Customs, dug into the budgets of the two settlements, examined landholding records, business deals, and tried to make economic sense out of the fluctuations on the Shanghai stock exchanges, both foreign and Chinese.

And he continued his explorations into the dark underside of Shanghai, its world of crime, of smuggling, the world of the opium trade, of arms running, the world where laborers were procured for the factories and prostitutes were procured for the tea shops of Foochow Road and the brothels of Blood Alley. "Crime has never attracted me," he wrote in *Typhoon* on June 10, and he remembered Rogers's warning that it might not be healthy to make too many inquiries into the opium trade.

But crime is part of the life of this city. As it is of most cities. Here, however, Shanghai's division into three jurisdictions— Chinese, French, and quasi-British—has provided a particularly favorable climate for organizations of criminals to carry on their trade. Or trades. For it's not just opium, as I've been finding out. The drug may be the most lucrative part of the underworld picture here, but it is only a part.

The people who bring opium in here are the same ones who are in the arms-smuggling racket. With a new warlord taking over every six months or so, there's a ready market for Mausers, Lee-Enfields, and Remingtons, to say nothing of grenades and bombs. They also run the prostitution rings. Not white slavery, whatever the papers back home may say, because there's little of that, apart from the desperately poor Russian refugees. Most of the girls are Chinese, recruited from the villages and towns of the interior. The youngest and prettiest are reputed to be from Soochow, for there's a belief that the lilting Soochow accent on a girl's lips somehow makes her irresistible to men. Whatever their origins, such girls are carefully trained by their mistresses, and can command very considerable prices, particularly for the first night that they go with a man. Even later on, the exotic services that the best of them can provide keep them much in demand, especially among the rich.

But these girls are the aristocrats of the profession. Most of the others—the ones the Chinese call "wild pheasants"—are castoffs from the cotton mills, or girls who've been driven to the city by the continual fighting in the countryside and have no other way to make a living than by selling themselves.

The gangs also run more conventional kinds of labor recruitment. Factory managers here, both Chinese and foreign, leave the hiring of workers up to their foremen. The foremen then make contracts with the gangs' labor recruiters to deliver them what they need: so and so many girls for the spinning of cotton and silk, so and so many men for heavier work. The recruiters go out to the villages to buy children; sometimes they promise the parents that the girls will have a better life in Shanghai, but most of the time no such excuse is needed. No family, in one of those impoverished villages of the countryside, wants to keep a daughter. Nor can they afford to. So the transaction, however phrased, becomes an outright sale. The parents get the money, the recruiter takes a percentage of the sale price, and of the wages paid by the factories. And the worker practically becomes a slave.

A week later, Simon found a chance to see the mills for himself.

Thursday, June 17, 1926

Hsiao-sha-tu is not a part of Shanghai that many foreign visitors see, or indeed would want to see. It's up in the mill district, one of the centers of our troubles last year, and it is here that Father Duchamp has persuaded his superiors to do some mission work. The day before yesterday it was he who acted as my guide on a visit we had planned some time ago.

To reach it, you cross the Soochow Creek, curling black and

filthy under its bridges, yet crowded with sampans, barges, and the flat-bottomed river junks that bring in food from the countryside. Thousands of people live aboard them, washing, drinking, cooking with the water they draw from the stream. Their lives look appalling to us, but worse yet is the condition of the slum dwellers north of the city, condemned to live in shacks of rotting wood and crumbling plaster that offer little protection against either the heat of summer or the cold of winter. Piles of garbage lie in the streets, spoiling in the sun; ragpickers go through them, as bony, gaunt, and disheveled as vultures, though it's hard to imagine that in this desperate poverty anything useful gets thrown away. Naked children, many of them covered with sores, play in the black and oily puddles that stand in the streets, or in the open drains that carry sewage down into the Creek. The yellow air is heavy: smoke from the mills, the smell of waste, rot, decay, disease, the stench of poverty. "When it rains," Duchamp tells me, "the gutters overflow, and the streets are covered with a slime that seeps in through the doorways. Impossible to believe that men and women can live in such conditions. Have you read Zola? I always think of him when I come here."

We turn through an iron gate that leads into a courtyard between two long, nondescript brick buildings that make up the mill. Standing outside, we can already hear the noise coming from the machinery; when we enter the mill, the sound has become deafening. One of the foremen meets us, clearly not happy that we are there, but under orders to show us around. He shouts directions above the din: "Be careful, don't get in the way of the workers, stay away from the machinery, it's dangerous."

Of course I've heard about the mills often enough. But nothing prepared me for what I saw today. Imagine a long room with high ceilings, windows so dirty that the light comes in only where the glass has been broken. The air is thick with dirt and lint, so that it's impossible to breathe properly. Row upon row of machines stand there, glistening with oil in the dim light, their shuttles moving dangerously back and forth. In front of them, with no thought given to their safety, are the women and girls, the youngest probably no more than six or seven, dressed in rags, black eyes staring out of their pale faces at the work before them, not daring to look up as we pass by. On a pile of cotton waste shoved into a dirty corner, I see something move. "A baby," Duchamp explains. "Its mother is one of the workers; she has no place to put her child, so she brings it here to the factory. Of course it's against regulations, but what else can she do? And there are others ..."

For the next hour we tour the mill, trying to take in this landscape of rapidly moving machines, of heat, of dirt, of danger, and of the patient workers who tend them. It's impossible to talk for the noise. At one point a high scream of pain rises above the din, a cry of human agony cutting through the relentless mechanical driving of the looms. The foreman scans the floor, no emotion on his face. The rows of girls and women do not even glance up. He points to the other side of the room, where an injured girl—she looks no more than thirteen—with blood streaming from her hand is being led away by two other workers. "Stupid," he says. "We tell them to be careful, but they're only peasants, not used to the kind of work they have to do here. What can you expect? No matter; we have an infirmary, and they'll take care of her." He looks at us expectantly, as if wanting to be congratulated for the solicitude his mill shows the workers.

And then what? I ask.

He's not interested in the question. "How should I know? She'll go home; perhaps if her hand heals, she'll come back. But even if she's crippled, it doesn't matter; there are lots more ready to take her place."

When we leave the mill, I am suddenly tired. Duchamp looks at me with concern, asks whether I am ill, and only then do I realize that my almost-forgotten wound is once again reminding me of its presence, that the pain is draining my strength from me. I think suddenly of the cool, peaceful rooms of the Shanghai Club, awnings rolled down to protect them from the summer sun. I think of the men who sit in those great green leather chairs, reading the stock and share reports in the *North China*, occasionally summoning a boy to fetch drinks. How often do they visit their mills and factories? How much do they know about the ways in which those factories are run? What do they care about that twilight world of poverty, fatigue, and danger, beyond their balance sheets and their figures of production?

"The owners have a lot to answer for," says Duchamp, as if

reading my mind. "Remember that this is a Japanese mill, and the Japanese are said to be the best and most humanitarian of the employers. They or the British." He doesn't need to add that all agree the Chinese are the worst.

What do you think? I ask him. He's worked here, has had a chance to see many such scenes.

He shrugs his shoulders. "When one reaches a certain level of human misery, there is little point in making comparisons." He pauses, then looks at me.

"Do you believe in God, Simon?" But he's not really interested in my answer. "If there is a God, since there is a God, He will call these people to account."

That won't help the workers much, I suggest.

"No," he says, "you are quite right. That is why God calls on us to help such people right now. Not simply to tell them that their sufferings will someday earn them a reward in heaven. But to make it possible for them to live in dignity, to live like human beings, not like animals. Here, now, in this world."

So, unlike many of the missionaries here, he talks with admiration of the work being done by the labor unions, the Kuomintang, even the Communists. His superiors don't like the Communists. "But," he tells me, "I have met some, at least some who call themselves Communists. They are good people, the ones who work in the factories, who try to organize the unions. And"—he adds this with an ironic smile—"sometimes they have trouble with their superiors. Just as I do."

The factory owners turn a blind eye to the conditions in their mills. They turn a blind eye to the way in which the labor recruiters from the underworld work. They've got to have the workers, after all. Meanwhile the gangsters who run the rackets get enormously rich. Even respected. Tu Yüeh-sheng, their leader, lives right here in Frenchtown, in a large house on the rue Wagner. He's known as a man of public spirit, a philanthropist, a man who's honored and admired.

His business is no secret; everyone knows it. Yet no one does anything about it. Why should they? Tu and his gangsters make sure that there will be a supply of laborers coming into the mills, a supply of coolies working the docks, and a supply of girls coming into the brothels. And above all they make sure that the foreign settlements will enjoy peace and quiet, and that Shanghai's violence will take place only in the Chinese city, away from sensitive foreign eyes. Then the foreigners can go on congratulating themselves on how well they run things.

The more I learn, the more I'm convinced I must meet Tu Yüeh-sheng. It won't be easy. I've asked Verdier at the French Consulate about it, and he evades the question. Monsieur Tu does not like foreign journalists, it seems; a private man, you understand, a modest man who prefers that his good deeds—the building of schools, of hospitals for the poor, and such—be done away from the public eye. And he never gives interviews.

"Still," says Verdier, "I will see what I can do."

The weather made the summer of 1926 particularly difficult for those living in Shanghai. "Almost every day the thermometer climbs over a hundred degrees," wrote Simon in his private journal on July 20.

Shanghai hasn't seen such heat in living memory, and the summer rains have failed in the rich Yangtze delta. This year it is not the warlords, but nature, that threatens the city's food supply, driving up the cost of rice week by week. The city stews under the pale yellow-white dome of the sky, and the stench of its juices dripping into the filthy drains, into the sluggish creeks that carry the wastes of three million souls, pervades every street, every building, every corner. In this stagnant heat, their fetid exhalations bring pestilence: a thousand people dead of cholera in the Chinese city so far, and more falling victim every day.

This is the season when the rich and the fortunate flee the city, traveling by sea to the cool of distant Korean or Japanese hill resorts, or the bamboo-shaded glades of the mountain retreats closer by at Kuling and Mokanshan. Some go to the beaches, and I've learned that E. has been carried off for a month by Muriel Ransom to a seaside bungalow at Peitaiho, up near the Shan-hai kuan, where the Great Wall descends into the sea after its two-thousand-mile march from the deserts of the northwest. Her editor has given her his blessing. After all, it's summer, and there's not much to be found on the society page when society has escaped the city.

Her absence makes life easier for me, for I no longer run the risk of seeing her, laughing and enjoying herself with other people. No doubt the Ransoms hope that in Peitaiho she'll meet a presentable bachelor from one of the legations in Peking—one of those suitable young Americans from Princeton or Yale, perhaps, who will enable her to forget me, and all that we have meant to each other.

Meanwhile I continue with my investigations. And I read the shipping pages in the paper, and begin to plan my autumn journey home.

So in the damp heat of July and August, Simon had tried to work, sitting at his desk in front of an electric fan, the shirt wet on his back, the paper on which he wrote sticking to his damp skin. (Matthew, reading this description, wondered with some apprehension if he'd still be in Shanghai in July, when summer's high heat arrived. Although it was still late spring by the calendar, the day already seemed oppressively hot, and while an air conditioner sat beneath the window of his room, it was a locally made machine that wheezed and roared in such a disconcerting way that he hesitated even to turn it on.)

The draft of *Typhoon Over Shanghai* had more to say about summer in the city.

We who are unfortunate enough to have to stay put in Shanghai must find what ways we can to deal with the heat. . . . Fans help, iced drinks help, a stroll after sunset in the park helps, but best of all is the swimming bath out at the French Club on the rue Cardinal Mercier, just north of the avenue Joffre. The new building opened in January, and it's quickly become the most popular spot in town—or at least the most popular respectable spot.

There is about its new quarters an ebullient gaiety and a grace that's missing in all those ponderous British imperial structures lining the Bund and the Settlement's Central District. And its appearance has an effect on the people there. You go to the Shanghai Club or the American Club for business, but you go to the Cercle Sportif for fun: to swim, to play tennis, to dance, or just to sit under the pergola on the roof garden with a cold glass in your hand, listening to the orchestra, watching the daylight fade in the western sky, and waiting for the first breezes of the evening. You go also because you can meet Chinese there, as you cannot at the Anglo-Saxon clubs, with their stolidly correct views about the proper relations among the races.

Across the street, as he read this, Matthew could make out the sound of the pneumatic drills destroying the building Simon had described sixty years ago.

There it had been, in mid-July 1926, that he had met Tu Yüeh-sheng.

And you go to the Cercle Sportif, because this is where the leaders of the French community hold their public celebrations. *Le tout Shanghai*, as our local paper puts it, has turned out for the observance of Bastille Day last Wednesday. A decorous observance it has been too, seemingly organized by the authorities to call up no memories of revolution that might be unsettling in today's volatile and unpredictable China. A hundred and thirty and more years ago, the mob hunted through the streets of Paris, baying for the blood of aristocrats, but today the old cry of Liberty, Equality, and Fraternity has given way to Law, Order, and Stability, and it is now these virtues that we celebrate politely under the tricolor that flies everywhere above the Concession. At Kouzaka Park there are proper games for the children in the morning, and when the band of the *Garde municipale* plays its afternoon concert, the *Marseillaise* no longer sounds a call to arms, but becomes rather a confident reminder of who it is that holds power. (Moored off the French Bund, its bright holiday flags flying in the summer sun, lies the darkly dangerous shape of a French cruiser. It bears the name of *Jules Michelet*, historian of republican virtues.) On Tuesday, after darkness has fallen, a torchlight procession flares along the avenue Joffre, and on Wednesday, for those favored with invitations, there is a dinner and a gala with fireworks, presided over by our new consul general, M. Naggiar, at the Cercle Sportif.

M. and Mme Verdier had asked me to join them for the occasion. The French authorities know how few of their countrymen there are who live here, sense that their Concession is becoming an anomaly, and that to keep it, they must cultivate friendly relations with foreigners such as I. More than anything else, more even than bolshevism, they fear the prospect that as their influence wanes in Shanghai, their little patch of territory will be swallowed up by the larger and richer International Settlement, and French amour-propre will be wounded.

So I went with the Verdiers to the new club awash with light and music in the hot summer night, the building hung with red, white, and blue bunting, the women in their light summer silks, the men in evening dress or white naval uniforms, their hair glistening with brilliantine. Two orchestras of small dark Russians played the latest songs from Paris and New York, occasionally reverting to Offenbach or Lecocq—"La Madelon de la Victoire" and "Bye-bye, Blackbird," with *La Belle Helène* as counterpoint.

In this gathering, I made myself as charming as I know how, both to my hosts and to their compatriots. And though I sought no reward for my good behavior, one nonetheless came my way. At about midnight, just as I was thinking of leaving, M. Verdier came through the crowd to find me chatting with the Baroness Kokovtsev (one of our recently ennobled White Russians, I suspect, but nonetheless a woman of charm and intelligence). With an apology to her, he carried me off to a private room upstairs, where some fifteen or twenty guests, both Chinese and foreign, had just finished their dinner and were taking leave of their host.

That man stood at the head of the table, bidding his guests farewell. Though I had never seen him before, I knew at once who he was. Gaunt and sallow, with a long head shaped like an egg, he had no chin, but cold, thin lips, a receding forehead, and hair cut short above it. And huge ears, startling ears, ears almost like the wings of a bat. That's the feature that gave him away: the Chinese know him as Big-eared Tu, Tu Yüeh-sheng.

Verdier presented me. "*Enchanté, m'sieu,*" we murmured to each other, "*chiu-yang, chiu-yang*"; his hand felt soft and dangerous in mine. He waved me to a chair and motioned to a boy to pour me some champagne. I'd already had enough wine for the evening, but I accepted it anyway, for politeness's sake.

We talked. We talked for about twenty minutes, helped by an interpreter, a small man with a pale and frightened face, for M. Tu had exhausted his knowledge of French in his greeting, and I found myself baffled by his thick Shanghainese dialect. What we talked about doesn't matter; most of it was inconsequential, conventional phrases of politeness echoed in French and Chinese. But that's not the point. I had a troubled sense of charm, and more than that, of tremendous power, a power that he was using to size me up, to fit me into the universe he inhabited, to see if I had any useful place in it. He told me about the orphanage he planned to build on the rue Doumer—"you see, M. Larsen, I was an orphan myself in Pootung, and if I can spare just a few children—no, just one child, a single child—the miseries I myself experienced, then I know that my life will have been worthwhile." Meanwhile Verdier beamed his approval, and I said nothing, but only nodded. He asked about my work, about the book I'm writing, about my friends in Shanghai. Then, glancing at his watch, he rose, and I had the sense that by then he had discovered all he needed to know about me for the present—and that a new entry would be made in his files, a dossier begun, should he someday have cause to remember me.

Shortly before this meeting took place, the political and military map of China had begun to change. In early July, the leaders of the revolutionary government in Canton had begun a great military drive, boasting that their armies would unite all China and bring her under the banner of the national revolution. Though at first it seemed to be no more than another of the endless summer battles among competing generals, even to the most jaded foreign observers in Shanghai it soon became evident that the Northern Expedition, as the Chinese called it, was not simply an ordinary warlord campaign that would be over in a few weeks or a few months. Led by General Chiang Kai-shek, and accompanied by Soviet advisers, the well-armed and well-financed Nationalist armies fought their way up from Kwangtung into the provinces of south and central China, driving toward the Yangtze valley and the rich cities that lay on the river.

Simon, watching the campaign unfold from Shanghai, had commented on all this in *Typhoon*, though Matthew learned little that he had not already known. But in August his concentration on his work was suddenly broken by Emily's reappearance in his life. She'd come back from Peitaiho, and, more important, had come back to him. Again the journal entry was in Larsen's scrawled handwriting.

Wednesday, August 25, 1926

We met, after she had telephoned, at our old rendezvous [he still had not said where it was]. Mme Vorontsov brought us tea, smiled at us, & said she was glad to see us back, just like the old days.

E. looks brown and fit after her month at the seaside, but also seemed tired, smoking incessantly, tearing the cigarette package into tiny pieces, screwing them up, putting them into the ashtray one by one. Most of the time she looked at the table, glancing up only occasionally to see what effect her words were having on me.

She told me she's decided to take me back, give me another chance. Of course I fell for it, no questions asked, just gratitude. At first. But then strangely almost resentful. Why's it her decision, not mine? Am I to have nothing to say about all this after what she's done to me for these last few months?

Has she forgiven me? or decided there's nothing to forgive? or is she asking me to forgive her? Difficult to make out. Or make out reasons for the change. Loneliness and boredom in Peitaiho? Perhaps—endless games of bridge after dinner, she said, & now she hates the game.

I gather that one evening, one of those presentable young bachelor diplomats from Peking made advances. More than he should have. And she didn't at first discourage him. So things happened. No need to spell them out, I could guess what she meant. I didn't want to, tried to put out of my mind the picture that flashed through it—E. in that resort hotel by the sea, late at night, someone else with her. I know her life's her own, she can make her own decisions. Still, couldn't help feeling that this was somehow different. That somehow the memory of our time together should have been strong enough to prevent this, whatever it was that happened. And I almost resented her telling me about it, wondered why she was saying it, didn't want to guess the answer.

She must have seen the look on my face, & it made her relent. Afterward, she hated herself, said it made her feel mean. But it also made her realize how different from this sordid passage were the times that we'd known together here in Shanghai. Was I still willing to try again?

Of course I was. All my resentment & mistrust vanished in the face of that simple question. But instead I asked her: did she feel she could trust me again? Childish question, of course, childish because it was almost like a boast, reminding her of what she'd discovered of my past. As if I somehow hoped to reclaim at least part of the power I'd lost listening to her own brief confession.

She looked at me and answered: More than she can trust any other man. Then reminded me that now I'll have to trust her too. Somehow that restored the sense of balance between us. "Maybe we're just a bad lot, Simon, you and I"—then she smiled at me, the first real smile of the afternoon, the old Emily smile.

CHAPTER SIX

Saturday, June 3, 1989

The picture flickered and wavered, lines crackling across the screen before it settled down and the voice of the announcer came on. Slowly the camera panned over the hundred thousand people who had pressed into Tiananmen Square the day before, where four young men had begun a new hunger strike to protest the imposition of martial law. Though the crowd looked cheerful enough in the bright spring sun, the weeks of living outdoors had begun to tell. Hastily pitched tents and emergency latrines covered the square, and everywhere there lay scattered piles of debris, litter, garbage.

Matthew, watching the American news broadcast as he was getting ready to leave for the institute, was struck by the incongruity of the scene. He'd seen pictures of this same space taken twenty years earlier, in the days when it had been filled by the millions of Red Guards who had made up the shock troops of the Great Proletarian Cultural Revolution. There they'd stood all night, waiting for the coming of dawn when, high on the red walls of the Tiananmen, the aging Chairman would appear out of the sunrise like a savior, and the crowd below would thunder out *Dongfang hong*, "The East is Red," waving their red books of quotations, and proclaiming a hysterical loyalty to the leader.

151

That was the sort of spectacle that Tiananmen Square had been designed for. Carved by the country's new leaders out of the city's living center after their rise to power, the square now exuded an almost obscene smell of dictatorship, by its very size and setting demanding such gigantic and well-disciplined rallies of the faithful. Yet today, for all its visual and architectural language of totalitarianism, for all the vast Stalinist monuments and palaces that flanked it, this great open space had been taken over by the ordinary citizens of Beijing: the people, thought Matthew, real people with real concerns, not that Marxist abstraction offhandedly dismissed as the masses. Around the square granite shaft of the Monument to the People's Heroes, they gathered by the tens of thousands, their banners and flags calling for democracy, for freedom, for an end to dictatorship and the corruptions of power, and for a chance to let China, their country, rise to a new greatness. Meanwhile to the north, the tall white figure of the Goddess of Democracy continued her steadfast and untiring challenge to the Chairman's portrait, and to the leaders who took shelter behind it.

Sketchy reports told of an attempt early Friday morning by several thousand troops to advance into the square from Chang'an Boulevard, only to be turned back by the crowds of men and women who came out to argue with them, and to throw up hasty barricades of buses, cars, and trucks, blocking the way to the square. Three people had been struck and killed by a speeding police car. Or so the story went, and whether true or not, more protests had followed. Meanwhile the ominous rumors of a troop concentration building around the capital continued. But the details were uncertain; since the declaration of martial law, the Chinese papers had fallen back on the safety of parroting the official line, while foreign reporters found themselves barred from talking freely to the demonstrators and their supporters.

Matthew stared at the television set with a growing uneasiness. Suddenly the telephone rang. "Wait, please," said the hotel operator, and then Laura's voice came on the line. "Matt, is that you?"

"Laura? How are you? Where are you, anyway? Are you in Pasadena yet?" She was planning to spend the summer in California, finishing the research for her dissertation.

"I'm still home, but I'm leaving tomorrow morning. Listen, Matt, I'm worried. What do things look like there?"

"Here? Everything seems pretty quiet. Sure, I've seen the news from Beijing. But there's no sign of trouble here. Not yet, anyway."

"What are you going to do? Are you going to stay? I saw Mr. Tao yesterday, and he doesn't think the army's going to wait much longer." Tao Keting was a visiting physicist from Beijing, spending the year at Harvard and Atherton. Matthew suspected that after his outspoken support for the democracy movement that spring, he might be trying to find a way not to go back to China after the academic year was over.

"I've only just arrived, Laura. Anyway, I can't believe anything terrible is going to happen. Probably the government's just going to wait the students out. The weather's getting hot, and it looks as if life in the square must be pretty uncomfortable by now. I mean, I think the networks are still trying to make a big thing out of the danger. They want to keep the story going."

Laura was quiet for a moment. "I hope you know what you're doing, Matt." Then: "What do other people think? Are there other foreigners there you can talk to?"

He laughed. "None that I've seen. Not even tourist groups. But this time I did call the consulate, so they know where I am in case there's any trouble."

"Well, that's some consolation. How's your work going?"

"I think I'm making some progress. With luck, I may even find out something about Great-uncle Simon. At least I've met some people who might give me some leads."

Silence again. "Matt, I hope you're going to be all right. Promise me, if there's trouble, you'll get out?"

"Okay," he said. "If there's trouble, I'll get out. Promise."

"Matt, I don't want anything to happen to you. Great-uncle Simon's not worth it, and surely your book can wait."

He laughed. "Publish or perish, you know. But I'll try not to do both."

Laura told him that wasn't funny, and after another minute's talk, they hung up. But her phone call had both surprised him and, despite all her worry (or perhaps because of it), comforted him. As much because she'd cared enough to make the effort, rather than forgetting him when he was halfway around the world. But of course her fears were absurd. Nothing bad happens on bright spring days like this, certainly not to college professors like him. His confidence returned when he left the hotel.

Outside, the sun was shining, the usual crowds already filled Huaihai Road, and by half past eight, the noise of traffic and the blasting horns of the trucks made everything look and sound normal once again. But all through the morning, as he made the long trip to the institute, as he read the dusty leavings of the past, he carried with him the sound of her voice, like the memory of a pleasant dream that lingers after waking, and gives the ordinary day a special radiance.

By the end of 1926, Shanghai was beginning to suffer from a fit of nerves. Despite all the predictions of the Old China Hands that the Bolshevik troops, as they called Chiang Kai-shek's forces, would be checked by the northern armies, the Nationalists had reached the Yangtze River in October, and in December announced that they were transferring their headquarters from Canton to Hankow. Six hundred miles west of Shanghai, Hankow was not only one of China's main industrial centers, but also a focal point for foreign interests and foreign trade in the Yangtze valley. To this city in December would move the new government and its cadre of Soviet advisers led by Michael Borodin, the spellbinding revolutionary who had done so much to help make the Nationalist success possible. And here too would come the communist and Kuomintang leaders, their two parties still allied with each other as they had been for the past three years. But every day growing more wary of each other, circling each other like gunfighters at the climax of an old western, each beginning to realize that in its own particular vision of China's future, there would no longer be room for the other.

General Chiang Kai-shek, however, had no intention of moving to Hankow. Commander-in-chief of the victorious armies that had stormed north to the Yangtze during the campaigns of the summer and fall, he thought the Nationalist government too much under the control of its radicals, too amenable to the wishes of its Soviet and Chinese communist allies. Remaining aloof, pleading that military necessity must keep him in the field, he set up his own separate headquarters in Kiangsi province, which his troops had taken in October. No one was yet talking openly about a rupture between Chiang's Kuomintang and its communist allies, and in the treaty ports like Shanghai, some of the Old China Hands warned darkly that the appearances of a split were simply a ruse, smoke blown in foreign eyes to blind them to the reality of the coming bolshevization of China.

If, some months earlier, Simon had been planning to finish his book and go home to America, all such intentions now seemed to have vanished. Everyone could see that with the revolution now having reached central China, Shanghai would very soon become its focal point. How could he finish his book if he were to leave in mid-chapter, without seeing the story through to its conclusion? If Simon, once again, had wanted an excuse to stay in China (and it was clear to Matthew that he did), he'd now found it.

No doubt too, the reconciliation with Emily Ransom helped, and Matthew, rereading the journal in the last few days with more care than he'd originally given it, found himself wondering more and more about the precise nature of the relationship between the two. Whatever she might have been like before coming to China, Emily by now was obviously very much a free spirit, what her generation would have called a new woman, and what Matthew's called liberated. It was clear that she and Simon had resumed their affair, one that seemed to be conducted largely in what Simon referred to as "our usual place," and though he gave no indication of where that might be, he apparently found it safer from the prying eyes of Shanghai society than were his own rooms. Nor, for all Simon's earlier resolutions, was it clear what the future might bring. Certainly there was no talk of marriage, at least in the journal, and Matthew could only guess that Emily was now satisfied with whatever might be the state of the relationship.

In any case, Simon, after his brief burst of confessional writing in his journal that summer of 1926, had now returned to the methodical analysis and recording of the great drama that was being played out before him, sketching out his ideas in his journal, and then retyping the pages to add to the draft of *Typhoon*. And it was clear now that, whatever else might have held Emily and Simon together, they shared a similar outlook toward the events that were now unfolding in China. Still restricted to her paper's society page, Emily was growing thoroughly bored with her job, complaining to Simon that she had no chance to do what she called real reporting, covering the kinds of stories that would allow her to use her growing knowledge of Chinese affairs. Simon, for his part, had begun to introduce her to his own circle of Chinese friends, many of whom he had met through Chu Hung-ying: the young writers and journalists, the intellectuals and activists, who made up so important a part of Shanghai's radical subculture in those days.

Simon had written about these gatherings, and though the entries were in his journal, Matthew guessed that, with Emily's name edited out, they might eventually have formed part of *Typhoon Over Shanghai.*

These meetings have certainly opened her eyes—and mine too—[ran an entry of Wednesday, October 27] to a side of Chinese life that's not normally seen from the villas of Bubbling Well Road or the shops of the Central District. She's now plunged enthusiastically into a course of self-education, and her sympathies, once aroused, are leading her to points of view that grow increasingly distant from those of her uncle and his circle.

So from time to time on late afternoons, the hour when John Ransom thinks his niece is being carried off by one of her admirers for tea-dancing at the Astor or the Majestic, we gather in Mr. Chu's room in a ramshackle building situated in a back alley near Dent Road. Small knots of young men appear, and sometimes one or two girls: students, young teachers from the city's colleges and universities, struggling newspaper reporters, junior employees of Chinese firms in the Settlement and Frenchtown. Many of them write for the little magazines and newspapers that blossom briefly before they go broke, or before the police get wind of them, raid their offices, and shut them down. They speak snatches of English, or sometimes a word or two of French, but most of the talk is in Shanghainese: I translate, with Mr. Chu at my elbow when my powers fail.

They are passionately devoted to their country, our visitors on these autumn afternoons, passionately partisan in their support for the Nationalist government in Canton. They talk of Kemal Ataturk, of Mussolini, and, above all, of Lenin: what such men have done for their countries, they themselves will do for China, building her into a great nation, a strong nation, of which they can be proud.

And yet much of the talk is conventional, the ordinary phrases of the political pamphleteer. Emily sees it, and her natural curiosity tries to get below the surface, to ask questions that they sometimes seem reluctant to answer. Gaining their trust is not easy. Her very appearance is against her: not only is she a woman (and even among these partisans of the new China, that's a drawback), but she's young, she's pretty, and she exudes the kind of self-confidence that goes with money, good education, and a certain kind of upbringing. Add to that her association with John Ransom of Standard Oil, and she's obviously worlds removed from these penurious Chinese students, these struggling teachers and journalists with dangerous ideas, in whose eyes she represents the whole world of wealth, privilege, and power that they are determined to drive from their country.

She understands this, and tries to overcome it, tries to stay in the background, tries even to look a little bit dowdy. Still, at best she and I must both seem to them as if we are no more than tourists, outsiders intruding briefly and without risk into a misery that doesn't concern us. And at worst we must appear outright threats, strangers who for uncertain reasons are trying to gain access to a half-secret world, a world best left in the twilight, away from the public eye.

He'd recorded one such meeting at some length, in an entry of Saturday, November 20, when Emily had been free from her duties at the paper. This particular gathering had taken place

... in a dingy teahouse on North Szechwan Road, near the factories and mills and slums of Chapei, just over the border from the Settlement. Chu Hung-ying leads us here, suggesting that some of his friends might talk more freely in these familiar surroundings. Emily's presence brings some stares, for women—at least respectable women—do not usually frequent such places. But among the advantages to being a foreigner in China is that you find yourself released not only from the obligations of the Chinese legal code, but from much of its social code as well.

A young man named T'ien is holding forth when we arrive. Pounding the rickety table with his fist, occasionally jumping to his feet to make a point, he argues that Chinese do not want the foreigners to leave the country. "China needs foreigners," he tells us, "and appreciates what she can learn from them. But foreigners must stop behaving as if they were running our country, as if we Chinese were here only for their benefit."

He reminds me of so many students I have known here and in Peking: about twenty years old, a boy's earnest face, large glasses, a cheap scarf wrapped around his neck to keep out the cold wind blowing through the open door. No doubt he spends his days in such political discussions as this, and he argues well, his ideas logical, coherent, persuasive, and absolutely serious. He smokes steadily as he talks, lighting one cheap cigarette after another, grinding out the butts on the dirty floor.

Others join in, and the talk goes on, rising in great clouds, like the steam from the tea that seems to fuel it, like the cigarette smoke that hangs heavy on the chilly blue air. Talk about politics, about the victories of Chiang Kai-shek's armies, about what we can expect when they reach Shanghai. Talk about the foreigners, British, French, Americans. And the Japanese, who are fellow Asians—will they help China? Or perhaps become a danger even greater than the Europeans themselves? Talk about communism, what it is, what it means, and whether it will benefit China. It is a Chinese form of communism they see, of course, not Russian; a way for China to cast off the shackles of the past and to build herself into a great and powerful nation, winning the respect of the world.

And as Russia herself has done, T'ien continues. But others warn that Russia must be watched—"today the Russians are China's friends," says one, "but they have their own reasons for being here. Just like the Japanese—or the Americans." A nervous but friendly laughter breaks out around the table as T'ien and the others rush to assure us that of course they do not mean Emily and me, and the tradition of Chinese courtesy overcomes, if only briefly, the fiery rhetoric that only a few minutes ago burned through the cold air.

The arguments, the smoke, the close air of the little room, dank and heavy, leave me with a headache, feeling groggy and depressed. Not so Emily, however, who is enthusiastic about what she's hearing. As the others rise to leave, she turns to Mr. Chu: What does he think is going to happen when the Nationalists reach Shanghai?

"Shanghai will be liberated," he says, "the warlords will be defeated. That will be the turning point of the revolution. But there are dangers in the way. Not all our friends trust Chiang—

they think he is becoming too powerful, too selfish. They warn that he will turn against the revolution, will ally himself with the warlords, with the imperialists. Some have even started to call him a new warlord himself." Mr. Chu speaks with his usual caution, but it is clear that he agrees with such views.

I remark that many foreigners still think Chiang is a Bolshevik; they call him the Red General. Mr. Chu laughs. "Yes," he answers, "the sorts of men whose view of China encompasses all that they can see from the windows of the Shanghai Club. But Ransom *hsiao-chieh*, Miss Ransom, and you are not like that. That's why I trust you with my friends here. And"—now he looks at us earnestly—"why we trust you to put their ideas down in what you write, so that Americans will understand us. Will understand we Chinese want only independence and justice. As you Americans did in 1776."

But many of my friends, Americans and others, see nothing of the sort. These days the papers are filled with stories of armed hordes sweeping through south China, throwing the countryside into chaos, trampling on the rights of foreigners, seizing property, stabling their horses in the mission chapels, using the mission schools as barracks, filling the mission hospitals with their wounded men. "Where the Nationalists control the Yangtze, trade has come to a standstill," Eric Massingham told me the other day. "Asiatic Petroleum, Brunner Mond, Standard Oil, Jardine's, all the big companies. They've either had to stop or see their ships come under fire in broad daylight on the river. Look at the trades unions in Hankow and Wuchang. Their demands are impossible, simply impossible. Not just against us, but against the Chinese employers too."

He paused to drive his point home. "And it'll happen here if we're not careful," he warns me. "But if your government and mine show enough backbone, old man, we can make sure Shanghai survives."

But what kind of a Shanghai will it be, I wonder, that comes out of all this? Easy enough for me to speculate about it. I am a bird of passage, I have no family here, no stake in the city. If things turn ugly, it will only force on me the decision I should have made some time ago: to go home. For some others, it won't be so easy. Shanghai is all they have, all they understand: a house, a garden, a business, money sunk into investments here in the settlements. Their friends, their clubs, their churches, schools for their children, all are here in Shanghai. If the city changes drastically, they'll be ruined. Then what? Massingham and Ransom and the taipans will do all right. Their sort always do. But for the lesser fry, it will be back to America or England, their pensions gone, to try to make a new start if they're not too old, or to retire to some little midwestern town, or some chilly gray village on the North Sea, nothing to do but watch the English rain pour down. It's a cheerless prospect for them. How many of them will be able to change enough to stay on here, to make a new life for themselves? Here, in a new Shanghai, run by the Chinese? Where foreigners no longer have special privileges, special exemptions? And have to depend on their ability to get along with the Chinese rather than lording it over them?

A few perhaps. But for most it will be very difficult. So we are already hearing talk about the need to defend Shanghai. Against what? We can't stop the Nationalist armies from taking the Chinese city. Then what? Will they starve us out? Unleash a new wave of strikes and a boycott, as they did last year? Attack the settlements? Images of the unwashed hordes rise in the imagination, soldiers and peasants breaking into our privileged sanctuaries: fire, rape, murder, pillage, the nightmares of men and women here, who cling uneasily to the edge of a vast continent they do not understand.

But if, as Mr. Chu says, some of us would simply look beyond the windows of the Shanghai Club and our comfortable houses, perhaps we would understand what it is the Chinese want. And perhaps we would sympathize more with their aspirations.

I should know now what it is they want, he tells me: I've seen the inside of the mills. Emily has not. But she doesn't need to, for her sympathies by now are thoroughly engaged on the Chinese side. She flourishes in these discussions. So much so that it is now I that have to restrain her. She mustn't let John Ransom hear her speaking to him as she does to me.

In early January 1927, the worst fears of men like Massingham seemed to be realized. Up in Hankow, revolutionary Hankow, a Chinese crowd, urged on by the Communists, broke through the lightly guarded defenses of the British Concession in that city, and occupied it. The British authorities knew that resistance was pointless, and within days the Concession had passed under Chinese control.

The effect on Shanghai was stunning, as *Typhoon* noted on January 10.

"BRITISH CONCESSION FALLS TO MOB!" The papers tell of British marines and bluejackets retreating passively to their ships in the harbor, giving up without so much as firing a shot! How can the stories be true? Has the consul shown the white feather? Is the admiral a traitor? You can almost reach out and feel the fire of quiet fury that burns in the halls of the Shanghai Club at Britain's humiliation. Can we count on our government to show a bit of backbone? Or is it too weak to send the warships up the Yangtze and teach the Bolsheviks a lesson?

Is there any pleasure greater than being able to say I told you so? All those people who've been warning us that the Nationalists couldn't be trusted now suddenly seem vindicated. In the Chinese papers, in the Chinese city, however, another story is put out: that British marines have fired into an unarmed crowd, and once again have massacred the innocent. It is May Thirtieth all over again. But this time, in this version, the Chinese people have triumphed, imperialist arrogance and imperialist aggression have crumbled. The British have run up the white flag of surrender, and the Concession is in Chinese hands.

As Matthew knew from his studies, neither of these stories was true. No shots had been fired, and the British authorities, far from being cowardly, had taken the only course that would avoid bloodshed, and had thus prevented a far worse outbreak. "A single rifle shot," noted Simon a few days later, "a single Chinese death, would have given the Nationalists a martyr, and the whole country would have burst into flame, just as it did in May 1925. But the outcome would have been far worse this time, because today the revolutionary armies—and they are good hard fighters—control most of China south of the Yangtze."

The events stirred the British government into action. Hankow's loss had been a blow to British commerce, and an even worse blow to British pride. But far worse, and far more dangerous, would be the loss of the International Settlement at Shanghai: a surrender there to revolutionary nationalism would shake the very foundations of the British Empire. "The foreign papers here condemn the events in Hankow as an abject betrayal of British interests," wrote Simon, "and in private some ask whether kowtowing to Chiang Kai-shek's Nationalists today will mean kowtowing to Gandhi's nationalists tomorrow."

Then, to the immense relief of many of Simon's friends, and the local English press, the British government announced in late January the formation of a Shanghai Defence Force, sixteen thousand troops to converge on the city, from India, from the Mediterranean, from Britain itself, to protect the foreigners against this new menace. Though it would take three months to build the armies up to strength, the first units began arriving from Hong Kong at the end of the month.

The last part of Simon's unfinished draft of *Typhoon Over Shanghai* came to an end with his observation of their landing.

Friday, February 1, 1927

The British here are rejoicing, for at last their government has seen the danger and is acting. They turn out in force to welcome the Tommies, as the troopships steam up the Huangpu to tie up at the Old Ningpo Wharf, and the men in khaki file down the gangplanks. Brass bands playing, they parade down the rainswept reaches of Broadway toward the Garden Bridge and the Bund. The streets are suddenly full of British soldiers, and on the borders of the Settlement, particularly up near Chapei and the North Station, barbed wire and sandbags surround the fortifications that they are putting up.

Many of my countrymen are disappointed, even ashamed, that Washington is not doing more, allowing Britain to take the responsibility for Shanghai's defense. "President Coolidge doesn't understand China's importance," Stanfield Frothingham tells the newspapers, while others blame the State Department for listening only to the persuasive voices of the missionaries rather than to the hardheaded and practical businessmen whose interests are now threatened by the bolshevization of China.

But what do they want? Don't they see that there's now a very real danger of war? And that we mustn't allow ourselves to be rushed into fighting to defend the British Empire? This storm sweeping across China today has all the force of history behind it, and to stand in the way would be not only wrong but also futile. We've only to look at the events in Russia for the last ten years, and to see the enormous progress that country has made, whatever one may think of her new rulers and the methods they have used. Magnificent as Shanghai is in so many ways, it's a creation of the past, built up by the British and others when China had no capacity for resistance. Today, whatever we foreigners may say, the Nationalists are telling us that China is no longer powerless, and that she is finally rising to reclaim her own.

On the very last page of the draft, the sentence about Russia had been circled in red, and in the margin there was a notation: "Too strong, perhaps?" Whether or not this particular sentiment would have survived when the book went to press, views like these, of course, were not popular in Shanghai. Though Matthew had no idea how openly Simon expressed them, they were probably well enough known so that he began to find himself criticized, even shunned, by men who had been his friends. That became evident in a scene that he had had with John Ransom about two weeks later, and reading it now, Matthew could almost feel the fury that came up from the pages of Simon's private journal. This was a passage, Matthew was sure, that was not intended as a draft for *Typhoon*.

Thursday, February 10, 1927

I'd gone to the American Club to have a look at some of the magazines from home, & he came up to me as I sat glancing through last October's *Atlantic*.

He had been hearing some things about me, he said, some things that he didn't like.

Couldn't think of any answer to that, so I simply put down my magazine & listened.

"They're saying that there are some questions about your politics"—he looked nervous, like a man who doesn't in the least like what he is doing but is determined to push ahead with it.

I told him I didn't know what he meant; surely my politics

are my own affair? Then realized the mistake I'd made: it sounded like the standard response of the guilty man, & in his eyes must have condemned me still further.

So he pressed on, given new confidence. "We're not living in the States. Perhaps there are some things you can do at home, and no one minds. But not here in Shanghai. Here we've got to stick together."

Same line that we've all gotten used to in the last few months. But I wasn't going to let him get away with generalities & asked him what he meant.

"Bolshevism"—the word seemed to soar toward the high ceiling and explode like a rocket, releasing a little spray of dangerous stars. Bolshevism.

"It's bad enough at home, but here it's an outright danger to us all."

I demanded that he tell me what he meant. Do I behave like a Bolshevik?

"No—but you have friends—Chinese friends. Nothing against the Chinese, of course, but you don't want to get too close to them & there are Chinese of the wrong sort ... after all, I've been here longer than you. . . ."

The same tired old Shanghai refrain: when you know China as well as I do, you'll agree with me. Will I ever have lived here long enough so that I'll find myself saying the same thing to newcomers? Ten, twenty years from now?

My friends? Is that what you mean by Chinese of the wrong sort?

"I've been told." He flushed.

By whom?

He looked away. "Can't reveal confidences, old man."

The English expression slipped out, sounding thoroughly self-conscious. Like many Americans here, R. has begun to adopt British ways, British expressions in his speech. Ever since he's been elected to the Shanghai Club, I thought, & hated myself for the cynicism.

Then we got to the real point. "Maybe your friends are your own business. But E.'s my business. I'm responsible for her as long as she's here in Shanghai."

Has she become a Bolshevik? I want to know. Then as soon as the sarcasm was out, knew I'd made a mistake.

R. blew up. "She's met your friends, your Chinese friends. And she comes home talking all that claptrap about how badly off the Chinese are, & how we ought to treat them as equals or go home. She's young, she's impressionable, doesn't understand what things are like here."

Then ordered me to stop seeing her, doesn't like what he calls my influence over her. I reminded him that E.'s of age, & has every right to choose her own friends.

A slanging match followed—I'm not proud of it, & I dare say R. isn't either. A lot came out. Accusations not just about my politics, but about the way I lived. No proper job, not playing my part among my fellow Americans. And Rhonda's name came into it too. What does he know about her? Is he the one who told Emily about her? Anyway, that's been all over for more than a year.

Finally I just walked out on him, leaving him standing there, staring at me. At home, I telephoned E. at the paper & told her what had happened. She sounded distracted; I'd called at a bad time, the office was in its usual late afternoon turmoil preparing the next morning's edition, she'd call me back, would I be at home? I hung up, disappointed. Of course I wanted her to flame up, angry at the injustice of Ransom's demand, wanted her to tell me to meet her outside the office on Kiukiang Road, to reassure me that what had happened would make no difference. I know it's unrealistic and unfair of me to have wanted her to make up her mind, there on the spot, when she was trying to think of a thousand different things. Still, I can't help feeling that if she's really the girl I think she is, she'd have given me an answer right away. Or could there be another reason for her silence?

Two days later, on Saturday, when Emily was free, they met at their usual place. The phrase, Matthew had now come to realize, referred to a rooming house kept by a White Russian woman in the French Concession. "It's drab, as such places are," Simon had written several weeks earlier. "Dark wood chairs, with stained green seat covers, a couch with cheap flowered cushions, and on the walls, framed prints of scenes in St. Petersburg: the Winter Palace, the Neva, the St. Isaac Cathedral. Not what I want for our meetings, yet its very appearance, darkly sordid in its secrecy, adds an element of romance. Above all it's safe, away from the world, away from the gossip that would surround us in my more visible quarters."

It had been a day of cold rain slanting across the city, borne in on a chill wind from the East China Sea, and threatening to turn to sleet by afternoon. Emily told Simon that she was sorry for having put him off, but said she couldn't talk then.

Prendergast [he was the paper's editor, Matthew knew] has just told her that she's as good as fired because of an article she'd written. An article about the situation here in China: the civil war, what's happened at Hankow, what it might mean for Shanghai. The sorts of questions we've talked about with Mr. Chu & his friends.

But there's more to it than that. She'd taken some of their ideas, & turned them into her own: Shanghai has gotten too used to having its own way with a weak country, & things are going to have to change. And the changes will be good for us too, because they will make us—Americans, Englishmen, Frenchmen—live up to our professed ideals about the way people should be treated.

I laugh at that, tell her that I'd like to have seen old Prendergast's face when he read it.

A knock at the door, & Mme Vorontsov's boy enters with a tray: two glasses, water, a bottle of Pernod. I take it from him, pour a drink for Emily, make one for myself.

It was awful, E. continues. "He called me into the office, waved the article at me. How did I possibly expect him to print such Bolshevik rubbish, such dangerous nonsense? I ought to be ashamed of myself. He'd taken me on because I'm John Ransom's niece, & he thought I could be trusted. On and on like that for about fifteen minutes."

In the end, he didn't quite fire her—but he let her know he'd given her the job as a favor to John Ransom, & if Ransom wants her out, there's no reason for P. to keep her on.

A few doors away, someone has put on a gramophone, and through the wall there comes the rhythm of Negro music. Incongruous, out of character in our tawdry setting for Russian exiles—but a reminder that we too, like Mme V., are thousands of miles from home.

The Pernod & the room's warmth bring the color back to

E.'s face, she begins to relax, sound more cheerful, holds up her glass for another drink.

I suggest that Ransom hopes he's about to be elected a member of the Municipal Council. And if he is, Prendergast wants to stay on his right side.

"But the worst of it is," says E., "that Mr. P. has told him about the article. Even showed him a copy of it. At least I think he did."

Ransom, of course, went through the roof. Not surprising, given his views about China & the Chinese.

There's more to it than that, she continues. Uncle John's been in a foul mood since Christmas. E. thinks that he's having money problems. If that's true, of course, it's not going to help him get elected to the council. So the article only made matters worse. He went at her, reminding her of all that he'd done for her, keeping her on in Shanghai after her mother went home, getting her a job on the paper, etc. etc. Where had she picked up these crazy ideas? Not that he didn't know.

Then he told her that perhaps she should go home if she won't have a job anymore. By now he'd calmed down a bit, said it wasn't to punish her, but it would be for her own safety. Shanghai's going to be dangerous for the next few months, & her family would be happier if Emily went back to the States. And so on, and so on.

Of course, for ordinary people there are no berths to be had on the outbound ships—every one of them is crowded with refugees going home from the upriver ports & the inland mission stations. So the ships home are booked solid for months.

But what's the use of being an important figure like J.R. if you can't make special arrangements? So he's found her a stateroom on the *President Polk* three weeks from today.

Of course E. doesn't want to leave and has refused to go. Why should she, when the biggest story in the world is unfolding right here, in front of her own eyes? And if Prendergast won't print what she writes, someone back in the States will.

I laugh, tell her it shows she has printers' ink in her veins. Always a dangerous sign.

But Emily, clever Emily, is already thinking of a way to stay on. "Simon"—this with a look of great seriousness—"from now on we're through." Then laughs at the disappointment in my face. "In public, I mean, Simon—only in public. I'll just let

Uncle John think I've lost interest in you, that you've gone out of my life. Because you're the real reason he wants me to go home, don't you see? But we can go on meeting here, as often as we like, because we know we can trust Mme Vorontsov."

She raises her glass, a toast to Mme V. The music on the other side of the wall is softer now, something sentimental, something sweet, a song from Paris that you hear in the clubs of the avenue Joffre: *"C'est jeune, et ça ne sait pas."*

Clever Emily, devious Emily. When she makes up her mind to do something, she generally does it. And I will play my part, because now, once again on this cold, raw evening which suddenly became spring for the two of us, I can no longer bear the thought of Shanghai without her. *Yün-yü nan wang jih yüeh hsin. . . .*

The seven simple Chinese characters with which Simon had ended this passage had sent Matthew to his dictionary when he first read them. "He could never forget his love for her, which was daily renewed," that work told him. The reference was to the T'ang emperor Ming Huang, whose love for the beautiful Yang Kuei-fei, over a thousand years ago, had cost him his throne, and had almost brought down his dynasty. And *yün-yü*, clouds and rain, particularly when associated with spring, can mean only one thing: a love that has been fully and passionately consummated.

The loud backfire of a truck in the street outside startled Matthew back into the world of today, and he realized guiltily that he'd almost dozed off, allowing himself to think about Emily and Simon, rather than concentrating on the reading he was meant to be doing. The documents in front of him were difficult to decipher, the Chinese characters rapidly and imprecisely drawn, the language almost telegraphic in its brevity. Sometimes the people of whom they spoke were identified only by a single character rather than their full names. It was easy enough for Matthew to tell who most of them were: "Yi" was Lo Yi-nung, one of the local communist leaders; "Shou" was Wang Shou-hua, the young chairman of the communist-run General Labor Union; and "En," of course, was Chou En-lai, who'd arrived in

Shanghai in late 1926 and had been put in charge of the military preparations for the coming insurrection. Zhao Shanling had helped Matthew with these names and some of the others. But there was another one, known only as "Hung," that neither Zhao nor Wang Baozhen had been able to identify. Matthew stared at the character—it could mean "wild goose" in one reading, "vast" or "broad" in another—wondering whether it could be an alias. That was unlikely; all the others had used a single character of their real names, after all. Somewhere, deep in the back of his mind, there was a flicker of sudden recognition. Then it vanished, and he couldn't recall it.

Shortly before noon Zhao Shanling appeared, apologetically reminding him that the institute was about to shut for the weekend. "I hope you had a good morning's work," he said.

"Thank you," said Matthew. "You've been very helpful." He began putting his notes away in his briefcase. "And I'm particularly grateful to you for these." Zhao had brought in a stack of photocopies of documents that he'd asked for several days before. Photocopies are hard to get in China; Matthew knew that Zhao must have gone to bat for him, and that they represented not only a gesture of goodwill, but also a gesture of trust. "I'll try to read them this weekend."

"*Bu keqi, bu keqi,*" Zhao replied, smiling at him. "Don't mention it. *Si wen tong gurou*—do you know the saying? All scholars are brothers. So we must help one another. I hope you'll find them useful. And I'll try to have some more of them for you on Monday."

Out in the street, despite the sun shining from the pale blue sky, the day was not oppressively hot, and Matthew decided to walk the two miles back to his hotel rather than fight his way aboard a packed noontime bus, or surrender to the luxury of a taxi from the Peace Hotel, a few blocks away in the old Sassoon House. Exhaust fumes mingled with the smells from sidewalk food stalls and street-corner restaurants, and high above the crowded street, long bamboo poles stretched from the windows, white and blue flags of drying laundry hanging limply in the humid air, lending an air of incongruous domestic intimacy to these old downtown office buildings. On the wall of what had once been the Shanghai Municipal Council building, a torn poster proclaimed its support of the democracy movement, while still affirming a prudent loyalty to the Communist Party.

Matthew, stopping to examine it, wondered what the ardent young revolutionaries, whose words he'd been reading that morning, would have made of this year's events. Here they had lived and worked, six decades ago, young and inexperienced men and women meeting in secret, trying to gain the confidence of a fearful people; how would they have looked on the enormous upwelling of sympathy for the protests against the government today? DEFEND OUR UNIVERSITY STUDENTS! read the banners he'd seen held up before the television cameras this morning. *Baowei women da xuesheng!*

Sixty years later, most of those once-young men and women had vanished, of course. Wang Shou-hua and Lo Yi-nung had died soon after the insurrection they had helped to lead, victims of the bloody anticommunist purges of 1927. Ch'en Tu-hsiu had lived until 1940, disgraced by the Party he had once led, his memory effaced from their history books which omitted his name. Even Chou En-lai, a survivor, and now canonized in the memories of millions of ordinary Chinese, had died of cancer in January 1976, only nine months before Mao himself had gone to his ancestors. How would such men have seen this spring's great popular revolt against the Party, the very Party for which they had been ready to sacrifice their own lives so long ago? Would they have recognized in today's cries for freedom any part of the cause that they themselves had served when they were young?

A phrase from Marx came back to him: "the development of the freedom of each will be the condition for the development of the freedom of all." A few of the veterans of 1927 still lived today. One of those brave young revolutionaries in Shanghai that spring had been named Yang Shangkun. Today he was in his mid-eighties, president of the People's Republic, a grim and frozen presence at official gatherings of the leadership. Today, too, as vice chairman of the Military Commission, he commanded the loyalties of those armies that were now taking up their positions around the capital. What must be passing through his mind as he looked east from the remote fastness of the Zhongnanhai, that citadel where China's highest leaders lived, toward Tiananmen Square? Did he recall the heroic days of his youth? Was there any resonance in his memory between that long-ago Shanghai spring of 1927 and the Beijing spring of 1989? Did he feel any trace of sympathy for those who, so many years later, still wanted to fight for a free and independent China?

History is what we remember, Matthew thought to himself: we as individuals, as a group, a people, a nation. By occupying Tiananmen Square, the students today had claimed a share in shaping that memory, for the square was the emotional heart of China. Not just China under the Communists, but China of the dynasties as well, for the Tiananmen itself, the vast Gate of Heavenly Peace, led into the heart of the Forbidden City, among whose temples and shadowy halls had lived and moved the emperors who had ruled China for five hundred years.

It was before the Tiananmen that the demonstrations of May 4, 1919, had taken place, demonstrations that had turned into a great national movement, a movement against the warlords, and against the foreigners, whose war to make the world safe for democracy had once again compromised China's nationhood. Chairman Mao had called May Fourth the birth of modern China, but a month ago, seventy years after that famous rally, on May 4, 1989, the regime's carefully controlled plans to commemorate this event as they wished it remembered had been overturned by the students in the square.

To the aging leaders in the Zhongnanhai, May Fourth recalled the heroic stand their generation had made against foreign imperialism, against warlord violence and corruption, against slavery to the demands of an outdated tradition. After years of struggle they had won those battles, and now theirs was the May Fourth they wanted remembered, a May Fourth that could be put into a museum, a relic of the past, safe, offering no challenge to the present. To the students, however, the rallying cries that had brought their forebears into the streets seventy years ago—for freedom, for democracy, for an end to corruption—still spoke to China's needs today. But in 1989, the despotism, the corrupt and autocratic superstitions that continued to rule their lives, came not from the ghosts of dead sages and bygone emperors, but from the outworn traditions of the Communists themselves. From the same people who had been fighting to win Shanghai for the revolution in 1927, thought Matthew, the men who today made up the handful of aging survivors of those distant struggles.

Much in China's future would depend on their historical

memories, on President Yang Shangkun's dim recollections of those heroic days, on whatever remnants there might still be of the vision that he and his comrades had fought for so many years ago. And on the echoes that he might still make out behind the passionate outcry from the young in these spring days of 1989.

CHAPTER SEVEN

Saturday, June 3, 1989

Sometimes it seemed to Matthew that actually being in Shanghai today made more rather than less difficult his attempt to recapture the city's past. So much still looked the same—the buildings, the streets, the river, the parks, all recalled the old photographs he had seen in books published half a century and more ago. Like the sort of recurrent dream in which one journeys yet again to an imagined country whose familiar landscape leaves an unnerving memory of reality upon waking, the sight of the city and its landmarks occasionally evoked in him the sense that he himself had walked the streets in Simon's day, and had known and felt that same mixture of excitement, uncertainty, and apprehension that had come with the approaching revolution.

Yet the Shanghai in which he found himself was obviously not the Shanghai of the past. Too much had changed over those many years, too much had happened to the men and women of that time to permit them still to occupy the kind of lost world that the physical appearance of their city even now suggested. But it was precisely that visual sameness that was making it so difficult for him to recover today a sense of the place that it had been sixty years ago and more, a sense of the city through which

173

had moved the men and women he was studying: Chiang Kai-shek and his communist antagonists, Tu Yüeh-sheng the gangster, ordinary Chinese like Chu Hung-ying and his friends, the foreigners like Simon Larsen, Eric Massingham, Emily and John Ransom, Stanfield Frothingham, and all those others who had lived there so long ago. And it was at such times that he was almost overwhelmed by a sense of his own effrontery in trying to order and arrange their lives, to reconstruct and, through his narrative, to give meaning to them, from the insubstantial and insufficient records they had left behind.

What had been the voices of the past—the street hawkers, the rickshaw pullers, the coolies with their carrying poles? How had people talked then—what had been the sounds of Russian, English, French, pidgin, standing out against the backdrop of Shanghainese? How had they looked and moved? What had been the smells of food, of dirt, of humanity? All those evanescent but still powerful evocations of the past are the property of no archive, and can only be suggested by the documents, letters, journals, photographs, that are the stuff of the historian's world. To rebuild in the imagination this city of the past, it might almost have been better to have stayed at home rather than to risk deception by coming to a place where so much still looked the same, and yet in which so much had changed.

The question was part of a larger one, as it is for all historians. How was Matthew to evoke a historical memory for a time he had never known, a place he had never seen, events he had never witnessed, people he had never met? The revolution of 1927 was very much part of modern China's historical memory. A *qiyi*, the Chinese called it, but though his dictionary translated the term as "uprising," or "insurrection," he knew that the word bears a moral freight that the English lacks, for it means a rising conceived in righteousness, a people united against their oppressors. André Malraux's Kyo Gisors had understood that meaning, when, on the eve of the rising, he dreamt of a Soviet China, a China turned communist for the sake of human dignity. Then had come betrayal: the bloody night of April 12, when Chiang Kai-shek had turned on his communist allies, his gangster squads of executioners spilling into the streets to butcher the very men and women who had welcomed him to Shanghai only three weeks earlier.

To write history, Matthew was coming to realize, is to engage in an act of translation. Take a story, or a poem; it's not simply a matter of turning it from one language into another. There's risk as well, for a matter of trust is at stake. How do you take the idiom of another time, another place, another voice, and render it as your own? How, when you put another's words into your own language, do you avoid breaking faith, betraying a confidence, a covenant that you have made with the original?

How far would the men and women of yesterday recognize themselves in the histories we devise for our own age? How is the historian to recover, from the scattered and incomplete shards of the past, the world that gave them birth? How do the meanings of words, expressions, gestures, change in the flow of time? How do you draw from the world of the past a shape that is comprehensible to the present? There's a question of integrity. The construction of the historian's narrative from those relics risks the danger of imposing on them a form that is not theirs: imagination can turn into invention, and when that happens, the covenant with the past is broken. Then history becomes false, for the historian's work is not so much to serve the ephemeral needs of the present as to enlarge, through the evocation of other times and other peoples, the present's understanding of the complexity of the human experience, the human condition.

Interesting as they might be, speculations like these were not going to get the job done. Back in his hotel, drowsy from the sun and the long walk home from the institute, Matthew considered the stack of photocopies that Zhao Shanling had given him that morning. Had he really asked for so much? Two hundred pages, more or less: most of them the records of the revolutionary underground in 1927, like the ones he'd seen that morning. The thickness of the pile discouraged him. Did he really have to read all of it? Two hundred pages of Chinese, some of it difficult, almost incomprehensible to him. You can skim through writing in your own language, he thought, but not Chinese, where every character has to be accounted for.

He felt oppressed by the room's heavy drabness, and allowed himself to glance at a photograph of Laura that he'd propped up on the desk: sitting on a rough stone wall, she smiled at him, swinging her long brown legs in the sunlight, while behind her the Chianti vineyards stretched off into an endless afternoon.

Memories of last summer filled his mind, to turn quickly into speculations about the present, the future. All morning long, the thought of her voice on the telephone had warmed him, the thought that she'd been been concerned enough to call. Now he wondered what that concern might mean for the future. They'd parted in May on friendly enough terms, but he still sensed that Laura's wariness had by no means disappeared. Furthermore, her years as a graduate student were soon coming to an end, she was already looking around for jobs—and then what? He knew that he didn't want her to leave, wanted her with him. Perhaps she'd land a position in one of the many colleges around Boston. But suppose she didn't? Did he want her enough to follow her wherever she went? To give up his own job, perhaps driving a spike through what for the moment looked like a promising career? Or might they become one of those two-career academic couples, he in Massachusetts, she in Oregon, seeing each other briefly during vacations, or when their paths crossed at academic conventions? The two of them had skirted around the subject on occasion. But then, he realized, even if they wound up within a few miles of each other, it still wasn't clear to him how she saw their future. If she saw their future.

But if she didn't, then why had she called? He looked at her picture again, and suddenly the prospect of going on with his work wearied him. Surely the papers could wait. It was a pleasant Saturday, and the institute was shut for the weekend, after all; why couldn't he at least take the afternoon off? Couldn't he ignore that quietly insistent voice from his conscience that reminded him he was there on a research grant: you're here spending someone else's money, use your time well. Sooner or later he'd have to begin. But why today? Tomorrow it was meant to rain. Then he'd have no excuse for leaving his room, and could begin to work his way through the stack that seemed to have grown even higher while he was thinking about it.

Of course his conscience got the better of him, as he knew it would. The same Puritan conscience that had driven Laura and him to the top of their alpine pass last summer rather than allowing them to spend the afternoon lazing in a sun-warmed meadow. Get to work, it told him, and it even held out a promise: the sooner you're through, the sooner you can go home. And see Laura, Laura, who's soon going to be in California, and who's just telephoned to find out if you're all right.

So he began by clearing a space on the desk, and in so doing managed to dislodge part of the pile balanced precariously on the corner. Damn, he thought as the photocopies cascaded to the floor, will I ever get them back in order? He leaned down to pick them up, resigning himself to the business of arranging them before he could start. Nothing is so discouraging as to make an unpleasant decision and then have to postpone carrying it through.

Fortunately, most of the papers were dated, so the job wasn't as bad as he expected. Then suddenly he came across a thick stack of papers written not in Chinese, but in English or French. Some were typed, others handwritten. What on earth were they? He'd asked for nothing of this kind.

He picked up the first sheet and began reading. Stunned, he was unable to believe what lay before him. A whole set of reports, some from the Municipal Police, others from the French police, still others from various foreign authorities. And all of them seemed to deal with Simon's activities during the crisis of early 1927.

The first appeared to be the beginnings of a dossier from the Municipal Police. "Larsen, Simon," it read.

> American. Born June 4, 1896, Philadelphia USA. Wounded in France, 1918. Author of "The Iron Ridge" [you didn't get that quite right, thought Matthew] describing his wartime service. Pacifist leanings. American police report no evidence of Bolshevik sympathies in U.S.A. Arrived in Peking, 1921 or 1922. Sometime teacher at Yen-ching University (American). Came to Shanghai, November 1923. Address 221 bis, route Père Robert, Frenchtown. Has taught English at St. John's University and Fu-tan University.

To which a handwritten note had been added: "Known to consort with Chinese of 'advanced' views among student and loafer element. Critical of S.M.C. since Nanking Road affair." After that was scrawled a date—December something. Probably 1926?

The next memorandum showed an even more direct interest.

Council Chamber
January 13, 1927

To: C.D.I. Givens
Shanghai Municipal Police, Special Branch

The overrunning of the British Concession at Hankow by the radical element of the Kuo Min Tang shows unmistakably that the Bolsheviks now control the new government established there December *ultimo*. It is to be feared that as the Cantonese armies approach Shanghai, similar outbreaks may be expected against the foreign settlements in the hope of provoking a forceful response, thereby giving rise to a fresh outburst of indignation among the natives against the foreign authorities. While naval landing parties and reinforcements may be expected to hold the Settlement boundaries against armed attack, there remains a danger of subversion from within, perhaps aided by foreigners with Bolshevik sympathies. With a view toward preventing such occurrences, will you please detail whatever men you can spare to watch the movements of the following:

Alfred Ingalls (British), 207 North Honan Road
Hilary Ordway (British), 134 Haiphong Road
Alexander Tchusov (Russian), 41a Medhurst Road
Boris Tcherepnin (Russian), 76 Hanbury Road
John Armbruster (American), 5 Tsitsihar Road
Gregor Scheiderhan (German), 72 route Voyron, Frenchtown
Simon Larsen (American), 221 bis, route Père Robert, Frenchtown
Kurt von Schlaudern (Australian), 16 rue Chapsal, Frenchtown
Serge Obermann (Russian), 417 avenue Joffre, Frenchtown

A copy of this letter is being sent to Captain Fiori of the French police, with the request that his men keep an eye on the residents of his Concession that are named above.

/s/A. H. *Hilton-Johnson*
Commissioner-General, Shanghai Municipal Council

Matthew read the documents with a growing excitement. Chief Detective-Inspector Patrick Givens had been, he knew, the head of the Special Branch of the Settlement's police, responsible for political intelligence and dealing with cases of subversion, and Major Hilton-Johnson had been commissioner of the Shanghai Municipal Police before his appointment to the council. But what had Simon done to make the police and the Municipal Council interested in him? Obviously, as the revolutionary armies drew closer in the winter of 1927, they considered him suspicious enough to be put under some kind of surveillance. But why? And on what evidence?

And where on earth had Zhao Shanling found these documents? Matthew had never asked for them, hadn't even known they existed. Presumably they'd been buried somewhere in the institute's archives, and Zhao had taken it upon himself to copy them, and to conceal the copies in the other material he'd handed Matthew that morning. "We scholars must help one another," he had said. Matthew breathed a silent prayer of thanks to Mr. Zhao's ancestors, and wondered what he could do to repay him.

> Hôtel municipale
> Conseil municipal de la
> Concession française
> Changhai, le 15 janvier 1927

Major A. H. Hilton-Johnson,
Shanghai Municipal Council
M. le Commissionaire,

J'accuse réception de vôtre lettre du 13ème [it began. Matthew skimmed it, translating as he went].

I will of course do all in my power and that of my men to take the proper steps to secure the integrity of the Concession against attacks from the outside or subversion from within. Please be advised that we have had Serge Obermann under surveillance since the disruptions of last October, and that he is known to have paid several visits to the Soviet consulate general on Whangpoo Road. The purpose of these visits is not known to us. Herr von Schlaudern has lived in Shanghai for many years, and while he was briefly interned as an enemy alien during the war, we have no evidence here to suggest any links to bolshevism. We will, however, watch his movements. Simon Larsen, the American, is well connected, and has several friends in high places, including M. Verdier of the consulate general. He is also known to have Chinese friends who are associated with the Kuo Min Tang, and has on several occasions shown himself to be friendly to the cause of the Cantonese faction in Chinese politics. Apart from that, little is known of his views. Perhaps the S.M.C. could inquire of the American consulate general whether the authorities of the United States know anything to Mr. Larsen's discredit.

Believe me, M. le Commissionaire,

/s/*Étienne Fiori*
Chef de la Garde municipale

Fifteen minutes later he came upon a document that was in some ways the most interesting of all.

Council Chambers
February 23, 1927

To: C.D.I. Givens
Shanghai Municipal Police, Special Branch

Last night, whilst attending the American community's annual celebration of George Washington's Birthday at the Majestic Hotel, I was approached by Mr. John Ransom, who, as you are aware, in all probability will presently hold one of the "American" seats on the Municipal Council. He was, he told me, concerned about one of his compatriots who, he had reason to believe, had formed some unwise and perhaps dangerous friendships with Chinese of advanced views. Upon my enquiring the name of the person to whom he referred, he at first demurred, but when I appealed to him in the name of the good order of the Settlement, admitted that he meant Mr. Simon Larsen. He has come to know Mr. Larsen quite well, he said, because of the attentions that the latter has paid to his niece, Miss Emily Ransom, who is employed by the American-owned *China Press*. Upon being asked for further information, Mr. Ransom said that Larsen (whose command of the local dialect is said to be very good) was well known for having consorted with a number of Chinese whose sympathies are said to lie with the radical wing of the Kuo Min Tang, and some of whom may even be bolshevist.

I reminded Mr. Ransom that since Larsen lives in the French Concession, our ability to find out more about his actions may be limited. Without telling him that we have asked the French authorities to place a watch on Mr. Larsen, I suggested that Mr. Ransom might wish to raise the question of his activities with the French authorities. He appears reluctant to do so, however, apparently believing that while the Shanghai Municipal Police can be relied upon in dealing with the case of one of his fellow citizens, the French police are worthy of no such trust.

Please let me know immediately if you have information from Captain Fiori or anyone else that would lend substance to these allegations against Mr. Larsen. In the meantime, I will have enquiries made of Mr. Paget, the American vice-consul.

/s/Major A. H. Hilton-Johnson
Commissioner-General, Shanghai Municipal Council

So, thought Matthew, that bastard Ransom had actually made an accusation against Simon. Not a formal accusation, but a kind of underhanded, indirect one that was likely to get him in just as much trouble, without Ransom's having to take the responsibility. Probably hoped that he could get Simon deported from Shanghai before Emily could see any more of him.

He looked at his watch. Three in the afternoon. All thoughts of going outside for a walk in the spring sunlight had now vanished. If he worked hard, he ought to be able at least to get a rough idea of what these papers contained by evening. He sat down at the desk and buried himself once again in the documents.

By the middle of February 1927, about the time that John Ransom had threatened to send his niece back to the States, Shanghai was developing a bad case of the jitters. "People talk in that bright and brittle way that betrays their nervousness," observed Simon. "The drink flows more freely in the clubs, and some people are quietly packing up their possessions and sending them home." Americans and Frenchmen complained that their governments didn't understand the danger in which Shanghai found itself, and resented their dependence on British troops.

Ben Rogers, the journalist, was less worried about the French.

Whatever might happen elsewhere in Shanghai, he predicted to Simon on February 16, the French Concession would come out of it all right.

I asked him what he meant. He shrugged his shoulders. "The French have ways of talking to the Chinese that the authorities of the Settlement can't imagine."

What French, and what Chinese, I asked him.

He shrugged again. "All of them—the police, the consulate, the French Council. They're in touch with the warlords, with Chiang Kai-shek. And—"

And? I prompted him.

"And with some less savory types as well."

Though I pressed him, I couldn't get any more out of him. But I remember Father Duchamp's strange story last year, about the arrangements the French police are said to have made with the underworld opium ring, and wondered what connections there might be with our political turmoil today.

Before we broke up to go our separate ways, Rogers asked me if I was still seeing much of Emily. I bristled at that—I like Rogers, but he's got no call to pry into my affairs. He admitted as much, but he also told me there's a story about that Ransom somehow has the idea I'm not fit company for his niece. Don't worry too much about it, he said. Ransom's feeling a bit edgy these days. He's apparently gone deeply into debt—to whom, Rogers doesn't know—and he's eager to hush it up because it might hurt his chances of being elected to the Municipal Council.

Ransom's problems are none of my business, & I don't care about them. But if Rogers is right, it would explain E.'s impression that her uncle has been worried by his finances recently. There are plenty of foreigners here, and Ransom may be one of them, who are tempted by the easy pleasures of Shanghai to live beyond their means—club memberships, horses, houseboats, entertaining—to name only some of the more public ways of running through one's money. And of course there are private ways as well, & there's no reason to suppose that R. is immune to the normal temptations of flesh and blood. Still, I wouldn't have thought of him as indulging in them, and I imagine he's done no more than simply to make a few bad investments.

One more disquieting piece of news from Rogers: Ransom has taken up recently with R. Sexton. Or, as he put it, "they've been seeing more of each other than some might think wise. Even though they're being careful not to let the world find out about it."

The news took me aback, though I hope I didn't show it. Maybe it's part of Rogers's business to know such things, and maybe he's passing this gossip on to me because he hopes that I can tell him more. But R. and I parted ways some time ago, and whatever I think of Ransom's private life, his domestic problems are his own concern, & I can't see that they should have any effect on Emily and me. Especially since, as far as Ransom is concerned, we are no longer interested in each other.

Simon himself, judging by his journal entries, was one of a handful of foreign residents who refused to be caught up in the sense of near panic sweeping through the city—though, as he had earlier admitted, he had no great stake in Shanghai, and could afford to play the role of disinterested observer of China's affairs. He was beginning to sound, Matthew thought, rather like some of the people he himself had met in Hong Kong, who refused to be panicked by the prospect of the colony's impending reversion to Chinese rule, concentrating single-mindedly instead on the opportunities that the city still offered for moneymaking. Simon, of course, was after information, not money; but like those people in Hong Kong today, he, too, enjoyed the advantages of a foreign passport.

In only one way, apparently, had the emergency impinged on Simon's life. His professional life, at any rate; his personal life and his relations with Emily were something else again. By late January he had noted, occasionally with some annoyance, that the usually dependable Chu Hung-ying was becoming more and more sporadic in his visits. And, Simon guessed, it was partly in order to make up for the lessons they had missed, that in mid-February—about the time of Simon's blowup with Ransom—Chu had brought with him one evening a friend who seemed particularly well informed about Nationalist politics, and about the ways that they might affect Shanghai. And was willing to talk about them to Simon. The man was introduced to him as Chang Shao-shan.

... a man of about thirty, with a fine, clear-featured face, marked by a prominent jaw and heavy eyebrows. He's a native of Shao-hsing in Chekiang, but tells me he was raised in Kiangsu province. He's obviously a well-traveled man, & as he talked it emerged that he'd studied in Tientsin & Tokyo before going to Europe, where he lived in Paris and Berlin. France, of course, has been a favorite place for Chinese students, at least those who can afford it, & Mr. Chang—neat, almost dapper, well turned out—was obviously one of those who could.

He's been in Canton for the past three years, and came to Shanghai last fall, where he now lives with his wife's family on the route Lafayette in the Concession. But it's not at all clear what he's been doing since then. To look at him, you'd think he might be a teacher at one of the Chinese universities. Or perhaps a businessman, or a journalist, or even a young army officer in mufti. Whenever I tried to discover what brought him here, however, he managed to turn my questions politely aside, and Mr. Chu was eager to change the subject.

Whatever may be his profession now, he seems to have—or to have had—a good many friends in the Kuomintang. He talked about the Nationalist Party, which he has come to know from his years in Canton, talked about the progress of the Northern Expedition, & about the state of Chiang Kai-shek's armies, for he appears to know many of the officers leading them. And he talked about the prospect of Shanghai's fall to those armies, for he has no doubt that it will happen in the next few months, and perhaps a good deal sooner.

Are the Nationalists going to try to seize the foreign settlements, I asked him. Will we see here a repetition of what happened in Hankow last month?

"The immediate task of the Kuomintang is to complete the present phase of the revolution by defeating the warlords and uniting the country." Even in Chinese the words sounded almost like a formula as they came out, words spoken many times before, suitable for a gathering of newspaper reporters. "Of course the settlements must be returned eventually. Shanghai is part of China, after all, just like Hankow, or Tientsin, or the other cities where foreigners live. Even Hong Kong." His mention of Britain's colony startled me, & I thought how E. Massingham & his friends would have exploded if they'd heard such a sentiment.

So I asked him what the foreigners can expect—the people whom the Kuomintang now denounces as imperialists.

He looked straight at me as he answered, with a directness that I couldn't help admiring.

"Imperialism by its very nature is doomed, & it cannot be allowed to continue in the new China. We do not say that foreigners should leave. But they must realize that they have much more to gain by cooperating with a new China than by trying to strangle it at birth."

I asked him the inevitable question, the same question I have asked Mr. Chu's other friends so often: what about Russia? What about the Communists?

"The Soviet Union is our friend. The Soviet Union alone has helped us. But"—and he looked straight at me again—"if the day ever comes when the Soviets try to dominate China, we will respond to them just as we do to any other imperialist nation. We will never again be the pawn of another country. Not even one pretending to be our friend. Not even Russia—or America."

By now I was fascinated, and had my notebook out, rapidly scribbling down his answers to my questions, though there was a great deal that he asked me, politely but firmly, to leave unwritten. From Mandarin, his conversation shifted easily into French, and then to Shanghainese, sometimes even to English. His vision of the kind of China he wants to see emerge from the civil war is not so different from that of Mr. Chu's other friends, the ones whom Emily and I have talked to at such length since last summer. But he brings to it a power of conviction, a persuasiveness of argument that makes those others seem, by contrast, nothing more than the green students they are. Not much older than they, he has obviously experienced far more of the world, & reluctant as he may be to reveal his own role in all of this, by the end of our talk I had become convinced that he not only knows some of the Kuomintang inner circle, but may at some time actually have been a member of that circle.

As I listened to him, I thought: this man should be a missionary, for everything he said seems utterly convincing, and a few men like this would do more to convert China than all the mission boards, the National Christian Councils, the Y.M.C.A.s, & the missionary universities put together.

Later, I realize: that's exactly what he is—a missionary. Even though his cause is not Christianity but the cause of China herself.

In Chang Shao-shan, thought Matthew, Simon must have sensed the presence of a kindred spirit, another man who, like him, had an experience of life beyond his years, a broadness of vision denied those whose time on earth had been more sheltered, more confined. He didn't seem particularly concerned when, two days later, Chu Hung-ying had admitted to him that Chang Shao-shan was an alias—or at least that Chang was not his surname. Chu had then begun to ask Simon a series of questions, most of them having to do with how the foreigners might respond to the revolution about to break over them, and Simon noted with some surprise that he had felt himself under examination, as if he were somehow being tested. He pleaded ignorance; he had no particular knowledge of such things, he said. Chu persisted; Simon had friends in high places in Shanghai, men like Eric Massingham and François Verdier. His own friends, he said, had been very impressed by the authority with which Simon spoke of the affairs of the foreign settlements.

Like Chang Shao-shan? I asked. Mr. Chu looked somewhat taken aback and then admitted that yes, his friend had been very interested—"it is important for them to know how the foreigners will behave when the Nationalist armies arrive."

So I pressed him. "The Nationalists want no trouble with the foreigners," he went on. "But of course crowds can get out of hand. As they did perhaps in Hankow. Or someone among the defenders might panic, and fire a few shots. As the police did in Nanking Road almost two years ago. Then there's no telling what might happen, no matter what orders the military commanders give."

Particularly, I suggested, if the Nationalist commanders themselves do not quite agree with those who are stirring up the crowds? He gave me a searching look, and told me he found that a very astute comment. "*Ming jen tien t'ou chiu chih—*" a nod of the head is enough for the intelligent man.

Events now began to move very fast. Hangchow, only a hundred and thirty miles south of Shanghai, fell to the Nationalist armies on February 17. Two days later the troops were moving up the rail line, and the papers reported them already in Kashing, only about sixty miles away. "The city has suddenly come alive with rumors," reported Simon in his journal (the pages, however, were carefully typed, probably for later insertion into the book).

> ... the revolutionary armies are advancing on Shanghai; the troops of Sun Ch'uan-fang, our local warlord, are already retreating to the north; a battle is imminent; there'll be no battle; Sun's commanders are digging in for a fight; Sun's commanders have already gone over to the Nationalists, bought by Chiang's silver bullets. And so on. The Chinese papers, heavily censored, have little reliable news, and the *North China* and *China Post* aren't much better.
>
> Nor have I seen Mr. Chu, who is usually so well informed about such matters; he scribbled a note to me yesterday telling me that he's fallen ill again, and apologizing for having to postpone our lesson for a few days. Strange. He seemed perfectly well a day earlier. But then, I suppose, Shanghai is an unhealthy place in the winter.

On February 21, the communist leaders of the General Labor Union called a citywide strike, ostensibly to welcome the impending arrival of the Nationalist forces. It was the largest such work stoppage since the strikes of June 1925—over a hundred thousand workers, dockers, tram drivers, rickshawmen, and others walked off their jobs. Just as they had two years earlier, factories and mills, shops and warehouses, lighters and godowns suddenly fell idle, and an apprehensive silence spread over the city like a winter fog.

Wednesday, February 23

Yet the peace is only superficial, for underneath the uncanny quiet lies a sense of excitement and anticipation, mixed with a real fear. We hear of isolated, desperate acts of violence in the last two days—skirmishes at police stations in Chapei and Pootung, a pitched battle near the South Station. From the Chinese districts, borne on the wind, comes the report of small-arms fire, rifle and pistol shots, sounding almost like the firecrackers that three weeks ago announced the coming of the New Year. But these sounds are sharper, more malevolent, more frightening. Last night we were suddenly jolted by a series of deeper crashes, as one of the Chinese gunboats in the Huangpu opened fire, and this morning the papers report that several shells landed in the French Concession.

As Matthew knew, the strike and the brief outbreak of fighting that followed had been part of an attempt by the Communists to take control of Shanghai before the Nationalist troops should arrive. Suddenly, however, for reasons that the historians had never explained, the armies moving up the railway from Hangchow came to a halt. At the time, Simon had suggested that the Nationalists might have outrun their supply lines. But others were speaking of treachery, factionalism, undercover negotiations between Chiang Kai-shek and his enemies, arrangements made for both sides to divide the spoils—"the usual stuff of warlord campaigns." Whatever might be the reason, the insurrectionists were now left helpless, and the police and the army put them down with a brutality unusual even for those bloody years. Newspapers told of military execution squads patrolling the streets of the Chinese city, seizing any whom they considered to be agitators, decapitating them on the spot, and then putting their heads on display.

In the journal's very last entry, dated Monday, February 28, Simon had described such a grisly scene, though it was impossible to tell whether he had seen it himself or had taken it from the accounts of others.

By now the troops have quieted the city down, the police have fought off their attackers. The gunboats, having briefly startled the city with their barrage, are silent again. Since then, most terrifying of all in the hushed city, have come the execution squads: each one a file of soldiers, led by an officer with a double-edged sword, red ribbons fluttering from the handle. For three days last week they prowled through the streets of the Chinese city with a ferocious intensity, hunting their victims. Just looking like a student was enough to get you arrested. No trials, of course, for those who are caught. The lucky are sent to jail; the unlucky are forced to their knees, down on the hard pavement, hands tied behind their backs, shivering in the cold, watched by the silent crowd. The headsman's bright sword raised high catches the thin winter sun; then it flashes swiftly down on their bare necks. A rush of blood on the street as the body falls; a sudden gasp from the watchers: enthralled, terrified, entertained? Who can tell? The executioner wipes his blade, motions to his men. They retrieve the severed heads, put them in wicker baskets, to be hung on lampposts, on gates, to decorate the bare trees. An hour later the crowds scarcely glance at them as they go impassively about their daily affairs, with no signs of pity or fear on their expressionless faces.

What are they thinking of? Why do they show no emotion as they walk beneath those terrifying ornaments?

If they really think nothing of what they see, that is most frightening of all.

How little we understand this country. . . .

And with that line, Simon's journal had come to an end. Or at least Matthew's copy did. He'd almost cried out in frustration when he first discovered it two months ago. Why should it break off there? Three weeks before the fall of Shanghai to the Nationalists, a month and a half before Chiang's bloody purge of April 12? He'd questioned Laura: surely there must be more, this can't be all there is. Laura had called her mother in California, her mother had looked again at the material retrieved from Aunt Kate's house back in Philadelphia. All to no avail. That was all there had been in the old trunk that had held what was left of Simon's belongings. Sorry; did it seem that something was missing?

Now, among the papers given him that morning by the resourceful Zhao Shanling, Matthew discovered the rest. There, with the other materials from the French police, were a hundred pages, more or less, written by Simon himself during that last month and a half before he vanished, from the beginning of March to mid-April 1927. Though his name did not appear on them, they were unmistakably his—even on the photocopies

Matthew could recognize the typeface of his old Underwood, with its broken downstroke on the capital R, which made it almost indistinguishable from a P.

Yet these pages had been kept separate from the main body of the journal. And somehow—for the moment Matthew could only guess why—they had found their way into the files of the police, kept there presumably with the other documents that had made up the dossier kept by the *Garde municipale* on Simon Larsen.

Why the police had found them interesting was immediately obvious. For in these pages Simon had described a surprising new role that he had taken on in the days after the failure of the February insurrection.

It had all begun with another meeting between Simon and Chang Shao-shan on Tuesday, March 1, 1927.

For the first time in a good ten days, Mr. Chu called last night. His absence no longer surprises me, & I can no longer doubt that he's been in some way connected with the events of last week. Why is it that I can't find the courage to ask him about his activities? Am I afraid of what I might find out if he were to give me a truthful answer to my questions? Partly that, I suppose. I like him & don't want to bring him into any danger. But it's also because whatever he and his friends may be doing is no concern of mine—China's problems are not my problems, and they are for the Chinese to solve themselves. Of course I'm interested in his views & those of his friends, just as I'm interested in the views of their opponents. But I don't take sides. Leave the emotions to others; my job is to examine and analyze, as accurately as I can, this great wave of violence that is now breaking over China, and to try to understand what it will leave in its wake.

E. makes it no easier. Her sympathies now are all with the revolutionaries, & she berates me: how can I just stand by & watch all this happen, without trying to help? Once, I might have answered differently: when I was her age, young and full of hope, before I had become acquainted with fear, pain, and death. Now I simply respond that this is China's quarrel, not ours, we mustn't interfere.

But she's impatient, & the reply no longer satisfies even me: at night the pain in my shoulder wakes me, almost as if it would break through the scar that marks it, and as I lie there, sweating in the cold, once again I see, as if in a dream, the executioner, the sudden gleam of that sharp sword, the severed heads in their baskets strung up high above the streets.

Late yesterday evening, Mr. Chu came, unannounced, bringing Chang Shao-shan with him. Both were impeccably turned out, wearing western suits, and looking for all the world like two young businessmen of eminent respectability, who, having finished their day's work, were now on their way to dinner and an evening's entertainment at the Palais Oriental. Only the fatigue in their faces betrayed a succession of sleepless nights, and suggested that they might not be entirely what their outward aspect proclaimed them to be.

This time, no pleasantries, no exchange of Chinese compliments and courtesies. With an almost American directness they got down to the point.

Chang said the strike last week had only been the prelude to a plan for a general insurrection in the Chinese city, a rising that would deliver Shanghai into the hands of the revolutionaries. It was timed to coincide with the advance of the Nationalist armies, & had it worked, the city would have fallen without a pitched battle. The police stations were to be attacked first, and their weapons seized, then there would have been an assault on the military garrisons left in the city. In the meantime, mutineers aboard the Chinese gunboats planned to seize those ships, and block any reinforcements sent by water.

I asked what had gone wrong.

"Many things," said Chang. "Bad planning; insufficient training of the armed units that have been formed among the workers; too few weapons; bad communications."

And betrayal. The plans to seize the gunboats had been discovered, & in the confusion of a cold and dark winter night, some of the workers' units never got the orders to start the rising, while others went into action before they should have, & were easily defeated by the police & soldiers. So last Thursday the leaders of the rising decided to cut their losses, called off the insurrection, and the unions told their members to go back to work.

Chang paused here, & politely asked: "I hope you find the information useful, Lai *hsien-sheng*?"

I agreed it was not the sort of story one found in the newspapers, & thanked him for telling me. Then waited for what would come next.

"I gave you the story to show my trust, Lai *hsien-sheng*. Now I need your help."

I protested: I didn't see that there was any way I could help. Or should help.

Mr. Chu intervened, repeating what he'd said two weeks ago: "You know lots of people in Shanghai. Important people. We have no designs on the foreign settlements. But we do wish to see Shanghai in the hands of the Chinese. Real Chinese, patriotic Chinese, not the warlords who have been running the city for so many years."

Chang glanced at Mr. Chu, who nodded, and I sensed he was telling Chang that I could be trusted, it was all right to lay his cards on the table.

"There will be another rising," he said. "Right now we are planning for it. This time we must succeed. We know who our Chinese antagonists are; we know their strengths and weaknesses. Perhaps we can persuade them to leave peacefully. But if we have to fight, we know how to defeat them. This time we will have more arms, better training, better communications, better intelligence.

"But what will the foreigners do? What orders will the authorities give those ten thousand troops who are now quartered in our city? We *must* know their intentions." He brought his fist down hard on the table and fixed me with a look of furious passion, like that of a man desperately playing his last card at the gaming table.

For a moment there was silence. Then he was once again the cool and rational tactician I had seen before.

"Some among us are convinced that the British will stop at nothing to keep the Nationalist armies from reaching Shanghai, that they are prepared to fight a war with China if necessary. Even with the Soviet Union. Others say that if we don't threaten the settlements, the foreigners will leave us alone. And even if the British want to fight, what about the others—the Americans, the Japanese, the French? We need more information about all of them too. If we know that we don't have to worry about the foreigners, it will be very helpful to us." He smiled, an engaging, almost self-deprecating smile, a startling contrast to his earlier intensity of aspect.

They both looked at me, expectantly. I protested again: how should I know the answers to these questions? How do they expect me to find them out? Anyway, I'm not Chinese, I'm a foreigner. Neither their government nor mine wants me to interfere in matters that are not my concern. I'm a private citizen. Not a diplomat or a general. And certainly not a secret agent—(I can't quite bring myself to use the word "spy").

Chang unimpressed. "Can you honestly say that foreign countries—including your own—have not interfered in matters that aren't their concern? We're not asking you to hurt your friends or your countrymen in any way. But we must know if they are planning to hurt us. All our plans depend on it."

I hesitated, of course. I was once what other men called a hero, and look what happened. They gave me a medal. And a year in a hospital. And memories that I am still not rid of today.

So I said nothing. But I was conscious of the winter cold that had crept indoors, a cold that the fire did little to keep out. My shoulder ached in the damp, and I wanted them to leave, I wanted to have a drink and go to bed, to forget them and their concerns.

Chang pressed on. "You know of the executions last week. Men and women—no, boys and girls, some of them— beheaded, right there in the street. And you saw their heads strung up above the roads—on walls, on gates, on poles. What would you do if you had seen such sights in New York? or San Francisco?"

I thought: I did see them, and I still see them. I don't want to think about them. That's not the China I want to remember.

But I'm a foreigner, I said. The excuse sounded even weaker than before.

"You are still a man," Chang said. "A human being. *Shih fei chih hsin, jen chieh yu chih*—'the hearts of all men can distinguish right from wrong.' Or perhaps you foreigners think that Chinese have different morals, different customs? That Chinese feel no pain? So that what's murder in America is all right in China?"

Mr. Chu broke in. "Do you remember *Hsiao* T'ien? Little

T'ien? in Chapei, a few months ago?" I did: the passionately eager young student with whom I had argued in the tea shop, a man with a gentle face and gentle manners, yet burning with indignation at his country's shame.

Mr. Chu said: "He was one of those beheaded last week."

I couldn't answer that. Silence, then Chang Shao-shan spoke. "To be neutral is to make a choice, Lai *hsien-sheng*. What is impossible is to make no choice."

I stared at the blackness beyond the window. It was very still in the room. From outside came the night noises of the street—automobile horns, the cries of peddlers, of rickshaw pullers. I thought of them shivering in the cold, thought of the rickshawman I had castigated that night I had first met Emily. Was he still alive, I wondered. Had he survived the searing summers and the icy winters that had come since then? I thought of the little girls herded together to work the looms of the Toyoda cotton mill. And I thought of *Hsiao* T'ien, and of those dreadful baskets decorating the streets of the Chinese city.

All right, I said. I will do what I can.

I wanted to add: only if you promise me that you'll keep this a fight between Chinese, that no foreigners will be hurt, that there'll be no attack on the settlements. But I know they're in no position to give such an undertaking, and I know that the revolution has reached a point where it has developed its own logic, its own direction, and is no longer under the control of the individuals who are trying to lead it.

And I know that at the deepest level of our existence, we are not Chinese. Or American, or English, or French. We are all human beings.

But ever since this morning, when I first woke, I have wondered: What is it that I have agreed to?

Despite his initial apprehensions, despite, as he put it, his dislike of deception, once embarked, Simon appeared to have gone about his new work with a determination that betrayed no sense of misgiving. The round of interviews he had made in 1926, when he had thought he was about to leave China, now gave him an excuse to see many of the same people again. Since then, there had been radical changes in Chinese politics; what more natural than for a man like Simon to seek their opinions on what those changes might mean for Shanghai's future? Especially a Simon who, in contrast to his earlier radical leanings, now let it be known that he understood the seriousness of the crisis, that he agreed with those voices among his fellows who were calling for stronger measures of defense against the revolutionary danger? For such a pose was obviously helpful to him. "So," he wrote early in March, "among men of my own kind, I have taken on the protective coloration of the embattled Shanghailander, speaking out against my government's passivity and pusillanimity, as so many others here do. I criticize its failure to recognize the gravity of our crisis here in Shanghai, and I praise the British for their courage in sending troops to our city—our city, mind you—to defend civilization against the forces that threaten it. And it has worked. I am greeted as a returned prodigal, someone who has at last seen the error of his ways, who can be trusted. Men with whom I've hardly exchanged two words in the last year now greet me effusively, clap me on the shoulder, call me a good fellow, and offer to buy me a drink.

"But all the time I keep my ears open, I listen carefully."

As he read passages like these, Matthew found himself surprised by how much of his life in the shadows Simon was willing to commit to paper. Obviously he wanted to keep a record for his later use—but equally obviously he must have been aware of the danger it put him in, should anyone find it. But why, in fact, should anyone find it? Simon Larsen was, outwardly, at any rate, a repected citizen, and in the China of those days, a white skin and a foreign passport must have seemed protection enough against any unwarranted search of his living quarters or private belongings.

Certainly, when he did reflect on the new position in which he found himself, he had no regrets about the agreement he had made. An entry in early March helped to explain why.

Tuesday, March 8, 1927

An incident, this morning in the Settlement: a small band of students, near the intersection of Thibet and Nanking Roads, handing out leaflets to any who will take them. They work rapidly through the crowd, as if they were depending on surprise to startle people into curiosity about their offerings, while behind them moves the usual bustle and activity of the New

World theater. They look thin and underfed, their padded blue cotton jackets of little use against the sharp wind that blows from the harbor, reminding us that we have yet to turn the corner from winter into spring. The handbills are written in simple Chinese and bad English, proclaiming the imminent arrival of the National Revolutionary Army, calling for the overthrow of the warlords, and for the return of Shanghai to Chinese control.

Suddenly, a detachment of Sikh policemen arrives. The students break and run, trying to lose themselves in the throng that is always here, at one of the city's busiest crossings. Then a man—a perfectly ordinary man with an ordinary red English face—abruptly thrusts out his foot and trips up one of the fugitives. Caught in mid-stride, he goes down, disintegrating onto the pavement, a look of astonishment on his face. Instantly the Sikhs swoop on him, their batons clubbing him on the back, on the head. When they pull him up by the hair, blood streams from his face, and he's marched off, hands manacled behind his back, into the ugly block of the Louza police station. Meanwhile, a little knot of bystanders clusters around the Englishman, congratulating him on the presence of mind that has suddenly made him an unexpected agent in the capture of a dangerous criminal. They are all foreign, of course; the Chinese crowds that have watched this little drama remain impassive, unmoved. Impossible to tell what they're thinking.

It's all over in an instant, and there's nothing unusual about it. Such incidents take place every day here. The prisoner will be given a hearing by the Mixed Court, let off with a fine if he's lucky, sentenced to jail for disturbing the peace if he's unlucky. Unless, of course, the Chinese police want him. Then he'll be handed over to the military headquarters at Lung-hua, near the South Station. And the interrogation will begin: Did you write these leaflets? If not, tell us who did, from whom you got them. Who are your friends? Where do they live? Tell us where they meet, where they work. Only when he's answered, or when torture finally leaves him no longer capable of answering, will he be taken outside and forced to his knees to await the executioner's bullet in the back of the neck, or the headsman's sword.

Such sights remind me of why I have entered into this secret life. How strange, then, that I should feel any sense of identity with the unknown man who was responsible for the arrest this morning. An ordinary man, but a man who, quite by accident, through no will of his own, found himself at the precise point in space and time where his fortunes intersected with those of another human being. Yet tonight he sits in his club, no doubt, regaling his listeners with the story of this petty encounter in Nanking Road, while the other shivers in a dark cell in Louza station, terrified of what the morning will bring. And I, because I am right here in Shanghai, precisely at this point, this winter of 1927, this time of war and revolution, find myself caught up in an enterprise I had not planned, in which I had felt no part, and yet which is now becoming the focus of my life.

Not only his apparent political conversion, but also Simon's reputation as a war hero helped him, for in Shanghai, military experience was respected, and he surmised an uneasy conscience among those who "though able-bodied enough ten years ago, had stayed in Shanghai running their businesses and amassing profits, while their compatriots were sent to the slaughterhouses of the Somme and Gallipoli." Moreover, he found some of those to whom he talked to be easy targets.

> ... people like Verdier, or Massingham, or the others like them. They tell me what I want to know, sometimes indeed more than I want to know. I am continually surprised by how freely they talk, these civilians playing soldier, these office managers playing statesman. They're untrained for their high duties, yet here in Shanghai today, one mistake on the part of these well-intentioned amateurs could plunge their nations into war, call up whole armies and navies, cause congresses and parliaments to meet late into the night, voting appropriations for campaigns to be fought and blood to be spilled ten thousand miles away on the other side of the world. They're unbelievably careless.
>
> Take Massingham, pleased as Punch at his recent elevation, at this moment of crisis, to the glories of a seat on the Shanghai Municipal Council. I talk to him, tell him of the book I am writing, adding how fortunate I am to be here in such stirring times. And to have the privilege of speaking to him. I let a note of unctuous flattery creep into my voice. I'm horrified; it

doesn't sound like me at all. Does it? Why isn't Massingham put off by it? Can it be that he notices no difference? Does he think this is the way I talk all the time?

That thought is even more appalling. Never mind: that's not the point. So I quiz Massingham on troop movements, the intentions of the army. But it's clear he's not well informed. That's not surprising, for General Duncan, the commander of the Shanghai Defence Force, keeps his own counsel, and is too intelligent to share his staff's planning with mere civilians.

Will there be a war between England and China? Some of Mr. Chu's friends think so, foresee a British occupation of the entire city, foreign troops fanning out across the flat countryside of the Yangtze delta, to keep Shanghai's wealth safely in foreign hands. Some of the British also think this will happen. Or at least that's what they hope for: from their command post in the smoking room of the Shanghai Club, these captains of the imagination spin visions of their Royal Navy steaming six hundred miles up the Yangtze, battle ensigns flying, to retake the Concession so ignominiously surrendered two months ago at Hankow. But they know it can't happen yet, for in winter the water is low, and they must wait until the Himalayan snows begin to melt, and the river rises, so that its channel becomes full enough to bear the cruisers and destroyers that will lead this armada. Wait till summer, they say, wait till there's deep water again in the Great River.

Meanwhile, the armies draw closer. The Nationalist troops are on the march again, moving steadily up the rail line from the south, and this time they aren't going to stop. Again, the rumors fly: of troops deployed for battle around the city, of silver bullets, Nationalist bribes to win the warlord officers over to the side of the revolution. Or at least to give up without a fight.

And that's not all. Chang Shao-shan speaks darkly about growing strains between the right wing of the Kuomintang and the progressives, as he calls them. From his military headquarters in Kiangsi province, Chiang Kai-shek exercises a control over the former, while the latter find their strength in the government that they established at Hankow three months ago. Both sides have their agents here in Shanghai, and while

Chang is circumspect in his discussions with me, he is also honest enough to keep his part of the bargain that he made: his information (carefully given, to be sure) on what is transpiring in the revolutionary camp, in return for the information I can glean about what is happening in the foreign camp.

I listen, I watch, I learn from both sides.

And, as Matthew discovered, he talked to no one about his new role. Except Emily.

CHAPTER EIGHT

Saturday, June 3, 1989

Except Emily. Because in Journal B, as Matthew now began to call the pages that Zhao Shanling had found, it was clear that she was becoming Simon's willing—perhaps even too willing—collaborator.

That spring, when he had first skimmed through the journal Laura had given him, Matthew had rather ignored Emily. His interests, after all, lay in the history of the city itself, and Emily's presence had never been much more than a diversion. She was useful because her appearance in Simon's life gave the historian a view of certain aspects of Shanghai's social code, with its double standards, its attempts—at least at her level of society—to marry the ethos of small-town Protestant America, or middle-class England, to the opportunities of a city where virtually no restrictions existed, and those that did could be easily circumvented. Simon's earlier affair, if that's what it was, with Rhonda, had probably been met with few disapproving glances, for whoever Rhonda Sexton might have been, she was obviously no green girl. Nor was she part of the tight little Shanghai American community, and men (as Emily herself had admitted) had to be allowed a certain latitude. Simon's taking up with Emily was, in the eyes of John Ransom and his circle, at any rate, something else again, and while the adventurous Emily might have felt no qualms, her uncle and aunt apparently did.

Now, however, Emily herself appeared to be becoming an actor in the city's history. Ransom may only have been using politics as an excuse when he ordered Simon to stop seeing his niece in February, and tried to send her home. But Emily, clever, devious Emily, not only managed to stay on in Shanghai, but in the new role that Simon had taken on in late February, she had become very much a supporting player. Sometimes, indeed, she seemed to have become the star herself.

Had Simon meant to tell her of what he was doing for Chang Shao-shan? Or had the admission come out because she had once again criticized his apparent passivity in the face of a crisis? Perhaps he'd tried to defend himself by telling her how he was acting. Or had he—more likely—simply needed someone he could trust, someone to turn to when doubts assailed him?

Impossible to know. But tell her he had. And once told, Emily became not simply a confidante, but a willing partner in his plans. Simon clearly had misgivings about drawing her in, and more than once urged her to forget everything, even confessing at one point in Journal B that he wished she'd heeded her uncle's advice after all, and had gone back home.

Simon, after all, had been drawn unwillingly into his own role. Reading his journal, Matthew found there a man who believed that whatever idealism he might once have had had been driven out of him by his experiences in France. Nonetheless, after living in Shanghai for four years, after seeing its brutality, its vice, its naked exploitation of the helpless, some residue of that old hope had come to the surface, and had led him to conclude that the Nationalists and their communist allies, whatever their faults might be, still offered China her best prospect. In that belief, he had been willing to shed his mask of impartial observer, critic, and analyst, and to take sides in the battle being fought out around him. Emily, on the other hand, had arrived in Shanghai during the troubles of 1925 with all her American ideals intact. But as Journal B made clear, what worried Simon was not so much Emily's sympathy for the underdog, as that she so obviously enjoyed her new role. He told her severely that it was no game they were playing, that there might even be some danger—not much, of course, but some—if he were found out. None of his arguments made the slightest difference.

And there were, of course, obvious advantages to Emily's position. Simon's connections gained him access to many places and many people who could unwittingly help him in his new role (and who, knowing of his book, perhaps also wanted to make sure that they would find a place in it). Emily, on the other hand, had succeeded in making her peace with John Ransom by the simple expedient of letting her uncle guess that she was no longer interested in Simon—and seeing no need to tell him that he had guessed wrong. Then, after Ransom was elected to the Shanghai Municipal Council in late February 1927, the large house on Bubbling Well Road saw many gatherings—social gatherings to be sure, but during which the important guests were apt to discuss important matters. And of course Emily was there with her aunt, to help entertain the other councillors, the taipans, the members of the Volunteer Corps, and the military officers—all of them the leaders of a foreign Shanghai facing the crisis of bolshevism.

Emily, in short, became a spy. Not the sort of spy who would abstract secret papers from briefcases, or photograph military plans with cameras disguised as cigarette cases, or send messages in invisible ink (though at one point she did suggest, at least half seriously, that she might use this as a medium of communication with Simon). But Emily was pretty, she was intelligent, and men two and three times her age found her a good listener. So she kept her ears open and her mouth shut, save for the occasional insinuation into these conversations of the kinds of questions that might elicit useful answers. And the men who visited her uncle were charmed to find a girl so fascinated by their work, and were flattered by her open admiration of the ways in which they conducted the great affairs that were their concern.

Such, in any case, was the version of the story as Emily told it to Simon, and as reached Matthew, filtered through Journal B. It all sounded too easy, however, and Matthew wondered (as Simon had also worried before him) whether the very eagerness with which she embraced this role might not have led to a suspicion on the part of the men in whose work she took such a great interest. "I keep telling her that she's got to be careful," wrote Simon on March 12, "that she mustn't risk everything by seeming too inquisitive about affairs that belong properly to a man's world. She just laughs at my concern, and tells me that

I'm almost as bad as her uncle's friends, worried by what will happen if women are allowed to meddle in such matters. You're just afraid, she told me this afternoon, that you'll discover we can handle them as well as you. Perhaps even better."

In any case, Emily had on occasion picked up some interesting pieces of information. It was Emily who learned that the Municipal Council and its American chairman, Stanfield Frothingham, were scheming with the British to try to associate the American marines more fully with the British defense of the International Settlement. And it was Emily who overheard a conversation between that same American chairman and one of his colleagues, in which there was talk of a clandestine meeting between Frothingham, Captain Fiori of the French police, and some Chinese, whose names she was unable to catch.

All these bits of intelligence, and others as well, Simon passed on to Chang Shao-shan, sometimes directly, and sometimes through Chu Hung-ying. How useful they were to the two men, to the other leaders of the Shanghai revolution, Simon could not tell. But the reports were no doubt carried back to those members of the underground, young men and women with earnest faces, who sat around tables in cold and ill-lit rooms in that late winter of 1927, plotting the rising that would bring Shanghai face-to-face with its revolutionary destiny. And Simon, putting together the bits of information he gleaned from Chu Hung-ying and Chang Shao-shan, was coming to understand that in their minds, the real enemy was no longer to be found in the armies of the northern warlords. For all their ferocity and their modern weapons, for all the White Russian units who fought with them for Chinese pay, those armies had been thoroughly demoralized by their earlier defeats. Many of their officers had already been bribed by Chiang Kai-shek's agents, and by mid-March the city's garrison commander himself was dickering with the Nationalists to save his own skin.

"The question," Simon had written in Journal B on Friday, March 18, "is not whether Shanghai will fall to the revolution, for that much is certain. The question is rather what kind of revolution we will see after that fall has come."

> ... Most foreigners here don't realize that, and they still expect a battle between the northern armies who hold the city and their Nationalist attackers advancing from the south. As

much out of wishful thinking as ignorance, they maintain that the northerners will be able to hold the line—for several weeks, at any rate, perhaps indefinitely. Massingham tells me he has seen intelligence maps giving the disposition of the Chinese troops, and is convinced that the northern units will be more than a match for the southern forces. He points to a photograph in the paper of the armored train, manned by White Russians, that now stands at the North Station, and says: the Reds have nothing like that.

And so, given a pitched battle, the northern forces might prevail. But there's not going to be a pitched battle. Or at least there won't be if the plans drawn up by Chang Shao-shan and his friends work out as they should. A couple of days ago I met some of them in Mr. Chu's quarters. Sitting there, smoking nervously, drinking tea to keep out the chill, they look absurdly young and inexperienced, quite unlike the pictures of bomb-throwing Bolsheviks with which the *North China Daily News* frightens its readers. Again they question me: what do I know of the intentions of the foreigners? Is it true that British weapons are being given to the warlord armies? Are the British going to provoke an incident and then attack the Chinese? Already they've moved their troops beyond the Settlement, out to Jessfield; do they plan to occupy the whole Shanghai district? What will the foreigners do? What do men like Mr. Massingham and M. Verdier and Mr. Ransom say about the prospect of a Shanghai in the hands of the revolutionaries?

I tell them what I can, of course, but for the most part plead ignorance: I know something of the intentions of the Shanghai Municipal Council and the new French Provisional Commission. But the foreign commanders, like General Duncan of the Shanghai Defence Force, and Colonel Hill of the American marines, are hardly likely to take a civilian like me into their confidence. I tell them: if the foreigners think that the settlements will come under attack, then they will fight back. That much is certain. But if you leave the settlements alone, there will be no trouble. They look at one another and nod. The foreigners want trade, they say, and will be prepared to work with any who trade with them, warlord or nationalist, southern or northern.

All these matters we have discussed before. But this time they ask me some new questions. Has Chiang Kai-shek been in touch with the Shanghai Municipal Council? With the French

Provisional Commission? With the consuls, like the Englishman
Barton or the French Naggiar? I shake my head, I don't know.
Do you think you could try to find out, Mr. Larsen? We know
the warlord armies will be driven from Shanghai. But what kind
of a city will we see then? A new, democratic Shanghai, with a
popular government, a government of the people, controlling
it? Or a Shanghai in the hands of men who masquerade as revolutionaries but who are really reactionaries?

Simon had realized, of course, that by this last phrase they
meant Chiang Kai-shek and his generals. Though the Kuomintang and the Communists were still allies, it took no great wit to
understand that the two parties were falling out with each other,
and that each was determined to control Shanghai. If Chiang's
armies got there first, the city would pass into his hands. Hence,
as they had a month earlier, the Communists were planning
their own insurrection to take control of the Chinese city before
Chiang's men arrived.

That much Matthew knew from his earlier researches, and
the Party documents he'd seen at the institute spoke of the
communist preparations: Chou En-lai's training of bands of
armed workers, the formation of propaganda teams, the recruitment of women's groups for first aid and nursing of the
wounded, and the establishment of a municipal government,
under communist control, that would have assumed power by
the time Chiang arrived.

How much did Simon know of their plans? Much of it he
must have guessed, pieced together from what they told him,
from simply keeping his ears open to the stories, the rumors,
that sped through the nervous city. Certainly the documents
that Zhao Shanling had produced had much to say about the
fears of the foreign councils and the foreign police for Shanghai's safety as the city prepared for battle. They pointed to
the growing activity around the Soviet consulate general on
Whangpoo Road, to the use of Soviet gold to subvert the increasingly dispirited soldiers of the warlord armies, and to efforts
that were being made to extract military intelligence from British officers (no mention, however, of Emily Ransom!).

By March 16, the final campaign in the battle for Shanghai
was beginning, led by the Eastern Route Army, commanded by
General Pai Chung-hsi, a brilliant military leader from Kwangsi

province, who was a recent convert to the Nationalist cause. On the nineteenth, his advance units had crossed the Huangpu south of Shanghai. Shortly thereafter, the warlord troops guarding the old walled city of Sungkiang, less than thirty miles south of Shanghai, gave up without a struggle, and the way to the city lay open.

The outbreak came on March 21, 1927. It had been a Monday, a warm, sunlit day with a promise of spring in the air. The night before, General Pai's vanguard had reached the southern limits of Shanghai, their arrival announced to a nervous city by the distant sound of heavy artillery fire. The real battle for Shanghai, however, was to be fought not between the rival armies, but rather in the shadowy world in which the underground, both communist and Kuomintang, had moved and made their plans.

That morning, the communist-led General Labor Union once again called for a strike to begin across the city at noon. Then, an hour later, the revolution began.

Simon had described the scene in the journal. Edited and re-typed with some care, it obviously had been intended for *Typhoon*.

Wednesday, March 23, 1927

In Hong Kong, midday is marked by the firing of a gun from Jardine's Lookout. Here in Shanghai, a black ball dropped from the harbor semaphore signals the passage of noon. Precisely at that point, on Monday morning, all Shanghai came to a halt. Utterly and completely. Imagine it: one moment, all the signs of the city bustling about its normal activity: tugs hooting in the river, trucks, carts, buses clattering through the streets, peddlers hawking their wares, the wharf coolies chanting their rhythmic singsong as they work their cargoes on the waterfront. The next moment, everything stops. Drivers desert their trams, leaving them to stand blocking the roads; coolies drop their carrying poles and vanish into the crowds; chauffeurs abandon their automobiles in the middle of the street, letting their angry passengers fend for themselves as best they can. Shops put up their shutters and lock their doors and even the sidewalk peddlers pick up and leave. All is still, and the harbor's sudden peace is broken only by the launches from the long line of foreign warships lying in the fairway.

It seems preposterous that this large and vital city should fall into such utter silence. But Chang Shao-shan and his friends have done their work well. It is the silence not of peace, but of anticipation. Near a tangle of barbed wire and sandbags a detachment of British soldiers stands guard. They pace nervously, rifles at the ready, their faces apprehensive under their steel helmets, not knowing what to expect. The quiet unnerves them; perhaps the older ones remember how, in Flanders, the sudden cessation of the German artillery would bring a few minutes' peace before the heaviest barrages started.

Today the apprehensive stillness lasts an hour. Then from the Chinese city, the sound of scattered small-arms fire announces the start of the insurrection. The rattle spreads—there are gunshots in Pootung across the river, there is fighting in Chapei north of the Creek. Occasionally we hear a louder explosion: the concussion of a bomb or a grenade. Chang Shao-shan's armed units are attacking the Chinese police stations; they want to seize these places, capture their stocks of weapons, and fortify them as strong points against any counterattack.

But there is little resistance, and no counterattack. The leaders of the rising have prepared the ground, and in most places the police give up without a fight, or with only token resistance. Poor devils, what do they have to fight for? Loyalty to officers who are ready to sacrifice them? To a general who, according to rumor, has prudently gone to ground in the Settlement even before the fighting begins?

By late afternoon it is finished almost everywhere. In only a few hours, all of Shanghai—Chinese Shanghai—has gone over to the revolution. Throughout the Chinese city there now flies the flag of the Kuomintang: the white sun set against a blue sky that the Nationalists have taken as their emblem.

Except in Chapei, as Matthew knew. There something had gone wrong. The police stations did not surrender easily, and the warlord troops had taken up positions in the North Station and several other big buildings nearby, where their machine guns could command the streets. By twilight the battle had been joined, and through the night the continual sound of rifle fire was punctuated by the deeper roar from the cannon of the White Russian armored train near the station. A fire broke out, reddening the night sky, and in the settlements, Simon wrote, "foreigners climb to their rooftops to watch Chapei burn. It is an entertainment for them, and they have no thought for the poor wretches caught in the fury of the battle." All night long, refugees from the flames and the fighting crossed into the Settlement. The British troops manning the lines tried to turn them back, but anyone who knew the city had been able to find one of the hundreds of little alleyways, courtyards, doors, that gave into the Settlement. On Tuesday, their supplies cut off, their generals melted away to safety, the last of the defenders gave up, rushed from their remaining stronghold in the North Station, throwing their rifles down on the street, and headed for the safety of the Settlement. And this time the soldiers let them through, Ben Rogers told Simon. "He'd seen it all, covering the battle for his paper, and tells me that the mob would have slaughtered every last one of the northern soldiers if they'd had the chance."

With that, the battle for Shanghai was over.

Wednesday, March 23, 1927

At Mme V.'s yesterday with E., to celebrate the successful end of our work with a bottle of champagne. More than a single bottle, perhaps? We both must have gotten a little bit tight, & started making up stories about our own contributions to the victory. As evening fell, they became more extravagant & outrageous, until we'd managed to convince ourselves that it was the two of us—not Chiang Kai-shek & his revolutionary generals, not Borodin & his Russian agents, not any other minor actors—who really deserve the credit for what's happened in these last few days. Will they give us medals, E. wants to know, & we write imaginary headlines: "Without Her We Would Have Failed: Borodin Praises Intrepid Heroine of Chinese Revolution." Or: "Defeated Warlord Blames Mystery Couple for Loss at Shanghai." E. thinks of Uncle John's face on reading such stories, and bursts into peals of laughter. Then she tells me I must stop worrying, & suggests that now that we've solved the problem of Shanghai, perhaps we should go to somewhere else, like Nicaragua or Mexico or India, and offer to do the same for them.

I promised I'd buy the tickets tomorrow if she'd come with me. But E. surprised me by suddenly falling silent, and I saw come into her eyes a look I've never seen there before, a look of longing, of inquiring, as if she were somehow measuring me, sizing me up, wondering whether to take me into her confidence before revealing one of her deepest secrets. Suddenly the afternoon's mood changed, our champagne-induced light-headedness had vanished, and E. fell into a reflective silence from which I was unable to rouse her before she had to go home. Once or twice she smiled at me, apologized for not being better company. Then, when it was time for her to leave, she threw her arms around my neck, and told me, in a voice that seemed strangely changed, that one of her wishes had come true, and she now felt closer to me than ever before.

Then she was gone, leaving me wondering about her behavior. Of course E.'s young, out of college not two years ago, & must be asking herself how she's managed to find herself in this position. How much more it must seem than what she'd bargained for—again I question what I've done, wondering whether I've been right in allowing her to become so deeply implicated in what has been a dark game, & one that so easily might have turned dangerous.

But now it's over, I'm relieved—though it was I who drew her into it, there were even more ways in which she took the initiative herself, sometimes against my better judgment. Anyway, the game is now played out, the danger passed, & we can retire from the field. But does she now have her own doubts about what she has done? Or is there now something else that she expects of me, wants of me?

Sunday, June 4, 1989

In its few folded pages, the *International Herald Tribune* described a whole world, a world outside Shanghai's gray and brown closeness, with its dusty summer-heavy air, and the impassive people filling the crowded streets. Finishing a cup of bad coffee, Matthew sat over a late breakfast, reading the weekend edition that he'd bought the previous evening. He read it all: about the millions mourning the death of the Ayatollah Khomeini in Teheran, the free elections being held in Poland, the political battles over the Speaker of the House in Washington. When he'd finished the news, he proceeded methodically through the editorials, the letters, the sports section with its stories of the pennant races and the French Open. The financial pages told him the latest values of exotically named investments like the Guinness Flight International, the Rothschild ECU d'Or Fund, and the Credit Suisse Hispano-Iberia Fund, names that conjured up promises of unimaginable wealth looked after by discreetly anonymous Zurich bankers, or tax lawyers in Guernsey and the Bahamas. He learned of spring auctions in the art markets of Paris and London and Milan, discovered where he might spend a country weekend within easy driving distance of the Boulevard Raspail or the Avenue Kléber (for all that it had been printed in Hong Kong, the *Tribune* still reflected its European provenance). Advertisements in small print told him of villas for rent in Umbria or Provence, of apartments for sale in Geneva and Verbier, and of attorneys with German names who specialize in quick and painless divorces under the laws of small impoverished countries in the Caribbean.

When he could no longer postpone getting back to work, he rose, paid his bill, and went up to his room, determined to make a dent in the pile of Chinese papers that Zhao Shanling had given him. It was Sunday, and he'd slept rather later than he'd meant to. While his mind was fresh, he would work on them; there'd be time enough later to get back to Simon's journal.

"Minutes of the meeting of the Propaganda Committee, March 31, 1927." Among those present, Matthew could make out the abbreviations for Ch'en Tu-hsiu, Chou En-lai, and four or five others, including the man named Hung, whose identity he had not yet discovered. By now Shanghai had been in the hands of the revolutionaries for ten days. Yet the insurrectionists, and the Communists who led them, sensed that time was no longer on their side. Chiang Kai-shek himself had arrived in the city four days earlier, and while praising the men and women who had led the revolution, was also issuing dark warnings against disorderly elements, calling on the citizens of Shanghai to go back to work and resume their normal lives. Meanwhile he built up his own military strength, bringing in more reliable units and transferring away from the city those he suspected of being too sympathetic to the labor unions.

Individual members of the committee reported on their progress on the state of affairs. Chou En-lai wanted more military training for his armed workers, and Wang Shou-hua complained of the difficulties in imposing communist control over workers who owed their positions to the Green Gang. Hung reported on what might be expected from the foreign police and the foreign municipal councils, where the imperialists were now spreading rumors of an attack on the settlements. (Could he be, Matthew suddenly wondered, Chu Hung-ying himself? Simon had never written out the characters of his Chinese teacher's name, but it made sense. Clearly Mr. Chu had been a man connected to the circle of revolutionaries plotting the risings that winter and spring. And a man who made it his business to know, or to try to discover, what the foreigners might do.) Like the others, he assumed that if Chiang should turn against the Communists, the foreigners would be on his side.

Two days later, on April 2, the Party's regional committee had met. The fear and uncertainty of its members was almost palpable. Chiang's troop movements were under way, new units loyal to the general arriving every day, and every day new skirmishes between his men and the armed workers who had formed the core of the insurrection.

Most worrying of all were Wang Shou-hua's warnings of the increasingly close ties between the Green Gang and the men in Chiang Kai-shek's entourage. Some days earlier Tu Yüeh-sheng had agreed to form an organization blandly called the Society for Common Progress, with its headquarters in the French Concession; it would act as a front for the recruitment of gangsters to do Chiang's dirty work for him, terrorizing those workers and union leaders who had gravitated to the Communists. Tu's plans were already having their effect, Wang reported, and the workers were demoralized, their loyalty to the communist-led unions uncertain. All of this, said Hung, was taking place under the benevolently protective eyes of the French police force, and Paul-Émile Naggiar, the French consul general, had himself been in touch with Chiang's emissaries, joining his voice to those of the other foreigners who were urging the general to suppress the Communists.

Matthew read steadily but slowly, checking what he was discovering against his other notes on the events of those weeks leading up to the ferocious purge that Chiang had launched on April 12.

The telephone's insistent ring interrupted him. "Hello?" he answered. "*Wei?*"

"Matt—it's me, Laura."

"Laura. It's wonderful to hear you." Again, the very sound of her voice rekindled all his hopes for the future.

But she ignored this. "Matt, are you all right?"

"All right? Sure." He was puzzled by the intensity in her voice. "Why not?"

"Matt, I've been watching television. The pictures of the massacre in Beijing. It's terrible. How much do you know about it there?"

Massacre? He was stunned. What was she talking about? "What massacre? Are you sure? Laura?" Stupid question, but he couldn't believe what she'd said. But he'd gotten up too late to watch the news that morning.

"All they talk about here is Beijing, nothing about Shanghai or anywhere else. But it's all over the news this evening."

"No, I haven't heard anything. It's Sunday, and things are pretty quiet." He found himself unable to think. "Are you sure you heard it right? What's supposed to have happened?" He still didn't want to believe it, hoped that the report might be wrong. Was anything going on outside? Impossible to tell from his room. The window gave onto a courtyard, and he couldn't see into the street beyond it.

"It must be. They showed pictures. On television, I mean. Horrible—tanks, machine guns firing into the crowds. They say at least fifty people were killed. So I called—I didn't know how much news you get there."

By now he'd turned on the little television set in his room, switching rapidly between the three channels. Everything was normal; on the American channel, as he thought of it, a game show was in progress—vacuous faces, stupid questions, canned laughter.

"I'll try to find out what I can. But, Laura, don't worry. I'm sure nothing will happen here." He wasn't sure at all, of course; given Shanghai's explosive history, there was no telling what furies might erupt if Laura were right, and the news became widely known.

"Do be careful, Matt. How soon can you come home?"

"Come home? I just got here. Look, I'll have to find out

what's going on first. I hope you're wrong, and things aren't that bad."

"Matt, they are bad. Believe me. It's all over the news this evening. On all the channels."

The line went dead for a moment. Then she was back.

"Something's happening to the connection. Listen, Matt: here's my number, where you can reach me. Here in Pasadena." She read it off to him. "Call me if you can. Let me know what's going on."

"I will. And, Laura—"

"Yes?" Again the line blanked out for a few seconds.

"Laura—thanks for calling."

"Matt—"

"Yes?"

"Matt—be careful. Please."

The line went dead again, this time for good. After he hung up, he phoned the American consulate, about a mile west on Huaihai Road. The Sunday morning duty officer, a woman, could tell him only that there had been reports of indiscriminate shooting in Beijing. "We don't know how bad it is. The Chinese haven't heard much about it yet. But they will. So play it safe— don't go near crowds, or places where crowds can collect; don't go to universities. We don't want Americans getting caught in the crossfire. And stay in touch, in case we put out an advisory." She took down his name and address.

Matthew put down the phone, still in a state of shock. The pictures of the crowds in Tiananmen Square the day before had seemed so cheerful, so good-natured; it was hard to imagine that the government would do more than simply wait the students out, knowing that sooner or later heat and fatigue would drive them home. Something must have happened last night: an accident, perhaps, a panicked response, and then rage and violence. Stay away from crowds, the consulate told him. Not very useful advice when all Shanghai is a crowd. And how do you tell when a crowd is about to turn dangerous? How did the British police officer, standing in Nanking Road on that sunny late May morning in 1925, decide that the crowd was about to turn ugly? What happened to make him give the order to open fire? Had he seen something, caught a movement, perhaps, out of the corner of his eye, something that signaled to his policeman's training that only force now would prevent greater violence later? Is that what had happened in Beijing? Matthew pictured a squad leader, perhaps surrounded by the crowd near Tiananmen Square, panicking and opening fire. But if fifty people had been killed, and lots more injured . . . No mere accident could explain that kind of terrible bloodshed.

He left the hotel and went out into the street. Saturday's sunshine had given way to heavy gray clouds, and a light rain was starting to fall. Maoming Road, outside his hotel, looked normal enough, but at the corner of Huaihai Road he saw the first posters plastered up on the side of the old Cathay Theater: "Beijing has become a city of BLOOD!" cried one of them, the last character drawn in brilliant red ink. Below it, written in another hand, was a lament for the dead and a condemnation of the government's cruelty, set in the stately phrases of classical Chinese.

The news is out, Matthew thought. He wondered if he should be worried, remembering the advice to stay away from crowds. But the street looked calm. Calmer than usual, in fact, since there were no cars or trucks on it. Then he saw why. A block east, at the corner of Ruijin Road, a crowd was gathering around a bus that sat disconsolately on flattened tires in the middle of the intersection. A large banner hung on its side: FANDUI XUEXING TUSHA RENMIN—Oppose the bloodthirsty massacre of the people! Red flags flew from its roof, and a group of students stood on top, making angry speeches at the passing crowd. One or two policemen stood by idly, not interfering, and most people seemed to pay little attention. In Shanghai, as elsewhere, Sunday is a day for strolling, a day for shopping, and most men and women seemed to be going about their business as if nothing had happened, seemingly oblivious, uninterested, or perhaps simply uncomprehending of what had happened in Beijing. Or just wary, not knowing what to believe, waiting until the government had spoken before deciding how to react.

He walked up the street toward Hilding's hotel, his mind a confused whirl of impressions. Perhaps he should have telephoned first to remind Hilding of the meeting they'd arranged two days earlier. But he wanted to see the Englishman, wanted to discover how much he knew about what had happened in Beijing. Maybe he'd have had some word from his daughter. Perhaps she was already back in Shanghai, to the relief both of her father and the worried Professor Wang.

Hilding met him at the door. "Have you heard the news?" Matthew asked. "Do you know what's happened?"

"A friend called me earlier from Beijing," said Hilding. He looked pale, and his hands moved nervously. "How much do you know?"

"I had a call from America. It's been on television there. And the American consulate confirmed that there had been shooting. But they don't know much."

"Ten to twenty people killed," said Hilding. "That's what I was told." Not as bad as the report I got, thought Matthew, but he said nothing. Instead, he asked: "Is your daughter back?"

"No, not yet. I tried to send word to her. But it's difficult. So much confusion in Beijing. I hope to God the message reached her." He stood there, looking at Matthew, as if he thought he might somehow be the bearer of good news. "I've tried to call up there this morning. But the lines are blocked, it's impossible to get through."

"I'm sure she'll be back soon," said Matthew. Then suddenly wished he hadn't. What right did he have to speak such false words? He knew nothing, could say nothing that would comfort Hilding. What came next was no better. "If there's anything I can do . . ." But of course there wasn't. It was an empty gesture, a formula.

But Hilding seemed to take it as an expression of sympathy. "Thank you," he said. "Mary's a sensible girl. She'll be all right. We've friends in Beijing she may be staying with. And she does have a British passport, thank God."

Matthew stood uncertainly near the door. "Shall I come back later?" he asked. "I don't want to disturb you if you have other things to do."

"No," said Hilding. "No. I'm sorry, I'm forgetting my manners." He looked at his watch. "We were going to have lunch, weren't we? Let's go, then."

They talked over their meal, Matthew steering the conversation around to Hilding's early days in Shanghai and to the memoirs that he was writing. The older man spoke rapidly and animatedly, but he was distracted, his mind clearly elsewhere. After lunch Matthew accompanied him back to his room. As

Hilding opened the door, the phone rang, and he jerked the receiver to his ear. A flood of rapid Chinese followed. Hilding wiped his forehead and hung up. He looked pale. "It's worse," he said. "That was a man I know at Xinhua—the New China News Agency. He says there were over a hundred killed. Many, many wounded."

Matthew was incredulous. "I can't believe it," he said. "There's got to be some mistake." Like many western students of China, he retained, almost unconsciously, something of the old faith in a nation that really had been reborn under the Communists. A people's government would never move against its own citizens. Hilding said nothing at first, but looked at Matthew curiously. "I saw the Cultural Revolution," he remarked dryly. "Thank you for joining me, Mr. Walker. It's a comfort to have someone to talk to on a day like this." He went on: "I'm worried. They're apparently looking for Meihua."

The name meant nothing to Matthew. Then he remembered that Hilding had mentioned her a few days before, as one of the student leaders in the square. "Liu Meihua? Mary's friend, you mean? The one you told me about—that she went to Beijing with?"

"Yes. The police are after her. They're looking for all of them. Wu'er Kaixi, Chai Ling, Wang Dan. Most of them come from Beijing." Hilding's eyes swept around the room as he talked, and Matthew felt uncomfortable, an intruder in no position to do anything useful. "But Meihua's a Shanghai girl. Mary's brought her here several times. She's been trying to teach her English. And Meihua works on Mary's Chinese. But I don't think they've made much progress. They spend most of their time laughing at each other's mistakes. But the two of them are like sisters. Even in their looks. Mary takes after her mother. Not me." He spoke proudly. "To look at her, you'd never know she was English."

"Will you call me when you hear anything?" asked Matthew. "And if I can help—" But he knew the words were useless, almost hypocritical.

Hilding nodded. "Of course. It's kind of you to concern yourself. But I'm sure everything will be all right."

Matthew left, walking down the dark stairs, out through the lobby where the same drowsy desk clerk was listening to Taiwan pop. Matthew wondered if he'd heard the news, wondered what he'd made of it. He felt helpless himself, wishing he could have said something to console the old man. What did he know of how it felt to be a parent, to have a daughter in harm's way? A sudden memory came back to him: of an ice storm that March, arriving unexpectedly late one afternoon, while Laura was driving back to Cambridge. The evening news brought reports of accidents, massive pile-ups on the highways leading to Boston; near Winchester a tractor-trailer had skidded and rolled over, crushing a car approaching in the opposite lane. Over and over he had dialed her number, listening to the phone ring in the empty apartment, long after she should have been home. Sick with fear, he imagined her injured, dying by the side of the road, had thought of calling the police, the hospitals. But of course he didn't even know her car's license number. Anyway, the lines would already be clogged with the reports of real emergencies, not just those that grew in the imagination. Finally, late that evening, he had reached her. She sounded cool and unperturbed: sensibly, she had pulled off the big roads when the storm began, waiting the weather out at a friend's house in Lexington. A wave of relief swept over him, followed by something almost like anger: why hadn't she thought to call him and tell him she'd be late, that she was all right? Laura had laughed at his worries, of course: how could he possibly imagine that she was in any danger?

But this very morning, of course, after seeing the television reports of the events in Tiananmen Square, it had been Laura who had telephoned him to see if he was all right.

Outside Hilding's hotel he found his fears evaporating. The streets looked normal enough, though a block away, at the intersection of Yan'an and Thibet Roads, some buses were stopped, and a small group of people had gathered outside them. They looked like the pictures he'd seen from Beijing, where the demonstrators had pulled buses across intersections to form roadblocks, hoping to prevent, or at least slow down, the army's threatened arrival. Apparently it hadn't worked. But here the scene looked entirely peaceful. He asked a bystander what was happening. The man shrugged. "*Huaile*. A breakdown, that's all. The buses are too old. It's like that all the time. *Meiyou fazi*"— the age-old Chinese expression. "Nothing to be done about it."

Matthew thanked him and walked on, heading west along Yan'an Road back toward his hotel. An expanse of gray-brown buildings, and above him the dusty green leaves were wet in the light rain that continued to fall. There were few people out. Were the streets always this empty on Sunday? At a kiosk he bought a newspaper: the Shanghai *Xinmin Wanbao*, New People's Evening News. There was the story on the front page: "Beijing Martial Law Authorities Suppress Counterrevolutionary Disturbance," announced the headline. A very small handful of troublemakers, the account continued, had tried to disrupt the good order of the capital, interfering with the people's safety and threatening the stability of socialist democracy. Martial law units of the People's Liberation Army had been ordered to clear the square, and now the situation was normal again. That was all there was. No mention of casualties.

Not much help there, thought Matthew. Because it was Sunday, there'd be no papers from Hong Kong that afternoon. But perhaps he could learn something from the news on television that evening. He still clung to the hope that the reports were mistaken. Or at least wildly exaggerated.

Wang Baozhen was waiting for him when he got back to the hotel. "I took a chance of finding you here," she said. "They told me you'd gone out. Have you heard the news?" He nodded, told her of his meeting with Hilding. "Did his daughter get back?" she asked. "I've been trying to find her at the university, but no one knows where she is." The first scattered reports of violence in Beijing had reached Fudan University late last night, she said. The students had already begun to respond: demonstrations, roadblocks, the hurried preparation of propaganda leaflets. He described the buses he'd seen on Yan'an Road, on Huaihai Road. "There'll be lots more by tomorrow," she said. "Buses, railings, concrete blocks; they're using anything they can find to stop traffic. Of course, a lot of the students have already gone home. Some of the schools have canceled classes. It's a way of getting them out of the way before they make trouble. But there are still a lot left."

"What do you think is going to happen?"

"They're afraid—we're all afraid—that the army is going to come in. As it did in Beijing."

Matthew hadn't thought that far ahead. For the first time he wondered what would happen then, whether he'd find himself trapped in the city.

"Are the roadblocks going to stop the army?"

"Perhaps they'll slow it down. But the students—and some of

the workers—want more than that. They want a general strike that will bring Shanghai to a stop. They think that then the government will be forced to give way."

"Will it?"

She looked close to tears. "I don't think so. Not if the reports we are getting from Beijing are true. Li Peng, Yang Shangkun— those men will stop at nothing to break the movement." She looked around cautiously, to see whether anyone was listening to her. "I've heard there are eighty thousand troops around Shanghai, waiting for orders to march. With tanks and artillery. Maybe it's only rumor. But who wants to take the chance? If they come, a few buses in the roads aren't going to stop them. The only thing that will stop them will be if the commanders refuse to obey the Party's orders to move against the people."

"That doesn't seem to have worked in Beijing, does it?"

"No. It's so terrible. After all we've been through, now to have this happen. All our work, all our hopes—I was so proud of those students in the square. But, Mr. Walker, on a day like this, I am ashamed to be Chinese."

She looked at him, and again he felt her toughness of spirit, a survivor's toughness. "You've read Lu Hsün," she went on. "Do you know what he said about the government firing on its own people, killing its own students?" Matthew nodded, recalling the words that Chu Hung-ying had quoted to Simon Larsen after the killings in Tiananmen Square in 1926: "I'll never shrink from thinking the worst of the Chinese. But this affair really shows a side I'd never quite expected. . . . I never thought we'd act with such appalling barbarism."

But again he was overtaken by a sense of utter helplessness. What could he possibly say? What was he doing here anyway? He had no business even being in China at a time like this. His research, his book, the pleasant little diversion from his work that he'd found in Simon's disappearance, everything that had brought him to Shanghai, suddenly seemed pointless, no more than a game, an intellectual exercise that he could engage in because he came from a rich and powerful country that had time for such curiosity. He felt like an eavesdropper, a touristic voyeur, an outsider spying on China's agony yet insulated from it by his nationality. The old unequal treaties, with their concessions and settlements that had protected foreigners like Simon, had long since gone. Yet foreigners were still different, still privileged, still able to witness poor tortured China from another world, secure in the knowledge that if things got bad enough, the consulates—American, British, French, German—would come to their rescue, help them to get out of the country safely and leave China to face her troubles alone.

Back in the hotel he wondered about calling Laura. Then remembered the nine hours difference: it would be two in the morning on the West Coast. Maybe later, when he knew more about what was happening. Maybe by then she would know more than he did.

That winter, he'd found the uncertainty of their relationship a factor that, even when he tried not to think of it, had continually unsettled his life. Like Simon Larsen after his break with Emily, he too had plunged into his work. But for him it was different, of course. Unlike Simon, he had no secret past that she'd uncovered, and anyway, she still came to Atherton twice a week to teach. So he continued to see her, though they still circled each other in that friendly but wary fashion that had characterized their meetings since the late autumn, neither one willing to make a clean break, yet each realizing that something had happened, and each waiting for the other to make the first move. To do what? To repair it? Or to make the break final? Even that wasn't clear.

One Friday afternoon in late January, he'd gone home, taking his books and papers with him, before going out to a party at Jane and Alex Brandon's. They were giving it, Jane had told him, to mark the start of spring term. "I know it's not even quite February yet," she had said. "But at least it's now almost possible to believe we'll get through to summer."

It was a cold day, and though the morning had been brilliantly sunny, by afternoon the clouds had come in, and the radio spoke of the possibility of more snow that night to add to what had come a week before. He walked to the Brandons' house, feeling the damp chill cut through the layers of clothes he was wearing. The party was already going strong by six-thirty, when he arrived, and he pushed the door open, knowing that no one would hear if he rang. Hanging up his coat, he went into the Brandons' living room, and the first person he saw was Laura. He hadn't even known she was there, since Friday wasn't one of her usual teaching days. But there she was, standing across the room, wearing a white turtleneck and a dark blue skirt, her hair shining in the light of the lamp near the fire. She was talking to Sam Goodman and Jack Blodgett, both of them in her own department, laughing and apparently enjoying herself. The sight of her, coming unexpectedly as it did, brought a sudden flush of remembered excitement, recalling the first time he'd met her, at a gathering very much like this, back in the fall of 1987. Then a wave of disappointment. Not that she was there, of course. But that she was there—what was it?—independently of him, unknown to him, at the sort of party that not too long ago they'd have gone to together. And she hadn't even told him she was in town.

Jane Brandon spotted him, and came up to greet him.

"Here you are, Matt. So glad you could make it. You'll find something to drink if you can fight your way through to the other room. That's where Alex set up the bar."

She looked over his shoulder as he spoke, as if to see whether anyone else was coming in, or whether any of her guests had to be helped. He liked Jane, an eminently kind and practical woman, and liked her physicist husband Alex, whom he saw now moving around the room in a somewhat detached fashion, pleasantly enough, but with the air of a man who'd like to get back to his books and his laboratory.

"Laura Donati's here," she went on. "I thought you'd enjoy seeing each other." Her voice had a slight rising tone to it, as if she were suddenly not quite sure whether they actually would enjoy it. She'd probably invited them both, assuming that they were still a couple, and now was wondering if she'd put her foot in it.

Before he could answer, Alicia Benson appeared at his elbow.

"Good evening, Matt. Forgive me for not shaking hands, but as you see, I'm encumbered." She held a drink in each hand, and was clearly carrying them to someone else. "Glad you're here, and that you've made it as far as the spring term. Someone told me you were buried in your book, and that's why we never see you anymore."

"Me?" He was surprised. He'd been working hard, true, but didn't think he'd turned into a recluse. "I haven't been spending much time on the book. Just trying to stay ahead of things with my classes." Last year, when he'd first arrived, Alicia, who was a veteran of seventeen years at Atherton, had taken him under her wing, and he remained grateful to her for introducing him to the academic life, explaining to him, with a refreshing honesty, the way things worked in the history department, and at the college. "The second year's easier than the first," she said. "At least I hope you're finding it that way."

"It is indeed. Marginally, at least." Last year, his first year of teaching, had been much harder than he'd imagined. A good thing perhaps that Laura had gone off to London when she did, leaving him on his own to struggle through the endless writing of new lectures, grading of papers.

"It gets better," she said. "Don't forget summer's coming. That's what we're celebrating tonight. The start of the spring term. It's our version of the winter solstice."

"Or the Chinese New Year. Anyway, I can't wait."

Over Alicia's shoulder he glanced at Laura, her face flushed, laughing at something Sam had said to her. Then she looked up and saw him, and immediately sent him a look, the sort of look, he thought, that said: come over and join us.

Alicia must have noted the exchange. "Nice to see you, Matt," she said. "Now, if you'll forgive me, I have to go deliver these drinks in the next room. And you look as if you could stand one yourself."

Matthew made his way through the crowd to the bar, finding a plastic glass of nondescript white wine, taking a few sips to drive out the cold. Moving uncertainly in Laura's direction, he found himself wondering whether he'd misinterpreted her look, whether she really wanted him to break into what seemed like a very lively conversation.

But she smiled at him as she saw him coming.

"Hi, Matt." A friendly greeting, no more, no less. "I saw you over there. Come and join us. What's it doing out there?"

"It's going to snow. At least that's what the radio said. I didn't know you were here today."

"Big department meeting," she said. "So my tyrannical colleagues forced me to come, when I could have stayed safe and warm down in Cambridge." She looked at Sam and Jack.

"Not guilty," said Jack. "We just like to see your smiling face around the office, that's all. Here's to the spring term and the prospect of summer in the future." He raised his glass, and they all drank to it.

The talk went on, idle talk turning to politics, to literature, to Atherton itself, clever talk, talk about everything, talk about nothing in particular. Matthew, who'd never been particularly good at such conversation, found himself feeling like more and more of an outsider, uncertain why he was there, uncertain of his relationship with Laura. She herself had somewhat retreated from the group by now, and he caught her looking up at him while she pretended to be examining her now-empty glass. He returned the glance uncertainly, but now saw the laughter in her eyes, and he knew she was thinking what he was: that left to themselves, the two of them would find better things to do than join in this pleasantly inane conversation going on around them.

"Let me get you another drink," he said, holding out his hand.

"I'll come with you," she said. "I've been standing by the fire too long." She turned to the others to wish them good-bye, and then followed Matt as he began making his way through the crowd.

"Matt," she said, looking at her watch. "I don't think I have time for another drink. It's late, and I'd better be going now. If I'm going to get home tonight."

Now that he had a chance of having her to himself, he didn't want her to leave.

"How about a bite to eat? Before you go? We could get a sandwich at Luigi's, or something."

"No thanks. I had plenty here. Wonderful appetizers Jane puts out. So I made my dinner of them. Anyway, I don't want to pull you away."

"You're not pulling me away. How about some coffee at least? Keep you awake on the way home."

She considered that for a few seconds. "That sounds good, Matt. But are you sure you don't want to stay?"

Not if he could be with her, he didn't want to stay.

"Come back to my apartment," he said. "I'll give you a cup of coffee and then you can be on your way."

She nodded, he helped her into her coat, and they made their farewells to Jane Brandon. "So glad you could both come," she said, and Matt wondered if she was glad to see them leaving together even if they'd come separately. "And sorry you have to go so soon." She looked around her and made a face. "I think I may have this crowd here all night, the way they're going on. I just hope poor Alex doesn't mind too much."

"You shouldn't give such wonderful parties, Jane," said Laura. "I wouldn't be leaving this gathering myself if I didn't have to drive back through the snow and ice to the city."

"Be careful," said Jane. "And maybe the snow will hold off till you get there." She kissed Laura and waved them both out the door.

Then they were alone, walking through the still night, crunching over the snow frozen on the path from last week's fall, the smell of woodsmoke drifting down from the chimneys of the houses around them. Laura led the way to where she had parked her old Datsun, a car that she'd inherited from an older brother, now spending its last year or so of life being eaten to death by the salt of the New England winter roads. The engine started under protest, but then began to run smoothly, and she drove the half mile to Matthew's apartment. He got out, felt in his pockets for the door key, thought for a panicked moment that he'd lost it, found it, and opened the door, switching on the hall light as he did so. He helped Laura off with her coat, laying it on a chair in the hall, and went into the kitchen to start the coffee. "Make yourself at home," he said. "What do you want at this hour? Decaf or the real thing? Or would you like a drink and something to eat?"

"No thanks." She sat down on the lone sofa and picked up a book. "I had plenty to eat at the party. And if I'm driving home, I don't want any more to drink. Just a cup of coffee—real coffee—would be fine."

He poured the beans into the grinder and pressed the top, filling the kitchen with a brief screeching roar. When it stopped, he heard music; Laura had turned the radio on, and the sound of a piano and violin filled the room. He didn't recognize the piece.

"Sounds nice. What is it? Do you know?"

"Yes," she answered. "It's Schubert. I used to play this. In the days when I still had time to practice the violin."

He came out to join her, and they both listened in silence. The music, in three-quarter time, rose, filling the room, the violin slow and sweet, but darkly serious above the arpeggios of the piano. Laura's eyes were closed, but he could see her lips moving.

"It's a set of variations on one of his songs," she said quietly. She sang the phrase. "*Sei mir gegrüsst, sei mir geküsst.* A love song." Then fell silent again.

He went back into the kitchen and came out with two mugs of coffee. Laura sat up, opening her eyes, reached for hers. "I need it," she said, smiling. "I was almost asleep."

"Are you sure you want to drive home tonight?"

She paused before answering. "I've got to, Matt. Don't worry. I'll be fine after this."

That wasn't what had worried him, of course. But he said nothing.

She looked at him, over the edge of her cup. "I'm sorry, Matt. I'm not being good company tonight. I'm afraid I haven't been good company to you recently." She sipped her coffee. "But you've been good putting up with me. It's just that I've got to get things sorted out. Stop and figure out where I'm going. But between my classes and my colonial novelists, I don't seem to have the time."

"Figured out? What do you mean? It sounds to me as if you're doing just fine."

"I've been thinking these last few months." She reflected for a moment. "No, that's not true. Maybe I've been trying not to think."

"About?"

"What have I been trying not to think about? Oh, about lots of things. Why I'm doing what I'm doing. Where I'm going. Where it's all going to lead."

"It's going to lead to a Ph.D. in English, and to everyone saying you're brilliant."

She laughed. "I don't think so. The first, perhaps. The second, less likely." More silence. The music, faster now, swelled to its final cadence. Then stopped, and the voice of the announcer broke in—educated, serious, a bit pedantic. Franz Schubert, Fantasy in C major, Deutsch listing 934. Laura got up and turned the radio off.

"Why do I want a Ph.D. in English? Do I want it? And what then? Maybe there are better things to do with one's life, after all."

"Like what?"

"Oh, I don't know. The possibilities are endless. Maybe I should go off and be an investment banker in Los Angeles. A schoolteacher in Appalachia. Another Mother Teresa. An automobile mechanic in Pocatello. There are all sorts of things I might want to do." She thought again. "Or maybe I should just get married and have four kids, join the PTA, see them through their homework, their piano lessons, braces on the teeth, acne, and all the rest of it. The world is full of opportunities. Yet here I am, married to Conrad, Greene, Forster, and company. Temporarily at least. Writing something that no one's ever going to read. Including maybe even my adviser."

"But you're good at it. Everyone says so. You should hear what they say about you in the English department. Your ears would be burning."

She flushed. He knew that she never quite knew how to respond to such talk. "It's not just my work. On the good days I love it; I can't imagine doing anything else. But—oh, I don't know. At other times I think maybe I just work away at it because it keeps me from having to think. About what's really important."

"Meaning?"

"Meaning, do I want this kind of thing? Do I really want to settle down to this sort of life for the next thirty years? I love Jane Brandon, and they were fun, all those people tonight. Most of the time I love my writing and I love my teaching. But I'm not sure I want to do it for the rest of my life. Or that I do it well enough to be good at it. Despite what they may say in the English department. Look at me; where am I going to be a quarter century from now? When I'm over fifty?"

Matthew was a bit surprised at this. Having made up his own mind to be a historian, to spend his life writing and teaching, he hadn't worried much about whether he'd made the right decision. Or what the other possibilities in life might be. I guess I could have been a lawyer too, he thought. Or an investment banker. Or even an auto mechanic in Idaho. But they all seemed unlikely.

"Then finish up Conrad and Co., and go on to something new."

"It's not just them. Or the Victorians or the modernists. Or even teaching English. It's a question of who I am, what I want. Or maybe how to make my life useful. It's different for you. You seem pretty well set in what you're doing. And that's good. But I'm not there yet. And—"

"And—"

"And it's different for a woman, anyway. You'll marry some nice girl and she'll look after you, cook your meals, make sure that your children are dressed and fed. No man's going to do all that for me. So if I do get married, what'll happen to my literary career?"

He ignored the ironic, self-deprecating tone in which she'd referred to her own life. He didn't want to talk to her about marrying some nice girl, wasn't at all sure that's what he wanted. And he certainly didn't want to talk about her marrying some man, nice or otherwise.

"But last summer? You seemed pretty clear about things then. About where you were going, I mean." And my part in your life, he thought, but didn't say it.

"Last summer was different. I didn't have all these questions then. I'd been in London, away from all this, away from you, away from my friends, concentrating single-mindedly on my work. The question of identity didn't even arise. And then along you came and we went to Italy. It all seemed to fit so well. Until a few months ago."

"What's the problem?" He still didn't understand. "Was it me?" He asked the question, even though he was afraid of the answer.

She thought for a bit before answering. "That's what I thought at the time. Now I'm not so sure. Maybe I was just blaming you when I should have blamed myself. I'm sorry if that's what I did. I still think—don't get me wrong, Matt—I still think you've got some figuring out to do yourself. Not about your work, your career; you seem pretty well launched, enjoying what you do. But about what else there is to life."

"But I think I know what I want."

"Maybe you do, Matt, maybe you do. Maybe it's simpler for men. But what I mean is, Matt, where are the rest of us going to fit in your life? Your family, your friends?" When he was silent, she took his hand, and went on. "Anyway, I guess what I'm trying to say is that it's not just you. It's me too. I've got some figuring out to do. For a while I thought you'd help me do the figuring. Or perhaps that with you I wouldn't have to do the figuring. But now I know it's something I have to do, and I have to do it myself."

She put her mug down, and looked at her watch. "It's eight-thirty. An hour and a half home. I've got to go. Thanks for the coffee, Matt. And for the talk." She gave him a rueful smile. "I'll try to be better in the future. Let's have lunch together next week and talk about something cheerful."

"Laura," he said. His mouth felt dry.

"Yes?"

"Are you sure you don't want to spend the night? And go home in the morning, I mean?"

"In your spare room?" He nodded. Was that what he had meant? "Well—" She went to the window and looked out. A few flakes were coming down in the light of the streetlamp. "The snow seems to be beginning."

"Then stay. I'd be happier."

She considered this, looked at her watch again, looked out the window. "Maybe I should." Then turned to him. "No, I've got to go. I really do. Anyway, I promised to see someone tomorrow. In Cambridge, I mean. So I'd better get back."

To see someone? She hadn't mentioned this before. But why should she? Matthew didn't have the nerve to ask who it was. A woman? A man? Someone with whom she was going to discuss her work? Or another teaching job? Or just a friend? He knew it was none of his business.

She picked up her coat from the chair and put it on. Then turned to him, took his face in her hands, and kissed him. "Dear Matt," she said. "You've been very good to me, letting me ramble on like this. Much better than I would be. But—you've got to see this—I don't want to get too attached—or even reattached— until I figure all these things out a bit more clearly."

"Maybe we can help each other," he said. "If you think I've got some figuring too."

"Maybe. Maybe. Good night, Matt. Thanks for the coffee and the talk." She kissed him again, and then was gone out into the cold, dark night, where the snow was beginning to fall a bit more heavily.

CHAPTER NINE

Monday, June 5, 1989

By the next morning, the cloud of uncertainty and fear building above Beijing was spreading south, driven by the reports and rumors flowing from the capital. Last evening, alone in his room, Matthew had seen the first video clips of tanks breaking into Tiananmen Square, running over the pitiful cluster of tents in which the demonstrators had been living. Tracer bullets carved red and yellow arcs into the night sky above the city, and an armored car, caught by a Molotov cocktail, flamed through the street, out of control. Then, in the dim greenish light in front of the Tiananmen itself, a camera caught the Goddess of Liberty, slowly toppling from her stand, crashing down onto the pavement, her hands still carrying her torch of freedom.

At eight o'clock, the satellite-borne television news from America reported a Beijing Red Cross estimate that twenty-six hundred had died, and thousands more were wounded. In daylight, the square was a smoking desert, where skeletons of burned-out buses sprawled across the streets, crushed corpses of bicycles strewn around them, while olive-drab helicopters thrummed and coughed above the city. Rumors spoke of soldiers rapidly cremating bodies in order to cover up the scope of the carnage. Foreign governments were urging their citizens to leave the capital as soon as possible, airlines arranging special flights to Tokyo. Meanwhile, in Washington, the cameras showed crowds of Chinese students gathered outside the embassy on Wisconsin Avenue, denouncing the massacre and shouting demands for the overthrow of Li Peng's tyrannical government. The State Department's spokeswoman calmly assured the press corps that President Bush "deplored" the actions of the Chinese military, and was closely "monitoring"—as she put it—the situation.

Deplored! thought Matthew, appalled at the staggering casualty figures he'd just heard. Deplored! Was that the best word the president could choose to reflect his country's reaction to what had happened? When the broadcast had moved on to other matters, matters of politics and economics, sports and stock markets, all those reminders of the normal world, he turned to the Chinese news program. The pacification had gone according to plan, said the announcer. The capital had resumed its normal life, and people could once more go about their business, thankful that their security and livelihood would no longer be threatened by the *jishaoshu ren zhizao de dongluan,* the small handful of troublemakers who had tested the government's goodwill for so long by their occupation of the square. The People's Army had dealt firmly but justly with this threat to the People's Government, and all Chinese could be proud of the actions of their guardians.

Yesterday evening, Wang Baozhen had told him to be sure to go to the institute on Monday. "Don't get there too early; if there are no buses running, they'll open late. Anyway, they're probably not going to want any foreigners around till they've had a chance to digest the news. But Zhao Shanling says you must see him. He has some more information for you, and he thinks this may be the last he can give you." Matthew had hesitated, uncertain whether he should go. "Mr. Zhao's been very helpful," he said. "But now—with this news—I mean, I don't want to do anything to embarrass him. Or the people at the institute." No, she assured him; the situation would still be very fluid for a day or so, no one would yet know how to react. "In a few days it may all change, we may no longer be able to talk so freely to foreigners. That's why he says you must see him now."

Outside the hotel, the city had fallen suddenly silent. Today there were no cars, no buses, no trucks blaring their horns and jangling their loose cargoes over the rough pavement. The scene, contrasting with the grim and dark pictures from Beijing, was one at once of extraordinary peace and extraordinary liveliness; it was as if the suddenly unencumbered flood of pedestrians and the bicyclists were now claiming the streets as their own. No longer needing to shout at one another to be heard, they talked in normal voices, and the whispered hush rose above them in a soft haze, echoing gently off the buildings, to vanish in the green branches that overhung the street.

By this morning, nearly every main intersection had been blocked. Deserted by their drivers, their tires flattened, the dirty blue and white articulated trolley buses sat like beached whales astride the crossings. Slogans and posters plastered their sides: mixtures of fact, of rumor, taken down from broadcasts by the Voice of America, by the BBC: a thousand people reported dead, three thousand, five thousand. Red flags flew above them, students with bullhorns stood on their roofs to harangue the passersby. On Huaihai Road, a large crowd had collected outside the Academy of the Social Sciences, where a leading liberal paper, the *World Economic Herald*, had recently been shut down by the authorities, and its outspoken editor fired.

Now, down the street, Matthew saw coming a procession of several hundred students, singing the *Internationale*, the leaders carrying the flag of China, others behind them holding banners proclaiming their loyalty to their country, to the cause of socialism, denouncing the corrupt tyrants who had opened fire on their own people in Beijing. Matthew, nervously remembering the consulate's admonition to stay away from crowds, nonetheless found himself swept up by the mass of people around him, moving aside to let the marchers go by. "Students," said a voice in English at his elbow. "From East China Normal University. Are you American?"

"Yes," said Matthew. "Where are they going?"

"They are marching to show their patriotism," said the man. "To show the government what they think of them." By now a group of people was gathering around them, calling out questions to him in English and Chinese. "How much do you know about the massacre?" "What does the American news say?" "What will America do?"

"Tell President Bush he must break diplomatic relations," called one. There was immediate disagreement. "No, that would hurt the people. But Bush must condemn the government, must condemn Li Peng."

Matthew dealt with their questions as well as he could. But he knew no more than they did, or at least than those who had been able to listen to hear the foreign radio broadcasts. Another band of demonstrators came marching down the road, like the first carrying red flags and singing the *Internationale*. But some in this group were also shouting political slogans: *Dadao Li Peng! Dadao Li Peng!* "Down with Li Peng!"

"Li Peng is a Fascist," said one of Matthew's interrogators to him. "Worse than a Fascist." It made no sense, of course. There was nothing fascist about the premier of China. He was a Communist, not a Fascist. Like Stalin, like Brezhnev. Even in democracies, soldiers fire on their own people. Kent State. Matthew had been ten when that happened. Old enough to remember the date. May 4, 1970. America's May Fourth movement, one of his professors had later called it.

But Kent State wasn't like this. What happened in Tiananmen Square had all the marks of a carefully planned military operation. The army hadn't fired by accident or out of fear, but by design. Clearing the demonstrators from the square was part of its purpose. But another part must have been to teach them a lesson. And not only them, but the people of Beijing, the people who had turned out by the hundreds of thousands to support them.

Away from the main streets, however, the city seemed remarkably calm. Here there were no posters, and except for the absence of cars and trucks, it looked like a normal day. The sun was breaking through the clouds left over from yesterday's drizzle, shops were open, and people, released from the normally crowded sidewalks, strolled peacefully down the middle of roads facing nothing more dangerous than a bicycle moving too fast. At Thibet Road, near Hilding's hotel, more roadblocks, more trolley buses pulled across the street. More speeches, more processions, more red flags. He thought about Hilding in there, wondered if he'd heard from his daughter.

It took him about an hour to reach the institute. Zhao Shanling was there to greet him, his face pale with worry, his strange darting movements more pronounced than ever.

"I'm glad you could come, Mr. Walker," he said. "Did you get my message from Professor Wang yesterday? Yes? Good." He took Matthew into the reading room, where they were alone. Matthew began to thank him for the materials Zhao had given him two days earlier. Zhao silenced him. "Some other time, Mr. Walker. I thought you'd be interested in them, and I'm glad they were useful. I have some more to show you today. But I'm afraid you won't be able to stay here very long. We're not very well organized today. It's been difficult for the staff to come to work, and we'll have to close early so they can get home." Matthew assured him that he understood. Zhao motioned to him to sit down. A young woman appeared with a new stack of manila folders and, a minute later, brought the cup of tea and the blue aluminum thermos. As if nothing had happened since Saturday. But today there was no pile driver hammering away in the distance, no raucous blast of horns from the streets below. Just the soft murmur of the crowds moving freely through them.

He tried to put his mind on the work before him. Some of the documents were simply the originals of the photocopies Zhao had given him on Saturday. But many were new. In French and English, occasionally in Chinese, most had to do with Simon. Some came from the police, French and English; others came from the Municipal Council, from the French administration, and a few pieces from the American consul general. They made it clear that John Ransom—now seated on the Shanghai Municipal Council—had continued his campaign against Simon, warning his fellow councillors, like Massingham, not to be taken in by Simon's apparent conversion to Shanghai loyalism. The French police had, somewhat grudgingly, set a watch on his house in the route Père Robert. "He has few visitors," reported the chief of the Sûreté in mid-March, writing to Chief Detective-Inspector Givens in the Settlement. "Almost every afternoon a man identified as Chu Hung-ying, a comprador employed by Racine & Cie., and who is Larsen's Chinese teacher, arrives and stays an hour or two. On Tuesday and again on Friday, he went to the café of Mme Vorontsov at 38 route Vallon, and met a *jeune fille*. She is believed to be Mademoiselle Ransom, niece of the municipal councillor in the International Settlement." Matthew wondered if Givens would have told Ransom about his niece's activities. Or might he simply have seen her meeting Simon as a testimony to the innocence of the American? "But we are seriously understaffed during the present emergency," the report finished, "and we need more than mere supposition to justify detailing an agent to watch M. Larsen's activities."

There was a petulant undertone to the report, as if the *Garde municipale* could not understand why they were being asked to waste their time on such an affair. Givens's reply to his French opposite number was noncommittal. "I realize that the number of suspects in the foreign settlements increases daily," he wrote, thanking Fiori for his information. "Mr. Ransom maintains his suspicions, but we have little else to go on." In other words, thought Matthew, John Ransom is throwing his weight around. The police are quite aware of Ransom's falling out with Simon, quite aware of the relationship between Simon and Emily Ransom (after all, there were no secrets in Shanghai). And, although Givens and his superiors can't quite come out and say it to a member of the S.M.C., they resent being asked to intervene in a private quarrel between the two men, when Shanghai is in turmoil, and they have more important work to do.

For—as they realized, as Simon himself was now coming to realize—the city's fall to the Nationalists was proving to be only the beginning of a more dangerous phase of the crisis. The Communists had engineered the rising that had driven the warlord troops from the city, and had proclaimed the formation of a new municipal government that they would control themselves. But Chiang Kai-shek's armies had now entered Shanghai, and while Communists and Nationalists still publicly professed an undying friendship, only the most credulous—Chinese or foreign—took these assertions at face value.

Simon, however, clearly believed—or at least wanted to believe—that with the entry of the revolutionary armies into Shanghai, his work was done. "I have no taste for the sort of deception I've been practicing," he wrote on March 24, nagged by the thought that he'd taken advantage of men who were his friends. More than that, he was eager to keep the impetuous Emily out of more trouble. That very day, however, there had come a serious outbreak of trouble at Nanking. Two hundred miles upstream, the city had fallen to the Nationalists, and in the fighting, several foreigners had lost their lives. Most of the others—businessmen, missionaries from the American-run university, consular officials, and others—had escaped to the riverbank, under the protection of a barrage laid down by British and

American warships, and there they had been evacuated to Shanghai.

Matthew, who had read much about the episode, knew that even today historians could not agree whether the deaths had been accidental or intentional, and Simon's journal had little to add to the question. "Panic again," he noted on March 26. "Every hour fresh rumors: Nanking in flames, the city pillaged, foreign women raped, a general massacre of foreigners by the revolutionary troops. Lurid reports from the Chinese: an unprovoked naval bombardment has laid waste large parts of the city and killed thousands of innocent civilians."

Though within a few days Shanghai had come to a more sober assessment of the story, the Nanking outrage, as it quickly became known, brought renewed calls for foreign intervention to keep Shanghai safe. America must act, Simon reported his countrymen as saying. " 'How can we stand by and let the British do our work for us? Send the marines, send the army, to protect this oasis of civilization from the hordes of barbarism!' Even some of the missionaries now think we've turned the other cheek once too often."

He also realized that wherever the responsibilities for it might lie, the Nanking affair was also bound to increase the tensions between Chiang Kai-shek's Kuomintang and their communist allies. Chang Shao-shan confirmed the view in a hurried meeting that Mr. Chu had arranged in a back alley restaurant off Peking Road.

Monday, March 28, 1927

There are men, powerful men, around Chiang Kai-shek, who have never liked the Kuomintang's alliance with the Communists, and are now ready to break it. The Shanghai rising showed the power of the Reds, they say, and they are now urging Chiang Kai-shek to move against the radicals before it's too late. He won't need much convincing, Chang Shao-shan thinks. If he's going to pay his armies, General Chiang needs the money that Shanghai's bankers and businessmen can put at his disposal, and he needs the revenues that Shanghai's trade and taxes—legal and illegal—will bring in. Of course, the bankers and businessmen are willing to help. And of course they have their price, and that price is the suppression of the workers' groups and the labor unions.

Nor, since the events at Nanking last week, can Chiang Kai-shek afford to provoke the foreigners. Now he's got to show them he'll be a firm leader, keeping the unruly elements under control, cracking down on the strikers, on the labor unions, on the armed workers. Otherwise he'll never get the backing of the rich and powerful men, foreign and Chinese, who run this city.

So, Chang says, the general is rapidly reaching his moment of decision. Will he accept the fact of a new Shanghai, a people's Shanghai, a Shanghai become the center of the Chinese revolution, indeed of the world revolution? or will he betray that revolution, turn against the masses, and make Shanghai once again the center of reaction?

What will you do? I asked him.

"At all events, we will defend ourselves," he said. "The revolution gave us arms, and we're stronger than we've ever been before. We have the people on our side too. If Chiang Kai-shek will not serve the revolution, then at least he must not impede it. We must make him understand this. But if he does not, if he turns against us, then we are ready."

Though I didn't want to hear his next question, by then I think I knew it was coming, and mentally I kicked myself for not having left before he had a chance to ask it. "Lai *hsien-sheng*, we still need your help. We know who our enemies are among the Chinese. But we must know more about the plans of the foreigners here in Shanghai. If Chiang Kai-shek strikes, will he have their support? And if he does, what form will that support take?"

I think he saw my hesitancy, my unwillingness to give him the answer he wanted. So he waited a few moments, and then reminded me of the sight that I've been trying to forget: those heads in their wicker cages, hanging above the streets of the Chinese city. "Are we to see those again," he asked me gently, "this time strung up there by Chiang Kai-shek's executioners? What will you do when you see your friend, your teacher, Chu Hung-ying, looking down at you with his dead eyes from one of those baskets, suspended from a telephone pole?"

I had no answer for that.

By the beginning of April, the breach in the revolutionary camp was evident to everyone. In Hankow, Borodin and the leftists were still in control of the Nationalist Government that had moved there in December. But Hankow was a city in distress, its trade and industry come to a stop, its new government rapidly sinking into a chaotic bankruptcy. Six hundred miles downriver, Shanghai, with its wealth, with its control over the commerce of the entire Yangtze valley, Shanghai with its millions of men and women, grim-faced and tired, but now at last given a reason for hope, was the key to the revolution's future. And there, in that city living on its nerves, the uneasy alliance between Chiang Kai-shek and the left continued. Chiang's armies controlled the military headquarters at Lung-hua, his emissaries parleyed with the representatives of the foreign settlements. But in the streets of the Chinese city, in the slums of Chapei and Pootung, in the tangle of stinking alleys that wound their way between the hovels where the poor lived, the armed guards of the Communists continued their patrols, recruiting, training, preparing to defend the victory they had won in the insurrection ten days earlier.

By then, Chiang Kai-shek's plans were almost ready. And Simon, patiently and methodically, returned to his game of deception, trying to learn what the response of the foreigners would be—the councillors, the police officials, the consuls, the military officers.

Saturday, April 2, 1927

The question is no longer whether, but only when, Chiang Kai-shek will move against the Communists. Any fool can see that. The *North China*, of course, is urging him on, and gleefully reports every clash that breaks out between the Nationalist soldiers and the groups of armed workers as evidence of the divisions in the revolutionary camp.

What the *North China* does not report is how heavily the foreigners—or some of them, at least—are involved. Even some of those who are the loudest in publicly protesting their neutrality. I find their hypocrisy sickening. But I'm careful not to show it. And they continue to trust me.

Look at François Verdier. I like him, I've always considered him a friend, a man with whom you can discuss ideas, books, music, and heaven knows, there are few enough like him in our narrow little world of the foreign settlements. But do his superiors in Paris know that he talks more than he should? A year ago I would have felt I was betraying his confidences. Now, after all that I've seen, I am not so sure. Anyway, are they really confidences? He's under no obligation to tell me as much as he does.

Yet would he talk so freely if he knew what was happening to the information he gives me? Of course he knows that it will find its way into my book—eventually. He tells me I may not publish it yet. And of course I don't. But in the meantime his news has other uses.

From the indiscreet Verdier, Simon had learned enough to realize that the French police, with the backing of the consulate, had been making arrangements to strengthen Tu Yüeh-sheng's Green Gang. A month ago, the consul general had cabled Paris, asking for a shipment of small arms, presumably for distribution to the gangsters. The French motives were simple: in a time of crisis, they wanted the help of the mob in keeping order in the Concession. And, from what Father Duchamp had told him, Simon had guessed that part of the bargain also meant continued French connivance in the lucrative opium trade that the gangsters ran out of the Concession.

Nor were the French the only ones making arrangements with the underworld. At roughly the same time, Captain Fiori, the French police chief, had arranged a secret meeting between Tu Yüeh-sheng and Stanfield Frothingham of the Shanghai Municipal Council, to enlist the council's help—or at least its benevolent neutrality—in Chiang Kai-shek's strike against the Communists (it was a conversation about this meeting, presumably, that Emily had overheard). And, as Matthew already knew, Chiang Kai-shek himself had enlisted the aid of the gangsters. "Preparations are being made by the Kung Chin Hui (Joint Progressive Society) to make a surprise attack on the General Labor Union" read one of the daily intelligence reports by the Municipal Police that Zhao Shanling had given him. "The attack will be made by members of the Green Gang with the assistance of soldiers in plain clothes."

All this information, and more, Simon had passed on to Chang Shao-shan and to Chu Hung-ying. Had they known what he was doing, his compatriots would have called him a traitor. But they didn't, of course. Except John Ransom. He'd been quite right in warning the police about Simon's activities. The question, of course, was whether he knew what Simon was doing. Or had he simply made a shrewd guess, motivated by personal animosity? An animosity that, as Matthew was coming to realize, might arise from more than simply a dislike of Simon's political views and their effect on Emily?

Tuesday, March 15, 1927

Usually I'm the one who tells Mr. Chu about the doings of Shanghai's foreigners. But today it was the other way around. When he arrived for one of our periodic meetings, which we still politely call language lessons, he gave me a piece of rather startling information.

Actually that's not so surprising. It's the sort of information that a Chinese is more likely to know about than a foreigner.

It has to do with gambling.

There are three kinds of gambling here: the respectable, the less respectable, and the illicit.

The respectable forms are reserved for the rich: betting on the stock market and betting on the horses. No social opprobrium attaches to the man who engages in these particular games of chance.

The illicit is reserved for the Chinese, particularly the poor Chinese, in the wonderful variety of games of cards, or dice, or counters, in which they are persuaded to squander their meager earnings, usually to the profit of a leader of the city's underworld.

And then there is the middle sort. Not quite illegal, but not quite respectable either, and certainly not something that missionaries—or municipal councillors—ought to be seen doing. So if you must do it, and if you're at all prudent, you do it not in the International Settlement, but in the French Concession, where the police look with a somewhat more tolerant eye on human nature's varied frailties.

If they look at all, that is, for in many cases it seems the police choose to keep their eyes firmly fixed in other directions. That's particularly true when the gambling establishment is run by a powerful figure. And that's the case here. The Chat Noir, in an alley off the rue Ratard, is one of the many semireputable dives that have started up in recent years in the foreign settlements. They're all the same, these seedy establishments: a Filipino dance band, Russian and Chinese girls in gaudy silk to entertain the customers, a few tables for cards, a roulette wheel. Except when an occasional brawl breaks out over money or over a girl, there's no reason for the police to pay much attention. They've got better ways to spend their time. Everyone knows that. And some whisper that the owners of the houses, indeed, make it worthwhile for the police, both European and Chinese, to look the other way should anything unseemly happen.

But in the Chat Noir, it seems that for the more favored patrons there's a whole second establishment in back, in a part of the building never seen by those who drop in casually looking for an evening's entertainment. Here, one imagines, the furnishings are more luxurious, and the girls better dressed, and more practiced in the arts of entertainment. Above all, the stakes at the tables are higher. And here, it seems, the upstanding John Ransom has recently been spending a good deal of his spare time.

To say nothing of his spare money. Which he's been losing. Or so Mr. Chu tells me.

Hence, perhaps, the rumors of Ransom's financial problems. Any troubles over money are bad enough for a councillor or a would-be councillor. But gambling losses are a far sight worse than the problems that come from simply making a few unwise investments.

All the more so when the creditor is both rich and powerful and has a somewhat less than unsullied reputation. For if Mr. Chu is to be believed, the Chat Noir is one of the many properties in the French Concession that's held by Tu Yüeh-sheng.

Not directly, of course. A philanthropist and patron of culture like Monsieur Tu would not, of course, concern himself with such a relatively unimportant holding as this unpretentious building in a back street. Certainly a man of his standing would never stoop to any activity that would take advantage of human weakness. But M. Tu is a busy man, who no doubt can exercise only the most general supervision over his financial empire. So, if his underlings should, by accident, happen to invest for him in the occasional gaming house (or the occasional brothel or opium den), then surely he can't be held responsible.

All the same, and speaking only for myself, I should not like to find myself deeply in debt to M. Tu Yüeh-sheng.

Among the police records that Zhao had given Matthew were several others that had to do with Tu Yüeh-sheng.

Shanghai Municipal Police
March 12, 1927

From: C.D.I. Givens

To: Major A. H. Hilton-Johnson

From information received, I have learned that the opium ring known to be active in the French Concession, under the control of the notorious Tu Yüeh-sheng, is about to try to extend its marketing of the drug into the Settlement on an experimental basis. To this end, the ring, which is already believed to have suborned several high officials of the French police, and perhaps one or two members of the French Council, may try to use similar tactics here. I have warned all officers to be on their guard, and to report to me immediately any attempts at bribery.

Another memorandum linked Ransom's name with that of Tu. Matthew had no idea who the anonymous informant might be.

March 13, 1927

Very Secret

From a source whose identity I am not able to disclose, but who has proved herself generally accurate in the past, I have learned that in the last month, Mr. John Ransom, of the Municipal Council, has held several meetings with Mr. Tu Yüeh-sheng. The subject of their discussions is not known, but is believed to have had to do with certain sums of money that Mr. Ransom is alleged to owe Mr. Tu.

A note had been scrawled in pencil at the bottom. The initials that followed were illegible. "Earlier this winter," it read, "Mr. Ransom was reported to have been in a condition of acute financial distress. Whatever may have been its causes, that distress now appears to be a thing of the past." Another pair of letters, also handwritten, and dated after the city had fallen to the revolutionaries, reflected a concern that the Municipal Council and its police were being drawn into waters that might be deeper than they knew. The first was from the commissioner of the Shanghai Municipal Police.

March 25, 1927

Very Secret

My dear Hilton-Johnson,

As you no doubt could tell, I was somewhat surprised to learn from you this afternoon that certain agents of the person whom we discussed were henceforth to be allowed free access to the Settlement without hindrance from the police. I have stated on several occasions my belief that my French opposite number and several of his colleagues have both unwisely and improperly allowed themselves to be drawn into this person's violation of the laws, both of the French Concession itself, and of the Republic of China, with regard to the traffic in narcotics. While I certainly can understand that in the present emergency the security and good order of the Settlement are paramount, I would be remiss in my duty were I not to state once more, in writing and with all the force that I may command, that I believe it to be a mistake to enlist the services of this person in the maintenance of that order. In my opinion, the forces despatched to Shanghai by His Majesty's Government, together with the Municipal Police and the Volunteers, are now sufficient to keep the peace, and it would be misguided were we, as our French colleagues have done, to come to depend on this person to do for us what we might better do for ourselves.

/s/E. I. M. *Barrett*

25 March 1927

My dear Barrett,

As you know, in ordinary times I would wholeheartedly agree with you. However, these are not ordinary times. What is now at stake, and will be for the next several weeks (not longer, let us hope) is not simply the well-being of the International Settlement, but of all Shanghai. It will profit us little if we are able to maintain the integrity and good order of the Settlement alone while the rest of the city is engulfed by the Bolshevik flood. Consequently such actions as those we have discussed must be taken in the Chinese city, particularly in Chapei—and for obvious reasons, our at least passive cooperation will be needed if they are to be effective.

I have discussed your views fully with Mr. Frothingham and Mr. Ransom, and they both agree that no hindrance of any kind for any reason should be placed in the way of a certain person's agents in the Settlement.

/s/A. H. Hilton-Johnson

Three guesses, thought Matthew, as to the identity of that "certain person." Barrett, an honest cop, didn't like the idea of Tu Yüeh-sheng expanding his underworld empire into the Settlement, but found himself overruled by his superiors. By this time, the gangster would already have had his meeting with council chairman Frothingham, and would have secured Frothingham's agreement to give him and his friends free run in the Settlement as long as the emergency lasted.

But what was Ransom's name doing in there? Of course he was a member of the council, and presumably all the members of the council were privy to the arrangements Frothingham had made with Tu Yüeh-sheng. Was there any more to it than that? Any connection, for instance, between the arrangements that would give Tu's agents a free hand in the Settlement and the sudden end of Ransom's indebtedness to Tu?

Simon, of course, couldn't possibly have known about the concerns of the Shanghai police. No matter; he had other sources of information.

Monday, March 28, 1927

Duchamp very agitated, having just learned—to his own satisfaction, at any rate—that the men who run the opium ring have been enlisted by Chiang Kai-shek for his battle with the Communists.

I'm hardly surprised, since this is very much what I've been hearing from Mr. Chu & Chang Shao-shan. But what's new is Duchamp's claim that the ring is also trying to pay off some of the Settlement's authorities, much as they paid off some of the French authorities (including the chief of police) almost two years ago.

He says they've approached Stanfield Frothingham & John Ransom among others, won't tell me where his information comes from, just that he's virtually certain there's something to it. And he wants me to do what I can to stop it. The arrangement in the French Concession has been highly profitable to the ring & the officials they've cut in on it. But it's also claimed a great many victims, & is turning the Concession into little more than a fief of Tu Yüeh-sheng's Green Gang & its underworld connections.

Duchamp's no Bolshevik, of course. In fact, he's often told me he doesn't believe there really is such a thing as Chinese bolshevism; those who call themselves communist do so only in order to appear fashionably western. But apparently neither his ecclesiastical superiors nor the French authorities agree, and his attempts to tell them of his findings in this case have been met with disbelief and resistance. Of course I've warned him that he mustn't expect me to do much better—I'm certainly in no position to tell the Settlement authorities how to go about their business. Even if some of them are my own countrymen.

Nonetheless, I'm curious enough to have sent Ransom a note today, asking for an interview with him. A purely professional one, of course, in his capacity as member of the S.M.C. It's been a while since we last met, and I don't think he'll refuse me. Particularly since I suggested I wanted to finish up my work, leaving it up to him to conclude that I'll be leaving Shanghai presently. He knows that I've been visiting his colleagues, & he won't be able to resist the temptation to ensure that future generations know his part in helping to guide Shanghai through this storm.

Tried to reach E. to sound her out about the plan first, but can't get in touch with her. Her office says she's taking a couple of days off to rest.

Friday, April 1, 1927

John Ransom received me this morning in his office in Kiukiang Road. It was the first time we'd met since our scene almost two months ago, and the occasion was one of chilly formality, pleasant for neither of us. Nor was it particularly fruitful. We discussed the measures taken to guard the Settlement and the prospects for the city under the Nationalists. Ransom still hopes, like many others here, that the revolutionary successes are only temporary, and that before long, the northern troops will be back in control, and the revolutionaries in headlong flight south toward Canton.

I asked him what the council and its police might do if Chiang Kai-shek moves against the armed workers in the Chinese city, as the *North China* and the other papers predict. Ransom immediately assumed the pleased look of a man in possession of the sort of confidential intelligence denied to ordinary mortals like me. But as befits someone in his high position, he was very circumspect (much more so than some of his colleagues!). I could rest assured—this in a lordly tone—that the settlements have nothing to fear, and that the Municipal Council has the matter well in hand. Of course there is information that I cannot possibly divulge, et cetera, et cetera, but when the time comes and this is all behind us, the world will see how prudent the authorities have been. Et cetera, et cetera.

Only when I pressed the point, and rather gingerly introduced Tu Yüeh-sheng's name into the conversation, did he look startled. Or was it my imagination? In any case, he recovered himself quickly, and assured me that while he had heard of Mr. Tu, he knew him only as a businessman and public citizen of the French Concession. He then began to question me, obviously wanting to know where my information came from. But I think that, in withholding my own confidential sources, I gave as good an account of myself as he had.

I asked to be remembered to both Emily and Muriel Ransom, and we parted with mutual expressions of regard. But I'm little wiser today than I was yesterday, and certainly know nothing more about his doings with Tu Yüeh-sheng—whatever they may be—than I did.

In fact, I have a disquieting feeling that it might have been more prudent of me not to have brought up Tu's name at all.

Tuesday, April 6, 1927

Saw E. this afternoon, who said she had some news to give me. She looked pale & tired, very apologetic for not having been able to meet me sooner, says she's not been feeling herself, & is unable to eat properly. But a moment later her old cheerfulness had come back, told me not to worry, she's been to the doctor, is in good hands, & everything O.K.

What she had to tell me was not so much news as a warning. Her uncle has said I've been making trouble and he's going to "take care of me." Thought at first he'd found out about us, but E. says no, that's not it—& somewhat unwillingly admitted the warning came via Rhonda Sexton. Astounding—I had no idea that Emily had met R.—she'd never told me. Then I remembered what Rogers had said about R. & J. Ransom.

E. remembered her words exactly. "It's no concern of mine what trouble S.L. gets himself into. But I've still got a soft spot left in my heart for him. So tell him to be careful, because your uncle John thinks that Simon knows some things he shouldn't know. And says that he's planning to take care of him."

E. also said Ransom no longer seems so worried about his finances as earlier. Doesn't know why—he says only that his ship's come in, & he's made some good investments. None of my business, of course, but I'd like to know what they are.

A few days later, Simon had had his last interview with Chang Shao-shan, finding him bitter and upset over the reports that the foreigners were ready to cooperate in Chiang Kai-shek's suppression of the Communists.

Sunday, April 10, 1927

... He expected more of the French, he said. The English—well, they'll stop at nothing in their blind attempt to uphold the prestige of a dying empire. But he'd admired the French, thought them more flexible, more realistic. Though no matter what might be true of individual Frenchmen, it's not surprising that the moneyed interests of Paris, with their links to London and Wall Street, can't risk the possibility of a revolution triumphant in China. Too much depends upon keeping China poor, inert, and obedient. Capable of being exploited, in other words, as she has been in the past.

Well, he told me, we are ready for them. And we have the people on our side.

But they hadn't, of course. Or not enough of them. As Simon realized.

Monday, April 11, 1927

Everywhere there are signs that the break is coming soon. Every day the foreign press grows more insistent in demanding that Chiang Kai-shek deal firmly and resolutely with the Bolsheviks, and no doubt he's getting the same message in private from the consuls and the businessmen and all the others who stand to lose if the revolution continues. That's the only way he'll get the trust of the men whose support he will need in his plans to rebuild China.

Chang Shao-shan and Mr. Chu may be confident that Chiang cannot prevail against the masses who have taken control of Shanghai. I admire their faith and their courage, but I am not so certain as they. What can an unarmed people, no matter how many of them there may be, do against a modern army fighting with modern weapons?

Last night, for the first time in many months, I dreamed once again of leaving China, knowing that this part of my life was over, and that the time had come for me to go home. But this time when I woke, I found that my dream did not vanish, nor did the fears that had grown in darkness evaporate with the coming of daylight, as they have done in the past. All today they have pursued me, growing in my imagination like a thick, heavy cloud that is about to burst, threatening to send down a black rain of destruction. After these few months of hope, the promises this spring of a new future, I am once again being haunted by those old memories that, here in China, I thought I had finally banished. In my dreams, in my waking today, those horrifying visions have returned, stronger than ever, almost tangible: the French countryside nine years ago, with its houses black and destroyed, the bodies of cattle lying rotting in the pastures, trees broken and dying, and everywhere, everywhere, the stench of devastation and death.

I've been through all this before, and rebel at the prospect of seeing such sights again. Only a few years ago, we embarked for France, full of hope and innocent in our youth and our enthusiasm, we who were going to rescue the tired nations of the old world from the despair and death into which they had sunk. Yet now I remember the terror and pain that waited for us. For in the end the old world was too much for us. Our hope, our enthusiasm, had changed nothing. Instead, it was we, or those of us who were still left, who came back changed, turned suddenly into old men.

Here in China, this winter and spring has once again been a time of waiting, of extraordinary anticipation. And for a while it seemed to reawaken in me all those old promises, those old hopes, that I had known ten years ago. With Emily, because of

Emily, I have recaptured my beliefs, my enthusiasms, in a way that I no longer thought possible. If Europe, poor, tired old Europe, was beyond our saving, perhaps here in the Orient a new dawn would break. We would help it come, she and I. And we did help it come. Or so it seemed, just a few weeks ago, as we sat joking with each other and boasting about our accomplishments.

Today, it seems once again that in reality we have changed nothing. History has its own painful logic, and we are helpless before it. In this land that is so old, so incomprehensible, so seemingly impervious to the trivial irritations of outsiders like ourselves, what possibility can there be of change? Once again our hopes have betrayed us, once again history is triumphing over our desires, our will. Strange that a Chinese like Chang Shao-shan can still believe in progress, can still believe that the course of history moves forward, toward a better future. Once I believed that too; but after the trenches of France and Flanders, such faith is no longer possible, at least for me. I do not like what is coming, and I do not want to see it happen.

I told Emily about my dream when I saw her today. For a few minutes she looked at me without speaking, and then her face, her lovely face, took on that strange new look that I have now learned to know. But I wasn't prepared for it when she burst into tears, telling me that she too has decided she must go home, and will sail from Shanghai in a few weeks' time. Her family wants her back in Baltimore, tells her she's already been away too long. And no doubt her uncle will be relieved to have her off his hands. But there are other reasons to go, because now for the first time since she's arrived here, she finds Shanghai grating on her, getting on her nerves, she finds that the sights, the sounds, the smells of the city that she once found fascinating now almost repel her.

Her mood has changed recently, I know, and I've been thoughtless not to have noticed earlier how the strain of the past two months has been telling on her. What seemed once lighthearted, almost a schoolgirl lark, has now taken on a seriousness, even a danger, that she hadn't foreseen. But when I reproach myself for having let her fall ill, she smiles at my worries, telling me no, that isn't it, I mustn't concern myself, and in a little while she'll be all right.

Today, when she left me, she warned me again to be careful.

You've got to look after yourself, she said, because in the past few weeks I've felt closer to you, more grateful to you than you can now understand for all you've given me. Again that new look, tender, wondering, but sad, came over her face. I'll tell you all about it next time we meet. I pressed her, but she wouldn't say any more, told me I must be patient, and let her have her surprise. Then she kissed me hurriedly and left.

I'm touched by her concern, but also worried, for never before has she been the one to suggest there's any need for caution, any danger that might befall us. All afternoon, all this evening, I have thought about her decision to leave Shanghai. It comes as something of a relief, for it will put her out of danger. Yet it's also helped me to focus my own mind, to consider what it is that keeps me here. And to consider the bleak prospect of life without her.

I will wait one more day. And then, if my mood hasn't passed, if the cloud hasn't yet burst, I'll finally do what I've so often dreamt of doing: buy my steamship ticket, and say my farewells to all those I have known here. And to put behind me a piece of my life, uncertain after all these years here just what it is that I have accomplished. And uncertain, at last, how to justify this long absence from my family.

Emily's leaving will make the decision easier for me, to understand that now, perhaps, at last it is time to go home.

And to ask her, at last, if she will be willing to share my life.

There were no more entries in the journal.

Early the next morning, Matthew knew, the purge had begun. Thousands of Tu Yüeh-sheng's gangsters, working closely with the army, had descended on the strongholds of the Communists and the workers, in Pootung, in Chapei, throughout the Chinese city. In some cases the workers' units were taken by surprise and disarmed with hardly the chance to fire a shot; in other places they'd managed to put up a brief resistance before the superior firepower of the troops and their underworld allies overcame them. The labor unions had enough fight left in them to put a hundred thousand workers into the streets later that day. There were more demonstrations, more marches, more bloodshed as the general's troops fired into the angry crowds protesting what had happened. All over the city, anonymous posters had gone up denouncing Chiang Kai-shek as a new warlord, denouncing the imperialists who had helped him carry out his massacre, promising that the Chinese people would rise against their new oppressors.

Even now, no one knows exactly how many died on April 12 and on the terrible days that followed. Matthew had seen estimates ranging from a few hundred to well over ten thousand, and he thought, with a startled apprehension of the present, of the uncertain and ever-changing reports that had been coming in from Beijing since Sunday. From Shanghai, the purges had grown ever bloodier, spreading to other cities under Nationalist control—Canton, Changsha, Nanking, Hangchow. Only in Hankow, that citadel of the left, did Borodin and his communist allies hold out for a few months. But by July, even they were gone, and Chiang Kai-shek had become master of China south of the Yangtze. A little more than a year later, in June 1928, when his troops drove into Beijing, he had proclaimed the unification of all China under the Nationalist banner.

Long before that, within a week or two of Chiang's strike against the Communists early on that morning of April 12, 1927, Shanghai had fallen quiet.

And Simon Larsen had vanished.

At two-thirty that afternoon, the door opened, and Zhao Shanling appeared, nervously apologetic for having broken in on Matthew's work.

"Mr. Walker," he said, "I'm afraid it's time to leave. We're closing for the day. Will you be coming tomorrow?" He would, Matthew answered, if that was all right. "Good, good. We will try to show you some more. I've spoken to the director, and he says that it is all right for you to take these copies with you. But please—you must not mention this to anyone. Not that it's improper on our part"—he smiled—"but still, we would not want everyone to expect the same treatment. We know that you've come a long way, and we want to do what we can to help."

Matthew put the papers into his briefcase and got up, thanking Zhao for all he had done. He wondered if he should come back; might his presence, as a foreigner, become an embarrassment, even a danger, to the staff? Somehow he was reluctant to ask, reluctant to try to discover Zhao's reaction to the terrifying events of Sunday; it would seem too much like prying, and once again he had the uneasy feeling of being a voyeur, a tourist of the emotions, watching, with an almost macabre fascination, the spectacle of China in pain.

Perhaps he misjudged him, perhaps Zhao wanted an expression of sympathy, even from a foreigner like himself, for the state into which his country had fallen. Perhaps he wanted to cry aloud, raising his voice to heaven, to mourn the dead youth of Tiananmen Square; perhaps, like one of those courageous old Confucian scholars under the despotism of the Ming emperors, he wanted to shout poems of classical curses against a government that would butcher its own people in cold blood. Zhao gave no such sign, however, as he accompanied Matthew out, making anxious little apologies for the need to shut early, for the disarray of the building, for the long walk back across the city that faced him—"there are no buses today, you see, no taxis"—bidding him farewell, and hoping he was comfortable in his hotel.

Two blocks away, on the Bund, a demonstration had been taking place since that morning. Matthew watched it now, a curiously quiet gathering of perhaps one or two thousand people, standing outside Party headquarters in the huge domed building that had been the Hongkong and Shanghai Bank. The iron gates outside the entrance had come down, and a detachment of soldiers, their bayonets fixed, stood guarding them, but neither being threatened by nor threatening the crowd. Along the streets men and women stopped to read posters, to look at cartoons of Li Peng dressed as Hitler, brandishing a machine gun in one hand and a large swastika in the other, and of Deng Xiaoping caparisoned as the old empress dowager, corrupt, senile, and cut off from the world of ordinary men and women.

Yet all through his long walk back to Maoming Road, he found himself amazed at the apparent impassivity of the crowds. Wall posters, in black and red ink, told of ever more frightening casualty figures from the capital. "Yesterday it was Beijing," cried one. "Tomorrow it will be Shanghai's turn." "The debt of BLOOD must be repaid!" Again that character that Simon had noted, drawn once again in brilliant red ink. Strike! strike! strike! Strike back against the tyrants of Beijing, strike back against the Fascists in the capital, a triple strike, a *san ba*, workers, students, shopkeepers, bringing the city to its knees, forcing the government to listen to the cry of the people. But stores were open, people moved in and out of them, buying things, looking at the displays in the windows. Children, urged gently on by their parents toward unknown destinations, licked sticks of orange ice under the afternoon sun, an occasional young couple strolled by hand in hand, stopping from time to time to listen to the students still manning the roadblocks. With the cars and the trucks vanished, it was as if the whole city had been turned into a giant pedestrian mall, and Matthew almost expected to see joggers, or Frisbee players, or kite flyers, as one did on Memorial Drive in Cambridge, closed to traffic on a summer Sunday afternoon.

Again he remembered Simon, writing in his journal of his wonder at the stolidity of the Chinese crowds as the headsman had made his rounds in that winter of 1927, at their apparently unemotional acceptance of cruelty, of disaster. Were they as unconcerned as they looked? Didn't they care about what was happening? Will we ever understand this country, Simon had wondered. And generations of Chinese intellectuals and political leaders in the twentieth century—Sun Yat-sen, the writer Lu Hsün, and others since then—had castigated their fellow countrymen for their unfeeling acceptance of their lot, their inability to understand the needs of the nation, the needs of society, for their seeming unwillingness to raise their eyes and look beyond the concerns of family, clan, and village. Yet there was another side as well: look at the young men and women who had taken to the streets of Shanghai in Simon's day, protesting against their country's shame and humiliation. It was they who had tried to make a revolution so many years before, and it was their descendants who had built the great democracy movement this spring of 1989.

A note from Hilding awaited him at the hotel. "No news yet from Beijing. Come to see me when you have time, and perhaps by then we will know something." Dinner was a lonely affair again, but he had been fortunate enough to get the last copy of the *South China Morning Post* at the hotel bookstore. Spread over the front page were pictures of the massacre, reports of thousands of dead and injured, and the stories spoke darkly of the prospect of outbreaks in other cities: Nanking, Hankow, and Shanghai, where the army was said to be poised on the outskirts, waiting for orders to move in and break the strike, should it get worse.

At ten, figuring it would be seven in the morning on the West

Coast, he tried to call Laura. No luck; the circuits were jammed, and the operator made no predictions about when he might be successful. He fought down his disappointment; he'd wanted desperately to talk to her, to hear her voice. And perhaps to find out from her more than he'd already learned. Despite the city's apparent calmness, the American news broadcast he'd seen that evening had renewed his worries. There had been pictures of the crowds of foreigners at the Beijing airport, waiting for flights to take them out: tourists, students, business families, embassy dependents, American, German, British, Australian. Here in Shanghai, the consulate had still not told Americans to leave, but was warning them to check in every day for the latest advisory. And if they were told to leave, Matthew had asked that morning, how would they get out? Vague suggestions were made of special flights; otherwise you were on your own. But every plane from here to Hong Kong was solidly booked for the next two weeks. And there was always the problem of getting to the airport; that afternoon he'd heard that those roads too had been blocked. Better to wait and see what happened.

That spring, he had still seen a good deal of Laura. There had been occasional earnest lunches on the days she came to Atherton, or occasional walks in the countryside, where patches of dirty snow lay melting under a sun that now began to have some real warmth to it, and the first green shoots were beginning to spring from the dark branches of the maples. Sometimes they met in Cambridge; Matthew would drive down on a Friday or Saturday to meet her on her home ground, and they'd have dinner, go to a movie, perhaps, or to a jazz club, or (for their musical tastes were eclectic) to hear a quartet in Jordan Hall.

Yet their relationship remained obscure and ambiguous and Matthew was never quite sure what the next step would be, of what might happen, of how the story would end, if Laura were to be more forthcoming. Sooner or later there'd have to be a resolution, but this was something he felt rather than consciously realized; trained into a mode of thought that encouraged a rational and ordered intellectualizing of the problems and possibilities that he met in his research, he was almost totally incapable of using that same talent to try to understand his own position.

By this time Laura had the end of her dissertation in sight, or almost in sight. Her grant application to the Sansom Foundation in Chicago had, somewhat to her surprise, been accepted, and she was now planning to spend most of the summer ensconced in the manorial splendor of the Huntington Library in Pasadena, working her way through literary manuscripts. "We can meet there when you get through in China," she'd said, and he'd already changed his ticket so that it would take him back through Los Angeles rather than Seattle. In the meantime, he taught his last classes, read his term papers, made up exams, and watched, almost without noting them, the indications of spring in the college landscape. There, the temperatures, rising into the seventies for the first time since October, brought the trees into bud, and worked a change among the students as well, so that winter's uniform cocoons of down parkas and characterless jeans gave way to shorts and T-shirts, while limbs that had been unseen for months now emerged, long and browned by the sun of a spring vacation spent in Bermuda or the Florida Keys. But whatever stirrings such visions might bring on, at Atherton Matthew's choices were limited, even if he'd wanted to exercise them, for most of his colleagues among the younger faculty were either married or otherwise engaged, and the sight of them together simply aroused in him a kind of wistful envy and revived, as summer drew nearer, a longing for something he had known a year earlier.

The loneliness grew on him as spring climbed into the skies, as the farmlands around Atherton turned from winter dun to the green of new life. Guides for gardeners sprouted in the window of the local bookstore, and sleekly expensive Italian racing bicycles replaced sleekly expensive French skis in the display of the Sporthaus, a downtown store catering to the high-tech athletic tastes of the Atherton students. Meanwhile, on the other side of town, away from the college and its visitors, black and red snowmobiles from Quebec and Japan gave way to aluminum and fiberglass motorboats hunched on the trailers that littered the parking lot at Johnson's Watersports.

For Chinese poets, late spring is the saddest time of year because of the very evanescence of a beauty that will so soon give way to the flat and dangerous heat of summer. As the time for his departure drew closer, Matthew realized that, excited as he was at the prospect of returning to China, particularly when an enormous wave of hope was sweeping the country, there was a side of him that did not want to go, that wanted to stay in Atherton to see the glory of a New England summer rather than spending it in the dusty streets of Shanghai.

And then, one day in May, his hopes came alive again.

He had been sitting in his study, ten days before leaving for China, trying to keep his mind fixed on the pile of blue examination books before him. He hated grading, was bored by the repetitious essays, bored by seeing his own ideas handed back to him with no criticism, no imagination. But he had no choice; they had to be finished. Otherwise the dean would be on his neck, and even though he might be nine thousand miles away across the Pacific, there'd be no escape. Fortunately, the weather that day was conducive to work. Outside it was drizzling softly, and the gray-green light of a wet spring afternoon filled the room.

There was a knock on his door, and when he opened it, Laura stood there, her arms full of purple and white lilacs, their smell filling the hall. "Hello, Matt," she said, shaking the raindrops from her hair, reminding him for a moment of an affectionate puppy come in from the wet. "I hope you don't mind my barging in on you like this, but the thought of you cooped up alone with your exams was more than I could bear. So I've brought these to cheer up your room. Watch out, they're wet." She brushed past him, carrying the flowers into the kitchen, and emerged a few minutes later, having arranged them in a vase, the only one he owned. "I won't stay long, I promise. But they look wonderful, don't they? I stole them from the bushes in back of Cushing." Cushing was the main administration building. "They've got so many, they'll never miss them."

"Stay as long as you like, Laura." He was unreasonably glad to see her. She looked almost like a figure in a pre-Raphaelite painting, he thought, just come in from an English garden in the rain. It had been one of her teaching days, and she was dressed for the classroom—a pale gray skirt, rather long, with a high-necked blouse—a uniform designed, she'd told him earlier, to keep the attentions of her male students fixed on the Great Poets of the Nineteenth Century and nowhere else. Matthew was by no means certain she'd achieved this goal.

"Are your exams as bad as all that? I still haven't begun mine yet."

"Fifty-seven essays on the victimization of women in Chinese society—footbinding, arranged marriages, the dowager empress, and Madame Mao. If I see the word 'patriarchy' again, I'll have a fit. But that's not what I meant. Sit down and stay awhile. Let me finish this one paper, and then I'll be sociable."

He went back to his desk, and Laura sat down, stretching her long legs out on his couch and picking up a book from the table. Matthew hurried through the rest of the exam, wrote some notes on it—"some good ideas; try to organize your arguments better; pay more attention to chronology"—and threw it on the pile of those he'd finished.

"What'd you give it?"

"B minus. The usual for honest effort and little or no imagination. But at least no mention of patriarchy."

"Man or woman?"

"Man."

"That explains it. He probably doesn't know the word exists. Or what it means."

"You'd be surprised how quickly even the men catch on. They know it's a good word to throw in, might make a difference of a grade point or so. Whether they understand it is something else again. After all, I'm in no position to judge."

They sparred with a mild and friendly acerbity, renewing an old skirmish over the claims of feminism and scholarship. Matthew had accused Laura of playing a double game—posing as a feminist in the den of males that constituted her department, yet refusing to succumb to the gentle but relentless pressure from the inhabitants of the women's studies program to fall in with their own views. "I don't want to play those games," she'd told him earlier that year. "They're trying to recruit me." In self-defense, she had begun to lace her speech with words from a vocabulary drawn from Derrida and Barthes and Lacan and Kristeva ("men, all of them except for one—women are too sensible to fall for that") thus surrounding herself with an impregnable armor of poststructuralism designed to frustrate any assaults on what she called her scholarly virginity. With Matthew, of course, she was more apt to press the claims of her sex. But at least she did it in plain English rather than in the language of literary theory, for which he was grateful.

Now she lay on the sofa, her head against his shoulder, looking abstractedly at a book of photographs of the French country-

side. "How I'd love to go there. Look at that, look at the light."
It was a picture of a Provençal hill town: ochre walls, tiled roofs,
olive trees on the slopes below the houses, a study in greens and
browns and grays and blues, carefully arranged by the photogra-
pher to evoke memories of Cezanne.

"Then let's go."

"We can't. You're going to China, and I'm going to California." Another photograph of a village in Savoy on a summer
morning, the snows of the Aiguille d'Argentière hanging, almost
as if disembodied, in the background. At least she hadn't said:
that's the trip we did last year, the time for that sort of thing has
passed.

"Some other time, I mean." Her hair, still damp, was like a
child's: it had a clean smell, the smell of spring, that she had
brought with her into the room. He turned her face up to his,
took off her glasses, laying them on the table, and kissed her: a
tentative kiss, the sort of kiss that's meant to test the waters.
But she returned it with more feeling than he'd expected.
Then drew back, and looked at him with her serious gray questioning eyes. He tried again, less tentatively now, and this time
there was a real passion in her response. She put her book back
on the table, then reached up and pulled his head down, nuzzling the back of his neck with her lips, her hands stroking his
back. He looked up, took her face again between his hands,
feeling the smoothness of her cheeks. Her eyes were closed
now, and when they kissed, he felt her lips moving under his,
felt her body stretched, taut against his, her arms pulling him
more and more tightly toward her, back, back to last summer,
to memories of Italy, of the Alps, now flooding his mind. This
is what it had been like then.

"Laura."

"Mmm." Her eyes stayed shut, her cheek against his.

"*Buona fortuna.*" It was what they had said to each other a
year ago, wishing each other luck when they had first begun to
realize how deeply into unknown territory their voyage of discovery was carrying them.

She laughed softly, remembering, and pulled his face down
against hers. "*Buona fortuna,* Matt." He kissed her eyelids, her
ears, under the smooth dark hair, the hair that smelled of spring;
then back to her open lips. This time their tongues touched, a
touch of exploration, at first tentative, then more confident.

Then, suddenly, she detached herself. "Stay there. I'm going to make you some iced tea."

"It's not hot enough for iced tea." He didn't want iced tea, or anything else. He wanted her back.

"It's quite hot enough for me. Do as you're told, and stay there." He heard her busying herself in the kitchen: the chinking of glasses, the kettle whistling, the shiver of ice wrenched loose from the tray. "Damn!" A glass shattered on the floor. "Don't worry, it's not one of your good ones." But he didn't have any good ones. A few minutes later she was out, triumphant, with two cold glasses on a tray.

What came next surprised even him. "Laura," he said.

"Yes?" Again, gray eyes watched him intently.

"Laura, I want you to marry me. Will you?" He hadn't meant it to sound that way, hadn't meant it to come out at all, at least not then, not without a proper buildup, a buildup of more than a few kisses and fitful embraces on a warm wet spring afternoon. But once the words were out, he was relieved to have said at last what had been in his mind so long. And surely in hers too.

She sat silently, looking at him, giving him no answer.

"Well, will you?"

"Will I what?"

"Will you marry me? Laura, this time I really mean it. I've meant it all spring, but—well, somehow it never seemed the right time to ask."

She got up and walked over to the window, looking out. Rain dripped from the trees; homebound afternoon traffic swished by on the road.

"No. At least I don't think so. At least not right now." But now she was smiling as she looked at him. The sort of smile that says: let's not shatter the friendliness of the afternoon by such questions.

But he wanted an answer.

"What's that supposed to mean? Is that yes or no?"

"Sorry, Matt. I don't know. It's the best I can do. Now, I mean."

"No now but maybe yes later?"

"No now, and I don't know what later. I just don't know."

"Why's it no now?"

But she wasn't going to give him a straight answer. Instead, she teased him, as if she wanted to bring him back to the afternoon's earlier lightness, before he had asked his question. "Sir, you have given me the greatest compliment a gentleman can pay—"

"Dammit, Laura, stop sounding like one of your Victorian novels. Why not?"

But she wouldn't be serious. "My mother told me never to marry a man who didn't have tenure. Untrustworthy, she told me."

"So you'll go fall for some gray-haired professor in his second adolescence? Like Steve Richardson?"

She laughed. "I think I'm too old for him. He seems to like them out of the cradle."

"Anyway, suppose I get tenure."

"That won't be for another three years at least."

"Maybe you'll get it before me. What then? What did your mother say about that?"

Again she deflected his question. "She said never marry a man who hasn't published his first book."

"What is this, some sort of professional hoop I have to jump through? Just to get married? And if I do publish it, what then? Is she going to say: 'Wait till the reviews come out'? Come on, Laura, I'm serious. Why won't you marry me?"

"Why won't I marry you right away?" Now she turned serious. "I think what Mother means is that marriage is a kind of tenure itself. And I'm not sure you're ready for it."

"What does that mean? I think I'm ready for it. I've been thinking about it all spring." He had; he just hadn't meant to tell her quite so soon. "Maybe you're the one who's not ready."

"Maybe I have to be ready to know that you're ready. I have to know that this isn't just another offer to play house for a while." She must have seen the hurt on his face, and looked unhappy herself. "Oh, Matt, I'm sorry, I don't know what I mean. I just know I can't give you a straight answer now."

At least it wasn't an outright rejection. So he couldn't be angry. And like her, wanting to salvage the remains of the afternoon, he now took up her earlier teasing.

"Wait till you wind up teaching English lit in some little cow college in South Dakota." It was the nightmare of every graduate student in Cambridge, almost as bad as not getting a job at all: going to a place where Lévi-Strauss meant only blue jeans, a place with no other deconstructionists on the faculty, a place where they still taught *The Tempest* (if they taught it at all) as a metaphor for the artistic imagination rather than as an allegory of imperialism and patriarchy.

"If I get a job at Cow State U., will you come out and join me? In Yankton? Or Mitchell?" He'd actually been through Mitchell once; that's where they had the Corn Palace.

Now it was his turn to dodge the question. "I'll finish my book and get tenure before that. Then your mother will be satisfied. And we'll have wasted several years. So if we're going to do it anyway, why not do it now? Or soon, at least?"

He saw that she was looking sad, and it was his turn now to make a joke out of it, to try to cheer her up. He thought for a moment. "Listen. Suppose I find out what happened to Great-uncle Simon. Would your mother let me marry you then?"

Laura laughed, and brightened. "All right, Matt. You find out what happened to Great-uncle Simon. And then at least I'll let you ask me again."

"Promise?"

"Promise." Again she looked at him intently. "Mother always said: if you can't marry a historian, at least marry a detective."

She kissed him again, long and lovingly. And the afternoon was saved.

All that had been only two weeks ago. Yet today it seemed a different world to him, and again there came the strange sense that he and Laura, in all their passages together, had been characters out of another time and another place, peopling not this world, with its gritty realism, but the imaginative world of the historian, the fictional world of the novelist. Laura in Italy, Laura on a winter evening, her face glowing in the firelight, Laura surprising him with spring flowers, damp with rain. He forced himself to think of a more prosaic Laura, a quotidian Laura: Laura when she was tired, pale, irritable, coming down with the winter flu, Laura when she was annoyed with him, Laura who was insecure, worried beyond reason by her work, her future, her life's direction. But his memory, even of such episodes, subverted all his attempts; her very presence had transformed these occasions, had showed him, as if for the first time, something denied to others. It was the self-absorption of the lover, of course, but it was also like looking at a painting of something perfectly ordinary—a landscape, a vase of flowers, a street in the rain, a woman bathing—transformed by an artist—

Bonnard, say, or Monet. To one viewer, it might seem no more than an exercise in arranging light, color, and form. But to another, it became an epiphany, an occasion of grace, and for the person who could see it that way, never would such simplicity seem ordinary again.

CHAPTER TEN

Tuesday, June 6, 1989

Faint as they were, the noises drifting in the open window from outside awoke Matthew at five-thirty in the morning. Huaihai Road, only a block away, was hidden from view by an old apartment house right outside his window. He lay there, listening to them, trying to make out if they sounded at all unusual. What were the normal sounds of Shanghai before dawn, anyway? What were the normal sounds of a city undergoing an abnormal strike? Would he know the sounds of danger if he heard them? What did a column of tanks sound like? He imagined a grinding roar, like a platoon of trucks hauling gravel up a steep hill—then gunfire, explosions, tracer bullets, screams. The television had showed army trucks hit by gasoline bombs, going up like torches, terrified soldiers leaping out into the midst of enraged crowds. Other images came rushing back into his mind as sleep vanished: the Goddess of Liberty at night, slowly tumbling over, disintegrating as she hit the ground, revealing behind her the threateningly benevolent face of Chairman Mao on the Tiananmen; people rushing for safety, diving into the alleys, behind walls, as the tanks and armored cars moved down Chang'an Boulevard into the square. Meanwhile, out at the airport east of the city, foreigners gathered, some of them wearing black armbands, tired children fell asleep on piles of cartons and suitcases, all of them waiting for space on flights that would carry them out of China.

So it must have been in the winter of 1927, as the Nationalist armies had driven into the Yangtze valley, moving in on Shanghai. Simon had seen the foreign steamers coming downriver in those days, loaded to the gunwales with refugees leaving the open ports, the up-country mission stations, thousands of them crowding into the safety of a Shanghai now guarded by British troops. Some had stayed there, waiting for the danger to blow over, eager to get back to the work of saving souls or garnering profits for Asiatic Petroleum or British-American Tobacco. But others, finding no room in Shanghai, had gone on to wait in Japan or Manila, or sailed back home to an uncertain future in England or America.

Simon's journal conveyed a vivid sense of the city's foreign colony in those weeks, its combination of pride and fear, its vision of itself as an oasis of civilization in a country overtaken by war, where Chinese hatred of foreigners now had become intertwined with the specter of red revolution. Men had left their offices, flocking to join the Shanghai Volunteer Corps; they had hummed songs like "Mademoiselle from Armentières" and "Tipperary," while their speech had reverted to the khaki idioms of France and Flanders ten years earlier. Pillboxes, barbed-wire emplacements, machine-gun nests, had appeared on the boundaries between the foreign settlements and the Chinese city, where sandy-haired young men from the English counties joined Sikhs and Gurkhas in a display of imperial unity. Every day, more foreign men of war had steamed slowly up the river, falling in line behind those already riding at anchor off the Bund: the gray cruisers and destroyers of the British and American China squadrons, ships like *Pittsburgh* and *Warspite* and *Defiance*, and the black fortress of the French *Jules Michelet*. The streets had been filled with British troops in khaki, officers jostling taipans at the Long Bar of the Shanghai Club, or in the public rooms of the Majestic, the Palace, and the Astor. On Sundays, they had crowded into the pews of Holy Trinity Cathedral and the Community Church, to listen to earnest chaplains remind them of the high duties imposed by the burdens of empire. Women, forgetting the worldly delights of Shanghai society, had thrown themselves unselfishly into the tasks of the home front, setting up canteens and organizing off-duty entertainments for these men suddenly set down on the rain-swept wharves of a winter-cold Shanghai, ten thousand miles from home.

Through this world Simon Larsen had moved. Curious that only John Ransom had earlier been astute enough to blow his cover, thought Matthew, and curious too that none of Ransom's colleagues appeared to have believed him, apparently preferring to think that he was simply angered by Simon's relationship with his niece. But whatever their earlier misgivings about his political views, the men who now found themselves responsible for the city's defense had apparently opened their doors to him. Not simply because they had believed in his conversion, but because, like Ransom himself, they had sensed that through Simon's writing they might make their little mark on history, on the ways in which the generations of the future would remember them.

And then Simon had disappeared. Right on the eve of Chiang Kai-shek's great purge. Why? Three months ago, when he had first read rapidly through the papers Laura had given him, Matthew hadn't thought much about the question. Simon living interested him as a window on the Shanghai that he, the historian, wanted to re-create; Simon vanished, or Simon dead, had seemed of interest primarily because his disappearance might reveal yet another facet of that city of the past. Yet in the last few days he'd found himself more and more neglecting the work he was supposed to be there for, giving his mind and his energies instead to Simon's doings almost seventy years ago. The horrifying reports from Beijing, and Shanghai's reaction to them, only reinforced a sense of history's immediacy, as if Matthew himself were witness to another act of that same drama Simon had seen, played out in this same city that looked so much like a stage set of the past.

So too Matthew had originally passed over the relationship between Simon and Emily. Simon's affairs were his own business, interesting to the historian only for the illumination they shed on a particular society. Yet it had been a relationship, he now had to admit, that was a bit more complex than he'd first imagined. Emily's warning that her uncle was out to get Simon—there could be many reasons for that. But what of Emily herself? What could explain the change in her behavior that had puzzled Simon that spring?

Tired and worried, she had fallen ill from the strain of her double life. Was that why she'd decided to leave Shanghai, to go back to her family? Or was there another explanation? Suddenly the light dawned. Emily Ransom was pregnant! Of course. It hadn't occurred to him when he was reading the documents the previous day. Any more than it seemed to have occurred to Simon, preoccupied as he was with the problems and dangers of his own position. The phrase from Simon's journal—when was it, early February? mid-February?—came back to him. "The cold, raw afternoon, which suddenly became spring for the two of us." That had to be it. Didn't it? The new look he had noticed in Emily's face, her eyes. And her recurrent bouts of illness, the ways in which the atmosphere of Shanghai had begun to repel her. Matthew was a bit uncertain about such matters, but wasn't Emily betraying the classic symptoms of morning sickness? So she was going home to have the baby. Even though she could have gotten rid of it. In Shanghai, though abortion was illegal, it had been—like anything else in that city—easily enough available. But obviously she'd wanted the baby—one of her wishes come true, she'd told Simon. Then why hadn't she told him she was carrying his child? Because she was too proud to seem to be trapping him into marriage that way? More likely, she was going to tell him when they next met. In that meeting that had never taken place, because Simon had vanished before they could see each other again.

Of course it all made sense. Or seemed to, anyway. What had happened to her? How had she told her family? What had happened to her child, Simon's child? Emily would be well into her eighties if she were still alive. And her child would be sixty-two. Somewhere back in America, Laura might have an aging and unknown cousin, perhaps still walking the streets of Baltimore, and living in one of those redbrick houses with the white stone steps that are everywhere in the city. She'd be surprised when she found that out.

He pulled himself back from these speculations. They were nothing but guesses, and in any case, Emily's fate was irrelevant to the book he was supposed to be writing. As indeed Simon's was. Wasn't it? Matthew was far too modern and sophisticated a scholar to believe that such accidental happenings, such accidental relationships between particular men and women, impinge on the course of history—at least the kind of history he was writing—and he had been carefully taught to scorn the kinds of popular treatments of the past that found room for such affairs. Nonetheless, despite the discipline drummed into him by countless professors, he had gradually found himself wanting to know more about Simon, about the way he lived, and why he had vanished. After all, as he had confessed to Laura, he read detective stories, and what's more, read them with an unashamedly clear conscience, feeling no need to apologize for such tastes. His scholar's mind (so he told himself) rejoiced in the ways that Lord Peter Wimsey or Philip Marlowe or Travis McGee assembled all those little scraps of evidence, those guarded statements, true and false, those suggestive silences and unspoken hints, organizing them finally into beautifully logical solutions. But it was more than the combination of adventure and intellectual exercise that he liked about such books. The attraction of the classical detective story, he had read somewhere (probably in one of Laura's lit crit studies), lies in its ability to picture a world in which, if the most appalling crime—the taking of a human life—is possible, the detective, by solving the mystery, nonetheless manages to reassure the reader that it is also a world in which such a crime will be found out and punished. The very violence that justifies the detective story's existence in the first place is itself an aberration, for the world in which the story plays itself out is ultimately proved to be a moral world, a world not only of justice but also one of logic, rationality, and order.

History itself had once described such a logical and moral world, a world explicable through the systems discovered by a Marx, an Acton, or a Toynbee. Today, however, historians devoted themselves to uncovering, piece by piece, and bit by bit, a very different sort of world, a world of uncertainty and indeterminacy, a world of irrationality and injustice (Hitler, Stalin, Idi Amin), and a world in which theory, rationality, even logic itself, had all been reduced to the level of ideology. No wonder some of them turned to detective stories as an escape from the appalling abyss they had revealed. Even to that fictional world, however, change had come: the beautiful logic of Conan Doyle's Victorian London and Agatha Christie's village parsonages had given way to the blurred gray country without maps uncovered by Graham Greene and John le Carré.

So it was that now, in the city where Simon had lived, where the voices of the past still spoke so strongly to those who would listen, his words had come to breathe an actuality, an immediacy, that Matthew had missed when he'd first read them, three months before and ten thousand miles away. Simon was no longer a ghost, but like that city in which he had lived, those people among whom he had moved, he was beginning to put on a humanity. No longer simply the disembodied recorder of another time, whose scattered writings the historian might incorporate in his work when they seemed useful, discarding and forgetting those that seemed irrelevant and beside the point, he had assumed a flesh-and-blood reality that had taken Matthew by surprise. And his love for Emily—particularly since, Matthew had now convinced himself, she was going to bear Simon a child—began to seem not something to be understood simply intellectually, or as a reflection of a particular social code, but as an outpouring of genuine human passion, desperately expressed against a background of danger and uncertainty.

So too the question of Simon's disappearance, which earlier had seemed a harmless diversion, something with no more reality than an episode in a crime novel, something to joke about with Laura—even though the joke had taken on a certain edge—was now becoming the focus of Matthew's attention. Simon's descent into the shadows, his willingness to take on the role of secret agent, his willingness, against his better judgment, to carry Emily on that voyage with him, meant that he had put himself in the way of danger. And the danger, whatever it was, had reached him in the end. Why? If the foreign police had discovered what he was doing, they might have arrested him, tried him, deported him perhaps. But none of that had happened. Either there had been an accident or someone had wanted Simon out of the way permanently. Perhaps when he had had a chance to read further in the papers Zhao Shanling had given him, he would discover a motive beginning to emerge, like the head of a plant that he couldn't at first identify poking its way through the drab brown earth of Shanghai early in that spring of 1927.

By six o'clock he'd given up the idea of more sleep. As the sky lightened, his worries subsided. Obviously the tanks were not grinding into Shanghai that morning, and the noises he'd heard were no more than those of the city waking up. He turned on the television set and got back into bed to watch it. Rather than a news program, at this hour the screen showed a series of unedited film clips, presumably being sent back by satellite to the New York studios for use in later broadcasts. There again were the families crowding Beijing's airport, telling reporters of their horror at what they'd seen; shots of infantrymen, on foot, in armored cars, firing at random at passersby on some of the capital's main thoroughfares; the debris, the carcasses of buses and trucks, and the smoke rising from the fires still smoldering in the middle of the square.

And then Matthew first saw the sequence that would soon provide the most famous image of those bloody days. A man, holding something—a shopping bag? a briefcase?—ran into the middle of one of those broad boulevards that intersect the city, right in front of an approaching line of tanks. With a courage scarcely believable, he raised his free hand above his head—in ordinary times, you'd have thought him a policeman directing traffic—in an appeal, a prayer, a supplication, to that murderous armored column to stop. And almost miraculously, it worked. Like a dog obeying its master's command to sit, the lead tank, seven tons of reinforced steel, its ugly cannon impaling the air around it, came to a halt, literally at the man's feet. The hatch opened, and the commander appeared—to threaten? to talk to? to plead with?—this solitary figure dressed in his white shirt, carrying his briefcase, looking like a man going to work on an ordinary summer day. Then suddenly it was over; three or four figures, civilians, friends of the man who had acted out this drama of lonely heroism, came running from the sidewalk, seized him, and hustled him away to safety before the startled tank crews could act.

Later that morning, Matthew would see the scene replayed, edited into the morning news from America, picked up immediately by the networks as a symbol of the movement's courage. The same broadcast carried the State Department's announcement that it was evacuating dependents from the embassy, and advising people against travel to China. At the Cathay Pacific office in the hotel, he stood in line for an hour, only to learn that there were no seats on outbound flights for another fortnight. He took the first he could get, and left his name on the waiting list for something earlier. No matter what happened, it might be well to have this insurance.

At ten o'clock, just as he was getting ready to leave his room, the phone rang. He picked it up.

"Matt, it's me. Laura."

"Laura—Laura, hi." It was wonderful to hear her voice. She'd been so much in his mind for the last week—not on it, but in it, living in the room that was his memory, moving about into whatever part of his brain was musing about the future, so that she'd always been with him, even while he was occupied with other thoughts, his work, his worries. A great wave of pleasure washed over him, pleasure at this thin electrical connection that brought her to him, pleasure too that she was concerned enough to have called him again. But hearing her voice left him tongue-tied, unable to think of all those things that he'd been storing up, that he wanted to say to her. Or was she about to tell him some even worse news that he'd not yet heard?

"I tried to call you last night. But I couldn't get through. All the lines were busy. How's everything in California?"

She ignored the utterly inane question. "Yes—well, it's taken me an hour to get through this evening. Matt—I hear they're telling people to leave China. Is that right?" He hadn't heard that; the consulate, when he'd phoned that morning, was still warning people not to go out if they could help it, and to stay away from crowds. "How do things look there?"

"I haven't been out yet today. But there hasn't been any real trouble yet. No tanks in the streets, no sign of the army. Things seemed pretty calm yesterday—some demonstrations, some processions. And all the streets are blocked, so there's no way to get around except on foot. Unless you have a bicycle, which I don't."

"Are you coming home?"

"I can't get a flight out of here for several days." That sounded better than two weeks. "And I don't want to take the train and have it go on strike halfway between here and Canton." Silence. "Laura? Are you still there?"

"Several days? Matt, I'm worried. I don't want anything to happen to you."

"It won't, I promise. I'm not brave, and I'm not stupid either."

"There's a rumor that some foreigners were hurt—maybe even killed. Maybe it wasn't Beijing, maybe somewhere else." He was startled; hadn't heard that.

"I don't think so, I think the consulate would have told us." Silence again. "Look, Laura, I promise: if they tell us to get out, I'll go."

"Call me, Matt. Let me know what you're doing." She gave him her number again.

"I'll try. There's nine hours difference between here and the coast, remember."

"Anytime," she said. "Day or night. Don't worry about waking me. I'll be here."

Outside, the streets remained blocked by the abandoned buses, great dirty hulks sitting low on their flattened tires across the intersections, while a large yellow bulldozer squatted in the middle of Ruijin Road. On windows, on walls, on telephone poles, the protesters had plastered photocopies of the front pages of the Chinese papers from Hong Kong. More cartoons and caricatures were there with them: Li Peng holding a bloody butcher's knife, Li Peng and Yang Shangkun with pigs' snouts, in Nazi uniforms, an aged Deng Xiaoping gambling at cards while tanks ran over harmless students in the background.

But there were no processions today, at least in this part of the city, and despite all the posters calling for a strike to bring the government to its knees, the life of the streets seemed almost back to normal. Except, of course, for the continuing uncanny silence, the absence of buses and trucks, the streets still taken over by pedestrians and bicyclists. And by now, even that respite from the usual racket of traffic had begun to take on something of the quality of a strange, almost frightening holiday from normal existence, as if the city had been unplugged from the machines that fed it and kept its heart beating, and might soon expire.

At the institute the staff were holding a meeting, no doubt to discuss the municipal government's latest proclamation. Matthew had seen copies in large black characters posted near the Bund. *Shanghai buneng luan!* "Shanghai must not fall into turmoil!" and it called on all citizens to keep calm and to maintain order in the face of the counterrevolutionary disturbances. Nothing was said of martial law, of calling in the army. Zhao Shanling had a guarded praise for Shanghai's mayor. "Zhu Rongji—he's not like his predecessor, Jiang Zemin. Jiang's a weak man, so he orders people about, won't allow any criticism. He's up in Beijing now. But Mayor Zhu is a better politician. So now he is appealing to the people of Shanghai. 'Do you want to protest?' he asks them. 'Then go protest. But as long as the road-blocks are there, the trucks and buses can't get through, there will be no food, no jobs, no way of getting to work. So decide if you want to protest. Or whether you'd sooner keep your job and get paid and eat.' "

"What's going to happen?"

"Shanghai people are very pragmatic. Especially since the Cultural Revolution." Shanghai had been chaotic back then, taken over by the radicals; no one wanted those days to return, Zhao seemed to suggest. "I think they would prefer to eat. Now they're just *faxie qing'gan*, blowing off steam."

Matthew found it hard to work that morning. Like Alice's looking glass, his documents invited him to step back into another world, the world of 1927, Simon's world, the world of revolution, and he tried to accept that invitation. But his own world, the world outside the institute's windows, was too compelling. Matthew was no coward, but, as he'd told Laura, neither was he foolish. He had no desire to find himself on the sidewalk the day the army decided to shoot its way up Yan'an Road or Huaihai Road; what he'd seen on television from Beijing had already made that decision for him. Yet reassured by the comparative placidity of Shanghai's streets that morning, so at variance with the terrifying pictures from the square, he had no desire to leave China unless he had to. Here was history in the making, after all, something that he was seeing take place before him, and a history, moreover, that bore an uncanny resemblance to the world that he was studying. The demonstrations: students marching, proclaiming the nation in peril, the readiness of young patriots to sacrifice themselves to save their country, a faith in the final victory of justice. The strike itself: the silence that had fallen over the city two days ago, like the silence Simon described just before the start of the great insurrection of 1927. The sense must have been the same then: an unreal hush, bringing with it a feeling not so much of peace as of anticipation, an oscillation between excitement and fear. The posters of protest: their large black characters, hastily scrawled on sheets of white paper, hanging on walls, on lampposts, denouncing the killings. The character that screamed BLOOD! written in brilliant red ink. The cartoons of helpless men and women crushed by their tyrannical rulers. Simon himself had seen signs that were practically the same, put up on the same walls of the same buildings in this city that had changed so little in half a century. Then and now, such pictures called up a long history of subservience by China's voiceless millions to their rulers: emperors, warlords, foreign imperialists. Then, the Communist Party had called on Chinese to rise, to change once and for all the system that for centuries had enslaved them. The system that had put the peasant at the mercy of the landlord and the money lender, that had allowed foreign imperialism to profit from China's wretchedness and poverty, the system that denied women any voice in their destinies, condemning them to lives of exploitation and despair, and driving them to suicide.

But today that same Party had joined the long procession of rulers, of emperors, landlords, imperialists, and generals, dim figures marching back into the mists of history and legend. Except that today the Party pretended to speak for the very people whose lives it now controlled, and over whom it was determined to maintain its mastery. To the age-old problem of domination was joined a particularly modern form of hypocrisy. Lu Hsün, thought Matthew, recalling that sardonic observer of Chinese weakness and self-deception, where are you now when we need you?

And the quietness of the crowds, thought Matthew as he walked home early that afternoon after the institute had shut for the day, men and women going about the ordinary business of life, drifting slowly along the crowded streets, unprotesting, uncomplaining, while events were being played out that might change their lives. Why don't they show their emotions, Simon had asked. Is it fear, is it self-control, is it self-absorption? Why can't I see what they are thinking?

Will we ever understand this country?

Matthew was back in his hotel in mid-afternoon when the phone rang. It was the desk this time.

"*You ren lai zhao nin.* There's someone here to see you."

"*Shei a?* Who is it?"

"His name's Wei. Wei Daoming. Shall I send him up?"

"Yes, please do." Matthew wondered what the old policeman's grandson could want. Did his grandfather want to meet Matthew again? Had he found something out? Or was Daoming going to make a hurried request for help in going to America to study?

Not a word about America. "My grandfather has found someone that you should see," Daoming told him. "If you're still interested in Lai Shi'an?" He sounded hesitant, as if the events of the past few days might have made such a matter of no importance.

"Yes, of course. I'm still very much interested. It's kind of your grandfather to take the trouble. Who is it?"

"He's a man who knew Lai Shi'an. His name is Chu Hungying."

The world suddenly came to a full stop. Matthew was dazed by what he had heard, completely unable to answer. Simon's Chinese teacher—could it possibly be the same man? He did some rapid arithmetic; if Mr. Chu had been, say, twenty-five at the time, he'd now be in his eighties. Well into his eighties, maybe ninety. "He's quite an old man," Daoming went on. "But my grandfather knows him, and says his memory is good. Do you want to meet him?"

Do I want to meet him! Matthew could scarcely keep the excitement out of his voice. "That's wonderful! Yes, of course I want to meet him. When can we do it?"

"Tonight, if you like. If you have nothing else planned?"

"No, nothing at all." He'd have dropped everything for the chance. "Where can we meet? Would he like to come here?"

"He can't. It's difficult for him to travel, since there are no buses." He said this almost apologetically, as if he expected Matthew to hold him and his grandfather responsible for the strike. "And it's too far for him to walk. He lives several kilometers away, up in Chapei. So he asks if perhaps you could come to see him. Do you know how to ride a bicycle?" Daoming asked this as if he expected rich Americans to have lost the use of their legs. "I can lend you one, and then I can take you to where he lives."

At six-thirty Wei Daoming showed up at the hotel's entrance, balancing two bicycles. "Here, you take mine. I've borrowed a friend's." His own was a Flying Pigeon. China's best, and made in Shanghai. Matthew knew Daoming was trusting him with what must be one of his most prized possessions.

They set off, joining the stream of cyclists up Maoming Road, setting a course that would take them gradually up to the northwestern reaches of the city. Luxurious though it might be by Chinese standards, the bicycle was big and heavy, built for stamina rather than speed or comfort, a thoroughly practical symbol of the new China. In the dusk, they pedaled along streets lined with block after block of the same dun-colored buildings—old western villas with their red-tiled roofs surmounting stucco or half-timbered walls, each one now inhabited by half a dozen families, and newer concrete apartment blocks, all of them decorated by clothes hanging out to dry in the humid air. In the cool of the evening, families sat outside, watching their children run in circles in the darkening streets, playing games, shouting at one another. Some carried bowls of food, spilling rice into their mouths as they ran, demonstrating a facility with chopsticks that Matthew could not help but envy. At one point he almost collided with a man who seemed to be repairing some kind of engine; finding no room on the sidewalk, he had taken it out into the street, where its guts now lay spread out on the pavement. Here, in these back streets away from the city's center, there were no marchers, no posters, no barricades, nothing to suggest that this was anything more than an ordinary evening in late spring.

A bridge took them over the black waters of the Wusong River, the stream that Simon had known as the Soochow Creek, and they passed into the western reaches of Chapei on Guangxin Road. Bumping over the tracks of the railway that led north to Beijing, Matthew could make out some dim figures in the twilight. At first he took them for a track gang still working late in the evening; but then he remembered he'd heard about groups of students who were trying to block the trains running into the city, and wondered if that's what he'd seen.

In Simon's day, when he and Father Duchamp had visited it, much of Chapei had been a slum. Many of the textile mills were here, and many of their workers had lived in tin shacks, or in filthy little houses no better than kennels. Four walls of cheap plaster and a leaking roof for the lucky, flimsy bamboo structures covered with mats for the others. It is still an industrial quarter today, overcrowded, dirty, a wilderness of buildings, old and new, large and small, with none of the broad streets and trees that grace the reaches of the old foreign settlements. By now it was quite dark, and the dim light of an occasional streetlamp did little to help Matthew keep his bearings. Daoming pressed on confidently, however, and finally jerked his bicycle to a sudden stop outside the plain gray box of a concrete apartment building. The doorway was framed with pale blue and white tiles, streaked with dirt. Somebody had made an attempt to bring a sense of individuality, some color to the otherwise unrelieved drabness; but to Matthew it managed only to look like the entrance to a particularly unprepossessing men's room.

Inside, voices rang in the unlit stairwell, and the air smelled of stale cooking, cheap tobacco, drying laundry, and drains. Daoming led him up to an apartment on the third floor. "Not very luxurious, I'm afraid," said Daoming, knocking at the door. "But Shanghai is a poor city." It was the usual statement of the obvious that Matthew had heard from so many others here, said with a note of apology, but at the same time a certain pride. For all its poverty, life in Shanghai—or indeed in any big city—remained the ambition of many who would never realize it. Only westerners who never knew its hardships could still see the life of rural China through the romantic spectacles of Taoism. Or Maoism.

Daoming spoke rapidly to the middle-aged woman who opened the door. "This is Miss Chu," he said, introducing Matthew. "She lives with her father and looks after him." Matthew was conscious of a vague note of embarrassment in his voice; even in the new China, an unmarried woman could be counted in some sense a failure.

The apartment they entered was small, shabby, and very, very tidy. A bare bulb in the ceiling threw an unforgiving light on its plainness—four walls of graying, aged whitewash, a small desk with a collection of books above it, a television set in a brown plastic case. But on the far wall hung a scroll on which had been brushed a sweeping and powerful running calligraphy, a poem that Matthew could not decipher. And next to it, an ink painting: modern, but done in the old style, three men in a pavilion surrounded by pines, cloud-hung mountains rising in the distance behind them, a sudden moment of transcendence in the gray anonymity surrounding it.

Chu Hung-ying rose to meet them. An octogenarian he may have been, but he looked ten years younger, and his eyes were as bright and as black as those of a Chinese child.

"I am glad to meet you, Mr. Walker. My old friend Wei Tiaoyuan has told me about you."

"It's very good of you to see me, Mr. Chu. I hope I'm not troubling you by coming to visit you."

"*Bu keqi, bu keqi,* don't stand on politeness. It is I who should apologize for making you come all this way. Do people still ride bicycles in America? I'm told that everyone there has a car."

Matthew was about to explain that many people rode bicycles for their health. But somehow the picture of Americans at home, got up in their black and yellow Italian cycling shorts, helmeted and T-shirted as if they were entries in the Tour de France, riding their thousand-dollar aluminum alloy machines, seemed out of place in Shanghai, where a Flying Pigeon represented the height of ambition.

"You've been asking about Lai Shi'an," said the old man after the exchange of preliminary courtesies. It was a statement of fact, not a question.

"Yes. I've been reading his diary. About his life in Shanghai. He spoke very highly of you."

"I taught him Chinese. Shanghai dialect too. He was a good student." There was a pause. "Can you speak Shanghainese?"

"No. Only *putonghua*—Mandarin. And even that not very well."

"You speak fluently, Mr. Walker. I can tell." Chinese courtesy is shamelessly flattering; even the simplest sentence uttered by a tourist, phrase book in hand, is enough to bring forth a torrent of unwarranted praise and admiration. But Matthew was proud of his linguistic abilities, perhaps a bit prouder than he deserved to be.

They talked in generalities for some minutes, again observing the conventions of propriety before getting down to business. "Mr. Chu," began Matthew. "I'm trying to find out about Simon Larsen. Particularly what happened to him. I know that he was in Shanghai in the spring of 1927. And then he disappeared. His family never heard from him again. They all assumed that he'd died. But they don't know when or where. Or how."

"Are you related to him?" The bright black eyes looked intently at Matthew.

"No. But a friend of mine who is his"—Matthew had to struggle through the range of complicated Chinese kinship terms, wondering how to find the word for "maternal grandniece," and hoped he got it close enough—"let me see his journal. And because I'm writing a book about Shanghai in those days, I'm curious about him."

"He was writing a book too. But I think he never finished it. He always said he was going to do it—next month, next year. But then always something happened to keep him from finishing it. The May Thirtieth Movement—you know about that?

The massacre in Nanking Road in 1925?" Matthew nodded. "Then came the Northern Expedition, the taking of Shanghai by the revolutionary armies—he would always say that he must see what was going to happen, that the book would not be complete without it."

"I think," said Matthew, "that he also knew that if he finished it, he'd have to leave China. To go home to America, to settle down. And he enjoyed living here. Maybe not finishing the book gave him an excuse to stay. But of course you knew him well, and I didn't."

"I knew him as well as I knew any foreigner. But there was still much that I did not understand about him. In those days we were young. We all thought we knew why foreigners behaved the way they did. Especially here in Shanghai, we thought they came to make money, to enjoy life in a poor country where food was cheap, servants were cheap, and one could get rich quickly. Now that I'm older, I know that human beings—Chinese, foreigners—are not that easy to understand, and the reasons they behave as they do are not always as clear as they once seemed."

"And Lai Shi'an? Why did you think he was here?"

Chu thought for a while. "He loved China. No, that's wrong. I don't think he loved China. But he was fascinated by China, fascinated by the way in which our country was trying to change, to turn herself into a modern nation. He saw it—how would you say it?—as an intellectual problem. And he set himself out to understand it. To understand it himself, and to explain it to others. To his countrymen."

"Like a scholar, you mean?"

"Yes. He would have made a good scholar. That's one of the reasons I liked him. I was educated by the Jesuits at Chendan— you know it? *L'Université l'Aurore*? And before that I had a traditional education in the classics from an old Confucian tutor whom my father hired to train me. Of course in those days I was eager to get away from Confucianism, to show how modern I was, how advanced were my views. And Christianity—back then we thought that Christianity was nothing but another form of foreign imperialism. But I was Chinese enough to respect and admire my teachers. The Confucians and the Christians. They both gave me a training for which I'm grateful. Even if I didn't always use it for purposes they would approve of."

Matthew said nothing. He followed Mr. Chu's look, which was now fixed on the landscape he'd noted when he first came in: the men in the pavilion, the cloud-hung mountains behind. "There are times, you see, when the scholar's life becomes a luxury. Or when the scholar, if he is a real scholar, knows he must act." Now he turned and looked at Matthew. "Lai *hsien-sheng,* Mr. Lai, discovered that."

Matthew waited, expecting him to go on. When he didn't, Matthew asked: "Do you remember when you last saw him?" (Here I go sounding like Hercule Poirot again, he thought. Where were you, Monsieur Chu, on the night of April 12? Can you account for your movements in those early morning hours, when Chiang's police and Chiang's soldiers and Chiang's gangsters smashed their way into the headquarters of the Communists, the labor leaders, the radicals, butchering so many of the men and women who had been their allies, their comrades in the making of a new China?)

"The last time I saw him? Yes, I remember it well. It was on April 14, 1927."

"In the French Concession?"

"Yes, in the French Concession. On the French Bund. At the *Taigu* wharf." *Taigu,* Taikoo, was the Chinese name of Butterfield and Swire, the English shipping company.

"So he left Shanghai that night?"

This time a long pause. "No, Mr. Walker. It was I who left Shanghai that night. On a steamer bound for Amoy and Swatow."

"And you have no idea what happened to him after that?"

"I don't think anything happened to him after that. He was dead, you see."

The memories of the old can wander, can play funny tricks. Was Mr. Chu off in a world of his own making? Was he playing with Matthew? He felt completely at sea. "I don't understand."

"Mr. Walker, I have never told this to anyone before. But I will tell it to you now. Lai Shi'an—Simon Larsen—was a brave man, a friend of China, and he deserves to be remembered. My friend Mr. Wei told me you are writing a book about Shanghai, about what happened in 1927. So make sure you put Lai Shi'an in it." Matthew nodded, unwilling to break the flow of talk. "How much do you know about what he was doing in 1927?"

"Just what I read in his diary. And a bit more that I've found in the records of the Shanghai police, both French and English. I know that you'd introduced him to a man named Chang Shao-shan, and that you'd made a bargain with him: Chang Shao-shan would give him information about the revolution, in return for Larsen's finding out what he could about the intentions of the foreigners."

"Chang Shao-shan. Yes, of course. Do you know who that was?"

Matthew shook his head. "I know it wasn't his real name. But he was obviously someone who knew a lot about politics, and about the general situation here in Shanghai."

"You've heard of him. If you have studied Chinese history. His real name was Chou En-lai. Sometimes he was called Chou Shao-shan. With Lai *hsien-sheng* he called himself Chang. At the time it seemed safer, you see."

Of course, thought Matthew, it all fits. How dumb not to have figured it out. Chou En-lai, who'd been to France and Germany. Chou En-lai, who'd been Chiang Kai-shek's deputy in Canton at the Whampoa Military Academy, training the officers who would lead the new revolutionary army. And Chou En-lai, who had been in charge of forming the armed workers' units for the Shanghai revolution; Chou, who had been one of the main planners of the insurrection, who'd almost been captured by Chiang's police after the April purge, but who'd managed to escape.

"Did Larsen know that?"

Chu shrugged, a very French shrug. "Maybe. I don't know. And if he did, what difference would it have made? Chou En-lai was not a famous man then. No one had heard of him. Except the police, of course."

"So Larsen gave you information about the foreigners. Was it useful to you then?"

"Yes. Very useful. We had to know, you see, what they would do when the Nationalist armies reached Shanghai in March. We had many sources of intelligence, of course, but Larsen helped to persuade us that as long as there were no outright attacks on the foreign settlements, the British would leave us alone. That meant that we could concentrate on our domestic enemies. The warlord armies. And didn't have to worry about the foreigners. Oh, of course, in our propaganda we made it sound as if the imperialists were about to attack us—it was a good way of rousing the people, and a good way also perhaps of keeping the imperialists from making a move."

By now Matthew thought he knew the answer to his next question. "I've been reading some of the Party documents," he said. "At the institute. There are references to a man named Hung. Was that you?"

"Yes," said Chu. "I wasn't a member of the Party committee. But sometimes I would meet with them. We all used single characters for our names. A kind of shorthand."

"But what happened then?" asked Matthew. "After all, Larsen was alive and well in early April."

Chu's daughter came in from the kitchen, carrying three cups of tea on a tray. Giving one to Matthew, she set the other before her father, and said something to him in a low voice. He smiled at her, but shook his head. Then went on.

"I'm coming to that. After the rising, after the revolutionary armies arrived, there was a great deal of strain between the Communists and the Kuomintang, at least Chiang Kai-shek's branch of the Kuomintang. You know that if you have read about the history of this period." Matthew nodded again. "We all knew that Chiang was getting ready to move against the Communists. But we didn't know whether he had any help from the foreigners. Larsen learned about certain meetings—meetings between foreign authorities, foreign policemen, and Chiang Kai-shek's agents."

"And Tu Yüeh-sheng?" asked Matthew. "The gangster?"

"I see you know a lot about all this, Mr. Walker. And, of course, with Tu Yüeh-sheng. Of course we had our own ways of finding out about Tu Yüeh-sheng. We didn't need a foreigner to tell us of the intentions of other Chinese."

"But it didn't work, did it? After all, the purge came."

"Yes, the purge came. We knew it was coming, but we weren't ready for it. Our masters made sure of that."

The Comintern, thought Matthew. The Communist International in Moscow, obedient to the orders of Stalin, who had refused to believe that Chiang might be one jump ahead of them, that Chiang could make the break on his terms rather than theirs. So the Kremlin had ordered the comrades in Shanghai to bury their arms and not to oppose Chiang. Openly, at least.

"So Chiang Kai-shek and his gangsters killed many of us that night of April twelfth. And killed many more in the days that followed. But some they did not get. They almost got Chou En-lai. And they almost got me."

Matthew waited for what was to follow.

"I spent two days hiding in the French Concession."

"In Larsen's house?"

"No. That would have been too obvious. We had been seen too much together. I was his teacher, after all. But in a place he found for me. A boardinghouse run by a Russian woman, on Huan-long *lu*—the route Vallon, the French called it. It was where Larsen used to go to meet a friend of his. An American girl."

Mme Vorontsov's, thought Matthew. Where Simon and Emily had met in secret during those years. "Emily Ransom?"

"I think that was her name, yes. Her uncle was a very important man. You probably know that." Matthew nodded. "So Lai Shi'an made the arrangements for me. The police were after me then. Chinese police, French police. He brought me some of his clothes to wear. So when I put them on, I looked just like a *liu xuesheng*, a student who'd just come back from America or Europe and had kept his western ways."

"So he helped you get out of Shanghai?"

"Yes. He bought me a ticket for Swatow on a *Taigu* ship that was due to sail on the night of April fourteenth. That evening he borrowed a friend's car. Came to the route Vallon to fetch me. He was going to drive me to the wharf, you see. He came dressed like a Chinese. So that at night I would look like the foreigner, he like a Chinese chauffeur. And Mr. Larsen and Mr. Chu would not be seen together. That way would be safer."

Matthew waited.

"We were wrong. As soon as we left the route Vallon, a car followed us. Not a police car, or an army car. But a large black car with two men standing on the running boards. Lai *hsien-sheng* guessed they were White Russians, bodyguards. Even today I don't know whose car it was. But I think it must have been one of Tu Yüeh-sheng's gangsters. Somehow they'd found out where I was staying. Lai Shi'an tried to lose them. He drove fast, and he was a good driver. But it was night, there were lots of rickshaws, of coolies, in the streets, and he had to slow down a lot to keep from hitting them. The other car stayed behind us. Lai *hsien-sheng* told me that he would take me up to the ship's gangplank, told me to get ready, to pull my hat down over my face so that I would not be recognized. Then I must walk up the gangplank slowly and deliberately. An ordinary foreigner leaving Shanghai. No one would dare shoot."

"Did it work?"

"It worked for me. I did exactly what I had been told to do. What I had not thought of, of course, was that just as I looked like the foreigner, so he looked like the Chinese. And as soon as I had reached the deck of the ship, there were shots. I looked around and I saw what had happened. The people in the black car with their bodyguards had shot my chauffeur. I saw him lying on the side of the quay. I tried to run back down the gangplank to help. But they were too quick. Before I could move, they'd taken the body, put it in the car, and had driven away. Very fast. Before the police could come."

"And—?"

"And that was the end. I never found out what happened. When I came back to Shanghai later, I asked. But no one remembered." He fell silent for a minute or two. Outside the door, voices rang in the stairwell. Through the thin walls came the sounds of television and radios: announcements, martial music. "So Lai *hsien-sheng*'s body was never found? The police never discovered anything?"

"As far as I can make out," said Matthew. "Of course there were investigations, but they came up with nothing. Or at least nothing that was reported."

"Probably we can guess what happened. The people in the black car discovered that they had killed a foreigner, a white man. So they had to dispose of the body. It wouldn't have been difficult, of course. Lots of people disappeared in those days."

It all fit, thought Matthew. It would help to explain everything. No report would have reached the American consulate or the French police. Or if it had come to Captain Fiori and his men, they might have thought it unnecessary to ask too many questions of their allies among Tu Yüeh-sheng's gangster friends. Particularly about a foreigner of dubious politics, a foreigner who'd made it his business to ask inconvenient questions about affairs that did not concern him. Simon was not the first foreigner to disappear in mysterious circumstances in Shanghai during those years, nor would he be the last.

"I've never told anyone else this story," said Mr. Chu slowly. "Any foreigner, I mean. But Simon Larsen saved my life. I don't know why he behaved as he did. I don't know why he should have done this for me, a Chinese. It would have been very simple for him just to say: your Chinese quarrels are none of my business, you got yourself into this dangerous situation, now get out as best you can."

Matthew thought: Simon Larsen had made the Chinese quarrel his quarrel, had become convinced that he could no longer stand by and watch it as an outsider, from the privileged safety of the foreigner's position. Something had made him become a participant, even if only a minor one, in the Chinese revolution. So he'd been willing to accept the risks that came with such engagement. The same qualities that had won him both a Bronze Star and near death at Saint-Mihiel. The qualities that he'd thought had been knocked out of him by his service in France, he'd found again, urged on by Emily, in the streets of Shanghai in 1927. And this time they had led him to his death.

Miss Chu came in, glancing at her watch, and saying something to the old man that Matthew didn't catch. He looked up at Matthew, smiling. "My daughter forbids me to stay up late," he said. "She's very firm with me, almost as if she were my mother. I tell her, it is a daughter's duty to obey her father. But now, it seems, I have reached a point in life where I must obey her."

She looked at Matthew apologetically. "I'm sorry," she said. "But he's under strict orders not to tire himself. And he should have been in bed some time ago."

"Of course," said Matthew. "And I must be going too." It was already past ten o'clock. "Mr. Chu, thank you very much for telling me this story. I know that Simon Larsen's family will be glad to know how he died. And that he was a brave man." He rose, then stopped. "One more question, may I? What were you doing during all those years after the failure of the revolution?"

The old man looked at him carefully, and Matthew was conscious again of those bright black eyes weighing him, as if calculating the answer.

"The revolution failed that summer. Here in Shanghai. But it did not fail elsewhere. That summer the Red Army was founded. And that autumn its troops reached Swatow, captured the city. They held it only a few days. But when they left, I went with them. I was with Chairman Mao in Kiangsi province after that, and with him on the Long March up to the northwest, in

1934 and 1935. Then the Party sent me back to Shanghai. I knew the city, knew the labor organizations here. I helped to organize the resistance against Japan during the war. And the resistance to the Kuomintang and the Americans after that. That was when I came to know Wei Tiaoyuan. We were colleagues, even though we did not always agree on politics." He smiled. "So you see, when you tell Lai Shi'an's family what happened, I do not know whether you want to tell them that the man he saved was a Communist. But I would do it all again if I were placed in the same position."

He rose to his feet, standing upright and looking directly at Matthew. "And if I were sixty years younger, I too would be in the streets, calling for a new revolution to save China." He held out his hand. "Good night, Mr. Walker."

Matthew stood with Daoming out in the street. "Please tell your uncle how grateful I am for being able to meet Mr. Chu. It has meant a lot to me, and I know will mean a lot to my friends at home. But now it's late. Don't bother to see me back—I'm sure I can find my own way now that you've showed me. Anyway, I've got a map."

"I'll take you back to the other side of the creek," said Daoming. "Then it's easy—here, let me show you." He unfolded the map and studied it. "Here," he said. "Look. Once we're over the creek, you can head south on Jiangning Road, and it'll take you right back to Huaihai Road."

Almost as soon as they'd turned out of the lane and were pedaling south through the dark city, however, it was clear that there was some kind of trouble. Ahead of them, a glow lit up the night sky. A light wind carried the sound of distant sirens—the police? ambulances? Matthew felt a pang of fear; it's happened at last, he thought, it's beginning, the army's coming in. He saw again those television shots of the tanks rolling down Chang'an Boulevard, the gunfire, people screaming, falling to the street. "What's going on?" he asked Daoming.

"Don't know. Probably just a fire. It happens sometimes."

The glare was getting brighter now, flaring up, silhouetting the dark buildings toward which they were riding. He heard people shouting. But there was nothing he could distinguish as gunfire.

Then, coming around a bend in the road, they saw it. Just beyond the level crossing on Guangxin Road, a train lay stopped, three or four cars derailed and on fire. Orange flames licked up out of open windows, lighting up the night, while beyond, a steam locomotive was panting and wheezing in the shadows. Matthew suddenly felt sick: were there still people in there being burned to death? A crowd broke and surged around the train, but the heat kept them at a distance—passengers who had fled, perhaps, or rescue workers, or just people who had come to see the sight? Had there been a collision? Or some other kind of accident? Then he remembered the dim figures he'd seen on the tracks a couple of hours earlier. Had they somehow managed to sabotage the train? To derail it?

By now the police had arrived, sirens bawling, blue lights flashing from their white cars. "Come on," Daoming shouted at him, "let's get out of here. We don't want to be found by the gong'an." Matthew needed no convincing, but it was too late; they were already caught up in the middle of the crowd, a mass of people, some of whom were trying to get away, others to reach the train, or to attack the police who were now moving in. He felt a sudden sharp pain between his shoulder blades; something or someone hit him in the back, knocking him off his bicycle and throwing him to the ground. Thoroughly frightened by now, Matthew thought: this certainly isn't my quarrel, I only want to get out of here. Above him the crowd was shouting—someone, trying to run, kicked him in the leg. He got to his feet; thank heavens, the bicycle was there, apparently unharmed, capable of carrying him away from this scene of fear and panic. Daoming was nowhere to be seen; Matthew called out to him, but he'd either fled into the dark or been carried away by the crowd, which by now was surging around Matthew, men and women shouting, throwing rocks at the police, who now charged in, swinging clubs. But not using guns; please God, thought Matthew, no guns, as long as there's no firing, perhaps things will stay under control. Still looking vainly for Daoming, he saw rails gleaming like tracers, curving off into the dark city, saw the faces of the people around him, lit by the fire, like characters in a Hitchcock movie, faces terrified, enraged, eager. But this wasn't a movie, this was real, he had no business being there, caught in this surging tide of violence. The pain in his shoulder—or was it his fear?—seemed to give him a new energy, and using his bicycle almost as a weapon, he managed to fight his way to the edge of the crowd. He had only one thought now:

to get out of this, to get away, to get back to the relative safety of his hotel. But his fall, and the turmoil of the crowd, meant that he'd lost all sense of direction. He remembered: I'm still north of the rail line, if I can get across it, at least I'll know I'm headed the right way. Clearly there was no hope of getting across near the burning train. He discovered a side road that ran parallel to the tracks, followed it west for about half a mile, and then came to a place where he could get over at another level crossing.

Then he'd have to find his way to a bridge over the creek, to get out of Chapei and back into Shanghai proper. But it's difficult to make one's way around at night; even in normal times, the city is dark, and there are very few streetlamps. Much too dark to read the street names on his map. A compass would have been more help. Heading in a direction he hoped was south, he found he had guessed right; the foul waters of the creek lay before him. A block away he saw a bridge, and crossed it with a sense of relief. All he had to do now was continue south and sooner or later he'd hit one of the main roads, Nanking Road or Yan'an Road, or Huaihai itself, and then he'd know his way home. Two men on a street corner pointed him in the direction of Jing'an Park, the old Bubbling Well Cemetery, about a mile northwest of his hotel. But he worried about Daoming, hoped that he had not come to grief in that wild, uncontrolled crowd that had ebbed and flowed around the fire.

By now he realized that whatever mystery might lie behind the burning train, the army was not coming into Shanghai. Or if it was, it certainly hadn't reached this part of the city yet. His fears began to fade; he no longer felt himself a fugitive running away from a crime in which he'd had no part, but simply a foreigner lost in a dark city perhaps, but no longer in real danger. But the image of those railway cars, the flames lighting them up inside, the heavy acrid smell of the fire, the mixture of hatred and terror on the faces of the crowd, stayed with him, and it was not for hours after he had finally reached the hotel at midnight, wrestling the bicycle up into his room for safekeeping, and stumbling into bed, that he was able to fall asleep.

CHAPTER ELEVEN

Wednesday, June 7, 1989

When he woke, bleary after a brief and fitful sleep, the sight of the bicycle leaning against the wall brought Matthew back suddenly into the reality of what had happened the previous night. The memory of Daoming came back to him, just before they'd been separated, shouting at him to get away from the crowd, and he hoped that he too had been able to escape from the melée surrounding the train. Watching the Chinese news as he dressed, he learned that some of the barricades had come down, dismantled last night by thousands of workers angry at the damage and disruption the agitators had caused. Or so the broadcast claimed. But there was nothing about the fire he'd seen just a few hours earlier. Though there was a report of hooligans disrupting rail traffic, the announcer, reading with her eyes fixed firmly on the text before her and never once looking at the camera, made no mention of the incident at the level crossing. Either the government hadn't yet decided how to play the story, or Matthew was simply reading too much into the affair, which might have been no more than simply one of the frequent accidents that upset the Chinese railway system. Yet that wouldn't explain the angry crowds he'd seen, or the violence with which they'd battled the police. He scribbled a brief note of thanks to Daoming, carefully avoiding any mention of last night's trouble, and left it at the desk, explaining to the clerk that the bicycle's owner might call for it later.

At eight-thirty, when he was back in his room, watching the American broadcast with its warnings of imminent civil war, the consulate called to say that there would be a chance to leave soon if he wanted to go. One of the American evacuation flights from Beijing would stop in Shanghai on its way to Tokyo, and Qantas was bringing in a jumbo jet the next day from Hong Kong. Australians would get priority, of course, but the remaining seats would go to anyone willing to pay the fare. "Are you telling me that I should be leaving?" he asked. No, not yet, said the voice on the other end of the line; but that advice could change anytime. In the meantime, stay in touch, wrap up your work here as soon as possible, and make plans to get out. And, of course, keep away from crowds.

Even though he might not be able to stay much longer, Matthew decided that nothing was going to keep him away from the institute that day. Chu Hung-ying's story last night certainly had the ring of truth to it, but Matthew was still unconvinced that Simon—no matter how he had been killed—could vanish from the face of the earth quite so easily as he had on that April night so many years ago. Surely those documents Zhao was obligingly providing had something more to tell him, something that would satisfy his curiosity about how and why Simon had met his end.

Today the roads were clear enough so that although there were still no buses running, he was able to engage the services of one of Shanghai's enterprising independent cabdrivers to take him to Szechwan Road. A strong-minded woman in her forties, she fired a series of questions about the news at him while navigating through a network of back streets to avoid the troubles on the main roads, before dropping him off at the institute's door. Clearly someone who took to heart Deng Xiaoping's admonition that to get rich is glorious, she charged him three times the normal fare for the trip. She also let it be known that she was available for a journey to the airport if need be; she knew how to get around the roadblocks, and would guarantee him a safe and timely delivery.

Up in the institute's reading room, above the still-quiet Szechwan Road, he leafed through the pile of papers that Zhao Shanling had brought him. In English and French, they contained comments by the foreign police and foreign councils on the swift series of events that had followed the fall of Shanghai to the Nationalists, and had led up to the purge. It was the search for this sort of information that had brought him to Shanghai, and by all rights he should ignore Simon Larsen and spend what time might remain to him right there. More time—he needed more time, time to listen to these voices from the past, to become attuned to their inflections, their tones, to understand what they were telling him. He read rapidly, taking notes on the important points, occasionally copying out a phrase or a whole sentence. But all the time he kept hoping that, buried within them, there'd be more news of Simon.

There was. The story began to emerge in a memorandum from Captain Fiori of the *Garde municipale* to the French consul general, Paul-Émile Naggiar.

Shanghai, 27.4.27

Acting on reports [from whom? Matthew wondered] that Simon Larsen, American, aged 31, may be missing, I detailed Lieutenant Péchinard to visit his address at 221 bis route Père Robert, on Tuesday 26 April. Taking with him one constable and one detective, Lt. Péchinard called at 15.45 hours that day. On receiving no response, he sought entry from the concierge, and on the authority of his warrant, searched the flat.

The search turned up little of interest. M. Larsen's finances are in good order, and there are no signs of indebtedness. His bankbook shows a balance of US $2,398.72 at the National City Bank in the Settlement. The last check was drawn to the account of Butterfield and Swire, and we are inquiring of the agents of that firm about the reasons for the payment. It is of course possible that he has purchased a steamer ticket, but although his friends report that he had been talking recently about returning to the United States, there is no evidence that he has left, or that he was contemplating a sudden departure from Shanghai. As evidence for that, I send along his passport, which was found in a desk drawer.

Among his papers were found copies of articles that he had written for various journals in the United States, a few from persons in that country, and materials that he was said to be using in the preparation of a book, the draft of which I enclose. It should be examined, of course, and if M. Larsen does not return, can be given to the American consul general with his other effects.

In short, the search found nothing that would help cast any light on Larsen's absence, and it can only be suggested that he has, for reasons known only to himself, chosen to drop from sight, or that he has been the victim of foul play.

Over in the Settlement, Chief Detective-Inspector Givens had nothing to add to the French evidence. John Ransom, Matthew gathered, was still making a nuisance of himself with the police, telling them that if only they'd listened to his warnings, they'd have been able to apprehend Simon before he had the chance to flee to Russia (Ransom seemed to be convinced that Soviet agents had spirited him out of the city before he could be arrested). Now that he'd disappeared, however, Ransom no longer wanted an investigation—it was too late for that, and the police had better things to do with their time.

Another memorandum from the French police, dated the last day of April, shed little more light on the mystery.

> It has been established that Larsen purchased a ticket for passage aboard the Butterfield and Swire coaster *Hupeh*, which sailed on 14 April for Foochow, Amoy, Swatow, and Hong Kong. The passenger manifest does not contain his name, however. It lists only seven foreigners, all but one of them missionaries and their families, who have been forced to leave because of the civil war. The seventh, an Italian businessman, M. Giuseppe Bentivoglio, is the proprietor of a well-known jewelry store on the avenue Edward VII.

Accompanying this memorandum, however, was another one of the same date that was marked MOST SECRET.

> In my formal report of the search of Simon Larsen's house carried out recently by Lt. Péchinard, I omitted mention of two items of particular interest found there, thinking it better to describe them separately.
>
> The first is a collection of a large amount of material, all of it in Chinese, emanating from the Kuomintang and Communist parties, both here in Shanghai and elsewhere. This includes several copies of the *Hsiang-tao chou-pao,* or "Guide

Weekly," the notorious Bolshevik journal believed to have been published in Chapei, which the Nationalists have now suppressed. There are also copies of propaganda pamphlets, handbills, and miscellaneous flyers, printed in the last few months, and intended to prepare Shanghai for the rising of March. Many of these items are already known to the police, and the others are being inventoried and translated.

M. Larsen is a journalist of a sort, and of course that fact might explain the existence in his house of a body of literature whose purpose is the subversion of the good order of the foreign settlements. Less susceptible of easy explanation is the presence of a confidential journal, which records not only M. Larsen's general observations about the situation as it has developed here over the last several years, but also sets forth in some detail his meetings since February with men who we have every reason to believe are Bolshevik agents.

There followed a brief description of some of the last entries in the journal, which Fiori suggested should be kept in the Larsen dossier at police headquarters. Then on May 20, Fiori had proposed drawing the case to a close. "Unless you object," he wrote the consul general,

> ... I will call off the investigation at this point. My officers and their men have already been overworked for months because of the emergency, and I cannot justify any further expenditure of time and effort in seeking the whereabouts of a man whose activities were, in all truth, becoming somewhat inconvenient in the Concession.
>
> Mlle Emily Ransom, for reasons that are now clear, is extremely distraught. She has told Lt. Péchinard that she saw M. Larsen for the last time on April 11, three days before his disappearance. Though he told her then that he might be returning to America before long, she had no sense that he was planning a precipitate departure.
>
> I myself have had occasion to talk to Mlle Ransom. Without revealing to her the contents of M. Larsen's confidential journal, in which she plays so prominent a role, I have nonetheless managed to suggest to her that her continued presence in Shanghai might pose some problems, not least to her uncle, M. John Ransom. Mlle Ransom gave me to understand, how-

ever, that she has already booked passage for herself aboard the
President Monroe, which will leave Shanghai on 4 June.

Should the American consul object that we have not done
our utmost in this case, it might be well to let him know, discreetly of course, that we are aware that Larsen has consorted
with Bolsheviks, and to show him, if necessary, the list of radical books and magazines seized from Larsen's domicile.

I would respectfully recommend, however, that on no account should you let him know of the existence of Larsen's
confidential journal, or at least of the entries that have been
made in it since late February, when Larsen appears to have begun his work for the Bolsheviks. There is certain information
that, if not properly understood, might jeopardize our good relations with the American authorities. Nor would it please M.
Larsen's family, in all likelihood, to learn that he had become a
Bolshevik agent. In any case, since the material may be of continued interest to the police, it should be maintained in the
files of the *Garde municipale*.

That, at any rate, explained the existence of Journal B among
the French police records. The earlier pages—everything up
through February 1927, before Simon began his double life—
must have been turned over with the draft of *Typhoon Over
Shanghai* and the rest of Larsen's personal effects to the American consul general. He would have sent them home to Simon's
family, without ever learning of the existence of the rest. Nor
would the French, of course, have mentioned it in the investigations that followed. Only Emily Ransom had been told of the
journal—or enough about it—to induce her to leave Shanghai
without making any trouble. But of course she'd already decided to leave, for reasons that had nothing to do with the
warnings of the French police, and which were none of their
business.

"Inconvenient," Fiori had said of Simon's activities. But the
word he used was *gênant*, which has more to do with getting in
the way, making trouble, than with being dangerous. Inconvenient, presumably, to the French authorities whom Tu Yüeh-
sheng was paying off so that he could run his opium racket in
the Concession. The chief of the *Garde municipale* had presumably discussed the matter with the French consul general, and
saw no need to spell out in writing his reasons for wanting to

drop the investigation. And the consul general apparently went along with it, for the only remaining message was a bland note a few days later from Naggiar to his "Dear and esteemed colleague" the American consul general, summarizing the evidence, and saying regretfully that the French police had come up against a blank wall. The last paragraph, by proposing that the American police be alerted to watch for Simon's appearance in the United States, managed to plant the discreet suggestion that the missing man might have criminal intentions.

And if the police had seen Simon only as a Bolshevik agent, there'd have been no great need for secrecy. No doubt the American consul might have been shocked to discover that one of his fellow citizens had turned traitor. But he'd get over it. Surely that wasn't a good enough reason to keep the news from him. Nor would a knowledge of Simon's subversive activities by themselves have jeopardized relations between the American consulate and the French authorities.

Was there something else, some other reason the French police hadn't wanted the American authorities prying too closely into Simon's disappearance? And why John Ransom himself now seemed to be discouraging any more inquiries? Where, in any case, did Ransom himself fit into all this? If he did fit? Ransom, who had gone into debt to Tu Yüeh-sheng? And whose debt had—apparently—been forgiven and forgotten so suddenly? Tu Yüeh-sheng was not the sort of man to act generously on a mere whim. Obviously he hadn't wanted to stand in the way of Ransom's elevation to the Shanghai Municipal Council. And that could only be because Ransom might be useful to him—or was already being useful to him. Matthew remembered Simon's feeling, when he met Tu, of being sized up, as if Tu wanted to know if he could use him.

Gradually the pieces were beginning to form themselves into a pattern in Matthew's mind. Having already bought off several of the highest-ranking officers in the French police, to say nothing of one or two of the French municipal councillors, Tu was presumably trying to extend his underworld operations into the International Settlement. And that would mean, presumably, buying off some of those authorities as well.

Ransom, in short, had been blackmailed. Racking up debts that he couldn't pay, threatened with an exposure that would have disgraced him, he had apparently agreed to become Tu's man on the council. And thus to give Tu Yüeh-sheng an entrée into the International Settlement. An entrée that he wanted, since it was just at that time that—according to the police—he was trying to expand the scope of his opium marketing syndicate. And against the better judgment of their police commissioner, Ransom and Stanfield Frothingham had agreed to let Tu's agents have free run of the Settlement.

Frothingham, presumably, had gone along with the arrangement because he knew that Tu and the Green Gang were about to join Chiang Kai-shek in crushing the Communists. But Ransom had seen it as an opportunity to pay off his debt to Tu. If the gangsters were to be allowed to operate in the Settlement as fighters in the war against bolshevism, what was to stop them from doing some other business at the same time?

And Simon, who already knew something about the French role in the opium trade, had now found out about Ransom. Or at least had smelled a rat and had made some very astute guesses. Then he had inadvertently let Ransom know that he knew. Ransom was in no position to take chances. And in a city like Shanghai, he had no need to take chances. All he had to do was to let Tu Yüeh-sheng's people know that Simon was dangerous. And they would take care of him.

If that supposition were true, then what did it say about Chu Hung-ying's story of how Simon met his end? Chu thought that Simon had died for his sake, to help him escape from Shanghai in the middle of Chiang Kai-shek's bloody purge. And no doubt Chu's name was on the general's wanted list, and the gangsters might well have gotten him sooner or later.

But was the killing of Simon merely a case of mistaken identity? Perhaps he'd been murdered not because Tu's henchmen thought he was someone else, but because they knew exactly who he was—a man who had found out more than was good for him about the opium syndicate's illegal operations, and about the way they were spreading into the Settlement. Was Simon Larsen the victim, in other words, not of the politics of revolution and counterrevolution, but of John Ransom's greed, and his need to cover himself?

After three hours of steady reading, Matthew now sat back, feeling immensely pleased with himself for having worked out a solution to the puzzle. Was his version true? He didn't know, had no way of knowing for sure. He'd need more evidence before he could convict Ransom in an American court (whatever happened to Ransom, he wondered). Or before he could write an account that would satisfy his fellow historians. All he had was circumstantial evidence, perhaps; but it certainly fit the facts.

Anyway, he could tell Laura. Then, suddenly, he was appalled at the thoughts going through his head. In his passion to find a neat solution to a historical problem, hadn't he lost sight of the human dimension to the story? Though Simon had vanished over sixty years ago, surely the mere passage of time didn't diminish his humanity. Or that of Emily Ransom, or the child Matthew was now convinced she had been bearing. Even when she'd learned of Simon's disappearance, she must still have held out some hope that he would come back to her, a hope that would have faded over the years, leaving only a memory in her heart. Wasn't he, Matthew, in danger of behaving like one of those fictional detectives he so enjoyed? So pleased at finding answers, at having people exclaim over their cleverness, as they lay out the solution in the final chapter, that they lose all sense of horror and pity for the victims of the crime? By now Simon and Emily had become to him more than two people whom he could use to help reconstruct life in that city of the past, more than two people whose story provided a pleasant diversion from the real work of history. They had, in these last few days, become real to him, two people whom he knew, and until last night he had found himself hoping that their story would have an improbably happy ending.

But there wasn't to be any happy ending. Weary from sitting, his eyes tired, Matthew stood up and stretched, and began gathering up his papers, separating them from the folders that Zhao had given him that morning, and putting them back into his briefcase. It was almost noon, time for the institute to close down for the lunch break. The morning had flown by, and in his excitement at the discoveries he was making about the events of the past, he'd managed to forget the very real events of the present. Voices came from the hall, a sound of excitement or agitation, but he paid no attention—it was none of his business, and in any case they were speaking a Shanghainese that he couldn't follow. Then the door opened, and Zhao Shanling came in, followed by Wang Baozhen.

Matthew could see at once that something was wrong. His

first thought—a self-interested one, he realized—was that Zhao's generosity to him had been discovered, and that there was going to be a problem about the papers he'd been allowed to see. He was going to have to give them back, not be able to use them. Perhaps even find himself in trouble—things like that did happen, he'd heard enough stories to know.

But that wasn't it at all. Zhao in fact said nothing, and it was Wang who spoke to him instead.

"Mr. Walker," she said in a careful English, and looking directly at him. "We've had bad news. Mr. Zhao and I didn't know whether to tell you. But I thought you should know. Xie Bona—Bernard Hilding. His daughter. She's dead. Shot."

Matthew was stunned. A foreigner? That was impossible. He'd heard nothing about it on the news. "When? How did it happen?"

"In Beijing. On Sunday. When the army went into Tiananmen Square."

Zhao remained silent, his hands moving nervously about, lighting a cigarette. He glanced out the window as if he half expected to see the armored column already moving up Szechwan Road below.

Matthew didn't want to believe it. Any more than he'd wanted to believe Laura when she'd called on Sunday. That poor man. He'd been so worried by what his daughter had been doing. Yet so proud of her too. "Are you sure? I mean, could there have been a mistake? How do you know?"

"Yes, we're quite sure, Mr. Walker. Early this morning some of her friends—students who had been in Beijing with her—got back to Shanghai. One of them had taken her to the hospital. She died just as they got there. He was with her, and saw it."

"And Mr. Hilding—does he know?"

"Yes. He's been told." There was a silence, during which once again Matthew remembered the night that spring when his imagination had seen Laura caught in the ice storm, her car crushed by the side of the road.

Then he asked: "How is he?"

"I don't know. I haven't seen him. It was another student who told him. The one who'd gone to the hospital with her."

Matthew thought: I've got to go see him. At least to say how sorry I am, to see if there's anything I can do to help. Or will I only seem a busybody? He hardly knew Hilding, after all—a man he'd met less than a week before, a man with whom he'd had a few conversations, talking about his past—and about his delight in the daughter whom he'd come to know after so many years, here to spend the year with him. It was bad enough to be an intruder on China's pain at this time. But Hilding's pain would be something else again, a deeply personal hurt, the ending of all his hopes for the future. What could Matthew say that could possibly be of any comfort to a man suffering from such a wound? And, to make it worse, a wound inflicted by the country he'd adopted as his own?

Never mind. He had to go. It would be inhuman not to look in at least. He thanked Professor Wang for telling him, zipped up his briefcase, saying good-bye to Zhao Shanling as he left.

He found Hilding sitting in his room, slumped in a chair by his desk, his face white and unshaven. Despite the day's heat, a woolen dressing gown hung from his bony shoulders. A few feet away sat a young man, probably in his early twenties. He too looked exhausted, and Matthew guessed that this was Mary's fellow student, the one who had brought Hilding the news of his daughter.

Hilding looked up at Matthew, his eyes dull with pain and incomprehension. "You've heard?" he asked. He struggled to rise.

"Please don't get up," said Matthew. "Mr. Hilding, I'm terribly sorry to hear the news. I came to see if there is anything I can do to help." He stood there awkwardly, aware of the insufficiency of the words, not quite sure what he should do or say next.

"This is Kang Kuangren." Hilding waved a hand in the direction of the other man, who had now risen to his feet. "A fellow student of my daughter's. He's just come back from Beijing. I'll let you introduce yourselves."

Matthew shook hands with him. "You were with Mary in Beijing?" he asked.

"Yes." He looked at Matthew, as if to size him up, wondering if he could be trusted. "I just got back last night. On the train. But there was an accident. The lines were blocked. So I didn't reach the university until about three o'clock this morning."

"An accident?" Had there been another one, then? "There was a train that caught fire. Were you on that?" He hadn't known that the train was coming from Beijing.

"Yes." Kang was surprised that Matthew knew about it, and

Matthew explained what he had seen. "But I didn't understand it. What happened?"

"I don't know exactly," said Kang. "I've heard there were people—students—blocking the tracks. Either the driver didn't see them, or didn't care. So the train ran over them. Some of them were killed. The train had to stop. Then the fire broke out. And there was fighting, when the police came. But we didn't stay, we wanted to get away as fast as possible."

Once again the fear and horror of the night came back, and Matthew felt sick. Those shadowy figures he'd seen on the tracks earlier in the evening—they must have been the ones run over. What could have induced them to stand in the way of the oncoming train? A desire for martyrdom? A hope that their death would inspire others? Or was it simply that they'd thought nothing could happen to them, that the train would stop?

"Who set it on fire? Do you know?"

"No. Maybe just an accident. Maybe it was the crowd, because they were so angry. But some of my friends think it was the police."

"The police? Why would they do that?" Matthew was puzzled.

"There were many people on that train from Beijing. And there were photographs and videotapes of the massacre in Tiananmen Square. We were bringing them back, to show people what really happened there."

"And the police got them?"

"Yes. Or they were burned up in the fire. Maybe a few were saved. I don't know." He looked at Matthew. "I heard there were several people killed there last night. Maybe we were the lucky ones." He paused. "And you too, perhaps."

There seemed no reply to that. Only a little while ago—just nine days ago, though it seemed far longer—Matthew had arrived in China. Now, suddenly, without in the least meaning to do so, he had become caught up in a confused and frightening turmoil that had already engulfed China's capital, and was threatening to sweep down into Shanghai. Now he sensed himself becoming, like Simon Larsen, not simply the detached observer of strife among other people, capable of a distant and impassive analysis, but someone who was rapidly being drawn into that strife himself. That morning, with the coming of daylight, the memory of the burning train, the flames turning the night sky red, lighting the faces of a frightened and angry crowd, had almost seemed to be no more than someone else's nightmare, a nightmare that he had blundered into by accident, and if it hadn't been for the dull pain in his shoulder, he might well believe the whole episode a dream. But now he knew it couldn't be gotten rid of that easily. It was no mere nightmare at all, but a terrifyingly real event, one that he could no longer simply try to forget and put behind him. Like it or not, he was finding himself in a world in which such things happened: a world in which an army had fired on its own people, and a world in which an old man had just learned of his daughter's death, the old man who now sat before him, stunned, trying, in his shock and hurt, to make some sense out of it all.

Matthew, of course, could leave China, indeed might shortly be told he had to leave, and a few hours of flight would see him back in another world. A world in which these kinds of things didn't happen, at least to people like him, a world of order and reason, a world of pattern and predictability. Just an hour or two ago he'd worked out a thoroughly logical solution to the puzzle of Simon's disappearance, imposing on those distant events the kind of rational and orderly explanation his mentors had trained him to give. And yet—and yet, for Simon himself, the last few days of life must have seemed anything but logical, must have seemed random, chaotic, purposeless, and terrifying. No logic, no neat little patterns there. Any more than there had been a few days ago, in Beijing. When the tanks went into the square. The violence, the shooting, the screams that he'd watched and heard on television. And the rage and terror that he'd seen himself last night, on those faces lit by the burning train.

No more logical pattern than there was now for the old man who sat before him in this bleak room, numb, unable to speak. Not just his daughter had been taken from him. For fifty years Bernard Hilding had lived in China, devoting himself to the cause of a revolution that was to transform the largest society on earth. He'd cut himself off from his own country, his own people back in England. He'd been called a dupe, a fool, a traitor. To the revolution he'd given up his wife, dead of neglect in a Beijing hospital after delivering his only child; and now, two decades later, that same child also lay dead in that same city, perhaps in the very same hospital, the victim this time not of neglect, but of a slaughter carried out in the name of the revolution in which he'd believed.

As Matthew sat there with Hilding and Kang, through the long hours of the afternoon, the story began to emerge. By late May, the original leaders of the movement, students from Beijing's universities, had tried to persuade the protesters to leave the square and go home. The imposition of martial law in the capital, the increasingly ominous reports of troops being moved into place around the city, had convinced them that the government would not stop at bloodshed, if that's what it took to clear the square. And many had left; fatigue, illness, fear, the worries of parents, had led them to return to their dormitories, or to go home. Those who'd stayed, including students who, like Mary, had arrived from other universities in other cities, now found themselves under the sway of a more radical group, young men and women determined not to give up, convinced that victory was almost theirs. It was these leaders who had arranged for the Goddess of Liberty to be brought into the square last week, as a way of raising the flagging spirits of their fellows; it was they who had made their brave and impassioned speeches about self-sacrifice, about martyrdom, if need be, to rescue their country from the plight into which it had fallen.

The first units of the army had approached the square at mid-afternoon on Saturday. That pleasant and sunny afternoon, when I was sitting alone in my hotel, thought Matthew, reading the documents Zhao had given me, trying to untangle the threads of Simon's life. Once again a few scuffles had broken out, but this time they were uglier and more serious, and by nightfall the demonstrators clustered around the Monument to the People's Heroes were fearful about what the hours of darkness might bring. Late that evening, with their nerves taut and strained, they'd heard the approach of the first armored columns moving in from the southwest. By the time the tanks and troop carriers had reached Chang'an Boulevard, leading east into the square, the sound of gunfire was unmistakable. Some had wanted to leave then; others were determined to stay, not only to make a courageous gesture, but also because they were convinced that the army would never open fire in the square, that symbolic heart of revolutionary China.

"They were very brave." Kang spoke softly, as if the tone of his voice could somehow bring comfort to Hilding. "Your daughter was one of them. We all admired her. They knew that she wasn't one of us, that she'd come from England, that she didn't have to put up with the danger of living in the square. And yet she stayed with us. She sacrificed herself for our country. Even though she could have left. I think we will never forget that."

Hilding looked up, grateful for what he was hearing. "I tried to get in touch with her, you know," he said, speaking now for the first time. "I wanted her to come back here to Shanghai. Twenty years ago, in the days of the Cultural Revolution, I'd seen what people—people in power—can do when they think they're being threatened."

"Mary wanted to leave," said Kang. "And I said I'd go with her, where I thought it would be safer. By that time I knew that if the army was willing to open fire anywhere in Beijing, it wouldn't stop when it got to the square." So with Liu Meihua and several others, they'd made a break for it, hoping to find safety in the side streets off the square. Then it had happened: just as they reached an intersection, two army trucks had pulled to a stop. About three dozen infantrymen climbed out of them, guns at the ready, and started shooting. People screamed. Some of the braver ones threw rocks and bottles at the soldiers. Kang saw three people, two young men and an old woman, fall dead in the street ahead of him. He grabbed Mary's wrist, and, with Liu Meihua following, tried to pull her into a *hu-t'ung*, one of the narrow alleys off the main streets. She screamed at him to let her go, she wanted to run up to the soldiers, to tell them to stop, to convince them that they were only killing innocent people.

"Then she was shot," he said. "There were bullets everywhere, a panic, and the soldiers seemed as scared as we were." With the help of Liu Meihua and one of the others, he had put her on the back of a trishaw, a bicycle-powered cart, and they wheeled her five blocks through the darkened streets of the city to a hospital. There they found the staff distraught, appalled at the carnage going on around them, appalled at the number of victims being carried in, so many that they didn't even have time to separate the dead from the living.

Mary had still been alive when they arrived. She kept asking for her father, wanting him to know that she was all right. "Tell him not to worry, tell him he mustn't worry," she kept repeating. But before any of the overworked doctors could reach her, she had died. A few minutes later, a detachment of soldiers broke into the hospital. As Kang learned the next day, they were looking for reporters, especially foreign reporters, ordering the doctors and nurses not to speak to the press, and particularly not to say anything about casualty figures. Matthew remembered the Chinese Red Cross report that twenty-six hundred people had died that night; yesterday, they denied ever having given such a figure.

Kang and his friends left at that point in a state of shock. Only as an afterthought had he remembered to take with him the knapsack Mary had been carrying. He had brought it with him now, and it lay on a chair, its pathetic contents spread around it: a wallet, a passport, a driver's license, a photograph of Mary herself with a smiling young man, presumably a friend or a fellow student at Leeds, a ballpoint pen, a bottle of drinking water, and a few clothes.

Liu Meihua and Kang had spent the next day in hiding, trying to avoid the army, as it began its cleanup sweeps through the city, continuing its apparently random and purposeless firing at clusters of onlookers. "A friend managed to buy us two tickets to Shanghai," said Kang. "There was such confusion at the railway station that we managed to get on the train. Even though by then the police and the soldiers were looking for Liu Meihua."

Matthew recalled seeing her picture that morning on the Chinese television broadcast, accompanied by a dozen or so others whom the police wanted because of their complicity in what the government now was calling the counterrevolutionary turmoil. At the time her name hadn't registered, but now he remembered that Hilding had spoken of her earlier, because she was Mary's friend. The photograph had showed an unremarkable young woman, barely out of her teens: a native of Soochow, said the announcement, now a student at Fudan University. Below it appeared the number of a direct telephone line to the police, and all good citizens were enjoined to keep a watch for these enemies of public order and socialist democracy, and to report immediately if they had seen them.

"Is she here now? In Shanghai?" he asked. And knew at once it was a stupid question.

Kang looked at him sharply. "She's with friends," he said. "With friends who can be trusted. Obviously she can't go back to Fudan. Or back to her parents in Soochow. The police are already searching the universities, looking for troublemakers. Maybe they already know that she's here in Shanghai."

"And what will you do now? Wouldn't she be better off out in the countryside rather than here? With all the police, I mean?"

"She'd be better off leaving China," said Kang. "The countryside's too risky. Maybe the peasants would hide her, maybe they wouldn't. They don't know much about what's been happening in Beijing." Or care much either, he seemed to imply. He spoke with the Chinese city-bred intellectual's typical condescension for the peasants.

Hilding looked up. "I know her," he said. "She came here several times. She was one of the friends Mary had made here this winter." He stopped, overcome by the thought. Or perhaps trying to refine from his memory some remnant of the happiness he had known earlier that year when his daughter had been with him.

Matthew nodded. "I remember your telling me about her," he said gently. "About the English lessons. Wasn't she the one?"

"Yes." Hilding was silent. "They were just the same age. They even looked alike. Almost like sisters."

And now the police are after her, thought Matthew. I hope she can depend on her friends. But how long could she rely on a public sense of outrage at the massacre to keep her safe? Already that morning there were signs that the strike was petering out. The demonstrators had been calling for a great upwelling of support, they wanted people, ordinary people, to pour into the street as they had in Beijing a few weeks ago, when the demonstrators had defied the authorities. They wanted the citizens of Shanghai to show their rage, their hatred for what the posters now called the *wei zhengquan*, the fraudulent regime of Li Peng, Yang Shangkun, and their henchmen. But it wasn't going to happen. As Zhao Shanling had said, Shanghai people are pragmatic, they accept reality as they find it, they don't fly in the face of the obvious. And it was obvious who had won the battle in Beijing. No point taking chances—especially when rumors spoke of another army lying outside Shanghai, poised to strike within hours.

"I wish I could help her," said Hilding. "I don't want to see—to see what happened to Mary happen to her too."

Kang looked at him. "She's got to stay in hiding. Either that or get out of China. But that's going to be very difficult with all the police looking for her. Perhaps your consulate could help. Or yours, Mr. Walker."

Hilding shook his head. "They're going to have enough trouble just dealing with their own citizens," he said. "I've already tried twice this morning to telephone them. To tell them about Mary. After all, she was a British subject, and they should know what happened to her. But I can't get through."

"The American consulate would never get mixed up in this," said Matthew. "Not a chance." He remembered the White House's strangely muted response, President Bush "deploring" the massacre. Picking up Mary's passport, he looked at her photograph. An intelligent face, not pretty, but pleasant, smiling directly at the camera. Despite her citizenship, despite her address in Leeds, her features looked thoroughly Chinese. Only her hair, worn fashionably short, cut almost like a boy's, looked western. She must indeed have taken after her mother, he thought; there was no sign of Hilding's gaunt English looks in that countenance. A pleasant, smiling, Chinese face. If she'd let her hair grow out, she would have been almost indistinguishable from her fellow students at Fudan that spring.

The thought, when it came, was beautifully logical. Probably it occurred both to him and to Kang at the same time. But it was Kang who spoke.

"Xie *hsien-sheng,*" he said. "Mr. Hilding. Do you really want to help her?"

Hilding looked at him, his face bleak. "What?" he asked. "Maybe once I could have. I used to have friends—in Beijing, men I could talk to, who would understand these things. But that was years ago. I don't know anyone in that group that runs things now." He shook his head. "They're not my sort of people." There were tears in his eyes. "How could they do it? I don't just mean Mary—I mean all those others who are being killed. Shooting their own people. How could they do it?"

"Xie *hsien-sheng.*" Kang persisted. He looked at Matthew, knowing that he understood. "Mr. Hilding. Look, don't call the British consulate just yet. Don't tell them about your daughter's death."

"But they've got to know. They must know. The British government should know. She was a British subject. Don't you understand that? She was British—not Chinese."

"Mr. Hilding." Matthew spoke now. He knew that he had no right to ask what he was about to ask. It seemed like a terrible imposition to make on a man who had just learned of his child's death. But he went ahead. "There's a chance—just a chance— that her friends might be able to get her out of the country. If they can use your daughter's passport." Kang nodded emphatically, relieved that Matthew understood.

At first Hilding said nothing, but simply looked at the two of them with a question in his face. Then he spoke. "I don't follow you. How? What are you thinking of?"

"I haven't seen either one of them," said Matthew. "But you said that they were almost like sisters. And your daughter's picture makes her look Chinese. Completely Chinese, a hundred percent." He picked up the passport, riffled through the pages until he found the Chinese visa. It was stamped with the date of Mary's entry into the country: September 28, 1988. The exit date had yet to be filled in.

"If they can only get her an airplane ticket," he said. "Somehow. To Tokyo, to Hong Kong, anywhere away from China. Then she could use this passport. Travel as a British citizen, at least until she's safely out of the country."

Hilding looked up at him, the incomprehension now fading. For the first time today a faint animation came into his face. "I see," he said slowly. "I see." He looked back at his daughter's passport. "What a good idea. What a very good idea." He paused. "And what a good thing that I couldn't get through to the consulate this morning." Then, briefly, the slightest of smiles broke out. "So often one curses the Chinese telephone system. Sometimes we ought to be quite grateful to it, I suppose."

But it was one thing to come up with a good idea, quite another thing to realize it. The passport would have to be delivered to Liu Meihua. Kang knew where she was; that should be easy enough. Provided, of course, that he wasn't followed. Though, since he hadn't been one of the leaders in the square, there'd be no reason for the police to look for him. Still, after she'd gotten the passport, if she got it, how was she going to break cover and make it out to the airport? Even if the roads were no longer blocked, that might prove difficult. Finally, there was the business of getting her a plane ticket. You could get on a waiting list, as he had, but that was chancy. How long could Liu Meihua stay in hiding, with her description and picture being broadcast several times a day? And how would she find out if and when a seat came available?

The next step was as logical as the first. But this time it wasn't

Matthew who thought of it. "Mr. Walker," said Kang. "Perhaps you could buy her a ticket."

"Me?" Matthew was surprised. He hadn't thought of himself having any role in this enterprise. But of course it made absolute sense. His own return ticket was on Cathay Pacific, a Hong Kong carrier. Much safer than flying on C.A.A.C., the Chinese airline. And Cathay's office was in the very hotel in which he was staying.

"You could take her passport," said Kang. "And buy the ticket. They won't question you. An American man traveling with an Englishwoman—with his English girlfriend."

Of course. It made perfect sense, he had to admit. The next step followed: that Liu Meihua would go to the airport with him. As his traveling companion. Two foreigners going through Chinese security control together. There should be no problem—assuming, for the moment, that Liu actually looked at least something like the woman in the photograph. But what if it didn't work? She was on the most-wanted list, and anyone who watched Chinese television would be familiar with her face and her description. He had a sudden vision of the two of them, seized by the police at Hongqiao Airport, Liu to be taken off into captivity, he to face what would at least be an unpleasant interrogation. And then what? Expulsion from China—that would be the best he could hope for. Did they put foreigners in Chinese jails? Labor camps? How much could the American consul help him there? How sympathetic would the consul be if he got himself into trouble trying to smuggle a known criminal out of the country?

But what could he say? The vivid television pictures of the tanks shooting their way into Beijing stayed in his mind. The outrage last night, those angry faces, lit by the glare of the burning train. "I'll try" is what he did say. He had to. How much choice did he have? How much choice had Simon Larsen had?

At about four that afternoon, Matthew left Hilding's apartment. The old man had recovered sufficiently by then to help the others in their planning. "Telephone me to say whether you've got the ticket," he said. "Then tomorrow perhaps we can figure out how you're going to get the girl to the airport. But it's going to depend a lot on how soon the two of you will be able to leave."

Matthew reached the airline office in the Jinjiang Hotel that afternoon just before it closed, joining a group of other foreigners trying to leave the country. But the walk alone back through the still-quiet streets of the city had revived his fears. Indeed, the very silence seemed now to suggest that the calls for a general strike were failing, and that the city wanted to get back to normal. Of course, if that were true, it lessened the risk of any attack by the army. But it also meant that the police, who so far had done little to interfere with the demonstrations, would begin to move in and arrest those whom they had decided were the ringleaders.

What on earth had he done in agreeing to go along with such a crazy scheme? In Hilding's apartment, everything seemed so logical, so rational, so easy to agree to. The sight of the old man, shattered by the news of his daughter's death, made it impossible to refuse. What right had he to complain of inconvenience, of danger—a very small danger, at that—in the face of such transcendent grief? By the time he was back in his hotel, however, the whole idea seemed thoroughly reckless, and the danger by no means small. Anyway, wasn't it all illegal? Not just under Chinese law, but under American law—wasn't there a rule somewhere that said Americans abroad should stay out of foreign political entanglements? Not only wars, revolutions, riots, but also helping criminals to escape? Matthew's only brushes with the law had come in the form of a few parking tickets, and he was also a firm believer that Americans abroad should not try to impose their own ways on other countries, but should abide by the local laws and customs, laws and customs as they actually were, not as Americans might like them to be. Besides, with Liu Meihua's picture now being played and replayed over and over again, sooner or later she was bound to be recognized. And if by some miracle they got to the airport safely, surely she'd be recognized by the security people there.

By the time he got to the airline counter, he was badly worried. That morning he'd gone to Cathay Pacific to ask for a single seat; now he wanted two. Would that make them suspicious? Would they want to know why? Did they report such strange behavior to the *gong'an*, the public security forces? Already he imagined the interrogation: a room with dirty whitewashed walls, covered with flyspecks, and brown stains looking disconcertingly like dried blood. Bright lights trained on him as he stood there, deprived of food, water, sleep. Like the opening scene in *The Last Emperor.* "Mr. Walker, how is it that you have so quickly acquired a traveling companion? Are you aware that you have contravened a particular clause of a particular paragraph of a particular subsection of the criminal code? Mr. Walker, I am afraid that we cannot permit you to leave China at present. As for your so-called companion . . ."

But of course nothing like that happened. The agent, a pleasant young woman who went about her work with a practiced, Hong Kong–like efficiency, tapped her keyboard to bring the information up on the screen, though surely she already knew the answer, having given it to hundreds of people in the last few days. "No seats yet, Mr. Walker," she announced cheerfully. "But come back tomorrow, and things may have changed."

"Could you put me—us—on the waiting list, please?"

"I already have you down, Mr. Walker. And—Mrs. Walker, is it?"

"No," he answered. "A woman—a foreign student who must leave Shanghai." He gave Mary Hilding's name. Would an alarm go off, bells start ringing, the police rush in? "She doesn't have a ticket yet. I'll have to buy her one."

"No problem, Mr. Walker." Some more taps into the computer. "May I see her passport?" He handed it over, and she checked to make sure the visa was in order. "All right, Mr. Walker," she said, returning it. "Come back tomorrow morning and we'll see what we can do for you and Miss Hilding. Next, please." Matthew gave way, his place taken by a pair of worried Italian businessmen who were trying to move whole families out of harm's way.

Nothing to do now but wait. How long? A day, two days, a week? The longer he was kept there, the greater would be the danger to Liu Meihua. And himself. But he'd passed the first hurdle. At least he'd tried to buy the ticket, and nothing had happened to him. Just like Simon Larsen buying a ticket for his Mr. Chu on a Butterfield and Swire steamer. Butterfield and Swire, Swire Holdings, it was today, the owners of Cathay Pacific. Checking at the desk, he was relieved to discover that Daoming had come for his bicycle. At least he was all right. Back in his room, he tried to settle down and read some of the papers Zhao had given him. But of course he couldn't keep his mind on them. Chinese terms, Chinese characters, that he knew perfectly well, sent him riffling through the pages of his dictionary as if he'd never seen them in his life. His left shoulder throbbed painfully from where he'd been struck the night before. He tried to keep his mind on his work, but the characters simply swam in front of his face, and before long he gave up.

At six o'clock, the Chinese television broadcast a statement by a government spokesman admitting now that there had been some deaths during the clearing of the square three days ago. Most of the victims were soldiers, however, and very few students had died. There were shots of the violence done to the army: an infantry truck on fire, gasoline bombs hurled at tanks, and a grisly shot of the charred body of a soldier who had been lynched and hanged from a highway overpass. In the face of enormous provocation, the army had acted with the greatest restraint, remaining true to its duty to serve the people. And the people were grateful; little children came out with flowers, men and women carried food and drink to the soldiers, thanking them for restoring order in the capital. The lies were told with no particular skill, yet Matthew expected that, as they were repeated over and over again during the weeks and months to follow, they would eventually come to be accepted by many—outside the capital, at least—as the truth. As history.

Then came the photographs of the ringleaders who were still at large. Blurred pictures of Wu'er Kaixi, Wang Dan, Chai Ling, and others from Beijing's various universities. Matthew watched them intently. A photograph of Liu Meihua appeared on the screen, and under it, her description.

"Liu Meihua, native of Soochow, twenty-two years old, student at Fudan University, majoring in history [Matthew had noticed that all these bulletins gave the students' major department of study, as if that would somehow help in their identification]. Height: 1.54 meters. Weight: 51 kilos." Then the voice of the announcer broke in. "Liu Meihua has been seen in Shanghai. Residents of the Lujiawan and Xujiahui districts should be particularly alert." Matthew's heart sank; how long could she last if they had already pinned down the district in which she was hiding? Here, in his hotel, he was in the Lujiawan district, and Xujiahui—Siccawei, Father Duchamp's Siccawei—lay just to the southwest, out by the old Catholic cathedral. He wondered if the report was right, if she was somewhere close by.

At seven, after a quick supper, feeling lonely and worried, he tried to call Laura. Never expecting to get through, he was surprised to hear the phone ring at the other end. Then her voice, still blurred by sleep, came on. "Hello?" it said uncertainly. Of course it was only four in the morning on the West Coast. Stupid of him not to have remembered. No wonder he'd gotten through so easily.

"Laura, it's me, Matt. Look, I'm sorry to wake you up. I know it's the middle of the night—"

"Matt? Are you all right? Where are you?" He could almost see her, lying there in bed in her white nightgown, rubbing her eyes, trying to make sense of this sudden encounter that had woken her out of a deep sleep. "Are you on your way home yet?"

"I'm fine, and I'm trying to get out of here. But, listen, there's been a slight complication at this end, and I may have to stay on a few more days."

"Complication?" She sounded wide-awake now. "What's that mean? Why can't you come now? They're saying on the news that all Americans are being told to get out of China."

"Well, in the first place, I can't get a ticket—"

"But there are special flights. I heard about it on the news."

"And in the second place—well, it's not that easy. I just can't talk about it now. But I'll tell you all about it later."

Silence on the other end of the line.

"Laura, it's just going to hold me up a few days at worst. Maybe not even that. Maybe I'll be out of here tomorrow. It all depends."

"Depends on what? I don't understand."

"Well—I can't say anything more at the moment. You understand, don't you?"

Outside his room, someone was knocking at the door.

"Not really. But I suppose I've got to trust you." Then, slowly: "Matt, don't do anything silly."

"I won't."

"Promise."

"I promise."

Then he remembered about last night. "Laura, you made me a promise too. Three weeks ago. Do you remember?"

"Yes—" Uncertainty. "Yes, I think so. Why?"

"Well, guess what. I've found out what happened to Great-uncle Simon."

"You have?" Did she remember that rainy afternoon, three weeks ago? "Oh, Matt, that's wonderful." She laughed; yes, clearly she remembered it. "Now I'll never get back to sleep. Thinking about it." There was a pause. "Oh, Matt, I do want to see you. I'm so glad you called. Even if it is four in the morning. Have I been awful to you? I'm afraid I have." Another pause. "I've been thinking about it a lot in the last few days. And worrying about you."

"Laura, no. Not awful, never awful. But I've been thinking too. About what you said. Ever since I've been here. You just helped me to see things more clearly."

"Things? About us, you mean?"

"About us, but also—oh, I don't know. There's been so much that's come so fast, I'm still trying to sort it all out. To make the connections. You, me. Great-uncle Simon. What happened to him. What's happening in China." Did any of that make sense? He wasn't quite sure what he meant himself. But somehow the threads had to be tied together.

The knocking outside became more insistent.

"Listen, Laura, I've got to go. But I'll see you soon."

"Let me know when you're coming, Matt, and I'll be waiting for you in the L.A. airport. And, Matt . . ."

"Yes?"

"I can't wait to hear all about Great-uncle Simon."

"I'll call you from Hong Kong. Later this week, I hope. Within the week, anyway."

He hung up. The knock came again. "*Qing jin*," he called, "Come in," and got up to open the door.

Kang Kuangren stood outside. He looked worried and even more exhausted than he'd been earlier. Matthew was surprised; he hadn't expected to see him so soon.

"What's the matter?"

Kang shook his head. "Not here," he said. "Come out into the street. There's something I've got to show you. Now, please."

Matthew followed him. When they were out in the middle of the crowd on Maoming Road, Kang said, "Not safe to talk in there. Better here, even if someone sees us."

"What's the matter?" Matthew asked again. "Has something gone wrong?" Then he remembered the news bulletin: the police perhaps closing in on Liu Meihua's hiding place. Kang had seen it too. He'd talked to his friends, and they'd decided that they couldn't wait, and that that evening she must be moved to Hilding's apartment, to stay there as his daughter.

"Is that safe?"

"Safer than where she is now. You know they're looking for her in this part of the city?" Matthew nodded. "Xie *hsien-sheng*—Mr. Hilding—says his daughter often used to come stay with him—for a night, for a weekend. So they won't be surprised to see her back there now. Did you manage to get her a ticket?" Matthew explained: not yet, but tomorrow he'd try again.

"Where is she now? How do you plan to get her to Hilding's hotel?"

Kang looked at him seriously. "Mr. Walker," he said. "You are our best chance. You've already done a great deal, and I know I shouldn't ask you to do more. But we think that if she travels in the company of a foreigner, she'll be safe. Or safer, at any rate."

He explained. In a couple of hours, when most of the city was asleep, a friend would pick them up in a borrowed taxi, and would drive them to Liu's hiding place, about two miles southwest, in the Xujiahui district. Matthew was to come with Mary's passport; if they were stopped by the police, what could be more natural than for two foreigners to be traveling together in a taxi? Both with proper identification, of course. "Try to dress as much as possible like an American," said Kang. Unlikely that anyone could mistake him for a Chinese, thought Matthew: six feet tall, fair-haired, and an obviously non-Chinese complexion. But then it would be dark, and they could take no chances.

At eight that evening, the friend turned up. His taxi was a Santana, a Shanghai-made Volkswagen, and a car that sounded none too healthy as they pulled away from the hotel and headed off through a warren of back streets in the old French Concession, avoiding the barricades that still kept the main roads restricted to pedestrians and bicyclists. Just like last night, thought Matthew, except that this time I'm in a car. On the whole it was better; his shoulder was hurting again, and he wasn't sure that he could have handled a bicycle across several miles of dark city. His meeting with Chu Hung-ying, his being caught in the melée at the railroad crossing, all that seemed ages ago. So much had happened since then, so much to change his position. At the scene of the fire he'd been an unintentional participant caught up in a protest with which he had no connection. Now, only twenty-four hours later, he felt as if he had been pulled into a conspiracy that grew out of that protest. No, not pulled in; this time he was a willing, if thoroughly nervous, participant, playing a role that he himself had helped to write.

"I'll leave you when we get there," said Kang. "Best if only the two of you are with the driver when you go back to Mr. Hilding's room." He smoked steadily, his fingers tapping nervously on the upholstery. As they crossed Urumchi Road, the car coughed, emitted a loud backfire, and stopped. The driver climbed out, threw up the hood, and was surrounded immediately by a crowd of curious onlookers, all offering advice about how to get it started. Then the driver (who was he? why was he doing this? was he a real cabdriver? Matthew didn't know) was back in his seat, grinding the starter. Nothing happened. He motioned three or four strong men to stand behind the car and push. They did. It worked; the engine fired into life, leaving them enveloped in a cloud of blue smoke. Valves, thought Matthew vaguely. He didn't know much about cars, and hoped they wouldn't turn to him as a technical expert from the West.

At Tianping Road, near the Xujiahui intersection, they stopped. Kang motioned Matthew to get out. "He'll wait here," he said. "Safer like that. Notice where you are so you can find your way back." Matthew looked around; a small grocery store, a shop selling clothes and shoes, a sign proclaiming the presence of the Number Eight Middle School. Nothing to distinguish it from a thousand other street corners in the city.

"Now," said Kang after he had led him a few blocks, turning several corners. "Wait here, please. Better not to come with me. If the police see a foreigner, they might start asking questions. And when she comes, talk English to her. She understands a little bit." They were in front of a small park; outside it were public notice boards on which copies of newspapers had been put up, and a group of men and women stood reading them. Matthew couldn't get close enough to make out the characters in the light from the single dim streetlamp. Nor did he want to draw attention to himself; having been told earlier to look as foreign as possible, he now thought that protective coloration might have been the best. Maybe what he really needed was a wig of black Chinese hair.

For a quarter of an hour he walked up and down the block, nervously looking around to see if anyone was watching him. But foreigners are no rarity in Shanghai, even in this kind of a back street. Anyway, hadn't he heard that there was a new Sheraton hotel here in Xujiahui? Acres of air-conditioned luxury, Swiss chefs, and two-hundred-dollar-a-night rooms? People here must be not only used to foreigners, but resentful of them as well.

Then Kang was back, and with him a woman wearing a pair of jeans and a light shirt, the universal student uniform.

The best approach was a direct one, he thought. Look like a tourist, sound like a tourist. "Hello, Mary," he said loudly in English, striding up to her and putting out his hand. "Long time no see," realizing with a start that the old banality was in fact a direct translation of a Chinese greeting. At any rate, it should establish his Americanism to anyone who might be watching or listening. "You're looking good."

Liu Meihua seemed startled for a minute. Then she took his hand. "Hel·lo—John," she said uncertainly. John? John? Why John? But of course the sound was a good deal easier for a Chinese than Matthew, with its unfortunate diphthong. She was a bit quicker on the uptake than he was.

"I've got a cab waiting for us just around the corner," he said. His voice was still unnaturally loud, a caricature of the American abroad. Just a couple of foreigners near the Sheraton. Nothing strange in that, even if they were among the last left in town. "It'll take us a minute to get there." By now Kang had melted away into the crowd. Matthew led her back the way he'd come, hoping desperately that he could find the waiting car in the dark, and thoroughly relieved when he saw the school again. During all this time Liu Meihua said nothing, and only when they were in the car (which fortunately started this time) and driving away did he speak to her in Chinese. He gave her Mary Hilding's passport, and explained the plans to her: she was to stay with Hilding, posing as his daughter, while Matthew would try to get her a ticket to Hong Kong as soon as possible. She said very little, whether because of fatigue or shock he didn't know. Only once did she show a small smile, and that was when she told him that her English was almost nonexistent. "I didn't study it as hard as I should," she said. "So it will be difficult for me to act like an English girl."

"*Meiyou guanxi,*" he said. "It doesn't matter." At least I hope it doesn't matter, he thought. "I'll try to do the talking. And if anyone sees you with Mr. Hilding, you can say you're speaking

Chinese for practice. After all, that's why you've come to China. Just be sure to make lots of mistakes, the sorts foreigners make. Like me."

She smiled again, relaxing a bit. But by now the car had started coughing ominously again, this time like a patient with severe bronchitis. And then it stopped. Stopped this time for good apparently, for the driver's ministrations under the hood were unavailing.

He cursed softly, and turned to Matthew. "You're going to have to walk," he said. "Sorry, but there's nothing more that I can do. And I don't think the police should find us all together here."

Matthew agreed, realizing he still didn't know the driver's name, or what his part in all this was. Another one of China's unsung heroes, choosing to risk his life when he could have stayed home. It was now a little past eleven, and he hoped that he and Liu Meihua wouldn't attract too much attention out on the streets at that hour. By now he was thoroughly lost, as badly lost as he'd been the previous night. But it was Liu Meihua's city, not his, and she seemed to know where she was going.

"We've got about three kilometers to go," she told him. "But we may not be able to follow the big streets." He continued to talk to her in English, and she answered monosyllabically in the same language. Or at least in what approximated English. Even though her answers didn't always make very much sense, he figured they'd be good enough to fool any members of the *gong'an* who might be tempted to investigate. Only when they found themselves alone did they slip into soft Chinese, Matthew shifting rapidly back to English if he saw anyone coming.

For about twenty minutes their passage through the darkened city was uneventful. The streets were still, and at one point a brief shower drove them to shelter in the open entrance of an apartment building. The empty pavements glistened blackly under the rare streetlamps, and for a few minutes the air seemed cleaner and free from dust.

"We're coming to Ruijin Road," whispered Meihua. "We've got to be careful here; there's a police station nearby." Matthew had seen it earlier; Ruijin Road, running north through the old French Concession, was also one of the streets that had been blocked.

As they came up to the intersection, they could see a crowd

ahead of them. Not demonstrators this time, and nothing like the angry mob he'd seen last night. But not ordinary pedestrians either. In the gloom Matthew could make out a man giving them orders. He was in uniform, police or army, he couldn't tell which. The image of dictatorship, he thought suddenly: silent crowds, working in the dark, commanded by men in uniforms. Meihua grabbed his arm and pulled him back into the shadows.

"What's happening?" he asked.

"I don't know. But I don't like seeing all those people there." She sounded worried. But not frightened, though Matthew could imagine the images that must be flooding into her mind.

"Stay here," he said. "I'll go see what's going on."

"No," she answered. "Don't go. You might be arrested."

"Even if I'm a foreigner?"

"Even if you're a foreigner. They wouldn't put you in jail, of course, but they might hold you for a while. Let me go. I can talk my way out of it if there's trouble."

He didn't want to let her go. But she insisted. "Just remember you're English, not Chinese," he told her. She already had Mary's passport with her.

She disappeared into the darkness, leaving Matthew worried that he'd given in too easily. It was crazy—her picture had been shown on television several times that day, and here she was going into the middle of what might turn out to be a very dangerous situation. But you've got to admire her guts, he thought, though courage wouldn't make up for his stupidity in letting her go.

Three minutes later she was back at his side. "They're taking away the roadblocks," she said. "Group of workers. They've been brought here by the police. All over the city they're doing it. So that tomorrow the streets will be open."

"Maybe we'd better try to avoid them?"

"I think so. The trouble is that sooner or later we're going to have to walk on the big streets. There are no back alleys here. At least none I know of. But I think it'll be all right. The police seem to be worried only about how to clear the streets."

How they were being removed became clear enough when they reached the intersection. What looked like an army truck had attached itself to one of the buses, and was now beginning to pull it away. It was noisy and slow; the bus's tires had been slashed, and it sloughed and bumped on its rims over the rough pavement, looking like the corpse of some great animal that had died in an inconvenient place. Obviously it was going to be some days before that particular vehicle would be back in service. A few minutes later they crossed Huaihai Road. It was full of people working quickly and with reasonable efficiency at the business of clearing it. But Liu was right. No policemen stopped them, or even bothered to look in their direction. Whether it was because Matthew looked like an American, he didn't know. Or care.

It was almost one in the morning when they reached the Huaihai Hotel. Fast asleep behind the counter, the clerk didn't notice them as they came in. This time the elevator was working, and Matthew saw Liu Meihua to Hilding's room with no trouble.

CHAPTER TWELVE

Thursday, June 8, 1989

Now he knew he'd have to leave Shanghai, he thought as he woke from an uncertain sleep in which one confused dream had chased another through the brief hours of the night. The point now was to get Liu Meihua out of the city as quickly and as easily as possible, before the reaction set in, before the public security squads began hunting in earnest for those who'd managed to escape their net. They'd already arrested many people, of course, but others were still at large, their pictures and descriptions broadcast on television: Wu'er Kaixi, the student from Beijing University who had faced down Li Peng at their meeting a couple of weeks ago; Chai Ling, the young woman who had emerged as one of the radical leaders; and others. Did they have friends too, like Liu Meihua, who would hide them, and perhaps try to spirit them out of the country?

But suddenly he'd become responsible for her. She had gotten herself out of Beijing, and had gone to ground in Shanghai. She'd depended on her friends, who had now done all they could. And now they were depending on him. How had he gotten himself into this mess? Certainly through no doing of his own. All he'd done was to respond to what others wanted him to do, told him to do. Yet, as the appalling reality of what had happened in Beijing sank in, he found himself glad, even grateful, that he had a chance to be useful.

For the last few days the pictures he'd seen on television of the shooting, the tanks, the crushed bicycles, the fires, the bodies lying on the streets, stacked in the capital's hospitals, all had made him feel his own impotence, made him feel a mere spectator in the face of tragedy. Now he was being told what he could do, no longer simply a tourist of the emotions, gazing at China's pain. Nor was he just helping Liu Meihua, a single human being trying to flee her country, but China as a whole, for by now, in his mind, she'd become a symbol—his symbol, at any rate—of China, and of the cause that had been crushed by the army just three days before. He sensed that the thought wouldn't stand much scrutiny, but found it curiously soothing nonetheless, seeming somehow to justify to him the appalling risk he might be taking.

At eight he was in line outside the airline office, waiting for it to open. "Good news, Mr. Walker. We have some seats today," the clerk told him when he reached the counter.

"That's wonderful," he said. "What happened?"

"Two special flights coming in today," she said. "Australian and American. And many people have decided to go with them instead. Do you still want two places on tonight's plane to Hong Kong?"

He made the reservations and went back to his room to phone Hilding. "Does Mary still want to leave this evening?" he asked. It seemed cruel to use the dead girl's name to her father, but he had to assume that someone might be listening in on the line. "If she does, tell her that she can come with me to the airport. The flight's at eight-fifteen. We can travel together and I'll see that she meets her friends in Hong Kong."

"I know she does, Mr. Walker." Hilding's voice sounded weak and very far away. "She'll be very glad to get there, I know." They talked some more about arrangements. Hilding first suggested bringing her to Matthew's hotel, since it was on the way to the airport. But Matthew didn't want her to go outside any more than she had to, and said he'd pick her up at Hilding's quarters at five. He'd have liked to leave even later. The airport was sure to be crawling with police, and the less time they spent there the better. But they had to allow some leeway for problems on the way, and in any case, an international flight would mean lots of formalities.

Almost as soon as he had hung up, the American consulate telephoned. This time, a voice told him, the advice was no longer simply to avoid crowds; it was to get out of the city, out of China. So much for any regrets he might have had at leaving his research in midstream; even without this new entanglement he couldn't have stayed. Nor did he know how welcome he'd have been at the institute in the forthcoming days. With the reaction beginning and gathering strength, the presence of a foreigner might well prove embarrassing. Zhao Shanling had hinted as much yesterday, and Matthew had no desire to make life any more difficult for him and his colleagues. Still, he must go to the institute to make his farewells, and to thank Zhao for all he had done. In any case, now that the decision was made, there was nothing to do but to wait until evening. And to hope that Liu Meihua would be safe with Bernard Hilding.

He wanted to call Laura again, to tell her he'd be on tonight's plane for Hong Kong. He looked at his watch. Ten-twelve—that would make it, let's see, seven-twelve in the evening in Los Angeles. A good time to get her. Unless she was out with friends, having dinner.

And a good time for everyone else to be calling as well, he thought a few minutes later when the operator was unable to get through to the States. Journalists, business people, worried families, were all jamming the lines, no doubt. He tried again in twenty minutes. Still no luck. Maybe he'd be able to reach her from Hong Kong. If all went well, and he was lucky enough actually to be there that evening, and not in some Chinese prison cell.

He had to talk to her. Yesterday when he'd last called he hadn't said half the things he'd wanted to say. He'd meant to tell her—what had he meant to tell her? Even now he wasn't sure himself. Simply that he wanted to hear her voice again? To tell her once again that he loved her? Just in case—just in case what? Just in case it might be the last time? But the thought, with its solemnity, seemed almost ludicrous, dated, like a scene from one of those grainy old black and white movies of the war years. Still, he couldn't possibly tell her what he was doing, what trouble he might be getting himself into.

Anyway, that was only part of what he wanted to say. Yesterday evening he'd told her that he was trying to make the connections. But what did that mean? That somehow, in these last few days, he'd begun to understand, a bit more clearly, what had come between them? What Laura had meant in putting him off? Yet he still couldn't quite put his finger on it, or explain it. Everything had happened so fast since Sunday, the fourth, the day of the massacre. His discoveries about the last month of Simon's life, about the decisions Simon had made, about the course he had chosen to follow so many years ago. The angry demonstrations he'd seen himself in the streets of Shanghai, and the nightmare vision of the burning train. And then the bewildering events of yesterday: learning of Mary Hilding's death, about Liu Meihua's flight from the police, and his part— unsought, unwanted, but nonetheless freely accepted in all of this.

The connections—what where they? Simon had been faced with a choice, and had chosen to act. And so had he. So many of those long talks with Laura last winter, he was now beginning to realize, had simply served to keep a distance between them, to keep them from talking about what really mattered to them. All those arguments—about relativism, about the indeterminacy of language, of knowledge—all of them now seemed dry, academic, beside the point, fashionably clever words suitable for dazzling students, perhaps, but hardly helpful in a world where real choices have to be made, where real actions have to be undertaken. "The model postmodernist romance," one of his friends had scoffed last winter after having him and Laura to dinner one evening. "You and that girl of yours. Both of you paralyzed into inaction."

The connections. Could he make them, as he'd done in untangling the threads in Simon Larsen's story? Fitting everything into place, like a detective in a mystery novel? But he wasn't in a novel. Nor was Laura. Perhaps it was precisely because of all that had happened in the last twenty-four hours that Matthew was now beginning to be able to see himself and Laura no longer as the disembodied and distant characters in a story written by somebody else, but as two real people, people as real as they had seemed to each other a year ago. People whose actions, whose emotions, could no longer be seen as contingent on a fiction of someone else's devising, but people with real identities, real needs, real longings. Painful as it might be, he had to admit that perhaps the problem lay with him: that he'd been trying to write Laura into his own story, to bring her into his own history on his own terms. If he had learned in the last few days the importance of respecting the integrity of voices from the past, surely he could learn to respect Laura's own integrity rather than to try to be a Prospero to her Miranda—or, rather, a Ferdinand, the sort of Ferdinand who had inherited his father-in-law's spells and continued to use them to hold the magician's daughter, even after she should have been set free, responsive now only to commitments openly asked and openly given. Maybe that was why Laura had held back, why she had either refused him or turned aside his suggestions and his offers with her teasing. And yet why she still had been willing to wait—at least he hoped she had—until he understood and was ready.

And he was ready now. He knew it. Now he wanted her desperately, wanted to tell her what he had realized about her, about himself, wanted to tell her so much that could never be spoken over the telephone. He'd have to wait. But not long. If all went well, not long.

Today the taxis were back at the main entrance to the Jinjiang Hotel, and with no trouble he found one to take him to the institute. The streets were clear at last, and there were even a few buses running. Though many of them, like the one he'd seen last night, probably had nowhere to go but the repair shop.

At the institute he found Zhao Shanling, and, full of apologies, explained that he had to leave Shanghai, that the American consulate had warned Americans to get out of the city.

"I understand, Mr. Walker," said Zhao. He seemed very calm today; no more of the earnest sandpiperlike movements of the past. "I'm very sorry that your trip should end this way, but I think that it's probably better for us too if you go. Things may be a bit confused in the next few months. Perhaps if you come back next year we'll be able to be more help to you."

"Mr. Zhao," said Matthew, "you've already shown me more than I could have hoped for." Zhao held his finger up to his lips and shook his head. Clearly he didn't want Matthew to say anything further.

"Don't mention it. And did you find out what happened to Lai Shi'an?"

"I think so," said Matthew. "Those papers you let me see—how did you find them?"

"It wasn't so difficult," said Zhao. "The French police—they arranged things well. Once I knew what I was looking for, it wasn't hard to go to the right places. Of course there may still be more that we don't know about. That's for when you come back. But I think you have enough to go on."

"More than enough. Easy or not, I'm very grateful to you."

"We scholars must help one another," said Zhao simply. "It's lucky for me that I should have been in a position to give you some assistance." He got up and walked over to the window, looking down on the street that was now filling up once more with the noise of traffic. "But let me say this."

Abruptly he went into English. "The day may be coming, Mr. Walker, when we scholars in China may need much help from you in America, and elsewhere." He looked worried, and Matthew could only guess that he was remembering all that he had been through in Mao's reeducation campaigns, wondering whether Sunday's massacre was going to lead to a new wave of repression, wiping out all the gains of the past few years.

"I'll do what I can," said Matthew. "We all will. I've seen much in the last few days to make me admire the Chinese people and their struggle." He knew the words were simply the safe clichés of communist propaganda, but knew too that Mr. Zhao would understand the meaning that lay behind them. "Good-bye, Mr. Zhao. Thank you very much again for all your help, and I hope that it won't be too long before we see you again in America."

"*Zuihou shengli,*" said Zhao, shaking his hand. It was the old slogan, used by Communists and Nationalists alike, in the days of the war against Japan. Victory will be ours in the end.

At three-thirty Matthew was back in his room, throwing his belongings into a suitcase. Down on the bottom went the papers that Zhao had given him, down where they'd be free from any casual inspection. If there were more than a casual inspection, he might be in trouble. Even if there was nothing illegal about his having them (and he hoped there wasn't), he still didn't want any awkward questions at this point, and he certainly didn't want to get the institute into trouble for going beyond the normal requirements of hospitality and scholarly cooperation. He looked around the room, opened drawers, checked the bathroom, trying not to leave anything behind. A warm afternoon wind, freighted with its city smell of dust, smoke, and food, blew in the window. He wondered when he'd be back again, felt almost a pang of affection for this dingy room, with its mottled carpet and water-stained walls, where he'd lived for the last ten days. Ten days in which so much had happened, ten days in which he'd learned to see things so much more clearly.

Downstairs, he paid his bill, not before reminding the clerk that the institute had negotiated for him a rate lower than the one the Jinjiang customarily charged. The virtues of *guanxi*, he thought. He'd already arranged for a taxi, and promptly at five was at the entrance to Hilding's apartment. Though the Englishman seemed somewhat recovered, Matthew, looking at his pale gray face, remembered their first meeting only a week ago, and was appalled at how much he'd changed in that time.

"Come in, Matthew." It was the first time that Hilding had called him by his first name. "I can't tell you how grateful I am to you for your willingness to see Mary safely out to Hong Kong."

It sounded oddly old-fashioned, almost as if he were a character from a Victorian novel, someone who could never expect that a young woman might be capable of travel without a man at her side.

"We've got a few minutes before you have to leave. Mary's just getting her things together, and she'll be with us in a minute."

Matthew, listening to him, wondered what kind of adrenaline must be flowing within the old man to give him this kind of courage and self-control in talking about Liu Meihua as if she were his own daughter. It was little more than twenty-four hours since he had learned of the real Mary's death. And yet he had suddenly found himself called upon to assume a role in a drama for which he must have had no stomach, pretending to a fatherhood for a girl he'd hardly known, calling her by his own dead daughter's name, pretending to a relief at her safe return from Beijing. All the time, as the initial shock wore off, the horror of what had really happened must be growing within him, a great tumor whose pain would increase day by day. A line from *King Lear* came back to him, when Edgar sees his blinded father approaching: "The worst is not/ So long as we can say, 'This is the worst.'" At the moment, Hilding, like Matthew, was doing what he had to do to meet an immediate need—that of getting a hunted fugitive out of the country. But once they had gone, once the aircraft had lifted off from Hongqiao airport and was flying south to Hong Kong, what would be left for him? Where was he going to turn for friendship, where would he find people to whom he could talk about what had happened? And, at a deeper level, how was he going to look back on the life he had led, on the cause he had served for so many years? Writing his memoirs—if he continued to do that—might prove to be therapeutic. But perhaps it would also raise the kinds of questions in Hilding's own mind that he might never have chosen to face—or had to face—before.

"Mr. Hilding," he began. "I'm so terribly sorry—"

But the old man held up his hand. "I know, I know," he said. "It's very kind of you. But not now." Did that mean he couldn't bear to talk about it? At least with a comparative stranger? Or was he afraid the room was bugged? Matthew didn't know, and couldn't ask.

"Tell me about your meeting the night before last," Hilding went on. "I had a hand in arranging it, you know."

Matthew hadn't realized that. "You did?"

"Wei Tiaoyuan called me up the day after you met him here. Wanted to know if I thought he could trust you. I told him he could, that you'd be discreet, leave his name out of whatever you might tell others about this. So he said he'd dug up a man who'd known your Simon Larsen, might know something about what had happened to him."

"He couldn't have found a better person. It was Larsen's old Chinese teacher. At least that's how Larsen knew him. But he also turns out to have been a member of the communist underground back in 1927. When I heard his name, of course, I knew exactly who he was."

"And was he helpful?"

"Extremely. He'd gone into hiding right after Chiang Kai-shek's purge in April that year. Larsen helped him escape from Shanghai, on a British steamer. But then Larsen himself was killed." He told Hilding the story: how Simon had been drawn into reporting on affairs among Shanghai's foreigners to Chou En-lai, how men like John Ransom had grown suspicious of him. And how, on that last night right after Chiang's purge, Simon had helped Chu Hung-ying escape, only to be shot by Tu Yüeh-sheng's gangsters.

"That was the last that Chu saw of Larsen. He guessed that when the gangsters discovered they'd killed a foreigner, they got rid of the body and hoped that the case would go away. Which it did, of course. There was a brief investigation by the police. But it didn't last very long. They were very busy and didn't want to waste time on it. By then, of course, they'd discovered that he'd been working for the Communists. John Ransom even managed to plant the idea that he'd been spirited away to Russia. By the Soviet consulate."

"And opium? Does that figure in the story?"

"I think so. But I can't prove it." He told Hilding of Ransom's ties with Tu Yüeh-sheng, and of his own suspicions that Ransom might have had a hand in Larsen's death.

"Tu had a habit of getting people into debt," said Hilding. "Then he'd forgive them what they owed. But there was always a price attached to the forgiveness. A most unsavory character. I never met him, of course, but I certainly heard a lot about him."

He fell silent. Then Liu Meihua came into the room, a slight, pale figure carrying a knapsack and a small duffel bag. It was the first time Matthew had seen her in daylight, and he was struck by how harmless, how innocent, she appeared. And somehow not like the impression he'd gotten from her the night before. Still in jeans, and wearing a faded T-shirt with the incongruous message PROPERTY OF BROWN UNIVERSITY ATHLETIC DEPARTMENT on it, she again looked indistinguishable from the ten thousand other globe-trotting students who crowd the waiting rooms of Kennedy, Heathrow, or Kaitak. No reason to suspect her of anything. Was that why she seemed somehow different today, different from the resourceful young woman he'd met in the dark streets during their flight from Xujiahui? "Good evening, Maxiu," she said carefully, smiling at him and struggling gamely with his unpronounceable name. "Thank you for taking me to the airport." If only her English were better. Each syllable was carefully formed, separated from its neighbors; it was like listening to someone reading literary Chinese, giving each character the same weight as the next.

He tried to reassure her. "Don't worry. I'll help get you safely to Hong Kong." But he knew that the words sounded boastful, and that he had no cause for such confidence.

She looked at him, and this time she seemed more like the Meihua he'd met last night. "Thank you. And maybe I can help you too." He was struck by the resolve in her voice. Was she reminding him that, whatever the government had done to her friends, this remained, after all, her country, not his? Or that, recent as her own initiation as a revolutionary may have been, she was still far more practiced than he, who knew of such things only from what he read in books? In any case, it was a gentle reminder that she was her own woman, and not simply someone who would fit into his plans, his version of what should be done. He was to become a partner in her crime, not a prince rescuing her from the dragon.

It was time to go. "Be careful, Matthew," said Hilding. "And you too, Mary. You've seen the television today?" Matthew nodded, trying to decide how closely the woman with him resembled those grainy photographs the police had been broadcasting.

He rose. "Mr. Hilding," he said. "Thank you for your help. I wish I could have done more for you and those memoirs of yours." He wanted to ask Hilding what his own plans were, but couldn't bring himself to invade the elder man's privacy.

"I'm going to go back to work on them," he said. "Maybe we'll meet each other again. I've been thinking a lot about the future these last few days. Wondering if there's a place left for me in China after what they've done."

"They" clearly meant Li Peng and his government. "You might go home, then?" asked Matthew.

"Home?" Hilding seemed not to understand the question. "I don't know where home is. I haven't had a home since I left Bradford sixty years ago." He thought for a minute. "But I still have family in England. Maybe it's time to go visit them. If they'll put up with me." Then, surprisingly, came a line of poetry: " 'Home is where, when you go there, they have to take you in.' That's one of your Americans, isn't it? Robert Frost?" he added when Matthew looked blank.

And then the two of them were in the taxi, Matthew and Liu Meihua, driving out along Yan'an Road, southwest toward the airport. In her careful English, Meihua told him of her stay with Hilding; how he had tried to find out all he could about his daughter's death, desperate to make absolutely certain that there had been no mistake, eager to clutch at any hope, no matter how slight, that Mary might still be alive.

"That poor man," she said. "I tell him his daughter's very brave. We all—*xianmu*—?"

"Admire," said Matthew.

"We all admire her very much. She is a great friend of Chinese people. Now we consider her *lieshi*—martyr?" Matthew nodded. Obviously the effort of speaking English fatigued her. And Matthew knew how frustrating it can be for an intelligent person to be reduced to speaking with what is mostly a child's vocabulary, making a child's mistakes. But she mustn't break into Chinese in the hearing of the cabdriver.

He changed the subject. "You look different today. Something's happened."

Now she smiled again. "My hair. I cut it myself this morning. Do you like it, Ma-xiu?" Suddenly she was a girl again, looking pleased that he'd noticed, perhaps even wanting a compliment from him. "So that I am more like the picture in the passport." That was it, of course; her hair was shorter, as Mary's had been when the photograph was taken. It made her look, in some indefinable way, less Chinese—or, like Mary, someone Chinese in features but with a foreign sense of appearance.

Traffic was still light, and in several places they passed groups of demonstrators marching with their red flags, carrying their banners of protest. But the traffic barriers were all gone, dismantled, and they had no problem in reaching the airport.

And no problem inside the airport. Even though it was crowded with foreigners leaving the country, even though, as Matthew had expected, there were policemen and soldiers everywhere. The customs men didn't even look at his bag, with its precious cargo of documents, as he checked it in at the Cathay Pacific counter. They were even less interested in Liu Meihua and her knapsack. To them, she was just another of the many foreigners leaving the country, like the crowds of Australians and Americans who'd passed through earlier in the day.

No problem, that is, until they got to passport control. That was the last hurdle, a little gate to pass through, where a policeman sat checking exit visas, there within sight of the waiting room for international passengers. Matthew let Meihua go first. She took out the British passport, holding it open to the visaed page, and showing her ticket to Hong Kong. The man flipped back to Mary Hilding's photograph, looked at it, looked up at Meihua's face. And then back at the photograph. He called one of his colleagues over and showed him the passport. They talked rapidly together for a minute. Then the second said in English, "You come this way please." Meihua, pale-faced, obviously terrified but very much in control of herself, went with him. Matthew followed them. The man tried to stop him, but Matthew said loudly in English, "Hey, you can't do that. She's traveling with me. If you're going to ask her any questions, I want to be there."

The policeman shrugged. Why not, after all? Then he led the two of them through a door into a small anteroom outside an office. He knocked at the office door and went in. A minute later he came out with another man, apparently his superior officer.

The latter came out, looked at Meihua and Matthew, and motioned them to come in, shutting the door behind them.

"I'm Captain Li Fenggui," he said. "Franklin Lee. Airport security. I'm delighted to meet some English people. I spent two happy years in that country not long ago." He spoke in English, handling the language fluently and without trouble. Oh, my God, thought Matthew, he's never going to be fooled by Meihua's primitive English. Somehow he was going to have to try to do the talking, to spare Meihua as much as possible.

"I'm an American, Captain Li," he said, holding out his passport. Captain Li took it, looked at the cover, and handed it back.

"So you are, Mr. Walker, so you are. And may I ask what has brought you to China?"

"I'm writing a book. About Shanghai and its history. So I came here to do some research for it."

"How interesting, Mr. Walker. And where have you been doing this research?"

Matthew mentioned the institute, adding that he had also talked to Bernard Hilding, Mary's father, hoping that the name would mean something. Hoping also that mentioning it would keep him from losing control of the situation, from giving in to his fears.

"I've never visited the United States, Mr. Walker. But I'd like very much to go. Especially after my time in England, I'd find very interesting the comparison between the transatlantic cousins."

Matthew's heart sank. There was no way, absolutely no way, that Meihua was ever going to be able to get by this man.

"And Miss Hilding? I see that you've been in China several months. What has brought you here?"

"She's a student," said Matthew. "She's been studying Chinese at Fudan University. On an exchange program. That's easy enough for you to check."

Captain Li held up his hand. "Please, Mr. Walker. Surely the day is past when women need men to speak for them. Miss Hilding?" He looked at her inquiringly.

"I am student," she said slowly and plainly.

Captain Li looked at her. " 'I am student,' " he repeated. "Yes. Well. I see." He thought for a moment. "Mr. Walker, would you mind waiting outside for a minute?" He opened the door and motioned to the guard.

"But I'm traveling with her," said Matthew. "The plane's leaving soon." He looked at his watch. "Couldn't you simply let us go to the gate?"

Captain Li smiled. "We'll try not to have you miss your plane, Mr. Walker. Anyway, it was late in leaving Hong Kong. So the passengers here won't be boarding until after nine."

There was nothing to do. Matthew looked at Meihua, trying to flash her a glance of encouragement, to keep her spirits up. But the guard hustled him into the anteroom outside, shut the door behind them, and motioned him to a chair.

He sat there, unable to move, unable to think, staring at the walls. They were bare of any decoration. In the old days at least there would have been a picture of Chairman Mao. And the whitewash looked dingy enough to have been put on back in Mao's day. Once again Matthew was reminded of those grim interrogation scenes in Bertolucci's *Last Emperor*, and of the prisoner's attempted suicide, slashing his wrists, holding them in a basin of dirty water that slowly turned red. He remembered Simon's description of the executed revolutionaries, their heads strung in baskets above the wintry streets of Shanghai. At least that kind of barbarism had long since gone. But another memory came back to him: five years earlier, traveling in China with two friends, he'd been in Xi'an, part of a large crowd watching what seemed to be a parade down one of the city's main streets. Then, following the ranks of policemen and soldiers, there had appeared four open army trucks, each one carrying about a dozen men with their heads shaved and their hands tied behind their backs, placards hanging from their necks announcing the crimes for which they had been convicted. Slowly the horrified realization of what he was watching had come to him: they were criminals on their way to the execution grounds outside the city, being shown off to the crowds before their lives were ended by a bullet in the back of the neck.

What on earth could he do? Though he was badly frightened, he tried to think rationally, to force his brain to make sense. But here he was, thousands of miles from home, in a country that was not his own, a country where he knew almost no one, had no one to turn to. And a country whose laws he was breaking. He'd never been in a situation remotely like this; it was the sort of thing that happened only in books. Or to someone like Simon Larsen. Suppose he stormed into Captain Li's office, the outraged foreigner, insisting that the two of them be allowed to leave? That might have worked in Simon's day, but not in 1989. What if he demanded that they let him call the American consulate? It would be shut now, of course, but at least there'd be a duty officer who could help. But how would the consul react when he discovered that Matthew was trying to smuggle someone—a wanted criminal—out of the country? And what if Captain Li insisted that they call the British consulate too, to vouch for Mary Hilding's identity? Then they might be in even worse trouble than they were now.

There was nothing, absolutely nothing, that he could do that made any sense. He knew what he'd known all along: that he could only sit there and wait, trying to keep his fears from taking control. He pulled out of his pocket one of the green Penguin detective stories he'd bought in Hong Kong. The foolish-looking but terribly competent hero was about to solve the case. Whatever it was, someone who'd been murdered, Matthew couldn't remember who. Or care. Or even keep his mind on the page. Through the door he could hear the sound of voices: the fluent Chinese-accented English of Captain Li, and Meihua's monosyllabic responses. Then silence for a minute or two, and when the voices started up again, Matthew realized that he could no longer make out what they were saying. Not just because they were speaking more softly now, but because the conversation had shifted to Chinese—not Mandarin, but the Shanghai dialect. That could mean only one thing—that she realized she could no longer keep up the pretense of being an English student. He could imagine her pleading with Captain Li, appealing to him. Not to let her leave the country, since that now seemed unthinkable, but perhaps to let her go home to Soochow, promising to stay out of trouble. And ready perhaps to turn in her friends as the price of her own safety? No—he rebelled at the thought. She wouldn't do that. Or would she? How did he know? Maybe she was even telling Captain Li about him, about the role he'd played, or tried to play, in her escape.

He looked at the guard, to see his reaction. Was he listening to what was taking place behind the door? Could he tell that Matthew's heart was racing, his mouth dry, that it was all he could do to sit still? But the man seemed thoroughly bored. No doubt he'd be glad when this last plane had come and gone, and he could head home for the night. The minutes ticked away. Longer and longer. They'd been in there fifteen, no, twenty minutes now. Was that a good sign or a bad sign? At least Meihua must be putting up a good fight. Unless Captain Li was simply enjoying himself, playing with her before closing in.

Half an hour after they'd gone in, when Matthew thought he could stand it no longer, the door opened. Meihua came out, looking pale, but smiling at Captain Li.

"All set, then, Mr. Walker," he said in English. "So sorry to have held you up. But one can't be too careful these days, you know. And Miss Hilding," he said, turning to Meihua. "I hope that you have enjoyed your stay in China. And do break away from your studies long enough to enjoy something of the beauties of Leeds." He turned to Matthew. "Miss Hilding is a student at the university there," he said, "but I find that she knows very little about the city itself. It is, of course, a testament to her hard work, I suppose. And she has learned her Chinese very well. Even our difficult Shanghai dialect." He smiled. "But all work and no play—I have told her that she should take some time off, have fun."

Matthew stared at him, unable at first to speak. Was this all a game? Then he said, "Thank you, Captain Li. I guess we'll be in time for our plane after all." He could hardly bring the words out, heard his own voice, thick with fear and incomprehension, and hoped that it sounded normal.

"Don't worry, Mr. Walker, don't worry. You'll be well in time. But I'll have the guard see you directly into the main waiting room anyway. To make up for the trouble we've caused you. Then you won't have to wait in any more lines. VIP treatment." He smiled. "In return, perhaps you could do me a favor."

"What's that?" asked Matthew.

"When you get to Hong Kong, you and Miss Hilding need not mention this episode. Particularly to outsiders. Perhaps the two of you could just forget that it ever happened. That'll make it easier for everyone. And, Mr. Walker—"

"Yes?"

"Please remember to tell your friends that Chinese have feelings too. And that not all of them behave the way the worst elements do." Matthew nodded, dumbfounded, unable to think of anything appropriate to say. "But then, I'm sure the same is true of America. Good-bye, Mr. Walker, good-bye Miss Hilding. *Yi lu ping'an*—have a good trip." He held out his hand, and Matthew took it; its warmth made him realize how cold his own must have been.

Captain Li went back into his office, and the guard motioned Matthew and Liu Meihua to follow him. A back door took them into the main international waiting room, and there he left them, rejoined with the other passengers waiting for the plane to arrive. Matthew felt weak with relief, unable to believe their good fortune. Did it mean they'd really done it? That they wouldn't be arrested after all? That in just over an hour they'd be airborne, flying south to Hong Kong and to freedom? That those terrifying visions of Shanghai prisons, of police interrogation cells, were nothing more than the fabrications of an overworked imagination?

And yet—it all seemed too easy. What if all this were simply part of a cruel game? A game whose last move waited to be played even as they were walking now among the long rows of fluorescent-lit counters that lined the lower level of the waiting room, counters filled with Chinese souvenirs, jewelry, food, drink, cigarettes, ready for sale to passengers with hard currency. Everything looked normal, even placid, the airport itself quiet and peaceful, waiting for the last flight out so it could close for the night.

He looked at Meihua beside him, desperately eager to talk to her, wanting to know what had happened. She caught his eye and shook her head, then stared straight ahead, leading him to a seat at some distance from the others in the waiting room.

He didn't so much sit down as feel his knees give way. Only then did Meihua speak.

"It's all right, Ma-xiu," she said in Chinese. She peered at him in the dim light of the room. "Are you ill? You look very strange. But it's all right now, I'm sure of it. You mustn't worry."

"He knew who you were?"

She nodded. "Of course he never said so. Directly, I mean. But it didn't take him long to discover I can't speak much English. Or that I didn't know anything about the university where Xie Meili—Mary Hilding—had studied."

Matthew was puzzled. Why had he kept her so long? "Then what were you talking about? You were in there at least half an hour." He saw no need to tell her how terrified he'd been, what visions had gone through his mind during that time.

"I know, Ma-xiu. And I thought about how worried you must have been. But I think he believed it would look suspicious if I came out too soon. As if he hadn't made a thorough investigation." She paused, then went on. "And he told me some things—"

"Things? What?"

"I was worried that he was going to ask me what I knew about the others. The others whom the police are looking for, I mean. But he didn't. Instead, he told me that the police must be very careful. There were too few of them, he said, to catch everyone. Some parts of the country were unguarded. And he told me where those parts were. Twice."

Matthew still didn't get it. "Why would he do that?"

"Don't you see? He was giving me information for the people I'll meet in Hong Kong. Telling me what are the safest ways to leave China. For others, who will come later. At least I think that's what he meant to do."

Matthew considered this, still wondering whether Captain Li was trustworthy.

"But he must be taking a terrible risk in letting you go."

"That's why we must do as he says. And not say anything about this. To anyone, ever. There are others like him, I think. People who want the news of what happened to get out. And they are depending on us, who were there, and who can leave China, to tell the world."

"It's not a trap?" He still couldn't believe it. "You don't think it's a trap of some kind?" He knew it made no sense; what sort of a trap could it be?

At that, she almost smiled. "No," she said, "no, I'm sure it isn't. In Beijing there were people like him, people who were in the police but who helped us, who were on our side." She looked at him again, a look now of concern. "Are you sure you're all right? Can I get you anything? Do something?"

Did he look that bad? He was almost ashamed of himself. If she, after all she had experienced, could be gutsy enough to stand up to what they'd been through that evening, surely he could pull himself together.

"No," he said. "I'm all right. Stay here. It's too dangerous for you to walk around." But he knew that what he really meant was that he didn't want her to leave him. It was almost as if he, who had started the evening as the rescuer, were now being rescued by her—rescued from the dragons of his own imagination, even after the frightening ordeal was over.

In the center of the waiting room a television set was on, showing a documentary of the recent events in Beijing. It was amateurishly done, without the slickness common to American productions. The handheld camera wobbled as it passed over long lines of burned-out vehicles, buses, army trucks, civilian cars, all of them, according to the announcer, destroyed by rioters. There were other pictures, like the ones he'd seen broadcast in the last few days: people throwing rocks and gasoline bombs at army trucks, the soldier's charred body hanging from a highway overpass, the personnel carrier aflame, running out of control, with its human cargo trapped inside: *junren hai zai nei*, said the voice-over, there are still soldiers in there. Pictures that suggested a mob gone out of control, violent, destructive, but gently and surely pacified by soldiers who exercised enormous self-control in the face of extreme provocation. A shot of the students marching out of the square, early on the morning of June 4, showed that the demonstration had ended peacefully and that there had been no shooting in the square. Despite what foreign propagandists said.

And then at the end, photographs of little children carrying flowers to give the soldiers, thanking them for all they had done to make the capital peaceful again. But the other pictures were missing: the tracers lighting up the night sky, the fires, the Goddess of Liberty toppling over and falling slowly to the ground, the crushed tents, the bodies of the dead and wounded, draped over bicycles, trishaws, handcarts, being carried to the hospitals. And no picture, of course, of the lonely man who had stopped a whole column of tanks by the simple act of walking in front of them.

Then, as soon as the report was over, there came on the screen the pictures and the descriptions of the fugitives still at large: Wu'er Kaixi, Chai Ling, Wang Dan, and the others. And then Liu Meihua herself, Liu Meihua, the history student from Soochow, still known to be at large in Shanghai. Matthew stared at the screen, appalled at what he saw. The picture looked exactly like her, exactly like the Meihua sitting next to him. Even with her newly cropped hair it was clear that she was the same person that the police wanted. And if he could see it so easily, surely everyone else around them could too.

Liu Meihua looked at him, and then rose to her feet. She nodded her head to indicate the presence of a couple of soldiers slumped in chairs nearby. But they too had their eyes fixed on the screen, seemingly uninterested in what was going on around them. Their faces showed no emotion; it was impossible to know what they were thinking, how much they believed what they were being told.

"Let's go over there," she said. "I think it's more comfortable." To him it looked no different from where they were, but he let her lead him over to a more remote part of the waiting room, where they could speak more freely. And there, convinced that there were no eyes watching her, no ears listening, she started to talk to him. "It wasn't like that, it wasn't like that at all," she said. She spoke Chinese now, almost as if she were already safely away from Chinese soil. Her voice was soft and unemotional, and he understood that she was trying to look like no more than an ordinary person carrying on an ordinary conversation. And that he must play his part by doing the same.

She told him what happened: what it had been like in Beijing, living in the square with the fears and the rumors, and the hope that against all the evidence, against all common sense, their cause would win in the end. She told him about the disagreements that had broken out among the demonstrators: those who wanted to leave, convinced that the government would crack down, and those who, like her, had argued that they must keep going, that they'd win in the end if they only persevered. And she told him about that final dreadful night when the army came in and the shooting had begun: how she'd been caught in the gunfire with Mary Hilding and Kang Kuangren, how the troops had fired apparently at random into the crowds. How they'd taken Mary to the hospital, only to watch her die. How they'd spent a day hiding in Beijing before being able to board the train that would take them back to

Shanghai. How the train had stopped in northwest Shanghai, and the fire had broken out, giving her and Kang a chance to escape into the night, just at the point when Matthew had found himself caught up in the crowd. And finally, how she had been hidden, out near Xujiahui, where Matthew had met her.

"The police knew you were there," said Matthew. "At least in that part of Shanghai. Someone must have seen you."

"I know," she said. "There was a television set I could watch. So I saw my picture and my description broadcast. I wondered how I could disguise myself. But I had to go outside that first day. Maybe someone saw me then and called the police." Chinese television was already carrying stories about loyal citizens who had used the hotline set up by the police to report sightings of troublemakers. In one case, a sister had turned in her own brother, and was being hailed for her patriotic act.

It was an extraordinary experience listening to her. She had been an eyewitness, a participant—no, more than that, a leader—in the greatest outburst of public opposition to the government in all Chinese history. And yet her story, and the story of the tens of thousands of others who'd been there, could be told only when she was safely out of her own country. And once it was told, who in China would hear it? What chance would it stand against the kind of story that the regime was putting out, the kind of story that they'd just been watching on the television set in the waiting room?

"Who are they going to believe?" Matthew asked Meihua. "In the future, I mean? Are people really going to be convinced by what the government's saying?" He nodded at the now-silent television set across the room.

"I don't want to think so," she said. "But I don't know. I think about all the things I was told. In school, in college. About all the things I believed. Maybe I still believe some of them—I don't know. But others I know are wrong." She thought for a while. "But I'm afraid that if lies are repeated long enough, then people will come to believe them. That's what they hope, of course. The men who run the government."

From the darkness outside came the distant roar of a jet touching down. The sense of relief among those in the room was palpable; the flight from Hong Kong had landed, the plane that would soon be carrying them out of China, its navigation lights winking in the night, now turning on the distant runway before taxiing up to the gate.

"But there must be lots of people in Beijing, at least, who will know the truth."

"Yes," she said doubtfully. "But Beijing's only a very small part of China, after all. And people—most people, anyway—are badly frightened now. They'll do whatever's safe."

They sat there in silence, watching the aircraft approach, its green and white body slowly becoming visible through the dark. "What'll you do when you get to Hong Kong?" he asked her. "Have you ever been there?"

"No," she said. "We have no chance to travel. But there are people there—student groups, and others—who've been supporting us. I have an address to go to where I know I'll be helped. In Mongkok. Do you know where that is?"

"Yes. It's part of Kowloon. And then what? Will you stay in Hong Kong?"

"I don't know. I can't think now. I'll see."

"I'm sorry," said Matthew. "I don't mean to ask you all these questions. I just want to be sure that you'll be safe when you arrive." He was beginning to feel sure of himself once more, becoming the rescuer again, protecting Meihua from her unknown enemies.

"Yes," she said. "I'll be safe with my friends. After that, who knows? Maybe the Chinese government will fall, and I can go home. Otherwise, I suppose that for a while at least I'll have to be an exile. But it is important that I tell my story—our story, the true story. Otherwise people may come to believe those lies." She nodded at the television set on the other side of the room. "Just as so many people believe all those lies that the Party has told us in the past."

By now the aircraft had reached the gate, and its passengers were getting off. There can't be more than ten or a dozen in that whole huge plane, thought Matthew as he watched them disembark, and he wondered how they must feel, stepping off the plane into the vast Chinese night, returning to a country where no one knew what turmoil might erupt.

They sat there, safe in the dim light of their corner of the terminal, talking softly, waiting for the aircraft to be refueled, to be prepared for its return. Finally the loudspeaker above them crackled, and a voice announced the coming departure of Cathay Pacific Flight 301 for Hong Kong. They rose, making their way toward the boarding gate, and were almost there when Matthew saw a soldier standing near the woman checking boarding passes, looking over the passengers filing into the aluminum gangway leading to the aircraft. For an instant, all his fears returned, and he moved to walk in front of Meihua, trying to hide her from view as best he could. Then, to his immense relief, just as the two of them reached the gate, the man, a vacant expression on his face, turned away to stare out the window at the lights on the runway; he too had the look of someone eager for the evening's work to be over.

Now they were inside the cabin, making their way through the crowds of other passengers to their seats. Meihua had a place by the window, and Matthew was next to her. In the seat pocket in front of him he found a menu telling him what to expect for dinner, and a folder advertising duty-free perfumes, cigarettes, brandy, Hermès scarves. A soft voice from the speaker above their heads urged them politely, in Cantonese, Mandarin, and English, to fasten their seat belts, and Matthew suddenly wanted to laugh out loud at the routine conventionality of it all, to laugh with relief at this comforting embrace of the world of the normal. Suddenly, in the everyday sameness of airplane travel, Shanghai seemed a million miles away.

But it wasn't, of course, for beyond the dark window, the brooding immensity of China stretched far off into the night. Next to him, Meihua sat staring out at the blue runway lights in the distance. What must she be feeling now, he wondered as the aircraft made its final preparations to leave? The doors were shut, and now they began moving slowly away from the gate. A few minutes later the aircraft was on the runway, gaining speed, the engines roaring in the night. Forty seconds later they were airborne, the ground falling away beneath them, pressed back into their seats as the plane began its climb through a thin layer of clouds that soon obscured the scattered lights of the villages below.

Even then Matthew still couldn't believe they were finally safe. His imagination, still not fully under control, pictured a special agent on the plane, watching them. Someone who was going to follow Meihua in Hong Kong, to find out who her friends were. Or would the Chinese air force come after them, shoot the plane down, the way the Korean airliner had been shot down by the Soviets six years ago? Or might Shanghai air traffic control order the aircraft back to the airport it had just left? Of course his reason told him that such speculations made no sense; but his reason was still fighting with his fears and his suspicions.

The cabin steward came by with a tray of drinks—orange juice, soda, wine, whiskey. Matthew, never a strong drinker, nonetheless took a glass of whiskey. It burned his throat as it went down, but it also gave him a new clarity of thought, so that for the first time since the encounter with Captain Li he began to see things a bit more plainly, to have them fall into place, to realize that his imagination had gotten the better of him, and that now, at last, they really were safe.

He looked at Meihua, sitting beside him. She'd said nothing since they'd left, and her face was still pressed to the glass of the window, as if she were trying to catch a last glimpse of the country she was leaving.

"Meihua?" He spoke her name tentatively, thinking perhaps that she did not want to be disturbed in her thoughts.

She turned to him, and he saw that she had been crying.

"Meihua, are you okay?" What a stupid question, he thought, after what she'd been through, after the events of the evening.

"I'm sorry," she said, still speaking Chinese, not even trying English. "Ma-xiu—you've done so much for me. Yesterday and today. Things you didn't have to do. I'll never forget it." She tried to smile, but the tears were still coming. "I've always dreamed of traveling. But not like this, not to leave my family and my friends. And not to leave my country like this, like—like a criminal. But it's all right—I'll be all right in a few minutes."

The drink was doing its work on Matthew. So was the aircraft's steady climb as it left Shanghai behind. On a screen in the front of the cabin, a yellow computerized map charted their progress: it showed the plane now near Hangchow, at an altitude of some seven thousand meters and still climbing, heading south-southwest at a ground speed of seven hundred fifty kilometers an hour. The display reassured him, made him feel himself again, as the flow of adrenaline that had kept him going that evening gradually subsided. He was in control again: of his fears, his nerves, his imagination, his destiny.

"My family," said Meihua. "What will happen to them? When the police find out I've left the country?"

There seemed to be no good answer to that question. "At least it'll be better than if you were still there," said Matthew, knowing it was small comfort.

Dinner appeared before them, little dishes filled with shrimp and snow peas, flavored with coriander and sesame oil.

"I've always wanted to see Hong Kong," she said. She seemed restored by the food. "At school, in our Youth League meetings, we were always told how terrible it was, how corrupt. Still a colony, so many poor people working like slaves for a handful of capitalist millionaires. Not like China, where everyone's equal. But then, whenever I talked to people who'd been there, they told me it's not like that at all, it's wonderful, a place where you can do anything, think anything, go anywhere."

"You'll like it," Matthew said. He described the Hong Kong he had seen, how different it was from Shanghai. Yet still thoroughly Chinese, built by millions of hardworking people into one of the world's great cities.

She looked at him. "Perhaps that's one of the reasons I began not to believe them. The Party members, I mean." She thought for a moment. "I think that we got used to them telling us lies. So we developed a sort of sixth sense about what to believe and what not to believe. But somehow it seemed not important."

Matthew looked at her inquiringly.

"Because it was easier to pretend to believe. And because we never thought that the government would—would turn on its own people. Kill them. Just because they were patriotic."

They talked softly through dinner, and afterward Meihua fell asleep, her head with its short hair resting against the window that kept the Chinese night outside. Matthew, watching her in the seat next to him, envied her ability to drop off like that; the evening's excitement was still too much with him. He leaned back, unable to read, but trying to make some sense out of what had happened in the brief period he'd been in Shanghai.

He thought of the soldier he'd seen at the gate, watching the passengers boarding the aircraft, and he thought of Chu Hung-ying and Simon on that last night they'd spent together in Shanghai. Of Chu's escape aboard a British steamer, and of Simon lying dead on the quay before his body was picked up and taken away. He thought about all the others—like Chou En-lai, whom Simon had known as Chang Shao-shan—who had faced danger and death in those years to bring about the transformation of the China they so passionately believed in, certain that they were helping her at last to escape the burdens of four thousand years of history. He thought about Bernard Hilding, of the years he had devoted as a foreigner to that transformation, and to the grief that had come to him near the end of his life, the betrayal of all his hopes. He thought about the drama that had been played out before the world that spring, about people like Liu Meihua and the other leaders of Tiananmen Square, who believed, equally passionately, that their country's transformation had yet to come. He thought about Chiang Kai-shek's betrayal of the revolution in Shanghai, in April 1927, when his troops and their gangster allies had slaughtered the Communists. And he thought about the communist government's own betrayal of its young four days ago, when in the early morning of June 4, the tanks had shot their way into Beijing.

He thought of the television broadcast they had just seen a couple of hours earlier, about the Party's attempt to incorporate the bloody events at Tiananmen into its own history, and to appropriate that history to its own uses. But whose property is history? A phrase from his reading came back to him—"history is a nightmare from which we are trying to awake," or something of the sort. James Joyce, was it? But surely, he thought, it becomes such a nightmare only when we allow ourselves to relinquish the understanding of history's meaning to others. To those who want to use that history as a source of power that makes possible the control of others, the sort of history that becomes no more than propaganda, a history that loses its integrity and betrays the memories of the men and women whose lives it purports to record. The sort of history that the Party was trying to write on the television screen that evening.

Perhaps we struggle not to fly from history, he thought, but to understand it, to master it so that it can't be used to master us. Wang Baozhen had come to understand that, after a lifetime of study, after a lifetime of bitter experience. In ways that had sometimes been painful, her own history had intersected that of her country, of the record that she was trying to describe. And from her own experience she had learned to see more clearly aspects of that record that, in happier times, might have remained invisible to her. And Simon Larsen, too, had brought to his understanding of China and its revolution something of the painful experience he'd gained in France, from his brush with death and his consciousness of his own mortality.

And here he was, Matthew Walker, in the night sky, nine thousand meters above Fukien province (the cabin chart told him that). What had he learned? If all travel is a voyage of discovery, what had this journey to the other side of the world taught him? About himself? About history? About humanity?

He looked around him, taking in the cabin of the plane with its three hundred and more people on board. Three hundred plus separate histories, separate memories. Liu Meihua's history, his own history. His reconstruction of those other histories: Simon Larsen's, Emily Ransom's. The history of Shanghai, of China. That distant spring so many years ago, this present spring from which they were escaping. All of them becoming part of the house of memory, the house that historians build, the house that we all build.

The connections, the connections between past and present, the worlds we imagine and the world we live in, the connections between ourselves and others. He was still trying to make them. They'd come, surely. But it was going to take time to absorb the lessons of the last few days. To understand them, when he had returned home to his own world, the world of books, of teaching, of writing.

And of Laura. He'd call her that evening when they landed, tell her that he was on his way back, that he'd be in California as soon as there was a seat on a homebound flight. Laura, whom in the last ten days he'd come better to understand—better, perhaps, than when he'd been with her. Strange that it should have taken this trip to the other side of the world, this confused rush of impressions that had swept over him, to make him begin to see more clearly what had been there all along. Laura, who would be waiting for him, Laura, who all along had grasped, better than he had ever done, what were the connections.

Then, like Meihua in the seat next to him, he slept.

An hour later he woke when the pitch of the engines changed and the wing flaps ground into position as the aircraft began its approach to Kaitak. Below them, there appeared the glowing sprawl of Kowloon, and on the other side of the harbor, the dim shape of the Peak hung with lights against the night sky.

ABOUT THE AUTHOR

Nicholas R. Clifford was on the faculty at M.I.T. and Princeton before coming to Middlebury College in 1967, where he teaches East Asian history. He lives with his wife, Deborah Clifford, also a historian and writer, in New Haven, Vermont. They have four daughters and, at last count, four grandchildren. Clifford is the author of three nonfiction books on China.